REPOSSESSED

OTHER BOOKS BY JULIAN COPE

Krautrocksampler (1995)

The Modern Antiquarian (1998)

SELECTED LPS BY JULIAN COPE

World Shut Your Mouth (1984)

Fried (1984)

Saint Julian (1987)

Skellington (1990)

Droolian (1990)

Peggy Suicide (1991)

Jehovahkill (1992)

Autogeddon (1994)

20 Mothers (1995)

Interpreter (1996)

OTHER SELECTED LPS FEATURING JULIAN COPE

The Teardrop Explodes, *Kilimanjaro* (1980)

The Teardrop Explodes, *Wilder* (1981)

The Teardrop Explodes, *Everyone wants to Shag
The Teardrop Explodes* (1990)

Julian Cope & Donald Ross Skinner, *Rite* (1993)

Queen Elizabeth, *Queen Elizabeth* (1994)

Queen Elizabeth, *Elizabeth Vagina* (1997)

REPOSSESSED

Shamanic Depressions in Tamworth
& London (1983–89)

JULIAN COPE

Thorsons
An Imprint of HarperCollins*Publishers*

Thorsons
An Imprint of HarperCollins*Publishers*
77–85 Fulham Palace Road
Hammersmith, London W6 8JB

The Thorsons website address is: www.thorsons.com

Published by Thorsons 1999 CE

10 9 8 7 6 5 4 3 2 1

A catalogue record for this book
is available from the British Library

ISBN 0 7225 3882 0

Printed in Great Britain by
Creative Print and Design (Wales), Ebbw Vale

CONTENTS

For Cally Callomon and Donald Ross Skinner

INTRODUCTION

Odin, Dva, Tree, Ch'terior, P'at,
Vachel zsiechick pagooliat,
F'droog, au whorechick veebig'eye-it,
Pre'ammer V'ziechicka Streely-hyatt,
Piff-paff, Oy oy oy,
Pagee-buy it Ziechick moy!

(in Russian)

The words above were the first I uttered as the lead singer in a rock'n'roll band, in November 1978. I'd been a child of *A Clockwork Orange*, doing Detente 'O'-level Russian from 1970 to 1974, and had spent the Glam of the '70s with a far more Krautrock prognosis than most. *A Clockwork Orange* is always played down in Glamrock essays because it doesn't conform to the lippy and fake homosexual stance, but its proto-Odinist combination of awesome frock-coated thuggery, poetry and mascara appealed considerably to my teenage pre-punk 'Hardpuff' stance. In *A Clockwork Orange*, Malcolm MacDowell was really playing the god Oder, a prehistoric precursor of Odin; an odd stinky poet and shaman, village seer and freak. The rock'n'roll singer is often an incarnation of Odin, either as Od, Ode, Oder, or all three. Odin was the One, the Singular, the Oldfather, the Allfather – but he was also the Wan, the Od, the Ode, the On, the Un-conventional. Because they don't actually ride its dizzying Muse, rock'n'roll writers study their subject from a southern Classical point-of-view. But male rock'n'roll is a pounding earth rhythm which incorporates the Violent alongside the Effeminate and the Poetic, denying nothing in a Motherfucking blaze of Pagan Paganinis. Look at the myths before the Vikings and you'll discover Odin at the root of all rock'n'roll, and most of all in Glamrock.

But the myths get changed by those that come after, sometimes even by those who were there. In the hot summer of 1996 CE, I recorded at the Old Mill at Rockfield Studios for the first time in 15 years. I've known the owners, Charles and Sandra Ward, since the beginning of my career and they both popped over to gossip and talk about old times.

'I've read your book, Julian, what was it . . . *Head-On*? Yes, I liked it . . . But what was all that old stuff about Gary chasing Dave Balfe with a shotgun? That was you with the shotgun. I remember the two of you zooming past my kitchen window! Oh, I got the fright of my life!'

I protested that it had not, in fact, been me with the shotgun but our drummer, Gary Dwyer. My friend the synthesist Thighpaulsandra was listening to all this with a big grin on his face. He has known all of us for years, and had heard the shotgun story countless times, as well as reading about it in the book. But I was amazed when Sandra constantly refused to accept my version of the story, until my protests became more and more directed just at Thighpaulsandra. Finally, and in desperation, I said:

'Thipe, if I'd really fired a shotgun at Dave Balfe, d'you think I'm the kind of person who'd try to hide it? Or would I yell about it from the rooftops?'

That clinched it for me. Though I have to deal in facts, I am a mythologist in everything and would love to tell you it was me with the gun. But it was not. Which clearly means that, as I've always argued, The Teardrop Explodes was never just Mad Me leading them over the cliff. It was Mad Julian, Mad Balfey and Mad Gary all unably supported by Mad Bill Drummond and Madder Colin Butler. I think Sandra Ward still doesn't believe my version of the story because she's had time to see it in context with the rest of my 'mad' reputation. So her mind's eye sees Julian Cope really running past the kitchen, because it's the kind of thing he should have done.

Repossessed is the story of what happened after all those people left me alone. It's mainly about me on my own or with my Muse and True-love Dorian. It's a weird story because I believe in the Weird, but I've always navigated with a Utopian eye and Blake's fear of Material Wealth causing Spiritual Poverty. Much of *Repossessed* takes place in my Scando-Keltic shaman brain, physically mirrored by the Midland landscapes around Tamworth, Fazeley, Drayton Bassett, Alvecote, Polesworth and Glascote Heath. Read it and understand how hard it was to share management with Level 42 and Tears for Fears.

No Mystical Gush – No Cheap New-age Fix!

Love on ya!
JULIAN (THE GLAM DICENN), 1999 CE

A SAFE HOUSE OF SORTS

For a few weeks there, the phone would not stop ringing. Our break up was big news and there was a lot of shit to wade through. I wouldn't leave Tamworth because too many people needed things from me, so Dorian and I reclused out. If I went to London now they'd all be persuading me to finish the dreadful third/turd album and tie up all the loose ends. I knew that I was safe up here in Tamworth, safe from a culture which was currently buying the hated Blancmange LP in droves, the same crap that currently hung transfixed on our wall by a 6" nail, vinyl and album sleeve alike. Underneath the blistered spiral burn marks from our electric hob, cartoon kittens squirmed with horror as they all stood listening to music on headphones – from the faces they were making, it was clear they themselves were listening to the Blancmange LP. "Never mind," said Dorian. "Americans don't have the dessert and pronounce the name 'Blank Man'." Nuff Said.

The Mill Lane house was a three-storey fortress which had been part of a quiet terrace until the development of recent years. But '70s council planning had gouged out the heart of these turn-of-the-20th-century houses and left no. 1 teetering on a small and ugly ring-road through the town. Its frontage was ultra-narrow and unprepossessing, but fell back to a considerable depth, creating inside a cell structure of small dimly lit rooms.

For a while, we lived on toast and tea in the bedroom. All my records and the stereo and my atrociously-finished flight case of cassettes were piled up in there. I was so used to hotels that I couldn't learn to spread out. We answered the door to no-one. I was so paranoid that I'd dive behind the kitchen counter if there was even a knock at the door.

Eventually, some time in early December, Paul King decided that it was time to sort out our finances. Our meagre £35 per week mysteriously rose to £100 despite our mounting debts. Dave Balfe made it clear that he had no desire to split up the group, as we were in debt. I told the bastard in no uncertain terms that the group did not exist to make money, that was a secondary inevitable part of the quest. The quest, Balfe. You remember that?

We will be remembered for our strength and foresight. We were not money-heads who insisted on releasing a shitty third album just to fulfil a contract. I'd felt like I'd already seen half of my favourite rock'n'roll groups in history

1

fizzle out with a final album that bore no resemblance to the spirit of the original group.

We would not be The Doors without Jim.

We would not be the Floyd without Syd.

We would not be the Velvets without Lou.

We would not be Sabs without Ozzy.

We would not be The Who without Keith.

We would not even be SAHB without Alex.

And we would not struggle on as The 13th Floor Elevators had been forced on, by business after the event, with one member dead of gunshot wounds and a lead singer only allowed out of the asylum to record albums. We would not even be Love with only Arthur Lee. The line ends here. Got me, Balfey? We were The Teardrop Explodes – probably the only group with a present participle in its name *and* two members at least who even knew what that meant! Come on, Balfey, it's like Peter Hammill said: "We have looked out on our heroes and they are found wanting." The only bands who continued for the money were '70s losers like Lindisfarne and '60s losers like The Walker Brothers. Scott had reformed them for Japanese tours whenever he needed the money – just like he'd lightly entertain you on his Jack Jones if the wad suited. What would have been the point of the whole Teardrop trip if we then continued purely for financial reasons?

Now, I told Balfe, we were going to have to do this right. We were from a scene which set great store by such romantic gestures. Would Echo & the Bunnymen live past their sell-by date and then drag on interminably as various original members left one by one? Hardly, my dear Balfe. And neither would we.

But as the meeting dragged on, Dave Balfe began to speak very unmythologically indeed. He was saying that we could "finish the album and tour it properly". Hold on, I've already split the group up. He was suggesting that we "could pay off a great many of the debts and split up in a year or so", as though we were some roof & guttering firm in financial difficulties. That he could sink to such depths of non-mythological thought appalled me so much that I, there-and-then, felt unbelievably weakened at having even been in a band with such as him.

"'Finish the album and tour it properly?' You misunderstand, my friend, there is no longer a group," I sneered. Suddenly, I perceived that I was a great being staring down at some vastly lesser molecular structure known as Dave Balfe. I was eternal and as big as a weather formation, and I had all the time in the world. I suddenly even understood Johnny Bug-Eyes Balfe. In his day-to-day mental landscape, poetic words such as 'Truth' and 'The Quest' had been eroded by constantly rubbing shoulders with ideas like Luxury and Publishing Deals. The scheming bastard was still Bill Drummonded up to the eyeballs. Balfe had never been anything but a fake Utopian and I was crazy to be looking for signs of a real one at this late stage.

But my body was still pierced by a thousand arrows when Balfe rose up to his full height of 3'11" and spluttered: "Well, don't look at me for paying the fuckin' debt, then."

And he would have none of it.

I was dealt a savage blow by that remark. Sure, I knew Balfe was a greedhead; I knew he wanted to be rich. But I thought he wanted to learn at the same time. After all, he and Bill Drummond had been the guys who had discovered the evil in me. And I had trusted them. I had stood to one side and taken their comments to heart.

Now I was totally betrayed. Betrayed by Dave Balfe's refusal to split the band until we were out of debt, betrayed by his insistence that we stay together for financial reasons. Every Balfe clause was financial. He'd even started writing songs for the third album purely for financial reasons. I've told everybody that the Teardrops have split up and here's planky guy trying to extend our sell-by date.

From very far away, right at the back of my head, I felt it coming . . . I felt it coming, clearer and clearer and, as different as night is from day, so my idea of sorting out the Teardrop debts was different from Dave Balfe's. And in as great and grand and almightily martyred a gesture as I could summon, I looked directly at Balfe and said to Paul King: "I'll take on the debt, the whole lot."

Dave Balfe looked at me. It was the look of a man who has faith only in this present life. The afterlife? We'll deal with that some other time. He waited for me to retract the statement, but I did not. Had he, maybe, misheard? No. He had not.

The gesture was over. The debt was real. It was presently at £85,000 and rising. Gary Dwyer was excluded from the debt. I thought it was only fair. He was burned enough by the Teardrop experience alone. Balfe found it hard to leave the meeting room. He couldn't believe his luck. How could Cope be so stupid? As he left, he made a vague promise to contribute money, should he ever earn it. I laughed inside. Balfe was a manager, a publisher and a recording artist, but I'd probably never see a penny.[1]

But rock'n'roll is gestures, and I understood that. Rock'n'roll is about willing your reality to change. And I was finally free of Dave Balfe *and* out of The Teardrop Explodes at last.

As I stormed out of Paul King's Outlaw offices, a song called 'Gone' by The Sunnyboys whirred and clicked in my head, its melancholy mystic sapping my physical strength, whilst simultaneously irrigating the most unused parts of my hidden mind:

"I'm not here to compromise, I've gone to the other side,
Oh, oh, oh, I've gone . . . Yeah, I've gone . . . Oh, oh, I've gone . . . Are you satisfied?"

---

1 I didn't find this out until 1996 CE but, hey, Balfe paid!

THE CUCKOO COCOON

As the Tamworth quiet of the winter mornings forced me awake, I would lie there in my grandmother's brass bed, inert and petrified. What had I done? Was I now doomed to disappear forever, aged 25 and a quarter? What was this yo-yo of emptiness that weaved itself around my sleep and jerked me into a living nightmare at 7.30 each morning? Here was I, struck down with shamanic depression, while Balfe had immediately gone off and set up a new label called Food Records, with the cynical fuck-you-up-the-ass '80s motto: LET US PREY!

Fuck, man, you invented the '80s. Learn from your mistakes, you gormless bug-eyed bushbaby! You've preyed on everyone these past years – d'you have to make such a Thatcherite celebration of it, you unmystical fucker?

I would fall asleep around 2 a.m. every morning, stoned out of my mind and ready to sleep through a battle. I was months behind on rest and now was the perfect opportunity. So why, why, why did I lie there each morning with a sense of loss so great that it made me insensible of anything else? Oh, such a loss of opportunity. Such a chance to get it right. And how wrong I had got it, how totally wrong. And lying next to me, cuddled up so close, this innocent and adoring girl slept peacefully, unaware of the maniac she had been saddled with.

By noon every day, there were no problems. Whilst the sun was up, so was I. And free. Free from stupid rock'n'roll, and free from the phone which never stopped ringing. Only it did. It stopped ringing pretty soon. In fact, I'd got so used to complaining about its ringing all the time that it took me a while to actually notice that no-one called us anymore. I was hurt. I was used to attention. How could I complain about how hassled I was if no-one hassled me? Who's that at the door? Some rabid fan who has travelled miles to catch a glimpse of me? Tell them I'm sick, I'm dead. Oh, it's the postman.

Eventually, the early morning fears became too much for me. Dorian and I started to go to bed later and later and later until we began to see the dawn come up. But by sleeping from 6 a.m. until 2 p.m., I freed myself from the loneliness and uncertainty of those early waking hours.

And now that I was free, I could do all the things I had wanted to do. I adored my parents and had always promised them a house in Epping Forest. I didn't have nearly enough money for that, but I did have a publishing cheque for £7,000. With all the debts, I felt very beholden to Paul King, but he was still a wealthy rock'n'roll promoter so we took out £2,000 in cash, booked two double rooms at a great hotel in Bath, and wined and dined my parents for three days. I had to spend now, before Kingy sussed that I had access to money.

But I needed to confront my parents in some way. My lifestyle was way out of line and they had no clue. I wanted them to know how their son lived.

I found the perfect opportunity during a conversation in the Bath Costume

Museum. My mother was telling me about a new friend of hers. ". . . so stage people naturally get very tense. Well, this old lady, you know she must be 85 and she's still remarkable looking, well, anyway, you'll never believe this, Julian." She spoke in the hushed tones of an excited schoolgirl. "She smokes hashish for relaxation."

I was amazed. Never before had I heard the act of skinning up a joint sound so sensible, so righteous. This is my perfect opportunity to tell her.

Quietly, I confided that I did the same thing sometimes.

My mother did not hear a word. She switched off immediately and said, "But not anymore, though."

And the moment was gone forever, as though it had never happened. I figured she really did not want to know and decided I had to live with it unspoken.

Bath was a mysterious semi-European paradise to me and I soon found an antique market full of furniture and curious handmade 19th-century model ships. The building was on a fairly steep slope that I was negotiating carefully, when the very corner of my peripheral vision was grabbed by the glinting of bright familiar colours. And just as the powder blues and salmon pinks of old Fender guitars had pervaded my teenage rock'n'roll dreams, so this unbelievable split second on a Bath hill telescoped me even further back to a pre-teen post-war time of two-tone high-gloss colours and bright petrol logos. For there at the entrance to the market was a small kiosk rammed to the rafters with old toys that I'd had as a child. The camber of the hill was as nothing as my gravity-defying body was sucked headlong into the gaping doorway of the market. Yahhhhhhhhhhhhhhhhhhhh!

For two hours I stared into the organised confusion of the toy stall, intoning endless cosmic platitudes to the stoic stallholder. I was so sucked in by the colours that millions of little memories all clustered together, creating ripe bunches of ideas which I handed to the poor guy in the form of questions, as though he were the Oracle of Toys sent in special civilian disguise to answer my oral inquisition. He was my best friend.

"We" discussed every model car which I had played with as a child in the '60s. I had been a child of Corgi Toys – small exquisite models of the then current common and exotic cars, finished in high-gloss colours and fitted out with windows, accurate wheels and interior detail. Ha, they were much better than Dinky Toys, the post-war leader which had started the whole craze off in the '30s then been overshadowed as I had come to toy-car-playing-with age in the late '50s. I had been a Corgi Toy snob, a future seeker with no time for the chunky finishing of Dinky's windowless blobs with agricultural-type wheels.

My mind mushroomed and sent me spinning back into those distant times and I was once again outside my parents' house in Glascote Heath, snubbing the old Dinky Toys with a prissy wave of my hand – a 10 year old in long shorts and flared nostrils. And then, I saw above me my old Corgi Toys Porsche Carrera 6. . .

As I opened the box, I glimpsed the blue plastic engine cover first and felt a rush which transported me back to a summer holiday in Cornwall in 1967. And I was nine years old again, sitting on the porch of a holiday bungalow on the beach in Porthtowan. The toy car which I had played so heartily with on the Cornish beach so long ago was now a gleaming and polished white ceremonial jewel in the cradling palm of my hand. Set down before me on the glass counter-top, the vibrant mid-blue and yellow box with its old-style printing still carried its original pre-decimal price of 7/9d, handwritten in faded black pen. As my eyes sank further into the ancient writing, now 17 years old, I imagined a proud Truro toy shop manager inscribing that price in what now seemed the deal of the century. The new price of £8 seemed unbelievably cheap considering that I spent more than that on a couple of Residents imports a month before. Why, it was just as though I had paid the stallowner a small rent to store them for me all these years.

As this line of reasoning continued, I felt an overwhelming desire to buy more Corgi Toys. Surely a man with spiralling debts and a publishing cheque in the thousands would be almost foolish not to take advantage of such a gift horse. Who knows how long Paul King could keep the bailiffs from my door? I had spent the latter days of the Teardrops avoiding the extortion of cocaine culture which had relieved Troy and Colin of £60 per gramme night after night after night. Hey, this new Corgi thing was nothing compared to that. £8 buys me a place for a genuine childhood artefact on the shelf by my bed. It's a drug which can't be consumed . . . *and* it represents my past, I reasoned with myself. Help yourself, Julian, you know this will help you.

I bought the Porsche Carrera 6, helped myself to three more rare Corgi Toys and took them all back to our room at the Hole in the Wall, where I set them all up on their boxes, just as the stallholder had displayed them. I got really close up to them until even my peripheral vision saw nothing but the four new old Corgis. Hey, from here it looked like that guy's stall.

I rushed back to the stall to buy any Corgi Toys literature, but there was none! The only toy book of any merit was an extremely expensive colour encyclopaedia of my beloved Corgis' arch-rivals Dinky Toys! Ech. I bought it in any case as a visible act of devotion to this new toy cause. We left Bath laden with furniture and toys – and I had a new hobby.

Paul King was in no hurry to get me working. He had signed a new group called Tears for Fears who were in the process of becoming huge. They had been Teardrop fans and signed to Kingy because of our connection. Outlaw Management was now run by Paul King, with help from Paul Crockford, Paul Darwin and Paul Scarborough, and getting bigger all the time.

Kingy told me to get my act together and ring him when I wanted to work. But the debt hung over my head like a guillotine waiting to fall. Every week, I would sit with the four Pauls and view new unpaid bills which had just come in – from the last US tour, from the Australian tour, from Colin's unpaid last-minute European hotel changes, suits against us (now me) for gigs cancelled and unfinished. And pretty soon it was up over £100,000 and travelling towards £120,000.

But in Tamworth I felt cocooned, and Dorian and the house became a wall between me and the outside world. The two of us had been through severe shit, but not together. No, that part of our life was just starting. I still kept so much inside me; I couldn't imagine anyone else respecting my way of thinking. When Dorian went to New York for Christmas, I asked her if she was aiming to come back straight afterwards. I wasn't sure that I was supposed to think it was a good idea and I told her so. She freaked out at me. Of course she was coming back. Was I crazy? I don't know. In my efforts to appear like the average uncaring rock male, I'd deluded myself that I had never thought our Love-affair that far forward before. But this young American was already my Muse and my Crutch. That I was not yet festooning her with this knowledge was probably, for the present time, entirely in her interests. I often forgot that she was four (long) years younger than me and my Oblivion of Experience.

THE LOVE-SONG KISSES FREEDOM

Whilst Dorian was in New York, I had a great idea. As a child of the '70s, I had learned Russian to "O" level standard and become so intrigued with the sound of the language that the very first Teardrop shows had opened with my intoning of an old Russian nursery rhyme. It had been a bit of a Glam-Prog thing to do, what with the *Clockwork Orange* "dryggu/droogy" connection, but the sound of spoken Russian over heavy clanging guitars had me by the balls.

More recently, the twice-translated poems of a Russian called Metranil Vavin had accompanied me on the final Teardrop shows, inspiring an unfinished epic poem in Pig German called "Krankenhaus", and I had been listening constantly to the *Block to Block* LP by a Russian band called De Presse[1] It was ragged and punky and instant, and full of those fantastic Glam Descends which had permeated all that early 'Good-bye to Love' fuzz guitar solo/end of 'Moonage

---

1 This LP was produced by John Leckie and released on the Siberia label SM1. I found it in the dump bin on the A&R floor of Phonogram Records. It still sounds like a cool mix of Joy Division and The Ruts with Hugh Cornwell singing!

Daydream'/Eno's 'Here Come the Warm Jets'/Mott's 'Roll Away the Stone'/ 'Rock'n'Roll Part 2'/'Pyjamarama' ilk. But only Magazine's 'The Light Pours out of Me' had seen a contemporary group dare to echo this enormous and Cyclopean sound. Why shouldn't I conjure up this forgotten clang – my new songs were certainly chock full of those Glam Descends and it would mean that I could side-step that '60s production which people always accused me of attempting (and failing). Also, that way I could achieve the urgency of Chicago's amazing version of Spencer Davis' 'I'm a Man' without people even clocking the fact! Get Down!

As my mind explored the possible musicians available, it suddenly became clear. Why shouldn't I make this really ragged album using DHSS as my group? The Department of Happiness & Self-Satisfaction were Tamworth's weirdest bunch of people and were known to enjoy singing cosmi-punk lyrics over repeated E major buzzchords. Joss had been at school with their leader Vince Watts, whose brother was B. Smith from The Flids.

I went to see them rehearse, but Joss had told them my plan upfront. Vince was so freaked out by the very idea that he spent the whole time soloing wildly in front of me. His overly-tall and gaunt Kid Strangeness gave way to a bouncy psychotic Jimmy Pursey-type (Gore Lummey Mate), which then metamorphosed into a lower-still Gollum-type of lifeform, whose most basic methods of communication I could not understand.

Finally, as a joke, they played the theme from *Top Gear*, the TV show about cars. When I told them it was an old Fleetwood Mac song, Vince couldn't think of a proper rock'n'roll way to react and behaved like a four year old with a late load in his undies.

But, for me, it was a life-changing experience. However crazy I was, nothing could have made me respond to a challenge in the way that Vince had chosen to do. Perhaps he had sussed from Minute One that he was not up to delivering what I required and so chose to fuck off in the most glorious and memorable way.

I'd love to think so, but . . . hardly!

Plan B, ho-hum.

But I would not be shaken from this new sound in my head. If my Glam Descend works only with me alone, then so be it. I started to pick up the guitar again and had bought a tiny cream Casio MT-40 plastic keyboard from Dave Balfe. I had nothing to do but play the guitar and look at the huge Dinky Toys book that I'd bought in Bath. I was secretly ashamed that the Dinky Toys in the sumptuous book had begun to pervade my waking thoughts. These were not toys of my childhood, yet the fabulous colour plates of '50s American cars and gigantic British delivery wagons had already obtained a place in my mythical mindscape which could not be shaken off. And because I felt so weird about my songs, I found it easier to sink into a soft couch of toy fundamentalism, where Dinky Toys v Corgi Toys was a way-of-life worth taking sides over.

I hadn't written anything that people had actually liked since 'You Disappear from View' almost a year earlier. In later Teardrop sessions, I'd play a song and it would be listened to and then dismissed. I kept playing the songs on acoustic guitar, but Balfe's comments still rang in my years. I had played him a song called 'Bandy's First Jump' for the third album, but he'd hated it. By that time, he seemed to hate anything with guitars in it.

With Dorian away, I was forced to keep busy. I couldn't drive a car so I was stuck. Stuck in this house with songs that no-one likes. I recorded them on to my ghetto blaster and listened back. I played electric guitar along with the songs and they sounded good. I should do something, really, I reasoned. But I was in Tamworth and this was nowhere. For a few days, I was frustrated, but the mood wouldn't go away.

I didn't know how to book a studio; that had always been done for me. But I had to record. It was the first time in ages that I'd felt that way. My mother told me about a teacher she knew. He had a studio. I thought it was probably a crap studio. A teacher? I'll ring him in a day or so. I sat in the Mill Lane house with my Dinky Toys book and some pot. Dorian was in New York and I knew I had to make the phone call.

What a snob I was! I went to the studio and it was brilliant. I was sooo surprised. The guy who ran it was called Steve Adams, a junior school teacher and ex-weirdo. The local taxi took me to this tiny cottage in Birchmoor, a village on the other side of Tamworth, near to Glascote Heath where I'd grown up. Birchmoor was a heath of great desolation and remove. As a child, my father had taken me on walks there, but I had always seen it as being "Beyond" my area. It was untamed and heathen, and the tiny houses squatted upon the moor.

The studio was in a house separate even from the rest of this remote village, and its bucolic position suddenly reinforced my solitary place out of the music scene. For this was not the Keltic drama of Rockfield – this was Dark Ages and Anglo-Saxon and on my home territory. Why, come daybreak, the Alvecote Mound would probably be visible just a mile to our south.

Steve Adams expected me to be big time and know about VU and all that studio stuff. I faked it for a while to make him feel better, but soon we were recording really fast and easily. I wasn't bothered about the sound. I put the drum-machine of my Casio into the Vox AC30 amplifier and played the song on acoustic guitar over its dry thumping. The song was a beautiful major-chord thing called 'Strasbourg' whose current arrangement was only one minute and 40 seconds long but featured a repeated Glam Descend link of considerable charm. Listening back to the empty song, I considered what Troy Tate might have contributed and set up the amp in a way that made me feel Troy-like as I recorded. I added a tight fuzz theme and distorted early Teardrop-type keyboard, then tightened the whole track up with tambourine. Ey-up, I was a bloody one-man-band. Balfe had made me terrified to pick up a guitar or bass anymore. Now look! And listen to this stuff . . . it's a moving fucking thing.

I was ecstatic. This was the sound I had wanted for the third Teardrop album, instead of those dumb programmed synthesizers. Synths should fart and squeak, but Balfe had kept his on Rhythm/Dribble. Fuck that!

I made a list of all my songs, things that I'd been scared to try. I'll try them! I can play! I can play! When Dorian rang me, I played 'Strasbourg' down the phone for her and she loved it. She loved it. I'm alive! I was dancing round the room. I played it to her again and a third time and danced all the time she listened.

In my sudden realisation that I could still be capable, we seemed suddenly so much closer and so much stronger that the most powerful lyric of the new song pulverised me with its truth:

"If I were France, and you were Germany,
What an alliance that would be."

When Dorian came home I was still high and we returned to the permanent twilight of Grandma Cope's bed for a few days. Dora pulled out a large box of her brothers' Dinky Toys which her mother had saved since the '50s. She told me that they were mainly battered but not broken, and she had wrapped up each one in tissue paper.

I opened every delicate package with a sense of awe. These were the famous Dinky Toys which I had seen in my book. I had been too young to play with many of them as a child, but they came rattling into my brain at 100 mph, sending me spinning back to my days as a five-year-old Don Juan, making the Tamworth–Lutterworth trip in the early '60s. Wow!

As a child of five, my parents had often taken me down the Watling Street to visit their friends Vin and Chris Peace in Lutterworth. We would visit fairly often, and I would divide my time between playing with the two boys and their fabulous Dinky Supertoys, and chatting up their 18-year-old daughter Catherine. Surrounded now by the same mesmerising force of die-cast metal memories, my twee five-year-old mind reasserted itself once more. In the lacquered assault of Dinky colours, my toy-fted mind time-surfed back 20 years to the public toilets at Long Street, Dordon, just off the Watling Street, where, as a precocious five year old, I had told my parents so many times that the red brick building would be our future home, once Catherine and I were married. Of course, my sweet parents never told me the baser functions of our dream-home and I was, cringingly, left to discover it for myself aged 10. And now, the domino-effect of feelings which each Dinky Toy precipitated came upon me as a rush greater than anything but love. For the roots of so many of these ancient toys linked themselves indirectly to me.

A Studebaker? I'd played with this very same toy at Uncle Neil's, when he was still unmarried in Cardiff. Its brutal wheels and windowless interiorlessness evoked thoughts of a Stone Age shuttle, whilst the matted tan and sand yellow two-tone colour-scheme reeked of my very early childhood in late '50s Britain and its colossally drab, almost Puritanical, versions of Americana.

As my brain surfed waves of memories on oceans long forgotten, I lined up all the Dinky Toys on the table. I surveyed all of them. Dinky Toys . . . Hmm . . . I walked around them and smiled. Then, over the coming weeks, I cleaned all 58 of them with deep love and a knowledge that they would never leave me.

My life had changed drastically. I had not rejected the world outside; I could just no longer live in that world.

I watched the growing success of Echo & the Bunnymen with a sense of sadness and distance. In 1981, I had, in various shapes or forms, appeared on *Top of the Pops* nine times. In 1982, zero. It was now the beginning of 1983 and I felt the world passing me by. Still, I had achieved my aim. I had avoided the inevitable slide of The Teardrop Explodes into tameness and oblivion. But no-one seemed to notice. I thought that everyone would rally around and say, "What purity! What a cleansing! Truly, this man was the Gun of Sod." But they didn't.

The press were bloody sick of me and my big mouth, sick of my ranting and pleased to get one such as me out of their faces. So they were even more sick when I insisted on writing my first press release, which read like an existential Mr Kipling advert:

Press Release – Spring 1983

Julian Cope, green eyes shining, steps out into the morning air. Dresses for comfort, his walk unlaboured; promises of something new. A special treat. Too, too many Teardrops have fallen. Now gone forever. The people he once knew are all far away. He is left alone – to sorrow and to melancholy. I asked Julian: "Are you lonely?"

"I am, my friend," he shot back. "I have toyed with this world too long." Now I am done. I leave him where he feels at ease.
In the furthest corners of your mind.
In the bear cage with spears in his side.
A tumour with a sense of humour.

At the Mill Lane house, we painted the video room all-black. I had wanted a sensory deprivation tank, but they cost £1,800. We painted the walls and the ceiling, fitted a black carpet and a screen of black glass in the window. It was our trip-out room – there was no sense of time in there at all. We sat in there for hours, watching *Animal House* and episodes of *The Monkees*.

There, in ultra-comfortable surroundings, we watched Pete Wylie dress as a Mary Poppins Penguin to perform his excruciating 'Story of the Blues', the worst song since 'Heartbreak Avenue' by The Maisonettes. Too fucking Lager! I blamed Adam Ant and the sooty Dexy's Midnight Runners for this Tarbuckian travesty. Wylie had been on a perfectly sound (if somewhat worthy) posi-drive trip of Boss-ian Clashness until those Pseudo-Kelts & Psemi-Clints had thrown a Spandau in the works.

Then the Bunnymen followed close on the "Toppy" trail with a song called 'The Cutter'. Bloody Hell. Too fucking Raga!

I lay morbidly fearful of *Top of the Pops*. Was this to be my life from now on? Peering fearfully at the uncoolness of more successful friends in a mute discontent of quivering impotent envy?

We had started to attract the Tamworth freaks to our house. First they hung around outside the front door, which was blocked up with furniture. They would try to sell us acid through the letterbox, which was uncool and stupid and *very* Tamworth. One time, when we didn't answer around 2 a.m., they walked off screaming, "Tell Julian he missed some brilliant acid." Great, just what I need, all the hobos, mongrels and village idiots on my scene.

A guy called Chippy used to shout "Duran Duran" at me every time I walked near him. The Chipman family was huge around Tamworth and I still cherished an enormous teddy bear which my father's neighbours, Mr and Mrs Chipman, had won for him at Fazeley Fair in 1929.

Fresh from Liverpool, everything to do with the name Chipman should have filled me with safety and a feeling of home. So it was even more disconcerting when Joss told me that Chippy had begun telling everyone that he'd "taught Julian Cope everything he knows". As a 15-year-old Krautrocker in Deutsche Tamworth, I had often wished to talk to Chippy, but the guy totally dissed me. As the only other freebass Krautrocker in Tamworth, he could have helped me out at a time when I looked up to him as a free-thinking mother. With his somehow punky Afro, Chippy could turn up at anyone's show and bring a truly burning vibe to the party. Aged 17, he'd turned Cott's group Klangkett into an Amon Duul 2 meets Aphrodite's Child live extravaganza with 20-minute looping freak outs of a similar intensity to *Yeti*'s title track and *666*'s 'All the Seats were Taken'. And all this at a time when my (Norris Brothers) Garage group, Softgraundt, were still struggling to replicate Can's 'I'm So Green', Krautrock's 'Louie Louie' on a learning level. He could have chosen to see the two years between us as an excuse to be benevolent, but, from his present behaviour, he had never been a big enough person.

But at least Chippy's friends were all cool towards me and seemed to enjoy having me back and wandering around the town. I'd see John and Richard Bujak smiling their enormous grins, like Kiss's Ace Frehley as the Cheshire Cat, and I'd be transported back to the Wilnecote schoolyard of 1975, where Richard nicknamed me Uncle Meat and told endless Hawkwind jokes which always ended in punchlines which derided the simplicity of Dave Brock's droning E chords.

One night, Dorian, Joss and I formed The Bujak Ujak Jak Ak Club and performed vocal-only versions of Ace Frehley's 'Shock Me' in the style of the Brothers Bujak.

I continued to record at Steve Adams' studio. I suggested he change its name to The Drug Attic, but he politely declined. The songs were coming thick and fast by now. I had hit upon a formula – just put everything on to tape that you can. I never gave Steve much time to sort out sounds; it would go down before we had a chance to get bored with it.

I had handpainted the little Casio keyboard that Balfe sold me. Dorian and Joss painted little scenes all over it, and it had become the basis for all my songs.

I was still alone, though.

I wanted a producer. Not someone to bully me, just someone to tell me when my head was up my ass.

THE REDISCOVERY OF STEVE LOVELL

I sat in Paul King's office whilst he made the phone call. I couldn't believe it. No-one wanted to work with me. They all told Kingy that it was not worth the grief.

Clive Langer had not answered his calls, he just left his answerphone on. But Clive had produced most of the Teardrop stuff! Clive loves me! Paul King eventually contacted Jake Riviera, Clive's manager. I sat in the room listening to the call turn into a slagging match. I heard Paul deny that I had been the cause of Clive's skin turning grey. But, even before he put the phone down, I gleaned that Jake Riviera was less than enamoured with Paul's idea.

I didn't like being in London. I felt exposed. If anyone recognised me, I was pissed off at the invasion of privacy. But if I didn't get recognised, I would brood all day. I understood how Lawrence of Arabia had felt when he came back to London and was compelled to dress like his legend and get in people's faces. I wanted to walk up to girls and foist myself upon them. Here's an autograph, you don't know me, ha ha ha ha. Hi, d'you want to know me? Aren't I a gross out, awlright?

Down Oxford Circus tube station we walked. Down and down. Dorian in her finery and me in the leather WW2 jerkin and red tie & dye tights. I heard a sound. Below us, a kind of subterranean art blues was unfolding. It wound along the corridors and came from the direction that we were headed. It was played on an echoey guitar and it drew me in. I never gave buskers money in 1983, as they played mostly 'Stairway' or 'Take Five' or some such. But this was mesmerising me. I felt in my pocket for a pound note and we turned the corner to face the guitarist. He stood, head down, his fringe over his face, a small amp at his side. I threw the money and he looked up for one second.

It was Steve Lovell!

Fucking hell, it was Steve Lovell!

This guy. Well, bloody hell, this is the guy that we used to adore from afar in Liverpool. Before the Bunnymen, before the Teardrop, Will Sargent, Simmo and I used to consider Steve the nearest thing to Tom Verlaine. Of course, Tom Verlaine was a guitar legend in Liverpool. And, though Steve had always played in crap bands, his guitaring had always been so pioneeringly emotional and truly nerve-shattering that we always just listened to *him*.

"Bloody hell, man. How are you?" I said, smiling like the sudden excavator of hidden treasure.

"Oh, 'iya man. I'm fine, I'm fine." He looked a little embarrassed to be busking, but it was definitely cool and we just took in the other's presence for a while.

It was hard to stay still in the flow of people, so we left with a smile and a wave, and I beamed my way back to Tamworth that night.

"Couldn't he produce you?" said Dorian. Dora, you're damn right he could. I'd even had a secret relationship with him already! In 1977/78, he had worked in Virgin Records. Steve had been the guy who supplied Yorkie with all those Human Switchboard EPs, Skydog reissues, lost genius like Second Layer's 'Courts or Wars' 45 and equally memorable but not-quite-essential-to-buy stuff that fills out a contemporary record collection and turns it into a cultural library. It was because of Steve Lovell that I could honestly say "I hate Gloria Mundi." In Eric's, Roger Eagle would never have dreamt of playing such uncool stuff. But the pragmatic artist in me always needed to hear it just to know it was bad. That's fucking Gnosis, man.

So Steve was just what I needed – someone who would be excited to work with me, not some over-experienced dickhead who thinks I'm going to kill them.

Paul King searched all over for Steve Lovell. It took two weeks, but it was worth it. Soon, Steve was up in Tamworth recording every night at the little studio in Birchmoor. We disrupted the hell out of Steve Adams' life, but he dug that.

I suddenly felt creative again. I never really thought that Steve would be quite such a vibe, but he was hysterical. A total Cainhead. All his girlfriend had been planks, and ugly planks at that. And being four years older than me, he had hit drugs 10 years before me – not having had the straight-edged beginnings of punk to help him out(!)

We recorded 10 songs in 10 short sessions for £38 per session and my spirits began to lift. Steve played guitar like a burning angel – he had a devastated inner-soul which could make Tom Verlaine sound like some wide-backed no-titted adolescent female.

I made brief sorties to London for business and the debt, but mainly I was holed up in the Mill Lane house with Dorian. When I went to London, I stayed at Steve's and copied his entire way of eating breakfast. I went back to Tamworth and just copped the whole thing, even his robe. I hadn't had a role model like Steve Lovell since my Teardrop guitar tech Mal had become my temporary guru Buchanan. But this time I hid my copying from Steve, because I knew it would weird him out, or, rather, Dorian second-guessed that any such behaviour would have me instantly producerless, and therefore rudderless, again. But I already knew that I could be a physical nuisance; somebody once said, "Julian Cope doesn't have a conventional sense of personal space." On a professional level I had to Back Off.

The Mill Lane house became a stop-off point for friends on the Liverpool–London run. Pete DeFreitas and Jake Brockman would turn up on their motor-bikes, escaping for a few days from the Bunnymen's heavy schedule. Johnno, whom I had known since before he was in Wah!, came to stay with us regularly. Gary Dwyer used the place as a chill-out zone after the group split up. His father had died one month after the split and then his marriage had failed after six months. Gary was totally fucked in the head. He didn't have the capacity to deal with it, so he would lash out at anybody. I couldn't really help much, as my head was as caned as ever, but I'd try.

I was still hung up on being evil. In the past, Balfe had told me that my songs tended to be morally unsound. That really upset me, as the main reason I wrote songs was as a learning process for myself, not as teaching process for others.

I was fed up with all the "Ra-Ra – Follow Me" shit that was around at this time. It was weird; I was stuck in Tamworth watching U2 get big. I was so removed from everything and this bunch of weaners that used to be the northern scene's biggest joke was socking it to them in America and selling themselves as precisely what they were not. So I was evil and U2 were good. Well, isn't that a kick in the ass. I've hung out with their girlfriends, man. If that was good, I think I prefer to be bad.

URBAN BLITZ

"I was dancing when I was 12 – I was dancing when I was aaah."

T. Rex, 'Cosmic Dancer'

But being bad was too easy. In the '80s music scene, it had become a kind of inverted snobbery. There was a group around at that time called Killing Joke. They were run by this tiny Jeremy Jazz dickhead who said stuff like "Charles Manson is cool", "Hitler was right" and "Staring Means You're A Visionary." I didn't want to hear shit like that. He even told our friend Patty that he'd put a curse on her and she believed him. Little Jeremy Jazz! Troy Tate had been in a group with him a few years before, said everyone called him by his real name, Jeremy, in order to piss him off. Now, Jeremy was "cursing" loads of people and forcing his trip on everyone. He'd begun life as a child-actor, a ragtime chimney-sweep known as the Jazz Coalman, and now he was coming on like the Anti-Christ. It shook me and it terrified me that this miniature goon was into pretending to be evil as a power trip. And here I was, stuck with *really* being evil and wanting absolutely no part of it.

I'd had my palm read when I was a 19-year-old punk, but had dismissed the woman as a henna-haired Old Hippy when she had told me that I would become a mean tyrant as I hit my thirties. I thought about Balfe's and Bill Drummond's constant proclamations about my evil mental state and I now wondered if the Old Hippy might have had something of value to tell me. I felt that there was a subdued power of badness within me, controlled for the time being, but waiting like an IRA bomb under a car. So long as I drove that car around slowly, I was fine. But let's just stay off the motorways, okay?

I decided that if I was truly evil, then I was going to be the nicest and most suppressed evil person in the world. Like Ozzy Osbourne's famously thrown peace-signs on the cover of *Black Sabbath Volume 4*, I would represent the victory of good over my true stained and cursed self.[1]

I was on an Midland Man trip with no respect for the city drips any more. No more hang ups about their preconceived stasis-of-cool. Another Midland

---

1 This issue clearly continued to worry me for long and sustained periods of time. My publicist recently found an article in *Just 17*, dated October 1988, which read: "Julian Cope's thrill at having a hit has been marred by his fears of getting older, since when he was 19 he had his palm read by a gypsy who told him that he'd be successful but by the age of 40 he would turn into a tyrant and everyone would hate him." So, five long years later, I was still talking about it.

Woden called Robert Plant had just filled in his 'Portrait of the Artist as a Consumer'[1] guide for *NME*, in which he had none other than Roky Erickson down as his favourite singer. I'd always "known" that Plant screamed that Roky scream, but now it made sense. Woden Texas and Woden Tamworth were central landmasses ruled by a bunch of existentialists in London/New York. Now I was back in the provinces, I thought, Fuck that.

Like Lou Reed and the Warhol scene slagging Iggy in '69 for his two-years-late-Byrds-do, I'd been the hick at Eric's who'd turned up like some Femmy Farmer's girl. Living my childhood on the wilds of Glascote Heath, I had seen the suburbs built right there before me on the stark hill-land. Our house had been the third to last house all the way to Polesworth. My childhood next-door neighbours had been cows. As a two year old, I'd named all the Jersey cows Gladys and the Fresians Mrs Moo. When I were a lad, this had all been trees and fields, when I were a lad.

Then, just as my teenage years had arrived, the roadmen had come and torn down Winnie's house opposite. They'd dumped all the bricks from her house into the pond next door, where we played. The newts and sticklebacks were probably not informed of this, but they'd needed to fill it all to flatten everything for the roundabout, which now lay at the foot of my parents' road, the size of four Olympic swimming-pools.

But the area had not been completely de-mystified until the arrival of the industrial estate right opposite my parents' house soon after I had left for college in Liverpool. Only at that moment had the land become truly subdued at last, as all-night security lighting around the aircraft-hangar sized Pirelli depot shifted the heathen bogeymen and ancient hillfolk off west to the darker more mysterious environs of Stoneydelph and Birchmoor.

But now, these rising feelings stirred me to a strange and long-coming fury and feeling of vitality. In existentialist London and Liverpool, I'd been hoodwinked into being an arthole by wily personalities who lived in stasis and fear. But now, in the reliving of those moments of pain and loss, I was like Alexander "Skip" Spence frrrrreewheeling across America with multiple personalities blazing; I was Iggy Pop the Igneus Fatuus, or "foolish fire", hanging from Iggdrassil, the heathen world tree of the Vikings; I was Sabbath's John "Ozzy" Osbourne, paranoid Woden on the edge of the sleeping village; Julian "Igjugurjuk" Cope transfixed on the pillar of Irminsul, a shamanic hedgehog with death

---

1 This pretentious variant on the usual "fave colour", "fave woman", etc. was excellent for revealing the hideous or unscrupulous sides of artists. The singer Jim Kerr, from then-popular group Simple Minds, claimed that his favourite album was Peter Gabriel's *The Lamb Lies Down on Broadway*. The real perpetrators of that sonic outrage were actually Peter Gabriel's group Genesis. But any mention of Genesis as a source-of-inspiration in 1984 was still a heinous post-punk crime to be obscured at all costs.

in his heart towards badness. A quiet village boy takes leave of his life and walks off into the mountains. Burn Baddies burn. Decadent Disco Inferno.

THE SHAMANIC JERKIN, THE "X" & THE STAIN

Incidents with such figures as the Coalman sent me running to the safety of my toys. Dorian and I would visit old toy fairs called "swap meets", where row upon row of picnic tables stood, groaning with the weight of rare and beautiful toy cars, boats, trains, robots, dolls and figurines. With Dorian's ultra-high heels, her remarkable bosom and her uncanny resemblance to sexy 1940s womanhood, we soon both got used to the stares of hundreds of middle-aged men, whose sexual thoughts had long ago been assimilated and submerged into the rush of weekend toy collecting. At first, I felt guilty about upsetting their routines, their quilted anoraks and their "wants" lists. But seeing the smiles on older men's faces was my greatest pleasure, as my darling Dora would come running up to me, saying excitedly, "There's a 40 series Dinky Austin for £4 on that stall!" When she even started bartering for me, I suddenly began to do the most unreal deals.

My parents also became more and more important in our lives. Their house was only five miles away in Glascote Heath and Sunday lunch became a regular 1 o'clock thang. It was so good to have them near. It meant that I had to act normally, as they wouldn't accept my weirdness. And neither of them had any clue as to the state I was in. Besides, how do you say to your father: "I think that I am possessed by a powerful evil. People that I respect have detected it in me. I have embarked on a series of drug binges, designed to destroy that part of my mind in which the evil lies. And by rendering myself psychically defenceless, the good people of this Earth will be alerted, should the monster within me see fit to rear its ugly head."

No. I couldn't do that. They'd have to put my mother in a rubber room, and my father too, maybe. They did not have access to the real poison in my life. And why should I subject them to it, what good would it do? No, it was enough to have my parents around. Just the wilfulness of their normality would be a strong psychological crutch for me. And their love. That was understood. It was strong and blind and devotional. And their friends loved me, too, so I figured that I must be good for something.

My father's friend, another John Osbourne, gave me his leather captain's jerkin from the D-Day landings. The bullet hole which ruined the line of the jerkin had been caused by the same slug which had killed the then Captain Osbourne's sergeant, who had been running up the beach beside him. As John Osbourne told me this story one Sunday afternoon at my parents' house, I thought of his two sons, much older than me, and wondered what I'd done to deserve a gift of such shamanic singularness. It was a blessed garment, handed to me by a blessed elder, for John was a very tall and impressively strong older man of intense depth and mysticism. He ended the conversation with a simple comment to the effect that I would understand the significance of this leather jerkin.

I went upstairs and stripped off my top, whereupon I proceeded to daub myself with the black shamanic "X" on my left lower torso.[1] My Teardrop-period "X"-trip would continue, for I now realised that it was not and never had been part of my Teardrop trip. It was more a part of me alone – a sign of my shamanic uniqueness, of my remove from everything. Like Captain John Osbourne's gift to me, the black "X" was in recognition of my oddness.

I took the jerkin off rarely over the next few years and never let the "X" wash out completely, topping up the black on a bi-weekly basis. I even adopted a sweatshirt of my brother's to accompany them, immaculate save for a single large stain across the chest. Photo-sessions of the period are ridden with the outfit and, in the high self-regard of the '80s, something as simple as the Stain would become the bane of *Smash Hits*-type photoshoots. To me, their seeing only the Stain was of immense significance.

GREG AND CELIA

Around late spring of 1983, Steve Lovell and I went up to Liverpool for rehearsals. We were ready to record my first album and I wanted to get simple again. At the Ministry, in our old room from way back, we thrashed through the songs. Gary played drums and Johnno and I alternated on bass and guitar. The songs woke me up; they had some great cacophony in them.

But Dave Bates was still my A&R man. He hated the songs and no, Steve could not produce! I fought and fought and got nowhere. He said we should try Chris Hughes out on one song. Oh yeah, Bates' mate, Chris Hughes. He was Merrick from the Ants and the producer of Tears for Fears, an un-righteous combination.

---

1 *NME* began their review of The Teardrop Explodes' 1982 Hammersmith Palais show: "With a big 'X', just like the ones lumberjacks put on trees waiting to be felled, marked on his ribcage in indelible black marker, Julian Cope breathlessly comes to the climax of his performance." I took this to be extremely significant at the time and was convinced that writers were picking up on my "signals". With hindsight, of course a writer's going to comment on some pop star with an in-your-face-black "X" on their belly.

I got Bates to make a deal. We try Chris Hughes out on one song. If it sucks shit, we use Steve. Ha ha ha. It sucked shit, intense amounts actually. Even Bates agreed. So Steve was the producer and we booked the studio.

In real terms, I was still doing nothing. My day to day was linear as hell. Breakfast at the Mill Lane house was always around noon. Followed by a spliff, endless tea and records, more spliffs, until bed. Sometimes, Dorian and I would be submerged until even later. We'd miss the bank and have no money and would have to search around for change. Then we would pile around to Rose Brothers Garage and buy chocolate for dinner, always Turkish Delight, Crunchies, Curly Wurlys, and milk for late night Horlicks.

I started to gain weight. Gradually at first, but little by little my body began to puff out. Dorian had been no cook at all when we first met. I had made all the meals and did the domestic stuff. I'd decided on that course after I found her just about to handwash my best wool jumper in boiling water. But now, she began to take over. And when we considered my unbalanced attitudes towards nutrition, it was obviously for the best. I loved food, but with the existential remove of a total Nowhead.

I was still obsessed by my father's way of shopping for food. If it was unbelievably cheap and close to the end of its shelf-life, my father would leap at virtually any awful offal offcut. Even here in Mill Lane, Dorian had recently had to run for cover as he slammed two half pig's faces on to our kitchen counter, triumphantly a-screaming, "Twelve and a half pence from the Co-op!" For all of its worth to Dorian, I might as well have just skinned it up. But my father's impoverished childhood would flood over into my life once more as I boiled up the two faces and slopped them into a deep bowl, wherein time would turn them into a jellified mass of meaty potted goo analogous to the 30-degree Silbury shape of a Neolithic hill altar.

I was into all these recipes that Dorian had inherited from her family. We porked out on home-made chocolate chip cookies and sweet apple pies; we always had something far-out in the house. I had no public face to put on. I looked like shit. Viking shit. My blond hair was matted and filthy, though I did cologne it occasionally, and I wandered around in long johns and my long leather shaman's vest.

Next door to us was a couple called Greg and Celia. They were mid-30s and weird as hell. We got fed up with keeping the milk in cold water in the sink. We wanted a fridge. Greg and Celia sold us this tiny old thing for £5 and that made us real neighbours.

This allowed them to confide that our music went on too long too loud and too late every night. Whoa, bad one. We conscientiously turned the music down and invented a very quiet game called "Door" to pass the time. With hindsight, the rules of Door are brutally simple, but this did not in any way stop us from playing the game long after we had reverted to being loud-gonzo-neighbours again. Dorian and I would sit facing each other in the black room, the bedroom door two feet away from us and parallel with us both. Joss the Referee would shout "One, two, three, Go!" and the first to look at the door was the winner. Pretty simple fun. And endlessly sustaining.

Anyway, our neighbours Greg and Celia had a sandy-coloured dog called Sandy, a fairly anonymous average family dog. One day, as I came down the entry at the back of our house, Sandy jumped out and bit me. Dorian laughed hysterically and so did our friend Lisa St. John, who was visiting from Boston. But I wasn't laughing at all, indeed I was hurting and my pride was wounded, and I knew that we couldn't have some biting dog around, so we had a conference.

"You'll have to tell them, man," said Dorian. I was totally weirded out at the prospect of confrontation, as the only kind I knew was laying Dave Bates out for releasing singles I didn't want, laying Balfey out for bullying me and sacking people in a heightened Odinist frenzy. How could I confront without over-reacting? These people are our neighbours. . .

Hmm . . . the problem seemed insurmountable but, nevertheless, real people had to deal with stuff like this. I went round and told them. Wow, it was easy.

Celia was mortified and behaved in the contrite and concerned way in which a neighbour should probably behave. But then it became harder, as Greg, displaying all the traits of a supreme adolescent ninny, said they'd have to put the dog down. I thought he was joking, but Greg was stoney-faced, so I guessed that irony might be dangerous to employ in this situation, and carefully told them, nay insisted, that Death of Sandy was not necessary. Unfortunately, Greg now took the point-of-view that Sandy the dog had to die in order to uphold the honour of the Greg & Celia family. Shit – they've got kids. But what an interesting technique – you dare complain about anything of mine and I'll destroy it right there and then. Self-loathing asshole.

Days passed and Greg confirmed that, yes, the dog had been put down. No more Sandy, end of story. Except that we'd occasionally be woken early in the morning by strange noises next door. And we'd look out the window and see Greg sneaking a dog into the car as he went to work.

I'd shout, "Dora, Dora, Dora, come and see this, quickly."

And we'd debate whether or not it was dead Sandy, even though it really had to be dead Sandy. And then we started hearing his bark at night. So we stopped talking to them because it was fucking weird and they were weird too. Finally, months later, they admitted they had kept Sandy and we started talking to them again.

When you have a reputation for being weird, but your neighbours are weirder, this is very reassuring.

ANIMALS HATE ME

And so Tamworth continued to fascinate me. It was supposed to be this nice normal town, but was really a microcosm of utter weirdness with its little Greg and Celia scenes and Vince Watts affairs.

One kid kept coming round. We ignored him for ages. But he eventually knocked at the back door, which we thought was very sussed indeed. So we started letting this kid in, and I really dug him.

His name was Mark Mortimer and he was a Mod. He dressed like a Mod, he rode a scooter, he loved the Jam and he talked obsessively about all things Mod. The reason I liked him so much was because he also hated Mod, thought it was uncool and asked not "How the hell do I get out of it?" but "How do I make it more Psychedelic and Utopian?"

Dorian and I called him "M", for the simple reason that Mark Mortimer lived in a spy movie. He brought all his photo albums around with all his little Moddy friends and their scooters and everything was captioned in the most impersonal way imaginable. "M. Mortimer with B. Lacey and C. Underwood. 1983." We got to know his friends from their photographs. Dorian and I would make up stories about them. We loved them; they had this timeless innocence, like some living kitchen-sink film.

"M" was famous in Tamworth for his unreasonable behaviour. He had once walked home through hedges in gardens, tearing through each one in an act of such terrific destruction that it even had his own friends gasping at the selfishness of the act. Mark was really out there. His most notorious act was to timidly ask an old couple for the use of their toilet, only to leave a little brown and steaming tapered gift in the middle of their immaculate bathtub.

But at least "M" was confused in a big romantic Roger Daltrey way. He led a photoreal life which caused all kinds of frictions, but it was great to have linked up with this junior truth-seeker who loved every woman that he met and humped their garden gates as they slept. He ran a psychedelic mod group called The Dream Factory and recorded one of his songs, entitled 'I Want To Tell you that I Love You'. Dorian's idea for the video was to simply film "M" singing "I want to tell you that I love you" to every girl in Tamworth.

"M" told us where all his friends worked and sometimes Dorian and I would stand outside Bacon's shoe shop and watch B. Lacey attending to some customer or other. Unlike Burdetts or other more traditional Tamworth shoe shops, Bacon's was a radical open-plan affair, situated in the equally radical Precinct, which allowed Dorian and I to huddle in the porch of Hamlet's Wine Bar and watch the sales antics of B. Lacey for hours on end. Once, M. Mortimer visited B. Lacey during work hours and our TV eyes telescoped them into our deepening mythological world. You can't beat your brain for entertainment.

Next to Bacon's was a pet shop. One day while we were watching B. Lacey it started to rain. We took shelter in the nearby pet shop and Dorian raced up and down the aisles admiring the birds and fish. I was just standing around in an I'm-only-in-here-because-it's-raining dither when a parrot poked its head out of its cage and violently bit me. As usual, Dorian went hysterical, but I freaked out. This was serious. First Sandy the dog and now this. Animals hated me, so this was indeed further proof that I was bad.

FREUR

And so our Tamworth existence continued. We were hermits on all but the rarest of occasions. Our only link to the past was through the TV. There was a new programme called *The Tube* which featured some happening musical act each week. I watched it faithfully, feeling so apart from what had been my every day.

The scene on *The Tube* looked good and I was jealous as hell, even though it was not what I wanted. It was a kind of Big in Japan jealousy, insofar as I didn't actually like the acts or the presenters, but I liked what it represented, which was dancing and being obnoxious in a Paula Yates "piss all over you" sort of way. But I knew that the cool I wished for was a falsehood anyway. Now it was a time of Jo-Boxers in their '30s boy-gangster-hat-on-sideways soul and Jimmy the Hoover's Venusian New-Age electro-skank.

But my mind was blown by the glam brilliance of Freur. This unfathomable bunch refused to take a name for their group, preferring a spirally squiggle like some kind of occult worm. Freur appeared on *The Tube* in electric blue outfits and space-perms to perform their magnificent 'Doot-Doot'. Dorian hated the song and reckoned that I only liked it so much because, like many of my own songs, the chorus kicked in with the words "And we go . . ." With me it was mainly "Ba-ba-ba". With Freur, they ended up going "Doot, doot-doot". Magnificent. Their drum-machine-led ensemble posed and pouted as early-Dalek I Love You music met beautiful choral vocals straight out of *The Yes Album*! Fucking Hell! The references were so left field that I could enjoy it without conceding the dubious similarities. And all of Freur's vibe was perched upon a designer bed of electric-blue early-Roxyness.

Oh, how high TV could make me at this time! I would sit for hours in our all-black TV room with its gleaming hand-made video sleeves on the shelves. I was removed from the TV world and an ocean away by now. With TV out of my life for so long, I liked it again as entertainment. Videos were so new that they pervaded my dreams. Again and again, I dreamed that I was walking on the once-undeveloped land around Glascote Heath, whereupon I would come across racks and racks of unattended videos just begging to be ripped off and hoarded by one such as me. But these dreams also scared me a little, for it was not since I had been a schoolboy that such obsessions had crowded into my dreams. Dreaming of videos! Get a grip. . .

Suddenly I was still further embarrassed about a memory of myself aged 12 when, as a Moody Blues fan, I had dreamed that I found the great lost Moodies album in similarly bucolic circumstances. In the dream, this 12-year-old Justin Hayward fan had sat studying the cover of the LP until it finally hit the run-out groove, at which point the dream began to mist up and I felt myself struggling to keep a hold of the magnificent and Blakean gatefold sleeve. And now I was dreaming of free videos in fields.

FEELS LIKE A CRYING SHAME

One night, I began the first of a series of terrifying recurring dreams. As if to remind myself of my lack of control over my previous situation, I continually dreamed that I was back in the Teardrop jeep, transformed in the dreams to a telescopic cherry picker whose hydraulic backseat always grew like a beanstalk into the sky as we zoomed through Monmouthshire country lanes of Rockfield proportions. Again, Alan Gill, Dave Balfe and Gary Dwyer were hundreds of feet below me, driving like cackling lunatics as I clung to my seat high in the air, screaming at them to keep away from pylons and low bridges, truly dread at the controls, and always in this configuration.

I knew that it had to be Alan Gill who was the secret ingredient. He had been the unique and moustachioed magician. Like Peter Hook's beard in Joy Division, Alan Gill's moustache had been accepted through sheer force of character and indifference to ridicule. That unbalanced line-up of the Teardrop was the closest to a mission by the Scandinavian gods as any rock'n'roll group had come, and my seemingly endless recurring dreams of shamanic soaring over the countryside at the hands of Balfe, Dwyer and Gill reminded me of my need for cohorts of some kind. Any kind. Please.

It was the dwarves who helped Odin out best, the elementals who were at too much peace within themselves to become monsters. I needed elementals around me to win again. It was time to record the album.

We were going to do it cheap and quick as hell. I had 10 songs and 10 days to finish the lot. I told Paul King not to expect a record that would compete with other contemporaries because I knew I just couldn't do that. I said that I felt I had two albums in me that were really just back catalogue – the term "back catalogue" was my most frequently used phrase. I just had to get them out of the way – nobody's listening anymore anyway.

Paul was fine about it, so long as I held to the plan. If I didn't learn anything, then I should forget the whole thing. And so we started the record.

WORLD SHUT YOUR MOUTH

His sticks were still clattering across the polished wood floor as Gary Dwyer stormed out of the studio. It had been a great take, but we thought there was a better one coming.

"It's no good, man. He's gone," gasped Steve Lovell, still breathless from the pursuit.

The backing tracks all sounded great. The only problem was keeping Gary in the studio. He freaked out badly at anything that required concentration and couldn't even play his parts on some songs.

We were recording in London, at the Point, a studio by Victoria station. The schedule was very heavy, but the pressure helped us make better decisions. We finished the backing tracks in two days, except for a song called 'Lunatic & Fire-Pistol', which had been overlooked during the Gary freak out. Steve Lovell tried to put the drums on, but his fills were leaden.

We kept everything as live as possible and I added shitloads of Gibson electric 12-string guitar on top. I had stuck the little painted Casio organ through my old Vox AC30 amplifier; it was reedy and thin and I loved it. The Casio MT40 had become so central to my songwriting that one song, 'Kolly Kibber's Birthday', was built entirely around the bass-drumfill and gaffer-taped C notes of the "accordion" setting. The song had come together simply by jamming endless guitar chords and exploring every possible harmonic move over the pulsating drone. All the songs came together except one called 'Wreck My Car', which I'd had high hopes for. But we kept to the schedule and I had my ass in gear all the time. Professional. Take that, Jake Riviera.

Troy Tate turned up. I hadn't seen him in months. He was so excited, almost foaming at the mouth. He called everyone "Baby" and said he was producing the next big thing, ho-hum. The day a group called The Smiths does anything at all is the day life's lava lamp spills over the hash cookies, I thought to myself. Even to Troy's face I was polite but doubtful, as Troy could get worked up about a fly in your sink.

But no-one else came down to see me. It wasn't like the Teardrop recordings with the inevitable entourage. Actually, Troy came down one more time about three weeks later. The main Smith had sacked him for spending too much time on the guitarist. Fuck 'em, man. Gives you more time to do The Railway Children.

I wanted to call the album *World Shut Your Mouth*. A guy called Andy Courtenay had used the phrase to describe the early Liverpool scene. I thought it was classic. Especially as everyone had forgotten about me. I was a voice crying out in the desert . . . Hey, in The Teardrop Explodes I was a voice in a desert. Now? I was humming the *Robinson Crusoe* theme and living in *Belle & Sebastian*. I was Noggin the Nog in my own halfway house halfway between Liverpool and London, between post-punk and absolution.

Many of the songs had been around for ages, but I rewrote at least half of them to accommodate my new-found blissful streams of experience. I piled lyrics in, stuffing them into any spare part of song. If an instrumental passage was too long, I stuck a refrain in. I only had *one* thing to say throughout the entire album. But I wanted to say that one thing over and over. Like the ever-ascending shut-that-man-up-somebody vocal excesses of 'Passionate Friend', this first Cope LP pasted any extra vocal asides it could over guitar riffs, keyboard sections, oboe incidents – hey, this Possible Future Taxi Driver was not going to get to 1990 and say, "Oh, I wish I'd put that bit in."

Dave Bates didn't give a shit about the album. He thought it was crap and I was crazy. His boss, Chris Briggs, didn't like it, but, as he didn't think it was crap, he became my A&R man. But no-one really cared. Without the weight of the Teardrop name I meant sod all. And no-one was interested in this guy making the cheap album as, by that time, I'd eroded the sympathy of my allies and confirmed the suspicions of my detractors.

People tend to imagine that an artist with a record contract is highly regarded by his entire record company. This is almost never the case. And sometimes you can hang around for years, waiting for the one guy who likes you to leave. Anyway, it was the summer of 1983 and Polygram Corporation had a lot of hits without me. They told me that I needed two more songs and they weren't in a hurry.

On the last day of that main recording session, a young friend of the tape op added the tailout drums to 'Lunatic & Fire-Pistol'. His name was Andrew Edge – just like Graeme Edge from The Moody Blues. Ha ha ha ha ha! Awlright! The main reason I'd been a huge fan of The Moody Blues when I was 12 was because Justin Hayward was the only singer tidy enough to make it past my mother's obsessively scrutinising eye. My first introduction to psychedelia had not been via the Barrett Floyd nor even the Beatles (whom I then considered to be Past-its-Shelf-life Laminated-in-Clarifoil-by-Garrod & Lofthouse dad rock kack). No. No. The real thing for me had been the proto-'70s artwork of Phil Travers' monumental sleeves for *On the Threshold of a Dream* and *In Search of the Lost Chord*. And Mike Pinder's 'The Best Way to Travel' was still the trippiest lost psychedelic trance song since Bill Wyman's Barrett-y 'In Another Land' from the Stones' disastrous *Satanic Majesties Request*.

Hmm. The Moody Blues thing got me thinking. At the end of the John Peel session of this same 'Lunatic & Fire-Pistol' song, Peel had asked over the radio: "Is that a Mellotron?" It was another Midland Man Moody Blues connection.

Now I'll have to go back and hang out for a while. Yeah, it's best to spend a little time getting these final songs right. Hmm . . . yes, yes. I've got an attitude and it's the right attitude.

And so we went home. Tears for Fears were big, so why should I bust my balls? Would Phonogram ever release this solo album or were they punishing me for splitting such a successful act? Ha ha ha ha ha ha ha ha ha ha.

The questions were seemingly eternal headtrips, but in Tamworth the sensible panoramic questions soon disappeared as I returned quickly to the vat of drugged wine that was my real life. The strong attitude that always pervaded when I was in London, surrounded by people who needed answers, left me as soon as I boarded the train at Euston station.

I could not maintain a clear head.

I could only reflect. And theorise.

Less than one year before, my world had been enormous. I could go wherever I chose. I'd been pulled screaming and kicking around the globe. But now my world was shrunken and deflated. *Tamworth* was my world. In a tiny house, spending my days with toys, I'd left the seething masses outside and found myself a new and fascinating land in which to focus my obsessions. I had taken a dive from enormous macrocosm to tiny microcosm, a huge and breathtaking 35,000-feet leap out of a plane and into a glass of water. These enormous metaphysical images pervaded my life.

And this new stage made little sense to me. I needed to give it reason. If I could not give it that reason, then there was no use staying around.

It also occurred to me that my situation was becoming increasingly like some metaphysical poem by John Donne or Andrew Marvell. I felt as though fate had left me at the corner of the world and was still deciding what to do with me. Metaphysical poetry is like pre-psychedelia. It takes the mundane and puts it on a pedestal. And I badly needed some kind of pedestal, no matter how much of it was my own making.

The days were gradually worn down by my routines, until each one lost its own individuality. Sometimes weeks passed without any day presenting itself to me as requiring special attention. In fact, whenever a special day did occur, I would do all in my power to make it normal and unspecified. A business day in London? I just ignored it. Visitors at the front door? Ignore them . . . Inspiration is everything in these situations. And so it became difficult to do anything. Why haul yourself over hot coals when you can stay inert in Zone 1?

So when the top floor toilet began to spill shit out of the overflow which then had to drop 25 feet before splatting onto the centre of our backyard, I ignored it. When Dorian hassled me about walking through shit, I cleaned the shit up occasionally and ignored the problem. I couldn't bear the idea of calling a plumber, or having a plumber round the house, so I told my father that the plumber was coming soon and ignored it.

THE ALVECOTE MOUND

Did you ever get the feeling when someone was telling you something that you intuitively knew already – and were really just being reminded?

Well, this was the place that I began to inhabit. It was a sort of sub-basement Gollum existence, but with a remarkably strong and upright backbone. Because, way down some obscure corridor in my soul, my own sense of uniqueness still remained powerfully intact. My eyes might have rolled back up into my head occasionally, but I decided that I should deal with the decay of my existence in my own way. I had seen examples of society's idea of good and bad. And I didn't like it at all. I was going to redefine what Good was – and BE it. It was all decided, then. I would escape the evil in my own way. I would never run to religion to solve my problems. And I could not bear to hide in the twilight half world of new cults like EST and Dianetics.

Joss was back from university. We would visit the Mound at Alvecote regularly. I held it dear to my heart in the same way that I cherished my childhood toys. It stood for innocence and peace, a time before I had knowledge.

I was growing to hate knowledge. Ha. What use is information if you don't learn from it? Information just fills up your brain like fast food fills up your stomach. Then it lies there and you're full, so it feels good, like you've achieved something. And I'd eaten so much fast food so quickly in these last years that I'd not even begun to digest it.

Of course, my brain was just too full of news and cultural information to let the mystic ever truly settle. I'd get angry with myself without giving my underground self a fighting chance. My cynical side wanted instant results to prove that it was worth going on – cynics are not world weary, quite the opposite. They are unformed humans who have prejudged situations before their actual experience takes place. They therefore don't actually experience it at all, just a fax of what they'd presupposed it would be like. I was like a *Sun* reporter who doesn't actually bother going round to see for himself, because he thinks he knows what the scene will be like in advance. I was cynical and presupposing, I suppose. Cynicism is not over-experience – it blots out actual experience. It is really closed-mindedness through the lack of genuine "experience", for we can touch the mystic in so many humdrum ways. Music easily. A view of an attractive unfamiliar member of the opposite sex. The smell of seasonal food out of season. It is always simple stuff like this which the cynic draws a veil over as being beyond what he considers worthy of "experience". Like rock'n'roll journalists who review their favourite albums for CD release, but can no longer summon up any enthusiasm, the cynic gets angry at the world for not being what he presupposed it was, which was based on too little information in the first place. And that was me.

And so, on top of the Alvecote Mound, I began a period of debriefing. Sometimes, the visits would last for hours as we stood unspeaking in the blackness and the wind. Despite its utter remoteness, there was nothing scary about that place. Even on an average night, though the nearest road was close to a mile away, it was easy to see the lights of Polesworth and those of Shuttington, Amington and Glascote Heath, where my parents lived.

The Mound was my Anglo-Saxon burial place. For me, it had the romance of Rainbarrow, that enormous tract of land in Thomas Hardy's *Return of the Native*. Ha. And better than that, the Mound was nothing. Really just a slag heap, barely 50 years old. I liked that. It was only special because I said so. Because I had decided. It was no church built by forgotten men. And there were no Sundays written in my calendar, no forced confessions once a week. I was the calendar; the Julian Calendar.

When I had first met Dorian in New York, she had asked if my real name was Julian Cope. She and her friends had thought it was a stage name. Now, I felt that I'd been given the name for a reason. I had to fight. I had to battle. And I had to cope. As the dictionary so succinctly told me, I was here "to handle a situation" and "to contend (against)" all that would be thrown at me. Dang.

Joss and I wandered around the Shuttington and Amington area at night, seething with adventure and Midland low-cunning. Our rush was standing tripping on the great Curve of the London–Liverpool line, beside the Alvecote Mound, and watching the lights of the express approaching from two miles away until they came crashing towards us, seemingly to crush our bones into splinters, only for the train to be four feet away and utterly safe. Joss loved to rearrange street furniture, putting road signs in the middle of humpback bridges and getting creative with traffic-cones. Beside the Alvecote Mound, we would lurk for hours beside the still pools of icy water and emerge from that zone in a feral state, dancing on the car-roofs of courting couples like weirdos without any brains.

DAVID BAILEY IS A VIDEO DIRECTOR NOW

At last we could finish the album. I had three more songs to record. Two of them were pretty old, but the final one I had just written. It was called 'Sunshine Playroom' and required the kind of drumming that was beyond Gary Dwyer. By this time, in any case, Gary was weird beyond words. I loved him dearly, but now it was time to move on. It was a mercenary attitude, but I wanted only to work with people who had their act together. I figured that some of it might rub off on me.

'Sunshine Playroom' is a ridiculous song. One day, I had started to sing along to the dumbest rhythm on my Casio MT40's drum machine the same lyric over and over:

"The sun in her hair, the sun in her eyes,
There's something that makes me want to go back."

Dorian and I laughed at it, and I always sung it in my Elvis voice, wobbling and sneering all over the place. Then it started to become a real song. I don't know how . . . it just kind of made sense. We laughed at it when we recorded it in Mickey Most's big RAK studio. We spent hours over the disco bass and roto-tom barrage of drum fills, and then laughed some more. But most of all, we had the biggest entertainment when Paul Buckmaster put the string arrangement on it. The guy was a lunatic. Professional, though.

I'd had these ideas for hellish harpy-like violins. He said he liked that idea, but "really Julian, I see it more like" and he made a violent and dramatic "V" shape in the air with his elbows. "Fine," I said. "Get *that* on tape." Then he came into the studio with a 24-piece string section, a 20-piece brass section, a young leather-clad boyfriend of about 25 and an enormously tall Japanese transvestite who was ugly-beautiful. I felt like a guest at my own session.

The arrangement of the song was still a mess, but it had somehow become my first solo single by general consensus. I don't know how it happened, but the finished version was disappointing as hell. The strings were shit, the arrangement was wrong and my performance never even got started. In trying not to let it get all slack and 'MacArthur Park'-ish, we arranged the originality out of it and sectioned it up too quickly for its organic good. Oh, who knows? I had this idea and it didn't happen right. Though 'Sunshine Playroom' was totally unrepresentative of me, that fact somehow appealed to my state of mind. I had a chance to confound again.

Then Bates got Bill Drummond and Dave Balfe in to remix it without asking me. Shine my fucking K.N.O.B.!!! Could you have shown your lack of faith in me to any worser enemas, Bates? I nicked one of Bates' poncy self-promo photos from his office and took it home. In order to psychically weaken Bates, I kept the photo sandwiched between multiple copies of Tears for Fears' latest abominable single, 'The Way You Are'.

Someone got David Bailey to do the video. Hey, I'm going to have a hit. Actually, David Bailey had decided that it was the '80s, so he must now be a video director, so Polygram gave him me to practise on first time. Weirdo Pop Singer, career on the skids = do what you want for £20,000.

It was not a great meeting. I brought Dorian along and David Bailey said he was surprised I wasn't a faggot and told me that the song was a desire to return to my mother's womb. Hmm . . . I hadn't thought about that. It threw me a bit, as I was on a strict psychological diet: sorry, no song analysis. Most of my contemporaries seemed to be looking too much up their own asses as it was. But I thought he could be right about the mother's womb thing and that gave him leverage enough to make me trust him.

But the video went the same way as the recording. Our Dave had just divorced Marie Helvin and married his new muse, whom he intended to get in all over the place. She had the starring role in my video and, once more, I felt like a guest. Unfortunately, what with the nicked bits of *Battleship Potemkin* and the Hammer Horror blood effects, La Bailey made the whole thing so violent that no-one would show it. So then he had to cut out the parts where I bleed, then the parts where the woman's baby dies in her pram, then the bit when my "mother figure" (his wife) ages in front of me. Finally all that was left was a piece of fluff with me singing.

Please don't show the video, I'll be a (bigger) laughing stock.

RELAX

Luckily for me, the video was "banned", though by whom I can't be sure to this day.[1] This instantly created a vibe, which caused the song to rocket up the charts . . . or rather, that's what I thought would happen.

Unfortunately, my old friends Holly Johnson and Paul Rutherford had a banned video out at the same time. And, more unfortunately for me, the song was no cobbled together letdown, it was fucking genius. Like 'Reward', Frankie Goes to Hollywood's 'Relax' hovered around the lower charts for weeks before

---

1 Perhaps Polygram didn't even bother taking it to TV, because they already knew that it was unusable. Devoid of its pantomime gore and evocative black-and-white footage, the "sanitised" video was the most boring film ever made and I even banned its release on a video compilation several years later.

it took its rightful stellar place. In the meantime, 'Sunshine Playroom' came out with a beautiful picture of Dorian on the front and it visited the charts for one week at no. 76. Worse than my worst fears.

I was expecting around 25% or so of Teardrop fans to stay loyal to me, but this proved to have been a huge inflated delusion. It was a brutal way to discover I had been forgotten. From speaking my ideas into records which had been blasted around over 200,000 British homes on *Kilimanjaro*, I was now virtually without a voice. I'd been clucking on and on for so long about how nobody loved me anymore that it had become merely a mantra – and I now despaired to discover that it was a reality which manifested itself in embarrassingly low sales figures.

Walking down South Moulton Street, in the West End, I happened to stare into a shop where Paul Rutherford was standing admiring himself in a new coat. Whoa, I was delighted to see him. I rushed round to the front door and ran right up to him. "Paul! Frankie's a hit! Yes!!! It's so good to see you! How're you doing?"

Paul, in all his ostentatious Paulness (which was a very beautiful thing), flung out his hands silently and luxuriously smoothed each lapel simultaneously with his fingers and thumbs. That was it, what more do you say? Paul + wealth = happiness. Oh, to be so fucking thick.

But I enjoyed the rest of the album recording, which was at Amazon Studios in Liverpool. We got a young guy called Steve Crease in to play drums and Ronnie François came up to play bass. It was fun, real fun. We all stayed at the New Manx Hotel again, and Jim hung out with us and, for a while, I could pretend it was a group.

We were recording an old Teardrop song, a slow funk thang called 'Pussyface' and there's a cool bit in the middle where everything breaks down and I scream:

"a-Take you to the top of the next victory
Oh I scream like Sky Saxon & The Seeds, but it's history."

Anyway, during the vocal take, I was sitting on a stool and squirming all over the place and the whole thing sounded great till it came to this one bit. I squirmed so much that I fell backwards off the stool as I screamed. When I listened back to it, it was brilliant. Steve Lovell had pushed the volume way up to make it clearer. I began to think I had a really cool album within my grasp. Some of the songs were disappointing, but it was much better than I had expected. At least it didn't sound like other people's records; that's all that interested me.

When Phonogram Records said the album could not come out until the late spring, I was totally pissed off and told them so. They wouldn't listen and didn't seem to care. I understood completely. If I was the managing director of some huge company, I'd have dumped me straight away. I was a total pain in the ass. But I had to be. I was born to take the piss. I couldn't acquiesce. Not at any time. And even though I had no mental capacity for it, I still, secretly, wanted to be a big star. I did not want to be some kind of cult figure. Cult figures suck shit. Even the best ones become enmeshed in the smugness of their own kiss-ass circle of friends and like-minds. The bad ones are 10,000,000 times worse. They actually set out to become cult figures – no more, no less. Well fuck that shit. And fuck all the shit in my yard.

But much of this mouthing-off was utter bravado. I knew that the record was going to have to search long and hard for its audience, and that, faced with oblivion, I'd acquiesce and take cultiness any day.

Who was I fooling anyway? The *World Shut Your Mouth* album jacket was ultra culty. Anton Corbijn photographed me, head bowed, at Alvecote Priory at 5.30 in the morning. Dorian, Mick Houghton, Anton, Joss and I had partied away until 3 a.m. so my face was puffed out and grey by the time the sun came up. Anton was only able to develop five worthy black-and-white shots; they were the only ones from the entire photo session that were considered acceptable to print.

There was a Tom Lehrer lyric that became my axiom: "Plagiarise, plagiarise, let no-one else's work evade your eyes." Tom had meant it humorously, of course, but, like Chip Taylor before me, I decided to take it seriously. From now on, it was alright to rip something off as long as I was not the first person to do it. The first person is the originator. The second person is the rip-off. The third person is just taking an established style. If George Harrison copies 'He's So Fine' for 'My Sweet Lord', which writer's gonna sue me when I write 'She's My Lord' with the same melody over the same chord sequence?

Soon after the album was ready, I wrote a new song. I had been jamming 'Louie Louie" on the guitar. I started to sing 'Get Off of My Cloud' over the same chords, then 'Hang on, Sloopy'. Then, out of nowhere, I sang:

"World shut your mouth, shut your mouth
Put your head back in the clouds and shut your mouth."

It sounded great. Why had I had that title for so long, but never written the song? It was so easy, it was stupid. Also, I could put it on my next album. I'd always loved the way The Doors' song 'Waiting for the Sun' had appeared two LPs after the album of that title. Same with Zep's 'Houses of the Holy'. How me.

And so I began to build up my new set of parameters, outside the Dante's Infernos of London and Liverpool. And around those two cities, great big psychological Exclusion Zones started to build in my mind. I could *never* be a part of them again.

I welcomed my exile. But I also resented it like crazy. Those bastards won't let me in, I thought, knowing that it was my own decision. I was a hermit living in the hills. It was a great and romantic self-denial trip. Ha ha.

I stayed in the house. I would be even more selective with visitors than before. I couldn't be seen by just *any*one. I felt like Alexander Pope in his poem 'Epistle to Dr. Arbuthnot':

"Shut, shut the door, good John,
Fatigued I said,
Tie up the knocker,
Say I'm sick, I'm dead,
The dog-star rages, nay, 'tis past a doubt,
All Bedlam and Parnassus is let out."

COMPLETE MADNESS

At first, my remove from the rest of my contemporaries seemed to be a singularly good thing. But, like my guru-ifying of crew members and certain shocked fans, my Teardrop slide from Martin Luther of Punk to heathen dandy had more to do with my natural celebration of the moment than any true fall into believing my own mythology. Hanging around with Mac had proven that, for it was he who had instigated the song 'B. Smith or Be Dead'. If Mac and his Grand Ennui could get worked up about some 16-year-old Tamworth punk, then I was not so riddled with grand mythological thoughts as I was often led to believe.

Dorian and I bought a video version of *Complete Madness*, Madness's greatest hits. Whoa, it was the greatest film ever and Madness were revealed at the best TV group since The Monkees. I thought that I had grown used to these videos, as they were regulars on all the pop and children's TV shows. But here, together in one package, the videos screamed out the genius of Madness. And even though there had been a strong Teardrop/Madness axis brought on through Clive Langer and the Balfe/Dwyer/Chas Smash link, those connections went off to the moon as soon as I watched *Complete Madness*. Now Madness were my new gods! Unbelievable individuals – I had a huge crush on them all. Dorian and I sat drooling over the video in the black room, my head doing endless reviews of each single, here encapsulated with exquisite thoroughness. I knew that there would never be better videos made than this.

Every member of Madness was a star, yet individual enough to take the lead whenever his time came. Between each video, every Madness member introduced the songs in his own inimitable way, and the idea that The Teardrop Explodes had been just me became more and more apparent. Chas Smash was good enough visually to be the leader of any group, appearing as a mysterious shadowy will o'the wisp character in their film for 'Grey Day' and causing me to rewind constantly to pick up on certain faces which he pulled. Chas' character seemed at war with himself and I felt a huge affinity for him. On 'Cardiac Arrest', Chas aped the final scenes of "Dr Zsivago", where Omaha Sheriff has a heart attack at the end, gasping for air and frantically trying to undo his tie. There was a magnificent moment in which all the members of Madness, dressed as workmen, sing soothingly to him from their fenced-off side of the street. The very last frame caught Chas' eyes as they looked directly into the camera and I would stare at the snapshot with happiness, rewinding over and over.

Suggs' genius came from his egolessness in bringing the characters of the songs to life. He mainly appeared as a sharply-dressed observer bemused by the songs and the characters within those songs. Shots of him roaring with laughter at the antics of Madness' flying sax player, Lee Thompson, or re-enacting a scene from some archetypal '60s series so endeared him to me that his facial expressions became a daily fix which I had to have. The bit in 'House of Fun' where Lee and Chas dress as old dears dancing in pinnies was rewound endlessly, as was Mike Barson's manic policeman at the beginning of 'Shut Up', where his piano falls out of the sky. Then there was the part where the impish Bedders bends down to get into the shot at the end of the chaotic 'Night Boat to Cairo', the fabulous Madness train-walk in all its versions and the weird light which pervaded the whole of the 'Embarrassment' video. Even the play dough faces of Madness' skinhead friends warmed the entire compilation and it all seemed hugely at odds with the po-faced Liverpool scene from which I had so recently fled.

THE MONKEES ARE MY FRIENDS

When Joss handed me 50 magic mushrooms for a trip, I told him in no uncertain terms that by my own incredibly high standards of excess, this was not nearly enough. Then we all retired to the black room for an evening of videos and hanging out.

These past couple of days, I had been working on a compilation of Monkees', Three Stooges' and Munsters' videos. With Letraset and my own felt pens, I was creating an artefact of retro-chemical power. Ha, I was no longer lead singer in a band. People could commission me to make harmoniously correct video compilations. A money-making scheme.

The 50 mushrooms which shouldn't have cabbaged a field-mouse began to insinuate themselves into my system, but around me things had got out of hand. Whilst Joss had been roaming around the third floor with his American girlfriend, Dawn, Dorian had suddenly become alarmingly off her head. It had happened when she spilt her low-cal ginger ale. The fizz and the foaming of the carpet had convinced her of one thing only – she had pissed herself.

Now she was crying and wailing like a three year old, tears running rivers through her eye make-up and her hair soaking wet and drooping over her face. I looked at her Gone Out. Man, she just looked gorgeous. I hugged her and tried to reason with her. She hadn't pissed herself; only she could feel it and smell it. But by now I had also become highly afflicted and I really made no sense at all as I stood in the doorway and looked down at this tearful figure on the floor. Then, she looked at the TV screen and smiled. The tears disappeared and she began to laugh. It was The Monkees! Now she was delighted.

"The Monkees are my friends. The Monkees are my friends."

Dorian looked up at me to share this joy. Then she immediately burst into tears again. Quickly, she turned back to the TV screen and The Monkees. She laughed and grinned her head off once more, chanting, "The Monkees are my friends, The Monkees are my friends."

This continued for quite a while. She'd look away from the screen and start crying, and only The Monkees could help her. Soon she was scared of being stuck watching The Monkees forever. Finally, Joss and Dawn could stand no more. They had to get out of here right now.

Once we were alone, the whole scene started to get very sexual and Dorian's autistic teenager qualities made me terrifically horny. We started to get it on in a big ass way, the mushrooms intensifying everything out of proportion. It was like the docking of two spacecraft ... time slowing down and down until we were locked in a metaphysical struggle. There was a knock on the back door.

JULIAN: *(curling into a tight ball)* "Who the hell is that?"
DORIAN: "It can't be Joss and Dawn; they've got a key."
JULIAN: "Shit. Who is it?"
(I sat on the bed, but the knocking continued, so I walked slowly downstairs, stopping twice to listen. As I got into the kitchen, Dorian switched the stair light off and I was in darkness.)
JULIAN: *(exasperated)* "Dorian, put the light back on."
DORIAN: *(crying, but almost laughing)* "Don't yell."
JULIAN: *(yelling)* "They'll think we're in."
DORIAN: *(laughing, but almost crying)* "But we *are* in." *(Switches light on again.)*
JULIAN: *(resigned, almost whispering)* "I'm going to the back door to see."
(From upstairs, Dorian switched the light on again. Then off. I walked to the back door and saw a shadowy figure.)
JULIAN: "Who's that?"

SHADOW: "It's Paul. You don't know me."
JULIAN: "Go away."
SHADOW: "It's Paul. Paul Gilligan."
JULIAN: "Go away."
SHADOW: "I've got some acid for you."
(I froze. I couldn't move. I knew that name . . . Joss had mentioned him
  before. He had acid for us? Why? We already had some.)
JULIAN: "Why? We've already got some . . . *(yelling again)* No! *(to no answer)*
  We're already tripping, so go away."

Upstairs, I shook Dorian and told her we must straighten out immediately. No
more of this. We're going crazy and we're attracting weirdos and it has to stop.
Now.

We sat in silence downstairs, drinking huge glasses of orange juice to bring
us down. That was it. No more. Then I remembered. Urgh! He was in our back
garden, so that guy would be knee deep in shit!

OF MODS AND MODIFICATIONS

"Let in thunder, let it whistle, let it blow like hell, I'm not really caring,
And my state of mind needs no repairing."

Alan Hull, 'United States of Mind'

As the winter trudged on, I was lost and forgotten in the depths of Tamworth.
It was over two years since *Wilder*, my last released album. I watched TV as
my more together contemporaries forged ahead with their "careers". It was so
depressing.

The Tube on Channel 4 was still the only music show I could watch. And
this week, when I switched on halfway through, they had some geek doing a
terrible version of Joy Division's 'Love Will Tear Us Apart'. There were these
awful '70s girl backing singers doing shit with their hands and making goo-goo
eyes. And people seemed to lap it right up. Oh, it's all too depressing to think
about, I can never be a part of this. Not even if I wanted to be. I watched in
a mixture of amazement and grief, lamenting the passing of cool music. Uh?
What? No, no, it can't be. . .

It was Paul Young. That singer on TV was Paul Young. Well, bloody hell.
He'd been the singer in a group called Streetband, a '70s one-hit wonder with
a song called 'Toast'. Now, he was aligning himself with the legendary and

shamanic dead Ian, and getting applause for it on *The Tube*. Its intolerable shallowness was all too much to even think about.

The nicer the music scene became, the more fucked up Dorian and I became. The only records on our turntable were either barely audible Skip Spence/Ed Askew/*Pink Moon* meets *Happy Sad* ambulance chasers or rampant frenzied pre-1970 guitar bands. I only liked over-achieving failures now. Utopian '70s music also grabbed me entirely by the poo-poo, such as early Roxy Music and most Krautrock. Futuristic sci-fi glam, such as Todd Rundgren's *A Wizard, A True Star*, Magma's *Mekanik Destruktiw Kommandoh* and, of course, the *Clockwork Orange* soundtrack also held a special place in my heart. But I became especially obsessed with The Misunderstood, a late-'60s Californian group whom John Peel had loudly championed, but who had subsequently been royally fucked up by circumstances. Their music was gut-wrenching and heavenly, so wired and inspired one moment, the next mantra-like and caught in the spell of walls of wah-wah and beatless cooing. In the words of the immortal Fred "Sonic" Smith, they were "forward-thinking motherfuckers".

I'd found a 1960s Elka organ with the words "United States of Mind" written in Dynotape across the top. I was amazed because these words came from an obscure Alan Hull solo LP from the mid '70s which I'd always cared about. The record itself was average but the double-LP sleeve had captivated me. It featured all of his friends and relatives and really cute nippers.

Joss and I formed a duo called The United States of Mind, after my Elka sticker, and recorded at Steve Adams' studio. It sounded mysterious even though we'd recorded the first song I had ever written, a song called 'Where do we go from here?' Joss and I turned it into a Casio psyche-out with Joss's arch lead vocals and unnecessarily Peter Hammillish vocal asides.

Pre-hippy, that was really my bag. But most of all pre-Manson and Altamont. I gave music a break if it had been recorded before this time, for I felt that it had at least been recorded in a Utopian headspace, or surrounded by a time of hope and of possibilities. I wanted to fill myself up from the gasoline tanks of the golden ages and rededicate myself to Real Good.

By this time the house had become a fortress. In my paranoia, I had moved furniture and bedding against the front window. I would ask Dorian's permission, but she never complained, knowing only too well that my hang ups needed to be temporarily assuaged. It was an essential psychological act. Even though we never opened that front door under any circumstances, my eyes needed proof of its impregnability every time I entered the room.

We were only nine feet from the road and only four feet from any fans who may have been staying in the garden waiting for a glimpse of me. That there never were fans in the garden anymore was hardly the point – such people clearly only ever leave temporarily, I fretted, so I had to be ready when they made their annoying and inevitable return.

The third floor was now our home. All the walls had been knocked out to leave one large room spanning the whole length of the house. Of course, I'd had no idea how to go about it, so my father organised the whole thing. His builder friend, Sid Woodward, turned it from three crappy little rooms into one long studio flat. When it was finished, we painted the en suite bathroom gloss red and sat looking out over the car park towards Ankerside and my beloved Anker Video. Hey, I even had a view into the rear of Tamworth Glass & Glazing, where I'd worked as a 17 year old. Awlright!

Vince Watts came around more and more, but I wouldn't let him in and always insisted on conducting our conversations through a sensibly paranoid slit in the door as his ultra-tall Kid Strange-like figure danced wall-eyed and Odinesque on the pavement outside. He had split up DHSS and was after a solo deal. One time he asked me if I could help him and I slammed the door, almost as a conditioned reflex, and apologised through our postbox. I told him his manner weirded me out.

Vince had taken to stripping in unusual places. One time, he was at the Castle Grounds and he saw some girls so he stripped. The authorities didn't realise he was anything more than a creep and fined him. But it was the beginning of a heavy Vince adventure, which often ended in a striptease for the poor staff of Anker Video. This was way too close for my liking – hell, the weirdos of Liverpool and London were supposed to have been kicked far into touch, and here's dear Vincent, keckless and unafraid.

Mark Mortimer was around all the time. This little Mod was a confirmed friend. I envied him and his mates, they seemed to have a simple unthreatened existence. Then one day his parents kicked him out and we said he could stay at ours! I couldn't believe I said it. Someone in our house overnight? Still, we chilled him out and gave him breakfast and I felt good about it, like an uncle or something. I was good at worrying about others. It just seemed to be my own life which was too weird to think about.

My brain still formulated alternative plans in case of an emergency. I was not completely convinced that I could stay in music. There were just too many factors – and I had a moral duty to keep away if I couldn't control the evil in me.

I suggested to Dorian that I could drive a taxi. I could handle that idea as a rock'n'roll concept – Tim Buckley had done it when he lost his Elektra recording deal. Of course, I'd be doing it in tame Tamworth, not La-la in Lost Angeles. Hmm . . . I didn't know how to drive. But I was thinking mythologically, and that was the main point.

But my big obsession was oil rigs. I was going to work in the North Sea for six months, bring home shitloads of money and rest for the next six. Then start the process all over again. It even made sound financial sense.

But then something happened which changed my mind.

NIGEL SIMPKINS

I was in London for a meeting at Phonogram Records. No-one really knew what should be done with me. The record company attitude was one of "humour him and maybe something will happen". It had got so that I could suggest quite reasonable things, only to receive a reaction of horror and repulsion. The more I suggested, the more they humoured me. They had decided that I was weird and that was that. "The press write that he's weird. He can't speak anymore. Apparently, Paul King gives him downers when he's at the record company to stop him wrecking the place . . ." Those kind of stories stuck. It had addled my brain just enough for everyone to think that it was irreversible.

All except one guy, that is.

His name was Cally Callomon and he had just become a product manager at Phonogram. I met him in Dave Bates' office and we talked and talked and talked. Shit, this guy was great. He knew everything I was into and treated me like a rational human being.

Of course, I responded with great style. How could I act weird with this guy? We communicated with the kind of vibration normally reserved for lovers and Dorian said she felt totally left out of the conversation. But Cally Callomon had a punk pedigree, an experimental pedigree, a Krautrock pedigree, the lot. He knew his music because he had lived it. For fuck's sake – this man *was* Nigel Simpkins.

Nigel Simpkins had released the first ever sampling record in 1978, to tremendous applause from the underground scene. 'Time's Encounter' had taken a drum demonstration record and added snippets of every hip record in the world to its Krautrock stew. Neu! Can, Stockhausen, SAHB, Amon Duul 2, Meryl Fankauser, Dr. Z, Soeur Sourire, Metal Urbain, Doctors of Madness, Runaways, Residents, George Harrison's *Wonderwall Music*, Pierre Henry, Charles Ives, Dashiell Hedayat's *Obsolete*, Hymie *Kangaroo* Downstein's classic Australian glam album *Forgotten Starboy*, it was all on that record, even Godley & Cream's *Consequences* and the T. Dream freak out from *Sci-Finance*, where Lulu first finds the guy's hand on the hot beach. The sleeve featured "Nigel" as a guy with *Madcap Laughs*-period Syd Barrett hair, wearing seven pairs of shades at the same time – it was an image that Robyn Hitchcock would copy a year or so later.

'Time's Encounter' had sold truckloads and never been off the John Peel show, though Cally treated it as an inspired joke at best. What? Throbbing Gristle had cited it as one of the most forward-looking 45s of its time and everybody had run to cop some of its trip. Planks all, said Cally.

Wow, so Nigel Simpkins had been Cally, eh! My head whirled with the day's events and I bored Dorian all the way back from Euston to Tamworth. "Wow, this guy, blah blah . . . drone . . . even *The Faust Tapes* . . . blah blah . . . Detroit, blah blah . . ." on and on and on.

Back home, I was so inspired. I made compilation tapes for him, picking each song with great thought and love. I felt good about myself for the first time in ages.

And Cally liked the album, *my* album, the one that had lain around Phonogram for what seemed like forever. I was amazed.

TALES FROM THE DRUG ATTIC

I had been hassling Neil Spencer, the editor of *NME*, that they needed to do something on true psychedelia, not the hippy garbage that was spoiling its memory.

"You need Max Bell to put a huge wad of material together," I said, "like that brilliant Tim Buckley piece he did in 1978." Max Bell's article had blown my mind and turned me into a Buckley freak overnight.

Long after I'd become friends with Max, I'd pester him as we lay stoned for hours on some bed, believing that a book of such exhilarating writing would be an instant classic. Now Neil Spencer called my bluff and said that if I was so concerned, why didn't I write it? Okay, you're on. My new Cally-fuelled attitude was ready to take on a mission.

I called the article "Tales from the Drug Attic" and laid into all the lame contemporary shit that called itself Psychedelic in 1983. Indeed, terrible retro groups were now recasting themselves as replica-psyche, in response to the Howard Jones-ness of the Like-to-Get-to-Know-You-Well '80s. But, unlike the English northern scene's coy refusal to ever accept a tag of Psychedelia, a crass new US scene was Wretchedly and Retchingly dubbing itself (get this!) The Paisley Underground. Oh, forlorn Intuitive Non-Career Movers! These deadly obvious groups were not pioneer music freaks, but cosy A-to-Zetros who had evidently all modelled themselves on The Byrds or the Pink Floyd 45s. They had names like The Jayne, Mardy Getz, Boston Mass, even The Dream Syndicate. That's fucking Lamonte Young's Tony Conrad/John Cale band!

At the behest of the *NME*, I had even bought an album called (get this again!) *Emergency Third Rail Power Trip* by the intriguingly named and greatly championed Rain Parade. With a title like that it had to be the fastest most manic thing since Love's 'Seven and Seven Is' . . . surely . . . Ho-hum. Track 1 began at 5 mph and got stuck in cross-town traffic even before the chorus – almost as pedestrian as Television's second LP *Adventure*. But not quite. Again, the vocals were by Raga Knobshiners from Hell, occupying far too much

Anglophile 'Bells of Rh*i*mney' airspace. Nevermind, my solo album will show you what hectic means – and it won't be stuck in the Sickstees either.

For the *NME* article, I decided that my mission was to kick all these psychedelic bandwagoners into touch, arrogantly dismissing whole chunks of '60s music as a waste of hippy time. Instead, I focused on 1965–66 as the classic period. I even subtitled the article "An Overview from Somebody who was Not There".

I loved the idea of the young American beer-drinking Rolling Stones copyists taking acid and losing their minds. It was so fucked up, so unintellectual and so innocent – every song was about losing a girlfriend. I wrote short intense hagiographies for The Seeds, The Misunderstood, The Chocolate Watchband and The 13th Floor Elevators, littering the article with lies and made-up bits to pad out the paucity of real information.

The article was great! In fact, it was the first great thing I'd done in ages, and I knew it. I was promised a front cover, but Sting had something to say that week so he got it instead. No matter! The Julian Cope Misconception of All-Things Psychedelic was in the shops.

In early December I'd seen a harrowing documentary about factory farming and decided there and then to stop eating meat. On Christmas Day, Dorian and I sat at my parents' house and watched my father serve us boiled sprouts, boiled potatoes and boiled mixed vegetables. Mmm . . . my favourite. My parents couldn't conceive of vegetarianism. My father passed me the gravy and was hurt and angry when I refused. I looked longingly at the roast turkey on the table. Birds are thick anyway . . . why not eat them? But I knew it was my stomach talking and I wasn't going to be beaten. We fought our way through the meal and I knew I was in for a long (and often lapsing) uphill struggle.

The rest of the festivities were far-out, though. It was my first Christmas as a serious toy collector and I felt like a child again: model cars, toy books, a remote-control truck. Wow, it was just too much for a guy to take in.

Joss was around all the time and we remembered hundreds of childhood incidents that gleamed like precious gems in my memory. When I rooted around in my parents' loft, I found our old Subbuteo log-book. Bloody hell, remember our Subbuteo Table-soccer? This miniature game had consumed us all through 1971 and '72. We remembered the leagues we had and the names of the clubs and the different colours. I had two clubs: FC Rialto, from some Latin country, and Gutenbad, definitely Germanic. Joss had AC Jesuit, a Catholic team, and Dinamo Ionion, from behind the Iron Curtain.

Ha, remember John Zsigo's teams? John was the kid across the road who just wanted to play the game – he wasn't interested in giving his teams names. We had to force him to do it. To show his distaste for all this, he'd picked the most prosaic names possible – Brooklino, named after his parents' house, and Pentonville Utd, from the Monopoly Board. The more we talked, the more surprised I was that we ever got round to playing any games. Other kids at school had stupid names like Manchester Utd or Chelsea for their teams, but our parallel Subbuteo universe was a microcosmic world of Soap Operatic proportions, a place where the game itself was just a game.

I had many stars in my teams. My $\frac{1}{76}$th-scale players all had characters of their own and a self-styled manager called Vernon Beburner. Whenever I played at home (my bedroom floor), the track-suited figure of Beburner would be on the sidelines, psyching out the other team. AC Jesuit had a star goalkeeper called Jeff Banks, named after the clothes designer. Joss's star striker was Denis Rocket! Wow, the memories flooded back. Joss had been a cool nine-year-old! I had Goalkeeping Hans Zodonckque. I insisted that he be called by his full name at all times (including the title "Goalkeeping"). Zodonckque had been cuckolding Vernon Beburner all through our Subbuteo childhood.

The memories went on and on and on. Our house was becoming a shrine to the past. My parents' loft was raided constantly for childhood junk, which would be cleaned up and hung on walls or put in my glass display cabinets. I couldn't handle the present day at all. It was moving far too quickly for me and my glorious times seemed long gone. If I was ever mentioned in the press, it was as some possessed fruitcake who was occasionally sighted doing weird things. The splendid Teardrop days of car surfing and Dark Ages boys' games now seemed so long ago as to have never really taken place at all.

So, I belonged in the past. It was official. I even began to accept it. And as I steeped myself in childhood memories, I found it easier for me to co-exist with myself. I could no longer compete. The Teardrops had often rambled and blown it in the quest for true experiment and free-consciousness, especially within the confines of the large concert halls which we had been playing. Compared with the roaming parameters of punk and post-punk thought, '80s audiences seemed to want some sort of Romanness of order. They didn't want danger and tension if it involved loss of cool, just a poised ABC fakery. On stage, groups like Echo & the Bunnymen and Dexy's Midnight Runners played each song with an apparently unrehearsed freedom which was, in fact, carefully and precisely worked out.

Of course, I resented that like crazy. It seemed so cynical to me to see McCulloch faking fits of spasmodic jerking on stage, when he was really about as shamanic as a 15-foot long prehistoric sloth. Still, what Mac didn't know couldn't hurt him. And I knew that if Mac had really followed my road, he'd have soon been foaming and drooling like a crazy. No, he was not built to endure – that was my end of the deal.

Then, on New Year's Day 1984, there was a knock at the front door. As usual, I ran into the kitchen and hid with my head in the crockery cabinet. As I stood in the darkness with my eyes screwed up, I heard Dorian say: "It's that young guy again, Donald. He and his friend want to talk to you."

Still crouching, I didn't know what to say. The kid had been around a couple of times already. Dorian had said I was out. Joss knew him. He was a Vince Watts acolyte and sometimes played in the dreadful DHSS. I sat there not knowing what to do. It was a life or death decision.

"Come on, Julian," Dorian said. "It's freezing. Let them in."

Okay.

Donald Skinner walked in with the quietest, most self-assured friendliness about him. Unfortunately, his friend, Matthew Lees, completely weirded me out. He was loud and obnoxiously up-front. In five minutes, I knew his life story and he was asking to borrow my Joy Division bootlegs. *Le Terme*? Great! Lend it to me!

Get this guy out of here. They left very quickly, but Dorian and I were entranced by Donald Skinner. We talked about him all evening, especially the way he said his name. "It's Donald."

Soon the house rang with young voices, and I felt as though Dorian and I had offspring of our own. It was Yorkie Part 2. Mark Mortimer and Donald Skinner spent nearly every evening with us. There were eight years between them and me, and I felt like a father and teacher with two kids waiting, like empty notebooks, to be filled up with stories and music and tales of groups they had never even heard of. I was only 26. But such an old 26. My life felt as though it was coming to an end. And before I went *anywhere*, I was going to tell them everything I knew.

Each night we sat at the top of the house, listening to The Seeds, Can, Pere Ubu, The 13th Floor Elevators, Television, Patti Smith, Faust, Tim Buckley, The Chocolate Watchband, Scott Walker, The Pop Group, on and on. I had to be careful not to go too fast. When a new record came on, I'd be almost beside myself with excitement. Wow, these guys are hearing this stuff for the first time! In a way, I was jealous of them. But I had built my record collection up over years, each one was a cherished part of me and I told the story of each song as we listened.

I was attracting my own scene. These kids inspired me far more than my own age group. They had done nothing remarkable yet and were stuck in Tamworth, but they had an enormous appetite for anything I shoved down their throats.

Also, they told me which stuff they didn't like. Carefully, at first, so they wouldn't hurt my feelings. But I soon found out that they hated Scott Walker. We were listening to 'The Seventh Seal' from *Scott 4* and Donald was looking at the LP sleeve. He looked bemused and his face held an expression of obvious distaste.

"Did he just see the film and then write this song about it?" Donald asked me.

Put like that, it sounded ridiculous. Scott Walker had been to see an Ingmar Bergmann film and been prompted to write this extraordinarily removed spaghetti western song. But Donald's youth refused Scott his metaphor completely and, after years of Scott being glued to my turntable, suddenly he sounded too camp, too existential and too ponderous. That voice! Donald studied *Scott Sings Songs from his TV Series*, and I knew it was all over between me and Scott. Okay, it's a general decision. Scott sucks existential shit. And he was deposed that very day.[1]

With the help of Donald and Cally, I began to draw up new parameters for my music. No more big emotions. Only tiny observations from now on. How could I honestly make world pronouncements? I was no longer in that world.

'REYNARD THE FOX' & THE GLAM DESCEND

Even though my first album had not yet been released, I decided on a title for its follow-up. It would be called *Fried*, a nickname that Dorian had given me describing my mental state. And I was happy. Happy happy happy.

This was beautiful music. This was the Saxon music of the Alvecote Mound. This was the Music of Woden and the West Midlands.

I felt inspired.

When *Fried* was released, people would love me again. It would be a cult classic AND it would be huge. I was certain of that. I just had to be patient for a while.

Everyone in the '80s music scene was making more and more impressive pronouncements about their forthcoming albums and shows. Wham! Madonna! Roman Holliday! Unlike anything you've ever seen before! Breaking every boundary thus far perceived! Challenging the very notion of entertainment! Fuck off!

I got so bored with this refusal to define any boundaries whatsoever that I decided to make the most restrictive rules possible. Like Dylan's 'Masters of War', in which the singer knows his own song "well before I start singing", I now utterly rejected any novelty. If it hadn't been done before, then I wasn't interested. I had an ancient and divine desire to travel the roads that were laid before. Tradition would reign from now on, starting with my songwriting.

I looked around for the most traditional song I could possibly write. The

---

1 Fifteen years have gone by and my love for Scott has, unfortunately, never returned. Yet my supposed affection for him is so ingrained in people that I would feel too churlish to inform most of those Scott-heads who bring up the subject. Blame Donneye *c.*1984.

first idea that I came across was 'Reynard the Fox', a theme so famous that there were over 400 versions in Germany alone! This was even better than 'Louie Louie', I thought.

Then that idea blossomed into an intriguing possibility which had me rolling around. I remembered the rhythmic genius of Thomas Grey's poem 'The Fox':

"The fox was strong,
He was full of cunning,
He could run for an hour,
And still keep running."

I played a blast of Glam Descending guitar chords from the tailout of the song 'Black Sabbath' (what the hell, it's also the same proto-Glam Descend as Sabbath's 'Iron Man'). Then I sang a version of Thomas Grey's 'The Fox', incorporating the name Reynard in the refrain. It worked first time.

My idea of tradition delighted me as I wrote and I next decided that I needed a monolithic riff for the main verse in order to complement the strange and unlikely Sabbath-ness of the chorus. Ozzy Osbourne was a proto-Reg Presley, so I listened to my Troggs' LPs for crassness, but none of their riffs were fast enough to rip off. I needed something as metal and brazen as 'In-A-Gadda-Da-Vida' or Blue Cheer's version of 'Summertime Blues', or even Pere Ubu playing Grand Funk Railroad. I listened to *Emerge* by The Litter, but none of their riffs were truly Dark Ages Brutal. Joss came around and immediately suggested the riff from 'I Can Only Give You Everything' – yeah, Bro', it fits the whole Sabbath chorus thing. And suddenly 'Reynard the Fox' was the first result of my new restrictions.

That February, I recorded a new BBC radio session for John Peel. I asked Donald Skinner to play guitar and Johnno to play the bass. The songs were incredibly simple, with very little going on, and I played organ and electric 12-string. 'Laughing Boy', 'Reynard the Fox' and "O. King of Chaos' were all unlike each other and all individually like nothing I'd recorded before, and far away from my forthcoming *World Shut Your Mouth* album. But that excited me and made me feel alive again. Hey, I thought, returning to my mantra, I was building up back catalogue whether people listened or not. If these LPs have to be my *TB Sheets* or *Starsailor*, then so be it. I have to record to prove that I exist at all.

'Laughing Boy' took its name from a Daryl Hall & John Oates song from their LP *Abandoned Luncheonette*. I loved the idea of naming such a Tim Buckley-esque *Happy Sad* breeze-out after such a lumpen teenage memory. The thumping piano song 'O. King of Chaos' was about a spirit that Lisa St. John and Patti Marsh accidentally conjured up playing on a ouija board in Boston.

The O. incident had gone on for months and seemed just one more reason for me to keep all occult types at a barge-pole's length.

At the Peel session, Donald Skinner played wild slide guitar like Glen Ross Campbell, the beautiful young guy out of The Misunderstood, who used to play cross-legged on the floor. I'd never worked with anyone as young or exuberant as this skinny blond-headed angel. Yeah, you're Glen Ross Campbell's kid brother . . . we've gotta call you Donald Ross Skinner.

THE MIGHTY FALLEN
"Out of place, out of time,
All your words drive me out of my mind. . .
Out of sight, out of style,
So far out I must stick out a mile."

Doctors of Madness, 'Out'

They hated it. They all hated it, every one of them. *World Shut Your Mouth* finally got released and they finally got to say what they'd wanted to say for ages.

Barney Hoskyns, the *NME* guy, was the heaviest. He said that I should stop making records altogether. His comments were so damning that my mate Bernie Connors rang me from Liverpool: "I read that review . . . What've you been doing, Copey? Shagging the guy's girlfriend?"

I didn't get it at all. This Barney Hoskins was declaring open season on me, yet he liked that redundant US Paisley Underground kack that claimed so much and delivered tasteless sub-zilchburgers of underachievement. The Rain Parade? On the train back from interviews in London, some guy sitting opposite me asked if I was Julian Cope. I said that I was.

"*NME* says that your album is a pile of shit."

Fuck you, Barney Hoskins, I seethed. If you don't become the greatest rock'n'roll writer of all-linear-time, I'm someday in the very distant future gonna deliver you a McGrathing from Hell!!![1]

Everyone who reviewed the album claimed to be fans with a bone to pick with me. They all loved my previous albums and why wasn't this one up to scratch? It was that hindsight thing again. The same people who'd slagged *Wilder* off for being so different from *Kilimanjaro* were now slagging off *World Shut Your Mouth* for being so unlike *Wilder*.

---

1 McGrathing – this term refers to my old friend and soundman Robbie McGrath, who had a very unique and penetrating way of dealing with male enemies such as managers and obstinate sessionmen. He now does sound for the Stones, so maybe Mick'll finally get to pay for Altamont.

The guy in *Sounds* called the album (and me):

"... bitty, incomplete and rather confused (and confusing) ... stuck in a creative rut, halfway between being famous and being a forgotten 'one hit wonder' boy ... a mixture of Syd Barrett and Gary Glitter ... an irritating pot-pourri of an album ... starting off like Mott the Hoople, careering into Blue Oyster Cult brashness ... and [will] send you running for your nearest Peter Hammill album."

I resented that like hell. Even back in 1977, Johnny Rotten's Top 10 had included 'Institute of Mental Health Burning' off Peter Hammill's *Nadir's Big Chance* LP, so don't come the prog with me – this was the same journalist who'd written that Ian Curtis "Died for You!" Get a Life! This guy had slagged me off for what he'd called our "glitterstomp" before, on the *Kilimanjaro* review. I loved glitter, but 1984 hated it. I loved Syd Barrett, but overachieving yuppie 1984 hated old underachieving Syd. I loved Mott and considered side one to be similar full-tilt glam psychedelia, but tense 1984 fucking hated glam and psychedelia. As for Peter Hammill, only Johnny Rotten, Cally and Fish out-of-Marillion and I were listeners. And Fish had been a Teardrop follower.

Shit. I was truly in trouble if they won't even allow me my '70s metaphor. But then, so must Cally be. We both listened to Van Der Graaf Generator's *Pawn Hearts* LP all the time (and irritated the hell out of Dorian when I tried to pass it off as very late psychedelia(!))

On Mr Sounds' own terms, all his put-downs had validity because I did actually try to create just that music that he so hated. But it was a heathen grind, so Up Your Puckered Artholes, ye grey urbanites. It seemed that 1984 wasn't allowing me to have such a wide range of feelings and the press were willing to stitch me up if I continued. Fuck that shit. I have all the time in the world. You think I'm Gesture Man? Eat Kack, Urban Knobhound. *NME* called me "incontinent with ecstasy". Now that's Awl-righttttt!!!!

There was a lyric on one song called 'An Elegant Chaos' that caused such waves of laughter and derision from certain quarters that I started to question my own sanity. You see, the words in question were my favourite on the entire album. They went like this:

"People I see
just remind me of mooing like a cow on the grass
And that's not to say
That there's anything wrong with being a cow anyway
But people are people
With the added advantage of the spoken word
We're getting on fine
But I feel more of a man when I get with the herd."

I knew it was a classic lyric. But if any writer wanted to cite examples of my weirdness, they would always quote those words. I could not understand it. It really upset me. I sat at home and read and reread them, looking for craziness, but always finding sense.

Mick Houghton had got as much publicity as he felt I could handle, but my brief sorties up to London were nowhere near enough to halt the slide into my new role as artistic and social pariah.

It was horrible.

I couldn't bear to be unhip. I wasn't used to it.

Now that I had the time to brood over bad press, there was certainly plenty to occupy my waking hours. At least when the Teardrop had fucked up in the past, everyone was divided about it. But now, it was a blanket dismissal. They *all* thought I was burned out and incapable of inspiration.

I approached the March tour with trepidation. They were going to get me whatever I did. Who? What if I'm imagining it? What if they'd all finally seen through my little game and sussed me as the evil bullshitter that I was? Or maybe what I have to say is redundant. Or maybe, even, I'm articulating it so badly that it sounds ridiculous. Yeah, that last one made the most sense. I'll have to be clearer from now on. Concentrate on saying things succinctly. I had to have hope in my beliefs or I would become lost forever.

As the British tour loomed ominously, Steve Lovell and I began to build a band. I had asked Johnno to play bass and Donald to play some loud guitar. Steve Crease, from the album session, would play drums. Everything had to be done as cheaply as possible, as there was no money around and Phonogram weren't even that into supporting a tour.

Paul King asked a guy called Andy Davis to play keyboards. He'd toured with Tears for Fears and was old enough to have been in Stackridge, a progressive rock group I had seen as a painted teenage hippy in Torquay in 1972. Later that summer, I had driven my brother and parents crazy with an endless refrain of a Stackridge song title 'Syracuse the Elephant'. I had never actually heard the song, but what a great title. Paul King figured that Andy Davis would be a sobering influence and I was pleased to be dealt such a "professional hand", after hearing so many old colleagues thinking up any excuse not to work with me.

I didn't want to do many old Teardrop songs. They were a bad memory and I couldn't rely on my past. I decided to play most of the new album, plus a couple of covers and two new songs: the gentle breeze called 'Laughing Boy' and the paranoid rock song called 'Reynard the Fox'.

But then, as rehearsals were just starting, Steve Crease was told to pull out. He'd been playing with a wimpy rock band called The Lotus Eaters, who had that minor 7th chicken-in-a-bedroom kind of 1983 sound. The guy who ran them was a knobhound called Jerry Eaglehead. The Lotus Eaters were big on Radio 2 and now the Eaglehead was telling Steve Crease that he couldn't be seen to associate with such as I.

This was all far too much for me. That a shiner like that had a say in my life made me want to beat him to death with a Dr Alimantado 12". What a bastard! I'd even lent him my red electric 12-string. Had I really done that? What a total plank! I wished dole and restart schemes upon the Eaglehead from all sides, and sought out another drummer.

Two weeks into rehearsals, everything was going fine. The songs started and finished at the right time, and everyone knew their parts. That was enough for me.

We now had this very sweet old geezer called John Dillon on drums. He was off his bloody head and 36 years old. Thirty-six. Oh, fucking hell. But no-one else would do the gig. John Dillon had lived through the '60s but didn't seem to have paid attention. He passed unsmokable menthol joints to horrified tokers and only ate grapes, as his insides were totally caned through drink.

But my real concern was Donald. With Steve and me on guitar, there was nothing for him to do. He'd never been thrown into anything like this before and spent most of the time behind his amplifier exploring the pot scene. I hated to sack him from the tour, but I had to do it. Shit, this'll probably fuck his head up totally. I got Paul King to give me moral support, and told Donald at the Averard Hotel. If it killed him to find out, he didn't show it. He was an 18 year old cool as ice man. Me, I was so guilty I gave him my new guitar.

At Bradford University, on the night of my first solo show, the vibration of intergalactic expectation did not hang in the air. I walked, uneasy and over-eager, up onto the stage and saw no-one in the audience whom I recognised.

So sure of myself before the tour, I had at the last minute chosen to open the set with an old Teardrop song ... *"I was a bouncing baby!!!"* ... and my next compulsion sent me hurtling into the heart of the crowd. The first four seconds of my new solo career looked uncannily like the dying embers of my departed career. Except, of course, for the size of the crowds.

One week into the tour, I was still not over the shock. I mean, I hadn't expected queues and queues of people, but these audiences were *tiny*. And some of the venues? I'd only casually glanced at the itinerary before the tour. I'd noted that there was a Lancaster show. Awlright! I'd played there loads of times, it was a 1,500 capacity hall in the university. Wrong! No-one had bought tickets, so the promoters had moved the gig to a basement in a pub. I'd spent the afternoon apologising to the band and now I was apologising to Rolo, the leader of The Woodentops, who were supporting me. Everyone was really nice and said that I needn't apologise. But I still felt stupid. I thought I was a rock'n'roll star.

Still, the shows clattered away fairly well. In Liverpool, a young student at my old college, C. F. Mott, said my wheelchair from the stitches incident was still there after seven long years. In Manchester, The Smiths sent me a load of flowers and that made me really happy. This was the group whose singer had sacked Troy Tate as producer. I still dismissed their music as rockabilly Polecat-trash but they were now gigantic and moving to people in a way that even I could understand.

The flowers made me feel remembered, but I was completely out of shape and had no sense of dynamics at all. Throughout the tour, I spent far too much time getting pulled out of the audience, and I'd get too excited during songs and break the mike-stands through the pressure I was feeling. During each show, Paul Crockford, the tour manager, glared at me from the wings. He was Paul King's affable 6'4" assistant and accepted no bullshit. But at every gig, another mike-stand would become first mangled, then dragged, then finally thrashed until it bit the dust.

I feared the London show more than I could bear. What if I fuck up? It was getting closer and I was not improving. Also, John Dillon's drumming had no sense of timing at all. He took all his cues from me. ME. I ask you. Some of the songs had kangaroo rhythm – bong-ga-bong-ga-bong – speeding up and slowing down all over the place. If I went into freeform, we would get started on a spiral and the whole band would be dragged down and down.

Oh wow. It was finally here. Hammersmith Palais, my London event. I spent the whole day looking for means of escape. I was reasoning with myself. Look. If Julian Cope doesn't show, it'll be half expected. If I do a crap gig, I'll be in deep shit. Maybe by not showing, I'll create more interest. Hmm.

I stood in front of the dressing-room mirror. There was now only a half an hour to go and I had not made my move. I couldn't run out of here, like it was an interview. I knew that. I owed Paul King too much. He had just informed me that he'd brought four BBC Radio producers to the show. Having started as a show promoter, Paul King very much belonged to an old school of show business and he wanted radio people to take his acts seriously. Kingy had worked hard at persuading these guys to turn up and he wanted to give them proof that I was no longer off my rocker. That way, they could start playing my records again on Wunnerful Radio One.

Shit. Pressure on. Gimme that whisky. I grabbed Johnno's Jim Beam and gulped it down fast. Then I rushed ape-like out into the other, smaller dressing room. Rat Scabies was sitting quietly. I flashed him a huge smile and wondered why he was there. As I struggled with my face, Johnno came in and did some cocaine with Rat Scabies. I didn't like that at all. Coke is very bad before a show; it gives you an uncontrollable attitude.

"'Ey, Copey, want a line of this?" Johnno held out a rolled £10 note.

"Yeah, deffo," I said, and hoovered it up my nose. Then I rushed out into the corridor and went to my secret place.

That afternoon, whilst I was assessing escape routes, I had found a trap door in the ceiling. I had climbed in and found a route that led right over the stage and audience. Now, I was lying flat and cruciform-like directly over The Woodentops, who were halfway through their set. They were going down incredibly well and I was getting annoyed. Rolo was climbing into the audience and kissing everyone. He had no top on and everyone loved it. Hey, that's *my* show, that's what *I* do! I was totally freaked out.

Paul Crockford told me it was a good crowd and the whisky made me feel heavy as hell. If anyone gives me shit tonight, er, Look Out!

Then I blundered on stage, my heart racing and my brain shouting: "Prove them wrong . . . You don't have to prove anything . . . Prove them wrong . . . You don't have to prove anything." On and on and on.

Halfway through the set and I was fucking up. I had lead boots on and my head was fixed to the floor. They hated me, of that I was positive. Sure, they cheered each song, but only out of force of habit. I mean, everybody cheers at gigs. I strummed the guitar throughout the set. On some songs, where I normally grooved and did my thang, I just turned the guitar volume down and mimed. It was my stupid security blanket and I wanted to cry. Why did I feel like this? What force took me over in these situations? Snap out of it, you dickhead. Come on. Now!

As the band stormed into 'Reynard the Fox', I finally peeled off my guitar. This was the last song and I was running out of time to be impressive. I stormed around the stage, still lead-booted but trying vainly to look natural. The song had a loose arrangement and we always fell into one of my rants at the end. This time, I could think of nothing. No thing at all. I clasped the mike-stand and pulled hard on it, hoping for divine inspiration. None came. We became caught in one of those dumb holding patterns as the band struggled along on C major.

Cacophony. I'll have to rely on cacophony and shut the fuck up. The tubular steel mike-stand started to bend under me and I grabbed it at one end and dragged it across the stage. The I took it in both hands and worked on the weak spot, to and fro, to and fro, putting more and more pressure on it until. . .

Snap!

The whole thing tore like a kid tears toffee, webs of weakened metal fanning out from the two broken ends. I hurled one piece into the floor and lifted up my black top. Then, quietly and methodically, I began to draw the metal wand across my stomach, all the time gazing thoughtlessly out into the audience. I could feel nothing, just the pulse of the ever-slowing music and the tickle of the feather in my hand.

Soon, I dragged my black top over my head. I looked up into the lights, then down. . .

Wow . . . my stomach!

It looked like Clapham Junction, hundreds of red lines cutting brazenly through the landscape of my belly. Certain deeper wounds sent the blood coursing down into my pants. My leathers were sodden and sticky.

Claudie, a Viennese journalist whom I knew well, stood crying in the photographer's pit, her mouth opening and closing. I was aware of people being lifted out of the audience by security guards. Johnno stood, mute and disgusted, playing his bass on automatic pilot, whilst the rest of the band and the road crew stood by bewildered, unsure whether or not to intervene.

And in the deafening roar of 'Reynard the Fox', I was finally and hysterically inspired. As I cut and cut, I began to quote Kenneth Williams as the dying Julius Caesar in the English comedy *Carry On Cleo*: "Infamy, infamy – they've all got it in for me."

"I don't care if it *kills* you, you dickhead."

In the silence of my Averard hotel room, Paul Crockford sat cleaning my blackened ripped stomach with cotton wool and the remains of the Jim Beam whisky. The pain was overwhelming. My stomach was 100 grinning bloody mouths which opened and closed in a horror of muted agony every time I took a breath. Paul Crockford ignored me as he continued his grim task. And Dorian sat quietly, occasionally glancing away from this pathetic spectacle, acutely aware of the harm that I had done this night.

The show had been a fiasco. After the blood ritual had reached its frenzied conclusion, I had bolted off the stage and rushed to the safety of my secret place high above the audience, leaving the band churning away in a C major grind of embarrassment and guilt. Up there in the grime and dust of the rafters, I had resumed my crucifix position and, as a final and contemptuous act, had poured water over the audience below me. There was no encore, of course. And no apology. By the time Crockford had lured me down, the rips in my belly were the trenches of some WW1 battlefield, screaming with a coagulated mess of filth and bloodiness.

I had fucked up most royally. I had failed Paul King. I had failed my band. They knew that I had copped out. I'd had nothing to say, nothing at all. And when this realisation hit me, I had crudely and most rudely changed the rules. I had stumbled into the fake trip of some tenth-grade performance artist.

But, underneath all that derisive puffing and blowing, there was a strange and anti-'80s glow about my behaviour. However hard I tried to play the contrite scallywag, my wanton actions on the stage of the Hammersmith Palais somehow quite appealed to me. And even though the show had been terminally boring, I knew that no-one there would ever remember that fact.

THE FLOOR KISS – THE CAR KISS

Anyway, the next day was a day off and Dorian returned to Tamworth. Today we were to drive to Fishguard, in west Wales, on our way to the Dublin show. And what a beautiful day for it. So, let's celebrate our misfortune and dance till dawn. Paul Crockford craned his spotty neck around 90 degrees from the driver's seat. He shook his head violently. "No. No way at all. I can't allow you to take acid on a day off."

As we stuttered and jerked through the London traffic, I felt strangely becalmed. Why did we even bother asking him?

I sat quietly in the itchy body sling that rode up from around my scars. I knew why. It was the guilt. Yesterday, I had blown it in a big ass way, that was for certain. But, you know, so what? At least I'd fucked up royally. Nothing half-assed. I'd fallen from a great height and shattered into 2,000,000 pieces on the ground. Yeah, when J. D. Cope blows it, he belows it.

"Paul," said Johnno, in his most reasonable and assertive way. "I don't want to annoy you but, speaking for myself, Mr Cope and Mr Lovell, we wish to take some LSD today."

And so we found ourselves, two hours and 100 miles later, buying everything that the Leigh Delamere M4 services had to offer. Lying in the back of the van, I was amazed at the shit I had bought: *The Best of Men Only No. 12*, a family-size Fruit & Nut bar, a Mars bar, a family-size Whole Nut bar, two Curly Wurlys, assorted packets of crisps and a modern die-cast model of a 1957 Ford Thunderbird made by Corgi Toys. Awlright!

Whilst everyone else built their spliffs, I lay back on the floor with my legs in the air, kissing the Ford Thunderbird. "Look at this," I said to no-one in particular, perhaps about the model itself, or more likely about my act of kissing it.

I was delighted by everything. It was fantastic. The acid had reduced my stomach wounds to a Crewe railway junction of minor itches and was now setting every one of my nerve endings aglow. I stared down into the centrefold of *The Best of Men Only No. 12*. Wow! She was incredible. Pages 50 and 51 were living before my eyes. I felt her tits rise to greet me and her elegant cunt stared deep into my eyes. Hey, Johnno, have a look at this. It's a phenomenon.

On the front of *No. 12*, a fantastic spiel advertised "wet lipped, smooth hipped, big busted, curvy thighed, round bottomed, high heeled, boa constricted, misty eyed, far from meek, hide and seek girls". I stared at the words from my dying fly position on the floor of the back seat area and recognised Desiree Cousteau, a porn queen who had appeared in every rock studio video collection that I knew of. But Desiree was older now, and harsher from her gruelling video sex-life. She snarled at me in a studded leather bra, and I felt myself rolling and tumbling into the pages of *The Best of Men Only No. 12*. I fled to the gargantuan beauty of Annie Ample's spread across pages 10 and 11, and basked in the sheer *Deep Purple in Rock*-ness of her cleft. In her unbelievable nakedness, this woman was as mysterious as if she stood before me fully clothed. Her mystery was fabulously beautiful and unfathomable, and I stared vacantly but religiously in an effort to understand it.

In the front seat, Steve Lovell was paranoid. His parents lived in west Wales. What if they came to see him? Johnno told him there were better things to worry about. Liverpool were playing later that day and if we didn't hurry, we would miss the match on TV.

Deeper and deeper into Wales we drove. The blue day was gone and grey Blakean storm clouds sat in high judgement, pitched on end across the horizon. But here I felt at home. Nearby was my birthplace and we were soon passing only a few miles from Rockfield Studios.

Yesterday's nightmare was almost forgotten now, though my belly was a plague of itches. Driving with a bunch of people I really dug reminded me of the cooler days in The Teardrop Explodes. Still crouching and cocooned on the floor of the van, I looked up at Steve Lovell and Paul Crockford. They were epic and amazing looking. Where were you when I needed you? The Teardrop Explodes could have worked with people like this.

It was wishfully-acid-addled-thinking, but at least the delusions were the product of my rekindled enthusiasm. Already, last night's show had been filed under "legendary" and left at that.

Droplets of rain began to mist the windscreen and my eyes fell down onto the perma-grin of Johnno, his eyes reduced to slits of enthusiasm. I felt good and took the spliff that John Dillon handed me. Cough, cough, cough, urgh, splutter.

"Ay, John. This is one of your disgusting menthol things."

"Oh yeah. Sorry."

A green 1958 Jaguar XK150 roared past us and I held up the toy Ford Thunderbird, mirroring the real car's movements. Rrrrrrrrrrrrrr. The rain was coming down in torrents and the Jag left a wake of white foam as it rushed along. It was deep into the trip and I was happy. It was an unthinking happiness. This time could be any time. I was happy just to be allowed to do this. At times, in Tamworth, I had begun to imagine a life without it.

Late afternoon, we pulled into a farm track and the van wheels spun crazily, looking for grip in the deep mud. The sun was out again, but the storm had left a quagmire to contend with. In the front seat, Steve Lovell crouched frozen with fear, his head below the dash. He was convinced that his parents had come to see him. Johnno and I sauntered into the bar, where the road crew were drinking and dancing. As I drove the toy car along the bar, it suddenly hit me: I didn't know where we were. What was this place?

The hotel was a huge old farmhouse on a steep, steep cliff. Crockford told me that there were old cottages surrounding the house. They belonged to the hotel and we would be staying there. Yes! I was excited and hassled everyone to finish their drinks. Johnno expressed a mighty soccer concern to the hotel manager, who smiled psychotically and escorted us up to our cottage. Don't act weird. Don't act weird.

Crockford and the manager led the way. Johnno and I were in hot pursuit, with the rest of them dragging along behind.

"Ay, Steve, there's your mum," laughed Johnno as a single sheep came around the corner. Petrified, Steve Lovell bent double and hid his face.

The hotel manager watched the scene but took no notice. He opened the door of the first cottage and we all walked in. Johnno promptly took out all the necessary shit and coolly started to skin up a joint.

"No, no," I screamed, as uncoolly as was possible, and smiled at the manager.

"Oh, it's okay. I used to do the lights at the Fillmore West in LA. You can do what you want here."

Then he began to skin up too. My head spun. I couldn't think. What was normal, what was not?

I took the Ford Thunderbird and held it in front of his face. "Would you like to kiss the car then?" I asked with the politeness of a 12-year-old Enid Blyton character.

"Er, no. No, I don't think so."

That night, I was happy. We all sat eating and drinking in the hotel bar, the sea crashing and violent way below us. I stayed around Steve and Johnno. I had no sense of normality at all. The road crew were getting out of hand and taking over the bar. Soon, everyone was doing Tequila slammers. I had two or three, but was content to watch as Ady Wilson and Johnno and D'Arcy pounded the glasses and glugged the lot down. Over and over. Over and over.

The night drew on and time began to exert its considerable force on everyone. Paul Crockford was a disgusting wreck and claimed to be sleeping in the same cottage as Johnno and myself. We staggered out and into the night, the acid trip of 12 hours reduced to a flicker of speed and drunkenness. . .

We heard the news from a roaring and farting Paul Crockford at about 3 a.m. Ady Wilson had nicked some kiddie's bike and driven fast towards the cliff in the darkness. In order to prevent a colossal fall ending in death, he had preferred to throw himself on to the scree-slope of loose rocks and boulders.

Soon we were crouched over him, concerned but crazy. His face was slit *right* through. Starting at his top lip, a rip carried on past his nose and up his cheek. He lifted the huge flap of skin back to reveal a bloody mass of gums and teeth. Although he was still drooling and crazy, he was in terrible pain.

I stood up and unwound my bandages. My wounds were ultra-violent looking, like a 25-bar electric fire tattooed across my lower belly. Ady sat up and put his face to my stomach. It was a perfect combination. D'Arcy grabbed his camera and snapped the gruesome twosome.

And then it was time for bed.

SECOND TIME AROUND

But soon the tour was a distant romanticised memory and it took me maybe two days at the most to get used to being at home again.

I sank into the old routine quite happily, whilst the *World Shut Your Mouth* LP consigned itself to the back catalogue. I checked that the D. R. Skinner ego was not dented too much and started to work on the *Fried* LP. I began to record acoustic songs on my ghetto blaster. Then I would take my electric guitar and build up drones over the click of the acoustic strings.

And then a funny thing happened. My decree absolute came through. I was free! The whole thing had dragged on for so long that I'd almost forgotten about it and I had now been separated from Kathy for over three years. On that day, Dorian and I rejoiced in every corner of the house. We danced jigs around the table and hugged each other.

"Let's get married," I said. What? Now? Dorian thought I was joking. We had already planned to have a Long Island wedding in the coming autumn.

"Yeah," I said. "But that'll be for everyone. You know, family and stuff." I worried about that. Weddings are notorious for getting out of hand, going on and on until the wedding couple are swamped with aunts and cousins telling them what to do. So let's have a quiet *secret* wedding just for us that no-one knows about.

We put up the bans and signed the legal stuff at Lichfield Register Office. We were so excited. No-one knew, no-one at all except Joss, who was my best man, and Donald, who was Dorian's witness. On the day of the wedding, we put on our best clothes and drove to Lichfield in Donald's mother's Mini. There was a short service and Donald took black & white photographs. Then we piled back into the mini and drove to Alvecote Priory for a wedding picnic. I was so happy. From the minute I'd seen her, I had loved Dorian and wanted her to be my wife. I resented being married to some other woman. It pissed me off to have made such a grand mistake.

We danced and toked and partied in the woods and around the picnic tables. Donald took more pictures and we drove home stoned as hell and psyched.

That night, Johnno, DeFreitas, Andy Eastwood and Jake all arrived from Liverpool. Eh-up, I mustn't tell them. I'm such a bloody loudmouth, though. I bit my tongue all through their stay. I never told a soul. This was a brand new feeling. It was Part 2. If Part 1 was a mess, here was the chance to clean up. I thought of Dorian and I thought of *Fried*.

I'll beat this craziness.

STONER

Through the spring of 1984, I was left alone by business and grief. The fortress at Mill Lane was chock full of toys and glass-fronted cabinets. Toys were all I talked about. Each weekend, we would pile into Joss's MG Midget and make for the latest swap meet. Then we would hurtle home with the loot, cover the kitchen table with it and marvel over each individual thing for hours on end. Sometimes Dorian would get so bored she'd just curl up in a corner and sleep through it all. Toys, though. When you get *in*to them, you just keep going in and in and in.

There was a car called a Volkswagen Karmann-Ghia. I had a Dinky Toy version and thought it was beautiful. Then one day I saw a picture of the real thing in a car magazine. Wow! It looked as though some Eastern-bloc country had built a sports car. I started to read up about Karmann-Ghias. They turned out to be just VW Beetles with a coupé body on top. We had to have one. I couldn't drive and Dorian only understood automatics, but I figured we could easily get around that.

The car magazines told us to see as many cars as possible before buying. We found one for sale in Birmingham and drove to see it immediately. It was incredible: dark green with an off-white roof. Forget the magazine's advice. I want this car!

We bought it that day and it broke down on the way home. No matter, it was soon fixed up and parked under a street lamp in the public car park opposite the house. Every night we would sit on the top floor and watch the car bathed in the glow of the light. For the first few weeks, only Joss could drive it. I always insisted that he park the car with the front wheel turned; that way it looked more racy under the light.

Sometimes we found footprints on the roof. Sometimes we found stuff written on the windscreen. It's funny, people associate pretty things with wealth so they want to hurt them. Huge 7 Series BMWs would be parked in the same place and never get touched.

Donald had moved to a hippy house around the corner from us in Victoria Road. We had heard that they were all witches, but I took that with a pinch of salt. There was a red light outside the house so urban legend was bound to develop. Then there was a national press blitz on the house – it even made the front page of the *Sun*. Half of its occupants were discovered dancing naked in Hopwas Woods at 3 a.m. one night. It rolled right over Donald. Nothing disturbed him.

There was a drugs dealer around Tamworth called Rick Wakeman, the same name as the keyboard prog guy. He'd had his surname changed by deed poll. People in Tamworth did shit like that. One night, this Rick Wakeman guy came around to the witches' house with his heavy friend. They smashed up all the furniture and broke one guy's arms. Finally, the heavy guy piled into Donald's bedroom, so Donald faked retardedness.

"Who the fuck are you?"

"I live in this room."

"Christ. Have a look in here, Rick. There's a guy who doesn't know what the fuck is going on."

The songs I was writing had hit a pattern. They just rolled along, no problem. Johnno and I began to record them at a little studio in Birmingham. We made extra-long versions of everything, as I was in the mood to groove. There was one called 'Mik Mak Mok' that was eight minutes long, and another, 'The Bloody Assizes', that had no form at all.

We recorded a new John Peel session to try out other songs. I came home with four brand new things, excited about every one of them. I was trying to de-write stuff. I resurrected this gawky riff that I had written in 1977 and wrote some lyrics for it called 'Search Party'. When John Peel played it on his show he said: "Some rum thoughts pass through that boy's head."

I was driven everywhere by Ady Wilson, the guy who had ripped his face open on the Welsh hillside. Paul King wanted someone in charge of me at all times and I trusted Ady. He drove at 110 mph at all times. But very safely. Or so he said.

And I was feeling good. I was married to Dorian now which made me feel more balanced. We became so used to each other that Dorian and I only noticed when the other was absent. Then I would sit inert in her chair, aping the things that she said and did. I would talk quietly as though she was there and that gave me comfort. One time, when she was in New York, I sat in my own chair and made up this song. I recorded it off the top of my head into my Walkman. It sounded great and the lyrics were fine. I just changed a couple of words and called the song 'Me Singing'. Wow. Everybody's gonna *love* this song.

And so, in every way, I began to work on getting back into the real world. I didn't really like my place here; it was too cosy. I still had this vision of pop music as a giant celebration of fucked-upness. I was sure that I could be big again, especially with this new music. It was so natural sounding, everyone was bound to fall for it.

I still attracted the weirdos and obsessives. I figured that was better than nothing, and some of them were very nice. When two American guys turned up on our doorstep, we actually invited them to stay. Dave and Robin were really nice guys. They told me that I still made people happy and that counted a lot to me. After they left, we kept in touch and then Robin sent me this beautiful old toy – a 1961 Ford Galaxie promo! Wow, my head was done in.

Meanwhile, closer to home, Vince Watts was getting weirder. He lived near my brother and Joss had a few tales to tell. One time, Vince needed firewood so he chopped up his piano. Then he tried to sell the wood to Joss as a piano.

I heard from Donald that Vince believed that Radio Moscow was in touch with him. The stories were so out of hand, I decided to reserve judgement until I spoke to him properly.

One day, as we pulled into my parents' driveway, we were greeted by the fantastic and worrying sight of Vince Watts talking to my father on the doorstep. My father stood, his head craned forward, trying desperately to understand Vince, who was rocking violently back and forth, his eyes looking skyward like some geeky version of Robert Newton's Long John Silver.

Dorian took my father into the house. I grabbed Vince's arm and we swung up the driveway out of the earshot of the others.

"Yer see, Julian," declared Vince, his eyes darting on each syllable and his voice emphasising each word in a shouted and hoarse whisper. "All those aerials are redundant. Unnecessary." He paused. "They've got it directly into my head . . . see?" And his eyes whirred around, as though he was transmitting. "Anyway. . ." he paused and looked around. "That's why I've got to sign to Virgin."

Aha, I thought. What the fuck is this about? Remember, Vince trusts me. His paranoia does not include me. In Tamworth, I'm the fearsomely weird Julian Cope. No-one is weirder than me. Except, that is, for Vince. And probably a couple of thousand other legendary no-marks of this twilight zone.

As it turned out, Vince was making pretty good sense. For Vince, that is. He had decided that he should utilise his direct brain link with Moscow to bring talks and peace with the West. Virgin Atlantic Airlines had just started their London–New York run. If he signed to Virgin Records, Vince had reasoned that he would get free trips to New York. He'd take his airwaves and save us all. It was quite beautiful, really.

You move back home. You see people from your past. You've got nothing in common any more. But you've got to talk. Well, haven't you? No. You don't have to do a thing. If they look as though they want to talk, do it. If it makes them uncomfortable, don't do it. It's not some kind of duty. It's not the difference between being a good person and a bad person.

I was beginning to learn this in Tamworth. I'd see someone that I knew and start to approach them. But they would have seen me and would already have looked away. Hmm ... a tricky situation. See, people think that once you've been on TV, you have no recollection of the past. So they don't want to attempt a conversation in case you've become some snotty twat who has forgotten what day it is.

One day, walking through Tamworth, I met Melvyn Jones in Market Street. Awlright! Melvyn Jones! "How are you doing? Where're you living? What are you listening to these days? Still playing guitar? What was that red solid body thing you had?" Bango bango bango.

I blasted old Melvyn Jones with questions and genuine concern. Why shouldn't I? This was the guy who came up with "Old Prick". See, when we were all 15 and still at school, Melvyn was one of those kids who had nothing to say. But he wasn't the kind to be kept out of conversations. Oh dear, no. If Melvyn felt that he was being ignored he would stand up and say, loudly and to no-one in particular: "He's here again."

Then we'd all look at Melvyn with resigned expressions on our faces and ask the inevitable question: "Who?"

Then Melvyn would smile broadly, taking in the attention he was suddenly getting, and say dramatically: "Old Prick."

He hit us with "Old Prick" at age 11 and we were still being subjected to it five years later.

When he left school at 16, I never saw him again. But I was haunted by "Old Prick". What made him come up with that? And I admired his staying power, too. To begin with, everyone had slagged him for it. But he just carried on and on and on until it became part of our routine. I had even told Dorian about it soon after we met. We were both fascinated by school memories and Old Prick became an important one.

Now a shrunken and balding 26 year old, Melvyn Jones was an unprepossessing sight in his anorak and glasses. Of course, I had to remind him of "Old Prick".

Ugh? He looked shocked, amazed that I remembered it. He was embarrassed. I felt stupid and sad. I'd locked him in my time-capsule in 1974 and expected him to stay in one place. As I left him there on Market Street, looking hunched and beaten by life, I said to myself: "He's here again. Who? ... Old Prick."

But in my real world, it seemed that the creeps were taking us over. They had divided us up, and now? Now they were ready to castrate the lot of us. But in the sneakiest way possible ... by giving us hits and feeding our egos and diverting the very thrust of our early intentions in Liverpool.

I'd been set up. Some force or another had turned The Teardrop Explodes into an advance guard of Quislings, tell-tales on the alternative scene, ready to dilute the general message by insufficient attention as to how we should communicate that message.

I saw old friends on TV. I saw everyone on TV. The airwaves were crammed with them. And each one had fallen for the falsehood that hits are good. Just as I had done. I began to feel guilty about that, as though I had inspired it.

Pete Wylie was having hits with his group Wah! Pete Burns was shaking his disco booty and turning into Greta Garbo. And now, Paul Rutherford and Holly were huge with Frankie Goes to Hollywood. And I was removed and in exile, far outside the city walls and unable to give them fair warning that they had been duped.

And yet, in a way, I liked the TV a lot. That was how I saw my friends. But the Melvyn Jones thing stuck in my mind. I wanted to rush around to everybody and tell them how I loved them. I've always loved you!

Running parallel with my fears of dilution was a feeling of intense celebration. It gave me a certain peace of mind to know that people I loved were doing well. Their success reflected my good judgement. Yeah, these are *my* friends. Cast out and alone though I was, the music biz still reeked of me. Or so I believed.

Late spring of '84 and Tamworth had started to draw me further and further into its small-town ideas. As much as we laughed at its scribblings, the *Tamworth Herald* newspaper consumed me. Its hellish blandness sucked me in and I found myself concerned with the same things as everyone else. Each week, Dorian and I would pore over the *Herald*'s pages, both delighted and appalled by the town's fixations. One week, the mayor would compare Tamworth's facilities with Stratford-upon-Avon or some such place of historical importance. The next week, the town's football team would be on the verge of simultaneous bankruptcy and cup glory.

In the "Music Box" column every week, the dashing columnist Christopher "Music" Jones would issue critiques of local bands that he'd been following. His writing style suggested that each pronouncement would be taken as a yes or no to the group's future. And accompanying each "Music Box" manifesto was a photograph: Christopher "Music" Jones of the *Herald* in all his Aryan coyness, shining and effervescent on the page. Oh, how we laughed. But how we loved it.

Of course, the *Tamworth Herald* was inflated and self-opinionated. But no more than any other local newspaper. There are stars on every street corner of this lickle planet. And some people don't want to look as far as Michael Jackson or Judy Garland. Instead, they want local heroes. Something that inspires them every day. It's like my brother Joss once said: "We're all in the gutter, but some of us are looking at the kerb."

I hated my position in the music scene. I was reliant on my supposed weirdness to keep people interested. And I needed the maniacs and obsessives to stay around, as the more reasonable of my fans had long since given up on me. I received letters from sick people with dead minds, each page of every letter reminding me of the way the world saw me.

A woman in her mid-thirties wrote to me regularly from Liverpool. Her name was Tracie Diane Prescott (middle name changed) and she was a heavy Catholic. The letters had started around November 1981, with Club Zoo. At first, she wrote only as a fan: "I love your music. You're my favourite singer," etc. But time moved on and so did Tracie Diane. Pictures of her family would arrive. And a bigger bunch of inbreds you could never care to meet. People who wore fully zipped-up anoraks at family functions. All her letters came to Outlaw Management and the family photos were a running joke there.

Then, I began to receive photographs of myself. Close-ups taken by Tracie Diane in cities like London and Liverpool. But how? She never made herself known to me. Yukko. What a creep. In time, her correspondence became intimate and fantastic. She confessed to being a virgin and wanted no sexual relations. She referred to herself as Mother Theresa and to me as Saint Julian. Together, we would save the world.

Never, not once, did I reply to her letters. At first, it was out of laziness, but as time moved on, I knew that putting pen to paper would open a can of worms.

Then letters full of sexual fantasies began to appear. Strained, writhing, religious nightmares. A violent and bloodied innocence, sheets stained with semen and sweat as I tore down her walls and entered into the very heart of her city. It was the height of everything gory and grotesque, and Dorian and I would stare for an age at the barely focused instamatic shots of herself that Tracie Diane included. They fascinated us in the same way that hastily shot blurred video news footage fascinates.

But then I got scared. I received a package containing a letter, a hospital name-tag and a certificate. In her letter, Tracie Diane said that she had got herself fitted with an IUD as she had decided it was time to lose her virginity. She was going to come down to Tamworth, murder Dorian and make love to me. P.S. The certificate was proof that she'd had it done.

We sat around in shock. Dorian laughed, but not very authentically. What kind of mind could think that a guy would want to fuck his wife's murderess? I think she was maybe goading me into answering her letters. We got paranoid for a long while, as I'd been reading Vincent Bugliosi's book *Helter Skelter* about the Manson Family. And people do strange stuff for attention. Outlaw Management started worrying, too, and stopped giving me her letters.

Stuff like that pushed me to straighten out. To exclude that obsession I had with ugly weirdos, I decided that I was into being Tamworthian. For a while, we moved all the trunks and folded beds and junk out of the centre of the front room. That way we could use the front door. It was very symbolic. Leaving by the front door meant normality. For a month, Dorian and I always used the front door. We loved it. It felt great to be normal.

Then, one day we stopped doing it. It didn't feel honest anymore. To me, it was as though we were playing at being normal, as though normal was good or something. It also suggested that we would now have to answer the front door when anyone knocked. Which we wouldn't. So that was false too. We decided to aim to be neither weird nor normal. We would be ourselves and become very good at that.

FUNNY FARMER

The summer brilliance of the 1984 sun dazzled my eyes each morning and lured me, semi-conscious and hungry, to the banks of the River Cam, where Brother Johnno and Ady Wilson would be sitting, drinking endless pots of coffee, smoking early morning joints and dividing up their toast between themselves and the gang of ducks which joined us, every morning, for breakfast.

We were staying at a hotel directly between Cambridge and Spaceward Studios – the place where we had, four days earlier, begun to record *Fried*.

Because of our unholy hours, the hotel manager had billeted us in the annex which was set on the river. At the end of each recording day, Ady, Johnno, Steve Lovell, Chas the engineer and I would stand in a row, at the doors of our riverbank homes, fumbling for our keys and screaming endless and enthusiastic goodnights at each other. Then we would sink into a heavily stoned sleep.

Between the hours of 3 and 11 a.m., there was no movement whatsoever. And then, that viciously pure and beautiful country sun would come rapping on our eyelids and, once more, drag us, insensible and complaining, to breakfast.

For *Fried*, I had a head full of ideas and a clear plan of action. It had begun with early strumming late '83 and had built up over the past months to a sound distinct and different from anything I had recorded before. I wanted to capture the pastoral flow of the songs. The crystal clear electric-guitar lines which Donald so effortlessly contributed was my first attack. Also, I wanted shimmery Hammond organ and lots of plucked acoustic guitar.

Initially, my blueprint for *Fried* was Tim Buckley's 1968 LP *Happy Sad*. I had travelled all over the world in the chaos of The Teardrop Explodes, but the security of my hotel room always cooled me out one step further when I played that particular Buckley album. Buckley also used jazz imagery and had lyrics like "Gypsy woman", which jarred with, and opened up, my tight-assed post-punk sensibilities – I'd never called a lover "Mama" in my whole life. But where his songs were inert with a sticky and hypnotic Tantric sex, my inertia was definitely brought on by a sapping of vital life energies.

•   •   •

The press now constantly compared me to Syd Barrett, the guy who had gone crazy after his early brilliance in Pink Floyd. Beside a brief teenage fascination with the *Piper at the Gates of Dawn/Relics* version of the Barrett Floyd, I had never investigated the Barrett solo albums, as they had been regarded by Mac, Simmo and most of the Liverpool scene as pretty hick stuff. Indeed, only the mystical Dan Brennan was a known Liverpool Barrett fan, and his famously Trolleyed mescaline experiences just about summed up post-punk's entire Syd Barrett attitude.

I began to read and ingest whatever scraps I could find out about Barrett, as it made me feel a little better about myself. Mick Houghton told me that the general public hadn't even noticed when Pink Floyd had sacked him in 1969. Mick said that those times didn't really regard individuals unless they were Jagger, Lennon, etc. Wow, Syd's situation was sad. An old baldy geezer unromantically flaked out and living with his mother in Cambridge, after years of performing ultra-visionary space-rock dressed in the guise of Dionysus. No wonder The TV Personalities had written a song called 'I Know Where Syd Barrett Lives" – it was a total freefall tragedy.

Intuitively, I began to look to Syd's predicament to help my own mirrored problems. Syd had put people off by acting like a mad crazy guy in front of the press. Right, I'll be extremely well-behaved in front of the press from now on. Syd had gone solo, recorded an album, formed a terrible new group, then followed the new Pink Floyd around, standing at the front of the stage and telling anyone who would listen that they were still "his" group. Right, I'll learn from that, too. I'll never be seen in public. That way, no-one can judge me.

So Syd became my anti-blueprint and my way of judging which behaviour was acceptable and which was not.

We were in Cambridge, also.

It wasn't because of Syd, though. Cambridge has a vibration similar to San Francisco and Amsterdam. It's one of the last bastions of free-dome.

And *Fried* was as free as I could ever be.

Yet, for every piece of savage venom directed at me as a Loser for the '80s, inside my deepest recesses, I still had the greatest hidden belief that I was an Eternal burning with 10,000 beacon fires. I knew my biggest problem would be summoning up the courage to get out there and tell people about it.

See, Phonogram Records were so uninterested in my situation that I was halfway through the album before they knew about it. Paul King had said, "Fuck 'em, Copey. Let's book the studio and do it." Sure. I had an album title and a bunch of songs: 'Land of Fear', 'World Shut Your Mouth', 'Reynard the Fox', 'Bill Drummond Said' and 'Sunspots'. It seemed as though it could really only go one way.

The nucleus of people was important. I needed certain trusted friends around at all times. Johnno was 21. I wanted him to learn about making an album. I figured he could be a future producer. Maybe my future producer. And Ady Wilson. He was my good-vibe and driver-supreme. He learned the entire Cambridge drug situation in one day flat. And Steve Lovell. I loved Steve and trusted him implicitly. Also, as an ex-acid head, it was easy to goad him into taking shit further than he wanted to.

I consciously made a point of only asking Donald down for a few days. He was on the brink of being sucked into my thing completely, but his independence was what I found most attractive. Hell, this was a guy who had sleepwalked nude when he stayed over at his friend's house, aged 14. Aged 18, he had lived with the Tamworth witches. No, Donald was an extremely impressive teenager. But whenever people had got too close in the past, I had dumped them pretty damn quickly. Donald deserved more. Hell, I deserved Donald!

In the main room of Spaceward Studios, the group songs sounded great: Johnno in one corner on bass, Steve on guitar and me, bare-chested and in red tie-dye tights, ranting around on the floor. A young guy called Chris Whitten came down to play the drums. But first he had to be persuaded by Steve Lovell. Chris had just left The Waterboys because he hated the petulance of their singer, Mike Scott, and said he'd heard worse things about me. I was determined to be a sweetheart all the time he was there. I was. I wanted him to go away loving me. Julian Cope, he would say to friends, is not weird or full of shit. That's what I hoped, anyway.

The basic group finished in two days. Chris Whitten left immediately and that's when we got serious about the whole thing. To truly capture the performance, the listener has to be able to *feel* what the singer is wearing. He should be able to see right into the moment of each song and say, "Yeah, that song takes place on the side of a hill" or "This song was sung when the guy was in a black, black mood." So you've got to help suck the listener in to your trip. You have to start at the record sleeve and end with the fade out of the final song. In the past, I had been content to decorate the studio a little and wear special outfits for recording. But not this time. This time had to be more. It was to be a complete trip from now on.

Steve Lovell was fixated by Brian Wilson of The Beach Boys. When I say "fixated", I really just mean obsessed. But I decided that he *should* be fixated. It was only right that my producer be psychotically *into* his thing. Steve put up a photograph of Brian Wilson in the studio. It hung in this shitty frame above the main tape machine. Every day, Steve would consult Brian on how the album was going.

I told Steve that he looked a little like Brian, which he didn't.

"Yeah?" Steve was surprised. He usually got compared with Martin Sheen or John F. Kennedy. "I'll have to put some weight on, man."

No, there was no need for that, I told him. Just wear your shirt outside your pants.

In the following days, Steve Lovell took on a true Brian Wilson persona. He let Chas the engineer make all technical decisions while he concentrated on sound and studio atmosphere. He combed his hair into this cool subnormal look and we moved a single bed into the control room. This last idea was mine and didn't work out too well. Steve hated being in bed all the time and seemed to do it to avoid hurting my feelings. It lasted a couple of days, but the bed remained for the duration of the album.

What was it in me? Why could I never just let people do their own thing? I always had to butt in and say no, non, this way, this way! I was horribly aware of it but I couldn't even consider changing my behaviour. That would have upset me.

And so, as the recording progressed, our cocoon splintered into two groups. And of course, I had to be in both of them. The control room became a hive of artistic activity: Chas at the controls, Steve in the chair, Brian on the wall and myself on the move. Johnno and Ady began to feel left out. It was inevitable, really. They became more drunk every day *and* more drugged out. I hung out with them in the back room, but then I'd go back to work, leaving them to get more destroyed. It was a Catch 22 thing. Johnno had nothing to do so he got out of his head. He'd be out of his head when I finally needed him, so I'd get pissed off and do it myself. Next time, I'd be less inclined to ask him. I'd just do it myself. As for Donald Ross Skinner, he was brilliant. He did his thing on all the songs and left four days later. Between his arrival and departure, the album changed shape entirely.

One night, Johnno and Ady were out scoring in Cambridge. They were due back at 7 o'clock but by midnight they were still missing. We were recording a song called 'Mik Mak Mok" and Johnno was supposed to play all the guitar parts. Finally, at 1.30 a.m., Ady walked in, sheepish but smiling his head off. He nodded a greeting and walked into the back room. I ran in and asked where the fuck Johnno was, and did he get any pot? Ady didn't say a word, just pointed outside and slumped down on the sofa bed.

Steve and I roamed out into the studio's schoolyard. In the farthest, darkest corner, Ady's car was impossible to make out. As we got nearer, though, I noticed that the passenger door was open and there was a loud snoring that cut the dead silence. Johnno's legs were still in the car, his feet crossed in a vision of total comfort. The rest of him was asleep on the floor of the schoolyard. He had obviously opened the door and promptly collapsed.

I was incensed. I had always insisted that people I worked with were more together than me. And now, here was Johnno acting the lead singer!

Steve and I grabbed an end each and hauled him into the back room. We lay him on the floor and I opened the blinds. That way, he would wake up all dehydrated with the morning sun blasting his eyes. Then we left for our hotel.

In the morning, it was all forgotten. I loved Johnno too much to keep it up. But the rest of *Fried* pretty much excluded his contributions.

Cambridge was a cool hang that summer. The sky was blue and the weather was up in the mid 80s all the time. I found an old toy shop down a back street and visited it every few days. One time, I picked up an old Corgi Toys gift set from amongst the garbage on the floor of the shop. It was incredible ... a set of Chipperfield's Circus vehicles that I'd had as a child. The guy in the shop knew old toys were worth money and he couldn't let me have it for less than £25. What a bargain! I charged out of the shop with my booty. The whole time in Cambridge was worth it just for that one buy.

Dorian finally plucked up the courage to drive the Karmann-Ghia all the way from Tamworth. She arrived a little freaked out but happy. Johnny Mellor and his girlfriend Chris came down for a while and the whole recording session turned into a party when Pete DeFreitas and Jake Brockman arrived on their Ducatti motorbikes with Andy Eastwood and his girlfriend Kathy. The little village square rang with the sound of late-night football and grooving from the schoolyard. We hung out and tripped and drank and danced at the studio and I was happy. Happy to have a distant and isolated scene, not aligned to anyone in particular and populated with everyone I cared about.

There was a primitive industrial video computer on which I spent hours creating endless rolling sprawls, each one reading the word "Fried", the colour and shape swelling and distorting and undulating like flock wallpaper during an acid trip.

By now, Phonogram Records had found out that I was recording. But they had decided to trust Paul King's judgement. Cally Callomon drove over from London all the time with ideas and scams for *Fried* which really excited me. I was flattered that anyone would have put in so much thought.

Spaceward Studios was so hippy that they undercharged us over 50% for the first half of the recording. It seemed that I could do as I liked and I began to feel comfortable at last. My friends and my surroundings altered the feel of the album completely. I felt no need to add extraneous noises or instruments, their presence made me feel comfortable and that became reflected in the emptiness of the record.

On one of our brief sorties to Cambridge, I picked up a huge old turtle shell from an antique/junk shop. It cost £30 and was brittle as hell. Back at the studio, I stripped off my clothes and climbed underneath it. Awlright! It was me! So much so that I laughed. Everyone laughed. It looked ridiculous but they nevertheless agreed that it was made for me.

So, in the true spirit of the recording, Steve Lovell insisted that I should sing from under the turtle shell. Imagine that! What a story to tell everyone!

We set up a low-level microphone and bathed the area in pale blue light to create a mood. Then I crouched down on my hands and feet as they lowered the shell on to my back. The music started and I began to sing. It was total shit. No power at all. No vocal range, either. It was like flying a plane with half the engines in the cargo hold. Oh, well. We tried it at least.

From then on, any visitor to the studio would be subjected to my turtle shell crawls across the floor. I spent hours in front of a large mirror, practising turtle movements – eating, sleeping, registering surprise and fear. It was wonderful. And I knew that this must be the image for the *Fried* album sleeve. But how to get it past the censors at the record company? I'd been given shit for the last album sleeve. And that was just because I was hiding my face! I told Cally Callomon the idea. He loved it. He told me not to worry. He was an ally. I stopped worrying. I knew he could make it happen.

Fried was almost finished. I had written a tiny and ultra-simple thing called 'Torpedo' on the Hammond organ. I added autoharp and this became the final song.

I'd sung all the songs except 'Reynard the Fox' completely nude. The record was more fragile that way and I felt sure that it would be noticeable to the listener. I wanted to subtitle the album "Tales of Pursuit", but that seemed like stating the obvious when I listened to *Fried* as a whole. We had worked hard and we had achieved. What it was, we did not yet know, but I was the happy dude. I sent Ady and Johnno to get some acid. It was party time.

I had already taken one tab of LSD and was trying to persuade my producer to trip out whilst we mixed a song called 'Sunspots'. But Steve refused on the grounds that it was going to be released as a single.

"Listen," I told him. "You have one tab, just one, okay? I'll take another at the same time. Just to *prove* how mild it is. Now that's gotta be cool."

"Alright then," said a worn-down Lovell. We swallowed one each and walked into the studio. It was time to work.

Bango Bango Bango!

A ha ha ha ha ha ha ha ha ha ha ha ha ha ha ha ha ha ha ha ha ha ha ha ha ha ha ha ha ha ha ha ha ha ha ha ha ha ha ha ha ha ha ha ha ha ha ha ha ha.

Oh, no! Laughing acid!

Ten minutes after we took the trip, my first dose suddenly hit me like a 747 knocking down a five-bar gate. Uh oh . . . How to tell Steve? I decided to cop out and ran screaming to the back room. And there I stayed for what seemed like the rest of my life, perched on the corner table and laughing my head off, with the vacuum cleaner gripped tightly in both hands as my only protection.

There was a beautiful arched window high up in the main wall. But I had never before noticed how filthy it was. Shit, the women will be coming to cook for us soon. I'll have to clean that thing before anyone can consider eating. I climbed up on the TV and crossed to the window ledge. Then, with the hose stretched to its fullest length and the hoover growling its disapproval, I began to vacuum the glass obsessively.

Forty-five minutes later, I was still up there. And still clinging. Below me, Steve Lovell was off his head laughing hysterically and slagging me off: "You dickhead, how am I gonna mix now? A ha ha ha ha ha ha ha ha. Come on, Copey. Oh, hiya. I'm the producer. Yeah, the one who's tripping. A ha ha ha ha ha ha ha ha ha ha."

Standing in the doorway, the two cooks watched Steve Lovell, fascinated. With Johnno, Ady and myself for comparison, they had always treated Steve as the boss. They had immediately accepted my need to clean the window, but Steve's behaviour was scaring them. Steve sensed this at once and ran back to the control room, where he intended to stay for the rest of the night. He sat on the bed and consulted Chas. "What would Brian Wilson do?"

"He'd chill out and trust the engineer," said Chas the engineer. Steve accepted this as good sense.

When I finally summoned the courage to re-enter the control room, it was awash with sound and Steve had found a "new beat".

"What the hell is this?" I asked, dumbfounded.

"It's 'Sunspots'." Chas sounded hurt.

"*My* song 'Sunspots'?" I found it hard to believe that anything could sound that way. It felt as though someone was stuffing my ears with marshmallow. And there was an awful grating noise of guys breaking off skyscrapers and using them as toothpicks.

"There's a new beat, man." Steve sat crouched over with his ear to the tiny mono speaker.

"Ignore him," said Chas. "He's been on this 'new beat' thing for bloody ages."

I listened for the new beat. Boom-clang, boom-clang, boom-clang, A-langa-langa-lang . . . It was on the clang, Steve told me. I listened and listened and . . . he was right!

"Yeah, Chas. There's a new beat. He's right."

Soon, Chas sent us out. All we could hear was the new beat. We couldn't hear one note of the song anymore. And then Steve forgot what the new beat was and I wasn't sure that I'd ever heard it in the first place.

Two hours later, we ambled sheepishly into the control room. Chas was hard at work and we did *not* want to annoy him. This trip was taking its toll on me. In the past year, I had considerably cut down on my LSD intake. Whereas in the Teardrop, I could trip for a week at a time, nowadays I was taking acid only frequently. In my space in the control room, I was a mess. If I ever came out of this, I would stop taking hallucinogenics forever.

The rhythm of 'Sunspots' was still impossible to make out. It moved like an old cutter through the sea.

"What d'ya think then?" asked Chas.

"Man ... I can't tell. Is it in the right key?" Steve Lovell was confused as all hell. He looked at me for wisdom but I was a blank page. "I'll ask Brian," he said and stood in front of the photograph.

At that moment, the Brian Wilson picture lost its footing in the shitty frame. It slid gracelessly out of its position and fell down behind the 24-track tape machine. Steve Lovell sank down on the bed. I stood motionless. Maybe it hadn't happened. We *were* on acid, after all.

"Man," said Steve. "What's going on?" He looked as though someone just proved to him that there was no God.

We rummaged around under the tape machine but could not find Brian anywhere. I was distraught, but not nearly so bad as Steve.

"Chas, was that weird?" asked Steve. "I mean, weird to you. . .? You're not tripping. So . . . was it weird or not? You know . . . to someone who is *not* tripping."

"Yeah. It was well weird," said Chas, trying to extract us from our twilight zone.

Steve and I hung around looking for more parts of the studio to clean until Chas shovelled us off back to the hotel just before dawn. The next morning was the final day of the album. 'Sunspots' sounded great – a hit single for sure. The album was ready and we done good. As we departed for our various homes, I felt sad as hell. *Fried* was going to hold a special place in my heart forever and ever.

SCAM KIDD

QUESTION: How do you get a picture of a naked guy under a turtle shell on the front of a major record label album sleeve in 1984?

ANSWER: Through lies, sneakiness and a wilful and sassy conspirator in the heart of that record company.

And so it was to be with the *Fried* sleeve. A covert operation followed by a *fait accompli*. And leading this conspiracy was Cally Callomon, a guy who turned out to have the most angles I have ever seen. In my Teardrop days, Bill Drummond pulled off some cool schemes. But Cally? Nere ... Cally shit all over Drummond for depth of idea and practical planning. And I had known him for almost a year before he revealed himself. He was clever. He understood my paranoia and gradually unveiled his enormous capacity for doing precisely what the fuck he wanted.

Cally and I were extremely similar. We were very middle class and we had both been bullied at school, singled out and hassled into intricate deceptions to make life bearable. But I was 6'2" and had beaten it by becoming the ever-smiling psychopath. Cally was only 5'8". He had, out of necessity, chosen the path of goofball and lovable loon. But underneath this front was a depth of character I had forgotten ever existed. He had the strongest sense of loyalty I'd seen in a man. Far more than mine.

Cally had been a class of '77 punk in London. But he would have suited the Liverpool scene much better. He was taking the piss out of the whole schmeer before most people had even heard of it. He had edited fake punk fanzines, deadly serious on the outside but poking vicious fingers at the scene's latecomers. He had no time for fakers and had started to dress like a psychedelic boy, as much to piss off the new punks as anything else.

He hated organised religion, too. So he edited a fake religious pamphlet called *The Humble Meek*. It was 90% dead serious with only tiny giveaways dotted hither and yon. The thing was even sold at religious bookstalls for a while. And he kept it going for much longer than was necessary: the sign of the true subversive.

If Cally Callomon had a problem then it was this: he was *too* sussed. He just had to take the piss. In the summer of 1977, Vertigo Records had wanted to release a punk compilation called *New Wave*. Cally was incensed. He saw that Vertigo had secured the rights to Patti Smith's first single, the lost genius of 'Piss Factory', and intended to use it as the main crowbar with which to prise the money out of limited Punk Pockets. Reading this as the beginning of the end, and having friends who did LP sleeves and knew A&R men, Cally infiltrated Vertigo as a temporary 'punk' consultant and set about suggesting a bunch of terrible groups who had nothing to do with punk. The lowest that he sunk was to include a bunch of Australian painted art-funk no-marks called The Skyhooks. Then he had grown a moustache especially for the LP sleeve and had a mate gob into the camera lens for the ultra *Sun/Mirror* clichéd Rentapunk. This is true and I have the LP still. As he had hoped, the album was released and treated as a total joke. But everyone, me included, bought the record just for 'Piss Factory' and had to learn to live with a moustachioed punk on the sleeve. It was a brilliant idea, but it had sailed over everyone's heads for this one reason – if you get as accurate as Cally's send-ups were, then rather than have people laugh at the result, you actually begin to influence people. Soon, Midland groups like GBH and Chron Gen would be un-ironically wearing moustaches, doubtless citing the *New Wave* LP as proof of genuine punk acceptability . . .

But no matter. Now we were a team. And with me as cracker of the aesthetic whip, there would be no room for cosiness or playful *cul-de-sacs*. I had no doubt that Cally and I could tame each other's weaknesses and become smiling *agent provocateurs*. The first Bourgeois-zealots.

· · ·

In Tamworth, one week later, Dorian and I sat transfixed. We were stuck in the property section of the *Tamworth Herald* newspaper, looking for a bigger house and trying to choose sensibly. Unfortunately, we had been struck a cosmic blow. The first place that we'd visited, a huge white 18th-century farmhouse called "Yew Tree House", had been perfect. Then we discovered that it was part of the estate of Sir Robert Peel, a former prime minister and creator of the police force. Now, we could think of living nowhere else. Months before, I had written the song called 'Laughing Boy', which had included the lyric:

"The king and queen have offered me the estate of Robert Peel."

It was a sign for sure. A big ugly signpost plainly pointing us where to go. We looked vaguely at other properties, but not with any real intent. The Yew Tree House lyric prediction had taken the wind out of our sails.

In London, Paul King became all-wealthy. Outlaw was becoming one of *thee* management companies. I was proud that I had helped get it started, but it got to me that these two little kids in Tears for Fears were earning all the money. Paul told me to chill out. The debts were still enormous, but they would come down eventually. And in the meantime, Kingy told me, buying a bigger house was our best financial move.

And so we put in a bid for the Peel house and it all began to roll. I was concerned about one thing only: space. My mind was busy reshooting that Belushi scene before the Toga party in *Animal House*. And in my head, my brain screamed out: "Toy Room, Toy Room, Toy Room, Toy Room . . ."

Every weekend, Cally drove up to Tamworth with plans for *Fried*. Its release date was set for late October and we wanted to be ready. We arranged the album photo session with an industrial photographer, an Italian guy called Donato Cinicolo. It would take place on Alvecote Mound, only 800 yards from the Priory, the sight of the previous album shoot.

On September 6th, we took a huge picnic basket and cameras up to the mound. Dorian organised the pot and our friend Nigel Dick filmed everything on his Super 8 camera. It was the perfect day. The sky was classically English in its vague blue-grey cloudiness. And far away in the surrounding villages of Shuttington and Newton Regis, the farmers had picked this day to burn off all their unwanted hay fields. As I clambered under the turtle shell and Donato began to shoot, we were amazed at this providence. The palls of smoke which, by now, stretched into harmony with the surrounding weather formations, provided a natural and incredible backdrop to the tiny and ugly scene on the Mound.

I had bought a largely wrecked red Triang toy truck from Bath indoor market. It had no front wheels at all. On its side, Cally's wife Jennie had painted the word "Fried" in childlike yellow lettering. Donato posed myself and the truck together. We had equal billing. That was its major strength. Like an absurd recreation of Stanley meeting Dr Livingstone. I knew that it was classic. Now . . . how to sneak it past the censors at the record company?

At home, however, we were having problems. The time to move was creeping upon us but we were hearing dubious reports about Yew Tree House. My father had suggested an independent search be made, concerning all the ancient earthworks and various amendments since the late 18th century. Ha. No problem. This house was chosen for us psychically! We were *fated* to live there. But I was not scoffing when Dorian heard from a local taxi driver that the house was haunted.

Sure enough, my father had heard the same story. Shit, we were only days from exchanging contracts. We had to go with it, we just had to. The Mill Lane house had already been sold to a young guy called Richard Cuttler, whose brother David had been head boy in my year at school. I liked Richard a lot and did not want to mess him around.

Then two days before we paid over the money, the independent report told us that our "new house" was a total disaster – flooring, sub-flooring, the whole place was built over an ancient mine-shaft. We pulled out at top speed.

In London, meanwhile, Paul King and Cally were getting their shit together. Phonogram Records had finally heard the album and were more than a little unhappy. But Paul King was in a mighty strong position. As the manager of Tears for Fears, he insisted that they bear with me. The whole album had cost only £19,000 to record and anyway, "Copey needs to do this at the moment. It won't be forever. Tears for Fears are already over £200,000 for this new one."

Cally put the sleeve together in his own time and presented them with the finished article. Photo costs: £215. Cheap, cheap, cheap, guys, just let it slide out. He designed an inelegant inner-sleeve and a poster too: a shot of me crouched and lonely in the Alvecote swamp. No lettering and mightily ugly.

So Kingy and Cally turned a series of most definite "no"s from the record company into a bunch of hazy "maybe, but probably not"s. And finally, through sheer Kingian determination and stubborn Callyness, *Fried* achieved its release date in the precise form that we had intended.

I was ecstatic. The record's strength was its gentle ugliness. I had great romantic visions that it would turn aside any public antipathy towards me. Shit, more than that. This could even be big!

Dorian and I prepared for our forthcoming "official" wedding on Long Island, New York. And prepare we must. It was to be a large Greek Orthodox affair at, get this, St. Paul's cathedral in Hempstead. We asked Dorian's mother, Helen, to hire us a 1949 Buick Roadmaster as a wedding car. If I was to have a big do, it had to be extreme.

At American weddings, the bride and groom give a gift, a "favour", to each and every guest. I thought toy London buses would be appropriate, so Cally, the scam kid, bought 100 of them from Matchbox Toys. He designed stickers for both sides of each bus. One said "Dorian and Julian Cope". The other read "Long Island Wedding 1984". And, of course, we never paid for them. It was just one of many details.

Cally was the King of Detail. If a Cope fan wrote to Phonogram, Cally would send what he called "bumper packs". He'd just find all the merchandise he could and send it for free. For a short time, fans would receive T-shirts, videos, promo singles, badges, posters, even albums, all together in the same package. Cally loved to blow people's minds. We trained together to utilise all kinds of reverse psychology.

JOHN THE BAPTIST

Paul King and Paul Crockford told me that I had to have a stag night. What? Whoa, I'll have none of that nakedness and strippers dressed as school-mistresses. That's the ugliest thing I could imagine.

After hearing all that, Kingy and Crockford planned a stag night of such un-me proportions that I refused to enter the place. Joss and I were tripping and were in no state to handle the social niceties of a London club, so Cally and Donneye negotiated with us for 40 minutes until we were persuaded in. But hell broke out immediately when two strippers dressed as school-mistresses entered the bar and came close to me. I took off and hid behind the chairs in a corner, while they took their undies off and masturbated with canes. I grabbed Joss and we hightailed outta-there. In my tripping state, I was a four year old with a sandpit mentality.

For the rest of the evening, I dodged in and out of restaurant back-alleys full of garbage bags and huge industrial dumpsters, while Paul Crockford's people tried to retrieve me. To send me bollock-naked and tripping on a train bound for Penzance, no doubt. They never did, so the fucking stag won for a change. Right on.

Then one day, I was dealt a blow. An enormous blow. I had to get baptised. In order to have a Greek Orthodox wedding, I had to be baptised. I couldn't think straight. Getting baptised was the last thing I wanted to do. God would think that I was trying to appease him. What a crock of bullshit! No way would I do such a thing to appease him. I'd made that perfectly clear to myself hundreds of times. My whole quest was based on beating evil myself. Running to God, even *appearing* to run to him, was more than I could stand.

A head spin. A tail spin. A body spinnin'. A-see the spin I'm in.

Dorian understood quite well – not everything, but enough to see the headtrips I was having. If I could not handle doing it, she said, we could call it all off. And she meant it. Awlright! This is true love talking. A great, selfless love aimed right at me. It gave me enormous strength and resolution. I decided to get baptised just for Dorian. I felt strong, too. In his heart of hearts, God would know that I was not doing this for him. I could be honourable *and* remain independent.

Fortuitously, I had recently met my old history teacher, John Fairclough. He had left teaching after 20 years to become a poorly paid junior cleric. I had always admired John Fairclough tremendously. His gentle Kenneth Williams English school of campness had helped to make my schooldays merely unbearable. Early that autumn, Dorian and I visited him in his little flat in Burton. I explained that I needed to get baptised, but not for religious reasons. I also explained that I was at odds with the Christian God and was using large amounts of drugs. John Fairclough soothed me. He said that baptism was only a first step, like filling out an entry form to join a club. It was confirmation that made you a full member.

I did some interviews in London whilst I considered my position. Yeah, I could live with it. It was just a test. I was being compromised by the Christian God to see if I could differentiate between my love for Dorian and my more selfish desire to understand my place in the stars. Ha. Gimme a break – of course I can.

It was the same situation with Yew Tree House – Fate was playing these tricks on us to test our mettle. They were Fate's diversions. To see if we could distinguish between true signs and these bogus ones sent merely to confuse us.

Whilst I was busy, Dorian and my mother had two weeks to find us a new house. Get anything, I told them. Honestly, I don't mind. After the previous wind-up, I was in no mood to fool around. Dorian found a place in Drayton Bassett, the other side of Tamworth, and promptly left for New York, two weeks ahead of me. She had shitloads of organising to do and I still had to get baptised.

On the actual day of the ceremony, I was nervous as all hell. With my wife away, every part of me seemed naked and defenceless. As I was about to leave the house, I was suddenly struck by a fear that my inherent evil would be exposed in church. I would have no protection.

I ran back in to the house and stripped off my jacket and shirt. Then, I took the thick black permanent marker-pen and, for the first time in over a year, daubed the black "X" back onto my torso.

At the church, everything went smoothly. The ceremony was simple and lovely, and John Fairclough's friends had all come down to lend support. But all the way home, I was ridden with guilt once more. The "X" on my side felt nasty. I hadn't needed that shit. My spinelessness repulsed me, as though evil had crept in around the back door.

THE BRITISH IN NORTH AMERICA

October 1984. When Dorian picked me up at New York's Kennedy Airport, there was a badness going on. As we trailed slowly down the Long Island Expressway towards Port Washington, I felt as though we were entering hell. The back-up of cars was all the way to the horizon, their tail-lights flickering in the filthy mist. I had not been to New York in ages and felt it consuming me like an outsize cancer.

For the previous two weeks, Dorian and I had spoken daily on the telephone. All was not well. Her father, Steve, was very ill. Close to death, Doctor Rubin had said. Could he make it through the ceremony? We honestly didn't know.

Steve Beslity had been at death's door for years. It was only his complete craziness and his undying love for a wife that he worshipped which had kept him going. The whole family had lived with the possibility of losing him since Dorian was nine years old. Now, he was struck down once more. And, as usual, fighting and protesting with all the obstinacy of an old donkey. He was uncontrollable. A crazy man.

See, Steve had always lived for the moment. And especially *this* moment. His life with Helen had been a roller-coaster ride, from the time they eloped when she was 19 right up to the present moment, when he was insisting on paying for an enormous Greek Orthodox wedding and party for his beloved daughter with money that he did not have. This was nothing new. It was just Steve's way. His whole life had been the same. He had written off car after amazing car, flown solo for 12 years with an illegal license (he never declared that he was diabetic), taken the family around the world at any opportunity, and devised schemes so far-out that his 30 different business partners either thought him genius or lunatic and the family could either be wealthy or broke at any given time.

I was still reeling from the news of impending death and bankruptcy when Dorian dropped the bomb: "Julian, I'm pregnant."

"Huh? How can you be? You're on the Pill."

"I know, I haven't missed a day." Dorian was on the verge of hysteria.

Shit, why now? Neither of us can handle this now. Babies have to be thought about. You can't go dropping them anywhere.

We cried and moaned all the way to Port Washington. Neither of us could believe it. Pregnancy is supposed to be so happy. We couldn't have a child where we were at. I was mad ... I'd kill it with my thoughts alone.

The house on the Island was total bloody hell. Awash with relatives pouring in to help out, to give advice, to render service, to get in the bloody way. Helen and Steve had roaring arguments in front of everyone. First, a rasping male voice in the bedroom would scream, "Hullun!" Then this beautiful Greek goddess of a woman would put her elbows together and clap with her wrists, all the time screaming: "Uh, uh, uh!" Then Steve would walk in, see her playing the performing seal and lose his mind. They didn't care. It even occasionally got a few people to leave. Steve was so ill, he just couldn't take the pressure at all.

Their neighbour, Mary Lou, was helping out with some of the arrangements. But she ran everything astrologically and tried to introduce her psychic into the proceedings. That weirded Dorian out because she was terrified of having it confirmed by someone else that her father might drop dead walking her down the aisle.

Then Yolanda came to stay. She was Steve's Hungarian half-sister. She'd been living in Hollywood for 50 years and still sounded like Zsa Zsa Gabor. "O, dahr-ling, I theenk yoo shood do eet this wey." Yolanda had her own line of expensive cosmetics in California called "Yolanda". She looked amazing.

And finally, Joss and my parents arrived. Nearly two weeks before the wedding. Great. They were utterly bewildered by events in the house. They were used to the quiet South Walean sobriety and fake decorum of our sweep-it-under-the-carpet family.[1]

Helen figured out a way to get them all out of the house. She gave Yolanda the mission of looking after them. Yolanda would bring them strong stewed English tea with lemon every morning at 8 a.m., and escort them around the sights of New York. It was weird. I had never seen my parents so lost . . . They looked like little kids on the first day of school.

The spectre of abortion hung over our every move. Happy stuff like the fitting of the bridesmaids' dresses, organising the seating arrangement for the reception, it was all tainted by *that*. I understood for the first time why aged aunts and uncles referred to extremely unpleasant memories with a raising of eyes to the heavens and the whispering of words in a stylised, almost humorous way. It was the only way to get through it. How else could you deal with something like *this*?

The Beslity finances were truly shattered. The day after the wedding, Helen and Steve were due to pack up and quit this private beach-front paradise and move into a tiny two-bedroom apartment. Meanwhile, my parents knew nothing about the problems that were going on all around us. I had never been able to tell my mother anything serious. Her solution to problems was to worry so much that *she* became the subject of concern.

Dorian and I desperately needed to be alone. But it was completely imposs-ible. Joss expected to be entertained. My parents expected to be entertained.

---

1 We had incest and in-breeding over three generations in our family, which is probably why they "treated us like royalty in the village", as my painter cousin John Uzzell Edwards wrote to me recently.

And so did Yolanda. I wished that they would all piss off and leave us in peace. Every day, the Beslity house become more and more littered with people; friends and relatives who understandably wanted to add to the happiness of the occasion. Of course, this was agony for Dorian, Helen and myself. We three alone knew the full story and, out of necessity, we became an emotional triumvirate, each dedicated to helping the other two get through this time.

Dorian began to look and feel pregnant to me. I ached to take her pain away and my recent exposure to God confused and angered me. Soon after my arrival in New York, I had told Dorian about the return of the black cross. I was concerned about the implications. What if I had no control over it? What if I am the Anti-Christ? Dorian refused to entertain the idea. Refused point-blank and said forget it. And that turned me around. I was to become a tower of strength in the next weeks. I loved this woman beyond words, beyond gestures and way down the road into true loss of self. It was beautiful because it was so easy.

So why was it so difficult? Over the coming weeks, the telephone did battle with pretty much everyone. No 1949 Buick? Get two '59 Cadillacs, then. Dave Bates can't be an usher? Fuck him, then, we only go back to the Beginning. I'd prefer Steve Gibaldi anyway. Hi, Cally. I got the *Fried* sleeve. It's perfect. No, no bulky gifts. Sorry, but it's all got to go back to England. Hello, Kingy, yeah, the house is going through fine. Can the office finish up all the details? Stax? Nere, no soul. Just bring the bubble gum and the garage stuff, okay?

A garage group called The Chesterfield Kings were going to do the reception, then we cancelled them on account of their being wholly inappropriate for anyone but the bride and groom. Suits got altered, dresses got bought, grass got toked and tempers got frayed. My father finally snapped one day and punched my brother out – an event as unlikely and unanticipated as the Queen posing for *Playboy*. Joss had not done a thing, but that was hardly the point, was it?

And in the midst of all this, the abortion got "taken care of". I have one message for those anti-abortionists who have the nerve to call themselves "pro-life". This is not a dainty world and no-one ever told you it was. The ultra-judgemental Lord Above is probably the guy who put you in this frame of mind anyway. If you can't accept reality, wheresoever that fundamental piece of earth exists, then Fuck off and live with the Amish. When you shoot a legal abortionist, your whole argument about the sanctity of life becomes null and void.

Somehow, October 28th finally rolled around. The wedding day. Joss and I slept at the apartment Helen and Steve would soon be moving to, got stoned and got ready. At around 2 p.m., our cream 1959 Cadillac Coupe de Ville arrived. Panic for a while, as neither us nor the driver knew where the church was, but we were soon on our way. . .

Have you ever seen *The Deerhunter*? Remember the wedding? With the '59

Cadillac and the Greek ceremony? That was *our* wedding; the same thing. At St Paul's cathedral, Hempstead, Long Island, Dorian and I stood together at the first altar. She looked like a little Greek doll and I was grinning like a fool. Steve, her father, had looked on the verge of collapse as he led her down the aisle, but he was too proud to fall over. The priest admired Dorian's thrift shop dress and began to sing his piece. High up in the Gods, at the back of the hall, another guy echoed every word that was sung. It was eerie and beautiful.

Concessions had been made as I was English. Everything would be sung six times: three in Greek, for the Holy Trinity, then three times in English for the same reason.

Then the priest fed us wine and led us dancing up to the next altar. We took the most unlikely route imaginable; the entire wedding party dipped and swayed around the stage. Matron of honour and best man, bridesmaids and ushers, each one trying to keep up with this jocular priest.

At the next altar, we were bound together by lace crowns linked with streamers. Dorian's Tante Mary placed them upon our heads and the priest fed us more wine. Then Joss handed over the ring and in 45 minutes it was done.

There had been no words. No "I do". Nothing. Instead, we had been bound together symbolically and spiritually. A fitting ceremony for our love. At the end of the service, the congregation parted and we danced down the aisle, grinning stupidly.

The rest of the night was a wild celebration. Dorian and I danced our way through the first song, by Frank Sinatra, and sat down to eat with Pink Floyd's 'Astronomie Dominie' ringing in our ears.

Someone showed us a copy of the *Melody Maker*. There was a news item on me. Under a turtle shell photograph was the caption: "Is it a bird? Is it a plane? Is it a twat?" Well, tonight nothing can faze me. I loved this wild family with its wild friends and associated crazies. We danced around tables handing out the London buses and everyone had a great time.

At the end of the reception, Dorian and I drove to our hotel and part-ayed! We had cut through the crap together and were even stronger for it. There was to be no honeymoon. We had said we didn't want one and, anyway, tomorrow we would be helping Helen and Steve move house. I didn't care one bit. For Dorian or Helen, I'd eat m'own shit.

KID STRANGE

In early November, we returned to England, our heads full of wedding and house moves. The Mill Lane house was wall-to-wall boxes, all labelled and taped with an obsessive precision. I had refused to be caught napping and insisted that everything be ready way in advance. At this time, however, I had only seen the new house once. The present owners, Mr and Mrs Shah, were a weird Indian couple who had told Dorian that he was a doctor and they had properties up and down the country. I visited the place again just before we moved in. The house was ugly as hell. But the vileness of the decor was mightily over-shadowed by an enormous pink bejewelled elephant in the centre of the huge living room. Oh well. We'll soon make it seem like home.

But the weeks rolled by and nothing happened. The Shahs became unavail-able and were clearly in no hurry to move out. Richard Cuttler was desperate to occupy the Mill Lane house and, as I knew him, it made stalling tactics particularly uncomfortable.

My paranoia level rose dramatically. Every night, we would drive over to Drayton Bassett to spy on our new home. Dorian would drive into Rectory Close and drive to the park at the end, where she would park the car behind the sports house. Then I would creep up the short driveway and peer into the front window. And every night was the same: shit, they haven't even moved the vases off the window-sill yet.

I could not think straight. They were doing this on purpose. I was on the phone all the time. Shit, why won't they get the fuck out?

I longed for simplicity. I longed for a life that was not hell-bent on answering questions. It seemed that every part of my life was a major cross-roads, but the drugs and the negative reputation that was building around me served only to make me question even the most basic and unremarkable event.

In the past, if a spider had crossed the carpet, Dorian would scream: "Julian, a bug! Kill it! Kill it!" and I would normally grab a piece of paper and get the spider to walk on it, then carefully carry it outside to safety. But now I was growing to resent their easy existence. Sometimes, I just squashed them. Take that, you lucky sod.

Whilst I was away in New York, my new album had deserted me. Rush-released to capitalise on the failure of the *World Shut Your Mouth* album, poor *Fried* had entered the charts at no. 85 and dropped out one week later. I was so sad. I'd really thought it stood a chance of being huge.

I would take the record out and study the sleeve whilst I listened to it. But I felt stupid. It was a stillborn baby.

I knew the album was good. So I realised that it must be me. *I* was putting everyone off with my supposed craziness. The music press never wrote a word about me, unless it was some damning and humorous description of my activi-ties, real or imagined. If a person becomes a little crazy, other people tend to think that it's a carved-in-stone craziness. "Keep away, he's off his head." And that starts the head trips and it makes you more crazy. It's a cumulative effect.

For example, one time I met a journalist in the Columbia Hotel. I was with Bernie Connors, and we were on our hands and knees on the third floor. We were pretending to be domestic animals because we were tripping. And Glen

Matlock, the guy who got booted out of the Sex Pistols, was following us around trying to make conversation. "I'm Glen Matlock, I used to be in the Sex Pistols," that kind of level. Throughout this strange scenario, this journalist was dead friendly, so I was nice to him. But, of course, only as nice as someone who is being an animal can be.

Time went on and I never saw the journalist again. Not until I was tripping out of my brain in a café. He walked in and I tried to act as normal as was possible. And all went well, until he ordered a cappuccino, which sent me to the moon in hysterics for the rest of the time we were together.

The outcome of this was that he could not write a word about me without shouting loud and long about how crazy I was. And I knew that, based on his experience, it was a quite reasonable attitude for him to have about *me* – but it was so unfair on *my songs*, because my songs are what I speak through, not my everyday life. Albums are like children and you don't want them to suffer at school because the parents have a bad reputation.

It was December 7th, the morning of the move. The Mill Lane house was completely empty. The removal men were on their five-mile journey to our new home in Drayton Bassett, whilst Donald, Joss, Dorian and I piled the last bits of paraphernalia into our rented Luton van. Then we waved goodbye to our old house and set off bumpily down the road, Joss and I balanced precariously in the back of the van, trying desperately to support our 10 million most fragile belongings.

The previous night, we had made a final reconnaissance mission to the new house. There had been no sign of movement whatsoever and the nik-naks were still in their usual places. I was extremely paranoid. What if they didn't leave? They had acted as though they were loaded, though. Shit. I couldn't sleep all that night. And now we were getting closer and closer every minute. I crossed my fingers and hoped for the best.

We arrived to a far-out sight. The Shah family was moving the entire contents of this huge four-bedroomed house in a small VW van. Uncles and cousins rushed around ordering each other to do various things, while nothing appeared to be actually getting done. It was moving to see a family all pitching in together, but their every action looked desperate.

Our removal men sat around whilst we all surveyed the chaos indoors and became mightily frustrated. The hours rolled by and we screamed delicately at them to please hurry the fuck up. By late afternoon, we had moved all of our belongings into the house. A few hours later, nearly all their belongings were gone except a huge pile in the middle of the living room. Dorian told them the house was now legally ours and they could pick up the rest of their stuff in their own time, but right now they had to vacate. And they went.

Apparently, moving house is considered by psychologists to be as traumatic as divorce and just below bereavement in the freak-out stakes. I believe it. My head was caned. And we couldn't find a thing. Boxes and boxes. All over the place. And all their bloody stuff to add to the confusion.

But by late December, a certain calm had descended on our household. Dorian and I were both weirded out in a good way. Drayton Bassett was even more of a village than we had thought and every morning we awoke to the sound of cows mooing and a cock crowing. The Karmann-Ghia was now hidden in a swanky double garage, so there was even more excuse to stay in. And it was harder for the Tamworth weirdos to find me.

I spent my time getting to know our new home and seeing what could be done to it. The Drayton Bassett house was a weird place. It stood at the end of a *cul-de-sac* and looked like an upmarket shack. Some guy had built all the houses in the close and made this one just for him. There was a tremendous lack of attention to detail, just *loads* of everything. And compared with the other houses, it reminded me of an overgrown and sub-normal older child that no-one could find the time to understand.

The living room was the perfect example: 36' × 26' of pure decorative hell. Imagine a fitted carpet that size in orange and tan swirls. And the ceiling had fake beams. Then there were the three huge modern bay windows with loads of tiny fussy squares of glass with patterns on it. Mercifully, the walls were painted white, but even they had been plastered with that swirly textured shit, probably by the three-year-old son of the builder.

We holed up in this place and decided to get to work. It seemed that I would have plenty of time now. A tour had been proposed for early spring, but everything had rested on the success of the new album.

As Christmas approached, I still felt the loss of *Fried*. I could not bear its easy defeat, especially as Cally had fought Phonogram throughout the whole campaign. As a symbolic gesture, I left the *Fried* truck in the middle of our new large back garden where it could rest in peace. And, in time, the grass grew high and it became almost lost from view. It looked beautiful. When visitors looked out of our ugly bay windows, their first sight was always of the rusting *Fried* truck in its dense overground grave.

The simple life that I had wished for was upon me. The move to Drayton Bassett ensured that no-one ever just dropped in. From this time on, a phone code was adopted. Two rings, ring off, then ring again. Our paranoia became more extreme than before. If anyone visited without a call first, we could not open the door. The two passageways at either side of the house had their doors screwed shut, then I piled up wood and junk behind them as a psychological security blanket. I covered up all the front windows; quilts and ancient curtains were tacked into place. And in the front bedroom, a little peep-hole was made so that I could rush upstairs to check out any unexpected knocks at the door.

Fortress Drayton Bassett was looking good. Soon, it was 10 times more impregnable that the Mill Lane house. And the extra miles from town really put off all but the most hardened friends and relatives.

How could we have lived *there* all that time? So close to traffic and people.

Two days before Christmas, the central heating went off. We were freezing and wondering why. Our friend Sid Woodward came around and told us we were out of oil. "Dr" Shah had not shown me the right way to check if there was enough left. But though Christmas with no heat was a drag, Dorian and I still had the best time ever. We were cut off from everyone and getting further away.

The new year came and went. The winter days of 1985 rolled by and the snow lay thick around Drayton Bassett. For a while, snowdrifts cut off the whole village, but we didn't worry. For months previous, Dorian and I had been stockpiling groceries around the house. Cans of all descriptions stood in boxes, hidden in the eaves of the roof, and there was endless coffee, tea and any other dried food you could name.

I was worried about the end of the world. But not on any "Hey Daddio, we're all gonna die tomorrow" high-priority level. In my great scheme of things, Armageddon was just one more thing to keep a check on and keep me awake at night. Nowadays, worrying was my only way of regarding a situation. Thinking and worrying were the same thing.

If someone visited, I worried about how long they would stay. If someone telephoned, I sat in a panic. Was that a code message or should we leave it? If a fan came to the door, should I be rude or just ignore him? If a friend wanted to stay with us, I would freak completely. The answer was almost always no, but Dorian and I would rack our brains for hours thinking up a believable excuse. We could not bear the idea that anyone would find out that we did not want to see them.

There were still certain exceptions, of course. The few people that I considered cool enough to accept our weirdness were held in such high regard that I counted the days between their visits. Johnno would come down all the time. And sometimes he brought Pete DeFreitas and Jake Brockman and Andy Eastwood. Any combination of those four guys turned up all the time. But it was never enough for me.

Pete and Jake kept me informed about the Bunnymen. I would casually ask about Mac, was he okay? How were the new songs? But the answers always worried me. Pete was not getting along with him and always referred to him as "that cunt".

Cally Callomon was my saviour. He treated me so normally that, in his presence, I *was* normal. We talked for hours on end about music and toys. He made tapes and tapes of stuff I should hear and I did the same for him. I loved the guy with a passion. His dumb sense of humour and his ability to laugh at anything was perfect for me. Dorian loved him as much as I did. The three of us began to conspire and plot. It became a Tamworth axis that gave me a feeling of worth again.

But then Cally would inevitably go back to London. And the positive feeling would seep through the doors and windows to be replaced, once more, by a thick haze of uncertainty and worthlessness. And yet each visit was a step forward. And each brilliant weekend added a power point to our score. It was as though Dorian and I had a kind of Cosmic Savings Account. And for every visitor through our door, we gained more points. It was easy to act normal around people but, gradually, we began to feel stronger on our own.

SPEED-WALKER

Then we got ill. Really sick. We moved the bed into the living room and we stayed there for two weeks with temperatures of 104. The weather was shitty so we drew all the curtains and lived on pills and dope. It was a really terrible 'flu and we couldn't eat a thing. Couldn't eat a thing. Brilliant. As soon as we were well, we weighed ourselves. We'd lost shitloads of weight! Ha. I'd been up to 12 stone, 4 pounds. "Bloody hell, said Dorian, "you've lost 10 pounds."

We decided to use the illness as a springboard to help us lose more weight. Now that I was down to 162 pounds, I decided to make 150 pounds my new target weight. Over the next few weeks, Dorian equipped us with calorie books and slimming magazines. We stocked up on health food and Dorian bought *Jane Fonda's Workout Challenge* on video.

Soon, our days were based around how many calories we took in and exercise. But I hated the Jane Fonda video and needed something better suited to me. Dorian had become the queen of mail-order slimmers and she sent off for a cassette of Ken Heathcote's *Fatigues*, specifically designed around Canadian Army exercises. It was totally crazily off its head. Ken had this terrible cheesy synthesizer music bouncing along whilst he whined and cajoled in his heavy Manchester accent: "Up, up, burn that fat . . . And you're there, with *Fatigues!*" Pete Burns' Dead or Alive had a huge hit with a disco song called 'You Spin Me Round' that March and his high energy always reminded me of the ridiculous sound of Ken Heathcote's *Fatigues*, the sheer pressure of its boinga-boinga beat sending me running for cover whenever I heard that sound.

Then one day, Dorian found an article on speed-walking. The guys in the picture had all these specialist clothes and looked pretty cool. That's for me. I didn't buy any dude gear to begin with. I wanted to be doing it for the right reason. So I assembled this mish-mash outfit with long johns and one of Dorian's fake fur collars for a hat. I worked out a route around Drayton Bassett and soon I was doing nightly battle with the village roads. At 7 p.m., I began my 10-minute breathing and stretching exercises, then I would grab my stopwatch and be off into the night.

Speed-walking is a killer discipline. It focuses your every attention on one thing: the desire to beat the previous night's time. The whole body is taut and pumping, thrusting along like some big phallic projectile. I was so turned on by speed-walking that it soon became an obsession. My warm-up exercises were taken rigorously in the unheated and freezing hallway. Then I'd put on my heavy knee-supports and start.

Every night, the same route. Out of the close and into the darkness towards the main road. Drayton Bassett is half a mile off the A4091 between Tamworth and the Belfry, where the Ryder Cup golf tournament is held. On the main road, the route became ill-defined in places. I tried to take the widest path at all times, to ensure that I didn't cheat myself. Then it was up Drayton Lane and back towards the village. At first, I would laugh every time I got to the streetlight where Jane Smith and I had had sex when we were 16, but time passed quickly and soon I associated the route with one thing only: speed-walking.

I walked two circuits each night. It was about four miles, but I was hardly ever out of sight of the house. Even in the enormous quiet of the pitch black night, I could still make out which were *our* lights. The rhythms of walking soothed me and I would chant songs in my head, great Gospel hymns to everyone I loved. Every song had the same rhythm, the rhythm of breathing and of the heartbeat.

Occasionally, I would set up a kind of Buddhist chant, also based on my breathing pattern. A long "aum" would come forth as I tried to control the air in my lungs, and I learned to chant whilst breathing out *and* in.

At two places in my journey, ugly and violent dogs presented themselves. At first I was a little wary and would pass with almost cloven-hoofed meekness. Then, as time went by, I became sneering and disdainful. I'd flare my nostrils at the dogs and cackle like Bluto in *Animal House*. But my temerity got me into trouble. One time, a vicious dickhead of an Alsatian followed me for half a mile. I shat out completely that day and only did one lap.

But each new day knocked seconds off my previous best time. I felt my weight first dropping and then shifting to different parts of my body. And as I got tougher physically, my mind started to refocus. Almost imperceptibly at first, but there, nonetheless. Throughout 1985, I could not justify missing even one walk. Like everything else in my life, the walks took on a near-religious significance. But they were sculpting a new shape for me within and without, and the post speed-walking me would never again become a faded slob.

KING OF BRITAIN

I was obsessed with everything. In the spring of 1985, I wanted *every*thing. The failure of *Fried* only made me more determined to establish myself on *my* terms. But what were my terms?

Well, I was bored stiff with craziness for a start. The only time I ever got mentioned in the press was as a crazy man. And if you *are* crazy, you don't get off on that too much. You see, sometimes, my mind *would* slip and I *would* be just the way I was portrayed. But other times, I'd *adopt* the role of loon as a joke. When *Top of the Pops* was on, the easiest way to piss Dorian off was to say: "Dorian, am I on tonight?" in a tiny, pathetic voice. "Oh fuck off, Julian. You haven't even got a record out," she would say, and I'd roll around laughing.

So really, all I wanted was to be treated as normal. And through being seen to be normal, I could think that I was normal and stop acting like someone I hated. I wanted this so badly. Almost too much. I was becoming obsessed with being straight. I tried watching bland TV comedies to see if I could enjoy them. I was looking for my perfect role model, I needed a role model badly. Thankfully, I had toy collecting. At least that was normal.

I decided that I wanted all the toys in the world. Toys had become symbolic of goodness to me and I wanted every toy ever made. Dorian and I would sit around and work out how to make a sound and legal claim on every toy in every collection, attic, toy room and shop in the world.

Then I remembered my bet with Max Eacock when we were 12 years old. I had bet him £5 that by the time I was 18 my official title would be "Julian Cope, King of Britain". Of course, this had not worked out at all. In fact, I still owed him the money.

When I had made the bet with Max, my mind had not really grasped the idea that my dream may not come true. I hated this, the realisation that certain things were just dreams after all. The moment that a man begins to think practically, he is lost.

Dorian suggested a compromise. I could aim to become "King of Toys". We hatched a plan that was quite inspired. I would issue an edict that gave me power over all toy collectors. We would construct a spiral staircase around Nelson's Column in Trafalgar Square and I would sit on a throne at the top of the column. Then, every toy collector in the kingdom, both adult and child, would, by law, have to bring their toys and present them to me. It was a wonderful idea.

Then one day I was standing in the car park of the Ankerside shopping mall in Tamworth, where Dorian and I had just done our weekly trek down the aisles of Sainsbury's. As I waited for Dorian to pull up in the Karmann-Ghia, I was aware of a guy in a quilted anorak and glasses staring at me.

"Er, excuse me, are you Julian Cope?"

The speaker was shy and ultra-straight. I told him that, yes, I was Julian Cope, but he seemed to know little or nothing at all about me.

"I'm a songwriter, see. D'you need any songs or do you do your own stuff?"

I looked at this sweet-looking dude. What a far-out idea! My mind reeled around at the prospect of getting a guy in to write second-hand observations about my life. But I said, very sweetly, "I don't think I need any songs written, thanks. Mine are a bit personal, really." Dorian pulled up and I left him standing in Ankerside.

All the way home we laughed at the idea of my using a Tamworth songwriter. Yeah ... I could get him to write an Oedipus song, and one about how my being called Julian affected my growing up in Tamworth, and all kinds of general songs about wanting to be other people.

But the memory of that meeting stayed with me. I remembered the gentleness of the guy and thought, over and over, about how much courage it must have taken to walk up to some singer and try and sell his songs and I was relieved that I'd been nice to the guy.

By now, I did have new songs that I needed to record. Throughout the spring, Donald, Joss and I visited UB40's studio in Birmingham. The studio was an old abattoir, an easily uncovered fact by virtue of UB40's naming it the Abattoir. It was on Fazeley Street, near to Fazeley St. Motors, named after the village of Fazeley, just two miles from our current home. We immediately renamed the house engineer Fazeley Saint Motors and introduced a new rule of speed-recording. I would play the song to Donald, who would immediately invent a drum pattern. We would then put the song down first take and add shitloads, all done in top gear.

Members of UB40 would come in to listen and hang out, but we got on best with their sound guy Ray Falconner. Ray would skin up a massive one and stay for hours. His brother Earl was in the band and the Abattoir had become everyone's hangout.

In a couple of weeks, we had an album's worth of material. But there was tremendous polarisation in the music. Some of it was even more ragged and unfinished than *Fried*. Other stuff, however, was rock'n'roll with riffs and an attitude a mile high. I decided that the more together stuff was to form the basis of the *Saint Julian* album, which should be ready in about six months.

UB40 did a really expensive video in which some modellers made perfect deathmasks of all their faces and then they swapped around heads and played other instruments to confuse the audience. After the video was over, the various members of UB40 carried the heads around then grew bored with them. But Donald and I loved the masks and when Ray Falconner gave us his mask, we were both so happy that we recorded loads of overdubs wearing "the Head".

In the meantime, I had all this other material lying around which became known as *Skellington*, a children's mispronunciation of the word "skeleton". It described the nature of the sketchy music and short songs perfectly. I played the songs to Cally. There were a whole bunch of recurring tunes, known as the "In-Bred Themes", which kept returning to one whistled or hummed refrain; there was an untitled piano-based dirge which began: 'And in the Abattoir I look for things that matter.' 'Phase Lee' was an unfolding melodic freak-out in the style of *The Faust Tapes*, and 'I Need Someone' was a pop song like Free's 'My Brother Jake', which had no place in my general songlist. There was even a very short fast psychedelic song called 'Prince Varmint', which I had tried to extend, but which somehow said it all in under two minutes.

Cally surprised me. He was not into it. Sure, he liked the songs well enough, but he told me that the attitude was a cop-out. A cop-out? Why the fuck is it a cop-out? "Because you're capable of so much more," said Cally. And he told me to listen to the song 'Saint Julian' and the newly recorded song 'World Shut Your Mouth'. "Anyone can copy their last LP," said Cally.

Wow, he was right. Completely right. I listened to him and agreed. Shit, yeah. We shelved *Skellington* and Cally suggested that I work hard at honing down my *Saint Julian* images. His belief in me made the work into fun. I finally had someone to act as a positive kind of friction. I decided to put all my frustrations at God and evil into this next album.

I loved the idea of *Saint Julian*. It was so perfectly representative of me, the white male middle-class asshole, whose life is so self-obsessed that he feels that he alone has the answer. And the title was presumptuous enough, too.

See, I hated the pomposity of U2. I detested their humourless earnestness and the singer's fake spur-of-the-moment muse. And their cynical use of God and religion to propel them to the top. And their "Follow me, 'cause I know God personally" rap had got under my skin and turned it a nice colour of green – presumably a combination of envy and septic, ho-hum. I secretly thought that God was probably no more likely to hang-out with the likes of U2 than he was to dine with Jim Jones, Anita Bryant or Jim and Tammy Bakker.

So, *Saint Julian* suited me. In order to explain my fears to the world, I had to take on the guise of the people I most detested. It was basic psychology, really. If you want to expose a fraud, align yourself with that fraud, then do your own thing very badly. Whilst you damage your own credibility, you also pull down all the others who are similar.

I answered the door to the Jehovah's Witnesses because I had the time. I talked to them constantly, trying to find out how watertight their arguments were. They weren't. They were at sea in a leaky boat. If I asked a question that they could not answer, they told me to have faith. Brilliant, I thought. Anyone with a Bible can play God. The modern evangelist is true rock'n'roll, full of sound and fury and signifying nothing.

I had a big problem, though. To explain my trip, I'd have to become enormous. I'd have to fill stadiums full of believing, mindless people. And that would take years of commitment to something I truly hated.

I had an unhealthy respect for the artist who sells out. Not everyone can sell out, even if they want to. Over the years, I had noticed that the strength of singers like Adam Ant and Billy Idol was their ability to sell their asses and still appear to be doing precisely what they wanted.

I, personally, did not have a clue. What *were* my strengths? What *were* my weaknesses? I was merely stumbling around the dark, doing my own thing. And even if I achieved this massive sell out, the sneaky evil spirit in me was guaranteed to creep out and start doing it for real. I felt sure that it must happen that way with many people. They start with high ideals and great intentions, then the physical rewards of this highly lusty and gratifying world take them over.

I was whirling around and around in a typical case of "up my own ass intellectual bullshit". It was the kind of thing that leads a person to conclude that the best way forward is to do absolutely nothing.

I needed a way around my problem. Then I remembered the guy in the Ankerside car park. Imagine if *he* wrote all the *Saint Julian* songs. If I gave him some titles and heavy personal subjects to write about, he could say what I wanted and give off a sense of distance at the same time.

Of course, I couldn't *really* entrust him with the job of writing my entire next album. I was too paranoid (*and* too greedy) for that. So, instead I hit upon the idea of imagining the way that he would write a Julian Cope song and doing it myself.

The guy in Ankerside became my God figure. I'd been visited by God and had told him nicely to butt out of my affairs. Now I was making it up to him by writing *my* problems, but from *his* perspective.

DIRK THE TURTLE BOY

One night Dorian woke me up crying that she'd just had this terrible dream in which she had given birth to a baby who was half turtle, half child. The turtle boy was called Dirk and she had adored him. Then the authorities had heard about it and imprisoned me. They had experimented on me, because of my turtle genes, and now they were after Dirk. She was pursued all over the world until, in the dying moments of the dream, she had been caught. Dorian awoke as Dirk was taken away from her and, though now awake, she was inconsolable. I was so moved that my wife could dream such tender weirdness, because I thought of her in terms beyond human.

Dorian's dreams often cast her in a male role, including one nightmare scene in ancient Rome in which she endured torture and castration. Indeed, compared with Dorian I was Wee Willy Winkie, so she completely understood my weird female side which was nevertheless heterosexual. The closest I could come to explaining myself was that I was a Lesbian in a Man's body. To me, the physical male was beautiful on a classical level, but chortlingly unsexy. My love of women erred on the side of fertility size and I had a bizarre waking image of myself as a huge cartoon Mothership, a smiling Ma Zeppelin with arms and a great belly, which increased in size as I dragged Dorian inside. Then I zipped up my great belly, heaved a huge sigh of relief and satisfaction, and roared off into the starry skies of outer space. The incident provoked a song called 'Planet Ride', which was later stripped of its most bizarre verses, but still contained the essence of my moment:

"See me living in the middle of England,
Set my course for the deepest heavens,
Dress me up like a rocket ship,
And drag you screaming into my belly – railing, complaining,
And I seal my girl inside 'cause she's my girl and I'm her planet ride."

INDOORS

Our routine bordered on the catatonic at times. We would wake around 11 o'clock and drift into the kitchen, where I would put the coffee on and Dorian would weigh out exactly 2 oz of Edam cheese for my breakfast. The I would make my own toast and Dorian her cereal. Every day was the same. Breakfast in the dining area until around 1 p.m., by which time the coffee would be finished and a spliff would be rolled. Then the day could proceed in one of two fashions. Either we could stay indoors nearly all day, then go out for a short time in the car. Or we could just stay in all day, full stop.

Every evening at 7 o'clock, Dorian and I would exercise rigorously then, most nights, Donald and Joss would come around and we would all get shitfaced. Dorian and I had a lot of sex, as well, particularly because the house was so new. I always get turned on by new places to have sex and the Drayton Bassett house had a lot of rooms to explore.

Sometimes, we would drive around in the Karmann-Ghia with the stereo blaring The 13th Floor Elevators or The Doors. Both groups make perfect driving music. We'd see the reflection of the car in a shop window and get turned on because we were in the most killer car in the world, so we would drive to some secluded place and I'd fuck Dorian on the back of the Karmann-Ghia. There was a white bridge, like a gentleman's folly, at the end of Drayton Lane. We did it a lot there as the traffic zoomed past, unaware of us.

Whenever we travelled by train, I loved us to fuck in the lavatories. Particularly the old British Railway carriages: they have these cold washbasins and loads of floor space.

But, ultimately, we were total routine-heads. On Saturdays, we visited toy swap meets. On Sundays, we had lunch at my parents. Sometimes Cally came to see us. Occasionally, I recorded with Joss and Donald.

I couldn't go anywhere new. That was too weird for me to think about. The prospect of a visit to a brand new place would fill me with such fear that I could not breathe. We can't go and that's an end to it, it freaks me out. And so everyone would acquiesce. They didn't want to cause bad feeling and, because they all thought that they were helping me, it became easier and easier for me to avoid things that I disliked.

Gradually, the psychological walls grew around the Drayton Bassett house and I believed that I could not go out. Of course, I *would* go to the places that I *really* wanted to visit. But it was more convenient to have people visit me and I became obsessed with staying indoors.

In the huge upstairs front bedroom the toy room was beginning to take shape. I had ripped up the shitty carpet and cheap wallpaper and painted the walls and ceiling grey. Then I had painted each floorboard with primer, undercoat and gloss, turning the whole floor into a blaze of pink and grey candy stripes. Each stripe took 20 minutes per coat, but I had all the time in the world to get it right.

Next, the cabinets came in and shelves and various display units. The whole place took on the appearance of an old shop and I had picked up ancient advertising material from all kinds of sources.

One day, a guy telephoned. "Hello. My name's Peat. Doug Peat." He offered me some old model car kits. I sifted though them and decided to buy the lot, because it would make my toy room look more like a real old toy shop.

Soon, all 70 kits were piled up with the rest of my junk and Doug Peat was our guest for dinner. He wore a suit, complemented Dorian on her cooking and took just the right amount of time over each toy in my toy room – that is, 20 minutes per toy. Dorian fell asleep downstairs, whilst Doug and I spent from 7.30 until midnight discussing various toys. Then, at the end of the night, Doug Peat played his ace: he was releasing a model of his own making onto the market. Wow, I was excited and crushed. I wanted my own toy company, too, or at least a name and a logo.

My paranoia increased as the toy room became more and more outrageous. But the Drayton Bassett house was a wild design. There were eaves running the full length of the house which linked the toy room with the music room. I built secret entrances for both rooms and boarded up the toy-room door. The only way to enter the room was by climbing through a hole in the music room and crawling the full length of the house. But it was not gross in the tunnel, because I spent so much time in it that it had to be well-furnished. And entering the

toy room from the tunnel was like coming out of the wardrobe into Narnia
... what a head trip! The whole room glowed with the souls of the children
who had once played with the toys I now cherished.

When visitors arrived, I would dim the lights and switch on all my battery
toys. Then I'd let them go crazy on the floor, a blur of flashing lights and
screaming sirens: Batmobiles, policecars, 747s, spacecars, robots, fire-engines,
everyone of them scooting around at the feet of our friends.

Dorian would come upstairs and find me staring vacantly into the overflowing cabinets. And although she would laugh at me, it disturbed her a lot.
But I felt peace in the toy room. It was my ultimate twilight world. And I was
at home there.

In May of 1985, for some reason known only to higher forces, Phonogram
Records chose to release a single from *Fried*. It was way past the event, of
course, and there was no reason at all to do it, but it least it gave me something
to concentrate on. 'Sunspots' was a great song, circular and repetitive, kind of
like Donovan the way it just prowled along with this gawky attitude. But both
Cally and I knew it couldn't be a hit. The record company wouldn't even give
it a 12" release, which was the kiss of death for any British single in the 1980s.

Instead, we contented ourselves with releasing the best ep of songs and the
most interesting package we could get away with. We decided to package it like
the European eps of the '60s, with a 7" miniature of the *Fried* album, carrying
the title *Smallfried* EP. But, at the last moment, Cally was told by the head of
marketing that the *Smallfried* idea was too obscure and that the 'Sunspots' lead
track would have to give its name to the title of the whole package. This solar
dimwittedness permeated the business and drove me crazy. In these situations,
I was in no position to have a hit and was not deluded enough to even think
so. But such corporate thinking did not even allow us to vibe up the few
thousands who *would* buy the record.

Instead, Cally acquired 100 toy cars. These were promptly turned into "Julian
Cope Mercury Promotionals" and sent to *Smash Hits* magazine. Then a bunch
of radio interviews were arranged. Soon, Dorian and I found ourselves driving
around England visiting all the major local radio stations. I knew that it was
wishful thinking to have any expectations whatsoever, but at least I had something to do.

Local radio in Britain is a law unto itself. The DJs are all stars in their own
area and expect to be treated as such. Most of the time, it's fine; they are usually
nice guys doing their thing. But sometimes you get a total twat.

At Radio Piccadilly in Manchester, there was this incredibly ugly death-dwarf
called Timmy Mallet. He was like some overgrown child star actor whose
self-esteem had been allowed to run wild. I knew that it was going to be difficult
to re-enter the radio scene and had been psyching myself up for days. But I
was still unpleasantly surprised when I walked into his control room and felt

an aura of sickly sweet repulsiveness rush into me, clogging my cosmic sinuses and bombarding my psychic shield.

"This is Wing Commander Timmy here. I have a problem. I need help. I need help from . . . aha . . . it's Captain Copey!"

Aaaaargh! What the fuck is this shit? In front of me, an ego of gargantuan proportions was playing out a life and death struggle and trying to include me. No way. I couldn't even speak.

I stayed just long enough to be obviously rude and we escaped into the night. Except that we had locked ourselves out of the car. Of course Wing Commander Timmy found out straight away. He announced it on the radio. Soon dudes from all over were arriving to try to help us. Finally, we escaped and I could breathe again.

No wonder I'd stayed away all this time. Guys like that . . . (drool) debase the very fibre . . . (gibber) of human existence. And joke about it as they do so. I got nervous as hell after that. It was a big deal being away from Drayton Bassett and I wanted to do good interviews without being paranoid for days.

GRAHAM NEALE EPISODE

Soon I was at Radio Trent in Nottingham, only 35 miles from Tamworth and with a guy that I knew from way back. Graham Neale had been at Trent for years. He was the John Peel of the station and I had done regular appearances on his show since 1981. He always asked probing questions and this time was no different. I soon chilled out and we talked for hours, playing most of the *Fried* album. His assistant, Lynn, brought me tea and biscuits and I felt like a real musician again.

But Graham was not himself. He asked all the right questions and made all the right comments well enough, but during the songs he hassled me about my ex-wife. Why did I leave her? Wasn't it a cop-out? Isn't it unfair on the person who's left behind?

"Come on, man," I said. "What's the problem?" But Graham persisted. He was far too interested in my first marriage and what had gone wrong. I couldn't even bear to discuss the subject. Then, as each song finished, the radio normality would once more return.

I left Graham Neale with ideas of a hit single on my hands. Maybe it could become huge accidentally. I had done some radio promotion and made an effort to be nice. Surely I deserved some success.

One week later, 'Sunspots' entered the charts at no. 78. Then it did an almighty sod-off forever. It was as though neither Dorian and I had even left the house.

I felt as though I had become musically unnecessary. And I still had an enormous debt to pay. A huge unpaid tax bill had come in from The Teardrop Explodes accounts, and it all fell on me. Sure, why not? I'll pay and pay. My life's routine was now a long-established succession of payments to people I did not know on behalf of old friends and colleagues who no longer wished to know me.

I saw it romantically and at a distance. All my publishing royalties and radio-play cheques and advances, everything, it all went into the black hole known as The Teardrop Explodes.

And then one day the strangest thing happened. I picked up the *Daily Mirror* and read the front-page headline: "The Tragic Triangle". Underneath was a photograph of a radio guy I knew with Lenny Henry! Whatttt? I read and I read and I thought, Hmmm, I know that girl in the other picture, but where from? And the story unfolded and I read the name and I turned the page and the truth went smack!

My sweet and concerned Nottingham DJ friend, Graham Neale of Radio Trent, had taken a hammer and murdered Lynn, his pretty assistant, who had brought me tea and biscuits all those times. Then he had hidden her body on the M1 and kept quiet about it. On hearing of her death, Lynn's new boyfriend had committed suicide. Graham was so appalled by the mess he had made that he hanged himself in his prison cell.

It was a bad, bad story. And Graham Neale was obviously the bad, bad guy. But my mind reeled as I thought of the deep conversation we'd had just weeks before. You know, he was there to interview me and my disturbed mind and all this miserable stuff. And he was Radio Trent's ambassador of cult music and Nottingham's fine upstanding rock'n'roll dude. And all the time, there was no-one, not one single person, who could see his pain and the trouble it was going to cause.

And I knew right then that I was living the best life that I could. And I knew for sure that my avoidance of evil was more than just a well-intentioned stab at goodness. But Graham Neale also reminded me that being unassuming and meek was not enough. Certainly, you can live life perfectly for 75 years. But what if, at age 76, you murder someone? What are you? You're a murderer – and you'll always be remembered as a murderer, hated, despised, with a life that will immediately be re-evaluated for earlier signs of your sickness.

I knew for a fact that I was going to have to try one *hell* of a lot harder from now on.

THE REALISTIC SYNTHESIZER

As Donald, Joss and I spent more and more time in Musical Exchanges, at the bottom of Birmingham's Snow Hill, so our access to its most secret keyboard departments gradually became easier. Beyond the area of chapel-size harmoniums and reed organs was a room of char-broiled solid body guitars, "rescued" from the legendary fire of a few years before. But one day I spotted a small analogue synthesizer sitting lost amongst the mass of '80s pre-set bullshit. It was a Realistic made by Tandy a few years before, a Moog Rogue with badge-engineering. We set it up through an amp and listened to the thing scream the place down. Then I paid £90 for it and rushed home alone to the toy room filled with inspiration. It was time to do an album there and then.

The Realistic Synthesizer was recorded "live" to cassette without echo, reverb or any FX whatsoever. After the undignified no. 78 chart position of the 'Sunspots' single, I was so determined to truly capture the moment and record the whole session as "an album" that even the choice of cassette itself became vital to the process. I eventually decided to record over a three-year-old Everest the Hard Way demo, left over from Zoo days, as this group was clearly going nowhere yet had endeared themselves to me through repeated listening to their tape in my toy room. And when the 37-minute toy-room performance of such primal pieces as 'Storm', 'Swarm', 'Scorn', 'Shorn', 'Spawn', 'Too Shy', 'Doot-Doot' and 'Jowett Javelin Arrives Too Late to Join the 40 Series' were over, the familiar sound of Everest the Hard Way blasted disjointedly out of the speakers, reminding me that the album was done.

DeFREITAS AND JOHNNO IN ANDY'S LANDY

The very next day, Dorian went to New York to be with her family. It was all a part of our routine and I accepted it. She had stocked the house with food. She had washed all my clothes. All I was expected to do was vegetate tidily until her return. Whenever this happened, I found it easiest to steep myself in a kind of romantic melancholy. That way, I could at least write songs about my situation.

We took the train from Tamworth and I arrived back from Heathrow Airport at around 9.30 p.m. The house felt hollow and enormous, and I curled up and sank into Dorian's favourite chair. I rolled a spliff and considered my actions for the forthcoming three weeks. I could not drive legally and found leaving the house alone to be a huge drag. I was unused to even being alone. I anticipated the forthcoming time with fear and trepidation.

As I sat quietly, I figured that Dorian would be halfway over the Atlantic Ocean by now ... I fell into a deep and melancholy sleep in front of the TV.

Then, at 11.30 that same night, the telephone rang and I heard the clipped rock tones of DeFreitas. "Julian, it's Peter. Can we come and visit you?"

Sure, bloody too right. Yeah, when? A visit from DeFreitas was overdue and I needed to see some real friends, people who had shared similarly driven experiences of goony fucking madness. Liverpool heads.

"We'll be down in a couple of hours in Andy's Land Rover. Okay? Johnno's coming and I think Jake'll follow us later."

And he was gone. I was so excited. Visitors! Wow. My melancholy was put on hold as I thought practically. Where would they sleep? What would they eat? I skinned up and sat nervously, a happy puppy awaiting the arrival of his favourite bones.

It was 1 o'clock in the morning. Where were they? It's only 100 miles. At 1.30, the phone rang. It was DeFreitas. "Julian, we need directions." They were about 20 miles away.

At 2 a.m., the phone rang again. "Julian, we need more directions." They were four miles away.

At 2.30 a.m., there was a blaze of light in the driveway and Andy Eastwood's orange Land Rover powered to a halt. DeFreitas, Andy, Johnno and some guy I'd never met all piled out. We hugged and they told me that Jack was the drummer in a new Liverpool group called The La's. As he spoke, Peter DeFreitas fumbled around in the pocket of his leather motorbike pants. "Sorry it took so long, man."

He threw a large block of black hash onto the coffee table, followed by a very mauled tablet of Moroccan, some keepers and a small tin of grass.

"I thought we were in some place we'd already been," he continued and dropped two wrappers of cocaine onto the table. One of the wrappers was almost empty and everyone was smiling, their nostrils quivering like crazy. I ran into the kitchen and put on some fresh coffee. Oh, happy happy happy. The sight of Johnno and Pete and Andy in my living room dispelled all worries about myself. Hey, I'm hanging with these guys. These guys came to me, I smiled to myself, feeling chuffed as all hell.

By the time I came back, everyone had skinned up large spliffs. We attacked the hashish and punished the coke and I was deliriously happy to be the rock'n'roll guy again. Pete had great stories to tell. The Bunnymen were getting huge world-wide and Andy and Johnno were working for them. I was so happy to see my old friends. It made me feel important to know that they would visit me and the night pulsed with adrenalin.

At around 3 a.m., Pete handed me a purple microdot of LSD. In my confused late-night state, I held it right next to my left eye and studied its every mini-millimetre. I had not taken one single hallucinogenic drug since my stag night over eight months before. Dorian and her mother had made it quite clear that they were worried about my central nervous system. But everyone swallowed their doses down, so I did too. Shit, it's not every day I get a visit from my favourite people.

The hours up to 5 a.m. were considerably interesting. Everyone but myself had consumed large quantities of Jim Beam whisky and German lager, and we all hit the grass in a very big way indeed. Then, as the acid came on, I showed them upstairs to the toy room, where my Realistic Synthesizer still arched and bleeped in the night. Over the next 20 minutes, I sought out and switched on all my battery toys and switched off the room lights. For most of the night, five stoned crazies stood motionless in the dark, as Batmobiles, fire-engines, spacecars and all kinds of wind-up electric toys performed around our feet. We wanted to leave, but we were trapped by the darkness.

Outside, it was getting light. And the dawn made everyone restless. We piled into the Land Rover and made for the Mound in Alvecote. Pete and Johnno had seen it before, but never in such ideal circumstances. The orange Land Rover struggled out of Rectory Close, through Drayton Bassett and on down to Fazeley. The straightness of the Watling Street weirded Andy out for several miles, but soon we had passed Wilnecote church and I was showing everyone the parts of Dumolo's Lane where I had been beaten up as a child. In Glascote Heath, we passed the house of my still-sleeping parents, then made for Poles-worth and passed down Robey's Lane, from where the Alvecote Mound could be reached along its damp causeway. . .

It was one hour later and we were paranoid as hell. Five tripping fools stood in the safety of the bushes on the canal bank near the Mound, whilst up on the tow-path the orange Land Rover was being searched by two policemen. They had noticed us soon after our arrival and soon spotted the crate of Jim Beam and piles of unlikely goodies in the back. Now we were shivering and cowering in the damp bushes.

As soon as the police had arrived, everyone had given me their drugs to look after. "You hide them, Copey. This is your area." Andy was so concerned about the whisky that his head kept sticking out of the bushes and it was only my greater experience which kept my tripping adolescent self from yelling: "Andy, keep your head down."

Finally, the police left. I couldn't move at all and stayed transfixed to my mooring beside the canal. Then, as Johnno and Jack eased their way out of their hiding-places, we gradually loosened up and started to calm down.

Johnno asked me where the dope was. Oh, yeah. Just along here. I searched every bush along a 50-yard stretch, then began to panic. This was my area and they trusted me. I extended the search to a 100-yard area, but still to no avail. Eventually, I was up to a 400-yard stretch and still couldn't find a thing . . . er, guys?

Then DeFreitas said he thought it was maybe around ... here. And he pulled out the entire stash. Oh, relief. Home, gentlemen dudes. My brain was fried up and good for nothing at all. This was like being on a tour of Europe or something.

At 7 a.m., Jake Brockman arrived on his Ducatti motorbike and the whole thing started again.

Wow, that weekend. Two days that shook my whole world. Not even a real weekend, just two days that felt like it. It sapped up all my strength and took all my energy just to keep up with the rest of them. I realised that I was already no longer equipped to do that stuff anymore. It affected me for weeks afterwards. I was at saturation point. From now on, I was determined to keep the fuck away from mind-expanders before my brain petrified into baking powder.

THE GIFT HORSE BITES MY ASS

On and on I walked. Night after night. Around and around Drayton Bassett. The weight was long gone and my legs were strong and shapely. Hey, I'm finally getting rock'n'roll legs! Our eating habits were obsessive and we were so tuned into health that we had become like new Christians. If my father even approached a piece of fatty meat, I would verbally slap him about and harp on about calories and heart rate. Dorian knew the calories of everything that went into our mouths and we tutted and fussed if Joss even brought biscuits round to the house.

We were preparing ourselves. Honing our attitudes down and getting ready to enter the real world again. Or so we romantically dreamed.

Where was this real world, though? There was nothing for me to do, nothing at all. I had a tape full of songs that had been accumulated from the Abattoir sessions and the BBC had recently recorded another four for radio. So why wasn't I busy?

The truth was Phonogram Records had no interest at all. Dave Bates had heard a special tape of my new songs and had given them a curt dismissal. Where was this new direction Cope promised us?

Shit. I was so pissed off. I had put four of my very best songs onto that tape. All really hard and melodic. And I had thought that two of them, 'Eve's Volcano" and 'World Shut Your Mouth', could make good singles. The other two, 'Saint Julian" and 'S.P.Q.R.', were equally tough sounding.

I got depressed as hell. I may hate Bates, but he does know his stuff. Fuck him. What *does* he really know? Nothing at all. And now he wants me to write some more songs! Well, fuck that shit. I'm passed the stage of having to prove myself to Dave Bates.

•   •   •

I was still reeling around when Paul Crockford phoned out of the blue.

"Er, is that J. Cope?"

"Yes."

"*Thee* J. Cope?"

"Yes, Crockford."

"The J. Cope who has just been invited to play in Japan?"

Huh?

What was he talking about? Since the Teardrop split, the only releases I'd had were in Britain and Canada. No-one else had been interested, least of all Japan.

But it seemed that I was wrong. Crockford told me that both solo albums had been released by Polystar and were actually doing okay. Certainly well enough to justify a short tour.

I freaked out. I mean just *freaked*.

I told Dorian and she freaked out, too. We were singing and dancing around the room like crazy. I started phoning people up and engaging them in polite conversation then dripping the news. Shit, I was happy. I thought this kind of thing was way in the past.

I rang Johnno. "You know how you're in Liverpool and on the dole with no money? Well, d'you want to come to Japan with me for 12 days and play bass and hang out and be treated gloriously?"

Then a huge argument with my brother Joss. He and Donald were in a group called Freight Train, which never did anything. They never gigged, never attempted to establish themselves and yet they were actually quite brilliant. I told Joss that I wanted to take Donald with me to Japan. No way, Joss said. That would split Freight Train up, so don't even ask him. Fuck, that's a hard one. I figured it was best to ask Steve Lovell to play guitar and hope Donald never found out about Joss's exertion of brotherly rights over me.

One week later, we were in Japan. Four days' rehearsal to learn the whole set and we had just enough songs to get by. My old friend D'Arcy was in charge of guitars and Steve Lovell had found some guy to play organ. On the 16-hour JAL flight, Johnno and D'Arcy had become Brits abroad and screamed around the plane, saki-ied to the max. Oh, come on, guys, let's be cool. I wanted us to be professional, reasonable and sweet, let's not make it reminiscent of the bloody Teardrop days.

After we'd been flying for 45 minutes, Johnno screamed: "Are we there yet?" The only time he'd ever flown before was from Liverpool to Belfast. And there'd been a stop-off in the Isle of Man for a rest.

I took two Mogadons to sleep through it all. Then I woke up in Moscow Airport completely unprepared. I had thought we were going via Anchorage, so I was wearing red tie & dye tights and the long shamanic leather jerkin. As we came through the armed guards at passport control, Johnno and D'Arcy shouted, "Comrades, comrades!" and fell to the ground in a hail of fake bullets.

Once out of Russian custody, I told them to be cool for a change. At the baggage claim at Narita Airport, Tokyo, I was told that my bags were still in London. Then, as we passed through customs, Johnno pointed to the drug-free, ultra-straight Chris Whitten and shouted: "Don't let him in. He's a fuckin' smack-head." Uh-oh, I thought, as Whitten was led away.

Japan was the headtrip of life. The women were beautiful and the place was crazy. They took all my idiosyncrasies for granted and one magazine had even awarded the *Fried* sleeve an award, the turtle being synonymous with good luck in Japan.

On stage, I cavorted and screamed, whirled and danced, necked with the front row and fell off stage every night. The more extreme I was, the more they dug it. Awlright! I was no freak show here. The speed-walking had so changed my body that I now walked the stage with an animal presence which I was totally aware of. My legs were entirely different and I strutted. We played 'Reynard the Fox' until all the bullshit disappeared – now it was streamlined and direct, and the poetic talk-down jarred less and less. And 'World Shut Your Mouth'' sounded anthemic and enormous. Shit, this could be the biggest hit ever.

I rose to the occasion and adored every moment. For 12 days in Japan, I felt like a star again. The kind of star that was worthwhile being. Young female fans waited in the futuristic foyer of the Roppongi Prince Hotel and showered me with beautiful gifts and letters of enthusiasm, books of philosophy, books of fables, little trinkets and tiny turtles.

There were two Julian Cope fan clubs, both producing handwritten magazines full of old interviews, line drawings and descriptions of Tamworth and the background to my songs. I had always said that I needed only one person to justify carrying on. Here was a whole bunch of people and I was deliriously happy.

My attitude to hygiene went from "lax, to say the least" to "shaved, showered and maybe a little too deodorised". Still, I could take no chances. Japan turned me around. Literally. They dug me for what I was. I made no apologies and found that I acted very professionally. Interviews were done with tremendous pleasure, accompanied by beaming photo sessions.

I walked everywhere with the young fans Luna Lure and Mineko and their gang of girlfriends. But there was tremendous rivalry. Whenever I left them alone, Mineko would kick the other girls and ignore Luna. I had forgotten about this shit, but I was happy that it was happening again, even for a short while.

My hotel room was full of toys and candy. And new flowers arrived every morning from various sources.

Japan is almost drug-free, but the place was so far-out that I hardly noticed. Also, it's so anti-vegetarian and so gloriously meatist that I should have been totally at odds with the culture. But now was not the time to play the right-on, pissed-off Western vegetarian pot-head abroad. Instead, I gorged myself on red meat until the death in my veins made me drunk and raging. I slugged the whisky and ate utter junk: three kinds of Mister Donut and fast-food BLTs with pinky microwaved bacon from Tokyo's idea of an American diner, a place called Jack & Betty Club: We Love Food.

The Japanese claimed to have a tremendous respect for the feelings of nature. One day, the temperature in Tokyo was 97 degrees, hotter than body heat. I put on my leather pants, jacket and boots and roamed the city. Oh no, said some of my fans. By dressing thus, you are showing a great lack of respect for the feelings of summer. Your clothes are totally at odds with summer.

I told them that I hated summer. Compared with winter it was no more than a fledgling, an upstart and a purveyor of naïve juvenile feelings. Humph, it takes no character whatsoever to love the summer. I said that I was wearing my leather to laugh in the face of summer. I am a Norseman without summer feelings.

The girls understood this and said no more. But it occurred to me that the Japanese way of thinking was utterly fascinating and worthy of being seriously ripped off.

Our last show took place on the fourth floor of a department store at 3 o'clock in the afternoon. This is a regular thing in Tokyo so we were determined to be fucking far-out.

The set was monstrous. I dipped and swayed and felt the power of each song coursing through my veins. During 'The Bloody Assizes', the keyboard player sat cross-legged on stage and played the guitar. I was incensed, but Johnno kicked his dumb ass around the stage and it only made everyone hotter. We finished the set with 'Reynard the Fox' and threw the entire contents of the stage into the audience. I turned around to see Chris Whitten systematically dismantling his (hired) drums and throwing the pieces into obscure sections of the audience. Awwwllll – RIGHT!

By the end of the tour, everyone was in sad shape. We had been wined and dined every night until we could eat no more. We had partied at these awful clubs where Western musicians and models drink for free. Places we wouldn't be seen dead in, were they in London. What am I saying? There *were* no places like that in London.

Paul Crockford was in love with *every*one and wore a red psychedelic Hawaiian shirt, lime green Bermuda shorts, which were a gift from Curt Smith, and patent leather Doc Marten shoes with no socks. As Crockford is 6'4", his presence in Japan was similar to that of a living Ralph Steadman cartoon.

D'Arcy and Johnno took full advantage of Tears for Fears' presence in Japan at the same time as us. They hit every club that would have them with D'Arcy's announcement: "Hi, I'm Sting and this is Curt from Tears for Fears." And it worked. They'd arrive everywhere with T-shirts and scarves to give away, drink all the free champagne and sod off.

On the last night, everyone stayed in. I chided them and called them weaners, but no amount of humiliation could drag them out. So, Johnno, D'Arcy and I raged hard around Roppongi. We hit an awful club called Tokio and we drank and we drank. Whilst the women were looking better and better, I was seething and snarling like a wild dog. Johnno said he was fed up with being broke. In full leathers and out of my mind, I stood up and announced, "D'you know what I do when we're skint? I ring up Paul King and ask for a couple of grand ... A ha ha ha ha ha ha ha ha ha ha ha ha ha ha."

By 5 a.m., even D'Arcy made no sense whatsoever and had to leave. Johnno and I were almost as incapable, so we hit every fast-food place in Roppongi for old time's sake. As the sun came up over Tokyo's party quarter, the two of us staggered from bar to coffee shop to bar to fast-food joint in a kind of wild zig-zag movement. Through hordes of street cleaners and garbage trucks and commuters and piles of rubbish, we trailed our way home. It was 8 a.m. and the last droplets of fun were squeezed out as early-bird fans laughed at our last desperate quest.

A few hours later, we pulled out of the Roppongi Prince coach park for the last time, our bus loaded with mysterious Japanese women and more still outside. I was determined to remember this feeling. Narita Airport was full of sad goodbyes and on the flight back to London, I downed the downers and prepared myself for a freak out.

"Hey, Crockford. In a few hours I'll be a no-mark again."

FREDDIE 'PARROT FACE' DAVIS
(PADDY 'FERRET FACE' DAVIS)

"Julian Cope? The difference between me and him is I'm a character from Shakespeare and he's a cartoon out of the *Beano*."

Ian McCulloch, 1985

Scared of everything. Scared of nothing. That's how I felt on my return from Japan. That country and its culture just oozed possibilities for me. For a start, it confirmed my suspicions that the art trip and the pop trip could run concurrently and work out fine.

All this insufferable bullshit that had come to represent "serious" music would make me gag and run screaming from the room. Every time Sting or David Byrne or The Eurythmics or some such did their thing on my TV, it was put across as a "soulful" and "world music" experience. But it came over the airwaves with all the sincerity of Emerson, Lake & Palmer doing 'Fanfare for the Common Man' or the Vanilla Fudge's reinterpretation of the Supremes'

'You Just Keep Me Hangin' On'. And the scariest part of all? Those people *mean* it. If they were just dabblers like Midge Ure and Richard Jobson, sure, I could take it. But I could feel the subtle shift as Sting moved from his role as Yo-Yo-Yo Bab Marli of de Noo Waihve to Spokesperson for the Third World. I could see the wheels turning. I could see old Sting a-thinking, I'm hanging out with Ziggy Marley, me. Better fuck old Andy and Stew off, and get some black dudes with the right credentials. To AU-THEN-TICATE MA SOUL!

I wanted to walk up and say, "Fuck off, String. You look like bloody Freddie Starr!"

Yeah, Japan had caught me off guard. It had allowed me to be a pop star again. And on my own terms. My own ridiculous terms. The Japanese were actually happier the more cartoony and two-dimensional I became. They seemed to see cartoons as more than merely a superficial representation. A bit like their attitude to robots. It was as though the best cartoons could be a summation of all the best in humankind. It made me *want* to be a cartoon. It made me *want* to project myself as two-dimensional.

Limitations. I had those in abundance. Now I wanted to *use* those limitations. I wanted to stand amongst all those enormous Western Artistes declaiming their world-changing strategies and scream: "I made this song up!"

Later in the summer, Patty and Al Jorgenson came to stay with us, with their new daughter Adrienne. Patty and Dorian had not spent a great deal of time together since the three of us had met in Albany, over four years before, so Patty arrived early whilst Al went to Berlin to record. The first days were wonderful as Dorian was so happy with Patty around that I could just enjoy watching the two of them being the way they used to be.

Then there was a knock on the door at 5 a.m. one morning, and a bedraggled fifteenager soaked to the skin announced that his name was Kenneth and that he had hitched from Glasgow to hide from his parents and see me. I freaked out at him and Dorian and I put him in the guest room to sleep. That night, Kenneth joined us all for dinner and we waited for Al to arrive from Heathrow.

Don't hold your breath. We stupidly tried to save money by sending a Tamworth cab down to pick up Al. When Dorian called the cab firm to confirm which terminal Al was arriving at, they told her that the guy had already left for London. "But it's only 2.30," said Dorian. "He doesn't arrive at Heathrow until 7 p.m."

"Oh, our driver hasn't been to London since 1966, so he's taking it easy and giving himself plenty of time."

Giving yourself over five hours to achieve 110 miles sounded like Dark Ages reasoning to the two Americans but I suggested that Al would at least be on time.

Of course, Al then arrived almost an hour early. We opened the front door to see Al hugging the taxi driver like a brother/lover and discovered that it was

Al's $25 tip which had caused the emotion, plus several lines of speed. Al said that once they had left the M1, he had become so amphetamine nervous of the dark that he had almost killed them both, throwing his arm across the chest of the taxi driver and screaming about racoons in the road. The driver had been so freaked out that Weird Al had hipped him to some speed and restored the situation.

When Al saw Kenneth and heard his story, he freaked out more. He was deeply impressed with me for having such devoted fans and deeply impressed by Kenneth's mystical attitude. He went into our bathroom and shaved his head that very morning, possibly as an act of fraternal weirdness.

But though we were friendly towards each other, Al and I never hung out together. I stood upstairs motionless in front of my toy cabinets for hours upon end. He just sat downstairs and aimed his dictaphone at our TV for hours on end.

In August 1985, we did two things. We ordered a miniature Schnauzer from a Sandbach kennels and Paul King flew us first class to New York.

It was the first time in my life that I had flown first class, a bizarre experience that involves eating so many courses of Fortnum & Mason's delicacies that there is no time even for a movie. It wasn't until then that I realised I'd been travelling cattle class my whole life. It made me understand why the people with big money seem so removed – it's because they *are* removed. The first-class section could be a different aeroplane. Handmaidens minister to your needs from the moment you step on until you land. And all the time, the outrageous hordes of Economy are just one skinny bulkhead away. It's like living on a deserted private island in full view of Hong Kong.

The New York weather was fantastic and Dorian's parents drove us out to Montauk Point at the very end of Long Island. The whole day rang with this amazing azure sky. The eastern end of Long Island is ringed with other tiny islands, each a community straight out of a Stephen King novel. We travelled on some of the Island ferries and I found a horde of abandoned '53 and '54 Studebakers.

Dorian's father was very ill and getting worse, but days like this soothed him. Steve needed to see Dorian and Helen together; their total love could change him from a raging old geezer to a most supreme dude.

I spent the whole day photographing old American cars and Steve accidentally exposed the film when he forgot how his own camera worked. Mind you, on the Montauk trip, he was driving like a crazy man – 80 mph or 25 mph. There were no in-betweens. Whenever I got angry, though, I'd remember the picture of him as a young man doing a handstand on the rail of the Brooklyn Bridge and I'd forgive him.

We were also in New York for business. Phonogram Records were certain to drop me, so Paul King had made an appointment with IRS, Miles Copeland's big independent label. But it wasn't happening. There were a couple of meetings, but they thought the new stuff sounded too like *Fried*.

I was dismayed. This stuff was for my rock album! How can they say it's culty. *Come on* – it's completely upfront and in your face! I was massively disappointed. It was almost a year since *Fried* had come out and I was nowhere, not even close to recording a new album.

No matter. I still had my mile-high attitude after Japan. I was going to succeed and I was sure of it.

Dorian and I spent the rest of our time in New York hanging out and doing family things. The Beslity family offers and demands a great deal of love and attention, and a lot of dinners were required to see everyone.

Back in England, Paul King had asked Cally Callomon to join Outlaw and look after my day-to-day business. Do it, Cally, do it! But Cally was hedging his bets. He wanted to stay at Phonogram, where he was sure of a salary. That way he could keep an objective eye on me.

A couple of days after we returned home, Dorian and I drove up to Sandbach in Cheshire to collect our new Schnauzer. He was the only boy dog in the litter and a bigger weaner you could not wish to meet. Dorian named him Smelvin and we gave him the unfurnished music room to sleep in. In two days, the place was transformed into 25' × 12' of tiny dog shit, piss puddles and little throw-ups in every corner. Schnauzers are a kind of battleship grey ex-ratter with the ludicrous moustaches of a turn-of-the-century Prussian general. For two weeks, we fussed and fought with this little rat-becoming-ratcatcher until one early morning in October. . .

I knew from the moment the telephone rang. It was Jamie, one of Dorian's brothers. Her father was dead. Shit, Shit, Shit, Shit, Shit. With the Karmann-Ghia temporarily off the road, I asked my father to drive us to Heathrow, but he refused to have his day disrupted. Instead Joss drove us to the airport in a rented car, two and a half hours of chilling silence. Now was not the time to placate or offer weak comment. In four hours, Dorian was on her way back to New York.

For two weeks while I waited for my wife's return, I nursed a small Schnauzer who was not yet old enough to have his necessary injections and consequently couldn't even leave the house. During that time, Cally warmed to the idea of working for Outlaw and Paul King told me that my finances were at rock bottom.

Another unpaid Teardrop Explodes tax bill had come in to add to the already suffocating debts. I thought of my bravado speech to Johnno and D'Arcy in the Tokio club and laughed. Big business debts can be a very removed and distant problem. The debts had been paid with money that I never saw, so it hadn't really felt like mine at all. That is, until now.

This tax bill was way too big to handle. No amount of creative accounting could hide this bastard. There was only one thing for it. I signed a new publishing deal with Virgin 10 Music and used the entire advance to pay the tax man. On that day, I hated Bill Drummond and Dave Balfe.

FOOD SHOPPING

Stuck inside the Drayton Bassett house and unable to drive officially, I started to get a little crazy. I made a couple of local hops in the Karmann-Ghia, but I had no real intention of driving without a license. My father's years of work with the Prudential had instilled in me a tremendous fear of passive law-breaking.

But my isolation was getting to me. It rendered me inert. I was soon out of food and even started raiding our fallout supply. As I speed-walked through the village, I knew that I could no longer put off the grocery-shopping trip. But I couldn't handle calling a taxi and I did *not* want to ask my father for help after he'd failed us so with the airport episode. The Co-op Superstore was only five miles away. Surely I could deal with that myself.

(The pathetic thing was, for what I required I could have probably got it all at the Drayton Bassett general store and post office. Failing that, I could have gone to the four shops in Fazeley, an easy two-mile walk. But we always did our food shopping at the Co-op. That was what I knew and, as a routine-head, that was the only place I could go.)

Days passed. Nothing. Shit, if I'd done the shopping two days ago, it would be done now. But I'll just put it off one more day whilst I consider my options again. How I hated this side of myself. What a total dickhead! My wife is going through total bloody hell and I can't even do the shopping.

Right. I'm ready. I'll walk to the Co-op Superstore. Tomorrow.

The next day was beautiful. I grabbed my new Japanese holdall, which bore the inscription "Pony Escape from the Herd" and began my walk. I had a plan.

I figured that there must be a quicker way to the Co-op. Following the main route was frustrating because you had to double back on yourself in order to avoid the river. Now I was psyched up. I had all the time in the world and I was determined to discover the new route.

I set off down Drayton Lane and came to the white bridge, the gentleman's folly where we occasionally had sex. I figured that by crossing the canal at the bridge and walking through this one field, I could definitely find a way to the Co-op. It would be a pastoral route, a green lane, and fun to boot.

I walked about 15 minutes and soon left the road far behind. I could hear a tractor but it was way in the distance. It felt great to be outside. I was wearing heavy black cotton pants tucked into black 16-hole US paratrooper boots with a thick black sweater tucked into the pants and a jacket.

After about a mile and a half, I heard water ahead of me, fast-flowing water in the area where I expected the river to be. So far, so good. Suddenly it was there. But much wider than I had anticipated and completely cutting off my path.

I knew that if I walked two miles down the riverbank I would come to the road bridge. But what fun was that? Instead, I turned to my right and started to look for some other means of crossing.

I walked and walked, but no alternative bridge presented itself. Instead, the river got wider. In fact, it got so wide that I turned back and by the time I returned to the point where I had first met the river, it did now seem quite narrow. I surveyed the torrent of rushing water, which had seemed so impassable only half an hour before. Now I believed I could probably jump that, no problem.

I took off my sweater and jacket and stuffed them into my black holdall. Then, in order to gain as much momentum as possible, I grabbed the bag by its strap and spun the whole thing round and round my head, whereupon I hoisted my belongings high over the river. They hung over the torrent for an agonising split second, then crashed down safely on the opposite bank.

Now, I have long arms and a powerful body and it was a heavy bag, but not once did I doubt that I myself would make it over, not once. I walked back about 30 yards, prepared myself and my heavy boots, and started to run.

I ran and I ran and I picked up speed, and as I got to the very edge of the bank, I launched myself with all my might – Up, up, UP – Go, go, GO. . .

If I had landed three quarters or even two thirds of the way across, I would have understood. But I actually landed less than halfway across the river. Suddenly, my body hit the water. My boots sank way down into the mud and I was stuck. The fast-flowing water came up around my chest, but the real concern was the thick syrupy silt which held my legs fast.

Slowly, I began to inch across, each step more laborious. The water was so cold and I was so fucked that I began to laugh. I was *no*where. I was still two miles from the Co-op and in no state to give up now.

Finally, I made it to the other bank. I dried myself off with my sweater and continued my walk. In front of me was the Reliant Car factory, the place that builds all those little three-wheelers. I walked all the way around it to find a final indignity: a small tributary which I was forced to cross.

That day, I left a thick trail of silt all the way up Bluebrick Hill and all around the aisles of the Co-op. I paid with a sodden cheque book, took my groceries and walked home. No taxi driver would have me and the silt trail was still with me as I passed the Reliant Factory on my return journey.

Shit like this had to stop. It made a funny story, but it's no way to live your life.

When my grief-stricken and heartbroken wife returned, we booked a suite in a Bournemouth hotel and drove down there in the Karmann-Ghia with Smelvin.

We visited Beaulieu Motor Museum and almost bought a battered '54 Studebaker coupé. The ponies and the scenery in the New Forest reminded us of our trip to Montauk only two months before and the whole episode was to remain fixed in our minds forever.

I will always remember the haunted expression on my poor wife's face, the awful distance and impenetrable sadness as the present and the past were in no way separate. Even as we lived through this time, I felt removed. It was like the scene in *Don't Look Now* when Donald Sutherland sees his already dead wife float past him in the gondola. Some periods of life are like that. Great chunks of the past come floating into view. You haven't yet lived them but, already, they belong in the past. You act them out because you know that it's real. But it's so removed. It's just something to get *through*.

I'd been talking to Dave Balfe. One of those conversations that we were destined to have every year or so: 20% nice and 80% trying our damnedest to get the other to see sense. Balfe was talking about our growing apart. He was lamenting the breaking up of such a particularly psychically similar group of people, namely our scene and favourite people within that scene. For me, it was way too early to be thinking in those terms. I was still too bitter towards him and Bill Drummond.

Balfe knew more details about Bill than anyone. All I knew was the geek was working for Warner Bros. and copping out in a big ass way. He had become "Bill Drummond, A&R Man and Fuck Up" as far as I was concerned.

Balfe understood my opinion but wanted to set the record straight. He still adored Bill and said that there were a lot of things that I did not know, things that could change my mind about him. This is the story Dave Balfe told me.

Why Bill Drummond Did What He Did and How It Affected Julian Cope

In 1976, Bill Drummond worked in the theatre as a set designer. He was engaged on a play based on *The Illuminatus*, the trilogy which claims to expose the world as a nightmare place, controlled by a group of Higher Fathers bigger than the Mafia, Freemasons and Church all put together.

When the play opened at the Everyman Theatre in Liverpool, Bill received a letter from the West Coast of America. The writer had seen and enjoyed the play, and was interested in Bill's designs. He said he would remain in contact and signed his letter "True Genius".

With the arrival of the punk thing, Bill Drummond decided to stay in Liverpool. As he became more and more of a figure on the scene, his correspondence with True Genius became stronger and stronger. And Bill's awareness of all things cosmic grew and grew.

Apparently, he had "found out" that one of the world's main "energy lines" started at the North Pole and ran through Reykjavik in Iceland, down through Liverpool, through the pyramid of Cheops, Egypt and down through New Zealand, ending at the South Pole. It was also said that this energy line cut through Mathew Street, making it a place of inspiration. This had been the heart of Liverpool music, with the Cavern in the '60s and again with Eric's in the '70s.[1] Bill Drummond had mentioned none of this to any of us at Eric's. But, then again, how could he have – 1977 was an anti-hippy, anti-drug, anti-cosmic, austere-as-hell exercise in Year Zero Rebirth. No-one would have listened, we'd have laughed in his hippy face.

So time went on, and Bill began to produce and manage The Teardrop Explodes and Echo & the Bunnymen. His correspondence with True Genius led him to believe that he too could achieve true genius. And Bill had a plan. It was a plan for attaining True Genius.

According to Balfey, he believed that the centre of Liverpool's power was near the Carl Jung statue which stood outside the Armadillo tea rooms, Liverpool. At that point, supposedly, five roads meet. They do meet, I guess, but you have to stretch it a little: at one particular point, you can stand *almost* at the start of West Mathew Street, Rainford Square, Button Street, East Mathew Street and Temple Street all at the same time. Carl Jung believed that Liverpool was "The Pool of Life" and "The Seat of Learning".

Bill Drummond planned to have Echo & the Bunnymen play a show in Reykjavik at the same time as The Teardrop Explodes were playing in New Zealand. The metaphysical energy coming down the "leyline" would create incredible psychic power. Bill Drummond would be standing in Liverpool, where the five roads meet, ride the power and attain True Genius.

And that was Bill Drummond's story. And that was the supposed point of the Australian tour. And that must have been why he insisted that the Bunnymen get the camouflage. And a whole load of other things that had fucked me up so badly at the time.

Bill Drummond never attained True Genius; he became an A&R man for Warner Bros. When the Bunnymen were in Reykjavik, we were only halfway through the Australian tour. But I had to admire his story. And I was pleased that there had, at least, been *some* reason for his craziness.

Also, Dave Balfe's account of this story made me feel warmer towards him. And it convinced me that my trip was not so strange after all. And whilst he was bemoaning the fact that we were no longer linked, I remembered the story that I had been told by Donato Cinicolo, the Italian photographer who was responsible for my *Fried* album sleeve.

1 This was Bill's story – I'm only repeating it in the general context of the book.

Donato Cinicolo's Story

Around 1971, Donato Cinicolo was a young art student. He was invited by a sculptor friend to drive to Essen in Germany to pick up a particular block of granite for a forthcoming statue. They drove there in a rare 1958 Borgward Isabella coupé, loaded the granite into the tiny boot and drove home. This was a peculiar detail, as Dorian's father had driven an Isabella coupé and I had spent my '60s childhood in the company of a 1961 coupé which had belonged to my parents' friends.[1]

Anyway, years passed. Donato and his friend lost contact. Many years later, they met once again and Donato reminded the sculptor of their journey to West Germany.

"What did you make from that block of granite we brought back from Essen?" he asked the sculptor.

"Oh, you should visit it in Liverpool some time," he replied. "It became a statue of Carl Jung in Mathew Street."

So Bill Drummond and Dave Balfe were still as linked to me as ever. I decided that it might be real and it might be bullshit. Whatever it was, it made me feel better – as though, somehow, our weird family was still together. It made Dave Balfe feel better, too.

Suddenly, Donato Cinicolo was photographing record sleeves for most of Dave Balfe's groups. So I wasn't the only one to take that shit seriously.

It was good to hear these stories. It made me feel that I was working towards something. *And* it eased my crazy soul.

Promise. The killer accolade. He showed promise. Like the graffiti in every English school lavatory which reads: "Here I sit, brokenhearted/Came to shit and only farted." Ho-hum. It was like being back at school again. But one of those progressive schools were it's up to you to do the work – you know, no-one forces you and you can hang around and waste your time if you so wish. But, ultimately, you come up with the goods or you leave.

I was no judge of my position in music. I had this romantic notion of myself as a tragic has-been, waiting to spring his biggest surprise on an unsuspecting world. But inside me, the images of that Japanese trip were working. In Japan, I was the turtle, a slow-moving and cumbersome creature, determined to find out at my own speed. A man must find his own speed, otherwise he is lost. And a man's first compromise leads to further compromise, creating a snowball effect.

---

1 This same coupé would end up in our Tulse Hill driveway from 1990 to 1992, only to be burned to a crisp when our estate exploded right next to it. See *Autogeddon* LP.

Yeah, for me, the road to enlightenment was an uphill cycle path with a maximum speed of 5 mph. And every day the hill was getting steeper. The road to narrow-mindedness was an eight-lane freeway, downhill all the way. It would have been such a pleasure to drive on. But I couldn't take the risk – there was no fucking speed limit at all.

A CAREERING SHOW BUSINESS

In December 1985, Echo & the Bunnymen were big, going on huge. So long as Mac didn't blow it by thinking he alone was responsible for their success, the Bunnymen were all set to race to the end of the '80s in the big league. But for now they were doing another British tour. They were playing Birmingham Odeon for two whole nights.

"Julian. It's Peter. We're in Room 832 in Birmingham."

I could hear screaming down the phone. Pete DeFreitas could have been in a club. There was weird music and chaos behind him. A lot of people were screaming my name and that made me feel happy.

> PETE: "Johnno and Jake are sitting next to me. D'you wanna have a word?"
>   *(Sounds of a struggle and a clunk and. . .)*
> JOHNNO: "'Iya, Copey. It's Johnno. We're on the eighth floor of thee 'Oliday Inn. Pete's got some fine Squaalo and truckloads o'pot . . . he, fuck off . . . Sorry, Copey. Are you coming over or what?"

I was happy as hell. I sang the *Bewitched* theme song over and over in my head: "Two nights, Two nights, Two night night night, Two nights. . ."

Two hours later and the maze of Birmingham's one-way systems was really pissing me off. The Karmann-Ghia windscreen was misting up and I was too hot. This fucking heating system is caned, it's either on full or way too low. How do we get into the Holiday Inn car park? See, we've passed it again . . . I told you to look out.

Why did they ask us to come? It's not like I even want to see the Bunnymen. I'll be jealous of Mac and pissed off at everyone for kissing his ass. And Pete and Johnno and Jake and everyone will be telling me what a twat he is. Then I'll feel better for a while, 'cause they'll like me better. Then the tour will carry on and go abroad and do really well, and all my friends will love me as a fading crazy memory, still stuck in the wilds of the West Midlands. And Mac will wander round oblivious to all this and not even be aware of anything but himself. Fucking hell. Dorian, turn the bastard car around. Let's go home . . . and we did.

Next day, Johnno was on the phone, angry as hell. "Come on, Copey. Don't be such a fucking cop-out bastard."

I told him about last night, but he was not at all interested.

"Listen, man. We come and see you all the time. No wonder you can't leave the house without freaking out."

He was right. I lay in a huge hermetically sealed vat of ideas and potential. What a cop-out I was! Johnno's words carried on for 20 minutes or more, until I was psyched for battle. Come on, Dora! We're off to Birmingham. . .

It was almost dusk as we arrived in the car park of the Holiday Inn. As we turned off the one-way system, the first thing that I saw was the figure of Peter DeFreitas, 400 yards above me, stretched, Christ-like and beautiful, over the eighth-floor balcony. Awlright! And he was dressed like the Don in the wine adverts, Castillian Spanish with a black brimmed hat and a gentleman's cloak.

Dorian and I raced up to the room.

Jake Brockman stood in the doorway, smiling. I hugged the fuck out of him and surveyed the chaos as a chorus of male voices blasted "Copey!" Pete lifted Dorian up and twirled her around. "You made it!" Johnno handed me a spliff and Dorian started to skin up along with everyone else.

Pete and I went out onto the balcony and I was home. As we stood quietly, talking about all things far-out and cosmic, Pete was looking totally beautiful. But he was unhappy with the Bunnymen. Andy Eastwood was not doing the tour, was not allowed to do the tour because of politics with Mac.

DeFreitas was like me. He needed all the people that he loved to be around him.

Meanwhile, the scene inside the bedroom was getting more and more intense. There were about 15 guys in the room, most of whom I didn't know. But Dorian was okay – Johnno and Jake were looking after her. Pete and I stayed on the balcony and gazed out over the bombed and burned-out ex-city centre of Birmingham: the ring-roads that left civic buildings stranded and alone, and the cast-iron monochrome rainbow pedestrian walkways that straddled the real city below, unsympathetic as a 100-foot high crane in a pub garden.

I stood becalmed and motionless. With these people, I was good. Of that I had no doubt. But if only I could be with them more. That night, Birmingham was where I wanted to be. As unclassically ugly as a West Midlands city can get.

It was a standard Bunnymen show, of course. Will, Les and Pete were heroic but Mac Von Däniken was all over the place and wildly out of tune. I was still so proud to be there. Of course.

I didn't see Mac, not even for one minute. He couldn't leave his cocoon to say hello to me. But why should he make any effort to see me? And why should I care? He's only completely on his own territory, only as safe as he'll ever be. He was on his tour trip. I understood. I still remembered Club Zoo.

•　　　•　　　•

Two weeks later. Bombardment. Pete DeFreitas was free from the Bunnymen tour schedule and straining at the leash. He turned up at the Drayton Bassett house with Sandra Pigg, his new woman, who had just starred in the film *Letter to Breshnev*. She had been a fixture of the *Brookside* programme, but I had never heard of her and was speechless that she'd chosen such a surname.

Pete DeFreitas had a plan. A real "Fuck off and begin again" plan. He was off to start his own scene, a scene that would evolve and develop rules and parameters as it went along. He said that he hated the suffocating restrictions of the Bunnymen, *and* the intrigue, *and* the bullshit.

That weekend, Dorian, Sandra, Pete and I did our thing. Whilst Pete schemed, his cocaine took a severe punishment. Johnno was in Ireland – but just a phone call away and up for adventure. Andy Eastwood was pissed off and poverty stricken in London. And I was running around the Drayton Bassett house, not quite part of it, but enjoying everything by proxy. If I couldn't leave home right now, I could sure as hell pretend.

The visit ended too soon. In a couple of days, DeFreitas was calling me from the Columbia Hotel, his plan already taking shape. He was forming a new group and everyone involved was to play a specific role – in Pete's mind, an enormous and grandiose one.

Tim Whittaker was down from Liverpool. He was to be the artist in the group and had been playing percussion for the Bunnymen. He had influenced everyone in Liverpool with his "Duck" paintings, which were based around a very loose theory, which most people rushed to misinterpret. Dave Balfe was so into it that he was trying to buy up every Duck that Tim had ever done.

Andy Eastwood was the biographer. He bought a 16mm film camera, a tape recorder and a large book in which to log all events. Pete adored Andy. They had worked together on the previous Bunnymen tours. Mac's insistence that Andy be excluded from this last tour had made Pete very bitter.

The planning continued. Johnno was in Ireland with his new girlfriend and a little reluctant to budge. He had insinuated himself into the family and was enjoying the country gentleman's life. But at this point, Pete clinched the deal. He booked four plane tickets to New Orleans, suites overlooking Lake Charles in the finest hotel he could find. Then he rang Johnno.

Then came a strange New Year party. Drayton Bassett 1986. A bunch of people who were not quite there. Mama Helena was over here to get away from the crushing loneliness of her first Christmas as a widow. She and Dorian would sit for hours, gazing thoughtlessly out of the window at Smelvin, who would run around in endless circles in the garden.

My brother Joss was here. And telling me that it was to be a very special year. Yes, I believed that it was. I knew that I had a fine album inside me – I just had to stay away from my detractors long enough to hone down my attitude.

Joss and I made promises to each other. We resolved to try harder as human beings, even become good at it. Resolutions, man. I need them.

On New Year's Day 1986, part of my heart flew off to New Orleans with Pete, Andy, Johnno and Tim. Pete rang me from the airport before they left and again when they arrived. Then phone calls began to come thick and fast. I was proud to be included in their trip. I don't think they realised quite how much, but I felt privileged. I'd been stuck outside the perimeter for so long. Whenever they visited me, they seemed to think our lifestyle was all by choice. But it was a horrendous drag to be so isolated. I hated it. Dorian hated it. And now, people we adored were really fucking going for it. Awlright!

In New Orleans, Pete was using his position as the Bunnymen's drummer to get free studio time, free use of instruments, free places to stay, free food and people to show them around. Still, within a week of their arrival, the cash was heavily depleted. But Pete had Bunnymen credit cards.

Time passed on. My life stopped. I became obsessed with the DeFreitas phone calls. Every day, they became stranger. And more and more of them. Occasionally, I'd hear Johnno for maybe 30 seconds – not quite as strange as Pete, but still way out there. By this time, Pete had metamorphosed into a character called "Mad Louis", Louis being one of his middle names. He was ringing only Jake and me, and hounding Jake to send more money.

Pete had bought a 1950 Dodge Meadowbrook in Forest Hills blue. I sat with my Chrysler book on my lap and looked at a picture of the same car, whilst Pete told me all the far-out scenes they were having. Then other people began to ring me. Me! Ha, I felt really cool. Mr No Calls was suddenly deluged!

"Uh, yeah, he's rung twice today already."

Ha Ha. All these people bouncing off walls, trying to find a way of stopping DeFreitas from spending all that money. But to me, it was a wonderful and absurd game. And a game that included me.

Pete, Andy, Johnno and Tim had this one-off group/cultural support group/ thang called The Sex Gods for quite a while, but the orthodoxy of the Bunnymen had precluded their getting too far. Now was the time to do it. Pete hit me with all the weirder angles first. He explained about the looseness of the music and the completeness of the trip and the psychology of it all. Then he went and spoilt it by bringing up the Duck. Of all the far-out and cosmic theories that I'd had shoved at me, the Duck was the one that truly made me cry "Enough!" Anyway, I'll tell you about it.

The Duck: A Tim Whittaker Theory

Tim Whittaker was inspired. A little crazy, but inspired. He used to play drums in a group called Deaf School, which everyone in Liverpool worshipped and I thought were shit. But for the past years, Tim had been painting huge organic works that had no end. (Dave Balfe once bought a painting that had changed so dramatically by the time he received it that he thought Tim had given him the wrong one.)

Tim Whittaker was a Liverpool guru. A quiet gentle guy who inspired all the drummers he met – DeFreitas, Gary Dwyer, Budgie – and also pretty much everyone else – Jayne Casey, Balfe, Bill Drummond, Tempo, the list is endless.

Anyway, around the middle of 1979, Dave Balfe and Tim Whittaker shared a flat in Grove Park, about 400 yards from my old place. Balfe turned his room into a shag paradise, with a high-level bed, sexy colours and seduction in mind. Everything was kept in neat order and Balfe would scream at you if you even dared to look comfortable.

Just down the corridor, in the same flat, was Tim's room. It was unpainted and had newspapers all over the floor. Tim had no belongings, except for a pair of slippers and a mattress. In that room, Tim would expound on his theory of the Duck. I heard it loads of times, mainly from Balfe, who'd bore everybody with it. On the outside, it seemed to be as simplistic as: "There is good. There is bad. And between the two lies the Duck." With a little pot in my system, I could dig that theory as much as the next man, but I never got in deep with it like a lot of people did. They'd become obsessed with it. I'd think I was missing out, listen some more, and still be unconvinced. And that was the theory and the story, no less, no more.

Except that the Duck theory continued. I moved to Tamworth and Tim Whittaker began to play extra drums with the Bunnymen, constantly reinforcing and upgrading his theory, insinuating it into people's consciousness with his paintings and his quiet talk. But *what* theory?

Pete DeFreitas, like many before him, was utterly convinced that the Duck was a symbol of ultimate good. It had been a powerful ritual animal throughout ancient Indo-European culture and appeared in many forms as a divinity itself. Wooden ladles in the shape of a duck had been discovered at a number of Neolithic sites in Latvia and Lithuania, and many scholars regarded the duck as the main sacrificial bird in Europe before the introduction of the hen.

But what was the sacrificial link between Pete DeFreitas and the Duck? Surely Pete had left the Bunnymen of his own free will and because he was bored to the very Core of his ardently Shamanic soul to be around such 24-hour-a-day wittering. Pete had just taken Tim's obsession and imbued it with all kinds of power and mysticism. By the time Pete was finished, the Duck had, in his own mind, become a shaman spirit which would descend upon The Sex Gods and fill them with an awe-inspiring Michigas, or Creative Spirit.

From my end of the telephone, and lacking the necessary Mythological Duck Files, it just sounded as though they were all taking large amounts of drugs. Crassly, I could only endlessly repeat in my head that classic Guess Who moment during 'Friends of Mine' when Burton Cummings screams: "I wanna do it to a duck in a ten ton truck and fade away." Not what Peter required at all. But I was sure that a great deal of the reasoning was classic hallucinogenic control-freak paranoia.[1] Like one extremely effective phone call that I received at 4 a.m.:

"Julian. It's Peter."

"Hi, Pete. It's 4 a.m."

"Yes. I know that. But I have to tell you *now*."

"Pete, it's January. I'm freezing. I'm standing in our bloody hall with just a T-shirt and no undies on."

"Yes, I understand this. But the way I see it, I have to tell you now. You're at such a low point, psychologically, that any knowledge that I have to give you will go directly to your brain."

And so, with our own lives on hold, the Pete DeFreitas story continued to act as a surrogate life, 3,500 miles away down a telephone wire. He wrote off the Dodge Meadowbrook on a tree and bought an old convertible. Then he met Michelle, the 16-year-old daughter of the New Orleans chief of police. Bill Drummond and the Bunnymen's tour manager flew to New Orleans, where they were confronted by an entire scene of people wearing shades, filming and working in the suites overlooking Lake Charles. When Pete finally turned up, he was in the back of his convertible, driven by Michelle, in leathers and mirrored sunglasses. Apparently, Bill Drummond was all set to bawl Pete out and ship him back. But when he saw what was going on, he was so into it that he could not put his heart into convincing Pete to return.

PETER DILEMMA

It was soon after that that everything got out of hand. New Orleans is a small place where everyone knows everyone. Huge debts were being run up, on top of everybody's goodwill. And Pete still refused to move to a less expensive hotel.

When Jake Brockman's father died, Pete was still hounding him for money. The drug reasoning had got way out of hand, and Johnno and Tim were getting scared. Andy told me that every time Pete made a particularly cosmic reference to the Duck, Tim would look paranoid and say: "Look, this stuff's got nothing to do with me."

And so, as Pete submerged himself, Mad Louis took over. He had spent all the money and the others just had their return tickets home. As they flew back

---

1 I'm now fairly sure that I was totally wrong about this. But only vats of experience and 20/20 Hindsight have clued me in. At the time, I was as sure D-F was derailing as the next poor sod.

to Liverpool, Pete took Michelle and his one remaining valid credit card and drove to Miami, whereupon her chief of police father gave chase to charge Pete with taking a minor over state lines. Awash with superfluous Duck Theory and in a state of panic and confusion, the two of them flew to Jamaica, where Pete hired a car. They drove to the far side of the island and rented a large house overlooking the sea. Finally, in his paranoid desire to stop moving, Pete went out and bought heavy darkwood furniture for the house.

Each phone call from Pete was lucid. He knew that he was acting weirdly, but still believed that the Duck had descended upon him. If he was to be a sacrifice, then we would probably soon find out. But I understood Lucid myself. I was totally coherent most of the time, but still managed to crawl into genuinely insane areas from time to time. The last thing we needed was to wait on Pete's next move. We should save the guy.

But I found myself in a strange position, because Pete had started to confide in me. Jake was too upset to even speak to him and I was supposed to be this great Utopian weirdo who accepted everything. But I didn't. If you're sober, you can tell me that you went to Jupiter on a singing hen and I may believe you. But if you're on drugs, then I won't believe you without incredible notes, photographs and colleagues' accounts of the journey. Drugs are great if you want to be fooled and Pete seemed to have slipped into a dangerous position between Enlightenment and Delusion. But how could I tell the guy without his thinking I was a non-Utopian No-mark? I was far too hung up to say a thing – and I was too made up to be included in the front-row of this mystery to rock the boat and have DeFreitas exclude me.

But with Andy, Johnno and Tim safely back in Liverpool, the possibly sacrificial Duck known as Pete DeFreitas was still being fooled by drugs in Jamaica. They had all fucked off home and used Pete's money to save their own asses. But these were the actions of desperate men, whose friend had now begun to stand in opposition to them.

And as Hurricane Mad Louis swept down the eastern seaboard of America and out towards the West Indies, certain defensive measures were being taken by worried observers back in England. The returning Sex Gods were, themselves, too frayed and shell-shocked to offer any enlightened insight into the current DeFreitas state of mind. Indeed, their very arrival back in Liverpool prompted an immediate and hugely judgmental backlash of righteous indignation from Bunnyfriends and relatives everywhere. However unfair it all was, Andy Eastwood, Johnno and Tim Whittaker were now social pariahs, every one.

Above: The Cope brothers at the Alvecote Priory arch; Summer 1983. (Photo: Dorian Cope)

Julian Cope at the Mill Lane house with his future usher Steve Gibaldi. The large grey Euro-style dustbins introduced in Tamworth during 1983 provided an ideal canvas for Cope's nocturnal psychedelic obsessions. (Photo: Dorian Cope)

Polaroid of Joss Cope at Alvecote Priory, Warwickshire, during a recce for the *World Shut Your Mouth* LP sleeve; Summer 1983. (Photo: Julian Cope)

Ex-Flid Joss Cope at the Mill Lane house, Tamworth; sometime in 1983. (Photo: Julian Cope)

Steve Lovell during rehearsals for the *World Shut Your Mouth* tour. (Photo: Ace Ventura)

Johnno during rehearsals for the *World Shut Your Mouth* tour. (Photo: Ace Ventura)

Twenty-four hours after Cope's infamous Hammersmith belly-slashing, his tour manager Ady Wilson slashed his own face to ribbons on a West Walean scree slope. (Photo: D'Arcy)

Dorian and Julian Cope's secret Lichfield wedding took place as soon after his divorce as was possible. The wedding picnic at Alvecote Priory was only attended by Joss Cope and Donald Ross Skinner. (Photos: Donald Ross Skinner)

Bottom right: Lisa St. John and
M. Mortimer ham it up in Ankerside shopping
centre; early 1984. (Photo: Dorian Cope)

Top right: Brother Johnno, Pete DeFreitas,
Andy Eastwood and Joe from The La's lie
trashed in Drayton Bassett, Staffordshire; 6
a.m. in the morning, Summer 1985.
(Photo: Julian Cope)

Bottom left: Lisa St. John in Tamworth, 1985,
with her then boyfriend Paul Barker of the
post-industrial freekbeat Robo-vampire O-So-
Bad (Zoso-bad?) Not-so-Bad Ex-Green
Gartside Wannabees Ministry.
(Photo: Dorian Cope)

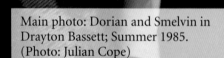

Main photo: Dorian and Smelvin in
Drayton Bassett; Summer 1985.
(Photo: Julian Cope)

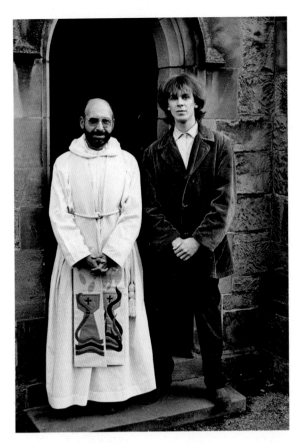

Left: Julian Cope with his old history teacher/new preacherman, the Revd John Fairclough, immediately after Cope's reluctant and hexed/X'd baptism in Burton, Staffs. Summer 1984. (Head Heritage Archive)

The newly-married Copes in a 1959 Cadillac Fleetwood limousine, outside St. Paul's cathedral (sic), Hempstead, Long Island; October 28th, 1984. (Photo: Deborah Padova)

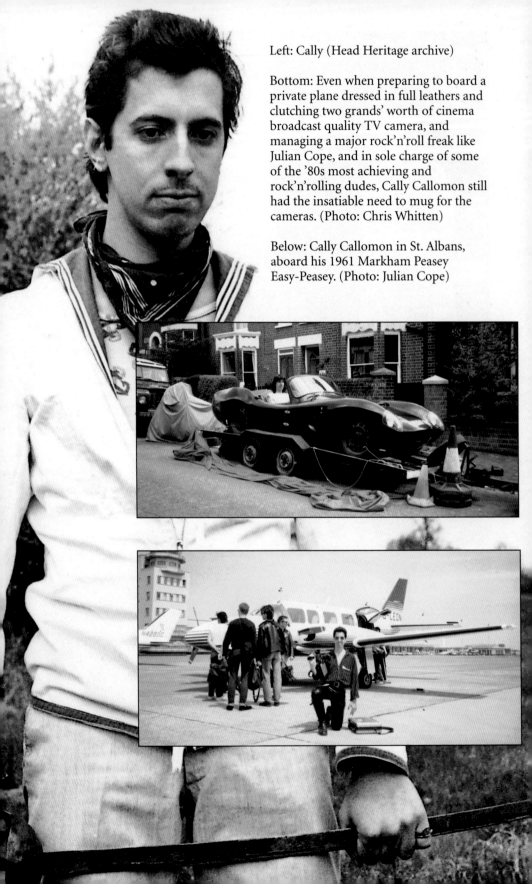

Left: Cally (Head Heritage archive)

Bottom: Even when preparing to board a private plane dressed in full leathers and clutching two grands' worth of cinema broadcast quality TV camera, and managing a major rock'n'roll freak like Julian Cope, and in sole charge of some of the '80s most achieving and rock'n'rolling dudes, Cally Callomon still had the insatiable need to mug for the cameras. (Photo: Chris Whitten)

Below: Cally Callomon in St. Albans, aboard his 1961 Markham Peasey Easy-Peasey. (Photo: Julian Cope)

Julian Cope's toys. When *Back to the Future* became Cope's favourite film, his 1985 obsession for toy DeLoreans mutated by 1990 into the need to bleach his hair, wear a white wunnsy and refer to himself as Doc, after the Utopian central character of the film. (Photo: Barry Douce)

POLICE DEPT.

PATROL

KEEP DANG! Cope looking fried during the
Fried photo-shoot; Autumn 1984.
(Photo: Donato Cinicolo)

Inset: The *Fried* sleeve.

The *Fried* truck took up residence in the Drayton Bassett garden, then became lost in
the undergrowth until retrieved by the new owners sometime in 1987. (Photo: M.)

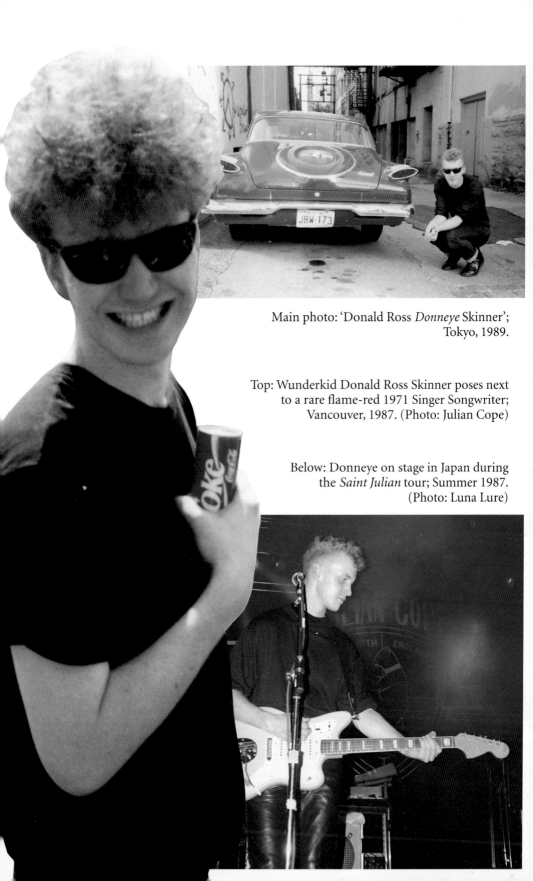

Main photo: 'Donald Ross *Donneye* Skinner';
Tokyo, 1989.

Top: Wunderkid Donald Ross Skinner poses next
to a rare flame-red 1971 Singer Songwriter;
Vancouver, 1987. (Photo: Julian Cope)

Below: Donneye on stage in Japan during
the *Saint Julian* tour; Summer 1987.
(Photo: Luna Lure)

Sometimes, the press were utterly split in their opinions of both Julian Cope and his work.

"The photograph enclosed is the most effortlessly beautiful picture of a man to grace these pages in five years. Mac must be seething, digging his fingernails into his palms."

Chris Roberts, *Melody Maker*,
October 22nd, 1987

"... all the divvies who thought they'd get into James or Run DMC and then heard how abysmal the records were have found an accessible and proclaimed-hip musical surgeon to smile limply to."

Chris Roberts, *Melody Maker*,
January 31st, 1987

"Given the choice between a 2,000-year-old geezer with long hair, sandals and 12 nosey mates and Julian, who would you choose for a date?"

James Brown, *Sounds*, March 7th, 1987

"A Post-Modernist Doll will soon be available in all good toy shops. One pull of the ring on its back and it quotes from Burroughs and wilfully wallows in a cesspit of its own making."

NME, February 14th, 1987

"World Shut Your Mouth ... how long before this emerges as the terrace chant of the season? Cope is still always first."

Melody Maker, November 8th, 1986

"Beached Whales of the Week: ...I dislike it. I dislike the manner in which the beat hops around, as if its ankles were tied together. I dislike the implicit scarf-waving..."

Melody Maker, September 20th, 1986

"...somehow this once again shimmering creature was coming back from the dead, an almost holy figure."

Sounds, December 26th, 1987

"... the only bloke ever to look odd because he's *not* wearing a turtle shell on his back... as unpredictable as a studied English 'eccentric' could be."

Sounds, April 18th, 1987

"He's always regarded himself as a launching pad for eccentric forays into the pop world, although he's never been able to whack up enough public funding to achieve anything but a 400 feet spurt into the air, followed by the inevitable dip in the trajectory and ignominious plop in the ocean."

Melody Maker, November 19th, 1988

"...he currently needs injections every 15 minutes and a wet-nurse to hold his nostrils and spoon feed him with broth every 30."

Melody Maker, November 12th, 1988

"Quote of the week from Julian Cope: 'My favourite shop is W.H.Smith. It's like a toy shop for me. I spend hours sniffing the envelopes.'"

Daily Mirror, May 4th, 1987

"Soccer manager Ron Atkinson appears on the new Julian Cope album."

The *Star*, April 8th, 1988

Just before The Teardrop Explodes split, Dave Balfe sold Cope this Casio MT40 for £40, inspiring such songs as 'Reynard the Fox' and 'World Shut Your Mouth'. The Gibson electric 12-string was bought from Manny's on New York's 42nd Street the same week that Cope met Dorian Beslity. Songs written on it include 'You Disappear from View', 'The Greatness & Perfection of Love', 'Trampolene', 'Shot Down' and 'When I Walk through the Land of Fear'. At the last Teardrops' gig it was thrown offstage; one year later its neck was broken by a London studio tape-op. In 1984, Cope's mother accidentally snapped the head off at the Mill Lane house. Cope even temporarily lost the guitar for eighteen months during the 1990s – but still it survives.

(Photo: Lawrence Watson)

Sometimes, the press were united in their opinion of Cope and his work:

"...Cope seems to be almost *glowing* up there... This aura isn't due entirely to clever lighting either – there's an unmistakable glimmer just above Julian's head and it shines brightly..."

Sounds, January 31st, 1987

"Non-manic types can only speculate as to what demons make this guy climb 40-foot lighting rigs and risk death by stroboscope, but it's certain that if he can keep this band together (and nothing in his past suggests he can), he'll have salvaged his reputation before you can say 'bless my cotton socks'."

Sounds, October 22nd, 1988

"The beauty of Cope is simply it's all a huge piss-take, frequently of the audience but predominantly of himself. Cope the thespian tackled a demanding range of roles – tripping acid freak, brain-addled rock star and sex-crazed stud – with the sort of conviction that must irritate the hell out of an inevitable handful of dimwits... We're being taken for the wildest ride conceivable."

Record Mirror, February 2nd, 1987

'World Shut Your Mouth' single review: "He's a bit of a genius is the lad... A very, very good record."

NME, September 20th, 1986

"Cope's current phase of activity may be his finest yet. But don't quote me on that."

Adam Sweeting, the *Guardian*, January 26th, 1987

" 'Mad', 'Bad' and 'God' are all words that spill irresistibly from adolescent lips at the mention of Julian Cope."

Time Out, October 5th, 1988

"And sizzling on each ray, like tiny bulbs of mercury on hot glass, dance the Qualities of Julian Cope. The confidence, the talent, the enthusiasm, the life ... and the infrasexiness. 225 volts of singing sex appeal. Julian Cope is the best songwriter in Britain."

James Brown, *Sounds*, November 8th, 1986

Rooster Cosby in 1988. His road excesses of the 1980s prepared no-one for his later graduation into the Jaki Leibezeit of the '90s. The most egoless player in rock'n'roll – and one of the best. (Photo: Head Heritage Archive)

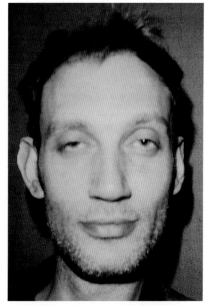

Rizla Deutsche AKA Gavin Wall. Known as 'The Two-Metre Man' in Cope's Japanese fan circles, it was Rizla who first reignited Julian Cope's Krautrock fixation. (Photo: Timothy Lewis Carroll)

Sid Mooneye AKA Mike Mooney in 1989. Adored by women and men alike, Mooneye leaves broken hearts around the world (When Courtney Love claimed to have lost her virginity to him in 1994, he strenuously denied it.) He plays guitar like Eddie Hazel but seems to have little regard for his own talent or that of the musicians he works with. A truly tortured genius. (Photo: Mika Anzai)

The unsinkable Mike Joyce proved to be a huge vibe during his time in the Julian Cope Group, even toasting new reggae versions of Smiths' songs during rehearsals – Girlfriend in a Coma, I hate the aroma! (Yoko Sato/Head Heritage Archive)

Andy Eastwood in 1989.
Singer, photographer,
writer, poet and traveller,
Easty came closest to
making it big with his
much-maligned Sex Gods.
His fastidious journal-
writing and camaraderie
helped to inspire Julian
Cope's '90s rebirth.
(Photo: Unknown)

The late and great
Pete DeFreitas.
(Photo: Unknown)

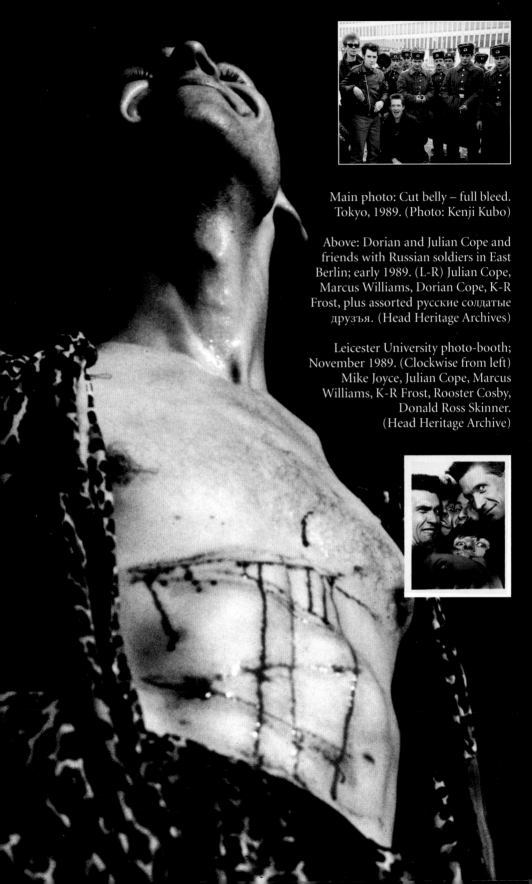

Main photo: Cut belly – full bleed. Tokyo, 1989. (Photo: Kenji Kubo)

Above: Dorian and Julian Cope and friends with Russian soldiers in East Berlin; early 1989. (L-R) Julian Cope, Marcus Williams, Dorian Cope, K-R Frost, plus assorted русские солдатые друзъя. (Head Heritage Archives)

Leicester University photo-booth; November 1989. (Clockwise from left) Mike Joyce, Julian Cope, Marcus Williams, K-R Frost, Rooster Cosby, Donald Ross Skinner. (Head Heritage Archive)

This tube of Japanese hair gel provided Cope with inspiration for one of his best known songs. (Head Heritage Archive)

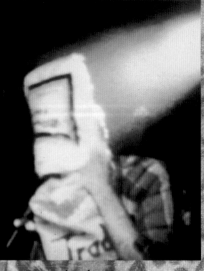

Bag on head, 1989. (Photo: Bruce Moreton-Cox)

Cope's 1989 chance discovery of the Safe Surfer condom at a Munich truckstop inspired one of the greatest guitar freakouts in rock'n'roll. (Head Heritage Archive)

The Journey of the Three Women. (L-R) Tante Mary Attubato, Dorian Cope, Helen Leli Beslity in Istanbul; Autumn 1989.

It was John Sinclair's 1971 book Guitar Army which reminded the lost Cope what a righteous trip rock'n'roll really was. (Head Heritage Archive)

STANDING ON THE VERGE OF GETTIN' IT ON

At home in Drayton Bassett, however, the bursting of the New Orleans bubble had prompted me into action. By now I had far more songs recorded than was necessary and The Sex Gods' attitudes had raised my own sufficiently to question everything.

Dave Bates introduced me to a famous A&R man, John Callodner, from Geffen Records. "He loves you, Copey. *And* the guy's a genius."

We sat in Bates' office, where I was subjected to the weakest schmooze of all time. "Yeah," said the Genius, "that song, erm . . .'True Love'. It's great. The arrangement sucks, of course, but it's a great song."

As I'd never written a song called 'True Love', the meeting did not impress me in any almighty way. The Genius had obviously barely heard of me and spent the whole time preening himself and coyly agreeing with the secretaries that, yes, he *did* look a little like John Lennon in his Abbey Road period.

Dorian and I stayed in to watch the *Challenger* mission at the end of January. It was a huge deal to Americans because of the presence of the schoolteacher Christa McAuliffe on the flight, the first non-technical member, and 1986 had been named "Year for Space Science". But the changeable weather conditions had meant long delays. And every delay just gave the TV more time to explore the life of Christa McAuliffe and show us her proud class making "Welcome Home" banners and cards. America's TV coverage was even more extreme.

But when the fourth attempt at take-off took place on that freezing January 28th, Dorian and I missed the live incineration of six American space heroes and returned one hour later to find media-land in mourning. The rubber o-ring seals which sealed each segment of the booster rockets had perished in the cold weather, allowing TV companies to repeat footage of the disaster every hour on the hour for days on end. I sat as guiltily fascinated by it as I had been by the coverage of the Aberfan disaster 18 years before. If they were willing to continue the reruns, I had to admit that watching the instant evaporation of a nation's dreams was freakily compelling.

Cally Callomon began to look at other record companies. I was starting to get freaked out. I'd had the idea of *Saint Julian* for over a year. And I seemed no closer to recording the thing. It was 14 months since the *Melody Maker* had used the headline "Saint Julian's 115th Dream"; it seemed as though other people had entire careers between the release of each of my albums.

In the spring of 1986, my public face was never more crazy. There were stories about my selling songs to workers on Paul McCartney's trout farm in the north of Scotland after the great man had refused to see me. I knew that I must reach out and haul myself from this mire before it was too late. Attitudes from the press rub off on the public and I started to feel pressure every time I went out. If I did *anything* remotely weird, everybody used it as confirmation of my craziness. If I was normal, they thought *that* was weird too.

They were wrong. Up in Liverpool, Pete DeFreitas was giving me a first-hand example of true inspired madness. Expelled from his group and now totally skint, Peter was back in the rent-free Bunnyhouse in Aigburth Drive and living on dandelion stew. He found it impossible to exist without a great deal of money. When he found 50 pence, he spent it on potato salad. When he needed heat, he paid Robbo to get firewood. Pete became convinced that he recognised the firewood, but never made the connection until he finally left the house one day and noticed that the substantial garden fence had been hacked to pieces.

SONGER

Hmm . . . I really wanted to tour. I wanted to get off my ass and work hard for a while.

Everyone at Outlaw said that I couldn't yet be trusted in Britain, so Cally looked for interest from abroad. Soon, a small tour of Italy had been arranged and Cally and I rang up Johnno and Chris Whitten and generally got very excited about the whole thing.

Then Malcolm Dunbar at Island Records got interested. Wow! I loved Island. They had helped get me through the dark days of the '70s. Pre-punk was a very uncool place to be, but Island had put out stuff by Roxy Music, Eno and John Cale, Nick Drake and John Martyn, and all kinds of weird reggae stuff. Somebody at Island's actually *interested*. I could hardly believe it.

You know, if you get treated like a crazoid for too long, that feeling starts to settle on you and it gets hard to shake it off. I just couldn't comply with other people's perception of me. It seemed phoney. And too cosy. I hated that Richard Hell attitude which insisted that the artist write from the point-of-view of the perpetual adolescent. On one hand, he had forced the whole question wide open with his Blank generation by telling us that Blank stood for "fill in your own description". But then he'd gone and spoiled it all by calling his band The Void-Oids, a veritable celebration of Blank as in DE-void. Plank. How could you develop or get anywhere with that tunnel vision?

My brother was already accusing me of changing the goalposts, but they were changing in front of me without any input from my end. There's a quote on the sleeve of *Freak Out* by The Mothers of Invention: "If your children ever find out how *lame* you really are, they'll murder you in your sleep." I had always worried about being lame. When I had first got to Liverpool, I felt really lame. When the Teardrop started I'd been lame as hell a front man and even lamer on my first solo tour. But now, after the Japanese shows, I was done with worrying. I didn't really care what anyone thought. I had entered a new phase – I'd become a Songer, one who sings of the things around him. The video '80s had every pop star thinking that they were Harrison Ford Coppolla – well I'm just gonna be a Songer. I felt like some forgotten Scandobard rising from the depths.

Then it all happened at once. Suddenly, Island decided that they really wanted to sign me. So Phonogram decided that they really wanted to keep me. With the Italian tour only a week away, Cally, Paul King and I spent all our time at my solicitors, tearing out hair and trying to reach some solution. The tour budget allowed the group only five days' rehearsals, so everyone was stuck indoors around the country, learning the songs from cassette.

Then Johnno rang.

"Hiya, Johnno."

"Hiya, Copey, how's it goin'?"

"Fine, man. Learnt the songs yet?"

Johnno sounded weird. He was not himself at all. Finally, he came out with it. All in one burst. "Look, I'm doin' this tour and everything, but I've got to insist that Pete does the drummin' and Ady does the tour managin'."

I freaked. I furry-freaked. You misunderstand, my friend. Deep inside me, I knew that it wasn't really Johnno speaking. It was a drug desperado operating Johnno's mouth and brain. But I was still hurt. These people. These people who are so different from the rest. I can't rely on them. Not even them. My head spun and I wasn't anywhere at all for a while. I couldn't even tell Dorian about it, but she could see that I was distraught. I was more embarrassed than anything. I felt so foolish. These guys that I adored. Wow. Bad one.

In two days, Chris Whitten found a friend for the job, a session bass player called Jeremy, who played for Joan Armatrading. The weirdness with Johnno was still doing my head in, but my mind was filled with Island Records and the unsigned contract. And the need to work Jeremy in at such short notice visibly helped me as practice in dealing with new people. The five days of rehearsals went incredibly well, and within two days we began to sound tight and exciting.

Soon we flew off to southern Italy, where it turned out that I had lots of fans. Awlright! Some heads in Rimini had put stickers of my *Fried* sleeve all across town, emblazoned with the words "Julian Cope is Coming – One Nation Underground". It looked great and important, though I had no idea what it meant.

The two young promoters took us around kiosk-size collectors' toy shops, and I picked up three extremely rare '50s promos of Chrysler show cars in tinplate and radiant blue plastic. Worth many hundreds of dollars in New York, they were here worth around £60 for the three. Just as I was leaving, Donald found three Ed Straker cars from the dustiest, mustiest corner of the shop.

Their boxes were perfect but dusty and these late Gerry Anderson Dinky Toys were still at their original price. I bought the lot, plus a huge and strange '60s E-Type Jaguar traffic control car, which negotiated its battery-driven way around traffic bollards and Belisha beacons.

The tour was mainly new songs in preparation for *Saint Julian*, so we played the shit out of the new songs and the audience was great. Soon, the music began to sound lean and amazing, and I felt a strange calm descend. Donald, Chris Whitten, Jeremy and I locked together as a group and Donald had turned into a psychotic guitar guy. We drank endless espresso coffees and smoked hashish out of a Coca-Cola tin. All except Whitten, that is, who still hated drugs with a loud and vociferous passion.

During one particularly full-on hash night, sitting with Donald and Jeremy in my hotel room, I was suddenly overcome by the most urgent and cosmic growl from under my own nose. My brow exploded into 40 rainbows and I went on a psychic downhill Cresta Run of such Winter Olympic intensity that I could hear Donald's whoops of glee in the far background, as my twisted lurching body squirmed and bounced around the room. My breathing was high-pitched and I brayed with assinine fear of what would come next. It was a feeling that would become gradually more recognisable over the coming 10 years, but there and then, right out of context and with nothing to compare it to, I thought I must have been experiencing some gigantic nerve attack as my soul moved three feet behind my body and stood gaping at the back of my own head. I felt as though I was in neither place at the same time, and my fluttering heart, caught between two worlds, struggled to maintain its beat. Yet the whole experience was both massively exhausting and inspiring. And at the end of the Cresta Run, I sat hazy and broken in the hotel bedroom – what was that all about?

MAGMA STORY

My tour manager Martin Cole had managed Faust and Magma, two of my favourite groups from the early '70s. Faust were the yippies who used drills and concrete on stage, and Martin regaled me with stories of their burning up stages across Britain. Having been at their Birmingham show, I was intrigued to remember that Martin Cole had been on the posters as co-promoter alongside Virgin Records. Martin told me about Magma's European tour in 1974. What a band. Magma were a Utopian Indo-European head trip who sung in their own language, Kobeian, and wrote epic percussion and vocal-based mantras about a huge personal mythology. Their albums *Mekanik Destruktiw Kommandoh* and *Kohntarkosz* had an almost *Fahrenheit 451* alternate reality about them.

Martin told us how the original group had come to a stunning and savage conclusion in Spain after a wild magic battle between Magma's leader, the percussionist Christian Vander, and the epically named bass player, Jannik Top. Vander had rented a hilltop castle for his own uses, which had annoyed Top's ego. He had rented a similar place within sight of Vander and the two proceeded to wage magic war upon each other. Martin Cole told of how he had ended driving from one castle to another trying to patch the band up, only to discover Jannik Top with serious chest wounds, screaming that Vander had caused him to tear his own chest open. Martin Cole is such a quiet man that I felt he was, if anything, downplaying this tale. His Magma story was nourishing to me – a great reminder of the strange and hidden world that I was quite happy to keep behind locked doors for the time being.

In Florence, we worked up this long quiet version of 'World Shut Your Mouth'. I can never normally see anything from the stage as my eyes are so bad. But during this particular sound check, I focused my eyes on the barmaid. She was the only person paying attention to me, gazing directly at the stage. My performance was brilliant. I showed off like crazy, singing and dancing and being every bit as entertaining as Mr Tommy Steele. On the way back to the dressing room, I had to walk past the barmaid. I even got a little nervous as I got closer. Only she wasn't a barmaid at all. She wasn't even alive. She was the wooden figurehead from an old sailing ship, which had been built into the bar itself. Bloody hell. I was too embarrassed even to tell Donald about that one.

But, at the end of the tour, I was in bliss. The whole of *Saint Julian* sounded great on stage. And on All Fool's Day, April 1st 1986, the Island contract was signed. I knew that the waiting and the going crazy and the yearning for work was over. All I had to do was to record the album and follow up with a frenzy of touring. Then I would change everyone's mind about me, once and for all.

THE TWO-CAR GARAGE BAND

The new Island deal had only been won from Phonogram Records at my expense, since my old label insisted on taking 2% of my first two Island LPs as payment for being allowed out of the contract. Unfortunately, this position quickly bred an attitude of "who-cares-how-expensive-recording-is-we'll-probably-never-see-any-money-in-any-case".

Unlike the *Fried* LP, which had not even been demoed, the *Saint Julian* demos which had been recorded on Phonogram time were used as blueprints for more demos in an attempt to further hone down the group to Cally's epic vision of a Two-Car Garage Band.

On Jeremy's return to Joan Armatrading, Cally co-opted James Eller to play bass and I felt the confidence of one who can trust his immediate surroundings. James had played all the best bass parts on *Wilder* and fitted into the group straight away. He had a Led Zeppelin sensibility devoid of ex-punk hang-ups which quickly spread to the rest of the band and saw our throwing of shapes dramatically increase during rehearsals.

In London, the band actually began to hang out as a unit and I found the whole thing inspiring until Chris Whitten came out dressed entirely in black leather – like me. We walked through Covent Garden and I felt like the bloody Quarrymen. But then, Donald started to wear black leathers, and Cally too. Hey, this is different – we're a band. I was the tense asshole, not Chris Whitten. Awlright! Rock'n'roll! People who wanna hang out with me and don't pretend they're too busy cleaning the car.

I asked Clive Langer to come down and listen to the band playing my arrangement of 'World Shut Your Mouth'. Island wanted it as the first single and I had honed the song down as much as I felt I could, introducing key changes into the solos to give the song a Sex Pistols heart-surge. Clive came! He was complimentary and told me that he would change virtually nothing, suggesting that we continue repeating the key change at the end. Yes. My songwriting mentor agreed with me – I was on the right track. Now I needed a producer to give it that 'Hang on, Sloopy' meets 'I Love Rock'n'Roll' gloss.

Malcolm Dunbar at Island suggested that we record with Ed Stasium, the Ramones' engineer, and played me some blasting garage band which Ed had taken into real Joan Jett territory. My mind was made up instantly. I knew that Ed Stasium would be exactly the right person for the job. Hell, his name is virtually Stadium, so how can we fail?

But we *couldn't* fail with a song like 'World Shut Your Mouth' and a Two-Car Garage Band. In fact, the song went onto tape easier than any song I had thus far recorded. At Livingston Studios in north London, I insisted on doing the vocals in full leathers, standing on top of a stack of specially-assembled flightcases. We lit the room so that light cascaded around me and lit up my tiny Matchbox Giftset, which I had bought in a Wood Green collectors' shop and set up across the floor far below.

Ed Stasium was a rock'n'roll doll with long blond hair and a smile like David Lee Roth's. He danced at the mixing desk, which I had festooned with toys, and held the vibe superbly, occasionally grabbing a guitar to suggest some simple but devastating lick. Ed had played all the lead guitar for the Ramones, as anything which was not a bar E chord was met by Johnny Ramone's stony "I don't do that stuff." So Ed had learned to make the most of even the most minimal flourish, a technique which he now employed with 'World Shut Your Mouth'. My Casio 202 had gone down during demo recording and a curiously entertaining sound kept bleeping out of the speakers. Now Ed recorded the distorted braying of the 202 and made the whole thing into a catchy electronic pay-off. I was intrigued. Surely this would be a hit – there was not a moment that didn't already sound like it had been Top 5. Gimme a hit. I need the dues.

But the band still needed a fifth member for live shows. I'd started crediting all my piano, synthesizer and organ overdubs to the imaginary Double DeHarrison, as keyboard playing was the last thing I wanted to be associated with. Cally suggested that we ask the keyboard player in Strawberry Switchblade, a great-looking guy called Frog from the nearly huge Farmers' Boys. But when Cally brought Frog down to Livingstone Studios, I was in the middle of freaking out and sat motionless under the secretary's desk the whole time he was there. No matter, everybody dug Frog immediately, so he was brought into the band and renamed Keith-Richard Frost in order to give him a brand new-ness. The band was finally a real band. Well, I could pretend.

The Two-Car Garage Band gradually acquired a new crew to go with it. A young guy called John Featherstone, who did lighting for The Smiths, said that he'd tour for free to prove how good he was.[1] This was a very cool and very rare gesture in rock'n'roll, and John's friend Rooster Cosby also came in to help with Chris Whitten's drums. As Rooster was normally in charge of Mike Joyce's kit, even the fastidious Whitten seemed at last set up. A big smiley fat geezer called Pete McKay became our mother hen and general driver, while Cally took Paul King's manager role on entirely. With Tears for Fears being treated like royalty in the United States, this worked out better for me in the long run. Kingy could get a little royal himself after he'd had his sizeable ass kissed across every coast of America, so I kept out of his precious way at those times and reflected on the yuppifying of the music business and its sapping effects on the true artists.

With the single on tape, the group made a brief sortie to Loco Studios in Caerleon, in deepest South Wales, in order to put together a suitably auspicious ep for the 'World Shut Your Mouth' release. Cally and I had chosen to clothe the single as a European-type high-gloss thing, repeating the same photographic image on either side. At Loco Studios, we now recorded versions of Pere Ubu's 'Non Alignment Pact' and The 13th Floor Elevators' 'Levitation', along with a new song called 'Umpteenth Unnatural Blues'.

The studio was run by a longhair called Tim Roller, who had programmed for PIL as Tim Carol Loose and recorded a recent Hawkwind album under the pseudonym of Bay City Roller(!)[2] Tim was obsessed with Peter Hammill and

---

1 Unfortunately, he was very, very good and now does Janet Jackson.
2 Roller's real name is either Timothy Carroll Lewis or Timothy Lewis Carroll. He currently uses the name Thighpaulsandra.

Kid Strange, and had seen both Van Der Graaf Generator and Doctors of Madness several times in the '70s, even fronting his own Glam-prog group Nancy Hitler. We got on like a house on fire and Tim pushed for wilder and wilder ideas, until a jam grew out of a duel between my Casio MT40 drum-machine and Chris Whitten's drums. It had the same prog-psychedelic beat as the end of Amon Duul 2's 'Green Bubble Raincoated Man'. We called the jam 'Transporting' and Donald worked in a clichéd space-rock riff of considerable charm, which James Eller followed sub-basically with his Moog Taurus bass pedals. Bay City Roller set my Selmer clavioline up out in the corridor, where I proceeded to record the whole track without headphones and with only a minimum of sound leakage through the door to aid me on my quest for tunefulness. The experiment paid off incredibly well, though, and my clavioline track was eerily melancholy and always just behind the chord changes of the other instruments.

By the end of the session, 'Transporting' had rightfully earned its future place as the intro music for the next two years of touring.

With Roller at the controls, we confidently launched into a late version of a recently-found song called 'Trampolene'. The demo was extraordinary – like an express train with a ZZ Top beard. I had found the song almost a year after I had perfunctorily left it lying in an old tape-player in the music room at Drayton Bassett, where I had recorded it, only to discover that 'Trampolene' was one of my favourite songs I had ever written. Aping the imagery of Chuck Berry's 'Maybellene' and Dolly Parton's 'Jolene', 'Trampolene' was a girl song about a brutal muse who takes the singer on a trip through cuckolded hell. I had written the whole song around a Chuck Berry E major Elevators' drone, which I had recorded onto my ghetto blaster, then played along over & over until the song took shape. But now, the Two-Car Garage Band transformed its arrangement into a spiralling and enthralling cosmic version of American southern rock, its splendid key changes and majesty totally at odds with the rest of its headlong rock'n'roll rush of careering scythe guitar.

Saint Julian was being transformed from a double-LP of themes and concepts into a far stronger fake rock'n'roll album, where the lead singer played the same role as early Alice Cooper – not the showbiz top-hat clown with anonymous backing, but the group of Detroit longhairs who had sung 'Caught in a Dream', 'School's Out' and 'Elected'. At that time, 'Alice' had just been a figurehead for an MC5-styled thing. It was a cosmic asshole role that I wanted to play and I knew that I could also mould the group that way.

The Dickhead Factor, which had been so central to the early Teardrop Explodes thought process, was now reinstated. I could play this role well. The leathers were on already and the blueprint was right in front of me. A young Midland group called The Mighty Lemon Drops had released a classic single called 'Like an Angel'. It was like the Bunnymen playing 'Reward' with a Wah! guitar sound. Donneye was big mates with them and they'd shown that the

Teardrop/Bunnymen/Wah thing worked in a uniform of Ramones' black leather. It was clean-looking and *Girl on a Motorcycle* in its pre-hippy lines. Cally adored it. Why not just take it back off them? We could even have them support us and get all the *NME* indie kids into us. They wouldn't think I was fucking crazy anymore because I'd be acting something that was natural to me.

With these thoughts in mind, I came back to Drayton Bassett and wrote an Alice Cooper-type song. First, I listened to *Killer*, the classic Alice LP which features 'Halo of Flies' and 'Under My Wheels'. I wanted those segmented stop-starts that Detroit groups do so well without sounding like Gennafuckings-iss. Once in that headspace, it was easy because I knew what I wanted to say and I knew it could be as rocking as Alice without people sussing that it was also a bit prog.

The song was called 'Shot Down' after an old Sonics' burn-out and took one hour to write from start to finish. I sat with my red Gibson 335 and played the intro, which flew into the main guitar riff, which then powered into B minor, at which time I grinned a big one. I let my professional Walkman record the next hour of ideas, until I had arranged the whole thing for my group, along with most of the lyrics.

When I took the song to the group, I told them about the Alice Cooper references (and a few Doors' comments to make Donneye comfortable) to show the weight of sound I wanted. This was 1986 and Smiths' fans were freaked out by a Gibson Les Paul. They thought it was too rock. But my group were all rock, except for Donneye, and James' references had always been Led Zeppelin.

So "Saint Julian" moved into another sphere entirely. He developed away from me, and independently of me, into some kind of two-dimensional rock star – something which I found to be a very manageable thing. I wrote a long poem about the nature of Saint Julian, an apologia explaining just how "Saint Julian ain't Julian". I knew that I was ready to do battle again, or face the prospects of there never being a better time. But I needed a peculiar form of armour this time and the Saint Julian image put several inches of psychic plate-glass between me and the 'real' world. As Mick Houghton had suggested at the time of my first solo album, it was really STOP THE WORLD, I WANT TO GET BACK ON!!!

NOT STING

"I've lived through The Beatles, I've tolerated Mick Jagger, and I even quite like Sting, but I'm afraid I draw the line at a clown on a piece of scaffolding."

"Outraged" of Dumfries, *Scottish Daily Record*

In late October 1986, I was back on *Top of the Pops* for the first time in five years. The combination of new record company and anthemic single had allowed 'World Shut Your Mouth' a place on everybody's radio and the disc zoomed up the charts. I'd even been on *Wogan*, which was the '80s equivalent of *Parkinson* (slicker & shitter). I felt like Reg Presley. A hip Reg Presley with a Joan Jett beat.

The chart was filled with credible mid '80s hits, like Cameo's 'Word Up', 'Walk This Way' by Run DMC, 'You Can Call Me Al' by Paul Simon and 'Don't Leave Me This Way' by The Communards. How exciting, we're on with The Bangles and fucking Nick Berry from TV. Fuck that. Who's the DJ? Oh great. Some young guy called Simon Mayo who's never even done it before. When I were a young man, they had a proper presenter, I thought to myself, like a man headed directly for Geezerdom. But I'd had years to mythologise the Teardrop performances in my head and I wanted it to be like that. I'd even hoped to do Toppy with Pete Burns and make an event of it, but his latest single had stalled the week 'World Shut Your Mouth' went Top 40.

The *Top of the Pops* studio was much bigger than I remembered it, possibly because I'd built a legend in my head of how famously small it was. I expected to be the size of a shoe-box. When The Bangles sang 'Walk Like an Egyptian', their singer, Suzannah Hoffs, wore a corset, and looked as though she was about to go solo any minute. Again, we were appearing as a four-piece to streamline the look and I rode the Iggdrassil mike-stand for all it was worth. But legendary it was not, and Nick Berry doing 'Every Loser Wins' at no. 1 really summed up the intense "blahs" of the whole thing. Why had I been breaking out in cold sweats in the run up to the charts every week? Had I fought hard with myself for this facile nonsense? It hardly seemed worth it. I should have just stayed indoors and accumulated more toys.

But when 'World Shut Your Mouth' stalled at no. 19 I was devastated. It was the most played record on Radio 1 – how did this happen? 'World Shut Your Mouth' is so much better than that, what a nothing chart position for the Natural Born Sibling of 'I Love Rock'n'Roll' and 'Hang on, Sloopy'. I suddenly cared far more about having a hit than I'd previously thought possible. I'd never had expectations as a solo artist because no-one had had faith in me for such a long time. Now I hated to see the record so close, only to slip out of our hands.

But I *was* a contender again and Island Records seemed to be just as hooting and hollering as me. Everyone there knew that 'Trampolene' would be a great follow-up single and the rest of the year was spent ensuring that the ep tracks and video maintained Cally's Two-Car Garage Band theory.

We decided to go to New York for Christmas. Dorian went a week before me, and was happy to be with her friends and family and have the opportunity to Christmas shop in New York instead of Birmingham. A few days before I joined her, she was shopping at Roosevelt Field, a large mall on Long Island, when she noticed she was being followed by a middle-aged man. He followed her in and out of several shops and she began to get nervous. She was about to confront him when he asked, "So how long has it been happening to you?" She told him she didn't know what he was talking about and if he didn't leave her alone she was going to scream. He then pulled out a business card which said "Channellers of Long Island". She stopped panicking that he was going to molest her, but weirded out for an entirely different reason, for Dorian had indeed had a "channelling" experience.

During the 'World Shut Your Mouth' single sessions at Loco Studios in Wales, in the early hours of the morning, I had been suddenly woken from a deep sleep by Dorian, who was crying hysterically, in a cold sweat with both her hands covering her mouth, and rocking back and forth. I thought she must have been having a dream, but I soon realised she was awake and something weird was going on. It must have taken at least five minutes before she was in a state to tell me what had happened. She had been awake and thinking about an article she had read the day before about a woman who was the "channel" for a man who had been dead for 500 years. As Dorian wondered if it could possibly be true, she said she felt a sudden jolt in the top of her head that went through to her stomach. Her mouth opened and a man's voice started to come out, as though struggling to be heard. Aware of what was happening, she quickly covered her mouth and screamed inwardly, "No, no, no!" There was a short conversation between Dorian and this presence, who explained to her that he would not hurt her, but Dorian was adamant that she did not wish this to be happening. Then it was over.[1]

So now here was this man at the shopping mall explaining to her that he knew she was "one of them" because of a great trail, a column of light, which she was leaving behind her. The man told Dorian that she had a duty to allow this shadowy side into her life and that if she were trained properly there would

---

1 The following evening, the overhead bedroom light started to sway of its own free will. At the time, we both put this down to that same presence, but Dorian now believes, with hindsight, that it was probably her own disturbed unconscious pushing the light to and fro. After the bedroom became the cooking area in 1987, no further unexplained events were recorded at Loco Studios. It closed in 1996 CE – I was the final customer.

be nothing to fear. Dorian stood there knowing that she faced a major life decision, but that agreeing could only consume her. After her experience at Loco, Dora reasoned that she had been particularly vulnerable to outside forces since her father had died. Indeed, she had had a couple of other weird experiences since her father's death. That explanation made sense.

The man in the mall did his best to convince her that there was a noble path ahead for her, but she chose not to walk it. She told me the story in great detail, but with no compunctions about having entirely rejected it.

We rang in the new year with New York phone interviews and photo-sessions. Travelling into Manhattan to Island Records was a big treat, as their offices were situated on 4th and Broadway, close to fabulous vinyl and old toy emporiums. Hordes of journalists filed in and out of the conference room, telling me that the 'World Shut Your Mouth' single was going to be a US Top 40. Awlright! At last! The video was being played on MTV constantly and I was offered an hour-long MTV special at the Ritz.

As the Ritz had been the venue where I'd thrown myself down the iron staircase in 1982, this idea appealed to me. The show was hugely promoted and sold out in advance, making me look like Lazarus back from the Dead in the light of the past few years' track record. What a difference a year makes. The Ritz show was storming and thunderous, and featured a sexy front row of women who wanted to have my children. They were all great looking, but my entire American family had turned up for this show and Dorian's brothers-in-law, cousins and aunts were staring on, bemused and intrigued. After the show, some of the women broke into the dressing room and continued their wailing: "Have my baby, Julian." My mother-in-law addressed them all firmly: "I'm his mother-in-law and this is his aunt," to which the women replied: "But we've come all the way from New England."

In San Francisco, we stayed at some Gay/New Age hotel on Geary Street, which was both compelling and repelling simultaneously. The staff were all incredibly arch and reminded me of the "Hotel 1969" in the Doctors' epic 'Mainlines', especially the bit where the "bellhop wears jackboots".

Within an hour of arriving in San Francisco, I had found a horrendous set of Martoy Chinese $\frac{1}{87}$ scale Hot Wheels rip-offs – 24 in a bubble-pack for $6.99 plus free roadway! I set these chromite nightmares up all over the floors and flat surfaces in order to combat the sheer '80s deluxe Existential-ness of it all and used the handpainted vase as a pisspot. The circular bath became a highly successful Hot Wheels wall-of-death and Donneye discovered a way of replacing the mini-bar Perrier with tap water with a gob of spit on the top.

We returned to Britain to film the 'Trampolene' video in Alvecote and Polesworth, close to the *Fried* mound. Cally got an MOTed Saab 96 on the video budget, tore off all the bits which stuck out and turned it into a white-walled silver UFO from *Fahrenheit 451*. It had to tow a big silver trailer which we were supposed to be performing inside, but the trailer was hired late and progress was deadly slow, as this big hulk caught on the narrow hedged corners of Alvecote railway bridge.

When we filmed the group sequence in a cornerless white environment with a circular rotating stage, someone brought huge amounts of cocaine and champagne, which was a hopeless combination for balance in such a featureless environment. I developed a terrible attitude and insisted that the Japanese make-up woman really tart me up. I looked crap. We all looked crap. Videos are crap.

Island had arranged for another TV special to be recorded at the Westminster Methodist Hall to be shown on BBC2, so we rehearsed new songs at John Henry's studio on the Caledonian Road.

When we were done, Frog, Donneye and myself found ourselves outside waiting for a taxi in the rain. As we stood shivering in black leather, a black cab drove up to us and stopped, then the driver peered out. He gave us the "V"s and drove off!

We were so pissed off that Frog took his Hackney carriage number in order to report him. "No," I said. "Let's celebrate the fucker and give him good vibes." When I got home, I took a magic marker and daubed "9918" in huge numbers upon my chest, where it would stay for the next year.

An hour before the Westminster Hall show began, I was caught in traffic on my way to appear on a new chat show called *The Last Resort*. The host was another new TV guy called Jonathan Ross and I arrived just in time to see him dressed as a gorilla. Oh, great. But Jonathan Ross took the gorilla suit off and made me look good and showed the *Fried* sleeve and talked about sex and all those unmiserable things, so I surged back to the Westminster Hall elated and invigorated and ready to rock.

The group was totally psyched for this show and played like rock monsters, but my voice was croaky and only vaguely in tune. I ranted and howled and threw myself into the orchestra pit, but the TV cameras made true freak out impossible – indeed, I broke a cameraman's arm by accidentally using his delicate long-boomed super-lens as a seesaw. But the camera team were all in the pay of Island Records and I had no reason to fear that it would end up anything less than mythological and totally Rock.

On January 17th 1987, 'Trampolene' entered the charts at no. 33, in the same confident manner as 'World Shut Your Mouth', then stuck at the no. 31 position for four long weeks. What was going on? How could it stall now, when there were gigantic posters of my face all over London? Every week, I expected the single to dislodge and start its fabulous ascent up the chart.

The press had loved 'Trampolene' and predicted a huge hit, *Time Out* stating flatly: "Nothing but the best of the week . . . Another hit from the forthcoming *St. Julian* LP", whilst *Sounds* had made it single of the week and said that I was "back from the wilderness to astound a largely unprepared public". So how could I fail now with all that potential riding on my shoulders? Yet by the time *Record Mirror* had written that 'Trampolene' "makes you feel that you could run 200 miles an hour" and *NME* had said it "makes you feel two feet taller just to hear it", the single was just another lost hit lying in my recent back catalogue.

Four weeks at no. 31 – what was the significance of that number? Damn! Damn! Damn! I waited in vain for the *Top of the Pops* call, but it never materialised. Instead, I had to content myself with dubious performances on excruciating '80s TV shows such as *Number 73*. I was bitterly disappointed.

But the vibe which had started six months before with 'World Shut Your Mouth' now proved itself on the release of the actual *Saint Julian* LP, which entered the album charts at no. 10. It was the highest album position I'd ever occupied and I was genuinely elated. I wandered around the West End staring at album racks full of the *Saint Julian* albums, their Top Ten stickers blissfully announcing my success to anyone who wished to look.

But the jacket of *Saint Julian* was totally unlike the marvellously upfront magazine-style of the first two singles, which Cally and I had slaved over and whose merits we had endlessly debated. For a whole month, we had attempted new and inferior takes on that familiar magazine-theme, until, with time and ideas running out, the album sleeve – any album sleeve – was demanded by Island Records.

The *Saint Julian* photo sessions were hastily shot in Richard Cuttler's scrap-yard, near Tamworth, by Peter Ashworth, a photographer friend from my days of hanging out with Soft Cell and Stevo. I told everyone that the Saint Julian character must look as though he's just beamed down and is having a quick snapshot taken. It now seemed entirely correct to temporarily extend the Tamworth connection and, as I had three years before sold our Mill Lane house to Richard Cuttler, so it was that Richard himself appeared on the back of the final sleeve, staring into the formidable heat of the smelting ovens.

But it was March 1987 and my genuine Tamworth days were truly over by now. I had been living once more in the Columbia Hotel and Cally told me that it was time for us to move to London full-time. Of course we should. If I'm walking around with "9918" on my chest, I reasoned that my London trip had already begun. Also, if the move had helped to straighten me out so much, surely it could do the same for my darling Dorian.

MAINLINE TRAINS COULD NEVER FIND DRIVERS TO RUN A SERVICE OUT TO HERE

"I could have been cabbaged for nearly a year . . . in fact, I probably was."

Dorian, 1999 CE

But what was happening to Dorian? All this time I'd been out of the crisp packet, she was turning into a chewy. She'd been willing me to be a contender for so long that it had never occurred to her that she'd be left in Drayton Bassett speeding her brains out and counting how many calories she had not eaten that day. And the next day. And the next day.

I think I have to explain why she wasn't allowed to be with me, otherwise it looks mean. But it had been so long since I had been attempting to compete that it was difficult for me to remain focused with her around. The *Saint Julian* sessions had turned into weeks, then months, and we were constantly changing studios. It was easier for my head to know that she was safe at home than to think of her wandering around London with Smelvin.

We had even talked of living in London, but only in an abstract kind of way. Dorian would look at property guides and say: "Elephant & Castle. Wow, doesn't that sound pretty?"

"Yeah," I'd say, in a removed way. And that would be it.

Dorian would come to visit me every 10 days or so to begin with, but as work became more gruelling and she became more culty the visits were less frequent. We'd talk on the telephone every day and she'd tell me how many times she'd done the Jane Fonda workout video or that she'd managed to put off eating until 4 p.m. Because her behaviour was ruled by speed and we were both pretty used to druggy behaviour, it never occurred to either of us that she had an eating disorder.

Barney and Bowie were Dorian's Tamworth connections – they'd been old schoolfriends of Joss's and often roadied for Freight Train. They would sell her as many of those big old-fashioned black & whites as she wanted, so there would never be any powder involved. Trust Tamworth to be a ready source of such archaic alchemy. Dorian would take a pill every two days, or every other day, and then smoke ciggy spliffs, drink Diet Coke and exercise. She'd been suspiciously excited by the World Cup during the summer of 1986. She knew nothing about football, so I couldn't understand why she was suddenly talking about it all the time. But watching it live from South America gave her a valid excuse to stay awake all night. And, as these were the days before British television had started broadcasting 24 hours, this meant a helluva lot to a non-sleeping speed freak.

I wasn't particularly worried about her, though, because I was still mad. Acting the part of a sane, dynamic rock'n'roll star was not bringing true sanity with it, but I did at last have one foot on the ladder. As we'd both been in the ditch, I knew it was important for at least one of us to be getting out. It was too much to expect that we could both get out at the same time. For now, it was enough for me to know her whereabouts. As long as she answered the phone each night, I was okay.

"SHUT YOUR MOUTH SINGER IN NO DRUGS DEAL"

But while I was in London, the bailiffs came around to our house and demanded hundreds of pounds from Dorian, telling her that the house tax had not been paid in months. My parents were there and my mother immediately offered to pay the debt, but my father said no, they shouldn't get involved. I hadn't relied on my father since I was 19 and he surely wasn't about to offer now. Phone calls to Cally only showed that we had no money and no likelihood of getting any. We had to move! What? Straight away? How can this happen when I've got such a good record deal?

Then, soon after the house sold to the first person who'd seen it, Cally discovered that we did have money. But for the past year Outlaw Management had been paying our mortgage twice a month out of two different private and personal bank accounts by mistake.

But Dorian didn't want to hear this and was fearful that I'd use it as an excuse to remain in Tamworth. Magical places with names like Elephant & Castle were giving her ideas. No way could she stay cabbaged up there for even another minute.

Some time in April 1987, we moved. Or rather, Dorian moved. While I was humping the Iggdrassil mike-stand on stage every night, she packed up my Drayton Bassett toy room, contracted house-movers and transported the entire household contents down to a small two-bedroomed maisonette at Albany Mews, near (you'll never guess) Elephant & Castle. Dorian and Smelvin followed the furniture van in the Karmann-Ghia, which struggled all the way down the M1 and came to rest in the Albany Mews parking space – the last time it would ever be drivable.

But Dorian had escaped at last and the problem of fitting 44 boxes of toys and the furniture of a four-bedroomed house into a tiny mews cubbyhole was, for her, something to be overcome at any cost. Along with other minor details which nearly brought the whole Albany Mews deal crashing down.

On the day that Dorian was supposed to sign the deal with the letting agent Yes Lets, the *Sun* ran a piece on their music page with the headline: "Shut Your Mouth Singer in No Drugs Deal!" It claimed that Island Records had insisted

I sign a no drugs clause in order to keep my contract and the owners of our new accommodation saw it and freaked out. Unbeknown to me, Dorian had to meet them and smooth it all out with "explanations".

When I arrived one week later, I knew I would have to compromise hugely. Our old living room had been big enough to run around – this whole space upside & down could have been covered in 10 seconds flat. The enclosed garden had plastic turf – I swept Smelvin's shit under it. I just couldn't get my head around the place at all and set about treating it as though it was the same size as Drayton Bassett. I set the huge pedal car in the centre of the living room and put the even huger jeweller's cabinets across the end, bringing the room in so much that it felt like one of the Victorian sitting rooms I'd known so well as a child. I set up every toy that I could squeeze inside the cabinet and piled boxes and boxes across its top, then set smaller model cars in smaller cabinets around the pedal car and pinned model planes to the ceiling. The second bedroom was ceiling high with toy boxes, but I still managed to find an area in which to spray paint the other old toys which I was restoring. In a toy-box I found the Head that Ray Falconner from UB40 had given to me and used it as a spray paint mask. I may be in London now, but life would still go on as always.

We soon discovered that Elephant & Castle was a letdown. But, at weekends, we would walk up Walworth Road, both nervous and excited to be in this city together for the first time since Bates' flat in the summer of 1981.

Signs on London buses were clearly put there to make everyone feel excluded and mystified. "No Graffiti" was self-explanatory, but what on earth did "No Tagging" mean? I asked a Slavic bus conductor on Walworth Road and he was as clueless as I was. That must be the way the city works – with everyone thinking, I'm the only one here who's totally in the dark; the rest all know what's going on. So everyone's too hung up to even ask. Divide and rule, I guess.

Dora was desperate to work in London. In her last Tamworth months, she had tried to find any kind of office work to keep her mind from getting slack, but the work was pitifully paid and full of ninnies. At least London would provide companions with a common goal. During a brief break from the schedule, I took Dorian to a temp agency, where she took a typing test and tried to jump out of the window in sheer fright, but was persuaded to do it anyway. She passed. Of course, she was a competent woman who'd learned how to type as a journalism student at New York University. It would all come back to her soon enough.

I kept cutting my hands and stubbing my toes in the new place. I was used to swinging my guitar around the house and singing all the time. Now, I kept smashing it into someone else's walls and thinking about the damage.

I was eager to get out and do some physical action when the Island 25 happened.

In April 1987, Chris Blackwell was celebrating 25 years of Island Records in a big party featuring all the current Island artists. There was a big double-LP out featuring 'World Shut Your Mouth' and, though it was a contrived family, I was proud to be a part of it. Even though Chris Blackwell liked to pose as a silverspoon ersatz black man with a posse of Ital-assrimmers, his record label suggested that he was much more, with its albums by Traffic, John Cale, Eno, Kevin Ayres, John Martyn, Nick Drake, Bob Marley, Burning Spear and all the '70s reggae artists whose on-the-One mysticism had so captured my heart.

On the day of the Island 25, we were playing at a Dutch festival called Tourhout. A guy came up to me after the show and said he had some toys for me. I took the box back to the dressing room, only to discover that it was packed with 1950s and 1960s European die-cast toy cars. I flipped out and wanted to run after him – you can't do this, it's too much. But I didn't. I just sat marvelling at each one as it came out of its individual tissue-paper wrapping. One hundred and twenty harlequin-coloured toys in fantastic condition. Whoa.

We flew to the Island 25 show by eight-seater single engine monoplane. Crossing the English Channel at 120 mph really showed me the vastness of the water and we seemed to hover indefinitely, almost birdlike, over the sea. We flew up the Thames estuary as the sun set and the streetlights came on. It really set my London heart on fire. The great bends of the River Thames were wash-cloths of brilliant blackness across the backdrop of millions of amber lights and even Chris Whitten's nervousness at flying in something so small was eclipsed by his awe at the path of our night flight.

The show was a big '80s letdown, of course. The groups just mimed their songs and shook their booty. But that flight was forged indelibly onto my mind.

The failure of 'Trampolene' and success of the *Saint Julian* LP was confusing to Island Records, but I was made up to have come this far. So when they said they wanted another single and video, I just used it as an excuse to buy hundreds of toys.

Cally and I worked out this elaborate plan to create a drive-in movie in $1/_{87}$ HO scale, and we visited a King's Cross toy warehouse which sold model 1949 and 1959 Cadillacs in boxes of 25. Gimme 20 boxes. I was in bliss and didn't give a shit about the single, 'Eve's Volcano'. Of course it wouldn't be a hit, so let's just have some fun.

We turned the sombre Outlaw offices into a papier máché mess, and built a huge drive-in with hundreds of cars. It looked magnificent – until the video bastards got to it. They melted half of the Cadillacs with TV lights and accidentally smashed the funfair, then sawed the car park in half "to facilitate close-ups".

I didn't want any of that shit. This was for my home – MTV would never play this video in a month of Sundays. They didn't. The single stiffed utterly. The video was pretty good, though. I kept rewinding it whenever the close-ups of the drive-in came on. Yeah, I thought, all those toys on that video are mine. Right On.

Cally started collecting those awful late '50s boy racer streamlined pretend Aston Martin/Ferrari copies. Real cars, not models. I didn't see the point in painting them British racing green or Ferrari red when they were all powered by modified 1940s Ford side-valve engines. But Cally loved the nerdiness of it all. He had a Markham Peasy kit car which built into a fair copy of a streamlined '50s racer. My favourite car at that time was a huge 1933 American show car called the Pierce Arrow Silver Arrow. What a name! It meant that Cally's kit car became known as the Markham Peasy Easy Peasy and I took a photo of him sitting in it still on its trailer outside his house. He was like Sid Vicious or Keith Moon in that way – unashamed.

We spent the summer in London parks and drank endless espressos at Bar Italia in Frith Street. Dorian was working for *Best* magazine and I met her after work every day and we would take the bus home to Albany Mews. Our lives were entirely different from our still-recent country existence. But the city was regenerating both of us and we knew that it was important to go with it. By acting like a rock star again, I was actually being taken seriously enough for it to work. And, on August 8th, it was proved to me that I was truly back when I even beat Mac in the teenage *Jackie* magazine's "Fight of the Year ... it's MACCA V. COPEY ... Jules, you're the champ." Right on.

GO ONE WAY, RETURN ANOTHER

A week into August, we arrived in New York early enough to pick out our hired gear at Sorry I Rented, an imageless rock'n'roll hire company in the meat packing district of Manhattan. As I needed my mike-stand and red Gibson 335 electric-12 string, Chris Whitten decided that he had to have his own drums, but the majority of the gear was rented on this most auspicious occasion of a genuine first American Julian Cope tour. And this gear was mostly a crap compromise – a fact that was only rubbed in that much more by the incredible detail, time and artistic attention which Cally had put into the designing of the laminated tour passes. Each laminate had a miniature pack shot of the first 13th Floor Elevators LP alongside a special logo of a Stuka flying towards the viewer and the script JU87 above. There was reference to Dude ranches, Dude this and Dude that, plus travel magazine views of '50s America. By now, the numbers "9918" had been carefully painted onto all the equipment in drop-shadowed battleship lettering. How had Cally found the time?

K-R Frost studied the wording on the back of the pass, then surveyed his motley keyboard set-up.

K-R *(To no-one in particular)*: "It says, 'Go one way, return another.' Should we kill him when he arrives? That's going one way and returning another. *(Poignantly)* Quite Nam."

DONNEYE: "Chelt – Nam!"

JULIAN: "Too different! 'Go one way, return another' doesn't imply death."

CHRIS WHITTEN: "Oh, honestly! It says: 'Enjoy the easiest of travel . . . with everything planned and all accommodation reserved and paid for in advance.'"

(As there had already been problems with our first hotel, this little in-joke which Cally had put together in his studio in St. Albans here smacked of underachievement and smugness.)

JAMES ELLER: *(Fake posh)* "A sacking offence, I fancy."

JULIAN: *(Fake Leeds accent)* "Aye, lad. Well into touch. *(Well-modulated Peter Sellers BBC type)* Go one way, return another. Arrive in the best state of employment. Exit stage left pursued by the Dole."

DONNEYE: *(Scots landlady)* "A refreshing lager beer of an idea, Copey, lad . . . but baggsy I'll no be the one to tell 'im!"

CHRIS WHITTEN: "It's poetic justice. All this Dude thing's got too out of hand!"

Starting in Vancouver, where I purchased a fine model of the *Loveboat* from the '70s TV series, we rocked all the way down the north-western seaboard with solo shows in Seattle and Portland. Awlright!!!

But this tour with Siouxsie & the Banshees which we had worked so hard for turned out to be a total letdown. The Banshees were playing 1,200 seater venues and not even packing them in, or out. Postcards of Robert Smith may have proliferated in tourist shops, but the Banshees were nowhere to be seen. I'd been led to believe that they were icons of Alternative Rock, with a guaranteed audience of thousands. Perhaps that was why Budgie was keeping his distance. Embarrassment causes some peculiar over-reactions. Budgie did say hello one time, which I felt was correct, as it was his tour, but he was no nicer to me than anyone else he'd just met for the first time and I was mortified to think that all my intended gestures of affection would now go unused.

Where was Cally? Every glance at the tour pass rubbed it in deeper. Underneath my pass photo were the words "Escorted Tour". So, Cally, where the fuck are you?

Night after night, the Banshees seemed to get a better sound than us, but everyone, including the Banshees' crew,[1] said we blew them offstage, even with our set reduced to 45 minutes. Of course, Rooster was now looking after Budgie's drums. But it was a stranger, glamorous be'mascara'd Rooster; a cackling, rootless Rooster; a screwloose footloose Rooster; a hidden agenda'd Rooster. Rooster on a Banshee trip was a remarkable transformation. For a start, he was hanging out with Captain Scarlet, the crazy 6'5" dreadlocked brunette-from-Hell who ran the Banshees' back line. Scarlet had a death-wish but could not die, so he caused mayhem at all points of the compass. On a beach in the Bay of Cadiz, Scarlet had once hired a jet-ski which he then proceeded to ride out to sea until the fuel ran out. Thinking that it was a genuine error, the French coastguard had refuelled the jet-ski, only to have Scarlet ride out of sight once more. When he ran out of gas the next time, he was arrested.

Now, together on the plane over to America, Scarlet and Rooster had caused so much trouble that they were arrested before they landed and jailed on arrival at LAX airport. They were abusive to everyone, including the passengers, the airport staff, the stewardesses, the police and customs officials, and Rooster was still clucking beyond the call of his nickname when he arrived at our hotel next morning. It was a remarkable sight and I was amazed how genuinely beautiful it can be to watch someone that far Off their Trolley. Rooster was wearing a ruff-collared shirt and a tailcoat, his hair was full Rooster red and his face was pretty with mascara and rouge and downered sleeplessness. He should've been on stage, not backstage, I thought. The guy was a fucking star.

But the disappointment of the joint shows was partly made up for by the intensity of our own club headliners. They were, in short, insane. The short support sets were horribly unsatisfying and our own headlining shows became demented things full of ringing freeform sections and stentorian paramilitary avalanches of take-it-downness.

My stage show was a writhing beanstalk-riding, self-fellating burn-out full of dramatic mike-stand climaxes and ridiculous pouts/grimaces. Acting the part of a sexy black-clad rock star was easy to do, or rather, overdo, especially when women in the front row demanded that I let them fellate me (an American phenomenon which never happened to me in Britain). Because it was not my natural trip, I had no way of knowing the parameters. Often, my Jim Morrison attempts would be more like stentorian bursts of Iron Butterfly meets

---

1 Rock'n'rollers as Gnostics: The Banshees' sound engineer on that tour was Tim Sunderland, a Scando-Druid of considerable proportions. Tim has mixed my front-of-house sound for years now and even accompanied me on my 1999 CE lecture tour for *The Modern Antiquarian*. When he read the unprovenanced W. G. Hoskins quote at the beginning of the first chapter, Tim told me immediately that the Hoskins book was called *The Making of the English Landscape*. None of my editors knew this, nor could we find Hoskins in libraries. Rock'n'rollers? Nuff Said.

Steppenwolf, whilst the Two-Car Garage Band was really only 65% Elevators/ Litter/MC5 v 25% Alice Cooper/Led Zep (with 10% TroublefunkadelicSly creeping in).

Many American journalists had no idea where the facial expressions especially were coming from, and, in typically American style, judged me as self-obsessed and humourless. One woman called my show a "chronic pouting and pretentious pantomime . . . so deeply immersed in its own melodrama that it begins to reek of tasteless self-parody". Fuck off, you Puritan twat. A "chronic pouting" baboon buffoon with his ass stuck in the audience is no "pretend" pantomime. It's bloody the Full Widow Twankey. No-one comes on stage with half a ton of galvanised RSJ unless they're doing the Glam Descend. As well as all the posturing, my eyes bulged as I gurned wildly, hopped on one leg, climbed speaker cabinets and wandered around on my knuckles. But she only noticed the "self-love". Sure, I was Diaghilev, babe-ee! But I was Jerry Lewis, too, so Up Yours!

In Toronto, Cally returned to the tour and we returned to the CN Tower. It's the highest free-standing structure in the world and, in a guilty state of forced camaraderie, we hung from the mesh to weird people out. But this tour was not what I'd had in mind at all and Cally's gung ho attitude irritated me. Problems? We'll just troubleshoot them all. Right. So why aren't we doing so, then? Placate me, Cally. Even if it's bullshit, I need to believe I'm not here for no reason.

"I'll come to Japan with you," said Cally. "There's an Aeroflot flight at half the regular price."

He began to come on all conspiratorial again. But, by now, I didn't want Cally in Japan. Why should he get to go to the great Japanese climax of the tour, when the bulk had been a royal shitstorm through the urbs & 'burbs of No-Mark USA? Even the Aeroflot thing smacked of Boy's Annual cheapo money-saving schemes, which only wound me up tighter.

And why are we playing Sag Harbour on Long Island when no-one under 60 will be there? Our New York show at the Felt Forum was a pro-Banshees fiasco, to less than 1,000 slash-lipped gothy no-marks waiting for me to get off. Last time, I'd played to more than this on my own at the Ritz.

As predicted, the Sag Harbour show was cancelled, as was the Ottawa date. By the time we played the Living Room in Providence, the irony of its name drove me into a violent sulk. In the south, our Miami show was really in St. Petersburg, where the rats go to die. The shops were closed all afternoon and the hotel swimming-pool became a weird combination of rock'n'roll flotsam & jetsam trying to have a good time.

The spectre of my inevitable thirtieth birthday hung like a sticky spider's web curtain across the long deep narrow valley of my life. For months, I'd been able to see it in the distance and there was to be no last-minute edging past it.

That night, I hung from the huge mike-stand with amazing grace and balanced precariously at the edge of the eight-foot deep orchestra pit. The

Miami show had a magic about it and I thought I was invincible, cavorting on the lip of that deep chasm and mock-fainting across the heavy iron beam footstands which bisected the main stalk of my mike-stand. Then, close to the end of the set, I lost my balance and flipped ungracefully over the edge of the stage and disappeared into the darkness. It was the end of the show.

My body was caned and numb, and the whole of my left side came up in a black cloudy bruise, but I'd been so grassed up when I fell that I had flopped down safely like a drunk. Tomorrow was a day off, so I opted to fly up to Washington alone and sleep my black bruises out. I was so glad to get off that tour bus – my whole sleeping area had become awash with these weird 1930s streamlined motor-coaches and sedans that I'd collected, and I'd wake up every night with lumps of die-cast metal sticking in my back. I was going to be 30 very soon – I was too old for this shit.

On that night in Miami, my group scored some vibrant LSD and jumped on to the Copeless tour bus bound for Washington. Donald later told me that a new atmosphere developed in the bus, after which James Eller and Frog both took the acid without quite knowing what it was. Neither had ever taken a trip before and neither had ever professed the desire to do so. Indeed, I had always felt as though I was foisting too much drug culture on them. But that Miami– Washington bus ride saw James and Frog both develop visible blue auras, which failed to completely disappear even after the trip. I was no longer some acid crazy who ranted and raged – I had cohorts in my own band who'd been driven to such acts of self-discovery.

Now, where was my fucking manager when I needed him? Here's my righteous group on the same trip as me and Cally's in fucking London or something.

Paul King flew in to see me with a proposal. He told me that Cally was incapable of doing the manager's job anymore and did I want him to take over again and refloat the project? I sat in the dressing room listening to all this, the whole left side of my body matt black from the high fall onto concrete, and felt as though Kingy was finally coming to save me. The jokey backstage pass conversation was coming true. "Sure, Paul. Look at me, I'm fucked up. Sack Cally and get me back on course."

I took no more calls from Cally for the rest of the tour and my bruisedness holed up with Dorian when we finally arrived in Boston, plotting Cally's downfall. But Dorian was hanging out in Lisa St. John's home town and expecting Patty to arrive any moment. She adored Cally and couldn't bear what was about to happen, especially as Cally became more and more frantic about phoning as he slowly realised what was going on behind his back. Like a dying fly with a limited amount of death kicks left, Cally was trying to get to me before I shut up shop once and for all and gave up on him forever. But the decision had been made and the regime had changed. And whether or not I was right to behave as I did, Cally's innocent tour theme "Go One Way, Return Another" had rebounded on him most brutally.

HOW WE RODE INTO FREEDOM ON WHIMSY & GREED

The Two-Car Garage Band arrived Callyless and unafraid in a Japan just waiting to be weirded out. The unfulfilled American tour drove us into a frenzy in a place where they didn't understand us and stood a good foot smaller. The attitude of two years before, when I had been grateful for the Japanese love, was gone. Now I arrived with my black-clad cohorts and my super crew, with one intention: to get satisfaction. To rock beyond our Role. To gorge ourselves – not to nibble Nippon, but to leap right on.

Our soundman was Mick Fussey, but everyone called him Lick Pussy, or Puss-ay, with an affected Frenchness at the end. He was the Roger Moore of rock'n'roll and women fell dead at his feet. He was the swarthiest man I'd ever met and once grew a beard from a newly shaven state in under a day. Mick lived with a pretty blonde model called Jo, a vegetarian for 10 years, and took great pleasure in sneaking bits of meat into her meals without telling her. Mick was euphoric because, just this past month, Jo had finally and inevitably buckled and returned to eating meat again. In celebration, Mick spent the whole time in Japan eating anything outrageous that he could find. And it was only when I saw him scouring the lists of dolphin steaks and tucking into monkey brains that the Japanese attitude to animals first hit me. Obscenities such as veal were nothing compared with the average Tokyo menu and a long-time fan of mine disgusted us when she one day defended Japanese cuisine with the exclamation: "But Julian, the dolphin is far too delicious not to eat!"

Jolyon Burnham became our minder in Tokyo and went berserk when some Japanese gangsters took exception to K-R Frost kicking their huge Mercedes. What a Toff! "Do you have a problem, old son?" inquired Jolyon flatly, as he held two gangsters off the floor down some tiny Roppongi street late one night. Truly off the ground. Right on. Of course, we were surrounded by the usual gaggle of women fans, who shrieked and yelled that we would get in big trouble. But we didn't, of course.

I saw a strange fake film poster for sale which really summed up Japan's love of the sound (and indifference to the meaning) of English. It read:

"FOR YANKEE GIRL
THE KIDS ARE ALRIGHT
DIZZY & MILKY
HYSTERIC AND THE 'GLAMOUR'
ALL TICKETS SOLD OUT"

A female fan gave me a metallic blue hair gel called Gelpop Perky Jean and I marvelled more and more at the Japanese attitude to our language. K-R Frost came up with a big carry-on bag whose logo proclaimed "We Are Not Nervous,

Even in Difficult – For We Have Beautiful BAG". Donneye's new bag bore the inscription "NewOneComingUp from Shiny Company" and there was a special kitchen message-board designed in Neo '50s, bearing the lines "Love-Message for Couple" and "My Message to Lovely You". Awlright!

We all became obsessed with this "Janglish" and searched it out all over the place. But most surprising of all was K-R Frost's unearthing of the Japanese *Fried* lyric sheet. For the Japanese had attempted to translate the part of the chorus in 'Sunspots' where I made the sound like a car going past. Instead of "Eee-ow, it goes away", it had become: "Indeed! It goes away."

The shows were insane and ritualistic, and probably not good on any other level than the reality which constitutes Japan. These rock'n'roll events were unlike any place in the world. The show times were absurd. First show Monday 6 p.m. Second show Tuesday 6 p.m. Third show Wednesday 3 p.m. It was loony land stuff. Who gets off work to rock at three? But come they did, and shriek, stamp, howl and coo they did also.

There was also a specifically Japanese phenomenon, which intrigued everyone and grossed Donneye out totally – girls would write notes to tell me of orgasms they had during the real obvious or long drawn-out songs. They would write this news in a flat, removed way and sometimes they even sounded just grateful. James Eller, Chris Whitten, K-R Frost and I would stand around with post-coital flared nostrils, staring heroically into the middle-distance. Hey, nowadays you can be approaching 30 and still get this response! Rock! These letters became a standard feature of this and all subsequent Japanese tours, so it was curious to hear tales of reserved Japanese audiences. We'd never seen any. They were wailing.

We were wailing, too. I took the band to the Lexington Queen, where Western rock'n'rollers and showbiz people drank for free. It was gross and none of the group believed me, but, once in, they were intoxicated. James Eller's *Hammer of the Gods*-trip had hit home with all of us, and we knew that 10 minutes in the Lexington Queen would have us surrounded by real rock women. Then Tears for Fears walked in with half of my old road crew – Ady, D'Arcy, Cliff and Robbie MacGrath – and the whole club was deluged by people who did business in the same London office as myself.

Weirder still, we went to see Tears for Fears the following night and the Japanese audience was a cliché of silence. This was the society which placed ambient white-noise machines in public toilets in order to stifle the noise of your plop. At the Tears for Fears gig, I suddenly "saw" the whole audience on the loo.

Unfortunately, seeing Tears for Fears made our last show insaner than ever. Their poor drummer, Manny, had to pitter-patter away to a reel-to-reel drum-machine and the sound from backstage was like some Polite Force production. In contrast, James Eller's Moog bass pedals now introduced many of the songs, whilst long metal endings drew each one to a stumbling conclusion, as Whitten and Donneye refused to consider making eye contact until they'd made enough racket themselves. I had developed a way of holding the huge mike-stand like a yoke and would swing it round and round and round before finally collapsing into the monitor speakers at the stage front. But what had been a knee-dropping kick-ass show in America had degenerated into a name-dropping kiss-ass show in Japan, as I threw in-jokes and non-sequiturs at the uncomprehending audience. Oh, and of course I sung, "Indeed! It goes away."

GOING BACK TO CALLY (NO GOING BACK TO CALLY)

By October 1987, *Saint Julian* was over at last and I turned 30. Suddenly, the three years of preparation were finally put into perspective and a lot of it felt like a meaningless waste of time. The Two-Car Garage Band which I had kept together at the expense of my best friend had turned out to be as ersatz as sticking a Granola bar up your rear end and offering it as a Toffee Crisp – the group disintegrated as soon as we returned from Japan. I should have seen it coming, especially as Chris Whitten had always told me he'd rather be playing for Funkadelic. Of course, with his stick-up-his-ass drum style, Chris was deluding himself as much as I had been. But now I was managerless and bandless and best-friendless and rudderless. Even my A&R man had defected to WEA. Was I angry? Were Kiss Unmasked?

I suppose I had progressed in career terms. We'd made it all the way to London, an unthinkable achievement two years before. Dorian was out of the Slough of Despond which had threatened to ruin her in Tamworth and she was now boarding an expansive new London lifestyle which gave her high expectations of herself.

But it was all without Cally. What a bitter and twisted blow!!! What had I been thinking of? What had made such sense in America was chicken-shit thinking in the cold light of London. Cally hadn't deserved to be sacked – he was the one who'd saved me from Burnt-out Oblivion Extinction. But it was the rock'n'roll business. And it was done. I was the best dressed Chicken in Town.

I bailed into preparing a new LP, which I wanted to call "The Great White Hoax", and returned to the pre-*Saint Julian* band of Donald and myself. The shock of sacking Cally brought on the self-defensive Great White Hoax image which said: "Don't trust me – I'll only screw you up the ass." Fair enough.

I was so shocked to be without Cally that it struck me once more just how unreal touring was. One ridiculous decision brought on by endlessly hectoring whinging session men had cost me the only guy to believe in me for years (of course they weren't "just" session men, just too fucking professional in their attitudes).

I could barely believe that the situation was irretrievable, but I soon found out it was. Within days of our return to London, I saw Cally from a distance just 200 yards west of Oxford Circus tube. As we edged ever closer in the hemmed in crowd, his distraught look and tearful eyes said it all, and the 10 words we exchanged were to be our last for many years before he was sucked up once more into the London Throng.

During the Japanese tour, Dorian had looked at 10 different houses and flats with an ever-more sinking heart. London house-prices had gone so far through the roof that people were rushing to secure anything, creating a dearth of housing in our price range. But she had finally found a quiet end terrace near a disused church on Tulse Hill, with double-parking (though we were carless) and an enclosed garden for Smelvin. Like the house-hunt which had ended in Drayton Bassett, I had seen none of these 10 houses and ran gratefully for the anonymity of 149A Tulse Hill. And on the day of moving, half of my road crew and the remnants of my band helped to transfer us the two miles from Albany Mews, pausing only for an hour-long search for Smelvin, who ran away as soon as we arrived.

Donald and I set up home in Granny's Studio, a Fulham 16-track run by a sweetheart called Ian Shaw. Donald brought down all the Funkadelic tapes which he had recorded from Whitten's collection and I found myself being drawn into his obsessions with putting the beat on-the-One.

Donald and I had seen Troublefunk twice in 1986 and had flipped out at their Parliament-style non-stop party gig. A Troublefunk remix of 'World Shut Your Mouth' had inspired us as Donneye and I became more and more interested in mixing Funk with Krautrock. Donald's bass style was by now a brain-popping mix of Larry Graham and Holger Czukay. I had written virtually no complete new songs, so I let Donald lead the way with beats and jams.

The demos rained thick and fast, and soon we had an amazing song called 'Caffeine', a eulogy to my second favourite drug, with an one-the-One beat that fused Kate Bush's 'Sat in Your Lap' with Can's 'Mother Sky'. We recorded a mightily melodic Krautrock bonanza called 'Ballad of King Plank', with a delightful chorus of OO gauge queerboys singing, 'A sonic train is on its way to meet King Plank, to meet King Plank.' That was me. I was King Plank or 'king plank, for sacking Call-eye!!!

We recorded an immense eight-minute on-the-One instrumental epic entitled 'My Nation Underground'. It was to be a colossal epic of Cecil B. De Mille proportions – a 'Montana Song' on-the-One. I had ripped the title off the American 'One Nation under God'. Funkadelic had more famously recorded *One Nation under a Groove*, whilst Pearls Before Swine had made *One Nation*

Underground. I allowed myself the third metaphor and the piece grew to Valhallic proportions as Donneye watched me add layer upon layer of keyboards and ideas onto his amazing electric vulture bass.

Other songs were slowly coaxed out of the mystic. 'Wanna' was a delightful Damo Suzuki-type groove that sounded like a 45,[1] whilst the only typical me song was a thing called 'There Goes the Neighbourhood' – an epic of reverb and a melancholy weepy in chugging '80s land. I was also convinced that two songs, called 'Ivory Tower Block' and 'I'm Not Losing Sleep', were certain smash hits and sang their choruses over and over again.

Then we ran out of pot. Completely. This situation was very unusual and put me in mind of being in Japan. I walked through the crowds of Fulham market and felt as though I were in some exotic north Japanese city. At first. Donald and I drank stronger coffee than ever and Donneye smoked ciggies with all the fervour of a modern addict shivering in some millennial corporate doorway. The songs temporarily dried up, but we still came in every day in order to establish some sort of desperately needed routine.

Eventually, the new A&R man at Island called me up to hear how the new LP was going. Chris Pain had managed the Pretenders for many years and his new job at Island had come as a surprise to everyone so soon after his being sacked by Chrissie Hynde. He sat down at the restaurant table and told me gently that he disliked every one of my new demos except for 'Ivory Tower Block'. I crumbled at the news and was not appeased by Chris wanting 'Ivory Tower Block' as a single. They were right. In the cold light of this discussion, I had quickly understood the Muselessness of this music. A song about Caffeine? I fucking ask you!

I had just told Donneye that we were dumping all the demos when Paul King called me and said we needed a meeting with Clive Banks and Chris Pain. I asked what it was all about and was distraught to hear that they were suggesting that I co-write songs with someone else ... Huh? The name put forward was Jo Callis from The Human League, whom I (barely) knew from many years ago. I was astounded by their cheek, but shaken by their collective lack of faith in me. Did they know something I didn't? Or had the new songs been so painfully underachieving? Whilst I was still made up to be capable of making records and performing again, they were all making plans for my big Sell Out. In their eyes I was thinking way too small. Gaaaa!

---

1 A new version of this song was released seven years later, as 'Girl-call', on the 1995 LP *20 Mothers*.

'CHARLATAN'

I tried to write new songs, but I was infertile as the arid desert and tense as a smoker. I burned around the Tulse Hill house, looking for forgotten cassettes and cursing the loudness of the neighbours. In our rush to secure a place which we could afford, neither Dorian nor I had noticed that our neighbours were the Nitcombers from Hell. Eight crusty doleys lived in a house the size of ours, blasting 'Money' by Pink Floyd at all hours of the night. When Dorian had gone around to complain because of my International Rockstar reticence, a 30-something Rizla git with staring Vince Watts eyes had greeted her brandishing a carving knife. Of course, Dorian was utterly unfazed by this and demeaned the guy for even thinking he was heavy, laughing in his face: 'And stop playing that shit music!' Over the next few weeks, the 3 a.m. reggae bass clung to our walls and worked across our ceilings, sometimes alternating with more repeated plays of 'Money', Pink Floyd's terminally uncool eulogy to the *Are You Being Served* theme-tune.

I was still wondering what to write about and feeling like "The Great White Hoax" was still my best shot as it was the closest to the truth thus far. Then I came across the original version of 'Trampolene', recorded in the music room at Drayton Bassett two years before. I played the tape again in order to understand how I had written the song over the recurring riff and boiled the kettle for some tea. But as I was making the tea, the demo of 'Trampolene' gave way to a new song, uncredited on the handwritten sleeve. I came in with my tea and sat, mesmerised, as a complete song spewed out its magical formula to me. It was called 'Charlatan' and its theme fitted my whole message of self-doubt and rudderlessness.

And so it was that the forgotten 24-month old 'Charlatan' became my flagship for the new project – an irony not lost on me. Even Island Records thought that it could be a big hit, but I just saw it as a way of getting that dreaded co-writing idea out of their collective mind. If you're not sure what you're writing about, the last thing a rock'n'roll hero needs is a co-writer. Uniquely meandering trash is one thing – but Diluted meandering trash is quite another matter.

THE NEIGHBOUR OF THE BEAST IS 667

It gets you out of doors, having Fucking Bastards for neighbours. But I was now being driven crazy on a Roman Polanskian level. Every morning, the cross-eyed punk next door would blast out 'Pulsar' from *Saint Julian*. Oh, great. Now, I'm being sent mad by my own music.

'Pulsar' is a primal headbanger of such base Odinist proportions that even the lead vocal follows the melody of the guitar and bass, like some one-handed punk Yardbirds. It begins with solo bawled vocals: "I've been awake too long and I'm wondering why I have to sell my soul for a piece of pie." But even though the song has great lyrics, it's in Ozzy territory for sheer melodic bankruptcy. That didn't stop the Nobby next door, though. I was left in the invidious position of having to play music to mask my own racket.

I was further incensed to discover that the Mohican Moron had spat in the face of our neighbour Joyce whilst I was last away recording. This was too much. Joyce was a respectable 60-year-old who had lost her husband soon after we had moved in. London seemed to operate by different rules. Like none at all.

The '80s were surfacing everywhere and in the most brutal fashion. But only now did it mean anything to me. We'd been the bad neighbours in Tamworth. In Drayton Bassett the house was too big to matter. At Albany Mews, it was too generally noisy to notice anyway, so it was only in the virtual silence of the area around 149A Tulse Hill which made 149B into Tulse Hell.

Having taken years to drag myself out of that unshaven five-skinner oily black abyss of Timelessness, I was now a rugged clean-shaven Romanised Born Again with NO time for slackers who reminded me of my former Ozzian self. My new byword was "Tense", for fuck's sake. "You've gotta be Tense," I'd say in every interview.[1] But, within the month, new barbarians descended on 149B. These guys were Proto-Iron Age *Mad Max* characters, with teeth missing and runny amber eyes. They parked their two gigantic bright yellow ex-Telecom vans in our parking spaces, dragging half of our hawthorn tree out by catching it in the tailgate. When I complained, *they* called *me* a hippy.

My recent past irked me and as I stood ear-to-the-wall listening for the unrocking rhythms of the dreaded Waters Floyd, I mutated into the unholy character of Juddge Mental. This ever-changing tribe/band/gathering never switched off or went to sleep. It just unfolded like the Bayeux Tapestry while we lived next door to it. There were too many people to take on, so I bought huge loud electric fans which whirred away throughout the day and night, and which would continue to whirr away all through our London days.

The only nice member of the Nitcombers from Hell was a young guy called Julian. He told me we should live in Wiltshire if we wanted quiet and tried to sell us his mother's house in Melksham.

The ever-changing moods of the ever-changing neighbours were to keep me forever on my London toes. I couldn't retaliate with noise and stoop to their level. There was too much of Mrs Do-As-You-Would-Be-Done-By in me for that, and, if anything, I played my music more quietly than before. But the

---

1 Like every existentialist arthole, I considered that what was good for me was good for everyone.

damage had been done and I subconsciously began to prepare a strategy for the day when I could get the better of those amorphous Plankton next door.

With Cally now out of the picture, I took the 2B bus everywhere in an effort to lose the soul-destroying effects of the neighbours. But the 2B was a horribly unpredictable entity to have to rely on so far from a tube station and missing one often meant waiting half an hour, only for three virtually empty 2Bs to appear at once.

That November and December I would meet Dorian in her ever more sexy business suits, then spend the afternoon trudging between the collectors' corner at Grey's Mews, off Bond Street, and the huge Hamley's toy shop on Regent Street. The dealers in Grey's Mews lived in a perpetual twilight which gave the toys a mystery found nowhere else and I would often arrive home with a strange-looking European toy in some mystery plastic. There was a huge '50s model of the politician Sir Anthony Eden made out of a bizarre soapy plastic which left abrasions on your skin when you touched it. What sort of child had received that as a gift? I bought it, of course. But I was 30.

An American game called *Capital Punishment* allowed you to take the role of Redneck or Wet Liberal (sic sic sic!) But either way sent the prisoner to the Chair. I bought a pair of Sooty shorts, with prints of the old early '60s TV character on yellow flannel. The size said "Age 4", but I couldn't resist and struggled into them in the men's toilet. The dealer was outraged. "They're collectable," he spluttered.

Old toys here were big business and commanded far greater sums than those at local swap meets. But I found real amazing stuff here and I had the time to search. A Welsh doctor called Colin Baddiel was my favourite dealer. He sold me a Corgi Toys Gift Set 15, which obsessively re-created an entire corner of the Silverstone racing circuit, complete with press box, AA and RAC boxes, and a play-mat. I spent two months making it to perfect '60s specifications, and marvelled at the ingenuity and patience that Corgi Toys had expected of an average 1960s boy.

Colin Baddiel, or Doctor Bad Deal as he was known, had a gorgeous wife, an exquisite Jewish beauty called Sarah. They always told me about their son David and what great expectations they had for him on the stage. I'd known Colin and Sarah since 1984, and we'd sit and talk for hours. They once told me of their experiences as LSD guinea-pigs in 1959. Sarah said she had regressed to her time in '30s Germany and had totally freaked out. Whoa, I was impressed and freaked out myself. I'd recently refused to be interviewed for a BBC documentary about LSD and here were two lucid middle-aged people putting a real perspective on it.

This conversation was a turning-point for me. I suddenly realised that the constraints of the Rick Sky Climie Fisher Brother Beyond '80s was warping my judgement little by little. Luckily, The Sex Gods had just signed to Island Records and I took a look at Andy Eastwood's inspiring sleevenotes for their forthcoming LP. Awlright! I'm having some of that! By this time, Pete DeFreitas had returned to Echo & the Moneymen as a paid employee, preferring to help finance The Sex Gods until they made money. A very heavy Gary Dwyer had become their drummer, whilst Mike Mooney AKA Mooneye was now lead guitarist. Their new album would be coming out around the time of my next one.

IF YOU WANT TO DEFEAT YOUR ENEMY, SING HIS SONG

Remember Mrs Do-As You-Would-Be-Done-By? Well, Fuck that! New people came to 149B as the Nitcombers moved out *en masse*. I broke in to see what we'd been living next door to and the stench was overwhelming. The house had been divided into umpteen tiny rooms, where unknown vermin three deep stood on each other's shoulders to nibble my ass. Cobwebs as thick as candyfloss hung down to chest level and the interminable 7/4 rhythm of 'Money' still ghosted throughout, caught forever in the '70s brickwork. With the two Telecom vans gone, the hawthorn just hung there limp, and the trashed front and back gardens now doubled as oil sumps.

I went back indoors and watched, Juddge Mentally, as the posh landlady of the house got out of a gigantic Mercedes. Shit, she was the problem. What a problem! Our other neighbours told us that she owned similar houses all over Lambeth. We'd landed in Hell.

I gave up on the unreliable 2B bus and bought a mountain bike from a guy in the Outlaw office. That way I could surge off up the drive when the neighbours' music sent me past the point. I needed the physical side of cycling to offset my need to attack the neighbours – especially as the new people were about 17 and were heavvvy white Tulse Hill Estate motherfuckers. I still complained long and hard. But I would dress weirdly before I went around.

Within the week, they and their friends had baseball-batted some poor sod right in front of our front door. A mate of theirs then towed his Renault 5 into their unused parking space and began to work on it all hours of the night. I found their music too inharmonious, too urgent and too loud. "Keep it down," I'd beg. The women they hung out with were 15-year-olds with love on their mind. When this happened one time, they went into the back of the Renault 5 and fucked right there. That was too much, so I went out and rocked the car violently until I felt sure they were sick. But they still knee-trembled in their doorway and they still left syringes on the path. Their friends still overdosed in front of their house and we would arrive in all weathers to see umpteen teenagers hanging by our porch, with their front door open and the noise of that inharmonious music I so detested. Every time they went out, I'd take an old Yale key and push it into their keyhole, then break it off at the core. At least it inconvenienced them. On special days, they opened every window, and partied all night. If we complained, they'd close a window. I'd dress weirdly especially to complain to them, then feel driven out of my own home and find myself cycling through Lambeth dressed like a right narna.

. . . And then they were gone. Silence. One whole hour followed by another. Then a whole day. After a few days, people came out of their houses once more. They looked at each other. What was that all about? But no-one was in the house and no-one was complaining.

Except me, that is. I lay awake at night without the fan on. I couldn't sleep for cold sweats. I'd put the fan on and be convinced that I heard melodies underneath, so I'd switch it off to check. Nothing. Then I'd find my unconscious mind seeping next door and wonder if they hadn't sent me mad already.

But finally it happened and I could breathe again. High octane lunatics descended once more on 149B and a new type of impossibly loud music began to twang at my earlobes. I was genuinely relieved at the newcomers' arrival, for my fear of the unknown had become way too much. But I also knew that I was back in Roman Polanski territory and dreamed constantly of ways to ritually burn the Anglo-Viking-Indian occupants and landlady in one magical night of Tulse Hilltop Suttee Hoo.

I decided to play the neighbours and the landlady at their own game. I could easily act as weirdly as they did and make their game-plan harder. I would divide them and conquer them all.

I knew that the neighbours had terrible plumbing problems, so I confronted the landlady the very next time her Mercedes pulled up. Being on their side would throw her off guard. To begin with, she presumed that I was complaining about them, and so she kissed my ass and told me what bad tenants they all were. I flung my bike to the ground and danced around her in a leopardskin minidress, a '70s thing by Funky, and accused her of causing misery. Get the picture? Now, she looked at the way I was dressed and backed off, but I pursued her and girlied around her, pointing dramatically to 149B, and repeating the word 'Misery! Misery! Misery!' until she jumped in the car and drove off. As I cycled up Ethelworth Court, she was still stuck in the traffic and freaked out when she saw me, though I had no thoughts of following her.

Two days later, her solicitor's letter accused me of being a bully on drugs and threatened me with the High Court. Shit! I'd absolutely misjudged the situation. What a plank I was. Softly, softly asshole!

'Ere, I forgave myself. How can I be expected to make judgements when I'm using her rules? I had refused to set up a Vox AC30 amplifier in the living room next to the neighbours' wall. I had refused to switch it on the maximum setting in order to play just one terrifyingly loud crash chord at 5 a.m. and leave them witless and waiting for a follow-on which would never happen. I was a good guy and I would win without being as loud as they were. But I thought of the *Watchmen* comics and their constant use of the Frederick Nietzsche quote: "Battle ye not with monsters lest ye become a monster."

BATTLE YE NOT WITH MONSTERS LEST YE BECOME A MONSTER

But it is dreadful for the artist to waste his magic on such negative thoughts and when Dorian suggested that I take the front bedroom as a toy room, I decided to make a proper job of it with a Scalextric layout in the attic. Dorian knew that I was going neighbour crazy and needed a reason to even stay in the Tulse Hill house at all. I wanted to move. I was loony.

Rooster came around and we designed an old-fashioned post-war Scalextric layout for the loft, the catalogue kind that utilises a 40-foot track in 10 square feet and still manages to house all the press boxes and pits and grandstands and genuine large crowd. We sawed it all together and papier màchéd bits and decorated with model land and installed all the hazard pavements, electric lap-counter and batteries of overhead lighting, not forgetting a celebrity area for my Airfix 1970 England World Cup squad (the same $1/_{32}$ scale gained them immediate free entry).

The loft was so small that each Scalextric player had to sit tidily and far from the others. So we designed a deluxe spliff carrier from the rare Scalextric Aston Martin DB5, whose roof I perversely hacked off and whose body I painted two-tone matt desert camouflage with whitewall tyres. A giant bolt thrusting through the passenger seat acted as the spliff holder itself.

Electric fans drowned any neighbour racket, and Rooster and I would sit for days on end holding endless series of 200-lap races, which became blurred memories of microcosmic hand movement and little else. Whole days could be spent in one position, until our backs were pulled and our eyes were bleary through lack of daylight, as we peered into the gloaming to pick out the trails of plastic virtual reality acting out their demented pattern in the valley hundreds of feet below. Every hour or so, we'd play a cleansing game of "Is there a problem, officer?" in which one of us would patrol the track in my Rover police car whilst the other drove the Aston Martin and lurked in tunnels and obscure parts of the course until finally confronted. Donneye would sometimes join us for the odd game and we'd all do speed trials in my oversized Eastern European plastic Lada with printed cardboard interior, but it was mainly a Rooster and me scene in a smoky room with zero brain movement.

And every day would end with Dorian's return home from work and our inevitable descent back into our unneighbourly neighbourhood of neighbouring neighbourhood hoods.

I briefly thought that I had met my match when two young Irishwomen moved in to 149B. The totalitaryan (sic) beats of yester-youth were now replaced by deep mystery and confusion in the forms of silence for days punctuated occasionally by drunken slurred shouts and the (not many) rocking songs on *Led Zeppelin 3*.

Deirdre and Panzie were both very young and outwardly quite opposite. Deirdre was quiet and unsexual, whilst Panzie was horny, pregnant and attracted to demented men in their late thirties, who loved to beat her mercilessly and leave before dawn. I'd greet her looking shell-shocked late mornings after a particularly heavy sesh-on and complain about the limited and extremely loud music.

"Oh, play something loud one morning to fuck me off, get back at me', she said to me once. No fucking way, plankette, I'd think. But I'd never call her "moron" to her face – the landlady incident had made me tread carefully. Until one night, that is. . .

On this particular night, Dorian and I had suffered no effects of excessive noise and were even relaxed enough to be prepared for a wholly peaceful night. The quiet of the close could be unnervingly unlike a city when the neighbours were out. Hey, it's 11.30. Let's go up to bed and read . . . BBOOOOOOMMM!!! Out of the top corner of 149B came the most distorted, trebly radio music right on the edge of feedback and loud enough to pierce enemy eardrums. We clapped our hands to our ears and ran about trying to escape from the din, but it was nightmarishly loud and even the kitchen offered no refuge.

I put soft wax earplugs into my ears and dashed around to beat the front door of 149B. Boom Boom Booom. No answer. No answer? What the fuck is going on here close to midnight on a weekday?

I dashed back into our house and put on dark clothes, boots and a black cap with ear flaps, then I rushed past the unquestioning Dorian, disappeared behind our line of houses and stole through the gap in the fence into the churchyard. The distorted radio music was still wailing sybillantly and mono-phonically, reduced to its most basic elements through the tiny buzzsaw speaker. Curiously, no-one was even out of their houses to check it out this wet post-stormy night and I struggled through the underbrush and hedges of the disused church on Trinity Rise which backed on to the gardens of 149A, B, C & D. I was a shocktrooper in a stupor.

Once over the fence, I grabbed at the back-door handle of 149B and yanked at it so viciously that it immediately came off in my hands. In horror, I hoisted the bent metal high into the damp dark of the churchyard and stood flummoxed before the seemingly unopenable door. But my heightened senses were fizzling and alert as radio antennae in the rain, and I spied the jettisoned tubular steel of a lawnmower accessory lurking under a pile of garden garbage. Here in the garden of 149B, my whole life's perspective changed as I regarded their everyday intolerables close-up and with such little time to act. I jemmied open the back door in half-a-sec and flung the makeshift crowbar off on a similar churchyard trajectory as the door handle. I was in.

Inside, the noise was unbearable and there was obviously no-one in. Triumphantly, I made for the upstairs bedroom to switch off the radio, only to stand suddenly frozen in my tracks before the front door. For there on the other side of the door, the lock was being turned and the door opened. There was Panzie with handfuls of food shopping. We stood staring at each other for about 100 millionth of a second, until I blurted out: "Oh, you're alright. Oh, shit. (*I'm breathless now.*) We . . . we heard the radio come on so late . . . and you being pregnant, and thought, well, she's passed out on the floor and there's no-one to take care of her. What are we gonna do? I've broken your fucking door, sorry. I'm so sorry (*backing out towards the front door*), really – it was that clock radio coming on. Whoa . . . (*Keep talking, nearly out.*) I'll see you tomorrow . . . (*hearty*) yeah. You're Okay!!!"

When I'd walked the five yards to our front door, I opened it to see a glazed Dorian. She'd heard Panzie's return and been unable to warn me. Now she was in shock. She didn't want any more neighbour problems and thought I was going to be in trouble. When I told her the story, she was delighted. Even better, the music was off.

Even better, Panzie decided that she was really touched by our being so caring and said she'd "endeavour" to keep the noise down. She couldn't tame it, of course, but we were getting a grip for the first time. 'Out on the Tiles' and 'The Immigrant Song' still affronted us at odd hours of the early morning, but Zep had definitely moved to a smaller stage after our face-to-face encounter. And as Panzie's pregnancy moved along, the two women became softer and easier to live around. But the monster behaviour was definitely getting to me – especially as it had reaped these early rewards.

GREY/AFRO

Despite the fact that they'd disliked my new song demos, Island Records were by now hassling me for a follow-up to *Saint Julian*. By March 1988, it was over a year since its release and they had put up with my protestations long enough and were now looking for a producer.

I wanted Donald Ross Skinner to produce but Clive Banks was having none of it – only tested employees were considered worthy enough. Then a strange thing happened. A staff producer called Ron Fair was hired by Chris Blackwell and foisted upon Clive Banks. I say "foisted" because Clive didn't like Ron at all and made it plain to everyone. Having been born into vast wealth, Chris Blackwell had always run the company like that and was far too shallow to see that such a move could be as bad, or worse, for his golden boy as it would be for the managing director with his hands tied. Then Clive foisted Ron Fair onto my new project, telling me that it was just for the 'Charlotte Anne' demo. I got on well with Ron, but the 'Charlotte Anne' demo came out like average shit and I wanted to dump him. No way! Clive Planks considered it a *fait accompli* and told me that we'd wasted enough time and I should go with Ron. End of story. I didn't say a word, just chuntered about a bit. I certainly didn't have enough opinions of my own to fuck Ron off. I was rudderless without friends, musicians or henchmen, except for the wondrous Donneye.

And so, in the greyness of Outlaw offices, the three of us worked up whatever we could from the few dismal ideas that I'd had and Ron even suggested a couple of covers that I liked. I asked Rooster to fill in on drums and percussion, and was amazed to discover that I had an untapped brilliance in my midst. Rooster had always explained quietly how he had followed Chris Whitten as chief percussionist in the National Youth Orchestra. But it was only now that I realised what that meant. I'd met Rooster as a member of the road crew – it had taken until now for me to register that I would serve myself better by employing him as a musician.

Over the next few days, Donald or Rooster played drums whilst Ron and I jammed on organ and guitars, or piano and organ, until we had the skeletal beginnings of an album. But whilst Ron was desperately trying to make enough music to fill two sides of vinyl, I was more desperately attempting to give gravity and truth to this slender museless excursion. I had decided to take the Andy Eastwood's Sex Gods' approach and supply copious notes without song lyrics.[1]

Ron Fair was a Los Angeles Jew with a typical self-deprecating sense of humour and a Bar Mitzvah organ style which Donneye and I immediately loved. He was addicted to old studios with archaic sound desks, so we chose The Who's *Quadrophenia* studio in Wandsworth, formerly known as Ramport. Its new owner, Richard Branson, had emotionally renamed it Townhouse 3, in order to sink its identity in corporate mush, but Ramport was an old Fort Knoxian church in a heavy council estate and forever oozed the ghost of Keith Moon. Huge percussion stands collected in dark corners and attics, whilst the church's original pulpit was available for all lead vocals and axe-wielding. It also meant that I could cycle down from Tulse Hill every day and bring Smelvin in a carrier bag around my neck. Right on!

---

1 The Sex Gods' LP had been held up by the clueless Chris Blackwell, who wanted them to change their name to something tasteful. The fool never realised what legends they'd already become as The Sex Gods.

I decided that the axis of the album would be the doubts expressed in two songs: 'Charlatan', now renamed 'Charlotte Anne', and a great hulking '60s thing called 'National Rockstar', then renamed 'The Great White Hoax'.

The on-the-One Cecil B. DeMille experiments were now entirely squashed in favour of a light '60s sound, which had a lot to do with Ron Fair's Randy Newman take on my love of garage psychedelia. He suggested we record a version of the Four Guys' 'Five O'Clock World', which was a kind of pre-American Breed shop-floor anthem with yodelling. Unfortunately, as it was a "new" old song to me, we were well into the recording of 'Five O'Clock World' before I realised that its candy novelties plus siren and shouting hid a song that sucked big logs. Too late. The best I could do was fiddle with the overdubs – the heinous fundamentals were structural and immovable. We even hired the early '60s singer Frank Ifield as guest ace yodeller, but his yodels were pathetic and impossibly varied. We kept asking him to end the yodels exactly the same each time. But he'd finish one yodel "Briddy-doo-ay" then finish the next "Beedley-ay". My mind was snapping with such arrant nonsense, and Rooster and I hid upstairs whilst Donneye and Ron cruelly milked Frank's session for laughs. When he had left, we returned to the control room to see Ron and Donneye hard at work with the engineer Hugoth Nicolson sampling all the crappest yodels then playing back these Celebrations of Underachievement for hour upon fucking hour, doubled-up with laughter at their singular non-vibe.

But I couldn't get into it in remotely the same way – Frank's yodels seemed to be a metaphor for these underachieving LP sessions. I'd stand before the magnificent marimbas and beat out the riff to 'Smoke on the Water'. I'd sit at the marvellous grand piano and make up fake reggae songs like:

"I was an Engleesh-man,
I go on holly-day to Jamaica,
I fly from Birming-ham
My mother pay but I do not take her."

Even Ron and Donneye would be pulled away from work when I played these things, and more hours would be spent on cavernous versions of Morris Albert's mawkish epic 'Feelings', as Ron entertained us with the Bar Mitzvah piano riffs of all time.

I started to use the crap songs and Scalextric to get around the paucity of real ideas, in denial of the real issue. Ron got a video camera in to give the album sessions a bigger sense of occasion, but it soon became used for watching close-ups of the Scalextric races on the main control-room monitor.

On National Scalextric Club day, we all piled into Hugoth Nicolson's Mini Cooper and drove to Milton Keynes for a day of bargain slot-cars. The next week was wasted as Hugoth had bought a fabulously rare German slot go-kart, which he proceeded to fuck up in its first Scalextric race and spent hours trying to fix. This gave Rooster and I the excuse to go to Homebase and buy all the necessary equipment for a giant Scalextric layout. With our recent loft experience, we built an 8' × 4' layout of 60 feet of track, which I immediately photographed and sent off to the National Scalextric Club to print in their magazine. We spent loads on populating the Scalextric and let the album lie fallow for a while. The 200-lap races sent everybody on a non-recording trajectory.

In fact, I became so unsure of the LP that my only way out seemed to lie in trawling on any and all ideas being bandied around. Girl singers? Sure. Strings? Definitely. Horns? Obviously. Whole hordes of session men and women beat a path to our door, but I lay under the mixing desk for all the non-Scalextric time and petted Smelvin.

I played virtually nothing on the LP and assigned the whole thing to Donneye – he even played drums on two tracks then built the rest of the tracks up around the rhythm. When James Eller sheepishly returned to overdub my original bass parts, he insisted on standing on a huge speaker cabinet in the control room. But this only reminded Donneye and me of our old camaraderie, and it was a deadly sesh. From under the mixing desk, I deluded myself that the decisions were mine, as bare tracks became huge teetering monstrosities with musical gable-ends and carved curlicues of aural icing. Ron Fair left no bar of the record untouched in otherworldly attempts to banish every Goyim feeling from the sound, whilst I led Rooster around every huger-than-huge piece of tuned percussion in Ramport and recorded him contributing great themes on vibraphones, marimba, multiple timpanis, one-and-a-half size kettledrums and Nile claves. Whilst Ron, Donneye and I had long discussed including Jewish string arrangements of massively sentimental proportions, the reality of that sound was so un-rock'n'roll that I had no field of reference, other than the Tiny Tim LP.

As Ron had often said about my Whiteness, I was from deep in the Goyim. In a feast of Ron's influence, I changed the lyrics round to suit the doubt of the Great White Hoax/Charlatan portrayed in the songs. Even The Shadows of Knight's 'Someone Like Me' had its Utopian barechestedness changed to 'I am *not* free', in an act of Norman thoroughness. I felt that perhaps every little cute extra act of detail could combine to hide the slightness of the whole trip.

But it was like painting the *QE2* with Airfix paintbrushes. Only one song even approached the initial vision which I had seen coursing through the project. Donneye, Ron, Rooster and I had somehow cobbled together many demo riffs to create a vast on-the-One groove called 'My Nation Underground'. It was a stomping and overloaded epic, but even this caused confusion when everyone heard my lyrics. They were all about killing everyone and in the most brutal, callous way. In the final scene, I sang: "It's hard to smell a fart when the deceased are caught below." It was an obvious way of saying "dead people stink" but it seemed effective.

But Donneye and Ron had worked so hard on the music that they hated such glory being used for themes of murderous intent. For the main body of the lyric, I copped out entirely and immediately. Where does it offend you? Change. Change. Change. I changed everything they hated, but made no effort to reconcile the new words with the old meaning. Hopefully, people would get it. Hell, I'm so full of shit – who gives a damn!

I reeled at the stance I was taking. I was amazed that one or two compromises had caused an endless saga of control taken out of my hands. This had never happened before and I was going to learn from it. At least the fart lyric had stayed.

Dorian went to New York for a fortnight and I was so bored in the studio one day that I grabbed Smelvin's bone away from him and he bit a chunk out of my finger. When I came back from Outpatients, he'd been put into the main studio and I went in to find him finishing off a nice blue chunk of Warfarin. As he'd eaten the whole thing, the vet said he'd only survive if I stopped him from moving for the following 10 days. Every day on the phone, I'd bullshit Dorian about how well Smelvin was, then cycle gingerly through Brixton with him sitting in a carrier back hanging from my neck. I kept him hot and overfed and cosy for 10 days and he survived. Awlright!

Then, at the behest of Clive Banks, we went to mix the wretched album at the impossibly expensive Genesis Studios in Surrey, where, on the next to last day of the mix, the huge deer-killing studio dog proceeded to attack Smelvin in a fit of pique. Though it was his third birthday, Smelvin looked like an ex-dog and one of his eyes was utterly crushed. The album was almost finished and so was he. But the vet stayed up with him for a whole night and Smelvin magically survived the ordeal. From that final-mix day on, Smelvin was known as Jeep, after Popeye's magic dog.

KICKS MY DICK INTO THE DIRT

After all the long months, *My Nation Underground* was sent around the world to Island world-wide, whereupon the response was fantastic and everybody said that it would be a huge record. Whoa! I'd not expected that at all. I came home one evening to hear a phone-message from Chris Blackwell and his New York MD, Lou Maglia. The message was so frothing-at-the-mouth kiss-ass that I saved it and played it around to everyone. Lou Maglia ended the message by saying that the LP "kicks my dick into the dirt"!

The only thing I liked about *My Nation Underground* was the fact that we'd put almost every song back on-the-One. I was always proud that the first two Teardrop Explodes singles had been on-the-One precisely because, at that time, it had been a symbolically unrock thing to do and we'd continued on-the-One until my garage rock obsession had started to affect my writing. Now, mine and Donneye's obsession with Funkadelic and Sly's on-the-One had manifested in a more clean epic for the title track, but it was still a mighty sound. Even the over-ornamentation didn't hide the fact that it was all recorded live and in chaos. But I had refused to take responsibility for the project and listening to what might have been was a pointless waste of time. For the foreseeable future, I had to promote an average album which everyone thought was bland enough to be huge.

Recording the album had already taken up most of 1988 and we rushed through the late summer/early autumn in order to finish the 'Charlotte Anne' video. There was no group, so Donneye, Rooster and Frog appeared in various guises throughout the filming. We auditioned bass players at John Henry's studio and picked the first one we met – a sweet young Rochdale nutter called Marcus Williams. Then Rooster suggested that we call Mike Joyce from The Smiths, who was so happy to play and such a vibe and quick learner that we actually felt as though we had the makings of a real group.

Island Records put all the machinery back into action and I was soon on *Wogan* once more. But the six-piece band looked unfocused and I was too much of a fairy. After my TV spot, Wogan's first guest, Auberon Waugh, slagged off my appearance as well as my performance. It was to become a fashionable thing to do and that week *Melody Maker* said I was "emaciated and feeble [on *Wogan*], warbling some palsy-ridden drivel about 'Charlotte Anne'".

The single stalled at no. 35 for two weeks and fled, leaving us all knee-deep in unsold CD-singles, 7 and 12, cassettes, etc. The late '80s was such a time of Greedhead promo-gimmicks that artists could only recognise their record company's intentions by the weight of promo and record formats which they threw at the public. Island had even had 100 special Cope leather jackets made, which I recognised immediately as High Expectations.

But, as this disaster unfolded, the *My Nation Underground* LP came out to unanimous disapproval. Some journalists sniffed a hype and took the opportunity to get back yet more snipes at my supposed newly-found sanity, *Sounds* magazine writing: "Julian Cope is convinced he's a turtle (to this day)." In October, *Melody Maker* wrote: "... he currently needs injections every 15 minutes and a wet-nurse to hold his nostrils and spoonfeed him with broth every 30." Then I became part of their weekly theme:

"He's always regarded himself as a launching pad for eccentric forays into the pop world, although he's never been able to whack up enough public funding to achieve anything but a 400 feet spurt into the air, followed by the inevitable dip in the trajectory and ignominious plop in the ocean."[1]

1 *Melody Maker*, November 19th 1988

New Musical Express followed suit with: "By now surely Cope must be spent with the drunkenness of ranting too much, too passionately and with no issue … Let the old times die."[1]

I had not got away with a thing. I'd been exposed for my Museless muse and was suffering horribly. The shows were awful and my performances were static tragedy. The new group was too big to really kick in until the tour was almost over, and the audiences found me fumbling and apologetic. Two hours before the Liverpool Royal Court show, I sat in my room and wrote:

> "If you can get through these nights in Liverpool, then you can get through anything … this isn't freedom. And what's coming up may be, or it may not."

When we arrived at London's Dominion Theatre, I was shocked to discover that it was seated. Argh! How had I not checked?

For that reason at least, the two shows were yet another disaster. At the end of the first show, my frustrations were taken out on the seated front row, who pulled me and my new tubular Iggdrassil mike-stand into their seats. Half of the seats collapsed, leaving people gasping for air. I got loads of shit for it, perhaps rightly so, I don't know. Can a Turd on a Bum Ride ever be really responsible? *The Daily Mirror* reported it thus:

"FANS BEAT UP HITMAN COPE

Chart star Julian Cope was recovering last night after being beaten up at his first London concert. The 28-year-old singer was mauled after he threw himself into the audience at the end of a sell-out show in London's Dominion Theatre."

What a crock o'kack. But I was in bed and I was depressed as hell. In the solitude of Tulse Hill I was disconcerted to discover that the serial number of *My Nation Underground* was 9918, the very number which I'd worn on my chest the whole of the previous year. Was 9918 a cosmic coincidence? Or were Clive Banks and Chris Blackwell in cahoots to weird me out? Or were they individually playing me off against the other? I didn't dare ask anyone because I didn't want to know the truth.

1 *NME*, October 22nd 1988

NOBODY OF THE YEAR

"NOBODY OF THE YEAR

He was everywhere and nowhere in 1988, disastrously memorable on *Wogan* ... Probably hoped to be 'Fruitcake of the Year' but even his mental instability is uninspired."

Melody Maker, December 24th 1988

In November, we took a bus to Europe and followed a depressing schedule of under-attended shows. I bought toys wherever I could and went crazy in Montpelier, where the local collectors' museum was having a sale. We visited the amazing Gaudi cathedral in Barcelona and marvelled at the juxtaposition of huge disco lettering and Jesus Christ on an RSJ. Atop the proto-mushroom trip spires, the purple, orange and pink '70s disco lettering read: "Hosanna, Hosanna, Hosanna" as the whole site took on the feel of a melting blancmange in an armadillo mould. Fifty-nine people came to a 3,000-seater shed in Toulouse and we did the best show in ages. In a packed club in Rennes, I found myself and my radio-mike in the men's room singing to a guy's dick.

In Amsterdam, the sound in the Milky Way club convinced me that there was an atonal harmony ringing through me and I stomped about in bovine confusion. Finally, I quit the stage altogether and screamed at everyone about the weird vibration. Then I pulled the band offstage. As the crowd got restless, most people considered the weird harmony to be in my own weird head, but I wasn't about to go back on. Then one of the Dutch crew found out that the whole left side of the stage vibrated in G flat. I had no songs in G flat and it was putting me off. I wasn't crazy after all and they just switched off certain speakers to get rid of the negative effect. But in Bielefeld in West Germany, the pointlessness of playing to 100 people saw me bouncing off rafters and changing the lyrics to fake Euro.

In Hamburg, Dorian saved me at last and we continued to West Berlin, which I had managed to avoid since the Teardrop's tripping Wall Pissing escapades seven years earlier. West Berliners were ruder than New Yorkers and lived in a permanent Bauhaus council estate of merely achieving drabness. The club owner came on like *Rock Follies* rather than *Cabaret* and freaked out when I used the extra height of the mike-stand to headbutt my way through the ceiling into the loft.

Next day, November 19th, Dorian, Frog, Marcus, Mike Joyce and I crossed through Checkpoint Charlie to lunch on the Unter den Linden, or East Berlin high street. Whoa. East Berlin had clearly got all the good buildings and we stared in awe at the indescribable Future/Past which we were experiencing. When we ordered coffee and cakes, they explained that the cake was just for show and not for sale. We settled for biscuits topped with old-fashioned cooking-chocolate, and sat shivering and Lilliputian in the unheated Third Reich-scale rooms. Russian troops marching up the Unter den Linden seemed unreal to us in their flimsy felt coats and hats, and I was determined to engage them in "O" level standard conversation. A young student called Philly helped us to talk to the soldiers, but they all wanted to discuss British cigarettes and smoking, whereas I knew a lot of transport words and kept pushing the subject back to Russian transport systems. *Avtobooce. Meenya zavoot Dyoolian. Ya eegrie-yoo na guitariyeh.*

In early December, we took Pan-Am flight 103 to New York and tried to forget the disastrous *My Nation Underground* LP. In New York, expectations were still high and I was welcomed at 4th & Broadway for what looked like a huge forthcoming campaign. I was assigned a very pretty independent publicist called Lori Soames, who said the album was gonna be massive. 'Five O'Clock World' was the first single and was already gaining airplay before its release. Unfortunately, Julian Cope singing 'Five O'Clock World' by now sounded as hollow as if Billy Bragg were to sing 'Psychedelic Ride'.

But just before Christmas, another Pan-Am flight 103 was blown out of the sky by Islamic terrorists, leaving bits of Jumbo strewn across the foothills of Lockerbie, in lowland Scotland. Years of Pan-Am 103 flights ensured that their stickers covered our luggage and we freaked out at the link. At Island Records' 4th & Broadway offices in Manhattan, staff were even more freaked out – Nona Hendryx and her Island Records A&R people had only just failed to get tickets for the doomed aircraft.

No-one in New York had a good Christmas as the repeated TV showings of collapsing hysterical relatives first hearing the awful news at JFK clogged the airwaves. This was closely followed by shots of the plane itself, especially the eggshell-quality of the 747's nose as it slumped lifeless on that tragic Lockerbie hillside.

Dorian, Mama Helena and I decided to cheer ourselves up by driving out to Jericho Avenue, where the Klumzics lived. All Americans decorate their porches with festival paraphernalia, and many festoon their bushes and trees with patterns of flashing lights, but the Klumzics lived in 365-day-per-year Christmasland. When we arrived, there were traffic jams around their house as people fought for parking spaces and stood in the middle of the road to get better photos of this flashing Winter Wonderland. The roof of the house was filled with various model Santas and reindeer-driven sleds, whilst the garden took un-Christmassy liberties with items such as rocket ships and even plastic Supermen and Spidermen standing along the gravel pathway, bedecked in tinsel and stars. And every pathway and paving stone, every sprig, spray or bud was here reduced to being merely a backdrop for festival flair, whilst disco lettering of the cheapest variety endlessly typed-out the halogen message: "A Merry Xmas 88 from the Klumzics ... A Merry Xmas 88 from the Klumzics ... A Merry Xmas 88 from the Klumzics."

As we drove home from Cousin Janet's New Year party out at Hicksville, Long Island, Dorian switched on WDRE and we were delighted to hear 'Five O'Clock World' as our first song of 1989. Perhaps 1989 was going to make a difference after all. Perhaps America was going to be important.

NOBODY OF THE NEW YEAR

But our return home was far worse than we could have imagined. The general world-wide failure of *My Nation Underground* had given the US company such cold feet that they now pulled out of promoting the album at all and denied me money to tour America. I only found out from Lisa St. John, who was told to stop designing the poster for my forthcoming Boston show.

In Britain, 'Five O'Clock World' was not a hit, so January 1989 saw me talking at length to Clive Banks, who wanted me to record a covers album. Or maybe form a group. Or maybe move to New York. Or anywhere.

My head was so brutally caned by Clive's lack of faith that I persuaded Dorian to check out New York apartments, which she did with unrestrained glee. If Island could pay to relocate us in Manhattan, I could at least start anew. But my conversations with Easty and Johnno and Mooneye freaked me out as I discovered the control trip which Clive Banks was on. All these months after *My Nation Underground*, The Sex Gods' LP was only now being released under the non-name (get this) The Balcony Dogs! Clive Banks and Chris Blackwell had managed to hold the album up for so long that the band eventually capitulated. But, of course, the barely promoted Balcony Dogs' LP had done nothing at all and now the group was spitting up. Three years' work was up the swanny because of the whims and well-rimmed quims of silver spoon shallow pool No-Marks. Well, fuck my old boots.

I knew at once that I was not going to be driven out of Britain by such as Clive Planks. I was gonna dig trenches and get stuck in. It was to be a war of attrition. Dorian and I decided that there would be no more contact with Island Records until Clive Banks started treating me with the respect deserved of a major artist. Dora suggested that we buy a computer and I try writing an autobiography. I wouldn't answer Island's phone calls or letters, just write and write and find out how it feels. I was so freaked out by Banks that the idea seemed perfect to me, even if it was just to get him out of my life. He had brought The Sex Gods to their knees and turned Ron Fair into a shadow of himself. I told everyone that Clive Banks was firing Live Blanks and that we shouldn't give a damn.

With thoughts of Manhattan living only recently banished from my mind, I felt it was desperately important to rebalance my British self, so Rooster suggested that we hold rehearsals at his Lewisham house. Rooster, Marcus, Donneye and myself were there joined by Mooneye, fresh from The Sex Gods' debàcle. We jammed and recorded a 15-minute blitz of Faust's 'It's a Rainy Day (Sunshine Girl)', which melded Detroit MC5 Stooges into pure on-the-One Krautrock. Whoa. Our obsessions with Sly and Funkadelic had been utterly emasculated in the mix of *My Nation Underground*, but here in Rooster's flat the group showed me how the on-the-One link between black funk and Krautrock could be approached without its being diluted, and I wrote a long set of lyrics entitled 'Hanging Out & Hung Up on the Line'.

When Donneye and Mooneye put together delicate new arrangements of 'Planet Ride' and 'Eve's Volcano', I asked Mooneye to replace Frog temporarily[1] for my soon-to-come Japanese tour. It was good to know that, however badly an album had done, the inevitable Japanese tour would psyche you up all over again.

Rooster's house set us up for genuine experiment because Rooster's friends were all genuine experiments themselves. Raja was a British army ex-policeman nurse (sic sic sic), who lived in the first-floor flat with another nurse, Polly. His hobby was eating food as long past its sell-by date as possible – for kicks. Holding it in was a major triumph to Raja, who would get the shit kicked out of him by Rooster for soiling the communal bathroom for days on end.

They had this mate Mark Shepherd. He used to come around, flop himself in the corner and only surface when a bong was going around. But one day he was pissing Raja off by claiming no hit from consecutive bongs. Raja rummaged around in the dirtiest corner of the massive living room for the largest, oldest, dirtiest, deadest spider he could find. He dumped it into the bong, with a camouflage of weed sprinkles over it and nudged everybody hysterically as Mark Shepherd did the spider in one. AND he said it had a kick.

At the end of March, I got a strange letter from three Japanese women who had spent Christmas in Tamworth. They told me that my song 'Reynard the Fox' had intrigued them so much that they had decided to spend Christmas 1987 in Tamworth, then take a taxi out to the Alvecote Mound and recite the song lyrics from the top of the Mound. They had enjoyed the experience so much that Christmas 1988 had been spent the same way and the Japanese English made their experience even more curious:

"Me, the Japanese, was so unusual in Tamworth they didn't look at me without curiosity. Most exciting for me was finding out the place you became a turtle.

---

1 Jill Bryson, Frog's wife and leader of Strawberry Switchblade, had a formidable agoraphobia which temporarily prevented his touring with me.

I asked the police Warwickshire and Polesworth founded out in 'Reynard the Fox'."

I found the idea of people acting this way strange but remarkable, and I could not judge them negatively. I had been smitten enough with the area to write the song in the first place. I realised just how well the Mound and its Polesworth environment had always worked for me as a surrogate Saxon burial mound. I loved that it had worked for others, that they had not come away disappointed. It seemed like something big.

BEAM ME UP, SCOTTY, THERE'S NO FOIL ON THE KIT-KATS

On April 2nd, my group, my crew and I sat at Terminal 3 of Heathrow, waiting to board the JAL Boeing 757 for Japan. This was going to be a real adventure. Mooneye's head was already blown at the prospect of being back to this magical place which had so adored him with the Bunnymen and The Psychedelic Furs, whilst Mike Joyce was freaking at the fact that he would be the "First Smith in Japan".

We'd been waiting for over an hour while Jolyon fidgeted and fussed to try and get the whole entourage upgraded to first class. Now, he was puffing and blowing and looking like he was getting nowhere. Sod it, I thought, and finally took Rooster up on his suggestion that I down a couple of his Attivan tablets. These were a prescription downer which really sorted out the men from the boys.

"No problems, maan," said Rooster. "You probably won't even feel 'em. I have to take five at a time before they even kick in. Know what I mean?"

Rooster is mad. Know what I mean? I woke up 18 hours later at Narita Airport, Tokyo, having been upgraded to first class and having benefited from none of it. Apparently, Jolyon had to take my first fresh orange juice away from me, as I was passing out before I'd even got my belt on.

I staggered out into the heat and light of Narita, where hundreds of girls were waiting for us, far more than ever before. It was only at this moment that I first realised what a coup having Mike Joyce in the band was going to be. It was also a very lucky time to be here – it was Apple Blossom time, a time of good fortune. What a shame I had such a short crap haircut.

We were all decanted into a magnificently chromed oriental bus, which was decorated inside with beads and curtains, giving way to an inner sanctum which had no seats at all. With fans in taxis and cars driving alongside us, we made our way to my beloved Roppongi Prince Hotel, where even more fans besieged us and I tried to take in the difference between the response here – seven sold-out shows – and the 59 fans who had turned up to see me in Toulouse just five months before. Rock'n'roll.

With Rooster, Joycey and Mooneye together in the same group, Jolyon knew that he had a hard time on his hands. They all immediately disappeared into the wilds of hidden Roppongi, surrounded by hordes of beautiful Japanese fans. This entourage was followed by the much younger and more impressionable, but equally hard-drinking Donald and Marcus. Jolyon sent our tour manager, Tim Hook, to go and search for them all, and I knew right away that this combination was made for Japan. Donald and Marcus were later discovered unconscious in the unlocked bar of a closed night-club, where the brandy chocolate, Bailey's Irish Cream and Malibu had lasted them all night long.

Our other Japanese secret weapon was Rizla Deutsche the Two-Metre Man. Rizla AKA Gavin Wall was our far-out Krautrock'n'Funkadelic Meister and super guitar/synthesizer Übertekhnician who got treated like a rock star in Japan. Rizla's heroes were Neu! and Can and we strolled around Tokyo together being tall aliens. In the evenings, the prettiest girls would cry hysterically over Rizla, Mooneye and Joycey, and often for much of the afternoons.

By midnight of the third day, I had finished all my interviews for Tokyo and was soon walking alone through the party streets of Roppongi. Of course, "alone" in Tokyo meant with a party of 20 women walking in my trail, laughing and talking, and helping me whenever I got lost. I was no longer hung up to be treated like a pop star once more, as it was only temporary and actually fantastic in very short doses. I bumped into Rooster and Mike Joyce, who was amazed and concerned at the single-skin wrappers around all Japanese confectionery. "Fucking hell, Copey, Good job The Smiths never played Japan. Andy Rourke wouldn't have stood it here." He held up the empty wrapper: "There's no foil on the Kit-Kats!!!"

And there in the main square at midnight was Mooneye with a gorgeous gay Japanese guy and a small Japanese businessman. Mooneye was not gay, but he'd already scored the pot and cocaine because of his looks, and was now on his way to find more exotic substances. I warned Mooneye that he was in Intolerant Japan and left him talking in the midnight heat.

But by the next morning, all of Mooneye's drugs were gone and we were all gasping to toke on a spliff. Tonight was the first show at a Tokyo club called MZA and there was huge pressure on us. Backstage, Mooneye absent-mindedly chopped up the parsley on the catering tables and remarked that a placebo spliff of parsley would chill him out better than nothing. We all jeered Mooneye wildly for this, but everyone's eyes were soon following him around the room as the parsley spliff kicked in. As was to be expected, Rizla had the first toke, then one by one everyone in the room had to check out the new Mooneye Substitute. It was cute and it worked, and we were soon running out of parsley and sending one of the gig runners down to a grocery store for an ounce of "Fresh".

The two shows at MZA were extreme performances, reflecting my group's weird personalities, especially in this alien landscape. At the rehearsals at Rooster's Lewisham flat, Donneye and Mooneye's version of 'Planet Ride' had its backbone in The 13th Floor Elevators' version of 'Gloria'. They put in call-and-answer MC5 vocal effects, then copped the sax solo from Faust's 'It's a Rainy Day' for the ending. It was a beautiful arrangement full of tense, urgent sensuality and the group boiled when we performed it in Japan. By the MZA dates, a minor-key rehearsal version of Count Five's 'Psychotic Reaction' had turned into a Cope "original" entitled 'The Angel & the Fellatress', a stop/go/stop/go song still linked by the former song's refrain: "And it feels like this."

This big group was so different from the Whitten/Eller/Frost group that it had appeared bulky in Britain and Europe. But a sleekness took over the Japanese gigs which can only be attributed to an increase in our god-selves. I'd never seen such a bunch of musicians change as now here in Japan. By the second MZA show, the group was so vibed up that I kept looking back from high atop my mike-stand throughout the show to check that I was not being upstaged.

Then, as the show edged to a close, I brought 'Reynard the Fox' to its penultimate climax only to glance back and see utter devastation around me. We were just at the part of the song when feedback and mayhem announce: "And then he reached down – and then he took the bag" . . . and Mike Joyce had thrown his entire drum-kit off the stage riser, whilst Rooster had thrown himself into his (rented) percussion, causing it to scatter all around the stage. Donneye was coaxing feedback from his red Fender 12-string by throwing it face-first on to his array of FX pedals, only to then purposefully stride over and retrieve it and start all over again. More simply, and perhaps more alarmingly, Marcus lay on his back with his bass turned down, bleating quietly to himself. I surveyed this devastation with amusement, bemusement and a sure-footed determination not to be upstaged by these genuine fucking lunatics. The last fast part of the song was now unplayable because the equipment was already trashed.

By this time, Mooneye had calmly and physically laid his speaker stack on its back facing the ceiling and was pacing around it when, suddenly, he turned and ran, guitar in hand, to dive into the audience. This was all too much . . . Hmm, hmm . . . Sir, you're jumping in *my* audience! Sirrah! Desist!

I pulled my top down in an obvious plea for attention and all eyes in the hall returned to me. Then, quick as a flash, I pulled up the top part of the heavy bespoke mike-stand until it came out of its sheath/base and revealed the rude untooled metal underneath. Then, I let this heavy metal run across my belly in a long series of "Z" motions until rivulets of blood were cascading down my belly. In order to alert the audience that this was a showbiz act rather than any genuine shamanic rite, I kept a huge smile on my face the entire time, but the normally unshockable Japanese audience was stunned by 10,000 bolts of instant Gore Reality. Many of them left the hall crying and some returned to the Roppongi Prince to find out if I was okay, whilst a sweet and strange TV disc jockey/animated glove puppet known as DJ Cookie announced on air that I had committed hara-kiri tonight, and, hey, how did it feel?

The entourage now moved on to Osaka and Kyoto. Rooster began to fall for a young Japanese woman called White Rabbit, whilst Mooneye became paranoid and was convinced that he was being ripped off by me and my management. But the group were such good friends that our nights were all spent together in hugely drunken celebrations, surrounded by more women than ever because of Joycey's mythical presence. Whilst Rizla's looks and height made him a star in his own right, here in Japan even my other tech, Baron Beetmoll Troy, was receiving attention from female fans and he looked like a member of some Dark Ages Viking SAS. And when our tour manager Tim Hook was adopted/co-opted by women fans as an auxiliary group member, I knew that this would be a tough tour to follow.

But Mooneye was weirding out again and just 10 minutes before the show in Nagoya he locked himself naked in the dressing-room toilet and refused to come out. Again, he was claiming that he'd been ripped off. I furry-freaked out. No-one, *no-one*, not even fucking Michael Mooneye, is allowed to be weirder than me on my own stage. Get on stage or I'll fucking kill you. Mooneye came out like a man who knew he could not fuck me up as a brother. Besides that, he'd just remembered that he'd already been paid the money. But he'd spent it already. Der.

We hugged and made up, and the band went out to play the intro to 'Five O'Clock World'. I loitered in the wings until the last moment then walked out star-like and elegant to cheers and screams, but, in the haze of the audience, I saw a group of bouncers really hitting two women who had dared to come into the centre aisle on my arrival. Without singing a note, I leapt off the stage and, in one Pete Townshend windmill, pummelled one guy to the floor in a single and dramatic movement. The crowd went wild. Fucking Right On.

By the end of the tour, the group members were in pieces. This group had a strange ability to hang out together, but the women and the extra vibe which Joycey and Mooneye brought in were almost too much. By the time we got to the Dohshin Hall in Sapporo, Rooster had dismantled all of the furniture in his hotel room and was casually walking naked around the hotel lobby. "Um, I've left my keys in the room?" he offered hopefully to the patrolling hotel manager, as implausible as a Santa with a ciggy.

Tim Hook phoned Dorian in New York and asked her to come home early from her holiday to meet me, as I had just freaked out and kicked the entire 14th-floor bedroom window (6' × 6') onto the pathway below. What a fucking joke. One minute it was there, the next moment half a ton of glass and steel was plummeting into what I thought MUST be a teeming street below. I shrieked and came to my senses looking into darkness below. No-one was killed, but I was in trouble for precisely 10 minutes, then off the hook. I shook all night with cold and the fear that I would suddenly take it upon myself to leap wildly out of the window. A perverse part of me felt sure that such an opportunity may well be a veiled invitation. What was I thinking? What was Japan turning me/us into?

The following morning, as we headed for the safety of Narita Airport, the Cope entourage was in a sad and deluded state. We'd been adored collectively for almost two weeks and now it was time to face reality again. We waved goodbye to the Japanese women who had inflated our egos so and prepared for a giant tantrum as the plane took off. I comforted Rooster, who was suffering from the loss of White Rabbit, and he topped me up with two Attivan tablets, which I sensibly didn't take until the upgraded food had begun to kick in. "I gotta Jap habit – gotta make a withdrawal."

CHINA DOLL

But the return to London was an enormous comedown for one so deeply interested in himself. Dorian had put herself out to return early from New York, but my head was truly caned from our Japanese obsessions. I had returned with every bag bulging with gifts of Japanese tinplate toys, including a special shippable bag which I had bought at the last minute in Kiddeland to fill with my 42 new Japanese taxis of all scales. As all toy collectors do, I convinced myself, I took out all of my previously bought Japanese taxis and displayed them together. Eighty-five Dinky Toy-sized cars take up a lot of room, but they were nearly all of the same colour so I just had to do it.

Rooster drowned his White Rabbit sorrows with me back in the Scalextric loft in more and more 200-lap festivals of speed. Now that The Sex Gods had split, Mooneye was around a lot more and we all felt desperate to continue the vibe which had begun in Japan. Like pathetic old war veterans who don't want the war to stop, we returned to Rooster's rehearsal room and jammed in true Nippon style.

In fact, so inspiring was this post-Japan rehearsal period that I was unfazed by Ron Fair's phone call in mid-April. Apparently, at this ultra-late stage, and with the LP long buried, Clive Banks had decided that I needed a third and final single from *My Nation Underground*, and could I record a new ep cheaply? They would even need a video. What? Why?

Though I was not talking to Clive Banks, I was excited at the prospect of recording and releasing new material. For even if the single was not a hit, I knew that three fine new pieces could shift the fans' perception of an album universally perceived as a dud. I told Ron that we should aim to record three new tracks for the *China Doll* ep. But rather than taking time in some cheap studio, I proposed that we should use the money differently and do it all in one day at Townhouse 3.

Ron was compliant but nervous. He made the point that using such a good studio would preclude paying many people. We could experiment, but we'd have to know exactly what we were going to do. Then I contacted everyone and discovered that people were busy when I needed them and my brief Utopia fell apart before it had started. Marcus had started working with The Mighty Lemon Drops, whilst Mooneye had just disappeared back into hidden Liverpool and I couldn't just offer Joycey peanuts because it was an ep.

But with a basic nucleus of Donneye, Rooster, Hugoth Nicolson and Ron Fair in the studio, the sessions for the *China Doll* ep were the greatest breath of fresh air in the studio since the Rabbi Joseph Gordan 45. Gone was the anally-retentive Ron Fair of the previous year, replaced by a who-gives-a-fuck-I'm-not-staying-at-Island-anyway guy with a point to make.

First, I recorded the epic Mill Lane song 'Crazy Farm Animal', an acoustic ever-changing ballad kind of like a prog-Donovan. Donneye played wild drums throughout my performance, but no-one else was around. Then, I added mouth-wah to the chorus and Donneye put a track of omnichord on to the second section, whilst Ron added a marvellous piano to the fade-out. Hold on, this was easy and not a problem at all. I was a good guitarist and got everything first take. Fuck, what was all that '80s shit when we were doing . . . *Nation*? I felt as though I'd been hoodwinked and the blinds were beginning to finally fall away.

We bailed into a hysterical live rant called 'Rail On'. It was a sort of Redneck Buddy Holly inbred thing with a melody stolen straight out of Black Sabbath's 'Snowblind'. But we were really cooking with gas by now and Donneye put down his beautiful sampled saxophone quartet for a delicate song called 'Desi', which we all added to quickly and mixed as we went along. By the end of the evening, the *China Doll* ep was completely finished. It had been recorded in the same studios as . . . *Nation* and mixed in the same studio as . . . *Nation*, using the . . . *Nation* team. Somehow, these facts made a huge difference to me. I'd had the right team all along, but the wrong attitude.

With expectations from a record-company, I was shit.

Without expectations from a record-company, I was great.

I called Jolyon up and informed him. Right, Bollocks, I'm not talking to Clive Banks again until he lets me do my thing.

I decided to reassert myself there and then.

BANGS – YOUNGER THAN THE NAZZ

An incredible tragedy happened at Hillsborough Stadium, Sheffield, on April 15th 1989, when the FA Cup semi-final between Liverpool and Notts Forest ended with the deaths of 96 Liverpool fans, all crushed together and asphyxiated before our eyes, mainly due to the cavalier attitudes of the authorities. It was the slowest, most painful British tragedy since the Aberfan disaster and living rooms throughout Britain watched it all unfold as the shocked commentators tried to come to terms with what was happening. On a personal level, Jolyon Burnham was devastated that Polydor Records felt the need to withdraw the first single by his new artist Carl Marsh. The song, released that week, was bizarrely entitled 'Here Comes the Crush'. It was to be Marsh's only release.

It was on our fifth anniversary, April 19th 1989, that Dorian gave me a soul-scourging and sacred document which changed my life forever and proved to me that my suspicions about rock'n'roll had always been correct. That document was a book called *Psychotic Reactions & Carburettor Dung*, a compilation of the LP reviews, interviews and musings made by the late Lester Bangs in various magazines, from *Creem* and *Rolling Stone* to *NME*. The book was an incendiary of the heart and had me standing 20-feet-tall by the end of the first chapter.

Bangs wrote as though rock'n'roll was a righteous place where the lone voice of the shaman could speak to the population through the universal medium of music. Unlike the cartoon yawnings of Nick Kent's *Dark Side*, Bangs flew the same flags as me!!! He was on the side of The Stooges AND the MC5. He championed Magma's notorious 'Ork Alarm', for fuck's sake. Amazingly, he gave and he didn't give AND he wanted to change the world!!! He didn't care that those two ideas were in opposition, he just rode roughshod over dualism completely. To those who said, "If you're not into drugs, you must be against them," he appeared to be saying "I'm a fuckhead – I need them, but I'm not such an egoist as to think that that means the whole population needs them." Bangs loved The Stooges because they were so Unrighteous and out to destroy. He adored Funkadelic and the Five because they were Righteous and out to replace. But he hated the self-righteous with as ass-kicking a passion as the Islamic fire which had burned to the walls of Vienna. Could I be overstating? No!!! The guy was fucking dead at 32 because of it. Younger than the Nazz.

Lester spoke in terms that thrilled me so because they were references which used the same vocabulary as my every day. He had a love of Richard Hell, which I initially bleeped out, but even Hell got lambasted for wearing his adolescence like a war wound. Bangs wrote in such hugely mythological terms that my psychic sinews rippled and flexed as I rediscovered my rock'n'roll self. I may have actually started purring during particularly pertinent segments and I sure as hell spent a great deal of time getting up, prowling round the house and looking in the mirror. Then, I would return to the book and sink back into the Bangsian Mystic. Aaaaahhhh!!! I'd thought that my *Head-On* rantings may have been a little shaky, but they were nothing compared to Lester Bangs. He'd start off talking about the Ramones and end up getting done for assault on his neighbour for his behaviour during the writing of the article. I was Odin, he was just Odd.

Then my eyes lit on his review of the Guess Who's *Live at the Paramount*. I knew nothing but the marvellous 'American Woman' single, a kind of 'Whole Lotta Love' meets 'L.A. Woman', but Bangs lured me in with cunning hints such as "the Guess Who is God" and the fact that their singer Burton Cummings was "the rightful and unquestionable heir to Jim Morrison's spiritual mantle". He also suggested that playing the live 16-minute version of 'American Woman' could possibly bring on heightened states of awareness and I understood that this was not a normal rock'n'roll writer at all, but one of my life's great gurus. Lester fucking Bangs. I'd known the name for years, but never had reason to check beyond the enormous piece on the Clash, which he'd done for *NME* in '77. But the Clash were nothing. And now, Lester was here as a man from the past – and showing me that I must forever look in unlikely places for revelation.

I got the Guess Who's live LP and Bangs was right. Burton Cummings WAS Jim Morrison. *Live at the Paramount* was a stone gasser, and made even greater by the fact that Burton Cummings was a genuine poet/freekazoid. He had choruses like: "We got cocaine and morphine, too, Lots of shit to get you high, Little pink pills that'll make you feel ill, Trucking off across the sky."

The greatest irony was the fact that the Guess Who had been booked to record their LP at the fabulous Carnegie Hall in New York. But farm-punk Burton had got so out of it that night that RCA had insisted they record the following night in Seattle! On the cover of the live album, the Guess Who are all glowering at the camera like their once-in-a-lifetime chance just went out the window while Burton grins up a storm in the middle.

So now Lester Bangs was my new spiritual advisor. Yes, I should have guessed. I was never gonna have some Eastern guy for my guru – I shoulda always known it would be this way. Don't get sucked into religion – save yourself for Rock'n'Roll!

SKELLINGTON

Just one week after the invigorating high of the *China Doll* ep session, I was called by an old music biz friend from early on in my career. He was a powerful man and had an unusual request. A new group had been signed to his label and could I play a Clive Langer-type role in the studio, rearranging and producing the songs? He said the group were big fans of my music and I could chose any studio I wished, but that it was all to be done in utmost secrecy.

Of course, I immediately chose Townhouse 3 with its Who-vibe and recent associations, especially as Tulse Hill was so cyclable late at night. By the next weekend, a Bank Holiday, I'd organised Hugoth Nicolson to be recording engineer again and Rooster to provide some extra percussion and conga playing on the sessions. We were all set up for the recording and hanging at Townhouse 3 when my friend's entire band got sick and failed to show up. Suddenly, I was left in an exciting position. Here I was – left with a Bank Holiday weekend's worth of free time with my favourite engineer and favourite drummer, at my favourite recording studio, with full catering and six reels of 2" tapes waiting to be filled. My friend at the record company was in Paris and no-one else from the company even knew we were here because of the secrecy.

I danced around and told everyone that we were finally going to be recording *Skellington*. The *China Doll* ep had inspired me so much that this piece of apparent serendipity, just one week later, showed me that now was the perfect time to do such a thing.

We had extreme time limitations – two days – but we also had the facilities of extremely high quality acoustics and recording equipment, and a deep know-ledge of the place. Studios are sacred space, so you soon remember where every percussion instrument sounds best, where vocals really bite and what unlikely corridor or toilet sounds better than the prescribed guitar room. I decided that any young band would have killed to have got themselves into such a position and that the main aim was to start recording and release *whatsoever* came out at the end of the studio time. The "moment" had clearly been handed to me – now I must deliver.

Of course, the problem of such dramatic and idealistic decisions is keeping your head long enough to define the terms under which you are working. What constituted a real album? Rooster, Hugoth and I decided that there should be a minimum of 13 songs in order to qualify *Skellington* as a "proper" album. The seven tracks per side on the first Ramones' LP obscured the fact that it was also 12 minutes per side. We decided that the 13 songs should all be short in order to be overdub-able in so short a time and that all overdubs should be "of the moment", with just one run-through permitted in order to remain on schedule.

With just my acoustic guitar at hand, without lyric book or even plectrum, I set myself up in my favourite booth. I decided that *Skellington* was going to be entirely judged on the vibe which we put on to the tape, so I got Rooster to set up opposite me in the same booth. The morning slowly kicked in as Rooster proceeded to skin up at a ferocious pace similar to my song recording.

First, I remembered a song called 'Doomed', which was catchy as hell and featured a sort of off-kilter refrain like Johnny Cash's 'Burning Ring of Fire'.

I could play it without a plectrum, so 'Doomed' became the first song to be recorded for *Skellington*. Next, I remembered an ancient song from even before The Teardrop Explodes. This song was called 'Beaver' and was extremely easy to perform, so I blasted through it and continued straight into 'Me & Jimmy Jones', a song in which the Christian God admonishes the Reverend Jim Jones for his murderous Jonestown massacre. Hugoth Nicolson found a crap plectrum so I decided to record 'Robert Mitchum' as it had easy and complete lyrics and a solid chord structure. I even rehearsed 'Robert Mitchum' but its roots as a McCulloch/Cope song from the A Shallow Madness days of April '78 were severely hidden by a very recent and sharp rearrangement/rewrite which I had given the song this past Christmas at my mother-in-law's. Now, it was a smart gem of a song with a fake French verse and a whistling solo, totally at odds with the first three tracks.

When I came out of recording 'Robert Mitchum', I called Donneye and told him to get himself over with as much gear as he could get in a taxi – we were recording *Skellington* and he had to be on it. We had even planned a very auspicious song for his first contribution to *Skellington*. It was an old Teardrop Explodes song from around Club Zoo time: 'Out of my Mind on Dope & Speed'. I had always threatened to record the song but never had the right vehicle for its inclusion. Until now.

While Donald was still at home putting a taxi of instruments together, we retraced our steps and put rudimentary overdubs on the first four songs. It was already decided that the running order of *Skellington* would just have to follow the order in which the songs were being recorded. We had no time to waste editing the thing at the end. I had no problem with that – it just meant that such decisions were being made far earlier than most people like to make them.

Hugoth's mother had left her trumpet in the studio these past weeks and Rooster said he had the East German sax in the car. Get 'em! We're gonna have an Iron Curtain soul band. I stood Rooster and Hugoth in front of a microphone and conducted their farts and squeals over 'Doomed' and 'Beaver', but by 'Me & Jimmy Jones', it was 'Enough Already!' With extra piano and Rooster's drums, *Skellington* was sounding like Skip Spence backed by The Plastic People of the Universe, or some kind of bucolic Fugs. Luckily, the whistling solo on 'Robert Mitchum' made it sound like a camp single, and as Donneye arrived I saw that we were steaming into this challenge and really achieving something.

'Out of My Mind on Dope & Speed' sounded like weak shit, but its charm was intact and I really had no more time to consider. I now had a list of songs and my lyric book, which Dorian had cabbed over from Tulse Hill. In rapid succession, recordings were made of 'Everything Playing at Once', 'Little Donkey', 'Great White Wonder', 'Incredibly Ugly Girl', 'No How, No Why, No Way, No Where, No When' and a couple of others. 'Don't Crash Here' finally made its debut, here in an economical 56-second arrangement. These songs were mostly years old and things that I sang at home for Dorian, as a joke, wind-up or for her entertainment. But shrewd overdubbing and harmony vocals had me dancing around like a loon.

We needed a final song. Rooster suggested 'I'm Comin' Soon', the most deranged song I'd made up in years. "I'll do it," I said. I sung it first take with Rooster literally holding his hands over his mouth to stop himself going hysterical. To make the song into an even more perfect ending, Hugoth copped a bird in a garden from a sound effects record, which we put on to a record deck then slowed down right at the end in order to reveal the artifice.

Skellington sounded stupendous for an album that had taken only one and a half days to invent, navigate, record and mix. Especially as five months in this same studio had produced the stasis of *My Nation Underground* one year before.

Now I had to cover my tracks at Townhouse 3. I knew that I couldn't walk out with the 2" 24-track tapes without creating a furore and I couldn't even tell my friend how well I'd used the recording time, as I knew he would have claimed the tracks for his own record label. Instead, after much musing over the problem, I decided to return the un-annotated master reels of *Skellington* to the vaults of my friend's record company, in whose inhospitable and corporate surroundings they would be certain to vanish forever. Then I took a reel-to-reel as my main master tape, along with a DAT and a large U-Matic video (which everyone in the music business loved at that time). No-one would ever be the wiser.

To celebrate the early completion of *Skellington* in one and a half days, I decided to spend the rest of the time recording Dorian and her tennis eulogy to Ivan Lendl. 'Go, Ivan, Go' was a Mo Tuckerish speak-along with the catchiest chorus of "Game, set and match, Lendl – Go, Ivan, Go!" As we flew through the recording process of this song also, I felt a new and singular me taking over.

THROUGH CORPORATE NIGHTMARES BY STEALTH

The recording of *Skellington* was as nourishing a thing as I had ever done before and I was now determined to claw my way out of this artistic canal and chase the river currents again. But the support which I was receiving from friends and musicians was far greater than that of my management. For the most part, Jolyon Burnham liked what I did well enough, but he had no all-out abandoned passion for it. Indeed, his pet project was Neil Arthur, the singer from the dreaded Blancmange, which summed up completely where Jolyon was really coming from. He also managed the embarrassing Shriekback, a *Rock Follies*-like eight-piece with a bald Sal Solo/Klaus Nomi singer and multiple harpies dressed like 'Video Killed the Radio Star' women. Other gems on his own roster were The Thrashing Doves and a rockband called King Swamp. Now, how could I get anywhere with my *Skellington* intentions, if my managers were this out of synch?

I told Jolyon that he should under no circumstances play *Skellington* to Clive Banks, as it would immediately compromise my position. "If you don't love it, Jolyon, how are you gonna convince Banks that it's even worth a shit?" But Shriekback were also on Island Records and that compromised me already. How could he blast Clive for me if he needed financial help for Shriekback? Though Jolyon could be a dangerous animal, I knew he was not psychically tough and obnoxious enough to deal with Banks' otherworldly Ralph Lauren-clad sneering to argue the case for such a malformed thing as *Skellington*. The great magician keeps his hand hidden from the corporate knobhounds until he is ready to play it.

I continued writing *Head-On* at all opportunities, while Island's chief video director Fraser Kent, along with Andy Eastwood and Pete DeFreitas, formulated plans for the 'China Doll' video. I was still unhappy with my ultra-short hair and told them that I didn't want a starring role in the vid. If the song was about Dorian, it seemed wrong to have me in shot without her. Then Fraser suggested that we get a couple in to play the part of Dorian and myself. Wow, that's a great idea. It allows me to do a video without all the travelling that such things entail. Awlright!

With The Sex Gods gone but their vibe still burning, Andy Eastwood and Pete DeFreitas had formed a traditional band known as The Divine Thunderbolt Corps, after the Japanese kamikaze pilots of WW2. The DeFreitas/Eastwood axis inhabited Paul Toogood's gallery at the Black Bull, in Fulham, where Tim Whittaker currently had a large exhibition. Tim was also playing drums for the DTC, as they had become known, along with Jake Brockman, who was playing acoustic guitar, Frank DeFreitas from The Woodentops on bass and Pete's girlfriend, Johnson, who had become the main lead singer. Easty sang and Pete played guitar, banjo and drums on a set of Negro spirituals and lost C&W numbers.

At the Black Bull meeting, we all decided to go for a simple road romance as the theme of the 'China Doll' video. Pete would be the motorcycling love-interest, with Easty as his colleague, then we would find a Dorianesque teenager to fall in love with Pete. The director, Fraser Kent was both my friend and an Island employee, so I would get what I wanted AND Island would trust him implicitly.

The night before Fraser, Andy and Pete left for France, The Divine Thunderbolt Corps played a fine set at the Black Bull. I say "fine" because everyone raved about it, but I avoided the show as I heard that Balfe and Drummond were expected. I was anything but churlish – I just refused to be weakened right now, just when I'd finally begun to navigate a route through my life.

Then a strange thing happened whilst Fraser, Pete and Andy were filming in France. I got a call from Paul King telling me that Levi's wanted me to write a traditional-sounding new song for their next advert. Whoa. I knew it was important because Paul King was taking time off from Tears for Fears to deal with it. I had, once before, been approached for some commercial, which Paul "You're in debts up to your ears" King had almost insisted I do. At the time, in a defensive attack, I'd arrogantly said, "Too small, Kingy, get me Levi's or Coke," sure that such a purist attitude would ensure that I'd never have to be tempted again. But I had obviously had my bluff called and the whole of Outlaw was down on me – "Don't let Copey get away."

Paul King, Jolyon and myself met the Levi's people, who said that their long campaign of classic '60s songs over new film footage was wearing thin as an idea. No shit, Sherlock! They liked my timeless/retro approach (their words/ thanks a lot) and wanted me to write something to fit in with a guy on a motorbike riding over Triboro Bridge in New York. I knew the New York cityscape as a second home and we came out of the meeting vibrating like loons. Kingy and Jolyon both agreed that I already had the right song in 'East Easy Rider'. When should we tell them? "Tell them straight away," I said. "Send them the song."

But when Levi's liked the song, I was troubled and couldn't get a grip on 'East Easy Rider' becoming a commercial. Shit, it hadn't even been released yet. At night, I thought about the image of East Easy Rider as its original metaphor for Andy Eastwood's and Pete DeFreitas' freewheeling fraternity which I so adored. I stuck it out for three days of soul-searching then rang Jolyon to tell him that the Levi's thing was off.

Jolyon was horrified and confused.

JOLYON: "Hold on, mush. We haven't even signed the deal with them. Don't tell them yet, for fuck's sake."
JULIAN: "Jolyon, if we haven't signed the deal, there's no problem."
JOLYON: "But if we tell them it's all off, they'll cancel everything."
JULIAN: "Jolyon, I *want* them to cancel everything. I just can't do a fucking Levi's advert."

Paul King was furious with me and raged about his office cursing me out in my absence, until I came in and made him see sense. Kingy, if I did the advert and hated myself, I'd destroy the months of writing I've done, and I couldn't keep piecing my musical thing back together. Cally's departure had been a disruption which Paul King had never sussed, but Paul had been with me long enough to know when I meant what I said. He backed off and we never again talked about Levi's. But to his credit he definitely digested the information.

Instead, Island Records had a giant vibe on the 'China Doll' video and I cycled over to Island Records to hang out with Fraser, DeFreitas, Easty and some of the Island staff. That night, Pete, Andy and I said goodbye to Satch at Island's back door and I stared, affronted, at Pete's preferred mode of transport. As much as I dug the symbolism of the large touring motorbikes which all three guys rode, Pete had managed to reduce his Ducatti 950 to the role of Morris Oxford/Austin Countryman hack/carryall, thus forfeiting all safety in the sheer enthusiasm of taking as many 'China Doll' videos back to Liverpool as he could.

Outside Island, as I remonstrated with Pete for his non-safety stance, he stared at me pie-eyed, smiling and unconcerned, both leather-clad arms hugging the white plastic bags with their stacks of videos in each. Easty doesn't do these things – why take your already-confused life closer to the edge? I only thought the last question, as Pete was still looking at me the same way I'd looked at people three years before. We all hugged and I was proud that they were taking "our" video to show off to the Liverpool scene. Awl-fucking-right!

HANNAH CANTRELL

By April 12th, the release date of 'China Doll', I discovered that I had reached page 50 of *Head-On* and was beginning to actively need the purge which such an exercise brings. I was running upstairs to write songs and stopping for poetry breaks and all kinds of wonderful stuff. Hey, I like computers if they let you write 25,000 words!

A fan of mine called Lois, who loved to besiege me with hundreds of postcards filled with obsessive, tiny writing, had finished her latest missive with an admonishment to me for now using a computer: "You can't beat an old fashioned typewriter." But Lois' postcard really pushed me in the opposite direction. The rejection of technology is only sound when it's done through understanding. Rejection through ignorance or belief in the natural superiority of the old ways seemed to me to be as bad as drably accepting all modernism.

For three days that week I typed and typed and saw the book really starting to unfold as a proper story. But *Head-On* was starting to so consume me that I had barely prepared for either the Eden recording session at the end of the week or the Richard Skinner session which followed just one day later. I hastily jotted down 'Robert Mitchum', 'Hanging Out & Hung Up on the Line' and 'East Easy Rider' as worthy of the BBC session, and decided that we should try to nail a version of The Sex Gods-inspired 'Double Vegetation' on the Eden session, as we had worked on that song recently in rehearsals.

Then, on June 14th, Johnno called me out of the blue and he was crying. I instantly knew why . . . Pete DeFreitas was dead. I only knew maybe three seconds before he told me because Johnno told me quickly, but Johnno doesn't cry and he also never calls friends in the morning. So it just had to be Pete. As soon as I knew, I saw Pete in my mind's eye so recently close and now so instantly beyond and out-of-reach, and a kind of 20/20 Hindsight told me that I'd known all along. I don't actually think I had a true knowledge that Pete was about to die, more a natural defence that almost instantly built around me to protect myself from such awesome and weakening news.

Pete had been travelling at 60 miles per hour when he was killed on the A51, near Rugeley, in Staffs. An old lady named Hannah Cantrell had pulled out without seeing his approach and Pete had died instantly. I regarded the name Hannah Cantrell with instant suspicion. It sounded like some archaic chant and I repeated it over and over, searching for a deeper meaning. Why had Pete died now? He was so together compared with his old ways. He adored his new daughter Lucy, and Johnson and Pete were at a better point than they'd ever been before. Why had Pete been killed? Why had he died so near Tamworth and why had he been travelling that way in any case?

The Eden session came only two days after Pete's death, and, as The Sex Gods' favourite recording studio, instantly became the focus of a huge outpouring of grief. As Donald, Rizla and Rooster set up the gear, Dorian and Mooneye arrived with Easty, Sola and Mooneye's old girlfriend Mary and her current boyfriend. Then Jake Brockman arrived with the rest of the DTC and the recording session collapsed into a courtyard of utter desolation.

I was about to tell the engineer to go home when Donneye suggested that we run once through 'Double Vegetation' and then call it a day. Perfunctorily, I strapped on my big blue Ovation acoustic and listened to Rooster's "1–2–3–4" with a feeling of utter remove. But then, quite out of nowhere, a righteous atmosphere suddenly invaded our immediate vicinity, and the song began to play itself – we were caught in the most delightful and enlightening moment that four musicians could have shared together.

This delicate and sad song had started from my jamming the Guess Who's epic 'Trucking off across the Sky' on acoustic guitar. 'Double Vegetation', which I had only ever sung to myself on my bike travels through London these past months, now unfolded with an exquisiteness far removed from the unpractised mess of one week before. Now, all the misery of Eden Studios rose up and co-agulated into one supreme energy which sieved itself through the song and left the most strange afterglow of Pete DeFreitas. It was not the drumming, nor was it Mooneye's tragic Will Sargeant-style tailout guitar. More strange than that, it was as though all the suffering in that courtyard had been channelled right into the four musicians' performance, leaving an indelible and collective impression of one group's core/*coeur* image of our recently passed-on Glowboy.

Just days later, the whole estranged Liverpool scene collected at the DeFreitas family church, in Goring-on-Thames. Paul King's car service arrived very late and so Dorian and I were forced to push into the church halfway through the service. I had no time to take in the fact that I was suddenly in the same room as Jayne Casey, Pam Young, Paul Simpson, Gary Dwyer, Ian McCulloch, Pete Wylie, Will Sargeant, Bill Drummond, Dave Balfe, Bill Butt, Jake Brockman, Mick Houghton, etc. But wherever I looked I saw grieving friends and grieving enemies and grieving families all fit to burst with despair. We piled out of the church into the sunshine and kept our individual heads down. After years of hearing Pete's negative comments about him, I had no interest in talking to Mac, whilst Wylie made the crassest of comments to no-one in particular about the fact that all The Crucial Three were together at last. But under what circumstances! Gimme a fucking break! Still, at least he'd forgotten to bring Midge Ure this time.

The reunion continued up at the DeFreitas family house, where cult characters swanned around uncomfortably and tried not to catch each other's eyes. If Pete's death was not enough to settle our differences, then maybe our differences were real. I surprised myself by deciding that I didn't have any problem with that, and Dorian and I left early. My relationship with DeFreitas had never extended to combinations of people other than Balfey and Gary Dwyer, or Easty and Fraser. I actually had few collective memories of him to share with the people here. Somehow, the Communion at Eden Studios had manifested Pete so strongly and vitally amongst those people who all currently loved him that I found this be-suited wake ill-suited and hard to take. But Pete DeFreitas had been an awesomely gregarious party host, quite unlike my hermit self. So when we left, it was mainly to celebrate Pete's uniqueness – his wonderful oddness. Because that was the side of him that was closest to me.

In the chaos of Pete's death, the fact that the *China Doll* ep had only reached no. 53 in the charts was lost on all but the management. But Jolyon and Kingy were distraught that Island could "only get the single to 53" and unveiled a plan of action without telling me. As proof positive that Outlaw Management had no idea about the nature of my act, Jolyon Burnham went into Island Records and calmly played *Skellington* to Clive Banks. Clive hit the roof. No, you can't release it on Island. It's shit. No, you can't release it yourselves, it would ruin Julian's career. No, you can't return Julian to the fallow in-grown arable land that he inhabited before he'd been manicured and pedicured for *Saint Julian*.

Jolyon and Kingy told me what they'd done and *I* hit the roof. Why even play it to that Corporate Knobshiner? How many hidden agendas did my management have? I decided that I would ignore everyone and sell the record myself. Hell, one of the reasons I'd always liked Island so much was because of its lax attitude to bootlegs. In the mid '70s, Dennis Brown had recorded the LP *War in a Babylon* for Island. But after he'd copped the money, he released the same LP in Jamaica, with new vocals and a new title: *Fire Fe the Vatican*. A precedent had long ago been created here at Island, so I decided to press *Skellington* on my own and force Island's hand.

I cycled over to Pete Flannagan at Zippo Records, in Chiswick, and asked if he could put out *Skellington* for me. He said he'd love to. I told him that I didn't have permission from Island Records yet, but I would get it, so he should go ahead with the artwork and test-pressing to see how it would sound and look. Here's a tape.

Just as I was leaving, I spotted a copy of John Sinclair's Detroit Bible: *Guitar Army*. Published in 1971, it was a hardback with rainbow pages with photos of the MC5, The Rationals and various posters and current Detroit activism. The book was not for sale but I wanted it more than anything in a long while. The inside was choc-a-block with wisdom and knowledge, all clothed in the hippest-looking hard cover that I'd ever seen. Why, if all books looked as heavyweight and as simultaneously Groovy as this book did, we'd all be reading five books a week! After five minutes of browsing, I knew that I couldn't leave the shop without *Guitar Army*. I was going to have to "borrow" this book on a very Revolutionary level. I left with *Guitar Army*, promising Pete Flannagan that I'd have it back within the week. As I mounted my bike, I thought to myself, Don't hold your breath.

But Pete DeFreitas' death at 27 oppressed me and I felt a deep significance in it. One incident at the funeral had sealed my feeling of cosmic fraternity with Pete. Just before Dorian and I had left, the young policeman who had found Pete's body told me that the only map which Pete had carried with him on his last night was one handdrawn by me four years before in Drayton Bassett. The policeman was extremely moved by the whole affair and felt that Pete had clearly used the map several times in those years and had preferred an A-road burn up to doing battle with the BMWs and white vans.

Now, my mind began to take on very real dreams of Pete and I saw myself enmeshed in his story as never before. I felt as though Pete were a sacrifice to us, an energy giver we were to mourn yet somehow feed off. How else could I explain his death? Even Bill Drummond would later write that Pete occasionally looked like the Duck which had so obsessed him. I couldn't articulate it to any of my male friends, but I knew that I had fed off that energy right from our magical mourning recording night at the aptly-titled Eden Studios.

There was a Hillsborough Disaster Benefit just around the corner, so I recalled Mike Joyce and Marcus Williams to summon up some of that Japanese energy.

The show at the Royal Court had to be amazing, so we decided to open with 'Hanging Out & Hung Up on the Line', which had by now become the best on-the-One Powerdrive of all time.

Mooneye was not available, but the show was a gas and throughout 'Reynard' I hung from the mike-stand with a plastic bag over my head proclaiming my own immortality: "I will never die!!! I will never die!!! I will never die!!!" The thunder of the band was back once more and I realised that I must make a truly experimental guitar album to accommodate such songs as 'Hanging Out & Hung Up on the Line'.

In London, Pete Flannagan gave me the artwork and test pressing for *Skellington*. The photographic front was an old shot of me in our Drayton Bassett living room, looking truly deranged, and I made the test artwork, or chromalin, into a proper sleeve with double-sided tape and shoved it in a heavy plastic album cover. It looked fantastic and I put it on one side of the living room, then ran to view it from the other side. After the gross Leslie Neilsen beauty of *My Nation Underground*, this was a pop art Psychomodo for the high mid '80s!

Everyone who saw it guffawed in fascinated horror. Ron Fair adored the idea and its sheer audacity, but he was finally beaten, he said, and was leaving for California. He'd had enough of the Banksian headtrips that had pushed him to the brink of worthlessness and that really boiled me over onto the hob. Now, the manslaughter at Hillsborough and the death of Pete DeFreitas combined in my head with the ruination and symbolic deaths at Island of both The Sex Gods and Ron Fair, and I was sickened. Everyone was dying and starting again.

Into my vision came John Sinclair's '60s image of the Greedhead – the Captain of Industry who keeps on at you until your conveyor belt is working at a pace right on the edge of your capabilities. Into my mind came Lord Buckley's '50s image of the Greedhead who has you unconsciously pushing shopping trolleys into other shopping trolleys and, therefore, working for the Man. In my crazy mind's eye, I suddenly saw Clive Banks up in his glass office as a grown-up cherub dispensing little bullets of hate to musicians and employees alike through a magical popgun – Johnno, Easty, Washy, Gary Dwyer, pop, pop, pop, pop. What an image I saw! Ralph Lauren wings! But it ran:

"Go quickly to your death,
Try not for one last lingering breath,
Tame your religious zeal
For knowledge and its bitter appeal.
Firing Live Blanks – Firing Live Blanks – Fire away."

Of course, I knew at once that I could never record such a negative song as this, for it would launch 1,000 dangers at Clive and, like John Cowper Powys' fear of his own power, could be the start of 100 major headtrips myself. I hated that I was writing such songwords about Clive, for they were clearly as I really felt and I could not stop this ruthless outpouring of poetic feelings. But, much more importantly, negative Clive feelings were pervading my waking thoughts just as Pete DeFreitas was currently appearing in my dreams at night.

Dorian and I decided to chase our blues away by going to stay with my mother-in-law in Port Washington. Perhaps a more distant perspective and a few exclusive moments with *Guitar Army* would further enlighten us.

BURTON'S CUMMING!

"What you gonna do, mama, now that the roast beef's gone?"

The Guess Who, *Live at the Paramount*

As the late New York summer sun burned away some of the protective fuzz which had grown around our psychic shields these past months, Dorian and I lost ourselves in the garage sales and thrift shops of Long Island. I was on a Sly and Guess Who quest which involved lots of searching but practically no exchanging of money. At one garage sale, I found the Guess Who's *American Woman* and *Wheatfield Soul* for 25 cents each LP. At the very next sale, I found two copies of their (crap) 100% average *Share the Land* LP for the same price, plus Sly & the Family Stone's *M'Lady* album and a Sly bootleg too!!! What? It was 25 cents like all the rest and I began to get greedy. When I got the bootleg back to Helen's flat, the album was a classic, but I knew in my heart that I'd have to give it to Donneye.

We drove up to Boston to see Lisa St. John, who freaked out at my Burton Cummings interest. She said that the re-formed Guess Who were playing her club the Channel in a couple of weeks and she'd already had to start thinking about doing artwork for the poster. Whoa! Lisa! I freaked out, you have to take their *American Woman* lettering and write: BURTON'S CUMMING! I knew Lisa would get it together – when Spinal Tap had played the Channel, she'd even remembered to lay out the rider buffet with pimentos only in every *other* olive!

I got back to my mother-in-law's and discovered that Lenny Kaye had called. When we got on the phone together, I was blowing his mind with fucking Burton, man. Talking to Doc Rock[1] about Burton "These Eyes" Cummings.

---

1 Though British fans grew up with Lenny Kaye as Patti Smith's right arm, Dorian and other Americans knew him much earlier as Doc Rock, a *Creem* and *Rolling Stone* writer, as well as compiler/definer of the entire *Nuggets* genre, which he anticipated by light-fucking-years.

I took a train into Manhattan to see Lenny Kaye and that sweetheart Dockest of Rocks had bought me an original *American Woman* LP. I explained that it wasn't great, indeed there was kack upon it, for days, but Burton had that yawp that Lester Bangs had found on their live LP and I couldn't rest until I'd found all the good Guess Who songs (Ratio: Great 20%/Crap 70%/Indescribably embarrassingly crap yet fucking going for it nonetheless 10%). Lisa phoned to tell me that Burton was not in this late-stage Guess Who after all. I was relieved and happy to know that he'd risen above such bullshit and went out to Mr Cheapo's to buy more Guess Who. Could there be much more? By the late stages of the Guess Who's career, Burton was sporting penny collars and a moustache and the guitarists changed by each successive LP. The ratio of good material went down to 0% until I couldn't buy them at all.

But Burton was at least keeping my mind very busy at this crucial late '80s time and I loved him all the more for it. As a role model he was like Peter Hammill – I loved the idea of him and, even when he was utter crap, it was interesting crap. Their 10-minute epic 'Friends of Mine' is like a medley of The Zodiac's 'Cosmic Sounds' with The Doors' button turned full-up. Only it makes you realise how good the *Soft Parade* title track really is.

But *Guitar Army* was washing all over and around me, and I was currently relocating my love of the provincial. John Sinclair's writing about Detroit was confirming all my suspicions about the deep mystical quest that the city's musicians had been making in the late '60s and '70s. The Funkadelic/MC5/Stooges sound that had so consumed myself and Donneye for the past two years had somehow so far evaded our grasp on record, but now I began to sink into the mystic of John Sinclair's writing and I knew that it was not the words which he wrote (which were often hoary clichés to an '80s mind), but the sheer force of his tumultuous pen which somehow transformed him into the rocking-est feminist anti-John Knox of all time.

I was halfway through Lester Bangs' incredible book when I came to a piece about The J. Geils Band where Lester gets invited on stage with the band to play a miked-up typewriter during the encore. Lester suddenly went into this astonishing bit about how he was coming on like a one-man version of the MC5:

> "I strutted up and onto the boards, Smith-Corona [typewriter] in hand, no trace of stage fright . . . I grabbed the mike and hollered 'Thankyouthankyou,' just like *Kick out the Jams*; I figured to include the whole riff – 'I want to see a sea of hands out there' – would be less than subtle."

I had no idea that anyone else had ever delighted in the Five's on-stage James Brown patter. But Bangs' writing was visionary and rock'n'roll at the same time, just like John Sinclair. He wrote about the mutation of Detroit rock as a visionary talks about enlightenment, and all at once I saw that rock'n'roll *was* enlightenment. Suddenly I understood that it was my historical knowledge that had got me through the *Fried* years of mean-mouthed critics, not just my intuition that it was the right way to go. I had always been able to centre myself in the knowledge that even *The Velvet Underground* and *The Madcap Laughs* had been dismissed as valueless in reviews of the time. And with Mick Houghton's publicist's knowledge always just down the other end of the phone, I had even been blessed with a knowledgeable elder to always set me straight.

How I grieved that Lester Bangs was dead. In my DeFreitas state-of-mind, all the great rock'n'rollers living and dead suddenly seemed equally precious, and I was flooded with enormous feelings of the moment, that moment in rock'n'roll on a wet Tuesday at 4 o'clock in the afternoon, when all of time turns away and a classic pop song is captured intact as it sparkles through the ether. I suddenly knew that it had nothing to do with waiting for inspiration – hell, the studio time was booked so the inspiration just had to be willed. Willed. Of course. I hadn't adored our time in Lubbock, Texas, because it was some known sacred centre. I'd loved it because Buddy Holly had grown up there. Rock'n'roll was a moveable feast to be set up not where the shaman deemed, but where the population happened to be. But did that affect the magic? Not at all. Jimmy Page had recorded *Zeppelin 2* in any toilet or corridor he could rent space in. Look at *Skellington* – it had coagulated out of the ether before our very eyes, merely because I had said, 'Let there be *Skellington!*'

Oh, yeah.

I suddenly understood what the Dadaist artist Hugo Ball had meant in 1917 when he had proclaimed: "Artists are Gnostics, and practise what the priests think is long forgotten." At school, they even beat "yeah" out of you and replace it with "yes", but the root of "yeah" is older and comes from the same root as the German *ja*. That's why Sloanies all say "Oh, yah!" From now on, this Gnostic rock'n'roller's songs would have titles like 'Yeah' and 'Yeah Yeah Yeah'. And another fucking thing – the rock'n'roller could turn anyplace into sacred space through sheer will, the will to say "Tonight this youth club is a temple" and the willingness of local youth to suspend all disbelief and say, "Okay, for tonight, we'll accept that idea. Partyyy!"

I told my mother-in-law about John Sinclair and Lester Bangs and asked her about historical movements similar to the Detroit scene. Helen told me about George Gurdjieff's incredible troupe of dancers whom he had trained in the early part of the 20th century and I was all at once consumed. Gurdjieff was midway between a druid and a rock'n'roller. He had astonished the over-worldy New York society audiences of the 1920s with his troupe of controlled Dervish dancers. On stage, sometimes 20 dancers would be spinning wildly, jumping, backflipping and all in unison at such a speed that those who wrote about seeing it came away in shock. Descriptions tell of Gurdjieff clapping his hands and the entire troupe all but hanging in mid-air.

I was still straight out of Existentialist school and it came as quite a shock to learn of esoteric headspaces being caused by physical exercise. But it resounded within me as a truth and when I really thought about it I gradually remembered many times of my own life when mystical states had been called up through physical exercise. Specifically, from Christmas 1985 when I had speed-walked every day for 15 months with the intention of entirely redefining my body. This had occurred, but more, for my mind had been so similarly toned up by the need to focus on this necessarily new approach that I had been galvanised into my most artistic period for years.

But I had forgotten all this. Forgotten. When we had gone to make a new start in London, the weight of the city's umpteen relentless pressures had given us shark's eyes from day one, when our Karmann-Ghia collapsed after the journey from Tamworth. But I knew there must be no more forgetting.

Reading George Gurdjieff defined a feeling that had lingered un-named within me. That feeling was what Gurdjieff had called "Being-duty". I was awake. And in my first fresh new days of wide awake-ness, it struck me as extremely poetic that these events had been congruous to the forthcoming new decade. I now realised that the rock'n'roll spirit had clearly manifested itself in earlier movements of art and literature and dance. Even Harley Earl's Utopian vision of General Motors in the 1950s had been guided by the same heathen rock'n'roll spirit which had driven the Kelts to become a nation of charioteers. But, most of all, I felt that the rock'n'roll writings of John Sinclair and Lester Bangs had set me Righteously on a devastating road of truth.

Because of my long links with Long Island, I still had great pull with WDRE Radio, the former WLIR, which had recorded the Teardrop's crazy snow-covered mescaline night at My Father's Place. So I called Dennis McNamara, who was now head of the station, and asked him if I could come and play some of *Skellington*. Of course I could, said Dennis, and I was soon on daytime radio sending 'Robert Mitchum', 'Doomed' and 'No How, No Why, No Way, No Where, No When' across Long Island and Queens.

The fact that *Skellington* now actually "existed" as an artefact was going a long way to getting it accepted. Its legend and the mugshot sleeve made it a real pop-artefact in the *Fried* tradition, but I was impatient to get it released. I stopped off at Island Records to see Lori Soames and was given a loose-leaf book of John Sinclair's poetry entitled *We Just Turned the Beat Around*. Awlright! Then I showed the album to Donna Ranieri and enough people to cause a rumour that the record really existed, explaining that Island had not yet said no.

Then Dorian and I took Helen up to New England to see Cape Cod and Lisa St. John in Boston. The three of us descended upon the white sands in boots and black clothes, the women's white makeup and my wan-ness causing one athlete-type to announce sarcastically: "A day at the beach!" But Cape Cod was a Fairyland Police State which sucked universal big-ones. It had everything just the way it wanted and strangers could just keep moving, which we did until we hit Boston.

Lisa took us out to see her friend Laurie Cabot, the self-proclaimed Witch Queen of Salem. Laurie was a fabulous-looking and truly Gothic sexagenarian, with black and purple robes flowing and big hair cascading. The force of her personality was extraordinary and I loved that she had affected such a change in Lisa. That power was a warm and all-consuming heat which she now gave off in the healing form of an inner peace.

But, for me, our meeting with Laurie Cabot was a confrontational reminder of what I must do. For I must act like the Gnostic rock'n'roller acts. Was not my literary rock'n'roll hero Lester Bangs telling me in plain, uncoded words that even the non-poet could understand:

"There are glints of beauty and bedrock joy that come shining through from time to precious time to remind anyone who cares to see that there is something higher and larger than ourselves."

Lester, I'm swooning. I had worried all those years about having no voice, but Bangs now made me see that "the world's forgotten boy" syndrome was righteous after all. Through the filtered or Domino effect of behaviour-rubbing-off-on-others, the one who dances at the world's edge eventually infuses the spirit of even the most central figures of society.

I would never become a Witch.

I would never become a Druid.

I was already what I was. A Shamanic Rock'n'Rolling Inner-Space Cadet. Something that the world had already accepted.

And on our Virgin Atlantic flight back to London, I underlined Lester's plans for my future, set out on page 221 of his *Psychotic Reactions . . .*:

"It may be time, in spite of all indications to the contrary from the exterior society, to begin thinking in terms of heroes again, of love instead of hate, of energy instead of violence, of strength instead of cruelty, of action instead of reaction."

THE JOURNEY OF THE THREE WOMEN

"It is the best of all trades to make songs, and second best to sing them."

Hilaire Belloc

Lester Bangs says. John Sinclair says. Lester Bangs says. Lester Bangs says. I came back from America with a head so full of ideas that I had to get a notebook and clear my mind of all this stuff. My notebooks had always been temporary affairs, scrappy and unproud things. But now the pages soon mounted up and I began to write smaller and smaller to conserve the notebook.

Everything I read or listened to was part of this new search for wisdom. My love of George Clinton and Sly and Iggy was now completed by their literary equivalents John and Lester. Clinton could veil his message in humour by having his female singers wail: "There's a tidal wave of mysticism surging through our jet-age generation. All designed to take us to the stars." You could tell that even his fellow singers had a problem singing the words: "Free your mind and your ass will follow – the kingdom of heaven is within", but he still forced those mothers on and on. Aim high. Take the risk. Now, here was the same thing in rock'n'roll literature, and it was freewheeling and fucking enormous. As Harley Earl had said during his designing of the 1959 Cadillac: "Go all the way and then back off."

All through the summer, I'd been listening to a long Troggs tape which the photographer Donna Ranieri had made for me. All the obvious stuff was there, but more. Donna had hit me with their 1969 "heavy" single 'Feels like a Woman', which blitzed my head like the Glitter Band playing "21st Century Schizoid Man". Now, I came upon an extended piece that Bangs had written about the Troggs, casting them in the role of proto-Stooges, and Reg Presley as the Ur-punk shaman of every garage band in America. The twist in my head from the unfolding *Head-On* story that I had been writing all year was making me super-consciously aware of the cute coincidences and acute serendipities that maketh rock'n'roll.

Bangs set out his stall and I knew he was talking to me when he talked about people only getting One Chance to say their piece and how many are put off altogether by the "people who would tell you only fools even try". I knew that I was the very first Post-*Animal House* Utopian and that counted for a whole other value system. I had time now. I had years.

To see it set out in this long-form of a Bangsian Idealism, I once again understood that Cynicism was a form of virginity, a kind of closed-mindedness which allowed the traveller to visit places without actually getting out of his pre-conditioned self and experience it. The strait-jacketed perception of many cynical reviewers, said Bangs, would not allow singers and poets their metaphor, and therefore strangled artists' work before it had a chance to breathe. This all made perfect sense to me. My most open-minded act in 1978 had been to open-wide my punk aesthetic to allow Tim Buckley the use of the word "mama" for "woman". Once I had done this "benevolent" thing, a whole flood of new emotions tumbled headlong into me out of the fountainhead which was Tim Buckley and his Unfathomable Muse. That was precisely Bangs' point. If you allow the poet his metaphor, even if it's just Iggy's insistence on the right to wear peanut butter, you do your*self* a favour and broaden your *own* horizons.

As the late summer of 1989 turned into the early autumn, our household was awash with a feeling of energy and vitality which we had never known before. But sadness and joy and out-of-reach-ness were mixed in with the incredible rock'n'roll revelations which were coming my way.

I was despondent at Dorian's forthcoming trip to Greece with her mother Helen and Tante Mary, even though I had been asked along and chosen not to go. And as the days drew closer to her leaving, the more I grew freaked out and agitated. Wasn't Athens the world's third most dangerous airport after Hgobben and Fibil-Billia Coo? Who were Britannia Airlines and did they even have a stand at Heathrow Airport?

As she packed up her bags for the airport, I picked my guitar up and played a sweet and urban and immediate song which I would later call 'Madmax'. She laughed at my refusal to go, knowing in advance that I would have had a great time, but I equated travel only with rock'n'roll tours and had no interest.

And so, that September, my Greek American wife and her Greek American mother and aunt flew off to visit Greece and parts of Turkey, with the words of 'Madmax' ringing in our Tulse Hill living room: "I'll be fine once you are gone, of that I'm sure . . . it's just the anticipation I can't stand."

But the Journey of the Three Women allowed me time to reflect on this new turn of rock'n'roll events and I sat down one evening and wrote a song called 'Promised Land' in virtually one sitting. The lyrics on the cassette tape poured straight from my head and I grasped the idea that inspiration could be, indeed had to be, summoned by the rock'n'roller. All of the Teardrop's best songs had been summoned out of the ether, whilst many of my own had appeared out of nowhere in an almost complete state. This must be the way to write again, I decided, and called up Mike Joyce. "Can Donneye and I come up and play in your basement for two days?" And we were off on the newest of trips.

In Joycey's house, the songs just tumbled out as I called them. I suggested we imagine a Bolan song and sung a song called 'Head' straight off. Donneye launched into a huge bass-line which became a song called 'Leperskin'. I showed Donneye a melodic bassline which I had cannibalised from an old riff and some 25 mph old bland song became the 2 mph dreamout 'Las Vegas Basement'. By the end of the two days, all this was completed, plus 'Pristeen' gained its shape and 'Hanging Out & Hung Up on the Line' was put back on-the-One. Donneye and I returned to London with heads full of ideas.

Dorian was still away for another week, so Donneye and Rooster brought around as much recording equipment as they could lay their hands on. They set it all up in the shed, which I had first carpeted across the walls, floor and ceiling, and we started to work hard from the moment the tape machine was installed.

But first we had a major weirdout. In amongst the shed full of boxes we found the Head. This was the Head that Ray Falconner had given to Donald and me four years before in Birmingham. But while we had taken Ray's Head as a gift and subsequently lost track of it in our house moves, Ray had recently been killed in a car accident. Rooster was weirded out just hearing the story of our recording in it, but Donneye and I were totally cosmically off keel at the news. We buried the Head in a corner of the garden and slowly forgot about it.

At least the late September sun put us in a total stony groove and I suggested that we record something epically ambient and unfolding, something that would provide an insulation from the neighbours' noise. Dorian and I had always wanted a long, long version of Sly's 'There's a Riot Goin' On' but nothing had yet been recorded which even came close. "How about a 20-minute version of 'Poet' meets 'Thank You for Talking to me Africa'?" I suggested. Donneye's clavinet was up there with Sly's and I knew it.

While I got caught on the phone, Rooster and Donneye put together an amazing 24-minute groove called 'Cherhill Down' with just bass and clavinet over drums. During the track, Rooster became a monster bass player while Donneye's clavinet glowed. The effect was so helpful to that night's sleep that I became obsessed with recording two new albums. The first would be a collection of songs, whilst the companion would be long unfolding urban grooves.

I got a call from Island Video, which was putting out a compilation of all mine and the Teardrop's videos. They asked me did I want to be involved and did I have a title? I remembered K-R Frost's brilliantly crap suggestion *Copeulation* and heard them wince at the other end of the phone. I left Donneye and Rooster in the shed for a couple of days working on a 25-minute piece called 'Nearer to Ya', and sat with Andy Eastwood and Island's chief video director Fraser Kent watching 16 crap videos at the Island Video offices. I said no way to the inclusion of the 'When I Dream' video and the 'Sunshine Playroom' disaster, but was oddly unbothered by the others. Hey, I've got over them. Looking back 10 years, it seemed quite a relief to discover the songs were all good and the videos merely nothing bad. The Bangsian yearning to escape from all this time was temporarily held back, as I realised I'd been around a long while in rock'n'roll terms. If I'd got away with all this tosh for so long, imagine how good it could get if I knew what I was doing.

When Dorian arrived home, she told me that she'd been to the Naval of the Universe. The Journey of the Three Women had taken them around the ancient temples of their native Greece and down into Old Greece, which was now Turkey. Islamic calls-to-prayers and staring-eyed men had weirded the three women out at all opportunities, but Dorian had clearly had a life-changing experience. It amazed me that the three of them had gone through all that with me at home. But I had learned huge amounts whilst she was away, so we were both Righteous and hanging.

THE ATONEMENT OF WASP

"The ultimate art is created not out of navel-gazing one's personal pain, but out of a clear perception of the unsentimental fact that, though we will all die sooner or later, not all life foreshadows that assignation."

Lester Bangs, *Psychotic Reactions & Carburettor Dung*

Reading *about* George Gurdjieff was easier than reading the words of George Gurdjieff and his story read like a rock'n'roll biography. Gurdjieff had said that the problem with modern art was that it no longer reflected the universal, being mainly more of a celebration of each artist's personal neurosis. I wondered what was the rock'n'roll point of getting ever more individual until, like Mahler, I was ruined from lack of genuine human responses. Fraser Kent had given me a copy of the epic Russian novel *Master & Margarita*, by Mickhail Bulgakov, which both devoured me and immersed me. It was startlingly individual and like nothing else, yet its language spoke across the ages and called out to me as a Universal of Experience. It lay inside me forever and I knew that the rock'n'roll which I was forever seeking out also did precisely that.

George Clinton was the modern master of this Gnostic style, integrating wild wisdom into the most unlikely settings. In Funkadelic's gigantic 'Good Thoughts, Bad Thoughts', George Clinton was claiming that: "The infinite intelligence within you knows the answers." He was calling down to me. Now I read the words of George Russell, the mystic also known as AE: "There is an ancestral wisdom in man and we can if we wish drink of that old wine of heaven." These words were almost 100 years older and digging the same groove.

I decided that my rock'n'roll trip was Righteous like the old Detroit scene, not Self-righteous and pious like the Christians. If I could get the information from rock'n'roll, then so be it. Where there were gaps, I would look for the nearest thing to rock'n'roll – appropriately comparative esoteric literature such as Gurdjieff, because he was rock'n'roll of his time, mixing equal amounts of the physical and the psychic.

•　　•　　•

The rehearsals at Mike Joyce's had gone so well that we booked time in October to record in the Pink Studio, in Liverpool. I went to stay with my friends Chris & Johnny Mellor, Donneye stayed at a friend's house and Mike Joyce drove over every day from Altrincham.

The Pink was a weird studio with a balcony all around and a kitchen high up on that balcony. We set up ambiently and I put my amp in the tiniest cupboard, so that the separation between its distortion and my clean acoustic guitar would be accentuated. Then we whizzed through versions of 'Pristeen', 'Las Vegas Basement', 'Madmax', 'Uptight', 'Head', 'You Can't Hurt Me Any-more' and 'Leperskin'. I added tiny amounts of organ and we left. The sound was unusual and still forming, but informing me that I had work of a special kind to do.

In November, Ron Fair called me from Los Angeles, where he had taken a job as the head of Capitol's Film Music division. He was looking for a song for a Richard Gere movie called *Pretty Woman* and did I have a song that could musically accompany a prostitute down the street? That night, I wrote a song called 'Drive, She Said' on a small programmable Casio keyboard. I'd always loved the challenge of writing to order and Ron loved the dinky automatic street strut cassette demo I sent to him. Within days, Capitol were paying for Donneye, Rooster, Marcus and Joycey to gather together at Greenhouse Studios, in London, where we attempted to record 'Drive, She Said'. But within hours, four new songs had been recorded and 'Drive, She Said' had taken on a new and dark sound, totally akin to the rest of the songs thus far recorded, but quite the opposite of Ron Fair's brief. I lost the film gig, of course, but each new explosion of recording gave me strength to focus on my own vision.

Late in November, a guy called Cliff Charleton from the rock'n'roll publishers Omnibus Press called me with interest in *Head-On*. I was made up that the news of my writing it had leaked out and knew that this would give me leverage with Clive Banks and his anti-*Skellington* scene. That morning, Pete from Zippo had sent me a white label of *Skellington*, along with a chromalin full-colour flat of the finished artwork. I promptly assembled the artwork into a real LP sleeve and filled it with the 12 white label. Then I cycled over to Cliff Charleton's office with the copy of *Skellington* on my back.

The meeting went marvellously and, that day, I must have cycled past 10 people who commented on *Skellington* and thought that it was a finished copy. Journalists, photographers, my publicist Mick Houghton – everyone thought it looked amazing and some thought it was already out. By the next week, the music papers had started to vibe on the mysterious *Skellington* LP and Clive Banks was furious. But I had been talking on and off about *Skellington* for over four years, and it was an idea whose time had almost come. It was just a question of precisely when.

•   •   •

At the beginning of December, one of my big Japanese fans, Luna Lure, sent me a box of 1,000 cranes. The crane is a symbolic paper folding and good luck charm – 1,000 in umpteen vivid colours is an exquisite sight. Underneath the cranes was a pile of press from my Japanese tour. The headline for the belly-cutting incident read: "Atonement of WASP". It really pissed me off that the Japanese had perceived it in such a Christian way. The white male still holds considerable portions of his pre-civilised self in check every day of his life, but I hated to be judged on it by a similarly barbarian society such as the Japanese.

But while I was musing on all this, Rooster's Sandra called me looking for her man, and I thought of that barbarian out in the West End, celebrating his birthday with Captain Scarlet and Kev the 'Ammer. He'd been gone for 36 hours and Sandra was worried.

When Rooster turned up, he was unrecognisable. He, Kev and the Captain had taken on all the bouncers at the Marquee club, who had called in mates from neighbouring Soho clubs as back-up. Rooster, Kev and the Captain were then beaten severely and left to sleep it off in an alley. On waking, the three began to beat each other up and fought together as one single many-armed lunatic all the way to the cross-roads of Oxford Street and Tottenham Court Road. Stopping the traffic, the Captain passed out with a collapsed lung, leaving Kev and Rooster to battle it out. Kev smashed Rooster's head into a bollard, but Rooster aimed a smart kick at Kev as he went down, breaking two ribs. When they had awoken in the cells, Rooster was convinced that he'd been in a traffic accident, until police explained that they'd long been observing the Three Stooges' "progress" through Soho.

On December 7th, on the day we left for New York for our usual early Christmas break, a gunman who "hated all women" shot dead 14 female students at the University of Montreal.

I needed this year-end more than ever and Dorian's mother brought home loads of Carl Jung for me to read. Jung? Why should I read him? Helen told me that Jung was mystical and had spent much of his early life convinced that he was crazy. I should read him, she said, because I was a poet and he brought poetry and science together.

One of the books was a collection of Jung's best letters to friends. I plunged into a letter to Father Victor White and found Jung slagging off Aldous Huxley's *The Doors of Perception*:

"I should hate to see the place where the paint is made that colours the world, where the light is created that makes shine the splendour of the dawn, the lines and shapes of all form."

I was open-mouthed at Carl Jung's rock'n'roll. Even in his denial, Jung wrote like the spoken passage on a Hank Williams song – he was a believer.

In a letter to the critic Aniela Jaffe, Jung wrote: "I often ask myself why by far the most of critics are so unfriendly and unobjective. Is my style so irritating, or what is it in me that the world finds so offensive?" This guy thought and wrote in a life-changing manner, yet he was more hung up than me. He told Dr Dorothee Hoch that laymen did not want to hear about "the visions of Theologians, as it would merely make them turn green with envy that such an experience never happened to him". How I disagreed. Reading Jung empowered me precisely because of where he had been and what he had seen. For it made me feel that at least those places truly existed. If I hadn't been there, at least he had. It meant that those inner worlds I often escaped to were cautiously habitable. When the priests and the artists had lost their direction, we certainly all needed Inner Space Cadets like Carl Jung.

It reminded me of the incident between the black activist Adam Clayton Powell and his local preacher in Harlem. Powell insisted on driving a black Ford sedan everywhere as a representative of the people. But the preacher came to him and told him to buy a Cadillac. "Reverend, that's the Man's car," said Powell. "How can you ask that of me?" The reverend replied that Adam Clayton Powell driving his Cadillac through Harlem would be a symbolic figure of achievement to every black man who saw him.

I sat in Helen's apartment listening to endless 'Cherhill Down' and devouring the mystical science of Carl Jung. I read Jung's essays as though they were epic poems and they resounded inside me so deeply that a new notebook bought on December 10th was filled by the 18th with tiny writing to page 50.

On that day, Dorian and I met Deborah on 34th Street, between 6th and 7th Avenues. Deborah was Dorian's oldest rock'n'roll friend and one of her bridesmaids, and was a huge born-again Christian, to the point of being almost mystically pagan about it. Deborah told me that she had had visions of "my pain" and that I had been "possessed by the Devil and wounded in many spiritual ways". I adore Deborah Padova and we have much in common in terms of sheer belief, but this day I was moved by her words, even though I disagreed. That night, I wrote a note in tiny writing: "P.S. Interesting that Deb looked foxier than I've seen her in ages."

IS-DEAD MEETS ISN'T-DEAD ON THE ROAD TO SALVATION

As we hurtled headlong towards the end of the '80s, I felt that my sudden notebook syndrome was creating the Moment in everyday life. The '90s were upon us, only two weeks away to the countdown to the Millennium! Whoa. I covered my notebook in heavy white paper and thought about symbolic things to celebrate the '80s/'90s Changeover.

Pete DeFreitas was in my dreams at night and, on December 19th, I wrote:

"Pete DeFreitas died on the A51, he left the highway, the motorway, the expressway; he chose instead to 'burn up' once more through the ancient tracks, more interested in the journey than the destination."

On December 21st, Dorian and I travelled up to Boston, Massachusetts, to see our dear friend Lisa St. John and promptly cancelled going to the Solstice party which was our official reason for being there. Instead, the three of us hung out in her Charles Street apartment, where we talked and talked and talked. Lisa's becoming a white witch these previous three years meant that she knew whole new areas of source material for my quest and we needed to be debriefed by someone newly steeped in alternative ways.

Amongst the endless questions, Lisa found time to put Dorian and myself into a deep trance, which was in itself a revelation. It was a very controlled version of a state that I had unwittingly used many times – and always found myself in during recording. But here was a key, a formula to activate what I had previously had to wait around for and achieve by accident. And during the trance I found myself hovering over the Alvecote Mound in Warwickshire. This was a perfectly real other reality and, according to my notes written later the same evening,

"I fell out of the sky in a total Blaze of fire, like debris of an aeroplane falling to earth – I experienced this in both first and third persons. I fell almost to earth but bounced . . . on an invisible jet of water in a fountain; ever-changing in height . . . I was bouncing, spiralling, flashing and generally scooting all over the place."

I was shaken and surprised by the intense physical exertion of the trance state we had experienced and was radiant with what felt like molten light. But the rest of the trance is secondary to what happened next.

The three of us were hungry and highly excited by our event, and fired up to go out into the snows of Boston and find food. I put my coat up around my ears, put on my Homburg, a hat which I had inherited from my late father-in-law, and walked out first to the top of the huge flight of stairs. By the time I'd got to the very top, Dorian was right behind me and Lisa was hurrying, after having locked the door of her apartment. She said something funny to me as I took my first step down the stairs. We all laughed and I actually stopped moving, preparing to answer her comment with a humorous reply. Balancing myself at the top of the stairs, I turned around to my left to address both Lisa and Dorian with my right hand waving in the air and my index finger out-stretched. But at a point when my hips had swivelled around about 90 degrees, time suddenly stopped, restarted at Warp 2000 speed, and another "self" of mine burned down the stairs in a thick Shamanic burning of bilious cascading light. It was a draining and outrageous magnetic experience, and my notes read thus:

> "At the bottom of the stairs, I was aged 15. I had dreamed this precise event when I was asleep soon after my grandfather Dad had died. In the dream, Dad was standing on the stairs, his right hand up to his face, apparently roaring in pain and confusion. At the time, aged 15 and upset at my grandfather's death, I thought that he must have been stuck in purgatory and unable to get through to the next world. Now I know very differently. That was not a dream about my grandfather. That was a dream about myself."

The borrowed black Homburg, the glasses, the long black coat and my right hand raised dramatically across my face, all had conspired to shoot this thunderbolt through me this day. Because Baptist funerals allowed only the eldest grandchild to attend, and that was me, the whole affair would have left a great impression on my memory in any circumstances. I had interpreted the vision in the dream to be "Dad" standing at the top of a staircase, between Heaven and Hell, apparently roaring in pain and confusion. But now I understood that my 15-year-old self had had a powerful and extremely positive pre-cognitive Vision. For here I was, a 32-year-old man, today realising that future dream. Never again could the world be the same – for certain of its hidden possibilities had opened up to me like off-duty clamshells.

The effects of all these shadowy outpourings of Light were such as to make me gather up all of the previous year's events, stir in the year's 400 pages of autobiography and add an extra 70 pages of notes inspired by the Boston experience. Whatever these events were, they were NOT me. I had never been a writer or keeper of neat notebooks, yet I now needed to write continuously. 1989 had seen a change come over me that was utterly consuming and coupling me with the cosmos. And the fact that it was becoming such a massively physical experience intrigued me even more.

EPILOGUE

When we returned home, I visited Alvecote Mound on New Year's Eve. I took with me a spade and a huge rock of DeFreitas' amethyst which he had brought back from Brazil in 1987. I buried the stone in the summit of the Mound to symbolically charge it across the decades and also simultaneously welcome Pete's spirit into the '90s.

My Uncle Neil and his teenage son Brychan accompanied Dorian and me, and I had a beautiful vestigial Vision, not turned full on, more like a current of truthful gas that coursed through me. It said to me that I had a path: you are a practical choice for the Saying of Some Stuff because you've already had an existentialist career for 10 years. In another 10 Righteous years, the public can judge you against your first un-Righteous 10 years. If the Righteous-trip is in any way True, comparisons between the two periods will be as night is to day. Therefore you are useful to others.

I'd read Gurdjieff's ideas of "Being-duty" and the moral code of the mystic, and had long regarded Funkadelic and the MC5's White Panther trip of Community Enlightenment as the ultimate rock'n'roll aim. In my new state of mind, being useful to others suddenly seemed to be of paramount importance. And time just expanded and expanded like a piece of Christo unfolding across the desert.

On that very last day of the '80s, I wrote: "I am happy this day – people *will* understand me. I *can* wait a great deal of time."

The Cast of *Repossessed* in 1999 CE

CALLY CALLOMON is a very successful freelance designer/consultant and lives in Suffolk with his wife Jennie and their two children Astrid and Dylan.

JOSS COPE is a video designer for children's TV.

ROOSTER COSBY is disabled and lives quietly in Bromley, Kent, with his wife Sandra and son Johnny.

PAUL CROCKFORD is a millionaire boxing promoter.

ANDY EASTWOOD continues to travel the world.

JAMES ELLER joined The The, then went solo. He lives in Bridgend, South Wales, with his wife and two children.

RON FAIR My much-put-upon American producer is now an LA businessman.

K-R FROST is a kitchen designer to rock'n'roll stars and still plays live bass with me. He lives in north London with his gorgeous ex-pop star wife Jill Bryson and their daughter Jessie.

BARNEY HOSKINS Strangest of all, the journalist who nearly made me give up music altogether in 1984 turned out to be just another average hack. Hoskins recently used Jim Morrison lyrics for both the title and subtitle of his own book, the 200-pages-too-brief *Waiting for the Sun: Weird Scenes in L.A.*, then slagged the genius Morrison mercilessly in under eight pages of this all too slight tome. He is a most self-serving rascal.

BROTHER JOHNNO After the collapse of The Sex Gods, Johnno took various jobs at Island Records then returned to self-imposed obscurity in Liverpool. Liverpool-scene friends say his present whereabouts are unknown.

MIKE JOYCE finally got his just rewards from the two major Greedheads. Nowadays, he lives comfortably in Manchester with his wife Tina and daughter Fay.

PAUL KING went bankrupt and lost everything in the summer of 1990, causing me further stunning financial losses. But he helped me through the '80s and if I saw him I'd hug him.

LISA ST. JOHN continues to be one of our closest friends. She left the Salem witch-scene behind in the early '90s and wed my brother Joss in a marriage-of-convenience. More recently, she designed all the maps for *The Modern Antiquarian* and currently lives in Maidenhead, England, with new husband Kentucky Jim Bennett and daughter Skye.

DONALD ROSS SKINNER lives quietly in London with his long-term partner Alison Diamond and plays guitar for Capri Hearse.

TIM WHITTAKER This most mystical of Liverpool legends died of cancer in 1997 CE.

CHRIS WHITTEN After leaving my band, Chris joined Paul McCartney's group and had to play 'C Moon' for two years. Then he joined Dire Straits and had to play 'Walk of Life' for three years.

INDEX

"One of the funniest, bleakest rock reads you could wish for ... And throughout, Cope never portrays himself as anything less than a self-serving, childish, whinging half-assed failure. He's wrong, of course, but it makes for insanely funny reading."

Select

"Not only is the arch-drude perfectly balanced mentally, but he has the longest and most detailed memory (or the most extensive and exhaustive diary) in rock ... As a glimpse of the essentially pathetic but amusing whims and eccentricities that lie behind the screwed down hairdos of rock musicians, it's equally essential reading. And as a genital-warts-and-all diary of madmen, it is simply supreme entertainment."

NME

". . . an enthralling saga of bitchiness, betrayal and unrepentant debauchery. It guarantees a full day's top entertainment to fans and foes, for whatever your opinion of Cope's vocal abilities or sartorial style, there's no denying he's a very good writer. From the moment he stops the bullying caused by his success in a school production of *Oliver!* by kissing the ring-leader to his band's dissolution in shame and degradation, there is not a dull moment. As well as pushing back the boundaries of personal hygiene and sexual licence, and proving once and for all that hallucinogenics should not be treated as a primary food group, Cope thoroughly demystifies the creative process: 'It needed a refrain, so we tried to copy the chorus at the end of The Doors' "Wintertime Love".'"

The Sunday Times ('Books of the Year')

"The picture it paints of Cope as a crazed and self-loathing Blakean rocker, torn between his delight in the rock satyricon and his wish to hide at his parents' home in Tamworth, is an appealing one ... a marvellously bitter-sweet evocation of college days, through to the final lurid collapse of The Teardrop Explodes, a group whose joyous and celebratory weirdness was one of the best things about the post-punk era. It's one of the best, most vibrant memoirs of punks' culture-distorting force yet produced ... An eye-opening and indispensable read for any fan of Cope or The Teardrop Explodes, *Head-On* is also a fascinating bit of madcap social history: an account that anyone who remembers the claustrophobic hotchpotch of late '70s Britain and the subsequent ballyhoo of punk rock will relish."

Q

"Visceral, ballsy, bitchy, brutal, beautifully written.
Book of the year.
Made my heart burst."

Observer

"Buy it."

Melody Maker

Head-On was ITC Music Media Awards Book of the Year 1994.

HEAD-ON

Memories of the Liverpool Punk-scene and
the story of The Teardrop Explodes (1976–82)

JULIAN COPE

Thorsons
An Imprint of HarperCollins*Publishers*

Thorsons
An Imprint of HarperCollins*Publishers*
77–85 Fulham Palace Road
Hammersmith, London W6 8JB

The Thorsons website address is: www.thorsons.com

First published by Magog Books Limited (A division of K.A.K. Ltd) 1994 CE
Third edition Head Heritage (A division of K.A.K. Ltd) 1995 CE
This edition Thorsons 1999 CE

The chapters "East of the Equator", "More by Luck than Judgement, Here Am I"
and "Bad to the Bone at Club Zoo" were originally published in *Select* magazine
in September 1992, entitled "The Hitler Diaries".

10 9 8 7 6 5 4 3 2 1

A catalogue record for this book
is available from the British Library

ISBN 0 7225 3882 0

Printed in Great Britain by
Creative Print and Design (Wales), Ebbw Vale

Thorsons Commissioning Editor-on-the-moor
MICHELLE PILLEY

Corralled, Ratified & Correlated by
DORIAN COPE

Edited by
LIZZIE WAYNE HUTCHINS

Commissioning Editor Indoors
BELINDA BUDGE

Executive Editor-under-fire
PAUL REDHEAD

Jacket Melded by
JAMES ANNAL

Repossessed Jacket Photographs by
DONATO CINICOLO
KENJI KUBO

Head-On Jacket Photographs by
CHALKIE DAVIES
CAROLE STARR

Liverpool Scene Photographs by
HILARY STEELE

Thorsons' Marketing
JO LAL

Head Heritage Picture Research by
JOANNE WILDER

All Live & In-concert Performances Arranged by
MICK GRIFFITHS
CAROLINE REASON

Photographs in Plate Sections Computed by
LISA BENNETT

Press by
MICK HOUGHTON
MEGAN SLYFIELD

CONTENTS

For Dave Balfe and Gary Dwyer

INTRODUCTION

I wrote this book in the spring and summer of 1989, when I was at war with Clive Banks, the then managing director of Island Records. Clive hated my just recorded *Skellington* album so much that he would not release it. I went into a sulk and refused to record any more music until *Skellington* was out. I needed to beat my blues, so Dorian bought a simple word processor and I poured all this information into it as quickly as I could – information from such a strange and distant Other Time that I lived the whole thing over again. Only this time I could escape when the nightmare got too out of hand.

Only a month into the writing of *Head-On*, my dear friend and brother Pete DeFreitas was killed on his motorbike at Rugeley, Staffs., on his way from London to Liverpool. At Pete's funeral, the young policeman who was first at the accident told me that the only map Pete had on him was a scrappy A4 sheet of paper with a hand-drawn map and instructions written by me. I had drawn the map nearly five years previously, when Dorian and I lived in Tamworth. Pete was only 27, yet had been the drummer with Echo & the Bunnymen since 1979. He died only two weeks after appearing in the video for my song 'China Doll', killed on the same motorbike that he rode in the film. His death shattered me and appears to have precipitated the complete change in direction which my life then took.

Since 1989, the whole world has changed. But I've reread this book and it's as clear as I'll ever get about that stuff. And it's not washing around in my brain anymore, which is a Major-League Vibe! So here 'tis!

Julian – Wessex, April 3rd 1994 CE

DOLPHINS – ON THE BRINK OF A DOUBLE-BUMMER
St. Ives Bay, Cornwall, Summer 1976

We were way out in the middle of the bay when the first dolphin broke the surface of the water. As he slid between us, my brother Joss stroked his tail and got dragged along and we were laughing and exhilarated. Then his mate came cruising and for a short while we were alone, the four of us under the sun.

God, some things are so incredible, but so unknown that they'll always be scary. These long suede submarines just below the surface of the water . . . It was a trip. And swimming in deep water is a trip too. I don't mean 20 or 30 feet, I mean right out in the middle of an Atlantic Ocean bay.

I spent a lot of time floating in St. Ives Bay that summer. I was wondering what the hell was going on. This "A" level exam failure had spent the whole of his 18 years in Tamworth in the Midlands – it seemed like 18 years of faking it which were about to catch me up.

My parents had wanted me to go to Oxford University and become the new Charles Dickens. Anything less was inglorious failure. Anything at all, except maybe becoming Shakespeare. So I had wallowed in the vat of "potential" that all my teachers supposedly saw in me and hid that I wanted only to play music and hang around with the freaks. Earlier that summer, I'd walked into the kitchen to see my mother crying and saying to my father, "Oh, Alan . . . What are we going to do with him?"

Oh. My exam results must have arrived. God, these people drive me crazy. They brought me up on reason – that once you find the reason, you'll see clear round the world. Well, I tried to understand them. Even harder, to respect them. But something always hauled me back – and kicking kicking kicking.

And so that summer of 1976 ended. But St. Ives Bay held my answer. My parents drove me crazy, but I saw clear round the world. And it wasn't me that found the reason. No, I was shown the reason. And swimming with the dolphins was swimming *next* to freedom. . .

BETWEEN THOUGHT AND EXPRESSION LIES A LIFETIME

Tamworth was in the grip of a dangerous malaise that had hung over it since 1946. Like the town in the famous sci-fi film *The Bodysnatchers*, its population had been replaced by clones. They all worked together, frantically trying to keep Tamworth in those good old post-war years. It galled me that I couldn't get to them. And I knew there was no point in trying. I decided to just do my time and hope that they didn't get me when I was asleep...

Every week Hutch and I would scan Lisa Robinson's 'New York' column in *Melody Maker* for sightings of all these weird sceneheads who had beamed down from another planet. Patti Smith and Lenny Kaye, Richard Hell, Tom Verlaine, the Ramones – these aliens, skinny and freaky-deaky, unconscious, unbelievable artist non-artists tripped my head and stuffed my head with 10 million dreams of this and that. Records? Nere. Didn't have any – not by those people, anyway. Hutch had the Patti Smith LP but the rest of them scared us as much as they fascinated us. Not the music, but their SCENE ... And sometimes Iggy Pop was there. And so was Andy Warhol. And I felt that I should be there too. But how? I mean, everybody in Tamworth called me a queer – so that qualified me. But how do I get to be interesting enough?

Resisting your influences is like walking over a minefield. You do all you can to keep out of their way, but every so often one blows up in your face and you just have to embrace it.

At age 15, I was Andrew Marvell and John Donne.

Aged 16, I was Jim Morrison in those leathers on the front of The Doors' *Absolutely Live* LP.

And these past two years, I was T. S. Eliot and John Cale. And Hutch was Lou Reed circa *Berlin* and Todd Rundgren at any stage of his career. We both had girlfriends we adored and the beermonsters *still* called us a couple of puffs. Mind you, we had fallen into a particularly cissified Daryl Hall & John Oates period these past six months...

And now I was off to some crap Liverpool college full of "A" level failures trying to continue some kind of higher education no matter what. To Hutch, I was leaving in triumph – I was getting out of Tamworth and that was enough. But I was scared stiff. What if I'm Billy Liar? What if I just fuck up totally and have to come home? People knew me as a psycho in Tamworth, but what if? And so the summer of 1976 ended, the "what ifs" still ringing in my ears...

The drive up to college was like some high-speed funeral procession, my mother alternately wringing her hands in grief and gnashing her teeth or relating for the umpteenth time how wonderful her college life had been. Joss and I sat in the back of the car, as we'd done since we were babies.

"Still, he's not actually going to be in Liverpool, more on the outskirts. And

most of the other students are teacher training types, so we won't have the old problems."

It was true. C. F. Mott College wasn't in Liverpool, not even in fucking Liverpool. Yeah sure, it looked like Liverpool on my father's *AA Road Map of the British Isles*, but on closer inspection, it was in a place called Prescot about 12 miles out of the city centre. That was like being in Watford and calling it London. Or being in Walsall and calling it Birmingham. Or being in East Berlin and calling it fucking West Berlin.

Why was I never in the centre of things? Everybody looked like total hicks and I mean total – Fruit-of-the-Loom sweatshirts and real-ale badges were all I could see. September 1976 was an uncool place to be in any case, but this place? This was my new home where I would flower and grow? I felt more repressed at that moment than at any time I'd experienced before. I could feel the prejudices seeping out of every pore. I always seemed to be watching . . . nobody would actually invite me in.

We drove in silence out of the college grounds, my father following instructions handwritten by a lecturer. Just to rub it in, I was expected to live off campus. I had qualified late at C. F. Mott College, Prescot, which meant I was excluded from their scene – instead I was going to stay with some family I didn't know.

After about five minutes, it seemed we were driving even further out of Liverpool. We passed through streets full of building societies and old town halls.

"It looks quite nice, darling," suggested my mother, as a fog of all-pervading gloom swirled around the car. We followed the instructions on to the M57 and the signs for St. Helens. My God, we were miles out. We drove and we drove and, finally, off the motorway we came. The conurbation was set out in front of us "like a patient etherised upon a table".

The Coopers' house was like any other in Whiston: large, double-fronted and with an entry between every other house. At one time, each had a small garden but, for most, this was now concreted over, just a place for two dustbins and a bicycle leaning against the front window.

We stayed in the car whilst my father rang the doorbell and a gaunt Irish-looking man opened the door.

"Mr Cooper?" asked my father.

"Yes," came the reply.

My father signalled to us and we reluctantly got out of the car. Joss and I struggled with my bags, but my mother was already mooching around inside to see what her child was heading for.

The long hot summer of 1976 was famous at the time. And unlike previous summers, it had had the good grace to stretch onwards into September. All this made entering the Coopers' house even more daunting. From the sticky heat

in the car, Joss and I made our way into the dim dank corridor of a mausoleum. The house was excruciatingly damp.

Mrs Cooper, a thin Irish-looking woman with skin drawn tightly over her cheekbones, welcomed us in. It was a look I would become used to over the years in Liverpool and even feel comfortable with but, here and now, my upbringing felt more middle class and isolated then ever.

Up the wide and worn and creaking staircase, the handrail was a vicious mid-blue over what had been polished dark wood, visible underneath from bumps and furniture removals. At the top was a shaft of brilliant light. Joss and I turned right into the huge bedroom. There were three enormous old single beds in a row along the near wall. In the middle of the opposite wall, a large and filthy fireplace. To each side of this were jerrybuilt fitted cupboards, handpainted with one coat of white gloss. Inside the shelves were unpainted wood with dirty newspapers on top, held down by drawing-pins as a temporary cover. But temporary like prefab houses – made to last a month and still there 20 years later.

Mr Cooper was beaming great smiles at my father, who nodded and chatted sheepishly. Joss sat at the end of the bed nearest the window and looked out. The sun poured in, clouded with dust, like it does in old houses, and I knew that I was seeing the room in its very best light. This was as good as it got.

In Grandma Cope's house, the air was dry, even in the room which wasn't used. When it was cold, it was a healthy cold. But this house was damp. The kind of damp that makes you wake up in the middle of the night sweating, only you realise it's not sweat.

Mr Cooper finally and graciously left. He seemed like a nice man. Probably a nice man who knew the people in his bedroom were thinking the very worst. We heard his steps at the bottom of the stairs and all looked at each other.

"Alan, he's not staying here. He's going to catch pneumonia."

I didn't say anything. I knew I had to stay, at least for tonight. I'd do what I always did – let my parents get me out of this one. And they would, like they always did.

We sat around for about an hour, not saying much. Then Joss got up. His jeans were soaking around his ass and all down his legs. I knew it was time for them to go and I made it easier for them than I wanted. We all hugged and kissed and hugged some more.

"Don't worry, boy. We'll sort this out in no time," my father said calmly.

I stood at the top of the stairs and watched them. Normally I would walk to the car with them, then wave frantically until they were out of sight. Now, I just walked to the dusty Victorian sash window and drew back the net curtain laden with greenfly.

As they drove slowly away, I raised my arm to make one dramatic drawn-out wave. My hand and wrist brushed against the glass and cleared an oily and

dirty trail across the window. The car moved quietly out of sight and I was alone. . .

SING, OLIVER, SING!

I was born in late 1957 in my grandparents' house in South Wales. Deri was a tiny mining village whose houses and chapels clung tenaciously to the sides of its narrow U-shaped valley. Of all the steep, steep streets in Deri, Glynmarch was surely the steepest, two long rows of miners' houses which rose severely upwards at a 1 in 3 incline. And only two houses from the very top was no. 20, the home of my mother's family, the Todds.

I was a late baby. Very late indeed. When my mother had decided to go back to Wales to have me, neither she nor my father realised quite how long they would have to wait. For weeks, my father travelled back and forth from their home in Tamworth in the Midlands. Nineteen-fifties Britain had no motorways at all and the 120-mile drive could take five hours or more. So when they finally pulled me out kicking and screaming on Battle of Trafalgar Day, October 21st, everyone gave a sigh of relief.

"Good God," cried my still teenage Uncle Neil, "he's longer then Brian Price!" and ran out to tell everyone in the village. As Brian Price was the captain of the Welsh international rugby team and the previous longest baby born in Deri, this was no bad thing at all.

And so my life started amidst rejoicing and much love. And that was the way it stayed for 12 long years. I was brought up in Tamworth as a delicate gentle boy who loved his family dearly and wished only to please them.

And please them I did. I was Julian, the only boy in the neighbourhood with that name. And such a nice speaking voice I had, not like the rest of them.

When my mother went back to teaching, I spent every day with Grandma Cope, whom I adored. Grandma was as tough as old boots. She'd brought up my father on the widow's pension due to her after my grandfather had died and had run the NAAFI canteen in Two Gates during WW2. All the artillery and troop movements from London up to the north west would take the famous A5, the ancient and Roman Watling Street which cut through the heart of England at Two Gates, two miles out of Tamworth. And when Grandma Cope took me with her to collect her pension, all the old ladies at the Two Gates post office would say, "Ooh, doon't 'e talk loovly?" And Grandma Cope would beam with pride.

Then, when I was four, my brother Joss was born. And for a while I was a little resentful. Not too bad, though. *I* was the firstborn and I had the confidence,

so I was the one who got to sing songs for the family and get all the praise and the special comments. But I was a nervous child. When my best friend, Paul Hill, had his fifth birthday party, mine was the only mother there – I just couldn't bear her to be out of my sight.

I adored my mother. She was a goddess – so beautiful and perfect that other women paled beside her. Her hair was black and her lips were full and bright red and she wore tight sweaters to show off her fabulous figure. She hated birds and insects, so I hated them too. She drank her tea black and weak, so I considered women who drank tea with milk to be of a lower social order. And all the men loved her and wanted her, but my father had her and that made me proud as proud.

Then, on my ninth birthday, October 21st 1966, there was a dreadful mining disaster at Aberfan colliery in South Wales. The slag-heap which had been pronounced dangerous by countless safety officers finally collapsed and buried the village school. One hundred and sixty-six children my age were killed and the pain was doubly felt as Deri, my birthplace (and second home), was only four miles away from Aberfan and a very similar mining village. The TV cameras and the wailing of mothers and the desperation of so many mining communities thanking good fortune that it was not their disaster ruined my birthday for years. I thought constantly of those dead children and became a very serious child.

In photographs as a 10, 11 and 12 year old, I appeared prissy and earnest. Life was a dreadful and serious thing. My Grandfather Cope had died when my father was aged 11 and I feared that history would repeat itself unless God was thanked daily. I often stood for hours gazing out of the back bedroom window in my grandparents' house in Deri. I thought about the Aberfan disaster constantly and prayed that my father would not die. Sometimes it became like a sick obsession – I could hear little devils calling, "He's going to die, he's going to die," and I would shut my eyes tightly and my nice middle-class mind would scream inside, "Bloody God . . . Bloody God!"

Perhaps I would have remained that way, were it not for something that happened just a few years later. . .

It's April 1970 and I'm surrounded by boys much older than me, all chanting and laughing and pushing and prodding me. I'm 12 years old and I'm thinking I may have made a big mistake. Six months ago, I had been asked to play Oliver Twist in the school's version of the musical. I had accepted and I was a success. Well, with my parents. And with the girls at school. And the teachers. Yes, I'm the pet of pretty much everybody in the school. Everybody, that is, except the guys, the dudes, the bad-ass mofos, the people who mean shit. So now I'm standing in the middle of a group of heavy 15 year olds all chanting, "Sing, Oliver, sing!" Every playtime it's the same – tears are running down my face and I'm trying my best to block out what is happening, to go back inside myself, to remove myself from this rude spectacle and watch quietly and calmly from

within until these people perhaps get bored, realise that it's the same thing every day with this one and eventually go away. . .

But gradually I began to think differently. The bullying took its toll on me for a while until, one special, special day, I had a Blinding Flash. In the corridor and on my way to a geography class, I was again confronted by the whole "Sing, Oliver, sing" gang. Their leader walked up to me, pinched my ass and said, "Ooh, he's gorgeous . . . Ay, Julie-Anne, you're gorgeous. Tell us how gorgeous you are . . . Give us a kiss, Gorgeous . . . Give us a kiss, Gorgeous. . ."

So I did. In one blinding, earth-shattering moment, I threw my 12-year-old arms around his stupid 15-year-old neck, clung on for dear life and began to kiss. Kiss kiss kiss slobber kiss!!

In about 30 frenzied seconds, my weakness left me, never to return. The "Sing, Oliver, sing" gang stayed away from then on. *Everyone* stayed away. Keep back, he's weird.

Psychologically, I became so strong from that incident that it changed my life entirely. As time passed, I felt almost as though I had been saved – saved from an early death and freed to run like a crazy wherever I wanted. By the time I was 14, I was totally free-spirited. I would conform only when rebellion over a situation could cause total sleeplessness in my mother.

And I was lucky. For mine was not a free spirit which had to prove itself. There was now no pressure felt to smoke or to take drugs. I had learned how to turn the wrath of tough Midland kids with strong ugly accents away from this smiling blond kid called Julian. After that, I was under no pressure to lose my "posh" accent or to conform in any way.

Those were my schooldays and they confirmed one vital piece of information: the way people see you is the way you really are.

ANARCHY IN THE UK

Brian Simpson was about 5'10" and slightly overweight. His hair was blue-black and his eyes were blue. He was young Oliver Reed as Bill Sykes and young David Bailey if he was played by Mel Gibson. Brian wore a ripped black T-shirt and straight black-worn-grey cotton drill pants. His shoes were black brothel creepers with faded lilac laces and he had an earring in his left ear. Girls flocked around him and real-ale rugby types hated but respected him. He was the coolest guy in college and the first true punk I knew. . .

It was November 1976 by this time and I'd found a group of music heads to hang out with. I'd stayed at the Coopers' house only one night before a friend of my parents drove me out of that place. Now I was just kind of dossing around people's rooms while I looked for somewhere of my own.

A guy called Chris Goodson became very special to me. He had a room on campus on the cool bottom floor of Prescot Hall. We'd spend hours talking about Can and Faust. And he had The Doors' albums and Love albums, and stuff that I'd never heard from the mid '60s. I heard *Goodbye and Hello* by Tim Buckley and *Electric Music for the Mind & Body* by Country Joe & The Fish. Nick Drake, Traffic, Funkadelic, who scared me, and very cool reggae. Even the sleeves of his Prince Far I albums looked a real heavy scene.

And on that floor I met other fuck-ups and reasonable people. Opposite Chris Goodson was Martin, a heavy-metal boy. Next to him was Ritchie Blofeld, who had Jeff Goldblum eyes and rocked himself to sleep at night. Ritchie was a totally sweet guy, even though his obsession with losing his virginity gave everyone sleepless nights. Next to Chris on the corridor was Pat Hickey, a very quiet and gentle boy who was totally hung up on his weird looks. He wasn't weird looking, of course – he really had a serene countenance, but what use was that?

So anyway, we'd all play our eclectic music to each other and think how cool we were and I'd see Brian the punk walking in from his lodgings with the first Modern Lovers LP and the Patti Smith album. He'd wear Richard Hell T-shirts and home-made reggae shirts. All I'd read about punk was music press slag-offs and reviews of the audience violence. But Brian had *The Modern Lovers*?

I loved that stuff but didn't even know it was punk.

One day, Chris took me to Candy's room on the eighth floor of Prescot Hall. Candy James was a year older than us and had the coolest room I'd seen in college. We sat around and listened to *Overnight Sensation* by The Mothers of Invention and everything was very laid back and grooving.

Then, after about five minutes, Brian Simpson walked in. He was a good friend of Candy's and slept with a girl on her floor. As soon as Brian opened his mouth I was entranced by him. He was from London and had followed the Sex Pistols all summer. Brian hated the Seditionaries side of it and was already wary that the punk thing would be ruined. Don't call it "punk", Brian said, that was just a press thing. The true punks never used the word. Also, said Brian, you don't need all the bullshit accessories. Look at Johnny Rotten. Just plain ripped jeans and ripped T-shirts. Brian said it was all attitude and facial expressions. And you had to look like that every day, not just changing to weird for weekends.

We talked about three hours constant. I had a huge crush on Brian from then on. He was turning me on to something very big. It sounded like some huge mythology that I was desperate to be a part of. Brian went to his girlfriend's room to get the *Ramones* album. Hutch and I had heard it in Birmingham that summer, but then it had just sounded jokey. It had reminded me more of The Banana Splits than a rock group – just cartoony. Even the Velvet Underground had songs and some of their music was really beautiful. . .

But now the Ramones sounded different. In Candy's room with a new attitude and understanding it was brilliant. The Ramones *tried* to make everything sound the same. It was a big joke *and* an art-trip. In Tamworth, we all played like Can because it was so easy to fake. It never changed because they were confident enough as musicians to play the same riff for hours. But the Ramones were different – they repeated themselves because that's all they were capable of. And that was a big, big difference.

So Brian Simpson laid it all out clearly for me.

And after that, things were not the same. It was October 1976 and more was happening. I was still stuck in college 12 miles from Liverpool, but now I had allies. We'd hang out in Candy's room and listen to John Peel sessions every night. It was the first term so we all had shit to do. Merely hanging out in Candy's room made a Lou Reed fan very happy.

Late October, we took a bus into Liverpool. We went to a store called Gimbles and I got my right ear pierced. I'd decided on the right one as that was a gay sign and I wanted to piss people off with my new bad attitude. Besides, Johnny Rotten had his right ear pierced.

We walked into Penny Lane Records and I freaked. Rows and rows of the coolest imports and weird stuff. And on the wall were lines of hip 45s. 'Little Johnny Jewel' by Television, 'Gloria' by Patti Smith on French import, Stooges bootleg eps and '30 Seconds over Tokyo' by Pere Ubu. I wanted everything and I could not wait. We looked through every record sleeve and just glowed. I was finally in Liverpool for real and maybe I could really be cool one day.

I saw weird-looking guys hanging around – some rock'n'roll, but some just weird. Zombie-like and deathly pale. And I was a farm-punk, with an earring, medium hair and flares. I was so freaked out. Shit, I'm not a weirdo at all. Bloody hell. I felt like ... what was all that shit I went through at school for? What would the heavies at my school have done to *these* guys?

I still agreed with Brian's idea of dressing simply but my head was totally done in by those people in Liverpool. I left with an MC5 45 called 'Borderline', a Snatch single and the first Richard Hell ep. It was all American – there was no English punk. Not yet. Brian bought nothing. He said he was waiting for the Sex Pistols' record. 'Anarchy in the UK' was due out next week.

BLINDING FLASHES

Once I heard this stuff, there was no going back. For about a year after October 1976 The Doors sounded muso, the Velvets sounded reasonable and Can sounded like hippies. I put on Television's 'Little Johnny Jewel' and couldn't

believe that they had the nerve to record it. It made The New York Dolls sound like Yes – the bass had no bass, the guitars had no power at all and the singing was awful. In fact the whole record was awful. And epic. And completely brilliant and we never stopped playing it.

Candy's room became the home of this new scene and it would be the place I sorted myself out in the coming months. In one intense meeting with Brian Simpson, I'd been hit by a blinding flash: I was going to play punk music. I wasn't going to stay in some crap college. I was going to play punk music.

I always set great store by blinding flashes. They are those happenings you get all the time throughout childhood and your early teens. A blinding flash is that first instant when something that you had always accepted as a world truth was suddenly revealed as being false.

Those world truths hit you smack in the face when you're a kid, when things that seemed imperative can be destroyed by one smart Alec kid with an older brother or a know-it-all father. You know, you're arguing with your brother about what Thunderbird 2's maximum load would be and Steven Urbicki's dad up the road says it couldn't even fly in the first place because the wings are too small. Or you see a Minic International 500 electric slot-car racetrack on top of your parents' wardrobe all through December, then you receive it as a gift from . . . Santa Claus on Christmas Day. In a blinding flash, the world has changed. And it will never be the same again.

And now I wanted to totally quit education. Brian Simpson had revealed that to me in a blinding flash.

CANDY'S ROOM

In November 1976, I moved into Candy James' room. I'd been away from home only six weeks but already it felt like years. I was a crazy man away from my parents and loving every single minute of it. I forgot about Tamworth and times past, and I forgot about Jane, my girlfriend of three years.

Candy and I loved to sleep together. There was nothing sexual – I was still getting over splitting with Jane anyway, but Candy was getting hassled by a guy called Murphy Philips. With me in her bed, it made things difficult for him.

We'd fool around with make-up and clothes, trying to work out some kind of style. The New York scene was really cool but we couldn't have long hair like Patti Smith and Lenny Kaye. It had to be more of a statement. One day I

stood in front of Candy's mirror and chopped off my hair. It looked total shit. Not punky, not anything, but it was a start.

Then Caroline Coon's review of the Pistols' single came out. It sounded fantastic and the Pistols were like bedrock on every level.

We rushed home and played it.

And played it and played it.

Brian thought it was the best thing ever and I agreed. But inside I felt weird. I was disappointed, but I couldn't admit it. I wasn't cool enough in myself to say I preferred 'Little Johnny Jewel'. On Tony Wilson's *So It Goes* programme, before 'Anarchy' came out, the Pistols were brilliant and messy. On the B-side, 'I Wanna Be Me' was classic and shitty. But 'Anarchy in the UK' was too perfect.

As the only two punks in the college, things became a little strained. Brian and I both lived on the eighth floor of Prescot Hall, a girls' floor. We'd take baths together in the communal bathroom and wander round the corridors semi-naked.

One time, we were drying off and dancing in the corridor. In the room next to Candy was a fat pretty girl, and her two dumpy mates sat in her room all day. They both fancied Brian and me, but Brian most of all. So he danced up to their half-open door naked and pulled his foreskin back. As his dick started to grow he knocked on the door, which opened slowly.

I was totally into this, and amazed, too, as no way would I have been cool enough to do that. He stood there grinning and the three girls came slowly out of the room. One of the ugly friends made a grab for the dick and Brian flashed into Candy's room.

Another time I was having a shower and Brian was in the bath opposite. We were singing and then I started laughing so much that I needed to shit. I stood there in the shower and just did two shits straight off. The high pressure shower would break them up, I thought.

We carried on laughing and screaming, but the shit didn't move. It's weird really. You shit every day for years and years, but you never really know the true consistency. It never comes up until you're stuck in the shower with turds at your feet.

First I moved them gently with my toes to the plug-hole, then I so delicately began to tread them in. All this time, we were screaming and shouting, and girls wanted baths and I was up to my ankles in shit. The plug-hole was blocked and there was no way I could clear it.

"Candy!" I screamed and she came running. "I need your toothbrush."

Candy came running again, this time with her toothbrush. I prodded the shit down and eventually cleaned it all up. Twenty minutes of cleaning and there were no traces.

When we got back to the room, Candy said, "I worried that you'd clean the bathroom with it."

Brian and I smiled and I handed her the toothbrush. Candy was a sweetie.

DUDE RISING

After about a month at C. F. Mott, I noticed a girl walking around with the weirdest style. My friend, Paul Ellerbeck, said she looked like Brunhilda coming out of Valhalla. Her name was Hilary Steele and she came from Leeds.

She was bleached ash blonde with masses of make-up. Her hair was very long and she had all kinds of decorations in it. She had a strong Yorkshire accent and took no shit. When rugby students and the real-ale brigade laughed at her, she screamed her head off and threw things.

One day, Brian got talking to Hilary and she invited us to her room in Eccleston Hall. The room was brilliant and I freaked – she'd redecorated her room with real cool colours and had food and a coffee machine. On her wall was a picture of Johnny Rotten looking angelic. We hung out and had Earl Grey tea and biscuits. Brian and I never had money. We did, but it was all going on records.

I talked incessantly and felt completely uncool compared to Hilary and Brian. They were cool and I was a yokel – just a farm-punk. Still, I got on with Hilary better than Brian did and we started hanging out together.

There was no sex between us. It just wasn't there. But I loved being with a woman. I was missing Jane so much and I was proud to be seen with someone as far-out as Hilary. Or as hip. See, Hilary had been to Eric's. It was *the* Liverpool club. Brian and I had twice been into Liverpool but both times failed to find it. We'd already missed the Sex Pistols when they played. The second time, we missed the Stranglers. Now we knew someone who could take us there.

College was becoming unbearable and I didn't go to many lectures because there was too much going on. The drama classes were okay because it was the late seventies and all the lecturers were hippies. They'd just get us to pair off with a girl and curl up together in a corner. And drama classes had the best-looking trippiest girls.

I'd pair off with Mary Ozanne and we'd fool around all afternoon. Then class would end and we'd go to her room and fool around in her bed. I thought she was very great looking – pale, pale skin and very blonde hair. We didn't have any kind of relationship, really, just around drama classes.

Being one of two punks increased my popularity with the real snotty women. But Brian and I were objects of total derision if we ate in the canteen and hung

out in the college bar. We didn't have to do anything, just be there. I still looked like complete shit, but weird enough to piss off the rugby types. So Brian and I would neck with each other for the good of our cause and set fire to T-shirts we were wearing – until I wore a college T-shirt I'd nicked. When I set fire to that, the beermonsters threw us both into the biology pool, which was half full of broken beer glasses. I wasn't badly cut, but enough for me to feel martyred.

By the end of 1976 I was working towards some kind of look. All I knew had been learned from Brian and I found it increasingly hard to get anywhere on my own. I didn't feel right, but at least I felt that I was on the way *somewhere*.

I wasn't with any particular girl at this time – I wasn't interested. The Jane thing had messed me up inside.

There was a weird sweet girl called Julia who was out in lodgings. Candy was away for the weekend and had offered her room 819 without telling me. Anyway, one night I came back from Eric's and walked into Candy's room. It was about 3.30 a.m. and I was surprised to find Julia there. But I was knackered and I didn't care.

I got in bed. I'd met Julia before, briefly, and as the bed was a single, it was inevitable we were about to meet again. But in bed with someone else, I wasn't comfortable. I'd developed some dubious habits in Candy's room. Like I always pissed into an empty milk-bottle and when it was full, I would hold it out of the eighth-floor window and let go. I'd just tell Candy it was punk and she'd be into it.

But lying in bed with Julia, I felt edgy. She was tiny, a very small frame and this tiny ass. I wouldn't have been interested had I met her normally, but she felt great. Lying on our sides, facing each other, we started talking. She had a pout when she talked and that got to me. We were talking with our mouths touching, very quietly, and our tongues would touch the other's lips. It was about 4.30 a.m. My dick was rigid, as flat against my belly as my dick gets. Julia pushed her stomach against me and rubbed up and down with it. She had a ridiculous baby-doll nightie on and I pulled her on top of me. Now she was sitting across me and I put my right hand between her legs. I'd never felt any girl so wet. In the half-light, I tipped her onto her back and pushed my face between her legs. It felt as though she was foaming and she made little gasps as I lapped her up. She was way skinny and seemed more like a little animal than a young woman.

About a half hour later, she got up exhausted and shattered. She sat cross-legged on the bed, her hair soaking, her fringe over her eyes, no clothes, just a skinny waif. Then she looked up mid-smile and purred over to me on all fours, like a cat, sniffing around my ass and my legs. I was lying on my back, totally obliterated. My dick was no longer hard, it was just being there. And this little cat-girl sniffed around me then took my head in her mouth while

I was still soft. She didn't use her hands at all. It was all mouth and angles.

That night, Julia blew and blew until I couldn't come anymore and then we slept till two in the afternoon. It was the start of an oral affair. We didn't hang out together. We just gave each other head. Sometimes we'd meet in corridors and get too turned on and have to sneak to someone's room. It only lasted about two months, but it was so cool.

ERIC'S AND THE ORIGINS OF THE LIVERPOOL SCENE

I spent Christmas 1976 in Tamworth with my family. My mother took my appearance to be the end of her son. I spent the whole holiday with my brother Joss, who was still 15. I told him my cool stories and we would go out with a spray gun and paint names and slogans everywhere. I sprayed "Hi" on people's garages as I figured you couldn't be pissed off by that.

But Tamworth itched me. I'd come back too soon and I'd seen Jane and that did my head in. I felt like a kid again and I wanted to feel cosmopolitan, like I was beginning to feel in Liverpool. Jane knew I was coming home and so she went out with my friend Cott and screwed the ass off him because she knew my heart would break. And it did. And I went back to Liverpool and tried to forget it.

It was freezing. January 1977 in Liverpool was ice and wind. The Damned were playing Eric's in two days. I went to an Army & Navy and got my first drainpipe jeans for a pound. They were in a skip on the ground floor full of jeans and pink T-shirts. The T-shirts were 30p so I bought one. Back at college, I wondered what to wear. Brian lent me a leather jacket and at least I had drainies, but my hair was still shit. Maybe we'd be the coolest. Ho-hum.

Eric's club was in Mathew Street, opposite where the Cavern used to be. Next to it was a pub called the Grapes where everyone went. You'd go there before Eric's but we didn't know this yet. The Grapes was full of scene characters that I wanted to know. One day. But now I was a nervous farm-punk and everyone seemed a million miles away.

The other end of the street was Probe Records. I hadn't been in, though. We didn't even know this area until Hilary took us. The whole place was loaded with incredible atmosphere – really loaded. People knew their shit and that made it more scary 'cause I was used to weirdos but not ones who looked so weird.

We walked into Eric's and I loved it. Hilary looked right. Brian looked right. I looked shite. But it didn't matter and I didn't care. I just loved it. In Tamworth I was a weirdo, but look at these people. They looked off their heads.

Eric's was a basement, a real basement with bass that climbed round the walls. That first night, they played 'Great Stone' by King Tubby and I hung out by the DJ. I didn't speak right away as he was transfixed, a guy about 38 with old, old clothes and a moustache. Right after King Tubby came 'Tail Dragger' by Howlin' Wolf, then 'Roadrunner', then 'Ask the Angels' by Patti Smith.

Finally I plucked up the courage to talk to the DJ. He was Roger Eagle. He ran the club. He had been born only for music and I couldn't tell whether he liked or hated me. But he talked to me and that was enough.

There was a jukebox in the other room. The records were the coolest I'd ever seen on a jukebox. It had Bo Diddley, Captain Beefheart, 'Louie Louie' by The Kingsmen, '96 Tears'. It was such a trip hearing these songs blasting out across the bar, with the PA blasting a completely different song in the other room. Roger Eagle could do no wrong.

Hilary and Brian were talking to some weird-looking people. An overweight girl, who was poured into her black outfit, was with the faggiest guy I'd ever seen. Both of them had bottle-black hair, white theatre make-up and bondage clothes. The girl was really sexy and her name was Lyn. The guy was beautiful and he was Peter Burns.

In Tamworth, I'd been considered a faggot asshole, not because I was gay but because of my manner, my name and my accent. Now it was turned around. I looked at them spellbound. This was the Liverpool I wanted. This was stuff that turned my head upside-down. I'd spent my childhood thinking bad, bad things every day. It had made me sick and it had made me determined. But now, I looked at these people and I thought, Fuck, I was right all along. I should have gone further. I should have walked around Tamworth like these people.

Peter and Lyn Burns were the first real "scene" people that I had come into contact with. They were both 17 and I loved them right away. In 1976, anyone who dressed weird was, normally, just a Bryan Ferry head or a Bowie head, weekend dickheads with white suits and old Steve Harley albums. But this was freakstuff.

I felt so overawed the first time at Eric's that I just sat and smiled. Sure, there were 90% uncool people in the club, but that night I felt like the uncoolest. In Tamworth, I'd been hip as hell. In college, I could piss everyone off. But here? I knew it was gonna take me a long while to make any mark. I could never get close to Peter Burns' act. I couldn't try. All I knew was I would look different next week.

THE SHOP IN CASEY STREET

Peter and Lyn Burns had a shop in Casey Street, a cobbled street in the centre of town. Up three flights of stairs, above a printer's or something like that. They sold shit punk clothing and some okay stuff. The shop was decorated thus: huge black PVC dustbin liners all over the wall and ceiling. Very *Daily Mirror* punk. But they had this side to them and I thought it was cute. At one end was a rail of tatty coloured string jumpers and a few sub-Seditionaries T-shirts with slogans like "Fuck your mother and don't run away". Then another rail of leatherette skirts and pants. At the far end of the shop was a large armchair and a couch at right angles to it.

The psychology was incredible. You'd walk in to be confronted with all these clothes, then have to run the gauntlet of the Peter Burns barbed comment as you walked the full length of the shop to pay him. I was lucky – I already knew him through Hilary – but he'd reduce young punks to jelly.

"What are you buying that for? It's crap." He holds the offending garment at arm's length and looks round to the supply of Safeway's and Tesco's carrier bags. He plops it into a bag and scowls at the kid, a look of unremitting contempt. And all the time, Lyn sits in the huge armchair, knitting. In fact, it seems like Lyn spent the whole of punk knitting. She reminded me of the women who sat at the foot of the guillotine – but painted and decadent in a big sexy way.

Peter Burns would never wear clothes from his shop. He and Lyn would be out with us sometimes and they'd see someone wearing their clothes.

"Ha ha ha ha ha ha ha ha ha ha ha. The state of her," Peter would cackle, in his camp posh-Scouse whinny.

We'd meet kids in the shop we had nothing in common with, except for our attitude. A young girl called Cathy Lynch, with bleached white hair cut close to her head, like a pixie. And an outfit she had to be strapped into. She'd sit next to Lyn, staring straight ahead, being very sweet but always down. A guy would leave the shop to a Burns insult and Cathy would whisper a special, personal insult of her own to him. You'd never hear what it was and she'd never offer it. I really liked Cathy, but I never knew her well.

Then, about three years later, she got raped in her flat by two black guys. They locked her boyfriend in another room. After that, she didn't survive. One morning, a guy found her in Lodge Lane dead. She had jumped out of a 14th-floor window in the block of flats where she lived.

Then I met Boxhead. Boxhead was a Ted. He was 15 and he hung around the shop. I'd say, "Hey, Boxhead, why aren't you in school today?" and Box would say, "Oh I say, why are you not at school, Boxhead?" in the poshest, most upper-class voice he could think of. So that's how I sounded to some people.

If you gave Boxhead a pound and a Marks & Spencer's carrier bag, he'd fill it for you. Everybody did it. Marks was only 50 yards away and he'd come back with cool shit, like Ocean pies and real upmarket stuff. And he never got caught.

I liked Boxhead. He looked like one of those Scots footballers who play for Man. Utd – small and wiry. And he always made an entrance. If you were leaning over the counter in Probe, you'd feel the sinking of teeth into your ass, or your pants would start smouldering, and you knew it was Boxhead. Almost no-one else had that greeting.

I was starting to see less and less of Brian Simpson. As the punk thing expanded, it seemed he was losing interest. I felt like we'd exhausted our clique. I needed to meet more people. Even if they spoke shit, I felt I needed to hear it.

So Brian stopped coming into town. I felt really sad. This was going to be a trip and I wanted people I liked to be in on it. I'd phone Hutch in Tamworth and get him to come up and stay. My brother would come up and party all night. Eric's was now a two or three nights a week thing. I was still officially in college, so my parents were giving me money. We'd be in college in the early week, just hanging out in Candy's or Hilary's rooms. Chris Goodson was into the punk thing in theory, but he thought the look was crap. I played him the Television LP. I'd borrowed an import copy from a guy and kept it 'till it came out in Britain.

A lot of British stuff was already starting to sound like shit. The Vibrators and Ultravox were prime examples. They were just rock with a new name and sung in David Bowie's "European guy" voice. Bleep Bleep.

Hilary started going out with a guy called Paul Simpson. The first time I saw him I thought he was a big nance, with his cool '50s suit with acid burns all over it. But it soon seemed we had a lot in common. One day, I went over to Hilary's and this Paul Simpson guy was there. I'd seen him around but never talked – I'd prejudged him as a fashion punk. Anyway, Paul carried with him a classic photo of a group called Tiger Lily. This was Ultravox two years before. They had long Cockney Rebel hair and big flared suits. The singer, John Foxx, was still using his own name, Dennis Leigh, and they had a song called 'Monkey Jive'.

If you're surprised at my remembering all this shit, you have to understand that my entire friendship with Paul Simpson began with our mutual hatred of fake punk groups. So getting the goods on Ultravox started a long friendship. We all loved Patti Smith and 'Gloria' was by now an anthem. The *Marquee Moon* LP by Television was a classic and so was the *Modern Lovers* album. But British music still had miles to go.

It was April 1977. Hilary and I started hitching around to see gigs. London, Birmingham, Leeds. Everything was starting to get good.

BEING SUCKED IN

Candy's room was becoming a haven for the college trash. There were more art types than I'd expected and one day I arrived to find a guy in my bed, well, in Candy's bed. And he stank. "Um, um, er, Candy wasn't here so I let myself in. I, er, I, er, I live in Rainhill, my name's Paul."

As unprepossessing a sight as he was, Paul Ellerbeck was about to become a good friend and a big influence. He was tall and skinny, with the most upper middle class manner I'd ever seen. He'd start every sentence with "Um, um, er" and carry on some lengthy discussion, normally about art or music. He had a huge black portfolio with him and we soon discovered that we were both John Cale-heads. I'd seen Cale in 1974 in Birmingham. What an event! His whole group is grooving like crazy as the lights go down. Cale walks on in all-black leathers. His first solo tour ever. He sits at the piano, prepares himself and ... sings completely the wrong lyric, screams "FUUUCK" and rushes offstage. It's 15 minutes before he can be persuaded back.

Paul Ellerbeck was just a natural punk. He didn't try at all. In fact he didn't care at all. His hair was matted and fair and greasy. Not overgreasy naturally, just through not washing. He wore straight cream Marks & Spencer's summer pants ingrained with dirt and a sweaty T-shirt, ribbed like those high street store cotton and rayon tops. He had a foul raincoat, each pocket bulging with pens, chequebook and card, keys and cash. Also his address book, which was tiny and made tinier through forcing it into no space at all.

I told him about my quest for total hipness and he said he was into the same thing. Paul Ellerbeck looked exactly like Subway Sect's singer, Vic Goddard. Only he'd got there on his own. He opened his portfolio and took out *Another Green World* by Eno and a copy of *Trout Mask Replica* by Captain Beefheart – instant friendship. Back in Tamworth, only the coolest could take *Trout Mask*. It bore no allegiance to any other music but itself. All the hippies found it impenetrable.

In Candy's room, Paul got turned on to the whole punk thing, but from our angle. And that was the point – forever talking and honing the angle down. Every time you'd explain it to someone, your own head would get a clearer view as well.

For all that punk meant to us, in *Melody Maker* and *NME*, 1977 was mainly headlines about Gentle Giant gigs and the new albums by ELP or Genesis. Nick Kent had these blazing articles about Iggy, but most journalists were fucking up, glamorising the violence and missing the direction.

See, unlike most social phenomena, all the punk violence was directed at itself. People weren't hurting others – they were hurting themselves to get at others. That's why I dug it so much. It was just like my cutting myself at school.

It was saying, "You want to hurt me? Well, fuck you. And fuck your friends, too, because I can hurt me more than you could ever hope to." Ugly girls got into punk. Instead of waiting to become the bait of lager-swilling A-holes, they painted their faces like masks and said, "Yeah, I'm ugly, I'm weird looking. And isn't it great?" The school faggots got into it because it screamed loud into the ears of the rugby boys. It embarrassed the fuck out of straights just to know that there were people out there who were so totally alive that they needed to wear such weird shit.

And that was punk. Unconfident and undefined and incredibly powerful. It was weak guitar sounds and repetition. Laughing at itself way before anybody else could laugh at it. And Paul Ellerbeck was as much a punk as Brian Simpson or Peter Burns, but very, very different. And that intrigued me. I started to feel less like a farm-punk and more like myself.

Back at school when I was 15 we had a group. Max played guitar and Gary Norris played drums and I sung, as I couldn't play anything. We were doing a gig and we had no bass player, so Kevin Plater, a guy we called Spud, bought a bass and faked the entire gig. When it came to the bass solo in 'My Generation', Spud just ran his fingers up the neck and pumped his right hand at double-speed. Everybody laughed, including the group, but four years later I still remembered it as a monument of cool.

And so it was that Paul Ellerbeck did join us and become known to our scene. Only, because Paul never washed and always wore the same clothes, he became known as "Smelly Elly". And as I got to know Smelly Elly better, I noticed certain repellent sides to his character. Like he would arrive but never leave.

One time, in March 1977, I'd hitched all over to see gigs in London and Leeds and I was staying in Tamworth and trying to patch up my relationship with my parents, which was falling to pieces, and my mother wasn't talking to me and all this miserable stuff. Out of the blue, Smelly Elly called and needed a place to stay on his way to Liverpool. "Mmm, umm, uhm, er, Julian? I'm in a phone box in, uhm, Hendon. I'm hitching up to see you, so stay by the phone and I'll keep you informed where I am." And he was gone. I spent that night asleep on the couch next to the phone. "Hi, I've come 10 miles." "Hi, I'm nearly in Rugby." No-one would give him a lift. The next morning, I found Smelly Elly at a roundabout walking in the wrong direction. He stayed for three days.

Joss and my father were laying turf one morning when Smelly Elly finally surfaced and my mother made him a huge breakfast. He walked out into the garden and shouted to my father; "I'd give you a hand, Mr Cope, but I didn't bring any old clothes."

He just stood there stinking in these shitty rags. My mother adored him and gave him loads of my father's Marks & Spencer's tops and summer slacks. He went upstairs, had a bath and came down with some of the new stuff on.

He looked exactly the same. Exactly. Paul Ellerbeck had totally his own style.

Women don't much like smelly men unless they are really cute. And even then, they'd prefer them to wash. The hip middle classes dabble in dirt. They think dirty means no money, which is supposed to be hip. They're so fucking guilty, they think debasing themselves in squats is like helping Mother Teresa.

Both of my parents' families were poor, really poor, and all I got from them was cleanliness is next to godliness. We don't own anything but what we have sparkles. So when someone comes into your house and puts their muddy feet on your furniture, or eats like a fucking pig, tell them to get their act together and grow up. That's the middle classes. I know because I am one.

WHAT'S HIP AND WHAT SHOULD NEVER BE

It was spring 1977 and my hair was coming together slowly. I wore fucked and faded black or blue torn Levis, an assortment of home-made screen-printed shirts and shitty faded sneakers. I'd tried wearing a noose around my neck, but that looked like London affectation. I'd seen pictures of London punks with johnnies hanging from their ears and fake wounds. It may have started there, but the northern thing seemed far truer to the attitude. London was getting more *Rocky Horror* and less Stooges every day.

Probe Records in Whitechapel was becoming more and more a scene focal point. But hang ups still had everyone keeping to their own cliques. It seemed like every clique thought they were the coolest and didn't want to be found out.

Geoff Davies ran Probe. He was about 34 with a dead friendly face and the acid tongue of life. One day, we were just hanging around Probe and a young heavy-metal boy walked in.

"Have you got the new Rush album?"

"What?" said Geoff, affronted.

"Er, have you got the new Rush album, please?"

"Yeah . . . why?" Geoff leaned over the counter, glowering.

The whole shop stopped. We all looked down in embarrassment for the boy. But he carried on. "Er, could I 'ave it then?"

Geoff Davies surfed in on his reply. "No, you fucking can't have the new Rush album. Where d'you think you are, Virgin Records?"

The beaten boy looked quickly round and walked out of Probe. We watched him negotiate the steps, as a quarter of Probe's customers fell down them at least one time. Then we all looked back at Geoff.

Norman, Geoff's assistant, said, "Oh, Geoff won't sell stuff he thinks is shit.

He has to stock it 'cause of the deal with the distributors. If I'd been alone, I'd have sold the kid his Rush album."

So Geoff Davies was the coolest. Another person I had to know. And Probe Records began its reputation for not suffering fools gladly. In fact, it suffered many fools, but the kind that normally got kicked out of record shops.

Roger Eagle had played a compilation of New York stuff called *Live at Max's Kansas City*. He'd return to a song called 'Final Solution' over and over. In the quest for faster and faster punk, many people were getting blinded. But my idea of punk changed everyday. I decided to buy 'Final Solution', a big decision as it was only on import. I paid over the £1.50 and was handed this 7" black-labelled hip-beyond-hip slice of garbage-metal. I held it in both hands and studied the label. It said "Hearthan Records" in silver lettering and the group name: PERE UBU. As a drama student, I'd already read the plays. I'd already dug old Pa Ubu, the character who bustled around with the squeaky voice and the weird kitchen appliances. Alfred Jarry, who wrote the Ubu plays, looked like Charles II and his work seemed to exist in no particular time.

When I was back in Candy's, I played 'Final Solution' over and over and over. There were no real chords. The bass held it together and that was only with three notes. The music burned from the souls of numb-people. It sounded like it was from deep in the interior of some continent I needed to visit.

The other side, 'Cloud 149', was a different trip. At first, I mistakenly took it as a pop song. Of course, it wasn't, but following 15 repeats of the A-side, it at least seemed as though real humans had recorded it.

And so began my obsession with Pere Ubu and the new American art-fuck sound. Television and Patti Smith were gods in my eyes. If a group sounded as though they could play, I'd find myself switching off. I introduced punk to various people in precisely the way I saw it. I pinned the Pere Ubu single on the wall – it was a sign of hipness only I could enjoy. It even looked alien, no centre, like an old juke-box 45, and writing credits with weird names.

By late April, all the English groups had their albums out. They had either already fucked up or were getting big. The Stranglers were uncool, but I liked their uncoolness for a little while, and they did sound like an American West Coast group. Most people said The Doors, but Roger Eagle told me that they were more like The Music Machine or The Seeds. I knew The Seeds' 'Pushin' Too Hard' from the *Nuggets* album but I'd have to wait till later to investigate properly.

All that was left, now, was the Clash. The first single was 'White Riot' – just a tinny Glitter-stompf and football-fan vocals. I was disappointed. I expected something more. But I didn't know what. There was tremendous peer pressure to like the Clash. They'd been around for ages but played nowhere. The album came out mid-April. You had to buy an early copy to get the red sticker. Then

you sent the red sticker to *NME* and they sent you a limited 'Capital Radio' single with no sleeve.

It seemed like every week you had to dig deep to find cash for some record that no-one could be without and maintain any credibility. Peer pressure. All the bloody time. It put me off the Clash album. How could you enjoy something when you had to have the free accessory that took weeks to come? Besides, the Stranglers had done the same thing and been royally slagged off for it. Ah, but the Clash were different from everyone else. I could see that, but it still pissed me off.

The Ramones were God, of course. Without them we'd have all been stuck in flares still. In April 1977, they played Eric's with Talking Heads supporting. 'Love Goes to Building on Fire' was Talking Heads' debut single. Everyone dug it and the club was packed. Talking Heads just kind of shambled on and did their thing. Then came the Ramones. The lights went down and they were there. I was standing to the right, in front of Dee Dee. 1–2–3–4 Vvvv-rowwwmmmm. Into 'Blitzkrieg Bop', 1–2–3–4, into 'Beat on the Brat', 1–2–3–4, 'Surfin' Bird', 1–2–3–4, 'Now I Wanna Sniff Some Glue'. . . It was incessant. On record, the Ramones were cartoons. They had a kind of weak sub-metal Spector vibe. But on stage? Dee Dee just kept on coming with those 1–2–3–4s. He held the show together. The Ramones were a paramilitary operation, like funny terrorists. For 'Pinhead', out came a placard with "Gabba-Gabba-Hey". Now, only the Ramones could get away with this, and even they were pushing it.

After that, I had no real wish to play fast thrash. The Ramones had done it. All you could do was go faster. So what? Musically, it was fundamentalism. You add one guitar solo and the whole trip falls down. Of course, they never would – the Ramones were perfect.

A GUY CALLED LAWRENCE GETS HIS

One weekend, Eric's was not open and I was at a major loose end. I went into town with Smelly Elly and Hilary and bought *Nuggets*, a psychedelic-punk compilation of '60s weird stuff that Lenny Kaye had put together. We arrived back in Prescot Hall and got a scene going in Candy's room.

I went down to see Chris Goodson and the others on the ground floor, but they had gone to some disco in the main hall to cop off. Back in Candy's room, we decided we needed beer and so Brian and I went up to the disco.

Weekends in Studentland just blew my mind. Hideous hordes of alcohol-blind knobhounds stumbled around the campus pawing at each other. These

people never went into Liverpool – they stayed on campus getting pissed for the three whole years of their course.

One guy, a Welsh student called Lawrence, was obnoxious to me. He had been for a while. He'd call out in the canteen about faggots and what should be done with them. Then he'd comment about punk being a rich-kid thing. Even his mates thought he was a plank, but he mouthed off all the time. Ignoring him made it worse, but I'd only allow myself a terse "Suck shit, Lawrence" and hope he would shut the fuck up. I wasn't there enough for it to affect me but we got enough shit in the street without some half-assed student heaviness.

We walked out of Prescot Hall into the semi-darkness of the college drive. The building was surrounded by trees and to the side was a playing field. I had 'The Night Time is the Right Time' by The Strangeloves stuck in my head. I'd first heard Roger Eagle play it at Eric's and since it was on the *Nuggets* LP we'd played it over and over that night.

Brian was wearing his burned college shirt and black jeans. I had on torn faded drainpipes and a cotton long-sleeved shirt, originally white but screen-printed over with factory shapes in red and yellow. On the breast pocket was a cloth Lenin patch. I wore it with the sleeves rolled part way up and the shirt-tail out over my ass. My hair was natural blond and spiky with gel and hairspray.

Walking up the driveway towards the disco, I had a real attitude. A *real* attitude. I felt too good for the place and we were doing a favour even walking around. I couldn't wait to get out of there, but while I was here I was going to piss people off.

"*I want to be-ee with you, in the night time.*"

A girl called Lesley walked up to us. She was very good looking in a snotty, haughty kind of way and men enjoyed her presence but she had a way of scaring them off. She joined us as we walked up the road, then she whispered to me, "I've got suspenders on." I shifted in my jeans and we carried on walking.

The college hall entrance was awash with piss-head students doing their ungainly piss-head thing. I stayed outside and talked dirty with Lesley, and Brian went inside to pick up some beer. We waited around under the awning of the hall. It was one of those '60s buildings, all concrete and glass, and the awning was supported by two painted metal struts. They were rusty in places, where the paint had flaked off. I leaned against one of them and it left a brown line on the back of my shirt.

Brian was taking ages and it was cold out in the darkness. In the hall, the disco played 'If You Leave Me Now' by Chicago and I thought about the Chicago guy who had accidentally shot himself. Then out of the hall came Lawrence and his little gang of buddies, all ready for a cosmopolitan night out at the scout-hut. They walked towards us and I thought, Don't say anything, Lawrence, knowing his reason for living was to bait me. As they trooped past us, each one seemed to beam us a gawky, nervous smile – except Lawrence.

"Alright, Punky? Are yew goying to grayce us with yoor presence?" came the boorish Welsh drone.

I laughed. It was the way he called me "Punky". That was pretty sussed. It was the best put-down I'd heard. So weeny. I reminded myself to use it in the future. Then I hit him in the face. It was more a slap with open knuckles than a punch. I never fought. I was never in the mood to hurt another person. Except for tonight. I don't know why, but tonight was a perfect night and Lesley was looking good and I was in the mood to stoop to Lawrence's level.

His friends stood around while I beat his face and knocked him down. He got up and I grabbed him by the hair. I dragged him to the metal struts that held up the awning, then I pushed his face against one of them and began to drag it downwards. The rusty strut cut into his cheek and blood coursed down his face. Lesley was screaming but I'd just gone mad.

Brian came out with the beers and Lawrence was slumped on the ground. He had blood pouring out of his mouth. He looked up at me through slitted eyes and said, "You've broken my fucking teeth, you bastard." Shit.

Everyone said Lawrence was a twat and he deserved it and good job. But it wasn't a good job because he was in hospital on a drip. And his jaw was broken.

And then, one week later, came two letters in one envelope sent from my parents. The first was on college notepaper and said: "Dear Mr and Mrs Cope, Your son . . . blah, blah, blah . . . fighting and breaking students' jaws, etc., etc." It finished by saying if I was found on the college grounds at all, the police would be called. The second letter was from my parents, who sounded shattered. I did feel bad for them, but I'd had no intention of staying in college and this would probably get me up off my ass.

MAY 5th 1977: A MEETING OF THE MINDS

On Saturday May 5th, I was woken at about 10.30 a.m. by Candy James bearing white toast spread thick with butter and marmalade, and a mug of milky tea with two sugars. It was part of an arrangement we'd come to. She would get up and go for breakfast in the college canteen, then, before her first lecture, she'd bring some toast back and make the tea in our room. It was a routine many months old and I'd been able to continue it indefinitely because of my enforced low profile on account of the Banning Order.

I'd been at Eric's all Friday night. We'd got a taxi about 2 a.m. and he'd taken us as far as we could afford. Hilary was away in Leeds, so we'd been dropped off at the Old Swan. Smelly Elly and I had walked the remaining seven miles, freezing but happy. One time, I'd got the driver to drop me off near an

alley, then I ran off without paying. But Liverpool taxi drivers were too sussed to risk it often. I'd heard about one guy getting run down by the cab-driver he did it to.

I lay on my stomach in bed and felt around on the floor for the toast. I took a bite and put my head back on the pillow. Then I sunk back to sleep with my hand in the marmalade. About 12.30, I woke again. No-one was there, and no music played, like it usually did down the corridor. I turned over on to my back and licked the toast off my right hand. I then remembered that the Clash were playing that evening, and I walked into the shower room and hosed myself down.

I stayed in the shower about 45 minutes and gradually came around. I'd plugged the hole and the water was now midway round my ankles. I sunk down into the shower. The heat and the pressure of the water cascading over my head forced me to breathe through my mouth. I stretched up from my still-crouching position and switched off the water. I hadn't brought any soap with me, but I felt gooood.

Around 3 o'clock, Smelly Elly walked into the room. I'd sat for nearly two hours wondering what to wear. As soon as someone arrived, I'd always be galvanised into action. And, suddenly, we had to be in Mathew Street.

I stuck on a faded yellow Big Youth T-shirt that rode up at the back, my faded sneakers and these really tight black-cotton drainpipes that were coated with weird oily rubber. The stuff came off every time I sat down, but they were so cool. It was hot so I just took my shittiest jacket and a pair of shades that, I thought, made me look like Patti Smith on the inside sleeve of *Radio Ethiopia*.

We jumped on a no. 10 bus for Liverpool. I carried nothing but the jacket. The cloakrooms in Eric's were crap. People just used them to have sex in. And when the main group was on, the crush in front of the stage was like the seventh wave going over you.

Of course, Smelly Elly was dressed as usual. He never paid heed to where he was. He'd dress the same whether it was a dinner party or a week's holiday. He wore a long mac and a V-neck sweater, and he held a carrier bag full of shit that would fall out if he put the bag down. Every week it was the same – he'd get up to dance and next to his feet, on the dance floor, would be a carrier bag full of shit.

Mathew Street was awash with brand-new punk-rockers. People we'd never seen before. Weekend punks, greasers, bikers, Teds, even hippies with make-up and Union Jacks painted on their faces.

It was the first real event. It felt like the public had heard too. But that was okay, because it was for the Clash and they didn't really suit the underground. Somehow it was even better if young kids got into the Clash because they had this heavy moral side to them. They were like Cromwell's New Model Army

marching into battle. I loved the Clash when Strummer was angry, but when they occasionally became good time, I'd automatically bleep it out of my mind.

We walked around for a while then left the area. There were just too many people. We hung out in a pub up by the Anglican cathedral and waited for the crowd to disappear. Eric's had a "No under-20" policy, which was great. It was okay for us, though, as you didn't need ID.

About 9 o'clock, we made the mile trek back to Eric's. We waited on the line about five minutes, showed our tickets and strode down into the lights and the bass-boom of Eric's. At the bottom of the stairs, Peter Burns and Paul Rutherford were ensconced on their thrones, the territory of floor just before the main doors. They would sit there, sometimes with Lyn and their young acolytes, and slag people off as they entered the club.

"Ay, Julian, Hilary's been looking for yer," said Peter, then to a girl behind me, who was wearing a leopard-skin pill-box hat, "Ay, gairl, worrav yer gorra dead cat on yer 'ed for?"

Smelly Elly and I fought our way up to the bar. Hilary had been home to Leeds. The 'White Riot' tour was there the night before Liverpool. I heard her sweet Leodian strains: "Julian, I thought I'd never find you. I only got back just in time. They were brilliant last night, it was fucking brill. Oh, yeah, this is Kath, me mate I've told you about. And this is Sue, she's come up from London."

I smiled. Sue was really cute, black hair and a great figure. She had tits like Siouxsie Sioux and a washed out white T-shirt. Kath had just split up with her long-time boyfriend and was at her first punk gig.

"The Slits are fucking brilliant, too," Hilary continued. "I don't like Subway Sect, though, it's just dead monotonous."

I was trusting Hilary's musical judgement less and less as time went on. It seemed too early to be splitting into musical factions. But it was happening naturally.

In the other room, the main room, the sound system had shut off. There was a sound of cables being plugged into loud amplifiers. I ducked out of the conversation and made my way through the crowd to the front of the stage.

In plain black shirts and casual black pants, the four members of Subway Sect ambled, sheepishly, onto the stage. The drummer had a tiny kit with one floor tom-tom. The guitarist had a Fender Jaguar and a plain yellow armband. The bass player was totally anonymous and the singer stood with his back to the audience eating a sandwich.

Drums and bass started together, a slow-midtempo beat: Boom-bum-bum-bum, Boom-bum-bum-bum, Boom-bum-bum-bum. . .

Then a single tiny guitar note: Bow, bow, bow, bow, bow. . .

For at least a minute, the riff held steady, then the lead singer carelessly turned half round, the mike in his left hand. With his right hand in the air, he crushed the remains of the sandwich into the ceiling and began to intone into

the mike. It was almost puritanical. I had no idea what he was singing about, but it felt as though he'd been into the future and was telling us about it. There was no chorus. Just the same riff throughout. I guessed the chorus must be the bit where everyone sung the same word over and over. The song finished and there was polite applause.

The next song was the same. A kind of three-note Stooges thing. But still at 15 mph. This time the guitarist played a chord for most of the song, but when the singer muttered, "Solo" into the mike, the guitarist returned to the steady Bow-bow-bow of the first song. The songs all had names like 'Eastern Europe', 'Parallel Lines', 'Don't Split It' or equally cryptic titles.

I watched, spellbound, as they played. They were the first group I'd seen where the musicians were motionless. But each one was wrapped up in the concentration of his fragile two-note part. They never fell to pieces. They always started and stopped together. But you knew that if, for one moment, one of them lost concentration, then they'd be horribly lost.

After about half an hour, they walked off, heads bowed, to more polite applause. Wow, my head spun. These guys were my new heroes. I rushed back to the other room to discuss how brilliant they were with someone.

"Oh, I thought they were crap, Julian. They've no songs," said Hilary.

"Oh, uhm, I er, erm, I thought they were, uhm, er, quite brilliant, actually." Smelly Elly was beaming. It was his ideal music, I could tell that. He'd been doing his minimalist thing in some obscure part of the club.

A bunch of guys I'd seen loads were going crazy about Subway Sect. Actually, most of them were standing looking at just this one guy, who was going crazy on his own. This guy was a bit of a loudmouth. I'd noticed him in Probe before. But his face was so animated, I stood and gazed at him. He wore a black leather jacket and black combat pants. He had a Clash T-shirt under the jacket, which was zipped halfway. His hair was a natural black and gelled into a boyish quiff. In fact, everything about him was boyish. He was the most enthusiastic person I had ever seen. Beautiful. On his leather was a home-made badge. It said: "Rebel Without a Degree".

In the main room, a guitar cranked out an ugly funk chord. The Slits were on stage. I rushed in to see a row of beer guts leering over the crash barrier at the front. The four girls on stage looked like four skinny sheaves of straw tied with rags. "Show us your minge," called a beerhound to Ari, the singer. She goose-stepped around and booted him in the throat. It even got applause from his mates.

The Slits was pounding, scratchy and tom-tom heavy. The vocals were like harpies calling to each other. The drums always followed the riff. They had song titles like 'So Tough', and 'Typical Girls' and Ari-Up, the singer, introduced the songs in voices alternating between white-reggae girl and Nico speaking Wagner.

I really liked The Slits. I didn't love them, though. They were too alien to me and too hard. I couldn't appreciate them, they weren't sexy or confrontational. They were weird chicks that just existed. I walked back to the bar and sat down in an alcove.

It was an event. This was definitely an event. I'd been excited to see the Clash. I knew it would be a big deal, but it was just hitting me. I was getting off more on other people's anticipation, and there was a hell of a lot in the club at that moment.

What if the Clash were crap? All the people here would freak. Everyone held them in such high regard, the pressure was terrible. I worried and worried, then I thought, Shit, what am I worrying for? I just couldn't imagine what *they* thought. This scene was supposed to be the great leveller, but I felt just the same about these groups as I felt about Can or John Cale.

Groups like Subway Sect were even stranger. They'd stand next to you in the toilet and you'd look at them. You'd think, Do these guys know what they are doing? Like weird cults, they trailed into Eric's, did their diffident thing and left.

I thought deeply about all this stuff, while the Eric's party raged. I could see Pete Burns' lot lying all over the stairs. Hilary was at the bar talking to her friends Sue and Kath and Lyn Burns. And the Rebel and his cronies were heading into the main room. It was time for the Clash.

There was no intro, no music or anything. The Clash walked on and just went, "Fuuuck Offff!" It was so funny, I started laughing at them. They were totally brilliant. It was just as cartoony as the Ramones, but blazing with colour. And they all moved in rigid formation. Joe Strummer was a maniac, on his knees and bawling his head off at the front row. As he got lower, the guys at the front also went down with him and from behind you could see everything. It was this weird tableau, one guy performing to about four guys, all of them crouching as low as they could get.

I noticed something particular about the audience. You could get lost in it. You could let yourself get carried anywhere you wished. The crowd was like a field of corn, swaying and dipping. It felt so good, I sunk deeper into the centre. And the Clash whirlwind blew across us and took our heads off.

This group was like one of those old Eastern-European wind-up train sets. You turn the key, put the engine on the track, the engine scurries down and picks up a truck, then the two of them zoom into a depot and pick up their load, which is just some lithographed cylinder. Meanwhile there's a little factory mill in the corner that also started the minute you switched on. The doors open and inside is a click-click-click-click. You peer in and there is a two-dimensional tin-man sawing the same piece of tin wood endlessly. In a far corner a signal gantry stutters its stop, go, stop, go. And all this from one wind-up.

That was the Clash. Strummer was the engine and Mick Jones was the truck,

both zooming round doing their own thing but each picking up the crowd, zipping it round and then dropping it back down. In his corner, Simonon endlessly sawed the same piece of wood.

In the very heart of the crowd, I was a madman. I bounced up and down, up and down. The pogo thing was a bit of an urban legend. People danced that way because there was no room. It was only after people heard the word "pogo" that the craze started. I tended to do whatever the group on stage suggested. During Subway Sect, I stood still and watched. The Slits made you move, like a skank, but more graceless than reggae. The Clash, however, suggested unlimited nuclear war. You needed a dance that described fire-fights in the Mekong Delta or the napalming of homeless children.

I didn't overthink my thing, I just did it, spinning wildly and, in the confines of the crowd, using up far too much space. I was in the mood to be the guy who pisses everybody off, you know, the dickhead who starts the crowd rocking from side to side. Most members of an audience don't think they, individually, have any power. It's not true, though. You do what you want.

I bounced ass off for about 40 minutes, but I kept reeling backwards into the same guy. I didn't look around, but I'd feel his toes under my feet. Finally he began to push me. Oh, I thought, he's alive after all. I spun around and with my back to the Clash I bounced up and down on the spot and stared him out.

It was the Rebel Without a Degree. We fixed each other with a blank face. My blank face was better, though, because the up-and-down movement forced my tongue out, visibly reducing my IQ.

The confrontation was passing. I mean, I liked this guy I'd never talked to. I could feel my expression getting more reasonable every minute, so I spun back around to face the Clash.

I'd managed to create a minor space around me by putting my hands on my hips. This turned my elbows into lethal weapons and everyone kept out of my way. There was a sudden surge in the crowd and we all went flying to the left. As the crowd righted itself, I elbowed my way back to my spot, but there was an obstruction to my right and I had to twat the person next to me. I heard a girl scream. It was Hilary's friend Kath. I didn't know her at all. We'd smiled at each other, but suddenly I was whacking her in the face. I felt bad, so I hauled her out of the crowd and into the other room.

"Are you crazy? They're all maniacs in there. Stay in here and watch or you'll get killed," and I was off, piling back into the rugby scrum at the centre.

The Clash were epic. They were totally fucking epic. My favourite music was always the weirder shit, but this was so upfront and such hard showbiz that I fell for it pretty much all the way. They did loads of encores, made loads of effort, then they were gone.

The club burned on free energy for the rest of the night. All the right-on guys loved Strummer. All the women wanted to fuck Simonon. All the secret

rock stars wanted to be Mick Jones. It was just garble, garble, for the rest of the night.

I saw a girl I knew called Jane. She was a bit of a punkette and she'd cut my hair about a month before. We nattered our heads off near the bar and she said she saw her boyfriend coming over. It was my friend the Rebel.

"Hiya, Pete, this is Julian. He's at college in Prescot."

So we were finally meeting. His name was Pete Wylie. And he talked and he talked and he talked. He was great. I knew that, instantly. Energy surged out of him. It was the first time I'd ever met someone and known immediately that they were fated to get somewhere.

Wylie's mates trooped over to where we were standing. They were an unprepossessing bunch. There was a straight-looking guy with glasses called Jim. Another guy with very long hair whose name I didn't catch. And behind them stood two other guys. These two were just kids. One of them was called Dave Pickett. He had a friendly face, like one of the baddies in *Thunderbirds* – remember how they had concerned frowns moulded into their foreheads? He was a mixture of embarrassment at everything and "Fuck off, you're all crap". I liked him immediately.

The last kid of the group was a total dork. He looked like Joey Ramone – thick glasses and long shapeless hair and huge purple Jagger lips. He was a bit nondescript in places, but he had great detail. Like his white ankle-socks and his baggy black pants were studiously at half-mast. His sleeves were a little too short, but just enough for him to have made it a conscious thing. If I'd met him cold, I'd have dismissed him as a non-head, but he was Wylie's mate and he did cut it in a weird kind of way.

"This is Duke," said Wylie. "He wants to be Dave Bowie." The idea of this guy ever being "Dave" Bowie was so off its head that I didn't even laugh. And Duke didn't retaliate. He didn't seem to need to answer.

We stood around in a circle and ranted. Pete Wylie was solar-powered, no on-off switch, he started and then he just went. But he did listen too. The others watched as Wylie and I talked.

Then Duke spoke. His one sentence in half an hour. Wylie listened intently, agreed, and carried on ranting. Duke, or the Duke, as people seemed to refer to him, had the lowest, strongest Liverpool accent I'd heard. He didn't speak in sentences. Just interjections.

Wylie would talk about places they all hated. Duke would agree by simply saying "Scummy" under his breath.

Wylie would talk about groups they all hated. Duke would dismiss them abruptly: "Bunch o' no-marks."

Wylie would get on his Clash-as-gods rap. Duke dismissed his entire argument with a simple "No way."

It was a classic comedy act and they'd developed it without noticing. As an outsider, I thought it was brilliant.

That night, we talked and exchanged addresses. I wrote down Duke's address under "D", Duke McCool. Of course, his name wasn't McCool. I found out later that I'd just misheard McCull. But I thought of him as Duke McCool for quite a while after that.

They all lived with their parents. Wylie was at Liverpool University but never went, Duke was doing his "A" levels and Dave Pickett was in the lower sixth form.

"D'you want to form a group?" Wylie asked me, out of the blue. He didn't know if I even played anything.

"Sure."

"Duke's the singer. He's got a great voice. Ay, Duke, be Iggy."

There was no answer. There was no need.

"Okay, I'll play bass," I said. My bass was back in Tamworth and I was completely shit, but I didn't know if these guys were serious or winding me up.

By the end of the evening, we were a group. It was all Wylie's trip. He suggested Arthur Hostile & the Crucial Three. Duke said, "Sod the bloody Arthur Hostile bit off, it's crap." So we were The Crucial Three. Wylie went on about how legendary we would be, and Duke and I went along with him, as part of the in-joke.

It was 2 a.m. The place was closing. Everyone had left but us and we were about to be kicked out. I hadn't even noticed. I was just transfixed by my new pals. Hilary came up and I casually introduced her before she dragged me off into the night.

We walked up the stairs of Eric's and I was dizzy from the evening. The cold air hit us hard, but we had a lift home as Sue had a car. Hilary got in the front passenger seat, next to Sue, and I got in the back with Hilary's friend Kath.

We followed the one-way system through Whitechapel, then round past the Royal Court Theatre, round back routes and onto Prescot Road. I sat in the back seat, head against the window, and tripped out on the night's events as the car sped towards Prescot.

CHERRIES

All down Prescot Road, I watched Sue's reflection in the rear-view mirror. From my back-seat position, I saw the streetlights catch her face every hundred or so yards. I was drawn to pale bratty-looking girls and black hair. But she and Hilary were involved in heavy conversation.

I started to make conversation with Kath. Hilary had kept me informed of a running saga between Kath and her boyfriend, Daryl, in Leeds. She was always running away from him, then going back, then running again. He'd make her dress normally for a while, then she'd freak out and dress crazy in front of guys he wanted to impress. They'd started to sound like a real pair of planks. He'd just voted National Front to piss her off and she was trying to break away.

With all this information from Hilary, I wasn't too interested in talking to Kath, but I was a nice kid, so I did anyway.

Kathryn Cherry was nothing like I'd imagined. She was sweet and bright and hung up about her boyfriend. She knew it was all over, but it had gone on so long, she felt bad about the wasted time. I understood. I felt empty without Jane. But this new scene was filling all my time and making it much easier. We spilled our troubles to each other in the back of the car and were still talking as we pulled into college.

It was about 3.30 a.m. and everywhere glistened with dew. Kath invited us back to her room. She was in the same hall as Hilary and the four of us made our way down the corridor.

Outside Kath's door, Hilary was suddenly exhausted and said she was going to bed. Sue was staying in Hilary's room, so she left too. I felt intrusive and made my excuses to leave. But Kath was so down to earth, I couldn't. I didn't want to, anyway, we were having a good time and I was speeding off the adrenalin of the night.

The room was like Hilary's, really cosy and well-stocked. We put Kath's nightlight almost under the bed, so we were just shapes, and she made tea and granary toast with Lurpak butter. I ate about eight pieces as well as her Camembert. We had more tea and I finished a packet of digestives and a Kit-Kat. I never ate for hours, or days if I could avoid it. Money was far too precious to spend on the stomach. So every time I'd hit some free seam of food, I made sure it all went.

It was about 5.30 in the morning. The dawn chorus had started doing their thing and Kath said she wanted to change. She stood up and turned her back to me. She was wearing black riding-jodhpurs and an old tiny lace top. I hadn't noticed at first, but as the hours passed she was becoming incredibly sexy. She pushed the jodhpurs down over her ass with both hands and rolled over on the bed. The jodhpurs were scrunched up around her feet and they were getting her nowhere. I grabbed them, one leg at a time, and pulled them off.

She was gorgeous. Her hair was long and auburn and it had been plaited, very efficiently, around her head. Now it was late and her hair fell all over her face. She had on these tiny panties and her legs were very long. She bent down to pick the tray of food up and the lace top rode up over her ass. She wore no bra and looked so unrestrained.

Some women just change personality without clothes. Women who hold

themselves together in their finery can burst a man out of his pants as soon as they stop trying. I love that about women.

As the sun was coming up, we lay semi-clothed, each one thinking of a reason to touch the other. Finally, I said, "You have a beautiful belly," and ran the tips of my hand across her stomach to the top of her panties. She lay on her back and I was crushed between her and the wall. I was wearing just my black pants and more rubber was coming off onto her quilt. She sat up and said, "Take them off," then she pulled her lace top over her head and threw it across the room. She got up and we prodded and pulled till my pants came off.

We lay in bed touching each other all over and she felt so good. Her skin was very fair, almost white. I started to lick her all the way down her body, but when my tongue reached into her pubes, I wanted to stay in that one place for a very long while. I lay there and just lapped her up. I lapped and lapped and didn't get bored.

After about an hour, she manoeuvred me over to her long mirror and in the semi-darkness of 7 a.m. I watched her give me head in the reflection. . .

ONE DAY AND A HALF OF THE CRUCIAL THREE

Peter James Wylie, 19, stood at the gate of his Walton garden waiting for me to arrive. I'd given myself two hours for the journey as Liverpool had no sense of shape to me. If I knew a route, then I would use it at all costs. It took me a while to realise that the different areas were all joined together.

Walton is lots of 1950s suburban council estates. Nice roads with neat gardens and pleasant semi-detached houses. Roads spilled all over and nothing ran parallel with anything else. When I finally saw Wylie, I knew I'd been close by for at least an hour.

My bass guitar was back in Tamworth, so I'd borrowed a black Les Paul copy with four clumpy strings. We came through the side door and Pete's mother said hello. I liked mothers and was always as nice as they could stand. It was still strange away from home. I mean, it was great and all, but you soon forget how to act around adults. I tried to act the way I'd want my friends to behave in front of my parents.

In the living room was an amplifier with Wylie's guitar plugged in. The three-piece suite was arranged in a circle and Duke McCool was sitting reading. This was not at all unusual to me. But within weeks, I'd realise the enormous one-off quality of the Duke's presence here. In fact, in all the years I knew him, this would be the one and only time that he was earlier than me.

Duke McCool, AKA McCull, AKA Ian McCulloch, looked up at me, unconcerned, and said, "Awright?" He had thick, thick glasses on the end of his nose, as though he never wore them normally. I'd never seen him with glasses on before, but then, neither had they seen me in mine. I would rather screw my eyes up and squint like mad than be seen in public with glasses on.

Duke self-consciously took his glasses off. I thought he was preparing to say something, but no words came, and anyway, Wylie had started.

"So can you play? I mean, you don't have to be any good. Me mate Spenner is coming round to drum later. We'll set up all those boxes for him." He pointed to the corner of the room.

Yes, I could play. But everyone was nervous of doing his thing in front of the others.

"Sing 'Salomine Shuffle', Duke," said Wylie and launched into a kind of 'I'm not your Stepping Stone' riff. The amp was clanky and distorted. I thought it sounded great, but Duke sat there and said nothing.

Wylie carried on riffing away, walking around, smiling, doing his Joe Strummer stance. He strode over to me, all leather jacket and guitar, and stopped a foot away. We stared, smiling, into each other's eyes and I figured he was paying me back for dancing on his feet during the Clash gig.

Pete's mother brought the tea and biscuits in and we all lounged around, talking about music. Immediately, I felt tuned into them. It wasn't only what they liked; we disagreed on shitloads. No, what appealed to me was their unreasonable attitude. We soon realised that we had the Velvet Underground in common. But Duke loved Bowie and I thought he was shit. Wylie and I loved The Doors. "No way," said Duke. "Morrison? What a pretentious turd."

Duke loved The Stooges. He'd kill for Iggy. I'd only heard *Raw Power* and thought it was bad glam. But I'd read Nick Kent articles and Iggy Pop sounded brilliant.

We ranted on. I got The Dolls thrown at me, so I threw Television back. Then Patti Smith – and the New York scene was God. Sometimes we completely agreed with each other, other times it was more like a tournament. If I had never heard something that Duke considered important, he'd squint at me with his mouth open. He couldn't comprehend that I didn't know it. He seemed to be thinking, You poor sod.

I felt quite the opposite. I always felt jealous. Shit, I'd think, they've never heard this. And I'd watch the awe in their faces as the song unfolded before them, and I'd long for that feeling, and I'd be desperate for new music to blow my head clean off.

And so The Crucial Three rehearsal whizzed along. Every so often someone would pick up a guitar. Then we'd each describe the kind of thing we wanted, as not one of us could get close with an instrument. No-one wanted a punk group. And no-one was in a hurry. Well, we *were* in a hurry, really, quite a big hurry. But not so much that we had to form any old group.

See, the punk thing had this kind of built-in obsolescence. When I first got into the idea, in November 1976, I thought I was way too late. But new people were finding the scene all the time. Now we figured punk would be over in a couple of months. We wanted something new.

I told Wylie and Duke about Pere Ubu. Wylie was far and away the most open-minded guy I'd met. I told him about Can and Faust, and started in on my Ambassador of Kraut rant. We both got loud and crazy, and were dancing around the room, and I was shouting about seeing Faust in 1973: ". . . and they had two pinball machines, right, one on each side of the stage, and a block of concrete in front of the drums, and they . . . Oh wow, yeah, the pinball machines were put through a synthesizer. And one guy with an acoustic, and all these kind of arc lights or something. And they came on and just started with, have you heard 'It's a Rainy Day' off *Faust So Far*? Oh, it's just completely brilliant . . . wow . . . I've got to play you it, it's like just drums to start, Bom, Bom, Bom, Bom, Bom, Bom, and mad piano comes in, Jang, Jang, Jang, Jang, just building up and building up, and then the vocals come in, right, over the Jang, Jang, Jang, like," I was singing now, "It's a rainy day, Bom-Bom, Bom-hom, Bom-Bom . . . Sunshine girl, Bom-Bom, Bom-Bom, Bom-Bom . . . It's a rainy day, Bom-Bom, Bom-Bom, Bom-Bom . . . Sunshine baby . . . on and on and on. . ."

Outside, there was a face at the window. Spenner and I didn't shake hands, we just kind of acknowledged each other with smiles and grunts. It was a weird age to be meeting people. I was 19, Wylie and Duke were 18, and Spenner, at 17, was still at school. It didn't seem like we should start shaking hands for years. Spenner, AKA Steve Spence, turned out to be a friend and acolyte of Pete Wylie. There were many of them around. He was this friendly half-caste schoolkid who dug the hanging out. His arrival prompted us to play music.

We set up the boxes between the chair and the sofa, and Wylie said I could plug the bass into his amp. I had no leads and the only spare he had was about 18" long, so I had to sit on the amp and play sitting astride it.

Wylie showed me the riff to 'Salomine Shuffle'. "See, it's like . . . A, C, D, F, round and round. Sing 'Salomine', Duke."

The Duke remained slobbed out on the couch and Spenner and I lurched into this cyclical riff. Wylie joined in and drowned out my bass immediately. Duke seemed no closer to actually singing so Wylie started up:

"When I get zits, I use calamine
And when I need to dance, I do the Salomine."

It sounded terrible, but I didn't know them well enough, so we ground along until it just petered out.

But the Duke was suffering from a typical Liverpool malaise. "I don't wanna

35

do sod all, if it's gonna sound crap," he muttered under his breath. I was liking the Duke more every minute. We were total opposites. He refused to commit himself at any time – I just jumped in and thrashed about.

"Well, sing 'I'm Bloody Sure You're on Dope', then," hassled the ever-insistent Wylie.

"There's no bloody song," Duke looked down. "It's just a title, Pete. When 'ave I sung it, ay? When?"

I didn't want it to end in a fight. We talked some more, but the atmosphere got a bit weird and I said I had to go.

On the bus back to Prescot, I had to rethink. In the club, Pete Wylie was impressive and authoritative. He had all these girls and kids around him. I'd mistaken Duke for an acolyte at first, but Wylie deferred to him constantly. They were balanced in a weird way and I was baffled. The group thing didn't bother me. I'd had too much fun to be pissed off by that. It was the psychology that I was fascinated by – Wylie was outwardly very impressive, but hung up on the Duke's opinion. Duke was outwardly a dork, but didn't seem to give a shit. He seemed quite at home in his own space. I decided I liked them both a lot and hoped something would happen.

STITCHES

The early May weather was fantastic. This day, Smelly Elly had come into college very early, finished his morning lectures and had one hour and a half free, in which time we had decided to visit the Oxfam thrift shop in Prescot.

Candy James was away at her parents', which always caused me tremendous problems, as the room also became Smelly Elly's the moment she left. Many people at college believed that his flat was an urban legend – Smelly Elly was never off the campus. He slept anywhere. Wherever he left his bag of shit, that was home.

As I had done none of the coursework, I had a tendency to forget that other people could be busy. So now he was waiting for me and my lateness was eating into his free time.

I rushed in. "Hi, Paul, Keith's lent me his Dolls' albums." I cradled them in my arms, along with a large hairdryer and some shampoo. I'd borrowed these from Terry on the first floor and had to return them as soon as I was finished.

I put the first Dolls' album on and ran the hot water in Candy's sink. Then I stripped off my T-shirt and stuck my head in the basin. 'Personality Crisis' blared out over the whoosh of the water in my ears. Smelly Elly's muffled voice stuttered away in the background. "Uh?" I yelled and switched off the tap.

"Uh, uhm, I was wondering how long you'd be?"

"Er, I dunno, about five minutes. Why?"

"Uhm, we were going into, er, Prescot today."

Shit, I'd forgotten – and he'd been waiting ages. I bombed around the room and got my T-shirt and sneakers on, then I found Candy's keys and put them, with my money, into my jeans pocket.

"When I say I'm in lurve, you best believe I'm in love, L.U.V.," David Johansen barked, and The New York Dolls grunted into 'Lookin' for a Kiss.'

I took the hairdryer, plugged it in and furiously began to dry my hair. It took me about a minute, then I smeared gel all over and shouted, "Ready."

We waited at the lift. We waited and we waited, then we got pissed off. We'd hear the lift two floors below, grinding away, but it wasn't making it to the eighth floor today.

"Stairs," I shouted, and started to run down the corridor. Smelly Elly followed and we ran, almost in unison, to the fire exit.

No-one used the stairs at all. The stairwell was square and from the eighth floor, looking straight down, it was the same effect as that famous Beatles photograph where they're all leaning on the rail and looking over.

Over the months, I'd had the stairs pretty much to myself and I'd devised a way of kind of holding the rail as far ahead as I could reach, then vaulting down a full flight of stairs, cornering wildly, and repeating the same operation, only facing the other way.

The trick was to use as few steps as possible on the corners. The momentum of the jump was meant to propel you into each turn. Sometimes, you could work up a rhythm that would almost beat the lift, but generally I just used this route for returning the various stuff I was constantly borrowing.

Today, I had rhythm. I'd bounce and dance my way down every flight, I'd let out the vocal equivalent of a loud guitar crash-chord. Brang ... Then I'd inhale, during the cornering and the jump, and repeat the whole thing again. Brang ... Higher and higher I jumped, down I crashed, skidding and cornering like a bastard. The stairwell was flooded with brilliant sunshine. It was all glass and concrete, and the college playing fields dipped and lurched with me as I flew along. Above me, I could hear the Ellerbeck steps growing softer and I thought how good life can be...

Bam ... I blacked out.

"Aaaaaargh, aaaaaargh. Sheeeeee-it! Fuck, fuck, fuck."

I was lying on the floor of the stairwell, after smashing my head open on a jagged part of the ceiling. Smelly Elly and a girl called Ginny were looking over me.

"Aaaaaargh, uhn, uhn, uhn."

My right hand had automatically reached up in an effort to halt the terrible,

terrible pain. I had to moan. I had to let out long "Aaaaaarghs" just to channel the energy somewhere.

As I lay there, I was aware of people all around me. I must have been on one of the women's floors, and girls were crying and freaking out, except for Ginny, who was being nurse.

A girl I didn't know came rushing through the fire-door with a huge wad of stretchy bandage. Ginny grabbed it from her and started to fix me up. She took one end of the bandage and held it by my ear. Then she took Smelly Elly's hand and pressed it against both the bandage and ear. Slowly, she wound the material around, until it reached my bump. She eased my hand away, gently. Blood pumped out of my head and coursed down into my eyes.

"Shit, we'd better call an ambulance," she screamed, and all the other girls used this as an excuse to have hysterics and run around crazily.

Whiston Hospital is only about one and a half miles from college. It's a typical bunch of buildings, put up at various times, but I'd already heard of it. Scousers called it "Wizzy Ozzy". Anytime you want to create Liverpool slang, take the required word, knock off most of the ending and add "y" or "ie". For "football", Scousers say "footy". For "suspenders", they say "suzzies". *Coronation Street* was reduced to just "Corrie".

Anyway, the ambulance dropped us in front of Outpatients and zoomed off. We made our way through the glass doors and into reception.

"You'll have to register," said a curt-looking woman.

"Uhm, er, it's my friend, he, er, he's in rather a bad way."

"Yeah, well, 'e'll still have to register."

"I'll register for you," he said, stammerless and with some authority. "Er, could you get someone to take care of him? He's in great pain. I think he might be in shock."

Maybe it was the white coat. Maybe it's the role that people take on naturally when they are concerned. Whatever, Smelly Elly was galvanised into action.

A hospital orderly, pushing a wheelchair, was commandeered and we set off down a maze of corridors. Finally, we burst through double fire-doors into an enormous room. My head was bursting and my mind was playing tricks. I could feel my pulse battering away in my head. I kept thinking I was losing gallons of blood.

A young Indian trainee whisked me in for an X-ray, then she checked the wound. It started about two inches above my right eye and continued backwards and upwards.

"Is is bad, doctor?"

By now, Dr Ellerbeck was examining the wound. The Indian doctor was unforthcoming, so he described it to me. "Hmm. It's bad, alright. It's, er, about 4" long and it's . . . it's quite deep. In fact," he stopped. "Well, it gets, er, deeper in the centre . . . I can see your skull."

Alright, Paul, that was enough. I'd been getting into the idea of a wound. I always thought they gave you character, but this one seemed a bit over the top. The Indian trainee continued to clean and a doctor passed through the room on his way somewhere.

"Oh, doctor?" said the young intern.

"Yes? What is it?"

"This patient is requiring an awful lot of stitches."

He walked over and looked into my head. "How the hell did you do this? Fight?"

I started to tell him, in glorious detail, but he was in a roaring hurry. He called to the trainee, as he left, "You should be okay for the stitches. I'll come and check on you in a while." And he was gone.

The young intern began her task. First she cut and shaved the area around the gash, then she threaded a needle. She was hunched over me like a mechanic. The pain was terrible as the needle pushed into my skin. I'd avoided stitches until now. Shit, what did little kids do? I grimaced and tried not to buck around, but finally I said, "I'm sorry, but this is killing. Is it gonna take long?"

"Oh, how stupid of me. I'm most terribly sorry. I'll spray some painkiller on it."

What? She's just gone ahead and forgotten the painkiller? My confidence in her was visibly reduced and Dr Ellerbeck took control of the situation. He stood above me, administering the numbing aerosol every few minutes. Everyone was taking him completely seriously, including me.

Thirty minutes later, the doctor reappeared. "How did it go?" he asked, approaching the scene.

"Oh, I'm nearly finished, doctor." The young intern had started hesitantly, but now seemed to be doing a fine job.

"Good God, woman, when did you last do stitches?" The doctor was very angry. "Look at this. You've only put in 13. And they're all spaced apart. You should have done at least 20."

They began to argue. The doctor ushered the young woman into an adjoining room. It was a very one-sided argument and we were quickly forgotten. No way was I sitting through that again. And Dr Ellerbeck was obviously thinking the same thing. I slid off the couch and into the wheelchair. Dr Ellerbeck grabbed my X-rays and pushed me and the chair out of the room.

Down the corridors we sped. We saw no-one. Then we rounded the bend into reception. We slowed right down to a nice NHS pace and casually passed through the rows of waiting patients. A kid with a knee bandage opened the double doors for us and we were out.

The wheelchair bounced and grated across the gravel, the attendant on the gate muttered his greeting and we passed through. We carried on, as doctor and patient, until we hit the Warrington Road. Then we stopped.

And I laughed my bloody head off.

HIP IS HIP, BUT HIPPEST IS THE TRIP

I was sitting with my brother Joss in the new alcove that Roger Eagle had built in Eric's. Where there had been three arches before, Roger had filled in the centre arch, creating a deep alcove with room for a table and seats for about eight.

Despite my paranoia, I was beginning to fit in. Peter Burns had looked so strange when I first met him that I'd felt pressure to look that weird. But he just did his glamour thing, got on with it and left everyone else to figure it out.

Roger Eagle, conversely, was a 40-year-old own-nothing "I sleep with my records" type. And yet, except for the petty bitching and the hang ups, each night at Eric's was like a homecoming – and here I was with 13 stitches in my half-shaven head.

Joss was up from Tamworth for a weekend of wildness. I'd promised him this trip for a while. He was 15, just, and I was causing a rift between him and my parents. I'd not intended this at all, but things were so good up here that I was desperate to share it with him. As the older brother, I'd always felt it my duty to look after him. We were very close and I didn't want my absence to affect him more than was necessary. Also, as the manic cuckoo had finally fled the roost, Joss had begun to feel the subtle downward pressure of parents, who were determined to "get it right" with this one.

I had collected Joss from Lime Street station around 3.30 in the afternoon and we'd hung around Mathew Street and Pete and Lyn's shop in Casey Street. It was fun for me, just showing him where we walked every day, flipping through the vast and seemingly impenetrable record sleeves in Probe.

I loved to give him bits of clothing that I'd picked out over the weeks in honour of his arrival. He would wear them with pride in Liverpool, then sneak them home and keep them hidden. My mother had an almost fanatical ability to turn our everyday clothes into dusters.

"I'm sorry, darling. I thought you'd finished with that old thing."

So now we were in Eric's and it was empty. See, the only way around the "No under-20" thing was to arrive before Roger Eagle, then lurk in the shadows until the place filled up. That meant getting in around 8 o'clock, around three hours before things started to happen. Doreen was on the door and she let us in free. She knew that getting in free was the difference between going three nights a week or going once.

As we sat in the alcove, I was getting off on being with Joss. There is something so thrilling about introducing someone to your thing. Watching their eyes and trying not to spoil it for them by saying, "Get ready, there's a good bit coming."

Joss was listening to the Buzzcocks all the time. Also the Clash and the Ramones. Fifteen and sixteen year olds loved that music. My brother had immediately formed Tamworth's first punk group. They were a two-piece called The Flids – local slang for kids with the thalidomide syndrome. Joss played bass and sang. Another kid, called B. Smith, played drums and sang. They sat at home and wrote chilling hung-up middle-England psycho-dramas. It's true. They hadn't realised it, but that didn't make it any less true. There were fully detailed descriptions of teacher/pupil love. There were endless pronouncements about girls at their school. One girl that they hated, called Tracey Stanisford, was anagrammed to Dirt-Sore-Cat's Fanny. It was all very detailed and it was set over this weak, weak Stooges sound. Joss played bass like Ron Asheton. He had to, as there was no other instrument to support him. While The Crucial Three were bullshitting each other, The Flids were back in Tamworth, churning out an album's worth of material every week.

The hours passed. Paul Ellerbeck had joined us in the alcove. Tonight the Spitfire Boys, the sole Liverpool punk group, were playing. They were weak and characterless, but they were doing something. Paul Rutherford, a 16-year-old cross between Patti Smith and Marc Bolan, was the singer. He was very pretty and danced his ass off every Eric's night. Pete Clarke, a guy from St. Helens, was the drummer. Paul had started to call him "Budgie" as a put-down and the name had stuck. The guitarist was a no-mark, who people slagged all the time, and lastly, my favourite, was Paul Anthony Griffiths.

Griff, the bass player, was a heavy gay and hysterically funny. In Tamworth, you were queer, not gay. Quickly, I adapted to cosmopolitan Liverpool. From now on, I'd remember, queers want to be called "gay". Except Griff, of course. He called himself a "queer". "Read William Burroughs, Julian. There's nothing normal about us 'queers'." Again and again, the weirder angle would be thrown at me. Each time, I'd take it in, decide for a while and file it away. To compound his theory, that his "queerness" was okay, Griff wore a home-made T-shirt with the inscription "Sodomy and Gonorrhoea – A Bible Story". He was about three years older than us, and three years was everything, at that age.

Tonight, Pete Wylie surpassed himself. My brother, on being introduced to him, asked why he had the name "Cliff God" chalked like a logo on the back of his leather jacket. He told Joss that he didn't have time to paint the name on, as the scene was moving so fast he might be someone else by tomorrow.

That was the first night in the alcove. And that was where I would stay, from now on. My eyes were so bad that I couldn't risk walking around. Besides, that way, they came to you.

Dave Pickett, Joss, Smelly Elly, the Duke and I sat around. I showed them my wound. It worked well, in context with my clothes, and I felt quite well coordinated.

Griff was hanging out with us, when Hilary rushed up. "Julian, Eagle's kicked your brother out."

Joss had left the alcove to make the 10-yard journey to the women's toilet and been seized by Roger Eagle and lobbed out of the club. I went up to see him, waiting in Mathew Street.

Joss was okay. Griff and Paul Rutherford let him in through the load-in bay and hid him in the dressing room. He stayed there until just before the Spitfire Boys went on. Then he came out front to watch.

I couldn't believe it. Roger Eagle saw him, immediately. Out he went. Then shit started. The Spitfire Boys refused to go on. Roger Eagle refused to budge. I reasoned with him. No reasoning. Paul and Hilary screamed their heads off at him. Nothing happened. It seemed like an hour – it was more like 10 minutes. Finally, Roger relented and my bewildered young brother walked in – to cheers.

All the people who thought Eric's was full of posey planks could, now, fuck off. The camaraderie shown for a little 15-year-old kid was unbelievable. From then on, as far as I was concerned, they could all do whatever they wanted.

DECISIONS

Everybody was thrashing about in the dark, trying to figure out what you should be into, what you shouldn't be into, which people you could trust and which people were saying things just to look good. And everybody thought everybody else had the answer, but was keeping them in the dark, as some mean joke. And if that all sounds confused, it's because we were.

I was born to apologise. I was a product of middle-class aspirations. The middle classes apologise all the time and there was nothing I could do about it. I'm sorry, but that's all there is to it. It took no time, getting used to the Liverpool attitude – it was so hard-faced, I fell deeply in love with it.

The music scene stretched all around Liverpool, but we were still just fans. Only now were we starting real plans. I was hanging around with Pete Wylie and Duke and Dave Pickett. Most people seemed to know Duke as McCull. He was never comfortable with Duke, so, gradually, we weaned ourselves off calling him that.

The first Crucial Three rehearsal seemed like the last. We'd talk songs and ideas, but it got embarrassing when people wanted to hear something. I just got pissed off with saying things like, "Oh, McCull's got a brilliant idea for a song called 'Spacehopper'." I needed to jump in. I needed to jump right in.

But nearly everyone's group was still at the talk stage. Paul Simpson introduced me to Les Pattinson, the guy with the *Thunderbirds* head. He built boats in Aughton. At first, I'd thought Les was a bit of a latecomer, a fashion-punk. But now, he'd got his act together and looked off his head. He had a black

nylon polo neck sweater on, with hipsters and a swinging medallion. His hair was very neat and platinum.

"I've gotta group called The Geoffs – I'm Geoff Lovestone and the other guys'll all be called Geoff." Then he sung us some great unaccompanied songs with titles like 'You, Me & the Sea', 'Outer Town/Outer Space' and 'I Can Face the World Now'. He told us that the music would be slow and Doors-y and that Geoff Lovestone would preach his songs, like Elvis Presley doing 'The Battle-Hymn of the Republic'. I listened in awe. By the time that he was finished, I was very jealous of his imaginary group.

Wylie had a friend called Mick Finkler, who looked like Mick Jones from the Clash. He was 16 and he loved Wylie, and Wylie lived for Joe Strummer. So they would walk around being Strummer and Jones. One time, we re-enacted the sleeve of the first Clash album, standing motionless in the doorways at Eric's, with me as Paul Simonon. Smelly Elly said that it was very Gilbert & George.

Then one night, during the imaginary groups period, I walked into Eric's and watched a group of guys I vaguely knew playing a set of shifting, colliding, New York-sounding music. They were called Big in Japan.

I thought they were cool, so I talked to their guitarist, Bill Drummond. He was about five years older than me, very tall and good looking. He had a soft Scots accent and told me Big in Japan had formed two days before. They were all okay musicians and they had just explored, on stage, their riffs, evolving as they went along.

I was impressed. I could play music like that. I could play a riff all night. In Tamworth, I'd had a group with my friends Max, Cott and Gary that was based on the Cologne group Can. We were called Softgraundt. It was our German period. We had once recorded a 20-minute song called 'Bumschen' on Cott's reel-to-reel. We would just repeat a simple bass riff over a shuffle-beat. Max played these tiny spindly riffs and I would repeat the song title, like a chorus.

Yeah, if music went in that direction, I'd be the man for the job.

At college, exams were bringing chaos to everyone. They all staggered round under books and files, with hardly a smile for me and my enthusiasm. Hilary and Kathy Cherry were doing their finals and told me to buzz off. In Prescot Hall, I was banned from Candy's room. The atmosphere on campus shook me into action. June brought the search for next year's accommodation. I had to find a place to live and someone to live with. Nearly all of my hip new friends were still going home to mom and dad at night.

Chris Goodson, Ritchie Blofeld and I decided to get a house as close to Liverpool as we could find. But I had a student problem, a problem that was turning into a phobia. You see, the punk thing precluded your being friendly

with students. Students were perceived as spineless, cop-out, do-nothing hippies. Hippies were even lower than that, since they revelled in their obsolete clothes and stank of patchouli oil.

But some of us punks were students. Indeed, all the ones with something to say were still in some form of higher education. Pete Wylie was at Liverpool University, the very place that had rejected me. What do we do? Walk around pretending to be thick. And then there were all the people caught in the middle – Chris Goodson was hipper, musically, than almost anyone else I knew. He soaked up all the stuff I played him, day in, day out, then blew my head off with Fugs' albums. But because he wasn't interested in the whole trip, Chris was to stay removed from the everyday physical threat of dockers and football supporters. He didn't tune in to the hang ups that were being aired.

See, as a 19 year old, I felt like nothing was truly mine. So when I got hold of this scene, I was pretty damn determined to make it right. Just hearing Little Feat or The Eagles wafting down some college corridor became an anathema to me. It was the music of passivity. In Liverpool, we felt a camaraderie with anyone who said, yes, there is an alternative to this bullshit. We would rush to the aid of any geek being threatened. I was on a martyr trip and everyone around me had to be on it too.

I'd explained this to Chris, over and over. Sometimes, I'd come back with a real attitude about stuff and I was at pains to show him that the friendship thing would always trash the "hip v unhip" question.

There was a line already forming to get a room in our house. I crossed off all the hippies and the planks, and that left us with just Terry and Sue McKee. We were all happy with this and that was our blueprint for a happy unhippy household. We found a big townhouse off Prescot Road, about two miles out of the city centre. If everything went to plan, no. 7 Laburnam Road would be our new scene in the upcoming months.

MONG-OUT

"I can put it away for you, if you want. Put a quid down now and we'll keep it for you."

The rich, reasonable tones of John Atherton wafted round me, as we stood, face to face, separated only by the counter of Probe Records. I looked down again at the mysterious shrink-wrapped sleeve. Imports, I bloody loved them.

Staring out of the red and black foreground was an Alfred E. Neumann cartoon Nazi, smiling blandly. In the background, tiny cartoon Hitler-couples jived and grooved together. In Teutonic lettering around the illustration was the announcement: "The Residents Present the Third Reich 'n' Roll". John

Athey, as he was known, had taunted and tempted me with this stuff before. It was a collection of mid-'60s US Top 40 hits. Only, there was a difference. The songs had been reduced to shells and they all merged together. Sometimes, one song would feature a solo from a completely different song. And it was all played on piano, string synthesizer, percussion and the most wacked out vocals since the Muppets. It all sounded as though it took place in some obscure Tibetan monastery.

And why did I like it? I mean, shit, the tunes were all changed, the rhythms were changed. They'd even managed to turn 'Light My Fire' into a kind of 'I'm Yankee Doodle Dandy'. 'Gloria' was sung by a dying man clawing his way through some Dali-esque desert. It was happening in some ideal world, where the nerds, geeks and born losers were all running the show. If the characters in *Waiting for Godot* listened to Wonderful Radio 1, I believe it would have sounded like this.

"Get it," said Griff, who was with me. I mean, I had the money and all, but it would leave me without the bus fare. It was 32p back to Prescot. I'd be left with 12p, so I'd have to get the bus part of the way then walk.

Griff had no money at all. I'd bought him coffee already and he still had about 10 albums put away indefinitely. Shit, I thought, I'll buy it. When am I next going to have £4.79 to spend on one album? I handed the money to John. And we walked out and down the stairs of Probe into Button Street.

So, how would I get home? These things happened all the time. I'd go in the shop to buy something that I considered vital, only to leave with something far more vital.

I'd started leaving the standard stuff for Wylie to buy. He had loads more money than anyone else, as he now worked weekends in Probe. I was worried about him. I really admired his enthusiasm, but he had started to waste it on the Clash and Bruce Springsteen. I mean, the Boss?

Paul Simpson and Les Pattinson were listening to weird and interesting stuff. They had a friend called Will, who looked like Johnny Ramone, but loved Television and the Velvet Underground. Along with Griff and I, they were the most determined to try something. I liked McCull a lot, but sometimes the bravado and hang ups got to me. So when Griff and I hung around, it was a joy to buy the most fucked up music and read the most fucked up books, and look fucked up whilst you did it. And today, I was looking particularly retarded. In the charity shop, on London Road, I had found this disgustingly worn dog-tooth check thing that used to be a coat. It felt like I was wearing an old ironing-board cover. My head, my hands and my wrists stuck out way too far, and my still-scrubland hairstyle made me look like a real monkey-head.

After Probe, Griff showed me a weird little shop in Whitechapel. It was called News From Nowhere and it seemed like a kind of literary Probe.

We looked through the rows of heavy comics and the enormous bound art

books, and Griff read me some William Burroughs. Like your average "A" level geek, I'd tried it before, but as *Nova Express* was mainly cut-ups, I'd given it five minutes.

But now, Griff read an excerpt from *Junkie* to me. He read in book form. He read some more, then he pointed out a book called *Leaving the 20th Century* by the International Situationists.

"This is where McLaren got all the Pistols' sleeve ideas."

There was a photograph of a modern family at home. Each person or object was captioned: "Nice man", "Nice woman", "Nice dog", "Nice house". It just went on and on.

The bookshop had a reading area, so we stayed and checked through everything. You could make your own tea in the kitchen, if you paid 15p. We didn't.

It was getting late, but I'd kept putting off leaving. Griff lived a 20-minute walk away, in Gambier Terrace, up behind the Anglican cathedral. Finally, we left the shop and walked round to the row of bus shelters opposite St. John's Precinct. Griff waited with me and two minutes later, I jumped on an H8 Crosville bus, bound for Prescot.

If you ever take a bus from Liverpool to Prescot, make sure you avoid the H8. It takes forever and it goes through Huyton. No, you're far better off with the 10, 9c or 176. Straight up Prescot Road. Forty minutes and you're there.

But now I was sitting over the driver, upstairs, at the front of the H8. I was sitting amongst a group of old men, on an inside seat. I sat utterly still, with my right cheek occasionally against the glass. In my eyes was such a look of bland unawareness that I appeared to be making the old men around me uncomfortable. I couldn't have that, as they were part of my cover, so I backed off on the psycho expression.

I had got aboard the bus fully intending to pay the minimum fare, then pretend to fall asleep. But, luckily, the bus was full of pensioners. The couples all sat downstairs, very politely and quietly. But old guys together are still a gang. And they still like to go upstairs and they like their part of the bus to themselves. So they sat at the front, on the outside seats, and talked to each other across the aisle.

I had to almost force my way into my seat and as I sat amongst these old guys I realised that I could be one of them. Well, not one of them, I thought, I'll just be with them. For 12 miles I pretended to be the backward son of the old guy next to me. He didn't know. He and his gang thought I was just weird.

Every so often, the conductor checked us, but I was way too convincing. It wasn't my acting. It was my look.

Also, it was one of those days when you do something, it works out, and then you wish that you'd known in advance that it was going to work, so you could have enjoyed it while it was happening.

END OF TERM BYE-BYE

At college, everything was shutting down. The exams were over. We'd secured the house in Laburnam Road. And I'd formulated a plan that wasn't pretty, but seemed likely to work. I was going to forget college, get a group together, write some songs and make a living. I had already told all my friends. I had to do it or I'd be slagged off as a dickhead.

My biggest problem was money. My grant had been so pitiful that most of what I'd been spending in Liverpool was from my parents. I felt heavy guilt about that. I'd turned 19 the previous October and now I wanted to run my own life.

Until now, I'd been spending my folks' money on records and hanging out. When I felt poor, it was because I'd overspent on bullshit. I knew, in my head, that it was a fake situation and I could not take myself seriously whilst it continued.

The summer in Liverpool brought a state of limbo to the scene. People went on holiday, families were visited, the Spitfire Boys went on a mini-tour and ideas were left to simmer.

I decided that I needed a job. A summer job. Anything, really, so long as I could make some proper money. That way, come September, I could go on the dole and spend my savings on equipment and extras.

I looked around Liverpool for about half an hour. There were no jobs. Oh yeah, I'd heard about this before. For a while, I was stuck. Then the Cope family rescue-squad came to my aid.

My father and I were talking on a college pay-phone. We were trying to patch things up, as it had all got way out of hand. My mother and I weren't speaking – I was turning Joss into a delinquent, putting guys in hospital and hanging around with such weird-looking people that she couldn't sleep at night.

"Look," said my father, "come home and work. I'll find you a job. You'll only be here six weeks or so and she'll get some rest."

I said that it was a good plan and we hung up.

It *was* a good plan, but it still bothered me. I kept wondering if I'd ever be free of them. Everything my father did for me made me feel worse. It was my problem and it was my guilt. I'll do the job and shut up, I thought.

I had seen Kathy Cherry occasionally after the Clash night. There was no romance, but we were good friends and I enjoyed our sex. Also, she became far more interested after Hilary's friend Sue gave me a lift down to Tamworth one time. At the end of a letter to Hilary, Sue had written: "All my love to Julian. Tell him that the shag in the lay-by was perfect."

Of course nothing had happened, but a person is far more desirable if you think your friend wants to bed them.

Within a week, my father had a list of potential jobs. He phoned me constantly, describing each one in detail. I wanted money. That was the reason for doing it. I wanted money and the least hassle I could get away with.

The end of term was looming large. I had no reason to be there. I'd left my stuff at Laburnam Road, as Chris would be there over the summer. I said goodbye to anyone who was around and took a train down to Tamworth.

SEWAGE

And so it came to be that in July 1977, I did arrive promptly at Alder's Paper Mills, be-punked and ready for work.

In Liverpool, I was verbally abused hourly and physically abused occasionally. In Tamworth, there was almost no abuse of any sort. Instead, there was disbelief. They just stared, as if to say, "Why would he look like that?" I might as well have dressed in a Mickey Mouse outfit.

It galled me that I couldn't get to them. And I knew there was no point in trying. I decided to just do my time and hope that they didn't get me when I was asleep.

The morning sun made the 5 a.m. alarm bearable. Indeed, from the first day, it appeared that the early shift was the best. Between the hours of 6 a.m. and 2 p.m., I'd normally vegetate. I hated sunrise, just because I'd never seen it. It had never seemed hip to be into mornings.

I quickly settled into my routine. I would wake at 5 a.m. and dress quickly. Than I'd ride Joss's racing bike the six miles across town to the industrial estate where Alder's Paper Mill was situated. We would work from 6 a.m. until 2 p.m. with a 9.30 breakfast and an 11 o'clock tea-break. Then I'd get back on the bike and bomb home to my parents' house in Glascote. The rest of the day would be spent with Joss, working out our thing.

Alder's is an enormous place. It's a part of Tamworth's history and has been there since my father was a kid. There are five main areas and in the six weeks I got to work in all of them.

The largest building was the size of an aircraft hangar. It housed the pulp machine, which was as big as a rugby pitch. The pulp got sloshed in at one end, then it travelled through these enormous gears and vats, bubbling and stinking its way to the end, where it miraculously turned into unrefined paper. The paper was thick and soapy, like thousands of square feet of old bath sponge.

I got to know this machine well, as I was soon invited to clean the fucking thing. I'd been working in the quiet of the machine shop, as a mechanic's mate. The mechanics were all bikers in their late twenties. They'd have their bikes in

the machine shop, fixing them up and taking total liberties. One of them gave me his old leathers and I'd tell them stories and stuff. My engineer was called Terry.

Then one day, we were called over to the pulp machine. They had shut it down, and it burbled and stunk like a swamp. We walked to a grating about 100 yards along the machine. Terry removed it and we crawled on our hands and knees into the web of gears and along under the main flow of pulp. The heat and the damp and the stench . . . I had to breathe through my mouth to stop myself gagging. The only light came from the lamps in our hard-hats and I felt cocooned, as though in some vast mechanical rainforest.

Terry told me that the drainage was all blocked. We were going to have to climb into the main sewer. I directed my lantern beam at the manhole cover. It was covered with a thick layer of rotten pulp. Terry hacked the pulp away with a claw hammer. He hacked and he hacked until the cover was exposed, then he heaved it open and we started to choke.

Whoever came up with the phrase "bowels of hell" had been down that sewer. If you collected all your neighbourhood's garbage and stored it in your house for a year, then dug up all the dead from your local cemetery and cooked them on stoves around your house, after a while, it would start to smell as bad as this did.

We stuffed our hands over our faces and searched for our masks. Down there, in the gloaming, everything soon became covered with a thick film of sticky residue. We decided to forget about the masks and began the descent down the slippery ladder.

I passed down Terry's enormous canvas bag and followed him. The sewer pipe was about five feet high and cylindrical. A river of sewage flowed silently along and we stood crouching, our feet struggling for grip on the sewer walls.

Terry had hung his bag on the ladder. He took out two lanterns and gave one to me. Then we walked along the pipe, looking for blockages. The worst was in a large pipe about 20 feet from the sewer entrance. It should have been flowing freely, but nothing was coming out.

Terry hung his lantern on a hook by the pipe and we climbed out of the hell-hole. Back over in the machine shop, Terry weighed me down with shovel, scraper, rake and a long thing like a hoe. I was on my own.

For three days, I prodded and hacked and cursed the sewage out of the blocked pipes. By 9.30 every morning, I stunk so much I had to have breakfast on my own.

It was overwhelmingly hot down there. I'd rest by sitting over the sewage, my boots jammed against one side of the pipe, my ass against the other.

Then one day, I awoke to Terry's voice calling down the man-hole. I was missing breakfast. I'd fallen asleep and slid down into the sewage. My body had acted like a dam.

Around that time, the Stranglers had a song out called 'Down in the Sewer'.

It seemed to be advocating hanging out down there. I know it sounds glamorous, but believe me, it sucks.

THE VIKINGS

That summer, I spent the weekends in Liverpool or London. One time, my parents drove me up to the house in Laburnam Road. We took up paint and carpet and bedclothes, and we transformed this dingy little shitty attic into a cool pad in about eight hours.

One Friday night, the Spitfire Boys played in Birmingham. Hilary and Kathy Cherry came down from Leeds, and we all hung out on our own, in a totally empty club. That night, we all left for London. Kathy and I were alone in the back of the hired Luton van. We lay on Budgie's mattress and fucked all the way down the M1.

After that night, Kathy and I kind of fell into a relationship. She was looking for her Daryl substitute. I was trying to forget Jane. And, over the weeks, she came to visit me more and more.

As the summer stretched on, my moods swung all over the place. I was excited at the thought of being let loose in Liverpool, but my mother continually expressed her lack of faith in what I wanted. She'd cry and say she couldn't sleep for worrying. I tried to appease her, at first. But this kind of thing had gone on all through my childhood and I wasn't going to give in. No way. If I fell on my ass, then at least I fell doing what I wanted.

Meanwhile, back at the paper mill, I was making £75 a week. It seemed like a hell of a lot, so I spent shitloads on records and gave my parents £20 a week for board.

I was working on the Strachan-Henshaw, this huge polished paper machine that stretched, like a gleaming metal crab, across half the length of the main workroom. I told the three other guys on the Strachan-Henshaw that it reminded me of the Mare of Steel, the massive execution machine in the film *The Longships*. I loved the Strachan-Henshaw, I couldn't stop saying that name.

The radio played continuously through tannoys: Radio 1 at full treble. One day, Sag, an enormous biker guy who wore a headscarf, climbed on to the Strachan-Henshaw during 'Radar Love' and started to dance. Then I got up there and danced, and then Sag's brother Tommy, he got up and started dancing.

We had the coolest team. Sag and Tommy used to bait me about "punk rock". They'd name all these shit groups that had hits and were really The Faces speeded up, then they'd say, "They're all fuckin' shit." Then, they'd look at me and expect me to say, "No, no, you misunderstand, my friend, this is the new

music." But I never would. So then they were reduced to slagging off my appearance, which made me laugh, considering that Sag looked like Henry VIII and Tommy had his hair cut by the council. And they were the coolest guys in Tamworth. But you had to work with them for a month to find out.

SCHICKSA

My parents hated Jane. My friends hated Jane. Whoever she went out with after me, that guy's parents and friends would have hated her too.

See, she was an obsessive. An obsessive who wanted only to be with her man. While we were alone, she was happy. We were at peace. For almost three years, we would hole up wherever we were and pretty much ignore the rest of the world. Yeah, Jane and I were together for almost three years.

But now, it was August 1977. And I had broken off with her almost 10 months before. In that time, Jane had stuck, pretty much, to the plan she said she'd implement if I ever finished with her. She had gone out with two of my closest friends and fucked them both.

Now she was gone. My parents were ecstatic. My mother said, "Every time I saw that stupid pout, I wanted to slap her face." That's why I loved her – she was one of the snottiest girls I'd ever known. And will ever know.

Time was passing, but she stuck in my head. Sometimes, it was such a drag that she was missing all this fun. I'd remember all the cat-fights we used to have. She'd stand an inch from my face and just scream her fucking head off. That was the standard argument, till one fight at a bus stop. It went something like:

"Well then, Fuck Yewww, Cope." She's an inch from my face.

"Fuck you, too, Smith." I'm really matter of fact.

"Fuck Right Off." She's pissed off at my composure.

"Ditto."

"Oh, Fuck Off Cope, Ditto?"

"Yeah . . . Anyway, I'm going." I smile my blandest smile and turn around.

By the time I'm 10 yards away, she's screaming her head off: "Well then, fuckin' fuck you, you fuck."

I turn around, to stare her out. I'm still walking backwards and she's turned and started to walk away. Two people at the bus-stop are caught in the cross-fire of "Fuck offs". And it doesn't let up, either.

On that day, we continued screaming the same two words at each other until the other was out of sight. That argument was a whole art-statement. A verbal *Metal Machine Music*.

I'd think about these things. No wonder I missed her. I mean, we got into

John Cale together. And she got me into The Doors. And she was the only other person I knew who'd listen to 'Soup' by Can and enjoy it, and know it. My friend, Maxwell Eacock, used to put on 'Sister Ray' by the Velvet Underground, then work in the garden. He said he knew it was good, he just couldn't take it.

Anyway, Jane was out of my life now. For good.

Then, one weekend, it happened. My parents were away with Joss in Norfolk. Kathy was busy in Leeds. I had nothing to do.

On Saturday night, I went for a drink in the aptly named Tweedale Arms. I was never a pub-head, but I was with Hutch, a guy who had helped make school life bearable. And we were having a cool time and acting really camp and twee, in honour of the pub.

Then Jane Elizabeth Smith walked in. She looked great. Actually, she swanned in, like she swanned everywhere. She stared at me from across the room, then she walked over to us. Still staring at me, in a blank pissed-off manner, she started talking to Hutch.

The atmosphere was black. Jane wasn't listening to Hutch. She wasn't paying attention to either of us. I think it was a coincidence that she came in and now she was here, she may as well spoil our night.

Finally, I told Hutch that I needed to talk to Jane. The two of us left him in the Tweedale and headed off to the Castle Grounds, and to crying and misery.

It turned into one of those nights. A "what if" night. We wailed and hugged in a children's playground for hours and hours, then we took a taxi and sobbed all the way to my parents' house. Amidst tears and confusion, we stripped the clothes off each other and had really terrible sex.

And it was over. The whole thing. The spell was broken and we could get on with our lives. Jane agreed. Maybe we'd just needed to finish it properly. Now it was over. I love you, Jane, wherever you are.

7 LABURNAM ROAD

The summer was drawing to a close and the shit in my hair and skin was, finally, beginning to wash out. Tamworth had resolved many things, both in my head and in my past.

I had two trunks bound for Liverpool. One was full of all my records, from the childhood Tom Lehrer phase all the way to the clang of the Yankee imports that I'd recently accumulated. The other trunk was chock full of household necessities and family heirlooms. My Auntie Sheila had given me a slow-cooker.

"Just sling a few vegetables in it when you go out. You'll have a stew ready when you come back."

My mother had packed piles of old sheets and blankets, and Nana, my Welsh grandmother, had sent these beautiful hand-made quilts. They'd been in the family for years. One was 90 years old. I'd never give my teenage son anything that special. I'd be too worried about his friends nicking it for use in dirty sexual liaisons and its being dumped in a hallway afterwards, where a cat could sleep on it for six months.

My parents remained baffled by my plans, but the decision was made and they didn't want to fight me. Jane was finally purged from my "wants" list and my friendship with Kathy Cherry had taken over.

This last event was still concerning me. I was lazy in love. I let things drift sometimes and we'd fallen into a routine that I had instigated after the final Jane episode. Kathy was a sweet girl, but I wasn't going to get serious.

Meanwhile, I had the house to myself. This huge house that could be so beautiful, I thought. The rooms were dingy through years of student grime. No way was this becoming a student household.

My room had a skylight. I'd always wanted one for the garret atmosphere. The sun tore through the glass in the mornings, but I wouldn't cover that skylight. Dammit, I thought, people would kill for this room. So, every day for a week, I woke up at 7 a.m. dazzled by Mr Sun. Then very early one morning, in a fit of pique, I covered the skylight with tinfoil and banished the morning for good.

As my clean, fresh, white room was right at the top of the house, I figured maybe the entrance to the room should look as good. I painted the stairway almost down to the next floor, leaving a jagged edge on the wall. It was like a demarcation line. Then I found a roll of '30s stair-carpet for £3 in a junk shop. I painted the bannister the same green that was in the carpet and hung two of my grandmother's paintings on the walls of the stairway. I really got my ass in gear.

Chris Goodson arrived a week later. He walked into my room and would not leave. He said he felt dirty in the rest of the house. We spent the next days fixing his room up and soon I was jealous of him. Then we formed a group. We were called Hungry Types which, on reflection, is a shitty name, but suited a group whose line-up was piano, occasional slide guitar and household percussion.

The piano was already in the house. Actually, it was in the living room. This was to cause problems later for the others, as the piano and I became inseparable. I couldn't understand their reluctance to listen to me and called them Philistines. Recently, I found all the Hungry Types tapes. They were right. I sucked shit. A piano is also a beautiful piece of furniture and I might as well have been playing the three-piece suite or the chest of drawers.

Anyway, for two clear weeks, Chris and I hammered away on the piano, while I played him my ever-increasing Residents collection. I played him *Meet the Residents*. The jacket is a piss-take of the first Beatles LP. The music, however, is all piano and voices and, wait for it, what seemed to me to be household percussion. Perfect. In two days, Chris' old cassette player had recorded about six LPs' worth of unlistenable shit. One instrumental is 25 minutes long and has me playing the same riff over and over, while Chris "shapes" the music with "found sounds". At least, that's what I'd say if I was Dave Byrne. I'm not, so let's change that "found sounds" to "slide-acoustic with coffee-mug bottleneck and any bits of the tea service that he happened to pick up".

I played Chris the 'Streetwaves' and '30 Seconds over Tokyo' 45s by Pere Ubu. He freaked out. We played them over and over. This was the kind of music that I wanted to play. It was rock'n'roll underneath, but stripped right down and replaced by a kind of ambience of industrial noise. The Pere Ubu 45s had no instrumentation on the sleeves. What the fuck was it?

I had lots of "What's that?" going through my head.

Every time I played *Nuggets*, The 13th Floor Elevators would come on. "What's that weird noise?" everyone would say, about this kind of "dooga-dooga-dooga" sound in the background. But we just did not know.

Sometimes I would face stiff opposition from the TV addicts in the house, as the piano was in the same room. I'd be forced to use severe psychology and invite them all to play in the group for the evening. I'd hand them things that were virtually inaudible and every so often I'd tell them how much they were contributing. Placate, placate. Except, of course, for Ritchie. Like some Solipsist from Hell, he'd scream out demented lead vocals whenever we needed to rock.[1]

Kathy Cherry was staying with me until she found her own place. She'd started to teach mentally-handicapped kids. We got on really well and would go down to Eric's together. Laburnam Road was only two and a half miles away, so we walked it all the time. Hilary was now with Paul Simpson. It had started just before college ended and we made a good occasional foursome. Paul had the use of his mother's car, so through September and October of '77 we drove around Liverpool all the time and I got some sense of the shape of the place.

When Paul and Hilary split up, he got this one-room flat at 14 Rodney Street. It was £7.50 a week. And it was in the centre of town. It soon became a hang-out and port of call for both the cool people and the crazies.

"Smelly Elly's up here. He's been here all morning. He's walking round the

---

1 Hungry Types recorded a song entitled 'Oh, Dear Ritchie' which listed all the fine attributes as well as eulogising the downsizable downside of Mr Blofeld. Seven years later, the melody and music of this song were cannibalised for the *Fried* LP's 'Search Party'.

flat, hitting vases and shit with a biro. It just goes 'clunk', and then he says, 'Uhm, interesting sound,' to himself."

I knew how to deal with Mr Ellerbeck. We left him upstairs and went to a café for breakfast. When we came back, he was sitting in Paul Simpson's armchair. Completely unfazed. I loved the guy, I really did. But only in theory. The reality of Smelly Elly did people's heads in. Kathy and Hilary hated him openly.

One day, at Eric's, he said to Paul Rutherford, "Before you and Paul Simpson were around, everyone called me Paul. But now, I'm just Smelly Elly." It was so sad and so true. I mean, what d'you say?

After about a week of her looking for flats, it became apparent that Kathy and I hit it off. I didn't invite her to stay, but I never told her to sod off. I just said, "Look, I'm poor, I'm starting a group, give me space and we'll be fine."

It was the typical non-commital male thing. And if it sounds unromantic, that's because it was.

TOO DECAYED

Sometimes, you wake up in the morning, you know you've had no sleep but this thing in your head keeps going noogy, noogy, noogy, and presents itself to you. You can even laugh at the stupid psychology of the exercise. It's just your brain, which you'd always thought was a cool brain (because it's your brain) and it's saying, "Be afraid. Be very afraid." It doesn't happen to everyone. It only happens to you and you can't tell anyone else as how the hell would they understand?

And that was me, every morning. The October sun would teem through the tin-foiled skylight and scatter restlessness on my sleeping form, like the magic sprinkles from the wands of Disney witches. At 7 a.m., I'd lie awake, looking up at nothing, waiting for 8 o'clock, when Kathy would wake and dress quietly for work.

What had I done? Where was this group? Shit, man, I can't play anything. Will anyone ask me to play bass for them? I'm sure I could. But who'll ask me?

My head would rage each day at this time. Then Kathy would leave for work and Chris would surface around nine. The feeling would slink away as the day established itself and I was free. Until the next day, when it would happen again.

I was creeping towards 20. Uncool. Nineteen was the punk age to be. All my friends here were 18 or 19. Except the others, but I didn't count them, I only wanted examples who fuelled my arguments against myself. You see, in one month, I'd expected to get this group thing all sewn up. Everyone felt the

same. We were known faces and if we got a group together, we'd play Eric's and be given help by anyone who could. And yet, all around Liverpool, groups were springing up, doing well and sounding like shit. Oh, man.

"We just haven't got a clue what to do."

We'd hear the same story every week. Someone is playing with so-and-so. Oh sorry, they've split up. Always different combinations of the same group of people.

Big in Japan had blown it for me. They now had a girl singer and Holly on bass. Much as I dug Holly, it seemed inappropriate for a jarring Television-sounding quartet to work with a crazy 17-year-old bleach-baby with "Dogsex" written in his hair. Also, the singer was Jayne Casey. She looked like Holly, too. They both seemed unfinished. Jayne had these off-their-head outfits, where her tits and her ass defied whatever the music told her body to do. Singing. Never. Jayne just opened her big mouth and screamed blue bloody murder. Also, and more to the point, I thought she was the sexiest thing in Liverpool, and I hated to admit it, even to myself.

I hung around with Paul Simpson, or Simmo, as he hated to be called. McCulloch and I were a little in awe of Simmo. His mother was a Spiritualist and she said that he was going to be world famous. He had his flat in Rodney Street and he did not a thing, but he spoke with such authority that I never noticed quite exactly how much he copied David Bowie. If I like someone, I tend to bleep out all their bullshit traits so I can get on with the job of liking them.

Anyway, McCull, Simmo and I became a gang, a triumvirate. We were well-balanced, although one would always feel jealous if the other two were together. I had a massive crush on both of them. They were delicate and queer looking, whereas I was too psycho to cut it when I pansied out. Anyway, for a long while we talked a good group. Then, amidst the talk, something happened.

One Eric's night, Wylie was talking to Peter Burns and they had an idea for a group. Then I said I'd play and a junkie-looking drummer called Phil Hurst also agreed.

Okay, we'll do one gig, just all the stuff we like, really quickly. Fuck all that "Is it good? What if it sucks shit?"

Suddenly, Laburnam Road was besieged with drum-kits, make-up and Peter's entourage. The household freaked out. Sue McKee was so offended by the Burns' collective appearance that she left the house during each rehearsal.

Wylie and I got a simple set together. We learned 'I Can See for Miles', 'Doo-Wah-Diddy-Diddy-Um-Diddy-Ay', 'Wild Thing' and 'Someone Like Me' by The Shadows of Knight. That last song I had found in a junk shop in Tamworth during the summer. Wylie had some riffs that we turned into songs. I had a riff I'd ripped off The Heartbreakers, which later became a song called 'Bouncing Babies'.

We hadn't even bothered to find out if Peter could sing.

"Course he can," said Wylie. "Look at him."

Wylie was right, the rehearsals were easy, Peter Burns had as snotty a voice as you'd wish to hear. Phil Hurst was a plank, though, and his looking like Richard Hell didn't help his cause any. Still, we had a set ready in about a week and the Laburnam Road crowd were still speaking to me.

A week later, we supported, wait for it, Sham 69, the latecomers of the revolution. Oh, cruel fate. Eric's was a sea of out-of-town swillheads, all ready for *Bob's Full House*. And we'd called ourselves The Mystery Girls, too. We strolled on stage to abuse and indifference. Wylie had a toilet-seat on his back and Peter did his best Wayne County-isms. We finished with 'The Night Time is the Right Time' and roared off the stage.

I'd played a gig. I'd played the bass at a gig. That was all I needed to know. I could do it.

The group split immediately. We dug it and all, but it wasn't what we wanted to do.

I turned 20 that week. I wrote a pro-teen song as a final statement. I called it 'Two Decayed' and recorded it with Chris. It just said: "I'm two decades old, two decades old, too decayed to know what's going on." It was all downhill from here.

IT'S A MOVING THING

As Kathy and I became a couple, we started to get stuff that couples want. We started to get pissed off at the lack of privacy in the house. We found hippies in the house, people we didn't want to know. My grandmother's chamber pot became a weapon against these people.

I've always got up three or four times to pee during the night. And I've always had a chamber pot, as a necessity rather than a luxury. Otherwise I'd piss on the floor and that's gross. Anyway, now the hippies were around, I just dumped the whole lot out of the skylight on the off-chance of hitting one as he arrived.

Then one night, Kathy and I arrived home from Eric's. There were hippies everywhere, sleeping on the furniture and on the stairs. As we climbed up towards our attic, there seemed to be more and more, and then we opened our bedroom door. A guy in our bed. A guy in our fucking bed.

"Jonathan Lee, get out of this room." I knew the guy. I knew him well. I even liked the guy, but I was pissed off as hell.

After that, we had to move. The washing up never got done. The place was a tip. I developed an attitude. I expected everyone there to welcome my friends

in, even though my friends could be pretty rude. I welcomed their friends with a pot full of piss.

Then we got a cat who would shit indoors. I decided to leave while we were all still friends. Kathy and I, and Babylon the cat, moved into a drab damp bedsit across the road in Prospect Vale. The dole decided that I was Kathy's common-law-husband and stopped my money. We lived on her £30 a week and food parcels from our parents. Baked potatoes and beans every night. Arguments would flare up. One of us was using up all the butter. Being poor is bullshit. Jesus Christ said that the poor will always be with us. No shit, Sherlock.

McCull moved into the Ellerbeck household in Belmont Road. He was into Smelly Elly in a big way. I thought it was great. Now we can start writing some songs. But although we were only about a mile apart, we'd still just meet in Probe and talk ideas.

Wylie drifted away, getting another idea group together. We felt left out. Wylie had the energy, the contacts, everything. We were really just jealous as hell, and lazy. Give us the deal. Give us the equipment. Tell us what to write about.

If one person started a group that looked like it had a chance, the rest of us would be so scornful of it that it would crumble under the pressure. Another group would start. We'd bitch to each other, so green with jealousy and feeling so left out that we became inert vegetables. Then the group would fail. Suddenly, the pressure was off. We'd welcome the failure back, praising his efforts and sighing with relief. We were a family again. We wanted the others to do well, but only if we could be included. The whole scene was so incestuous that it was suffocating itself.

This imaginary conversation, between imaginary characters, is the best way to describe it:

"What d'you think of Wylie's new group?"

"Am I in the group?"

"No."

"They're crap."

And so on, and so on.

By Christmas, no-one had moved. You never do, when you spend all your time watching the others. The phrase "chill out" was still not invented. And we were all anti-drugs, so we just stayed tense as hell.

I spent Christmas in Tamworth. Kathy went to Leeds. On December 27th, at Eric's, the Spitfire Boys played their final show. The end of 1977 signified the end of punk. It was over just in time, too. The punk scene moved to a club called the Swinging Apple, along with the dickheads and the Nazis and all the other counter-revolutionaries.

Eric's became a snobby snotty little scene. And I was as snotty as anyone else. You always are, when you're on the inside.

GROW YOUR HAIR

The leathers I'd waited so long for. The hair I'd worked so hard at. The whole thing was over. Mark Smith was right. Get your V-necked sweater on. His girlfriend, Kay, writes hippy poems at the end of his letters. He addresses me "Dear Jules Verne". Is that the work of the tortured artist? Would a faker have the nerve to allow that sort of thing? You're damn right they would. Mark Smith's a genius. Did you see The Fall the other night? Sod Mo Tucker, Una Baines is the new heroine.

The Fall shot through us all. But not like they hit McCull, Dave Pickett and myself. We were goners. They didn't even have records out. You had to see them live to hear them and I saw them 28 times in 1978.

That was the brilliance of Mark Smith. His proximity. All the uncool thoughts you'd have, he'd say. I was ashamed of my songs at this time. They were so educated. Not wordy, but too pleased with themselves. Then Mark Smith writes 'The Mess of My Age' and I think that's educated too. But it's wise, so it's OK.

He should have worn leathers occasionally. That would have freaked us right out. McCull and I were in awe of Mark. He wouldn't pull a star trip, which was kind of more starry in a way, because then he was even more like the person you wanted to be. And that way, he pulled a lot of shit out of us that we were scared of with the others.

With hindsight, I'll say that the main reason anything started to happen was because of Mark. He had very shamanistic qualities, a particular ability to draw the best from people.

January 1978, I came home with a prize beyond prizes. It was *The Modern Dance*, the first album by Pere Ubu. Probe got it the week it came out in America. It had no UK release date. Maybe there was no point yet.

A whole album. And it was a classic. It started something in me which affected everything I did after it.

It starts with this metal yowl called 'Non-Alignment Pact', a classic "girl" song with the most Stooged-out riff. In fact, the record sounds like The Electric Prunes, The Troggs and The Stooges all got their songs rerecorded for the *Eraserhead* soundtrack.

Simmo, Will Sargeant and I shit. Just a million ideas in one record. McCull arrived late and said he hated it, but it wasn't Bowie, so what did he know? What about his "first one at school into The Stooges and the Velvets" claims? He was just like everybody else. I've sussed you Mac, I thought, you seek approval from others before you decide if it's okay to like it. Oh, this was a drag. His hating Pere Ubu could mean only one thing: he was a plank. I had to form a group right now.

I rushed around to Griff's flat and formed The Nova-Mob. Griff had the new Suicide album and was on a similar trip to me. We looked up names in William Burroughs' *Nova Express*. It had to be Burroughs as he was so fucking trendy, nobody had got round to realising he was brilliant as well. I'd see real dudes carrying his books. I'd think, Yeah, I really believe *this* guy. These guys read their Burroughs books as often as they played 'The Celebration of the Lizard' or 'Vitamin C' or 'Sister Ray'. In other words, never.

You get into the very middle of Burroughs' trip and no way is it not drugs. The same way as the film *Blue Velvet* is drugs and hanging out of a helicopter is drugs. But I digress.

The Nova-Mob was a huge hit with everyone. Pete Wylie joined and said we should all sing. Then Budgie joined. He said he wouldn't use a drum-kit and we all rushed around finding metal and pipes and stuff. We rehearsed every day in the coffee shop in Kirklands. We'd buy one coffee each and talk the songs together.

I had an epic called 'Passendale' which we all got excited about, but it never quite got written. Griff was still entranced and obsessed by the International Situationists' book *Leaving the 20th Century* and we sat for hours staring at all the strange literature sent to us from San Francisco by the Residents. Even the packaging and the franking on the stamps fascinated us.

"Ignorance of your culture is not considered cool," proclaimed the Residents. Awlright! If the music was taking too long in coming together, surely we could immortalise ourselves in some other way.

We released a limited edition T-shirt. Big in Japan were Liverpool's biggest group, so their singer Jayne Casey was emblazoned across it. Then we started a petition to get Big in Japan to split up. We were going to be the pettiest group in the world.

Of course, Bill Drummond was into the whole thing and told us we needed 14,000 signatures, then they'd split up. We got about nine. I was pissed off. I mean, where was people's pettiness?

Finally, we called our own bluff and headlined one night at Eric's, after Penetration, the main group, pulled out. We did one song, a 15-minute chant that went:

"We're in love with beauty, we're in love with wealth,
 We're in love with mental health."

It grunged on and on. It was crap. McCull hated that one. It took me ages to live it down. To top it off, Budgie sold us out and joined Big in Japan. Still, Wylie and I were back in the fold and everyone could rest easy again.

Mac and I made our peace. Even the briefest musical sortie was a help. But I now knew I wanted a group, not some art statement. Even my favourite Hungry

Types pieces had those which were most songlike. All through the spring of '78, we sat in the Prospect Vale bedsit, banging out ideas. Simmo played boxes, radios, anything that came to hand.

And Mac sung.

He grew bored with being precious and just, one day, started to sing.

His voice was brilliant. Very Lou Reed, very Iggy, but his own thing.

We played each other's songs or beat new ones together. Mac started playing 'Stepping Out' by The Fall. I improvised a melody for it. Next day, Mac had written words. "It's called 'I've Read It in Books'," he said. Shit, we thought, this is easy.

I gave him my heaviest, heaviest, straight out of 'Funhouse' riff. "It's called 'Stammheim'," I said. He wrote the words in five minutes. It was recorded in ten.

After that, it was easy. We had loads of songs. Acoustic stuff with titles like 'Robert Mitchum' and 'Jefferson Davis', and war-zone riffs that I'd write, with maybe one or two notes in the riff. Mac would lie on the floor and just repeat the ass off those words.

'You Think It's Love' was my pride and joy. I ripped off James Williamson big style on that one. We recorded a 12-minute version, complete with Mac shrieking like Iggy on *Metallic K.O.*, "Take it down, take it down, lemme in," until I get crazy and my amp falls on him.

"What a maniac," cackles Mac as the distortion envelopes him. I was excited as all hell. We could be the fucking pig's business if we carry on like this.

We called this writing group Uh?, a Dave Pickett expression and an intentionally lame name. See, this was work. We knew something could come of it, but we weren't in a hurry. Simmo didn't write. He kind of postured on our behalf. If Mac and I got too embarrassing, he'd rush out and buy milk.

"Eh, Julian, 'ave got this song, 'Iggy Pop'." Mac was deadly serious as he showed me the most low-grade riff of all time. It was Buddy Holly doing 'Surfin' Bird':

"Uh-er, Iggy Pow-uh-op, Uh-er, Iggy Pow-uh-op,
At the high-school hop, at the high-school hop."

It was a lost classic. It really was. I'm not sentimental for the most part. I know what is good and a lot of this stuff did suck. But, just sometimes, it was fucking brilliant.

Never again. No way would I fall for the serious artist schtick. If you repeat the words "Iggy Pop" for long enough, sure it's art. It's a homage, the way a homage should be sung. None of this "Here's a clever lyric." No, these guys love Iggy so much they just repeat his name, with gleeful intensity, for five minutes. I'd love to record it, but I can't. Only fucked-up teens should do that kind of thing when it's pure.

• • •

Mac and I hitched around to see The Fall all that spring. Dave Pickett was at school and Simmo was too hung up. He wasn't going to be mistaken for a groupie! I'd slept on the floor of Piccadilly bus station to see Pere Ubu's first UK show. And they were fantastic. If I was as cool as Simmo, I'd have missed out on half the important shit.

We played tapes to Mark E. and Mac would hide in the loo. I had no shame though. If I was a plank, Mark E. would have sussed me. Besides, who cares?

One night, the three of us walked back to Mark's flat in Prestwich. Mac started singing, "You don't notice time on the Bury New Road," so I did mouth-slide-guitar and Mark added extra words. Months later, I remembered that with a fondness that almost pissed me off.

Simmo and Will Sargeant had Industrial/Domestic, a noise group with two guitars, through echo units. We joined up the two groups one time at Will's house and recorded a version of 'Satisfaction' and the Big in Japan theme song. Will played way off key all the time. It sounded great, but I thought he was so weird that I couldn't tell if it was intentional.

I used to get crazy around some people, especially anyone who thought I was too much. I really dug Will, so I'd dance around him, and he was quiet, so it did his head in.

But I couldn't back off. I just loved this scene and these people so much. When I was around them, I was always drunk with glee. It was a problem I had.

JUST A SHALLOW MADNESS

The months stretched out and spring was here before we had really done anything. Kathy and I were living on nothing and weeks would go past when Mac, Paul Simpson and I would sit, inert, in the Prospect Vale bedsit. We'd walk most of the way into Liverpool to save money.

I had loads of records put by in Probe. I found all The Seeds' albums for £1.70 each and was paying off £1 per week. Mac and I wrote loads of goofy songs, but nothing usable until one day in April when we wrote 'Robert Mitchum' and 'Jefferson Davis'. They sounded okay and it finally happened. We played on stage. Me, Mac and Dave Pickett. Uh?

Wylie had joined a Dolls/Heartbreakers group called Crash Course with a new scenehead called Andy Eastwood. While Mac and I took turns to slag off the name of his group, Wylie invited us to support them at Kirklands.

We agreed. Until the last moment, when Mac was close to shitting out. First

he was really late. Then he wouldn't sing, he'd only play melodica. Sod it, man, I'll bloody sing.

We did 'Jefferson Davis', 'Robert Mitchum' and 'Louie Louie'. Mac had on a coat that Mark Smith had given him. My hair was all grown-out rootsy bleached and I had a shit anorak on. I thought I looked way hip. "No way," said Mac. "You look like Justin Hayward." He was right. Uncool.

Mac had a guru called Arrow. Maybe I met him, I can't remember. This guru wrote poems and one poem was called 'A Shallow Madness'. Mac suggested it to me as a new name, so Uh? changed their name and Simmo joined, on the condition that we dumped half the songs. He thought the 'Robert Mitchum'-type stuff sucked shit.

Mac and I thought Simmo was going to be huge. It was in his destiny, his mother said. We heard that all the time. It started to creep into our consciousness and both of us began to believe it. Having Simmo in the group made us feel confident.

Once Mac and I got comfortable together, we'd be dancing and grooving. I thought anything Mac sung was great. I thought any riff I played was great. Simmo was the voice of reason, he was the big No. He told us what not to play. And it worked.

We all thought that Simmo should play a keyboard of some sort. We looked around for a cheap organ and after sorting through our meagre choices Simmo bought a second-hand Gemini organ for £60 that made everything sound like '96 Tears'.

I showed him the riff to 'Evil Hoodoo' by The Seeds. It's only three notes. Simmo reduced it to two notes, and he and Mac wrote a song straight away. It was easy. Mind you, there were no real words or a chorus, but these things took time.

With Dave Pickett on packing cases and me on distorted guitar, A Shallow Madness rolled into low gear, where we stayed for a while. But we were finally, slowly, moving.

In the incest pool that was Liverpool, there had become a pecking order. Nobody liked it, but nobody complained too much. We were in that pecking order and there we'd stay.

Yet every new group that failed gave its members one less chance in the eyes of everyone else. In Probe, Geoff Davies and John Athey would sarcastically ask the name and line-up of each group that we put together. There were so many combinations, it seemed like I'd played with everyone in Liverpool. Yet I'd still made hardly a sound.

At the very least, Big in Japan were a real going somewhere group. I'd watch them with such jealousy, I couldn't stand what they had become, but it was such entertaining bullshit. I admired Bill Drummond a great deal and still had

a thing for Jayne Casey's ass. Of course, I couldn't tell Simmo or Mac about this, I felt bad enough about it without telling my arbiters of cool.

Then one day, as I walked home down Prospect Vale, I was verbally accosted by the most cartoon woman I had ever met. I was only about 200 yards from our bedsit when this fat bleached-blonde beehive woman screeched at me, a banshee wail so piercing that she reminded me of the Mrs Cutout character from Monty Python. "Have you seen our David?" she cooed.

I said that I hadn't.

"Oh, he's up at the Empire, he's been to see the Boomtown Rats."

Ah, I thought. She'll be thinking I'm one of those punk rockers. The conversation dwindled. I never got closer to her than 20 yards, so I walked home convinced that the wail was her only method of speaking.

Then, about three days later, I got to meet "our David". He was 16, carried an armful of punk 45s and was short and fat in the same cartoony way as his mother.

"I've just bought The Adverts' album." He talked in a delicate nervous boy's tone, so I withheld my opinion of The Adverts.

"Yeah? I've just come back from seeing Pere Ubu."

Our David looked sweetly and uncomprehendingly at me. I found out later that he was making his first tentative steps towards cool music and some kind of hip quotient. Everyone at school hated him. His parents were divorced, so they each gave him money to assuage their guilt. He seemed pretty aware of his own shortcomings and I took him under my wing. It was like writing in a brand new book. I schooled our David in the way I would have wished to learn. I made him lists of stuff to buy and I lent him my records, on pain of death if they were not looked after. In fact, I felt stupid about the last proviso – when I got to see his stereo, it was about 500% better than my hairdryer-with-a-speaker.

In a few weeks, I had created a monster. He had all The Doors' albums, the Residents, the Velvet Underground, The Seeds, The 13th Floor Elevators, Pere Ubu, Suicide, Patti Smith, The Mothers of Invention, Television, Love, Captain Beefheart, on and on and on. I flipped out. Suddenly, I had a record library in my street. Our David the librarian even had more Doors records than me. And mostly still shrink-wrapped. Each LP that I had lovingly searched out over the years, then paid virtually nothing for, he had bought brand new.

He would walk into our flat and say, "What's this you're playing?"

"Oh, it's 'Mother Sky' by Can. You lent me it yesterday."

All my friends would slag him off. But he was so slaggable, I didn't see the need. I dug the little kid. Every time I played him something, his face would glow. He genuinely loved this stuff and if we couldn't like him, he would be a lost soul.

Wylie, he of the barbed tongue, immediately nicknamed him Yorkie, after the chocolate bar commercial. "Because he's good, rich and thick." And Yorkie he became.

And in the great scheme of things, Yorkie became our means of progress. His mother let us use their cellar in Prospect Vale. She charged us £1.50 per week and made us tea and toast. When we were totally skint, Yorkie would give his mother the money. Of course, we had to call her Gladys, a name I'd always had a problem saying without laughing, but Gladys Palmer was a sweet and crazy woman.

The chance meeting with Gladys and Yorkie put us, suddenly, way ahead. We had a basement. We could set up the equipment and leave it set up. It was June 1978 and our attention span was getting longer.

Then one evening I switched the TV on. *Granada Reports*, our northern magazine guide, started. Tony Wilson, the presenter, started to introduce this new group. I looked up and recognised them as Warsaw, a bunch who had played Eric's a million times and would never get better.

"Ladies and gentlemen, please welcome Joy Division."

I watched them. Casually, at first, as a name change usually meant sod all. Then I noticed something. They were good. I mean really good. The song, 'Shadowplay', was raw as hell, but in a dangerous and suppressed way. They had layered solarised film over the group's performance. It was an event.

Of all the groups, Warsaw seemed to me the unlikeliest. The only guy who'd even tried to champion them in the past was Will Sargeant. Every so often, he'd walk up to me during a Warsaw set and say, "Have a look at this. They're getting good." Then I'd saunter in, listen to their new Pere Ubu-bass sound, agree in principle and walk out.

It seemed like Will was right. The next day, Liverpool was buzzing. Joy Division, in one TV performance, had become a force. Also, Tony Wilson had signed them to his new Factory record label. I told Yorkie to buy everything so far released on Factory and we checked it all out.

I started to call him Yorkshire. It had more dignity and helped when others were mean to him. Mac hated him. He was quite willing to use Yorkie's situation but Mac never had any desire to turn people on to music. He had bad hang ups like that: if he was into something good, he'd keep it completely to himself. But if anyone was into something before him, he had to hate it.

I remember one conversation clearly. Mac said he was into the Velvet Underground in 1972. I said I thought I'd bought mine around the same time. It was the double-album compilation with the Andy Warhol coke bottles on the sleeve. I had bought it for £1.25 in Torquay, along with a Litter LP for 25p and a shit blues album by Zephyr, also for 25p. Then I thought, No, no, if it was Torquay, it must have been 1973. Yeah, I was 15 and I was working in a hotel.

Mac roared, "1973! Bloody 'ell." I'd never seen anyone so pleased with their one-upmanship in my life. It was almost worth losing just to see him so happy. Heaven help Yorkie, who'd just last week bought the entire Velvets' catalogue.

The middle of June, we saw a group called Dalek I Love You. They played Eric's one night with sofas and lamps on stage, and their set was a weird combination of uncool and brilliant. Like the guitarist had a moustache. Uncool. And the bass player was a total sissy, with a lisp and cutesy fringe. But they had organ lines, like The Seeds, and Doorsy bass lines. The bullshit on stage didn't work, but along with the psychedelic guitar and Suicide drum-machine, it all helped to create their own thing.

Back at rehearsals, their performance caused uproar. Mac was very late and the rest of us got talking about Dalek I Love You. When he arrived, Mac refused to even mention their name.

Simmo and I decided to bait him. We'd asked Pete Wylie's young mate Mick Finkler to try out on guitar, as I felt more comfortable on bass. Mick had the same reservations as us, but admired what Dalek were trying to do.

Mac got a cob on, the Scouse equivalent of "totally pissed off", and went home. The four of us – Dave Pickett, Mick Finkler, Simmo and I – all raged on about his attitude. And he was bloody late all the time. And he'd stopped coming up with stuff. And Mick Finkler was playing real cool chords and we'd done shitloads with him, until Mac had arrived.

It all welled up, the frustration at getting nowhere, the pettiness of trying to be cool all the time. Shit, man, we were getting so cool we weren't allowed to do anything. Who gave a shit, anyway? Have you seen The Pop Group? They're the coolest fucking uncoolest band in the world. Even Warsaw have got good. So, let's Go!!!!

Big in Japan split up. We were all sad now. They'd been really good in their own way. Still, they were all back in the fold.

Dave Balfe, the wimpy bass player from Dalek I Love You, had joined Big in Japan just before they split up. We all hated him because he'd shagged his way into the Liverpool scene and exaggerated his lisp in front of women. He had had every good-looking woman we knew. It was alright for Wylie to do that, but Balfe was an ugly plank. He and Bill Drummond were starting a record label. I thought that was a shame, as I'd wanted to do something with Bill. They were releasing a Big in Japan "farewell" record. What a drag. I hated Balfe. Even Jayne Casey nicknamed him "Smurf", and she was shagging him.

Meanwhile, rehearsals ground on and on. We'd write music while we waited for Mac, then Mac would hate it. Then he'd go off to see Smelly Elly's sister. It was a first affair thing for him, so I understood.

But we were not so close any more. I was now 20, long away from home, living with a woman and getting snottier. Mac was living with his mother, 18 years old, preoccupied with getting laid all the time I'd known him. Man, were we out of synch.

I wanted the group now. I told everyone. I got heavy and said I would sing if McCull didn't get his shit together. They said I couldn't sing. I couldn't. Not

a note. *And* I thought I was Sky Saxon. *And* the guy out of Pere Ubu. I didn't care. Mark Smith couldn't sing. Patti Smith couldn't sing. There was a long tradition of us.

I loved Mac. It did my head in to do it. It was my first guilt trip. I could tell Mac wasn't happy. He wanted a rock group and we were too stumbling. I didn't want it to end our friendship and I thought it wouldn't.

It was the end of A Shallow Madness. I asked Mac to leave so he kind of took the name with him. Rehearsals were weird. We had no name and no singer. I had to try now, as I'd kicked up such a fuss. I just hoped I wasn't as shit as everyone thought.

IT'S JUST LIKE SLEEPING GAS

Dave Pickett was a crap drummer. We loved him dearly, but it had to be said and I had to say it. It was the middle of August and he wasn't getting better. We told him the group was going nowhere and split up.

That week, Paul Simpson and I were looking for group names. We'd keep a name about a day and get bored. We were The Soul Giants for about four hours, but it soon sounded crap. By September, Mick and I were round at Simmo's every day. We needed a drummer and a name. Then Simmo got his comics out.

There was this story, in a *Super D.C.* comic, about a battle in Central Park, involving Namur, the undersea god, and the superhero, Daredevil. The whole story comes to a climax as the sun blots out and suddenly, for no reason at all, the Teardrop Explodes.

It made no sense, the story made no sense at all. We tried to figure it out and we couldn't. But it was a great name for a group. I loved it. It was like The 13th Floor Elevators or The Chocolate Watchband. And no-one had a name like that. September '78 was all short dour names. Ours was far-fucking-out.

That night, at Eric's, I asked Gary Dwyer to join our group. He was a big mate of Pete Wylie and he had talked about learning to play drums. Gary modelled himself on Rocky. He was 6'5", with dyed black hair and an enormous black coat.

In the deafening roar of Eric's bar, Gary said, "What are yer called?" When he heard the name, he looked down at me and said, "You've gotta weird one there, Julian."

He was right. And it looked like we might have a cool one, too. Gary brought a drum-kit down that his auntie had inherited. So we now had a real kit. And Gary could play this rhythm that Budgie had taught him.

Simmo, Mick and I had been worried about asking Gary. He knew absolute shit about music, but we were desperate. It turned out to be the best thing we could have done. Gary worked us really hard. He got good in about four weeks and asked us when the first gigs were.

Gigs? It's only October. Gary said we needed to play live or we'd never get better. I couldn't believe what he was saying. He'd only started playing drums in September. No way would we be ready this year. I was scared shitless. Sure, it sounded good. But only in comparison with how crap we'd been in August. I shuddered at the thought of playing on stage. This was our last real chance. I was convinced we had to do it right.

We had written a couple of songs by this time. One was called 'Camera Camera', built around this one skinny cyclical riff. It needed a refrain at the end of each verse, so we tried to copy the chorus at the end of The Doors' 'Wintertime Love'. Simmo and I wrote some pop-art images down and I intoned them over the song.

Next, we wrote 'Sleeping Gas'. It started with my bass riff, which I had ripped off from 'Ain't It Strange' by Patti Smith. The song had started from a bass & drums jam one month before between myself and Dave Pickett, who had promptly given the tune a classic post-punk name: 'Sleeping Gas'. Mick played these two spindly chords of D major and B flat, and Simmo just pumped away on two notes. But when Rocky Dwyer heard the song, he tried to put a disco beat to it and it became this low-grade dance song. We recorded a 45-minute version of 'Sleeping Gas', a whole side of a C90 cassette, with me singing anything, then I took the tape home, worked out what the words were and came back with a finished song. I showed Simmo a D minor chord, which he held down throughout the instrumental passage.

That week, with pressure on from Gary, Candy James got in touch with me. She'd hired Eric's for a party on November 15th. And would we play? Shit, it was three weeks away and we had about four songs. Okay, but we won't be very good. She didn't mind, she said, and that was that.

I rushed to Yorkie's to tell everyone. They flipped out, but we had to do it. We just had to go out there and be judged. It was easier at a party, but all the regulars would be there. Oh, well.

Mac and I still hung around all the time. He felt left out when we were rehearsing, but the friendship was stronger than that. Then one day we were all in the upstairs bar at Kirklands. Will Sargeant was pissed off, as Simmo's preoccupation with the Teardrops had meant the end of Industrial/Domestic. He and Mac got talking, a conversation I never heard, and a pretty low-key one I'd imagine, as they were the two most emotionally autistic guys I'd ever met. All they had in common was rejection by us lot. I knew it was hard on both of them, but my hang ups couldn't stop us this time. They started playing together and that eased our guilt.

The end of October came and we had two weeks to be ready. Shit, my singing was the worst. If we'd never known Mac's voice, maybe it would have been better. Keep trying, keep trying.

The set was now 'Sleeping Gas', 'Camera Camera', 'I've Read It in Books', my old Stooges rip-off 'Stammheim', a terrible slow McCulloch/Simpson thing called 'There Go the 70s' and a song called 'Seeing Through You'. It lasted about 30 minutes if we droned the fuck out of everything and 15 minutes if we didn't.

Then Mac told me that he and Will were getting places. They had jammed for hours along with Will's drum-machine. One night at Eric's, Geoff Lovestone, AKA Les Pattinson, told Simmo and me that he had a bass. He'd bought it for £30 and had written a bass line. He was scared to ask, but he wanted to join Mac and Will. We said he should ask them, they could support us in a week's time.

Les joined and Smelly Elly suggested names like Mona Lisa & the Grease Guns, the Daz-men, and Echo & the Bunnymen. They opted for the latter and the November 15th show was scheduled.

I had mixed feelings about the name. I wanted us to be the only group with a long psychedelic title. They never would have dared if we hadn't gone first. Still, Echo & the Bunnymen was a brilliant name, and Will was also a big 13th Floor Elevators head, and we still felt guilty, so who cared? We'd be a bigger force with both groups.

At Yorkie's basement we learned 'Evil Hoodoo' by The Seeds and wrote an instrumental thing for the start of the set. We had a few days left, so we sat around and tried not to shit ourselves.

Kathy found us a flat in Devonshire Road, in Liverpool 8. Wylie lived there and so did Hilary. It seemed like the place to be.

We had the seven-room top-floor of a Georgian house. It was £15 per week. I told the dole that I lived with our friends Ally and Chris, and left some clothes and stuff at their house to make it look convincing. The DHSS believed us and so we could afford the flat.

Les Pattinson brought his van and he, Yorkie and Simmo helped us move. We couldn't afford a bed, so we nicked the one from our bedsit. We had to leave something in its place, so Yorkie and I searched around. We found a double mattress on a skip and dragged it back to the bedsit. It was damp and filthy. It fitted perfectly into its surroundings.

NEED A VOICE

We sat in the Eric's dressing room, being cool. It felt weird. Eric's was home, but the dressing room? It didn't feel right. Only I had been in there before and then I'd scurried out as soon as I could.

Wylie came in, beaming and yelling that it was going to be great. All my friends from college were at the party and our hip, hip Eric's mates were waiting to judge us.

The Bunnymen had one song, built around Les's bass-riff. It was time for them to go on. Mac didn't want to, yet. The time passed and they had to go.

Will walked on stage and switched the drum-machine on. It started its insistent surf Suicide-y hiss and Les came in with his simple dum-dum-der, dum-dum-der-der-der bass. Will's full-on echoed one-note guitar followed and the almost-blind Ian McCulloch took up his stance at the mike. He did not sing.

Mac's sister, Julie, noticed that he was sweating so she passed him a Kleenex from the front row. Mac thought someone was attacking him and stepped back, quickly. Then he started his low repeated vocal, squinting into the darkness . . .

As they walked offstage, I rushed up to them. "That was totally brilliant. Shit, it was legendary." I was given to outbursts like that, in those days, but I really meant it. They were so simple. They played four notes, no chords, just four notes in the entire song. Man, I was jealous. If only I had a voice. Shit.

I don't much remember our set. It was good and people dug it, but mainly I just thought, The Bunnymen are brilliant and we're a real group at last. Simmo copped out of doing 'Evil Hoodoo' and we shortened 'Stammheim', as it was sounding like crap.

We arranged another gig one week later, again at Eric's. Roger Eagle said nothing about the music. I figured he hated us, but he put us on again, so I guess it was okay.

The Bunnymen went into songwriting mode and put off playing live for a while. We wrote two more songs for the next week's gig and I met Dave Balfe in Mathew Street. He'd heard that we were pretty good and said that he and Bill might want to record us. Hmm. I wasn't into Balfe. And we could hardly play. Gary had been drumming for nine weeks. My voice was shit. We didn't have enough songs. Etc., etc.

I kept up the excuses until after the next show. Bill said he wanted to do a single. He had time booked for December 6th. I wasn't sure and we'd been kicked out of Yorkie's while he sound-proofed the place. Bill said we could rehearse in the basement of Penny's café, where he worked. That way, he could hassle us.

Okay. It was a tentative okay, but my ego was all fired up. We would

be recording our first ep after only 11 weeks together. That appealed to me.

We moved into Penny's damp basement and worked as hard as we could. Bill Drummond came down with tea and advice every hour or so. We all thought 'Sleeping Gas' was a classic and Bill wanted it as lead track. We also wanted 'Camera Camera' for definite and a song called 'Seeing Through You'.

Dave Balfe came down to the basement. He wanted to check out our stuff. I told him to sod off and keep out of our affairs. I didn't like him and I didn't trust him. The Big in Japan ep had been re-pressed in secret. The rest of Big in Japan were all totally pissed off.

December 6th arrived. Yorkie and Les Pattinson helped us move our equipment up to the studio. It was a tiny four-track, above the café. We set up and played through the songs.

Without the cavernous reverb of the basement and Eric's, everything sounded so flat and weak that I got pissed off. Balfe said he was the producer. I told him to fuck off. We were producing it. "You're just the engineer, Balfe," I told him.

I insisted that he put loads more bass into the sound and reverb all over the vocals. He did that, then changed it back while I was playing the backing tracks. We played everything live and then I was to re-record the lead vocals.

'Sleeping Gas' sounded perfect. I insisted that we keep the first take. Balfe said it was shit. No way, I thought it was the best thing ever. I went into the studio and fell asleep on top of the drum booth. In the other room, Dave Balfe turned purple. Bill Drummond and the rest of the group just sat there. Finally, Balfe came in and said that he was paying for it, so do the bloody thing again. He was paying. I said nothing, then, "Okay Balfe, you fucking bread-head. We'll do it again. But you're a twat."

We piled back in the studio and did another take of 'Sleeping Gas'. Balfe was right. It sounded 10 times better. I acted as though it was my idea, to piss him off, then we recorded 'Camera Camera' and 'Seeing Through You' in a couple of takes.

I was nervous about recording the vocals, so everyone cleared out of the studio for a while. I sung my ass off, all the songs, really quickly and no mistakes. Everybody came back in and listened. Gary thought we should try another singer. Mick and Simmo were polite as they told me it sucked shit. Balfe said it was as good as I'd get, I just couldn't sing.

We had to get an ep out of the session, as Bill and Balfe had paid £35, which was their budget. We decided we could live with everything but 'Seeing Through You'. It was pathetic, weak and out of tune. We had an hour left, so we recorded one of Simmo's dreary instrumentals in as long as it took to play it.

We had three tracks for the ep. They were in tune and not speeded up too much. I hoped that everyone was deaf and couldn't hear the vocals.

Balfe asked his mate Alan Gill from Dalek I Love You to do the record

sleeve. We wanted it to look like *The Savoy Session* with a piano drawing on the front. The rest of the group wanted photos on the back, but I wanted total enigma. Mick Finkler was only 17. He wanted a photo as proof to his mates. So did Gary. Oh, well. My photo was taken so far away that it could have been anyone.

You know, your first record, it's the most special. I wanted it to do well, look great and be legendary.

The group was exhausting me. I wasn't used to work. Kathy and I went to my parents in Tamworth, where we spent a long pork-out Christmas. I told my mother the name of my group. She gave me her best withering look and said, "Oh, you'll get a long way with that name."

OF PENNY LANE AND PIES ON THE FLOOR

Jamie Farrell, 17, lay back in the armchair, checking every inch of the *Sleeping Gas* ep. He took the record out of its sleeve and examined the Zoo label for the hundredth time.

"It is, though, isn't it? I mean, you can't count Big in Japan. This is the first one, 'cause it's you lot ... and you lot are our lot. Know what I mean?"

Everyone in the room knew exactly what Jamie meant. There was a pride about the brand newness of the record. And even if they were not yet in a group, many of them felt that this was proof that they all could do it. The camaraderie was becoming very intense.

In December, Pete Wylie, Mick Finkler, Ian McCulloch and Gary Dwyer had all moved in together. Their flat, in Penny Lane, had become the central hang-out scene.

The place was a madhouse. Wylie was the shag-monster of Liverpool and had new woman every day. Jamie would be there, along with Tempo and Kevin the Drunk. Tempo was a great-looking rocker from Keighley whom everyone loved and Wylie idolised. His real name was Steve Tempest and Wylie was forever trying to form a band around him. And every night Kevin the Drunk would fall out of the second-floor window, landing in the awning of the Polish grocer who lived underneath. The grocer would freak and Bill Drummond, who lived about 200 yards away, could hear the chaos from his own home.

They lived on chicken pies and beer. One time, I heard a crash and Wylie rushed in. Gary had dropped all the pies on the floor. We went in to help him clear up, only to find Gary eating off the disgusting floor.

As the only Hebrew member of the scene, Mick Finkler was christened Kid Bagel by Wylie. At that time, all the younger guys adored Wylie; he could do

no wrong. Pete was on his Jim Morrison trip. Full leather outfit and hair grown out. Even with our groups, Mac and I were still hung up about the "power of Wylie". If ever I got too worried, Mac would dismiss my fears with a shrug: "Ay, don't worry about Wylie. He's just a dough-head."

Early February 1979, I walked down Rodney Street towards Paul Simpson's flat. The normally stiff and ultra-cool Simmo was hanging out of the window, waiting for me. He waved a newspaper and as I got closer, I heard him yelling, "Single-of-the-week, single-of-the-week!"

I rushed into the flat, where he had laid out *Sounds* and *NME*. We were in! We were good! They liked us! And Giovanni Dadomo, a guy I quite trusted, had said things I only dreamed about:

> "Absurdly basic, thoroughly hypnotic, stripped to a minimum rock'n'roll. 'Sleeping Gas' is the killer; sturdy, danceable as disco, reggae, 'Louie Louie' or '96 Tears', and sounding like nothing else I've heard."

'96 Tears'. I could not believe it.

We all walked around with swell-heads, being dead modest and faking surprise. We'd played two gigs and had single of the week. All-fucking-right.

We walked down to see Bill in the café. He was smiling his head off. "Tony Wilson's been on the phone. He wants you to do 'What's On' this week. He's been ringing Eagle all day, but I only just found out."

Shit, we were getting to play on TV. My head spun. I was still shocked at being in a group, and now all this.

Granada Studios were 30 miles away in Manchester. Dave Balfe drove us, with Bill in the front seat. Piled in the back was the group, Wylie, Jamie, Mac, Dave Pickett and the equipment. Yorkie wanted to come, but meanness precluded it.

We partied down the motorway and hit Manchester with a real attitude. Fuck everyone, Liverpool is the music scene. Our record meant one thing to everyone in the van: anyone can play.

It was ironic that the four group members were the worst musicians there. Except for Mac, who was equally inept. It was the start of a dangerous trend. I mean, Jamie and Wylie could play solos. They felt a pressure to go off and de-learn everything.

At the studios, we were shown around the *Coronation Street* set. Wylie and I were addicts and we nicked shitloads. Then coming through the gates was the legendary Eddie Yates, the greatest character on the programme. Wylie ran towards him, screaming, "Eddie, you're a god!", then he fell on his knees before the great man. Edward the Bemused cast his eyes towards the rest of us and smiled. Yes.

In the studio, Dave Balfe spluttered and argued with technicians, as the amps and drums took the stage. We occupied our time by writing "Fuck" almost invisibly on all the Granada TV logos that were used between programmes.

Eventually they were ready and we ran through the song. We'd decided on 'Camera Camera' as it didn't need reverb or too much of an atmosphere. There was no recording. It went out live. We waited and we waited. We all shit ourselves. Then we were on. "... a new group from Liverpool. Please welcome The Teardrop Explodes."

Outside Probe Records, young kids came up to us. They asked Simmo if he was in The Teardrop Explodes. He signed an autograph and they walked off happy. Hmm, I was maybe a little anonymous for a lead singer.

That night, with TV still coursing through our veins, we supported Wire at Eric's. Roger Eagle gave us £5 for expenses, with a curt "You're not on TV now."

The Teardrop Explodes' entourage began its inevitable drift around the north. I felt like we were enormous already, but according to Balfe there were other places to conquer.

We played Manchester's Band on the Wall club on Mark Smith's 23rd birthday. It was strange to be on stage with him in the audience. I still felt that I had loads to prove to him, especially as Mac had got a name-check on the B-side of the new Fall single.

Wylie sat in front of the drum-kit to prevent it moving forwards. John the Postman ranted throughout the show: "Brill, more, louder, lou-der!" Members of the Manchester scene were there to check us out.

The whole set was held together with attitude. We were shit. Bill and Balfe wanted us to get tight. To us, tight still meant starting and stopping together. We played Leeds and York, and Mac came with us at all times. It was like still having him in the group.

The Bunnymen had recorded a dreadful version of 'Monkeys' for a Liverpool compilation, featuring all the old guard of "fun groups" and hippy bullshit. Luckily for us, our track, 'The Tunnel', was erased by the dickhead engineer. He recorded The Naughty Lumps, a student-punk group, over our song by mistake. The Bunnymen had no such luck, so it had to come out.

It made no difference, really. The Bunnymen were beginning to sound great. Bill and Balfe recorded their single in March. The A-side, 'The Pictures on My Wall', had a beautiful "troika-chase" majesty about it. Their version of 'I've Read It in Books' was on the B-side. Simmo and Bill added backing vocals and hand-claps. It was a lot straighter than our record. Much poppier and very melodic. But I was jealous as hell of Mac's voice. Even though it was Bowie-ish,

it sounded so rich and ominous. Also, the drum-machine made them 10 times tighter than Gary's lumpy drums and my ragged bass.

'The Pictures on My Wall' was released on May 5th, Mac's 20th birthday. It got brilliant reviews and was also single of the week. We started to play shows together. That way, we could appear bigger than we were. We alternated headline and support every night, and the crowds started to get bigger and bigger.

The first 5,000 run of the *Sleeping Gas* ep all sold out and Bill and Balfe pressed up another 5,000 in late May.

In late spring Paul Simpson decided to leave. He wanted a show of his own and couldn't see me giving him enough room as the Teardrop became better. He was right. I'd begun to control the direction and kept everyone on a tight rein.

We had shows all the time and Dave Balfe said he wanted to play organ. Mick and I were reluctant as hell, but I had to admit that Balfe was good. He learned Simmo's two-note parts in half an hour and made us rehearse songs over and over. We still hated him, though. He was uncool as hell and rude to boot.

In early June, the second 45 was recorded. We went into an eight-track, at Amazon in north Liverpool. We wouldn't let Balfe play, so I did the organ on 'Bouncing Babies' and Gary and Mick played organ and atonal piano on the B-side, a horrible song called 'All I Am Is Loving You'.

Simmo had bought a copy of *Nite Flights* by The Walker Brothers for £1. Their music was incredibly inspiring. On two of the songs, Scott and John Walker sung these beautiful weird harmonies over a backdrop of atonal piano and a motorik Doors-y beat. So we tried to make 'All I Am Is Loving You' sound sad and wistful, like Scott Walker singing in purgatory, but my voice was particularly off that day and the whole thing was a resounding failure. The three of us admitted it to ourselves, but of course in public we said it was brilliant.

Kathy and I were happy at 20 Devonshire Road. We went to the rent tribunal and they reduced the rent to £12.50 per week. I got a royalty cheque for £33 from sales of *Sleeping Gas* and we bought a carpet for the bedroom.

I got a name-check on The Fall album in a song called 'Two-Steps Back'. The lyric was a reference to magic mushrooms:

"Julian said, how was the gear?
They don't sell things to you over here."

I was pleased as hell, but I was very anti-drugs at that time and could never remember any such conversation.

New groups were appearing in Liverpool. Andy McCluskey, a hippy we all

called "Leo Sayer", had formed a group called, get this, Orchestral Manoeuvres in the Dark. It seemed like everyone was jumping on the long-name bandwagon. I'd seen Andy McCluskey in a group called Pegasus. They'd done a bunch of heepy toons, then he introduced the "most important song of the decade" and they played 'Anarchy in the UK'. Gary said they had two hopes of getting anywhere: Bob Hope and no hope. We were on Zoo Records and fuck everyone else.

Lyn and Peter Burns had moved in to 20 Devonshire. They had the ground-floor flat. Sandwiched between us was an old couple and their son, Dave the Moron. He'd play ELO at anytime of day, so I retaliated by playing my ancient harmonium at 2 a.m. The old couple's bedroom was under my music room and I'd pedal like crazy and sellotape all the white notes down.

Kathy had some time off in August, so we got married. I don't know why, we just did. Actually, I do know my main reasons. Frank Zappa and Marc Bolan were both married at 21. It seemed like a cool thing to do. Most of the Liverpool scene were gay or promiscuous as hell. Being married seemed like the most non-conformist thing that we could do and I was always a man of great gestures.

Dave Balfe said I was a stupid twat and it would never last. He kept on and on at me until one day I said to him, "Balfe, she's only my first wife." Yeah.

YMCA

And so, in early July, our second record was released to hip, cool reviews and a second single of the week. 'Bouncing Babies' was a great song, but a very average record. I'd had the riff since late '77, but when I fell in love with The Pop Group's 'She Is Beyond Good & Evil', I ripped off its staccato rhythm completely.

If I heard a good riff, I'd use it in our songs. Sometimes, I'd take two bars of a song and repeat it over and over. Then I'd add my lyrics and melody. I'd write down every interesting comment or idea that I heard and give the person six months to use it. After that, I'd figure it was public domain and work it into my own songs.

After a while, I started cannibalising all of our stuff. Now I was obsessed by 'Louie Louie' and the dance-beat. If you listen to the music of The Doors and The Seeds, they use the same riffs and rhythms over and over. As my voice was still horribly weak, I would concentrate on repetitious lyrics. Insistent, always insistent.

• • •

The Teardrop and the Bunnymen were playing all over the north. The Zoo package was hip shit and we got good quickly. Neither group could bear to support and the Bunnymen were so miserable all the time that I used to psyche them out. When it was our turn to support, I'd walk into places and say, "Dump City, Bill. Bagsy we're on first." It didn't work often, but it wound them up just enough.

Of course, after one week in the band, Dave Balfe had started acting like the leader. He gave us such shit in rehearsal that we kicked him out. Ged Quinn, a sweet weirdo with a Tom Waits fixation, joined us for five gigs but Balfe was driving us to the shows and told us Ged sucked. Bill Drummond agreed so Balfe rejoined with, ha ha, promises to back off.

Then, out of the blue, The Teardrop Explodes got their first front cover. We went out to buy a copy of *Sounds* and there were Mick Finkler and me on the front. We couldn't believe it. A journalist called Dave McCulloch had done a little interview and a month later we were on the front. It made a huge difference. The guy was a plank, but he had good intentions and made us sound important. He turned on the people who'd dismissed us as bleak northerners.

We'd play the Factory in Manchester all the time. There'd be weird shitty new-wave support groups. One time, A Certain Ratio supported us. They were just these four little guys, three with guitars and one with a noise machine. They were crap, but unusual.

Then Kevin Millins rang us up. He ran Final Solution, the major alternative promoter, and wanted to do a big gig at the YMCA in Tottenham Court Road.

Bill Drummond had kept us away from London. He didn't want us playing shitty pubs. We weren't ready, anyway. But this seemed like a good idea. Final Solution picked weird places and then decorated them, and they were always the place to be. Besides, Joy Division were playing. I loved them. Let's do it.

The Bunnymen drove all the equipment down in Les's van and we all piled into Balfe's car. He had use of his father's Citroën, which made us all resentful as hell.

We arrived at the Y-Club mid-afternoon. It was the entire basement of the YMCA and the stage looked huge. I really didn't know London at all. We wrote London groups off as lame fashionaries. All that Mod stuff sucked shit. It was the time of The Jam and parkas and weasel-faced Paul Weller copyists.

We saw Joy Division rehearsing. They sounded Godlike. I'd lent Peter Hook my bass amp at Eric's two months before and I couldn't work out how he got that roar. We sunk into the background for the rest of the afternoon and just got into being in London.

Essential Logic, this London free-jazz thing, were headlining. Joy Division were second on the bill, then us, then the Bunnymen. Mac was nervous as hell, but that gave him an edge and made him snottier. They were all pissed off at

our being above them on the bill and aimed to blow us offstage. At the end of a song called 'Happy Death Men', Mac sang:

"Neil Young never sounded like this,
The Velvet Underground never sounded like this."

I thought they were pretty crap platitudes to be singing last on the bill. But, you know, it was the right thing to do. You always remember that kind of shit.

Just before we went on, Balfe told us to be brilliant. Of course we'll be brilliant, you plank. I told him not to mouth the words as he played keyboards. He had a tendency to do that shit and it looked crap.

We walked on and opened with a song called 'Second Head'. Mac and Mick Finkler shared a bedroom in Penny Lane. One night, Mac was woken by a sleeping Finkler shouting, "How's your second head? Oh, very good, very good," over and over.

The song was built round this sinewy bass line and tonight it sounded brilliant. We pounded along. It was just a great gig. I was wearing these weird three-quarter-length camo pants and had bare feet. The London audience had caught on to northern grey and I wanted to look different. Even Balfe was happy. I introduced 'I've Read It in Books': "This is a cover of an Echo & the Bunnymen song. Only ours is fab and better."

Then we finished with a totally psychotic 'Sleeping Gas'. That song just had the most Germanic disco-beat. I'd start goofing on the vocals and Balfe would fade in waves of noise from this little synthesizer we'd just got. We built the song up and up, then bam, we walked off the stage to cheers, Balfe's spluttering white-noise repeating and repeating. It was cool.

After that, we just hung out. Joy Division weren't the total all-out assault that they could be, but they were pretty damn good. Later that night, I bumped into their singer, Ian Curtis, and said he had a cool group. He had this deep sad Iggy Pop lament quality when he sang, but he spoke in the most gentle high-pitched Manchester accent. I couldn't reconcile two such different characters in one man. But he was a nice guy and he was doing his extremely cool thing.

Back in Liverpool, the reviews began to come in. They all said the same thing. The groups were all "unorthodox, but rarely inaccessible" and our songs "suggest something more sinister and disorientating underneath". Awlright! At last people could see northern music as more than grey coats and long faces.

Late summer, Bill got us a publishing deal with Warner Bros. It was enough for both groups to get a weekly wage. We were professional musicians now, so we swanned around Liverpool and told everybody, real casual like.

Uh, Look Out!

PRESSURE ON

And then it happened. Seymour Stein at Sire Records wanted to sign Echo & the Bunnymen. We went into the Zoo office in Whitechapel and the place was just going crazy. I was still reeling from our publishing deal. The Bunnymen on a major? What about us? That's all I thought. What about us?

Bill Drummond told me it was time to do something about my role as leader. Apparently I still moved and looked crap onstage. He said that Mac's look had interested Seymour Stein.

I was outraged. Totally freaked out. Balfe and Bill had no answers for me. I was blind and running, looking for excuses. Why was I no good? Why didn't I move? Oh shit!

Bill humoured me with the best wind-up of all: "Julian, the Bunnymen need Mac's lips. But when you make it, it's just gonna have to be the music that does it."

Oh thanks, Bill. Thanks a fucking lot. In my mind, I saw them, all my so-called friends. They were tiny, standing on a mantelpiece. I raised my arm up to one end and brushed the lot into oblivion.

I felt bad. I knew what I was. I was one of those ugly snob musicians who want to be recognised on their musical merit alone. You always want people to ignore your looks if you look crap. "Just take me for my music."

I'd fallen for real basic bullshit. I'd de-glamorised myself to the point where even my wife told me to look more like Paul Simpson or Les Pattinson. During the previous two years, I had looked alternately great or shit. But always good. Now I was becoming Bad Head Personified.

I spun around in a bewildered haze for a few weeks. Of the Bunnymen, only Mac was outright mean. I guessed that his real feelings were finally coming out, now he was on the verge of trashing me.

Devonshire Road was a sanctuary for a bloody long while. I couldn't think straight. I consoled myself in simple ways. Like the fact that the Bunnymen had to get a drummer to please their record company. Huh, cop out. Like the fact that Mac considered me enough of a rival to have to get back at me by swanning around in a new coat. And me, the one who introduced them to Zoo, always hoping the Bunnymen would do well. I was a saint and they didn't even notice. Huh.

I wallowed in self-pity and equally bullshitting thoughts for quite some time. Of course, it made no real difference in the near future. We were bigger and better than Echo & the Bunnydroppings any day of the week.

Mac used to call Simmo "Joe Bowie" in an effort to deflect the Thin White Duke comparisons away from himself. Have you heard the Bunnymen's new Peel session? Uncool. Not even a good Bowie rip-off, more like Mick Ronson, if you ask me.

I was filled with vitriol. A man possessed. Kathy suggested I change my look. I'd kind of become rigidly asexual. Kathy was never crazy about my looks and gradually it began to erode my confidence. If your partner is always telling you to try to look more like your close friend, it whittles away at your confidence. I loved Paul Simpson, but I never wanted to look like him. I dug his Fascist Bum-boy look, but I could live without it on me.

Balfe and Bill were down to earth at least. They told me that we'd get a deal, just forget the glamour, Julian, some of us aren't meant for it. Yeah, it's bullshit in any case. Who wants to be glamorous?

And so the fire raged on into the autumn of 1979. There were more groups like us every day. Paul Morley had coined the phrase "post-punk" to describe our kind of music.

The Teardrop and Bunnymen both played together at the Leeds Futurama festival. It was hell on earth. The groups were all hippy bullshitters with long coats on. And dickheads with a single straggly plait at the back of their ugly scrubland hairstyles. A group called The Monochrome Set came on and did some terribly English songs, with white suits and an early progressive rock stance. Fuck right off.

With pressure on, Mick Finkler and I wrote a great song. It was called 'Treason', and it was about rivalry and freaking out. It had the best chorus I had yet written and we said it was a hit.

Bill thought it was great. He rang his old friend, Clive Langer, who was now a big producer with Madness. Clive came up and thought we were crap. He humoured us for a while, but Gary put pressure on him. Gary had been a maniac for Deaf School, Clive's old group. He told Clive how much it would mean to him, and Clive just felt bad and said, "Okay."

As the Bunnymen signed to Sire, The Teardrop Explodes drove down to London to record their third single. It was our first 24-track session. We had a day to record 'Treason' and the B-side, which was our version of 'I've Read It in Books'.

The studio was below a launderette. We piled in and played the backing tracks over and over. It was lifeless, and Gary and I kept slowing down, speeding up, losing our place in the song, all this miserable stuff. Then, on the 23rd take, Clive said, "Yeah, I think that's the one. Come in and listen."

We went in. It was just bass and drums. Clive had taken my guide vocals and Mick's guitar out to check the rhythm track. I thought it was rubbish. How could he tell, with the bass and drums exposed like that? Better trust him.

We added all the other music really quickly. I can't remember doing any singing, so it was probably quite traumatic. I have a tendency to bleep out memories that are too much of a drag.

By 3 a.m. we had two sides of a single recorded. We slept overnight in a shit hotel in Sussex Gardens. There were prostitutes outside and the beds were shit. I wasn't used to hotels. We always drove back to Liverpool after gigs, as they were too expensive. I fell asleep with London's prossies echoing in my head. I was still angry at everything. This place sucks shit, get me out of here.

DAVE BALFE, WHAT'S GOT INTO YOU?

And so, whilst we were recording in London, Echo & the Bunnymen auditioned their one choice for drums, a 17 year old called Pete DeFreitas. Dave Balfe knew him. He shared a flat with Balfe's brother in London. I didn't really notice Pete. There were five years between us. I was married and had just turned 22. All that concerned me was Balfe's role in everything anyone did.

He'd insisted that we sign our Warner publishing through Zoo, giving them a cut. Okay, that's cool. Bill would do anything for me, so why not? But then, Balfe wanted to manage us. Sure Balfe, be our management, record company and publishers. You plank. I hated the guy. He wanted to be a full-time member of the Teardrop, but had an allegiance only to himself.

If I had an idea, I'd discuss it with him, get into it, go round to his flat and then ... if he was doing Bunnymen stuff, he'd put the idea on their song. The Bunnymen were always thick like that. They'd complain and moan about Balfe, but never do anything. I'd say, "Why don't you just twat the guy?" but they never would.

One time, we were coming back from a gig in Bristol. Pam Young, a Jenny Agutter-type, had arrived from Sheffield to become Zoo secretary. She was sitting in the back with Mick Finkler and me. Bill was in the front and Balfe was driving. I told her loudly and in great detail what a satanic son-of-a-bitch Balfe was. I started flicking his ears as we drove up the empty M5 and singing petty anti-Balfe rhymes.

After 10 minutes of this, he pulled onto the hard shoulder and told me to get out. This appealed to me. It was coming up to 3 a.m. and we were in the middle of nowhere.

Standing outside the car, I looked in on Balfe. I smiled.

"I'm not fucking coming back," he spluttered.

"Oh, I'd better leave my shoes in the car," I said. The road was wet and there was virtually no traffic.

"I'm going."

"Okay, David." I did a little jig in the middle of the motorway and waved them off. "See you in a while."

I started to walk up the motorway. I should have brought my jacket, I thought. I carried on gingerly. My feet began to freeze, so I took my sodden socks off and held them in my hand.

I figured they'd be back in 10 minutes. I had no watch, so 20 minutes seemed like an hour. I kept walking and walking. It was just like a bad hitch. I was cool. Certainly Nth degrees cooler than Dave "Smurf-features" Balfe.

Still no sign. I sat on a motorway crash barrier and raised my aching red feet in an effort to warm them up. No car, no Balfe. I began to grow uncomfortable. I mean, a twat like that. Maybe Bill couldn't persuade him, but surely Mick could. I mean, Mick hates him almost as much as I do.

Finally, a car screamed by in the opposite direction. It was Balfe's Citroën. Ten minutes later, he had found the nearest intersection, made the turn and roared up to me. I was freezing cold, soaking wet and beaten.

"Hi Balfe, where are you going?"

"Get in, Julian, I'm fucking pissed off as hell. I wouldn't have come back if Bill wasn't in the car."

Bill leaned over from the passenger seat and looked up at me. He told me they'd driven 25 miles before he could persuade Balfe to turn around.

"You know, I'm fine walking, Balfe. If I were you, I'd get off home. This has been quite an evening for you."

I was pushing my luck, I knew it. Any minute now, he'd be off for good. I got in the car, "as a favour to you, Davie," and we drove off on full wind-up power.

And that was the turning-point. From then on, I respected Balfe. He had a good measure of the psychotic in him and I realised how hard it was to be in his position. Of course, I'd use his uncoolness and red-faced rage against him whenever I could. But autumn was the start of the unlikely axis: Julian David Cope and David William Miguel Balfe. Er, Look Out!

The big chill started slowly. I still didn't trust Balfe. But I had, at last, grudgingly admitted to myself that he was good.

I took records and a lyric book around to his flat in Grove Park. He made tea and I played him *Scott 2* by Scott Walker. It was a record made by a total obsessive. Scott sung in an absurd voice, Tony Bennett on Valium. The music was lush and grossly over the top, and depressing as hell. We listened in silence. Side one ended. I turned the record over and played side two. On and on, the dark despairing camp grotesqueness of Scott Walker coagulated the atmosphere. Finally, the record ended.

Dave Balfe was moved. He was sucked in from the start. This was his music. Good God, let's make music like that. He got up and walked to the window. A pissy day in Liverpool presented itself to him and Balfe's mind switched into gear.

After that, we could talk to each other. We weren't any nicer to each other, but we understood, now.

HEY, MAN, THAT'S A FUCKING JOINT

As I walked down into the dressing room of Nottingham's tiniest club, I smelled something weird and looked over at Mick Finkler.

"Hey, man, what's that? It's a fucking joint. That's a fucking hippy joint, you bloody hippy. Fucking hell. I mean, fuck."

Mick ignored me and passed the joint to Balfe. Oh great. So now we're fucking The Grateful Dead or some shit. We might as well forget the whole thing. I was so anti-drugs. I thought the Clash had sold out when they'd got on their spliff and reggae trip. Now I was the bass player in bloody Hawkwind.

I went to the Bunnymen's dressing room. We hung out and I felt better. Pete DeFreitas, their new drummer, was so young. I felt old next to him. God, I just wished that I could relax. I was so tense all the time. Everything was so bloody important.

"This is for the hippies in the *bairnd*," I drawled, after the first song. Then we waded into the set, my head still raging. The songs sped by and I paid no attention to pace or tuning.

"Okay, this last song is 'White Rabbit'." We launched into a tense amphetamine version of 'Sleeping Gas'. It wailed on and on. I closed my eyes and drifted off, repeating over and over, *"It's so ethereal, it's so ethereal, it'ss oh eh-teer-eeal."*

About three minutes into this needle-in-the-eye rant, Balfe rushed over to centre stage and shouted, "If you don't stop messing around, I'm fucking leaving."

Oh, he was awake, was he? The song ended and Balfe and I had a slagging match on stage. We continued the argument through the encores and into the dressing room. I told him that he sucked intense amounts of shit and went home with the Bunnymen.

It was like old times again. We all shared a hatred of Balfe, so we spent the whole journey cursing his stupid lisp and his general uncoolness.

It was December 1979. Wow, a new decade coming. I was married and I had a cool group. The third single was ready for release and this time I was happy with it. Not just happy – I thought it was brilliant.

The Teardrop and the Bunnymen played a Christmas show at Eric's. It was a total party. We knew that the rivalry was beginning to pull us apart. Both Mac and I were starting to think that the other was becoming a prick.

Both groups came on at the end and we did a version of the Velvet Underground's 'What Goes On'. Mac and I danced and sang together, and hugged and camped it up. We were Liverpool's symbol of camaraderie and attitude.

Kathy went home to Leeds for Christmas. She couldn't bear it without her parents. I went to Tamworth on my own. It was fine. I don't know. I was just

troubled, that's all. I played *Scott 4* all the time. It's Scott Walker's most intense record. It just lies there on the turntable, brooding.

My brother Joss had passed his driving test by now. We drove around Tamworth and he cheered me up. We sat in the car, in the rain, in the car park of Alvecote Priory, singing 'Angels of Ashes', one of Scott's most chilling songs.

I wondered about being nice. You know, what it really was.

I COULD SWING FOR YOU

"Yeah? Well I've heard some of it and it's crap. And they've ruined 'Villier's Terrace' as well. It just churns along."

I was talking to Yorkie in his basement. I was smug as hell. The Bunnymen had started their album in South Wales and it sucked a big one. A guy called Pat Moran was doing it. It sounded as though he'd got them all to play as loud as possible, then done the crossword.

I was still licking my wounded heart over the Bunnymen's record deal. Bill and Balfe had tried to get us a deal with CBS, but the A&R man, Howard Thompson, said we were a good group but I couldn't sing and I looked terrible. Balfe enjoyed telling me that last bit, but they were both worried. We were getting bigger all the time, but the major companies thought we could never cross over, so it was not worth the effort.

The Bunnymen album was cancelled for a while. Everyone agreed that they should start again. It gave us a breather, as we had no money to record. The Bunnymen started turning up at Yorkie's with new guitars and amplifiers. Mac's clothes were getting flasher. They were getting away from us.

I wanted that record deal. It was on my mind, night and day. I wanted what Mac had and I Could Not Wait. I CAN NOT WAIT. What's the point of having a great record if it can't get in the chart?

I'd go home to my harmonium every night and pump out these great dreary laments. On into late evening, I was there, on my own. "No, it's okay, Kathy. Yeah, you go to bed, it's cool."

In public, I was the Happy Guy. Record deals? No, I'm not sure if we want one, really. We've got more control if we stay on Zoo. Bill says he'll pay to record our album. You see, if you've got your shit together, you shouldn't have to rely on big business. And on and on and on.

While we waited for 'Treason' to be released, I spent some time with Pete Wylie. He'd walked into the tea-rooms in Mathew Street when I was there and told me he had a group called Wah! Heat. It was the first good new group name

I'd heard in ages. Everyone was now obsessed with long rambling names. Pete felt lost in the wake of the Zoo triumph and I was worried about him. If I felt bad about Mac's record deal, I wondered, how must he be feeling? We'd gone off and left him. Pete was doing fine, though. He wrote a few crap songs and watched us get hip in the music press. But now he appeared to have snapped out of it. Roger Eagle's partner, Pete Fulwell, had played me some stuff. It sounded great.

Wylie rang me up and said that Wah! Heat were playing their first gig and would I play organ? I was really happy. I'd love to do it, man. I'll come down. In the gloaming of Eric's, Wah! Heat cranked out their noise. I walked in and hugged Wylie. It was like being free. They'd brought in an old Farfisa for me and I just had to do my thing. No directing, no voice problems and no rivalry.

I knew 'Better Scream', as it was the forthcoming single. I learned it quickly and added a Doors-y solo to it. It was a great song. It's got an ominous veil over it. I had wondered if he was talking about *The Illuminatus*. We played it over and over that day, and I never asked him.

One song was called simply 'Tempo' and I knew it had to be named after Wylie's Stuart Sutcliffian mate Steve Tempest. Wylie had initially formed Wah! Heat around Tempo's bass playing and vibe, but Tempo was a legend, not a bass player, so Pete had eulogised him in song instead.

A few days later Wah! Heat played their first show. It was great. I stood crouched over the organ, concentrating and watching Pete Wylie. There was a real anxiety in him and on a song called 'Somesay', he stood stock still and steamed, just like he'd completely seized up. "Some say our ideals are jokes, some say on our words we'll choke." Both I and the audience were totally absorbed. He had no records out, but Wylie had a following in Liverpool without that shit. He'd lost his Clashisms and had a set full of snotty strung-out bitch-ballads. Pete Wylie, the gothic Glen Campbell.

Uh, Look Out!

TREASON

And so it came to be that every day the atmosphere in the Zoo office became worse and worse. I couldn't bear to be in there when the McCulloch thing was happening. We avoided each other as much as we could.

Bill had called Mac "the new Frank Sinatra" in *NME*. He also said I was pretty good, too, in a patronising half-assed way. I needed Bill. I needed him even more at the moment, but the Bunnymen needed nursing all the time. I wanted us to do a film. Nothing expensive, just to get down what was happening with both groups. "Yeah, yeah," said Bill. And that was the end of that.

But I was getting desperate. Balfe and I spent our time in Callan's, a military shop in Whitechapel. We bought heavy-duty belts and US parachute boots really cheap. I had a few entire outfits, because they were so cheap.

Balfe said we should buy a vehicle. Yes! I'd seen this fantastic armoured car up by the Anglican cathedral. Find out where that guy got his from. Okay. I just felt that we needed something cheap. If we had no major record label behind us, surely we could appear like we had money.

It was difficult to haul all these things together. Every day I was more hung up and tense. Mick Finkler hated the idea of dressing the way Balfe and I did. Gary had started to, but tended to turn up dressed in entire outfits. He was obsessed by Robert Mitchum and would dress like a military general or an American sailor. I'd say, "No, man. It's got to be four people in the same kind of clothes, or we'll look like a showband."

Then, in early March, *Sounds* rang us to say that 'Treason' would be single of the week. Yes! We felt as though we had made it, as they'd rung up to tell us. We rushed out to buy the magazine as soon as it came out.

The singles review was way out. Wah! Heat had half a page on their 'Better Scream' 45 and our single had another half page.

Dave McCulloch, the journalist in question, had written his head and his ass onto the page. He called us "one of the most important bands in the country" and summed it up at the end: "Everything, the skill, the delivery, the touch of quaintness, the confidence, the commitment, points to a record of classic nature."

My head reeled. It was the first record that I was proud of and the review said what I wanted to hear. In the Wah! Heat review, we were even called "the already near-legendary The Teardrop Explodes". Awlright, this is the kind of shit I could believe.

Coming in the wake of what seemed like continuous rejection, everyone's response to the 'Treason' 45 lifted my head way out of the mire. The record was no. 3 on the Alternative chart for weeks and by the time it had finished had sold 25,000 copies. So stuff your major labels, I thought, we're going to do an album on Zoo.

It was time for us to tour. Of course, the Echo & the Bunnymen tour was going ahead first. Naturally. They had Warner Bros. backing them. I was resentful as hell. Our gigs would be in the same places, but theirs would look better.

Not necessarily, though. Anyone could do stuff with money. The Bunnymen have never had one single non-musical idea in their head.

We spent our days in Callan's military shop. I knew Carl, the main guy, really well. I'd go in and spend hours buying pre-1947 US flags.

"That's worth about £15 now. You can have it for three," Carl would say. "Here, get this entire World War 2 tank outfit. It's only £8."

God, the stuff in there. It was a lifetime's supply of stage props and stage outfits. I'd take Mick Finkler. He dug the stuff, but was worried about us becoming showbiz. I knew what he meant, but we would do it properly, keep the stage as the main military motif and keep our clothes as low key as possible.

I was reading books on Vietnam – *Nam* by Mark Baker and a thing called *From Five Miles Up*. I'd ripped off shitloads of ideas from that book. We had a new song called 'Went Crazy'. The song title was a chapter heading about the way soldiers lost their mind. I had used a rhyme from the US military as the middle-eight:

"Oh, if you have a daughter, bounce her on your knee,
Oh, if you have a son, send the bastard off to sea."

It was a cynical, mean little rhyme. I changed "bastard" to "blighter" to suit our Englishness better.

Everything was coming on fine. First the two Zoo groups would tour, separately for the first time. Then the Bunnymen would record their album, again in Rockfield in South Wales, and we would follow straight after that and do our album.

I was busy enough to forget my obsession with record deals for a while. Dindisc were interested, but they'd just signed Orchestral Manoeuvres, so they could piss off. A & M claimed some interest, but I think Bill and Balfe were just trying to keep my hopes buoyant.

One day, walking through Whitechapel, I bumped into Pete Wylie and Johnno, one of his young mates. I said I'd see them in Probe, but I had to pop into Zoo. The office was 20 yards away, across Button Street. I ran into the Zoo office and laughed my stupid head off.

Bill Drummond, the greatest guy of all time, was sitting on his own in the office, surrounded by scrim netting. You know, the camouflage netting that they put over tanks. It covered the entire office and it was brilliant. I didn't say anything, I just flopped down on the floor, among the chaos of the nets, and said, "Bill, this is Godlike." Who needs a bloody record company advance, when you've got ideas galore?

Bill was quiet. He wouldn't look at me. I asked what was wrong. Nothing could freak me out, this had made me higher than I'd been for months.

Bill said quietly, "It's not yours."

I didn't know what he meant.

"It's not for you. The scrim."

I couldn't work it out.

"Julian . . . It's for the Bunnymen tour."

Bill did not look at me. His voice trailed off. He had fucked me up the ass.

He had fucked me up the ass and then cut off my balls, and then? He'd sucked my brains and served them to Echo & the Bunnymen.

I was dead.

FUCKED UP THE ASS AND TOLD TO ENJOY IT

"One thing you can't hide, is when you're crippled inside."

John Lennon

I walked out of the Zoo office onto the dingy second floor landing of Chicago Buildings. I made for the stairs and climbed up and up, to the top floor, and found my way onto the outside balcony. I looked out across towards Church Street and I sobbed and I sobbed. I could not think. A black, black desperation enshrouded me and the most evil of evil thoughts flooded into my mind, as though any moral dam in my head had been smashed and swept away by the torrent of vicious unthinking treachery that had taken place.

Oh my God. I wished evil and mayhem and destruction on each individual Bunnyman, four guys who were still unaware of the chaos they were causing. But that made it worse. They didn't know about the scrim and the camouflage. Bill hadn't told them his idea. It was our thing, man. It was my fucking bastard idea.

I stayed on the roof. I was embarrassed as hell. Shit. Now Mac was going to have the best stage set ever. The guy who'd laughed at my camo and swanned around in his funky new gear was going to tour in MY OUTFITS. WELL, FUCK MY SHIT, McCULLOCH!

I stayed up there, in just that one position, for what seemed like hours. Then I caught the 73 bus back home to Devonshire Road. I went into my music room and glowed pure evil. The embarrassment. It just flooded over me, again and again. Then there'd be a seventh wave that just carried me deeper down, and over the rocks.

I cried. I kicked the hell out of things.

But, most of all, I stayed silent and motionless, and looked straight at the floor of my room. I stared and I stared until my eyes saw only directly in front of me, and darkness clouded the edges, and a tunnel formed, and I slipped into a mood of total inert psychosis.

And I sat there. And I thought that I would stay very quiet for a very, very long time.

That night, there was a noise in the hall and Kathy stuck her head around the door of my music room.

"Bill Drummond's here. Are you gonna speak to him?"

I was sitting in the same place I'd been all day. Bill walked in, his tall frame stooping and sheepish. He sat next to me and we both stared at the same patch of wall. There was silence for a couple of minutes, but I felt comfortable with it. Then Bill began to talk.

"I'm sorry, Julian. I should have told you. I do feel really bad." He fumbled for words. "It's just . . . well, it seemed perfect for the Bunnymen. And . . . well, we couldn't have afforded it for the Teardrops anyway. You know. I wanted it to be right."

I sat there. I understood him. It was a typical Zoo bullshit. He just liked the idea and had to do it now. If it was the other way around, the Bunnymen would have missed out. Balfe and Bill were so pleased with themselves that they were treating both groups like pawns. I could hear Bill talking in the background, but I wasn't listening. Eh, who cares? The Bunnymen are like sheep anyway. If Mac's given any idea, he thinks it's his own by the next day. They can all sod off.

Drummond got up and prepared to leave. He said some confused stuff about how they were a group, and how he loved groups, and he had this vision of them as The Rolling Stones, and how The Teardrop Explodes wasn't a group, never was, and I would always do precisely what I wanted. Then he said I was more talented than them, but he could direct them because they were not so wilful and they let him get more involved.

He finally left. I sat alone, again. Bill Drummond had said only one thing that I had heard. He had said I was more talented than them. He had said it for sure. Maybe he had said it to help ease his way out of a sticky situation? I didn't think so. He had said it so matter of factly that I believed him. Whether or not it was the truth, it appeased me.

There are certain marker-posts in everyone's lives. And this was one of mine. That day I stepped over a problem and into a new phase of possibilities. Yeah, I'll give them their camo, I thought, trying to belittle the very thing I'd been so desperate for. It'll be their gimmick.

And in a muddy and confused way, I felt almost good.

BE WARY OF PEOPLE WITH KNIVES IN THEIR BACKS

It was the final and absolute end of our innocence. And any thoughts we may have had that all this was still a game had now to be buried forever.

Mick Finkler and I had written all the main songs, but I felt that he was lacking ideas. The first year had been chock-a-block with riffs and stuff, but lately I

had been bringing in all the songs. Gary would sit reading *Sounds* magazine in the corner of the basement, occasionally looking up to see if we were struggling or getting somewhere.

Then, out of the blue, we wrote a song called 'When I Dream'. It was our most melodic yet, built around this circular bass riff. I sung the whole song pretty much off the top of my head, in one go, anchoring the words with the bass and drums. I wanted it to sound like The Seeds. Around this time I was listening to their live album *Merlin's Music Box* almost exclusively. I have periods like that. Sometimes it's good to steep yourself in one style.

We played it to Balfe, who added a sparkling toy-piano part. It sounded like a single and I wanted to write more, straight away, but I was frustrated by Mick. See, he would play only his own guitar lines. I found it frustrating to have a song turned down only because Mick could not think of a part. His snobbery and hang ups were losing us valuable songs.

I turned more and more to Balfe. He was excited and wanton. I said, "Let's fuck all the art-shit. Let's call the album something ridiculous." Balfe suggested "Everybody Wants to Shag The Teardrop Explodes'. Gary and I loved it.

Mac was getting into the "I'm a great artist, therefore I'm serious" angle, the very thing we'd always laughed at. No way would I fall for the art-trip. Round at Balfe's flat, I played him the *Forever Changes* album by Love. We'd been compared to Love in some interviews and Balfe wanted to hear them. It was another revelation for him. Beautiful acoustic guitar melodies under the most righteous trumpets in the world. But sneaky messed up lyrics that were gross in places. Arthur Lee, the songwriter and leader of the group, was a heavy dude.

Balfe wanted to use trumpets. He'd already contemplated a full orchestra in the wake of his Scott Walker schooling, but we figured trumpets would less easily swamp the group sound.

My hang ups were worked overtime as we got no nearer to a major record deal. We went on tour and it was great and all, but not the same as with a deal.

We played to more people than the Bunnymen, but their tour was so well advertised that it appeared as though they were bigger. That did my head in.

The live show got more psychotic throughout the tour. We were getting more used to stringing songs out and taking them down. Grooves would churn on and on. One night, at Bath University, the keyboards broke down halfway through the set. I gave Balfe my bass and played Mick's spare Fender copy. We played drony jams for about half an hour and I recorded the whole thing. I was getting into spontaneous shit. It was only 50% good but I liked the pressure.

In Glasgow, we played a packed and minuscule club called the Bungalow Bar. Aztec Camera were supporting. We were told that their singer was 12.

We had to play an hour's set! We decided to extend everything and were still working on it when Bill Drummond got a phone call.

It was Tony Wilson from Factory Records. Ian Curtis, from Joy Division, had killed himself. We couldn't say anything. I freaked out. He was one of our peers. He can't die. That's fucking ridiculous.

Halfway through the set, I quietly announced the horrible news. People didn't react. I don't think they could believe it. You come to enjoy yourself, I guess. Not to hear that kind of news.

During 'Sleeping Gas', I sung a Joy Division song called 'Novelty' over it. It was just for me really. It made me feel better, a bit anyway. Ian Curtis, man. What a sweetie.

'Treason' was selling loads, but in alternative shops. The new Echo & the Bunnymen 45, a great song called 'Rescue', was at no. 62 in the BBC chart. Yet it sold less than 'Treason'. That blew my mind. It just was not fair.

By the time we finished the tour, the Bunnymen were ready to start their album in Rockfield. Bill Drummond and Dave Balfe were going to produce it, under the name The Chameleons. They got in everywhere. Ian Broudie, a friend, had already produced two tracks for the Bunnymen album, then been kicked off the case.

We bided our time in Liverpool, then drove down to the studios, a few days before we started our album.

Rockfield Studios are about five miles outside Monmouth. The B4233 cuts its way through a shallow V-shaped valley with farmland and woods on either side. About a mile before the village of Rockfield are the studios' many buildings.

On the top of a steep hill, to the right, is a large white farmhouse. We drove up the narrow lane slowly, as both sides were obscured by thick hedges. At the top of the hill, we got out of the car and I looked back across the valley.

On the other side of the road was the studio. It was about a half-mile away. I put on my glasses and could just make out the figure of Les Pattinson walking across the courtyard.

We took our stuff into the white house and chose bedrooms. I looked out of the back window and saw Will Sargeant standing at the farm gate. At the back of the house, the land slopes away and down to the River Monnow. I dropped my bags and ran down to see him.

"Will, how's it going? Is it a classic or what?"

"It's crap."

Will was obviously very upset. We began to walk slowly down to the river. "Fucking Dave Balfe. He has to clean everything up. He has to make it poppy." Will spoke slowly and bitterly.

I knew what the main problem would be. Balfe had little regard for people's feelings and someone as gentle as Will would have no defence. I could threaten

and scare Dave Balfe, but Will would just bottle it up and slowly freak out.

We walked about a mile along the river towards Monmouth. I tried to console him. He was inconsolable. He wanted to sound like Television. He wanted sharp angles and swooping chiming riffs. We carried on along the river, like Winnie the Pooh and Piglet, his mind blown by events in the studio, my mind blown at the anticipation of events in the studio.

Soon, the Bunnymen were packed and gone. I heard their album. It was brilliant. Just brilliant. It *was* like Television and it chimed like crazy. I was jealous, and nervous about some of the production.

In typical Zoo fashion, Balfe had put our hallmark keyboard sound on their record. Also, on their *tour de force*, a song called 'Happy Death Men', he'd used fanfare trumpets. I was consoled only because the trumpets sounded shit. They were like cheap synthesizers, all reedy and horrible.

The Teardrop record had to be finished in two weeks. Drummond had remortgaged his house to pay for it. It was an act of extreme faith and we had to deliver.

We started slowly. Compared with the Bunnymen rhythm section, Gary and I were a liability. Balfe and Bill grew impatient. On the 20th take of a song called 'Poppies in the Field', Dave Balfe shouted at us, through the headphones, "Come on. That sounded fucking crap. Pete and Les were doing it in one take. Two at the most."

His brilliant use of psychology brought the session to its knees and I walked out. It was like that for the whole album.

When Mick recorded his guitar parts, no-one was happy. What had sounded great on stage sounded prosaic and unimaginative in the studio. We told him to change it. He sulked and said it was perfect.

We ploughed on, more concerned with finishing in time than making a great record. Balfe added too many keyboards to make up for the lame guitar. I sung my best, but it just felt like work.

In two weeks we were finished. We left the studio with knots in our stomachs and a sense of loss. A first LP is an event. An accumulation of all the ideas you ever had in your life. I had put no more than 10% of my ideas in. They were either suppressed through lack of time or not taken seriously.

Our album needed an early release in order to get Bill's money back. Tim Whittaker, a Liverpool legend and flatmate of Balfe, painted a mandala as the album sleeve, with the title of the record right across the top. It looked really good, in an independent sort of way.

Bill cut the album and we listened to the acetate, a facsimile of the finished record. It missed by miles. I wouldn't say anything, though. If I had my act together, we would have a deal and we wouldn't be in this mess.

Then came a breakthrough. Phonogram Records were interested.

"Phonogram are crap," I protested. "They don't even have paper labels." I was very purist. I refused to sign to a record company with plastic labels.

"Oh, fuck off, Copey." Balfe didn't want to hear that shit.

But Bill did understand. We both had a powerful sense of the aesthetic, on whatever level it was. "I don't want you to sign to Phonogram either, Julian. The guy who wants you is a real dickhead, but he's a big fan. You need that. You need someone who'll kill for you."

He was right. But Phonogram? Who do they have that's cool? No-one. I could think of no-one. Bill said that he'd use Phonogram's interest as a carrot to some other companies.

Time passed, and we had Dindisc and A & M vaguely into us. But the Phonogram guy was not to be put off. He had said something that made Balfe and Bill laugh a great deal and they told me as though it was the most ridiculous thing ever: "Guess what, Julian? The Phonogram guy thinks you can be a pin-up."

They laughed so much when they said it that I laughed too. By now I'd been slagged off by so many record executives that the idea of myself as a pin-up sounded as ridiculous to me as it did to everyone else.

Then I thought about it. The New York Dolls' albums were on Phonogram's subsidiary label, Mercury. Yeah, we'll record for Mercury. And I'll be a pin-up. Uh, Look Out!

LOSE YOUR SENSES

And so the pressure mounted. The pressure to get things right. The album was definitely not great. Someone is to blame. Find a scapegoat! Someone called Mick Finkler. I twisted and turned, I had to get this right.

Balfe and I were looking to blame somebody. Who better than Mick? He'd been a drag from the start to the end of the recording. He couldn't write songs anymore. He was holding us back, the bastard.

As the negotiations with Phonogram moved along, the anti-Mick feeling mounted in the Teardrop camp. Gary was non-commital in public, but quietly he agreed with us. If Mick made a simple mistake, we came down heavy on him.

Just as in any gang, once we all decided that he had to leave, anything he did made us think he was a dickhead. It wasn't his fault, it's just the way it goes. Mick was getting friendly with Wylie again. Huh, what a plank. Mick wore something crap today. God, he's so uncool. On and on it went.

Balfe got a little out of control. Any time Mick left the room during rehearsals, he'd say, "Sack him now, Copey. We should film it. Yeah, that'd be far-out. Film it in the Zoo office. I'll do it, it'll be historical."

Then we'd all dance around in the embarrassment of such a loathsome but tempting idea.

We got a call from Ruth Polsky in New York. After a first possible American trip had been aborted at the last minute, we didn't have high hopes of playing there soon. But now she was confident. And this time, she just wanted the Teardrop and no Bunnymen.

Yeeeess!

We've gotta do it Bill, we've got to. Imagine getting to New York before we've got a record contract. It would be the coolest.

Fuelled by these possibilities, we all realised that the Mick situation had to be resolved. Of course, he found out about New York and got all excited along with the rest of us. We knew we had to do it now. We even had a replacement lined up: Balfe's friend, Alan Gill. His group, Dalek I Love You, also had a contract with Phonogram Records. His album was released soon, but he wanted to join the group.

I decided to tell Mick Finkler the bad news, but I insisted that Gary, Balfe and Drummond were there, so Gary wouldn't crumble when Mick asked him on his own.

Two weeks before the New York gigs, we had a meeting at Zoo office. When Mick arrived, we had been there a while, getting composed. We thought we looked dead heavy, so when Mick walked in, I said, "I've got a bit of bad news. You're sacked."

Mick burst out laughing. He didn't believe us. True, Gary told Balfe that he was sacked every other day. It was a group joke to sack people.

I tried again. This time I was firmer. I didn't want to embarrass Mick. It was a crap thing to be doing, especially with the timing of the whole thing. Finally, Balfe said, "Look, Finkler, you're fuckin' out of the group. It's not a joke, alright?"

Mick, understandably, freaked. He launched into a tirade about Balfe, and how he'd ruined the group, and all kinds of miserable stuff that you just blot out of your memory as it goes on and on and on.

Mick had been in the group almost two years. He'd co-written all the songs with me. I spent pretty much every day in his company. After that day, I saw him only two more times in my life. I guess that's what groups are like.

HURRAH

And so it was that in July of 1980, The Teardrop Explodes arrived in New York, with our manager, Bill Drummond, and our mate and photographer, Bill Butt. All the guilt and defensiveness of the previous months were forgotten while we came to terms with America.

I had never even flown before. I wanted us to present a very cohesive image to New York. We were hip as hell in this city and this little hick wasn't going to blow it.

Of course, Gary jumped into a cab on our arrival and said, "53rd and 3rd, bud." He didn't want to go there, he just wanted to say it. Within 24 hours of being in New York, the group was transformed into a transatlantic rock'n'roll machine.

Except for me. And even I was trying hard.

Ruth Polsky had booked our sleeping arrangements. The two Bills were staying in the Iroquois Hotel on Columbus Circle. It was a hip dump, but mainly it was near the club.

Ruth farmed the rest of us out to women she knew. I thought I was mis-hearing her when she started to put us in different cabs, but no. Suddenly Alan Gill was on his own and bound for Brooklyn. Balfe was assigned to a woman in the East Village. Gary refused and ran off to the Iroquois, where the two Bills had an extra bed.

And me? Suddenly I was being driven downtown to 15th Street by a crazy Hispanic taxi driver. It was far-out. I was determined to enjoy it. Shit, I had my US military police outfit with me. I'll wear it tomorrow, I thought.

I arrived at the apartment on 15th and 5th. What a cool address, I thought, as I handed the driver $20.

"That'll do okay." He drove off. Wow, my first rip-off. And I've only been here one hour.

The next minute I was in this strange apartment with some strange woman. We talked and I looked around for another bed. There was only one.

I flipped through her records. Hmm, pretty hip. All the Velvet Underground. All The Doors. Hey, you like The Seeds? I passed her a Seeds 45 and we talked whilst it played. What a drag, I thought. I wished she was better looking. At that moment, I'd forgotten that I was married. I just wanted to hang out in some NY apartment and make love with The Seeds playing.

That night was too weird for me. I got the ugly girl sexual gross-outs. Next morning, I dressed in my MP outfit, grabbed my stuff and fled. I could see the Empire State Building in the distance. Eh, I'll walk, it's a doddle.

Forty blocks I walked, sweating and unaware, through heavy neighbourhoods that thought I was a real MP. I even wore my crowning glory: a military police

helmet. That walk gave me a short sharp lesson: don't presume that you're cool everywhere. Cool has context. Walking 40 blocks in a military outfit is dead uncool.

We were shown around by pleasant women who thought we were quaint relics from the past. Our everyday language included words like "awlright", "far-out", "it's cool", and so on. But they told us gently, and in private, "Actually, people don't say that kind of thing anymore."

It was weird that our speech bothered them. New York 1980 was a place of hang ups. We're all new wavers, right? And now these hip English groups speak like hippies, right?

That night, everyone but Balfe was in the Iroquois. There were three beds, so we figured it was fair to alternate between floor and bed. I slept in a walk-in cupboard and woke mid-morning to an empty suite. Everyone was doing their thing, so I found a bar and ate pastrami-on-rye for the rest of the stay.

Balfe and Gary scored LSD and partied and got laid and came back to the hotel in a murderous mood. I was still anti-drugs, but being with Alan Gill had started to ease my opinion. I hardly knew Alan, except for rehearsals, but he was going to be my biggest influence yet.

Balfe surged into our room, transporting like a bastard. "Way-up, how's it going?" The Balfe bug-eyes were blazing.

In the other room, I heard Gary talking to Paul Gambaccini, the American DJ. There there was a yell and a crash. We legged it into the other room to find Bill Drummond hanging on to the legs of Gary Dwyer. The rest of Gary was hanging out of the 12th-floor window. Bill Butt and Alan helped to haul him in.

Gary was unaware of his situation. Again, he began his uncanny Paul Gambaccini impersonation. Alan and I hauled ourselves back into the bedroom. Don't mess with drugs, I thought. They'll only fool you.

The rest of the trip was fine. Everyone but me tried cocaine and fine American weed. I was too hung up. The shows at Hurrah were good but not great, except for a version of Aretha Franklin's 'Save Me'. That was brilliant and went on for hours.

At JFK Airport, they all finished the cocaine in the toilets, like true groovers should and we boarded the plane for England.

MAKING OUR WAY TO KILIMANJARO

And so the party which had begun in New York continued on the other side of the ocean. We were a different group. We signed to Phonogram one week later and I was a different person.

Alan Gill was my guru. I loved the guy. He was about three years older than me and had an ultra-quiet confidence. He didn't give a shit, he even had a moustache. And this at a time when moustaches and beards were considered the uncoolest of the uncool.

Phonogram gave us money to re-record parts of the album, so we trotted back to Rockfield with a new attitude.

The first night we were there, Alan Gill said to me, "You know, Julie, you're too tense."

I'd never been called Julie before and, to this day, Alan is the only person I would accept it from. I agreed that I was too tense, but I wouldn't smoke pot, mainly because of the tobacco.

"Listen, Julie. I'll skin up a pure grass joint. You try it and maybe you'll be less tense."

For a while now, I'd been watching with interest as the three other members of the group had begun to fool with drugs. I was not into them myself, but I began to appreciate what they did for others.

Bill Drummond told me not to take anything. He said I was bad enough straight. Think of what a pain in the ass I'd be. I told Alan Gill about Bill's fears and he shrugged his shoulders. He told me that I was a tense asshole most of the time and said I needed to relax properly. Okay, that seemed fair enough.

He built this fine long spliff and passed it to me. I had *never, not ever,* smoked a cigarette. The idea had always made me sick. Why was I doing this? I hate drugs, they're bullshit.

I sucked hard on the joint. I didn't cough, as I thought I would. I sucked again, a massive toke, then passed it to Balfe. It tasted really good and when it came around again, I had a real heavy go on it.

I sunk lifelessly behind the couch and the rest of them started to laugh. My head cleared up. My aching, which had been there since my early teenage years, started to evaporate. Out of the top of my head I could feel all my little devils flying off. They were all muttering to each other about how I'd been saved.

Yes, I was saved. I felt clean. I was 22 and I felt free. Not hippy free, just cooler about myself. I realised that it was okay to be me. Uh-oh, revelations time.

"What d'you reckon then, Julie?"

"I reckon you should skin up another one, right now."

Alan looked over at me, and told me that the joint I'd just smoked contained the tobacco I'd been avoiding all my life. It wasn't pure grass at all.

"Fuck it, man. I don't care. Just keep them coming."

And so it began. It was the turning-point. The first time I had ever liked myself. That version of the group became a total hang-out experience.

•　　•　　•

We rerecorded huge chunks of the album. When I sang, I wanted it to be an event. Hell, you don't record your first album every day. "Hand me that spliff, I'm going to do all the singing dressed like Lawrence of Arabia."

Actually, I'd seen Sky Saxon, my hero from The Seeds, dressed like T. E. Lawrence in a picture. That inspired me. The vocals sounded 10 times, no, 50 times better.

Alan added backward guitar and we knocked out all Mick Finkler's clumsy riffs. We were making a real record.

And then one day Dave Balfe arrived with LSD. We were all sitting in the white farmhouse on the top of the hill. We had all decided to take it together and I was excited at meeting the true "psychedelic" experience.

In one review, a music writer had said: "It's time Julian Cope stopped messing around and started to write some real psychedelic lyrics." Until that time, I'd considered my words to be merely pop-art images. But the arrival of Alan Gill and the constant references to acid in our reviews fascinated me. At last, I was ready to trip. Everyone told me how the walls would melt. I'd see God and nothing would be the same again.

Dave Balfe, Gary and I all took it at the same time. We sat around and nothing happened. We waited for an hour and a half, but still nothing.

Then, out from his room, came Alan. He walked right up to me, his eyes blazing, and said, "Fucking hell, Julie. You've given me scabies."

His face was satanic and I ran into the other room. I heard Balfe say, "Oh great, Alan. He took his first trip an hour ago. Well done."

Alan came in to apologise, but I was scared of him. His face, man, it was bulging with evil. And I probably did give him scabies, too. I felt guilty as hell.

Gary and I stuck together. We looked out of the picture window across the valley to the studio. We could see Bill Drummond and Bill Butt in the courtyard. They were walking up the lane and making for the farmhouse. As we watched them getting closer, I got excited. I got so excited at the prospect of them coming to see us that I couldn't bear it. I turned to Gary, and said, "Gary . . . they're coming to see *us*." I couldn't believe it. Two guys that I really liked were coming to visit us. I hadn't seen them since, well, since this morning.

My stomach began to move around. I clutched at my belly and looked across the room. What I saw astonished me. Dave Balfe was drinking a glass of milk. And worse than that, he had the milk bottle on the table. Oh my God.

I wobbled over to him and stared at the milk bottle from about a foot away. The milk scared me. It clung to the sides of the bottle and I knew that if I looked away, we'd be in terrible danger.

I sat guarding the milk for quite a while. Balfe ate two bowls of cereal and was about to pick up the milk bottle. It was so lucky I just happened to be there.

"Don't touch the milk, Balfe!" I screamed.

"Sorry, Copey, I didn't realise." He walked into the kitchen and returned with another bottle.

There was danger all around us. I gazed over at Gary and shouted, "Gary, look out!" In the nick of time, he realised that he was sitting on a pillow. I ran over and grabbed it. I picked it up and threw it across the room. Gary thanked me. And we hugged emotionally. Still hugging, we moved crablike to the pillow and began to kick it. Kick, kick, kick. Then I realised.

"It's okay, Garfield." I called him that sometimes. "It was dead already."

The pillow lay lifeless. I knew it wasn't a dead pig. It just looked so much like one. I started to cry and Gary saw me and he began to cry too. We sat in a corner, crying and hugging each other.

Bill Drummond and Bill Butt walked in. They looked around and surveyed the scene. Bill Butt handed me a letter. "This'll cheer you up. It's from Julie Mac."

I tore the letter open and read the first line carefully. Wow, I thought, this is the best letter ever.

Gary started to talk to me, but I was lost in the first line of the letter. "Shit, Gary. Now I'll have to read the letter all over again."

I restarted the letter, but someone else bothered me. It was Balfe. "I'm going down the studio with Alan. Coming?"

No, I didn't think so. Alan was weirding me out and I still thought I'd given him scabies. They left the house and set off down the hill. Gary and I hugged as we watched them get smaller and smaller, then we looked at each other and laughed. Ha ha ha ha ha ha ha ha ha ha ha ha ha ha ha ha ha ha ha ha ha ha ha ha ha ha aha aha aha aha aha aha aha aha aha aha aha aha aha aha aha aha aha aha aha aha aha aha aha aha aha aha aha aha aha.

After about 15 minutes, the two Bills couldn't bear to be around us. As they left, we apologised through our crazed and hysterical laughter.

The phone rang. It was our sound engineer, Harry. Gary spoke to him, as I danced around the phone. I grabbed the receiver and listened. Harry de Mack has a strong Manchester twang. "Eh, are you two fookers on drugs?" It was the funniest voice I'd ever heard and it was coming out of a tiny speaker in the phone. I slammed the phone down, and Gary and I collapsed again.

Aha ha ha ha ha ha ha ha ha ha ha ha ha ha ha ha ha ha ha ha ha ha ha ha ha ha ha aha aha aha aha aha aha aha aha aha aha aha aha aha aha aha aha aha aha aha.

On and on the trip went. After two hours, I had to leave Gary and walk to the studio. I edged down the lane, one step every other minute. After an hour and a half, I was about 25 yards from the house. I'd look back every five minutes and Gary would be in the same position at the window. His face was pressed up against the glass and he was laughing and pointing at me.

The house was white and jolly. The windows were eyes and a mouth. It

smiled at me, like a Disney house. I felt warm and safe, so I sat down in the lane, with the house still in view.

I started to read Julie Mac's letter. I'd got to the end of the first line, when I noticed something incredible. My right hand had a deep cut in it. The cut had been healing over the past days, but now it was suddenly open again. I looked into it and as I got closer, I noticed the face of Will Sargeant. If I moved my finger, the cut would move and Will's face would smile. I watched, fascinated. The slightest movement and I could change Will's entire expression.

After a while, a bunch of cows stuck their heads over the fence and mooed at me. I looked at them. They were such gentle beasts and we hung out for ages.

The hours passed and I stayed in my one position. Will's face entertained me and the cows. Every hour I'd make an effort to read beyond the first line of Julie Mac's letter. It didn't seem to matter, though. What she had written in the first line seemed like perfect philosophy.

I heard voices and up the lane walked Balfe, Drummond and Bill Butt. They hauled me up and we walked the 25 yards into the house. Alan arrived soon. He was not satanic, in fact he was very sweet. "Sorry, Julie. I was dead uncool."

I was fine. My new guru liked me again. Awlright.

The night rode on. We were all safe in the smiling white house-on-the-hill. I tried to eat with a knife and a fork. I tried to walk without laughing. But, somehow, that all seemed way in the past.

In the following days, a new Julian David Cope emerged. I didn't worry about everything the way I had. I worried only about the things I could control. I trusted Alan Gill. He was quick in the studio and not hung up. The album was beginning to sound really good.

I walked around the farmland in my Lawrence of Arabia outfit. One night, just as I was crossing the road at the bottom of the hill, I heard a car coming around the corner. I began to run, so that I would be moving fast as the car's headlights hit me. I zoomed past with my arms flailing above my head. The car swerved to a stop. I froze. I heard two people freaking out. Finally they drove off and I continued my walk from the studio.

We'd wake up early every morning. Gary and I would take acid, as we had both finished our parts. Then we'd ride down to the studio on imaginary horses. I called mine Dobbin. Gary called his Bumhead.

The weather was fantastic. I felt good about myself at last. The LSD was clearing my mind of the deep evil I'd begun to feel about myself.

We drove back up to Liverpool for a few days. I was uncomfortable with Kathy. She didn't know I was getting into drugs. I didn't feel guilty, just pissed off that she wasn't going to enjoy the benefits. Also, my volte-face on the subject of drugs could not be easily explained. I had been a posturing oaf to Mick Finkler. I was way up there in the "I don't need drugs" Sanctimonious Dickhead

stakes. The only way that I could've explained away my raging hypocrisy was to have denied half the stuff on which our relationship was built. I decided to avoid immediate conflict by not telling my wife.

We bought a 1954 Austin Champ jeep. It was painted green, with a Rolls Royce engine. We drove back to South Wales in it, wearing full military gear. It did eight miles to the gallon and cost us a fortune.

I was so comfortable. It was the best time in my life, I decided. I had felt so tense for so long. I felt it slipping from my shoulders, a little more every day. I was becoming loose.

The album was finally finished. It was September. The Bunnymen's record had been out since the summer. They had rave reviews and were doing incredibly well. Still, we had our record deal and I was stoned and happy.

We decided that "Everybody Wants to Shag The Teardrop Explodes" was too stupid a name. Also, it lost its irony if I was to be a pin-up, ha ha. Les from the Bunnymen suggested *Kilimanjaro*, and so it was.

We drove to London in the jeep to sign the Phonogram record contract. Bill had put a clause in the contract that allowed paper labels on the first 10,000 of every single that we released. I couldn't bear those injection moulded records, yucko.

I finally met the guy who thought I could be a pin-up. His name was Dave Bates and I liked him immediately. We had kind of met before, when he first wanted to sign us, but we had all gone back to his hotel that night and thrown shit out of the windows. Then I'd had a bath fully clothed and flooded his bathroom. When we left his hotel room that night, all I'd been wearing was a pink carrier bag around my waist. But that was before we'd wanted to sign to Phonogram and I tended to be gauche around record companies that didn't impress me.

Now it was different. I was cool. I was far too cool to let any record company control me. As far as I was concerned, it was Phonogram Records? Uh, Look Out!

They hung a flag over New Bond Street, in honour of our arrival. On it was our new logo and the *Kilimanjaro* legend. Stuff was moving fast.

'When I Dream' was our next single. The album was out in October and we had a tour, too. And I had moved in two short months from Drug Puritan to Acid King.

It didn't seem dangerous. It didn't seem right. It was just the only thing I wanted to do. If it makes you more bearable, then Right On!

FALL OUT WITH ME

And so the four members of the Teardrop started a period of intense learning from each other. Whether this particular combination of people could last was another matter.

I was writing, separately, with both Dave Balfe and Alan Gill. Although Balfe had suggested Alan as Mick Finkler's replacement, there was no real friendship between the two. In fact Alan went out of his way to avoid getting close to Balfe.

For a couple of weeks, I made the trek to Alan's house in Oxton. It involved taking a ferry across the Mersey, and two buses and a walk. Alan's flat was mainly equipment. Keyboards littered the floor, drum-machine, effects pedals and tape-recorders lay on any available flat surface. In his sideboard drawers lived two rabbits and his pot.

Alan and I drank strong tea and smoked pot till it confused us too much to record. We put about three ideas on tape in all the time we worked there. One day, Balfe got jealous, so he came over with Pete DeFreitas and we picked magic mushrooms and did no work.

On finishing the album, I'd told Bill we had no songs at all for a second one. It was a drag, because we couldn't think of a good follow-up to 'When I Dream'. We needed one soon to help lift interest in the group. The album was doing fairly well, but only as a cult. I wanted to be big. I wanted to be fucking huge.

The relationship with Balfe was still very edgy. In rehearsals, he was a total bastard, making us play songs again and again, and arguing over any tiny little decision.

One day, I'd been pissing Balfe off. In a big ass way. He was almost mute with rage at the end of the rehearsal. I had a prized Television bootleg with me and I started to leave with Balfe.

"Where d'you think you're going?" Balfe asked, unsmiling.

"With you. How else d'you think I'm getting home?" Balfe and I lived only 600 yards apart.

"You can get the fucking bus. You were a dickhead today and you can't have a fucking lift."

Alan and Gary watched as the crisis mounted at the bottom of the stairs. I told Balfe how he was, one day, going to get his and started up the stairs. Then I stopped. I thought for a minute. Then I started to walk back down the stairs.

"On second thoughts, Balfe. You're going to get it now."

I charged towards Balfe, but he moved away to the cupboard. In seconds, I'd caught him and was beating his face severely.

"I'll give you a lift, I'll give you a lift," he squealed and that made me hit him harder.

When Balfe was good and beaten, a smiling Gary Dwyer stopped the fight and we drove home together.

It was constant assault, both verbal and physical. And they were always confused one-sided fights, because of the drugs.

Dave Balfe always needed three capsules of everything to everyone else's one. We'd be gibbering in no time, but LSD could not obliterate his sense of reason. He was convinced that he was right, even on the most ridiculous points.

It began to get on my nerves. We spent all our rehearsal tripping or skinning up huge spliffs and rolling around the floor.

We would have lunch at Brian's diner in Stanley Street. It was the coolest place to eat when we were tripping. I'd sit and watch in hysterics as the chicken levitated off the plate. There were whole gangs of guys in Brian's high on LSD and admiring the acrobatic food.

Then one day, we were preparing for a John Peel radio session. The unassuming Alan Gill walked into the rehearsal room and said he had a song. It needed lyrics and a melody, and it was called 'Reward'.

I loved the name and watched as he showed me the bass line. Then he showed Balfe the organ line and we jammed on it for 10 minutes. It was brilliant. Like a spy theme and completely breakneck. One part was an obvious hook and in no time I sung the chorus: *"Until I learn to accept my reward."* We jammed some more and I said I'd finish the lyrics in time for the Peel session.

The next day, I was standing in the BBC studio, in London, preparing to record vocals for our new song. At my feet were all the other members of the group, looking up to give me inspiration. I started my first vocal take: *"Bless my cotton socks, I'm in the news."*

There was uproar. At the end of the take, Balfe said he hated that lyric. Then he said he loved it. Then we all realised that the song was brilliant and got really happy.

Then we went on tour and the whole scene went down the toilet. We fought every minute. Alan couldn't bear to talk to Balfe. I shared a room with Alan, but I blew his mind because I required constant attention.

The shows were brilliant, but only because of the tension. I never took acid on stage at this time. We got very high on pot and then some amyl nitrate turned up with some fans. They were following the tour, so we were guaranteed to be fucked up for the entire tour. Amyl is for weak hearts. It sets your head racing and your temples bulging.

In the middle of the tour, we recorded *The Old Grey Whistle Test*, the BBC's long established 'rock' TV programme. We arrived at Shepperton Studios, which is owned by The Who. After four hours of waiting, we walked out to the stage.

But first we inhaled amyl nitrate and I kicked the dressing-room door down. I wasn't trying to be rock'n'roll. But amyl makes you Hulk-like.

My senses heaved to and fro as we were introduced and the whole group bounded into a song called 'Ha Ha, I'm Drowning'. It was dreadful. My voice was shit, the guitar was deafening me, and the brass, oh man. These two young trumpeters we'd hired were the absolute crappest of the crap.

The first song ended and I said something in fake French. As soon as I said it, I thought, Uh? Then off we were again, into a contemptuous version of 'Reward'.

GET OUTTA YO-VILLE

In Yeovil, the show was cancelled. We waited around and two long-term fans gave us some weird blotter acid. The evening was free, so Alan Gill, Balfe and I decided to take the acid at the hotel.

It was an ancient place. A beautiful old inn with a huge bar and low-ceiling corridors. We all sat in Gary and Balfe's bedroom and took two tabs each.

Gary said he wasn't going to do any. "We're doing too much," he said. "I'm off down the bar." And he was gone, for an evening of heavy drinking with Harry de Mack, our Mancunian tour manager.

We settled down in front of the TV to watch Charles Bronson in *Streetfighter*. We smoked a few joints and waited for the acid to start.

The film was a really intense '20s scenario with Charles Bronson doing his regular stoic thang in a flat-cap and braces, and we all soon got sucked into it. I'd almost forgotten we'd taken acid, when, Brang! The whole room was flooded with the film. *Streetfighter* spilled into the ambience and we all became characters in the film.

Alan got paranoid and buried himself in his headphones, so Balfe and I went out into the corridor. It was about 9 o'clock and we wanted a drink.

We started slowly, inching our way along the floor. The corridor was bouncing up and down. It was like walking on a trampoline. I held on to Balfe, who was now clasping at the wall to keep his balance.

Slowly, and ever so gently, we made our way to the bar. It was miles down the corridor. I started to build a slow rhythm and Balfe copied me. We danced down the tunnel, with its shimmery lights. It was so beautiful. I had to stop and gasp.

A young guy walked past us towards the bar. I stopped him and touched his face, "This light goes on in here."

He looked at me, concerned, then carried on down to the bar.

We manoeuvred slowly to the stairs, but Balfe could go no farther. I told

him to wait, I'd bring him a drink. I was very worried about his safety. I felt very protective of my friends and I also felt extremely attractive.

Down the stairs I walked. Hmm, I thought I had real purpose as I moved through the huge room. I wouldn't wear my glasses, as they weren't right for someone this attractive. Because of this, I squinted slowly past each table, quizzically checking every person.

My stomach oozed and rumbled as I approached Gary's table. Harry de Mack was with the most disgusting woman I'd ever seen. She looked like a hammerhead shark. I tried not to look too grossed out as we were introduced, but I found myself staring directly at her.

The others all looked wonderful to me, but through my totally distorted perception, I realised that they were all pissed out of their brains.

I looked at Gary and he was pointing at the stairs. Then I roared with laughter at what I saw. Sweating and bewildered, Dave Balfe was making his way slowly towards our table. He looked so funny and unattractive that I had to run into the men's toilet. There were five or six guys peeing and I rushed past them to the mirror. Wow, I looked great. I was so attractive. I stood and pulled faces. Hideous distorted grins. Very, very close to the glass. The guys in the toilet looked great, too. I decided that Balfe should come into the toilet, then he'd look attractive like me.

I left the men's room and strode aristocratically to our table. Balfe was sitting, red-faced and uncomfortable, next to Harry de Mack. The hammerhead shark was disgusting him, too, and I tried to take his mind off it. He told me he couldn't handle the bar and could we leave. He was freaking out. He was quivering all over.

The drunks at the table grew very ugly to me and Gary was way too tall. And then the meanest thing happened. Harry de Mack casually poured his lager over Dave Balfe.

The hammerhead shark started to laugh her head off. Harry brayed like a donkey. He *was* a donkey. But a vile drunk one. Laughter echoed around my brain and everything around me shook and shook.

Dave Balfe was a jelly. A jelly who could neither move nor speak. He sat and waited to dissolve and I realised my friend was in danger.

How dare they? I'll save you, laddie. I grabbed his hand. We surged out of the bar and up the stairs. Good God, we were moving like the wind, flying gracefully along the corridor towards our home and safe resting-place.

We burst into Balfe's room, where Alan Gill lay tripped-out and inert. His head lay back against the pillow, his headphones half off.

Balfe rolled a joint to calm us down. It took him about 20 minutes. First we couldn't find a cigarette, then Balfe couldn't sit up without sliding over onto his back.

We began to calm down at last and were happy in our black shelter, the darkness wrapping us in a blanket of safety. Then Gary burst in. A drunk and

disgusting Monster Gary. He towered above us and laughed crazily. Alan didn't notice him and carried on oblivious. So Gary slipped out the "Frank" from down his filthy and disgusting underpants and pressed it into Alan's face.

Alan woke in a frozen horror and screamed his bloody head off. While he freaked out, Gary cackled and dashed out to Harry de Mack's.

Around us was a scene of total emotional devastation. We just stood around, impassive and bovine. Each of us looked to the other for a way to normality.

Balfe was more composed than Alan or me, so we listened intently to what he had to say. Either it was genius or Balfe was bluffing, but he suggested that we take up the carpet in the corridor. Alan was still trembling, so Balfe and I left the bedroom and got down on our hands and knees in the hallway.

The carpet was thick and we sunk into it as we worked out how to un-fix it from the floor. Working on either side, on our hands and knees, we began to systematically yank out the carpet-tacks. The corridor stretched out in front of us, but we worked intently and vigorously. We made slow steady progress and within the hour we were outside Harry de Mack's room. Behind us lay the empty corridor. Next to us was the huge roll of luxurious carpet. We smiled at each other, satisfied.

Two feet appeared in front of me. It was the same young guy that we had danced past earlier. He was the hotel manager and what were we doing?

Neither of us could speak. We were overcome. Then Harry opened the door. He looked down at the roll of carpet, the bare corridor and the hotel manager.

"They're looking for the electricity socket," he said, unconvincingly, and we dashed into his room, where Gary, the hammerhead shark and her friend were drinking. We wondered why we were here. It was hell. Had we taken all that carpet up for nothing?

Harry was stuck outside with the hotel manager. Gary was drunk out of his mind. The shark and sharkfriend were making us sick. I had an idea. It was time to persuade Gary to do Sacky Bill.

Gary Dwyer had a few very weird trips. Sacky Bill was one of the grossest and one that he did to freak people out. We warned the shark as Gary pulled off his shorts. Then he grabbed his ball-sac and dragged it up his belly, over his dick and almost to his belly-button. It looked like a pet tortoise with a tarpaulin over it.

The shark screamed and Harry rushed in. Balfe and I rushed out of the room and down the corridor. That was it for me. I needed to be alone. I needed my own thing. I went into my room and lay down flat on the floor.

All the lights were off. My body was aching, so I pulled off my pants and shoes and lay on my back with just a T-shirt on. The gravity pulled me down like an electro-magnet. I tried to move, but I could not raise my head or my legs. As I concentrated, I could feel every tiny movement in my body. I could feel my heart bumping away, as though I were in there with it. I could feel my blood coursing through my veins. My arms and legs stretched out. My hands

stretched to their tips, and then my fingers and thumbs stretched even more.

I lay there in a cruciform, stretched to my maximum size. And I was a city centre. A centre designed to control the traffic's flow. My heart was sending the blood out of the main veins and out into the suburbs. I could tell when they turned around. The tips of my fingers glowed inside and redirected them. This endless stream of traffic mesmerised me and I lay motionless for hours. Occasionally, I would look up into the night sky of the ceiling, but I'd soon sink back to the city centre.

And so the night drifted on. Until the early morning sun eventually brought a burning grey into the room. And the LSD began to wear off, and I felt hollow inside. Like an ex-human who needs to be filled up, a real blank sheet.

And that was The Teardrop Explodes in autumn 1980. We had a great time, but it was too much. Either we couldn't bear each other or we had the best time in the world.

At Leicester University, we split up on stage. I told the audience that the rest of the group were all twats and fuck them. We left the stage, screaming into the mikes at one another.

The tour was a disaster. Sure, people came and we sold places out. But by the end, only Gary and I were still talking.

SPLIT (Parts 1–4)

Alan Gill left the group. In five months, he'd written a new single for us, saved the LP and turned me into a raging lunatic.

I felt savaged. My guru was gone before I could thank him. Bill Drummond was suggesting a guitarist called Troy Tate even before Alan was gone. Of course, we needed to keep the momentum and I felt happy to try anyone, but it was moving too fast and I couldn't keep pace with all the changes.

Troy Tate was great looking. He was dark haired and a little older than us. When he walked into the rehearsal room, he walked up to me, and said, "Hi, baby." I liked him at once.

We made a racket and he clanged his guitar the way I liked, so he was in. Within the week, we were firm friends.

Unfortunately, his niceness once more reminded me of Balfe's ugliness. It was almost Christmas. Kick Balfe out. He's a horrible person and I hate him. I told Bill Drummond, who fought for Balfe to no avail. Troy also fought the best he could. No way, I was the boss. Gary agreed. Fuck him off, the uncivil bastard. Let's get a new organist. And we'll get a new bass player, too. I'll just

sing. We'll just teach the new guys the songs and keep control over them.

Troy had been in the group one month, but I treated him like an original member. Things were moving so fast, the regime needed new friends. A coup could happen at any time.

Just before Christmas, we made a film for 'Reward', which was to be the next single. We invited friends down to the Liverpool docks, mainly the Bunnymen and Zoo people. Mac didn't turn up. We were way apart by now.

Don Letts made the film with Bill Butt. It was an end of the world scenario, with our jeep zooming all over the place. We appealed to Troy's and Les's sense of bravado, and filmed them miming trumpets on a creaking platform 200 feet in the air.

Balfe wanted to be involved, but I wouldn't let him. There was a sense of camaraderie in the making of the film, but I was fooling myself really. Christmas 1980 was the beginning of my power trip and I insisted that Yorkie and my wife, Kathy, be in the film.

The video was brilliant. 'Reward' was to be released just after Christmas, very early new year. We still needed a group, though. I could think of no-one.

Over Christmas, Dave Balfe moved to a small cottage in Rockfield. He went to live with Sian, the manageress of the studio. His head was blown from the past couple of months and I was alternately trying to kill him or telling him he was great.

Bill Drummond told me that we had to hold auditions for the bass and keyboard player. I was not interested in their ability, so I entrusted Troy with that task. Also, I told him to pick someone bearable, as I couldn't tell any more. I was interested in anyone who felt even vaguely okay.

The week 'Reward' was released, Troy, Gary and I sat in a small studio at Nomis, a shit-sterile overpriced rehearsal complex in Olympia, London.

We had 32 bass players to try and 14 keyboard players. The three of us were quite unprepared for it. I'd never done auditions in my life. How can you tell who's the right guy? I took a small hit of acid and left it up to Troy. I was wearing my Lawrence outfit and holding an acoustic guitar. Troy settled down with a six-pack and we began.

The bass players were nearly all shit. I'd picked a new song to jam on. It was called 'The Culture Bunker' and gave away little of our style. That was the point, as I wanted a guy who'd listen to the song.

But as the afternoon wore on, I became restless. Some of the bass players weren't even allowed to play; their appearance alone could put me off. Some stunk of cologne and my heightened sense of smell told me not to trust them.

A young guy called Rolo McGinty walked in. His name sounded great on acid and he was cute as hell. He jammed for ages but he wasn't as good as me

and I wanted someone better. We made a good friend, but eventually picked a small Londoner called Alfie. He wasn't the best, but he funked his thang well enough.

The keyboard players were an even more unprepossessing bunch. I just picked the first guy I could bear to look at. His name was Jeff Hammer and he looked like a record company type, totally uncool and wrong for the hip Teardrop Explodes. I didn't care, though. I was crazed and gibbering and wanted to get out of that room.

Two days later, Bill Drummond and Bill Butt drove our two new boys down to Rockfield for rehearsals. Apparently, the two Bills took it in turns to weird them out with drug and mayhem stories.

BEST BEHAVIOUR

Meanwhile, Rockfield was swinging. The Bunnymen were staying at the white house whilst they recorded new songs and The Teardrop Explodes were camped at the old mill, a beautiful grange belonging to the studio.

The mill was about a mile and a half from the studio. The road between the two is quiet and it soon became a racetrack for the two groups. Our proximity drove us back together and Les Pattinson would thunder down the mill lane in our jeep. We'd see Pete DeFreitas and the two Bills hanging off the back as they swerved and tumbled down the last half-mile to the mill.

There was a Dutch group working in the smaller studio and one night we organised a raid which left them with no food or drink. Their guitarist walked in to see a devilish Bunny/Drops combination ransacking their living quarters in full commando gear. Even Dave Balfe was hanging out with us. Somehow, his being sacked only one month before made no difference to me. Balfe lived two miles away and if he was absent for more than a day, I'd send Gary and Bill Butt to find him. We'd hang out and trip and smoke at the mill. Endless psychedelic scenes by the river would drag on into the evening and I'd be sad that the hanging out wouldn't translate into working together.

We knew we had to be on our best behaviour when the new guys arrived. Troy told me to be nice. Of course I'd be nice, I was a smiling fool, wasn't I? In fact, Bill Drummond had just informed me of a new Bunnymen song. It included Mac's mean observation: *"That golden smile could shame a politician."* Bill had only casually mentioned it, but the hallucinogenics in my system focused on that one line and I *did* feel evil and mean.

One afternoon in early January '81, we were furiously skinning up joints in the main living room at the mill. Gary Dwyer and Troy Tate were also drinking

heavily. Paul Simpson, our old organist, was down for the week and his girl-friend, Jeanne, was sitting around waiting for Balfe, who was writing songs for her. Of course, Balfe was with myself and Pete DeFreitas. This precluded our working on anything at all.

Gary, Balfe, Pete and I took hits of LSD in front of the TV and watched *Attila the Hun* with Yul Brynner. The film was particularly colourful and very soon Gary and I became scared of Yul Brynner's tunic. It was too bright and we had to sit behind the sofa. Every so often, we would peep out to see the film, then dart back in.

My head blazed with pleasure. My stomach felt so good that I just had to hold it and cradle it like a baby. My fingers were long and straight, proud and strong. As the full weight of the drug hit me, I pressed and prodded everything around me. I was becoming too excited about everything.

Jeanne came in with a tray of drinks to pacify us. She gave us a clear liquid that she called "Diamond Tea" and it tasted like angels' tears.

Gary told me he felt very posh, behind the sofa. I agreed. His power of suggestion was overwhelming and soon we were garbling on in ridiculous upper-class voices.

Balfe told us to shut the fuck up and that scared us. We had to leave the room and I was upset at having annoyed Balfe. In the confusion of the LSD, I wanted him to enjoy himself and not feel left out.

Pete DeFreitas decided to wear my bedsheet like a Roman toga. He made a laurel crown from a branch and also wore huge US Army boots. I named him Pulsar for the obvious reason that he looked like the cartoon mule from *Tom & Jerry*.

Then the two Bills walked in with Alfie and Jeff, the new organist and bass player. Best Behaviour. I smiled a huge and meaningless smile at both of them, then grabbed Gary and Pete.

The three of us ran into the huge dining room. At its centre was a large oak table, which Gary climbed on and made his home. He told us he was a mountain lion and that we should stay away, or he'd go "Bair-sairk . . . and I mean bair-sairk."

Pete and I got some cereal from the kitchen, then I ate a grapefruit with some camembert. Oh! What a snack. And you'd think a combination like that would taste disgusting.

Meanwhile, Gary the mountain lion was asserting his authority on the dining-room table. He repeated his threat that no-one could come near him and I took this to be a challenge.

I began to run round and around the enormous dining-table. Every time I ran past the den of the mountain lion, Gary would stretch out his right paw to grab me and I'd scream. Round and round the table I ran, each time screaming in that fright that children have when a friend suddenly gives chase.

I ran barefoot around the table, cornering wildly and slipping and sliding.

Up the main straight I ran, towards the kitchen, banked sharply to my right and then curved away up the back straight. I'd pass the fireplace and bank early for extra acceleration past the mountain lion, who was in his lair on the corner. Then I'd repeat the whole thing over and over.

Around half an hour into the run, my bare feet began to burn and rub on the carpet. The more I thought about it, the more my head whirled with this one unassailable problem.

Paul Simpson had been standing in the doorway between kitchen and dining room, watching events with interest.

"Simmo, get some milk in a bowl," I shouted, as I thundered past. Each lap took about eight seconds and I was pounding along. My senses were glowing and electrical and I yelled at Simmo, as he returned with the bowl of milk, "Now throw it on the carpet. It'll cool my feet down."

This he duly did, but it was no good at all. How stupid of me.

"Simmo," I shouted as I thundered past him, "it's too slippery. Go and put some Rice Crispies in the bowl."

Lap upon lap I ran and, finally, Simmo poured the mixture onto the patch of carpet at the most dangerous bend. Phoosh, my feet were cooled as I ran through the ford of milk and cereal. I had the upper hand on Gary now and I ran easily past his outstretched paws. Pete would run with me occasionally, but I was on a solo trip.

One and a half hours into the running, Gary was still doing his growl and his swiping of the air every eight seconds. We had a peculiar rhythm going, and I counted over and over as I ran.

Then, in the recreation room, a door opened and Les from the Bunnymen walked in. He viewed the scenario, asked no questions and began to run with me. It was so cool, as I needed a pace man just at that moment. We ran and ran, but the door to the recreation room was still open. Out of the corner of my eye, I could see Bill Drummond and Ian McCulloch staring at us. I tried to act normal, but a black and powerful force emanated from them and began to slow me down.

Round and round I went, my feet getting heavier and heavier and slower and heavier and slow-er anndd sslowwer anndd sslower . . . and stop.

I couldn't go on. The force they created together was too powerful. I felt debauched. I felt like a kid caught by his maiden aunt who does not approve. I stood guilty and awkward, then I ran into the kitchen and hid.

I waited, curled up in a ball in the space between the fridge and pantry. I was safe here. After 20 minutes they left. Things gradually got back to abnormal and I visited the two new guys.

They were in the recreation room, playing ping-pong. I tried to make conversation, but found myself diverted by the vapour trail of the ping-pong ball. Soon, I was staring at the net, vacantly caught in their game. They seemed comfortable enough, so I told them I had to go into the attic. I got up to leave,

but my legs were crablike and I was forced to walk in an ungainly sideways meander. I apologised to them profusely and left the room.

Back in the living room, Balfe had things his way. Pete and Gary had settled down to build a joint, but were in conference about each stage of the process.

I grandly announced that we were all going up to the attic to hang out and picnic. To my surprise, the others got up and did as I suggested. We walked into the kitchen and grabbed tins of baked beans, cheese and beer. Of course, this all took quite a while, but soon we were making our way up the winding and scary staircase towards the attic.

At the very top of the house, in the musty and dusty land which no-one had visited for years, we plopped down on the floor and began our picnic.

Remember how I told you that Balfe was taking charge downstairs? Well, this carried on in the attic and it was doing my head in, so I pissed in his baked beans and we argued till dawn.

REWARD

In the midst of the Rockfield trip, our second single for Mercury was released. It was called 'Reward' and it had nothing to do with the present. Between its recording in November 1980 and its release in January 1981, the entire Teardrop Explodes thing had changed dramatically.

Each week, we'd wait for our chart position. I didn't think it sounded like a hit, I just dug the song a lot. Out in the wilds of South Wales, the music business seemed a long way off. But I was still a nervous dude every Tuesday, when the charts were announced.

Slowly, the record inched its way to no. 41. We all got dead excited, but we missed *Top of the Pops* by one place and the next week 'Reward' slipped down to no. 45.

Oh well, I wasn't that bothered. See, you don't prove anything by selling records, I thought to myself.

We were rehearsing for an East Coast US tour. The main problem was assimilating the new guys into the group. They both looked wrong for the part and were both southerners, somehow lacking the bile and vitriol that made my Liverpool friends so bearable. I'd end up taking the piss out of them. Then I'd feel bad about it, so I'd placate them way too much. Rehearsals came to a stop, as Gary and I would be overcome by the power of the acid that we constantly ingested.

Troy was fantastic. A total gentleman, who sat with his tray of drinks and just bleeped in or out of conversations, depending on whether he could take it or not.

And every night, Balfe would be over. The new guys are crap, Copey. The new songs need this or that, Copey. And from under my throbbing head, I could hear a distant common sense being spoken.

Then? The impossible happened. 'Reward' went back up to no. 41. We were on *Top of the Pops*. We learned the night before and celebrated all evening. Balfe wasn't there and we all felt bad that he wasn't going to be involved.

The next day, Bob Proctor arrived in his Chevrolet Camaro. Troy, Gary and I were travelling in his car. The new guys'll be okay with the equipment van. Let's go!

We zoomed past the studio and on towards the M50 to London. As we passed Dave Balfe's house, we looked at each other.

"Yeah?" I asked.

"Yeah!" chorused Gary and Troy.

We turned off the road and up to Balfe's house. Bob Proctor beebeebeeped his horn and Balfe's dumb head came round the front door. From the car, I yelled, "We got *Top of the Pops!*"

Balfe looked pleased, but sad to be missing out.

"Come on, you dickhead. Come and mime the trumpets."

Awlright! Balfe was ready in a flash. By the time we had driven the three miles through Monmouth to the motorway, he was in charge. He handed Gary and me some LSD. They took theirs immediately, but I held off until we were almost in London. Surging and guzzling petrol, the great red shark of a Camaro thundered towards showbizland.

By the time we reached the BBC TV Centre in London, everyone was fucked up. Troy and Bob Proctor were pissed out of their minds. We'd had a bit of a spliff and amphetamine party in the confines of the three-seater Camaro, and the trips had begun to kick in.

We seethed out of the car and moved as one gibbering person towards the dressing room. Tony Hadley walked elegantly down the corridor.

"Hey, there's Spandoo," cried Balfe, and I danced around the singer, psy-chotically friendly and encouraging.

We piled into the dressing room. It was large and bright. The whole of the *Top of the Pops* studio was beautiful. I kept finding areas and inspecting them inch by inch.

Dave Bates, our A&R man, was down to look after us. He was mildly concerned that we were off our heads, but the whole group was in such a friendly mood. I mean, *Top of the Pops* is normally a big snob scene. We found that out soon enough. But for now, we're the friendliest dudes in the business.

Waiting around was not a drag. We got to see Toyah lisp her way through some piece of kack and we got to dance on the stage during our rehearsals. The acid made us happy and nice. We gushed around the place like inbreds at a New England dinner party.

Then we were on. Troy and Balfe were miming trumpets and sliding all over the place, even before we'd started. Then our announcement and away we went.

Ber-ber-ber-ber-ber-ber Doo der-der detder, Doo der-der detder ... *"Bless my cotton socks I'm in the news ..."*

Suddenly, the song sounded like a massive hit. *Top of the Pops*, man. It's total bullshit. But it's brilliant. I loved it. Let's be huge.

Afterwards, we partied at some club, as you do. Women were nice to me. Men complimented me. I just sat there drooling all night.

Dave Balfe copped off with a great-looking woman, which somehow completed the evening for me. Psychologically, I found the best way for me to shag around was to do it by proxy. So I always helped Balfe to score. That way I wouldn't feel guilty.

We all piled back to Rockfield and rested for the next two days. We felt goood. We were off to America any time.

My wife came down. It was nice, you know. I kept off the drugs completely, as she didn't know about it. Instead, I'd make do with smoking enormous amounts of Balfe's grass. I hated that, though. You know, your wife should know your whole trip. Kathy was missing my metamorphosis and I resented it like hell.

In the days before we left for New York, I got really sad. I mean, she enjoyed our being successful, but I wasn't running to involve her. The last days before the tour were such a drag. I didn't want to go, and we said see you soon, and cried and all kinds of miserable stuff.

Then I was off. 'Reward' was climbing up the charts and we were going to America to miss the action. I packed my old doctor's case. It's about 9" × 24". I wasn't into carrying much stuff around. Also, in those days I had a rather lax attitude towards hygiene and one pair of everything did me fine.

See you, Kathy. I'll be back in two weeks.

DON'T HOLD YOUR BREATH

I was standing in a corridor at the Taft Hotel in New York. I had on just a pair of leather pants and had been in the middle of a shave. Alfie, our new bass player, was standing next to me. We were both wondering whether to do anything about the catfight that was going on in the room opposite. We were on the fifth floor. There were prostitutes and weirdos hassling us, and I knew I was really in a pit.

The Taft Hotel is the place where Holden Caulfield has a very bad time in

The Catcher in the Rye. It's recently been knocked down, which makes me feel old in a good way.

Anyway, the crashing of furniture and the breaking of heads somehow spoiled our first night's sleep in New York. We got up early, and drove to Albany, in upstate New York.

The journey was spent smoking American weed and bullshitting Jeff, our new keyboard player. Jeff was a big Christian. He read the Bible in the van, which did my head in. Then I thought, Well, he's not interfering with me. So chill out.

I'd spoken to Jeff about twice and we had nothing in common. He was an okay guy, though, and I knew we'd scared him big style with all the drugs and stuff. Shit, it was only eight months since I'd freaked out over Mick Finkler smoking a joint. Remember him? Since then, I'd changed the group and myself so much, it seemed like that had been a different person. And that was why I now sat talking to Jeff. It was a guilt fuelled by all the weird things that were changing me, the drugs, the scene and my rapidly expanding position. Jeff was my idea of *supernormality* and I wanted some of that, too.

Soon we were in Albany. I'd no idea how far we drove from New York. I guessed around 30 miles. My sense of my surroundings were confused more each day.

I missed Balfe, but Troy and Gary were impeccable companions. Also, I really dug Bob Proctor, our tour manager. He looked like a rocker Van Morrison, very abrupt, Liverpudlian drawl, totally sarcastic, mean, surly and cool.

Albany is the state capital of New York. It's all ring-roads that lead you out of there. It's kind of like Birmingham – the traffic authorities want to keep your car moving in the hope that you'll soon get sick of their fair city and get the hell out of there.

We drove up to J. B. Scott's. It was *the* local club and it seemed like everyone had been there – Ritchie Blackmore's Rainbow, the Ramones, Tom Waits, posters of shows on every square foot of wall in the place.

Huh, I thought. They're going to see the real thing tonight. I checked through the set. I hadn't spent much time teaching the new guys the set. In fact, Troy had never learned half the stuff. I'd just taught them loads of new songs because they excited me. In the dressing room of J. B. Scott's club, I realised, for the first time, that I was now in charge.

"Did we learn 'When I Dream'?" I asked.

"Uhm, no. I've heard it, though," said Alfie. "How about you, Jeff?"

Jeff knew the song, so we learned it during the soundcheck. We had done nothing during rehearsals. I was so tripped out on getting control of the group that I'd forgotten it was also my job to teach them shit.

The evening dragged on. We ate pizzas and did coke in the dressing room. I was an alien here. What if I didn't cut it? At least Bill Butt was doing our

lights. Also he was filming everything, which gave us a feeling of self-importance.

This was my first show without my bass guitar. I was shitting it. What if I was a total dork? What if, what if?

Outside on the stage, all the lights went out. Over the PA came our intro music. It was 'Kilimanjaro', a strange and beautiful piece, that sounded as though it was recorded in a volcano on some Pacific atoll. The final seconds ticked away and the rest of the group trooped on stage. I followed quickly and picked up my new Fender electric 12-string.

I started the set with a new song called 'Like Layla Khaled Said' about a beautiful Middle Eastern terrorist girl. The song moved into its Arabesque groove and I stood oblivious of the audience. I was fine, hidden behind the guitar. My hair was long and blond, and I stood pretending to be Tim Buckley, one of my favourite singers.

"*. . . just like Layla Khaled said.*" Brang. "Thank you. Good evening, Albany. We're called The Teardrop Explodes and this is a modern classic. It's called . . . 'Reward'."

The guitar was put away. I was on my own. The crowd was grooving away, but I'd noticed two girls at the front of the stage. They were both brilliant looking and were hip as hell. They stood right in front of me and stared.

One was tall with a long face and crazy long hair. She was skinny, and stood tall and confident.

The other one was much shorter. She had punky black hair, with a fringe right over her face, dark eyes and the palest skin I'd seen. Her lips were bright red, in a kind of baby doll way, and she wore an adorable pink dress. She looked about 15 and I adored her immediately. I performed every song to her. During a new song, called 'Screaming Secrets', I lay down on the floor and sung looking up to her.

Of course, I was hung up as hell. I thought she was way too gorgeous to be really interested in me, so I figured I'd better just enjoy the set.

By the time we walked offstage, I was sad. I'd seen this perfect piece of woman. It was a total drag. Fuck, I'm married.

And there's this bratty-looking 15 year old outside, who looks like my ideal.

I sat, head bowed, on the floor of the dressing room. We were okay. Not great, but we did the set properly and I had a groove. We smoked endless killer US weed and the others took cocaine.

Then Bill Butt walked in. With my 15 year old and her mate in tow. Oh fuck. They're just groupies, after all. I felt stupid. Of course they *would* be, wouldn't they? They must do this every day.

I glowered in the corner and looked the other way. Bob Proctor offered them coke, which they took. Huh, groupies, man.

Whilst the skinny one took her line, the adorable one pushed herself up

Cope in Tamworth; March 1977, after hitching to the Roundhouse with Hilary Steele to see the Stranglers with Cherry Vanilla and the Jam supporting. Note noose and handcuffs, also big badge which read 'I hate Students', even though 97% of all Cope's Liverpool punk mates were students or sixth-form schoolkids. Liverpool fundamentalism soon made these accessories a no-no. (Photo: Hilary Steele)

Afghan coats, Krautrock and patchouli. The pre-punk Cope, aged 18, with Jane Smith at the photo-booth in Tamworth bus-station; August 1976.

Lyn and Pete Burns at Eric's Club; March 1977. They were the couple that had the most immediate impact on Cope on his arrival in Liverpool. Pete Burns later made it huge with his '80s group Dead or Alive. (Photo: Hilary Steele)

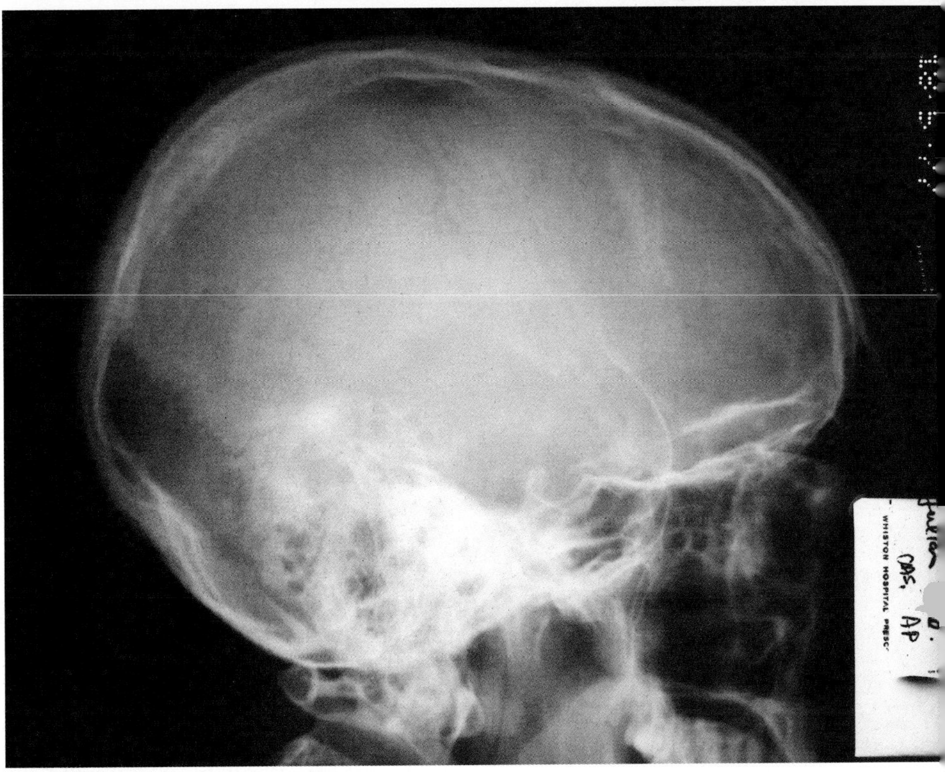

This X-ray of Julian Cope's head is dated 18.5.77 and was taken from Whiston Hospital by Cope in an NHS wheelchair pushed by his friend Smelly Elly.
(Head Heritage Archives)

Rentapunk at Simmo's house; Summer 1977.
(Photo: Paul Simpson)

Ian McCulloch and Julian Cope at Simmo's Rodney Street flat in Liverpool centre; February 1978.
(Photo: Paul Simpson)

Hilary Steele and Pete Wylie in the hallway of their adjoining Toxteth flats; Summer 1977.
(Photo: Jane Wylie)

The Uh? gig; April 1978. Ian McCulloch (out of frame), Dave Pickett and Julian Cope. Note Cope's post-punk fall into accidental Justin Hayward look.
(Photo: Wren)

Yorkie AKA David Tracey Palmer in his basement; Spring 1979. Aged 16, Yorkie and his mother Gladys agreed to let Julian Cope's band rehearse in their cellar, thus creating 75% of the new Liverpool scene's prime movers. Yorkie's 1979 position as motivator and patron can never be overstated enough – though he himself only became a popstar in the late '90s with the group Space.

The first photograph of The Teardrop Explodes appeared in the October 1978 edition of the free magazine *More Or Less Monthly*. The photograph, taken by Andy Eastwood, was captioned 'Funerals a Speciality', as the group had not yet played live and the editor was anticipating yet another of Cope's merely temporary, underachieving horrible rackets.

EASTWOOD 78

Funerals a Speciality

The Teardrop Explodes

The Teardrop Explodes' first press shot; January 1979. (L-R) Mick, Paul, Rocky, Julian. (Photo: Kevin Cummins)

Kevin Cummins took this photograph in Manchester, in October 1979, on one of Bill Drummond's co-headlining tours, designed to make the Teardrop and Bunnymen look bigger than they were. Gerard Quinn took over from Dave Balfe for five brief gigs until Balfe forced him out by sheer weight of personality and pestering the fuck out of Cope. Quinn later formed The Wild Swans with Paul Simpson. (L-R Top row) Will Sargeant, Les Pattinson, Rocky Dwyer, Ian McCulloch, Gerard Quinn. (L-R Bottom row) Mick Finkler, Julian Cope, Pete DeFreitas.

Turner Hous[e]

Granada TV, Manchester:
February 1979

The source of *that* name –
Daredevil No. 77
(Marvel Comics, June 1971)

Yorkie's typed and amended
Teardrop setlist; Spring 1979.

On Cope's first wedding day,
Kathy Cherry wore black and
Cope insisted on cutting the cake
on his own; August 1979.
(Photo: Alan Cope)

JULIAN COPE - VOCALS, BASS

FULL NAME:	Julian D. Cope
BORN:	21/10/57 in S. Wales
STARSIGN:	Libra
HEIGHT:	6' 1"
WEIGHT:	11 stones
EYES:	Blue
FAV. COLOUR:	Red
FAV. FILM:	Eraserhead
FAV. SINGLE:	Alone Again Or - Love
FAV. L.P.:	The Modern Dance - Pere Ubu
FAV. ACTOR:	Michael Ansara
FAV. ACTRESS:	Helen Mirren
FAV. FOOD:	Calzone
FAV. DRINK:	Whisky
FAV. CITY:	New York
FAV. ANIMAL:	Cat
FAV. BAND:	The Doors
FAV. MALE SINGER:	Scott Walker
FAV. FEMALE SINGER:	Nico
FAV. TIM BUCKLEY L.P.:	Happy Sad
FAV. SHAPE:	
FAV. PHASE:	"Groik"

DAVE BALFE - KEYBOARDS

FULL NAME:	David Iain William Miguel John Balfe
BORN:	2/10/58 in Carlisle
STARSIGN:	Libra
HEIGHT:	6 foot
WEIGHT:	150 lbs.
EYES:	Hazel
FAV. COLOUR:	Pink. Green.
FAV. FILM:	Breakfast at Tiffanys
FAV. SINGLE:	Jackie - Scott Walker
FAV. L.P.:	Rubber Soul - The Beatles
FAV. ACTOR:	Barry Fitzgerald
FAV. ACTRESS:	Audrey Hepburn
FAV. FOOD:	Tuna fish pie
FAV. DRINK:	Pernod and black
FAV. CITY:	New York
FAV. DRUG:	
FAV. ANIMAL:	Gary Dwyer
FAV. BAND:	The Beatles
FAV. MALE SINGER:	John Lennon
FAV. FEMALE SINGER:	Pet Clark
FAV. PHRASE:	"Fab Gear"
LIKES:	Jewish/black girls. America.
DISLIKES:	Stupidity. Happiness.

GARY DWYER - DRUMMER

FULL NAME:	Gary Andrew Dwyer
BORN:	28/8/59. Petrol Station/Highooal/ W. Virginia U.S.A.
STARSIGN:	Virgo
HEIGHT:	6' 6"
WEIGHT:	15½ stone
EYES:	Blue green
FAV. COLOUR:	Sky blue
FAV. FILM:	Rocky 1 & 2
FAV. SINGLE:	My Way - Frank Sinatra
FAV. L.P.:	Roxy Music 1
FAV. ACTOR:	Sylvester Stallone, Robert Mitchum
FAV. FOOD:	Shirley Maclaine
FAV. DRINK:	Egg on toast
FAV. CITY:	Whisky and dry
FAV. GROUP:	Edinburgh
FAV. MALE SINGER:	Blondie
FAV. FEMALE SINGER:	Frank Sinatra
FAV. PHASE:	Debs Harry
FAV. NAME:	
LIKES:	Buff Manilla
DISLIKES:	Raw sausages. Echo and The Bunnymen. (Note: Except the drummer.)

ALAN GILL - GUITAR

FULL NAME:	Alan David Gill
BORN:	1/1/56 in Liverpool
STARSIGN:	Capricorn
HEIGHT:	
WEIGHT:	
EYES:	11½ stone
FAV. COLOUR:	Brown
FAV. FILM:	Black
FAV. SINGLE:	Blazing Saddles
FAV. L.P.:	Hot Love - T. Rex
FAV. ACTOR:	White Album - The Beatles
FAV. ACTRESS:	Tony Randall
FAV. FOOD:	Shirley Maclaine
FAV. DRINK:	Steak
FAV. CITY:	Milkshake
	New York
FAV. BAND:	Amphetamine sulphate
FAV. SINGER:	Beatles
FAV. OTHER COLOUR:	John Lennon
FAV. PHRASE:	Light black
LIKES:	"Girls up her"
DISLIKES:	Being happy
	Being sad
FAV. JAN AND DEAN SONG:	Turkey' Trot
FAV. ANIMAL:	Piglets

The remarkable Alan Gill.
Note that Cope, still a Puritan,
is the only one without a
'favourite drug' listed on his
1980 Polygram Popfile.

So In Love! Gary Dwyer gives the 'V's to Jeff Hammer, the Teardrops' Christian keyboard player; Rockfield Old Mill, Welsh Border. (Photo: Julian Cope)

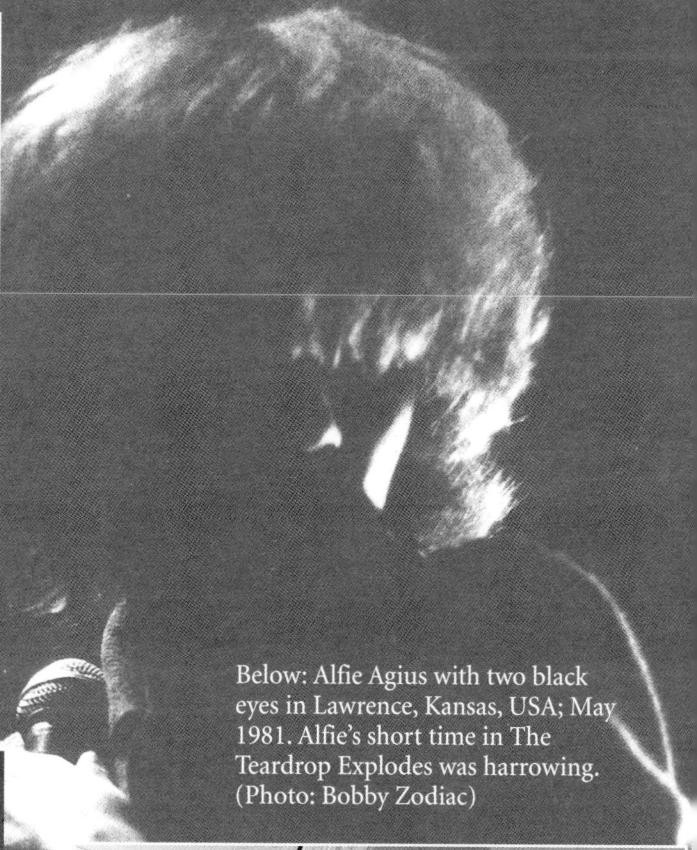

Below: Alfie Agius with two black eyes in Lawrence, Kansas, USA; May 1981. Alfie's short time in The Teardrop Explodes was harrowing. (Photo: Bobby Zodiac)

Left: Rocky Dwyer AKA Jimmy Luxembourg tripping at Rockfield Studios; Autumn 1980. (Photo: Bobby Zodiac)

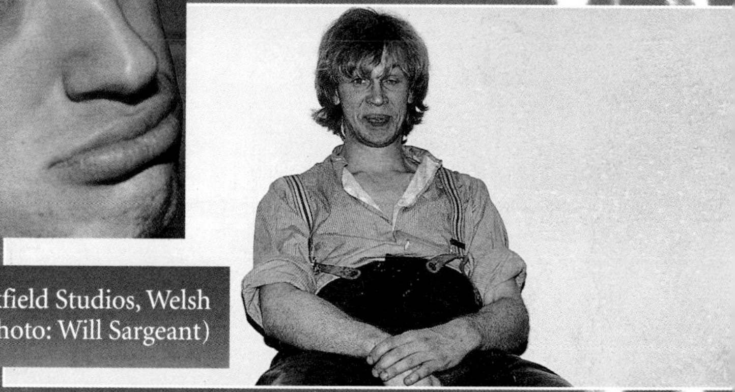

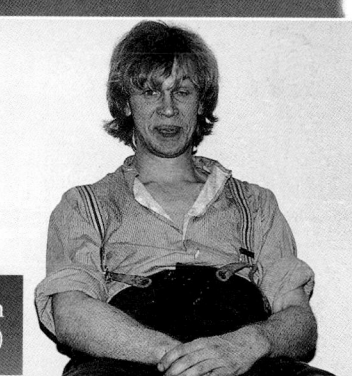

Right: Cope tripping at Rockfield Studios, Welsh Border; Summer 1980. (Photo: Will Sargeant)

Dorian Beslity in New York, aged 19. (Photo: Laura Levine)

Below: Mush-mouthed in Manhattan; March 1981. (Photo: Laura Levine)

Below: The Droyd AKA John Wilson. (Photo: Julian Cope)

Above: Dave Bates' first signing to Polygram was The Teardrop Explodes. In 1981, he presented Cope with a remix of The Doors' 'Hello, I Love You' with Bates singing harmony to Morrison. Later signed Tears for Fears and Scott Walker. A Genius and Lunatic. (Photo: Polygram Publicity Department)

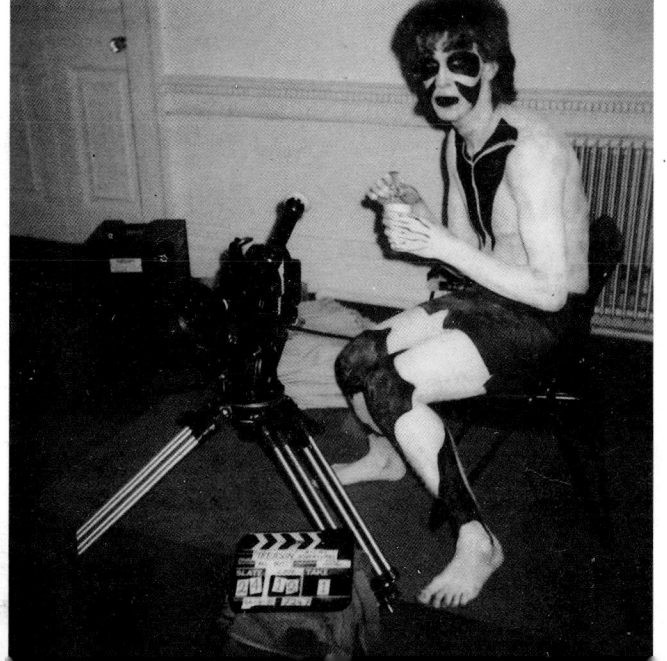

Left: In the video for 'Treason', Julian Cope wore Kiss make-up on Pall Mall to weird out the German tourists. (Photo: Jackie O.)

In 1981, Julian Cope appeared on many magazine covers.
In 1982, he appeared on none.

'Damn the Rules!' Dave Balfe looks secretly disappointed to be photographed with his biggest fan Carmen the Cadillac. (Photo: Buick McCain)

Pete DeFreitas

Above: In 1980, only Mick Houghton and The Teardrop Explodes used the word 'shag'. (Photo: Dorian Cope)

A Columbia Hotel Room 311 scene. (L-R) Pete DeFreitas, Julian Cope, Dave Balfe, Mick Houghton. (Photo: Dorian Cope)

Club Zoo conference; November 1981.
(L-R) Unknown, Julian Cope, Bill Drummond. (Photo: Kevin Cummins)

An extremely blank Julian Cope at Club Zoo with Pete Burns and his friend, the punk singer Sunny Periods. Sunny is experiencing the first Sony Walkman, whilst Ian Burden from The Human League parties in the background. (Photo: Kevin Cummins)

All X'd up! Bathtime after the Queen support show at Milton Keynes; Summer 1982. (L-R) Dave Balfe, Ronnie Francois, Julian Cope (obscuring Gary Dwyer), Ted Emmett (trumpeter) and Troy Tate. (Photo: Kevin Cummins)

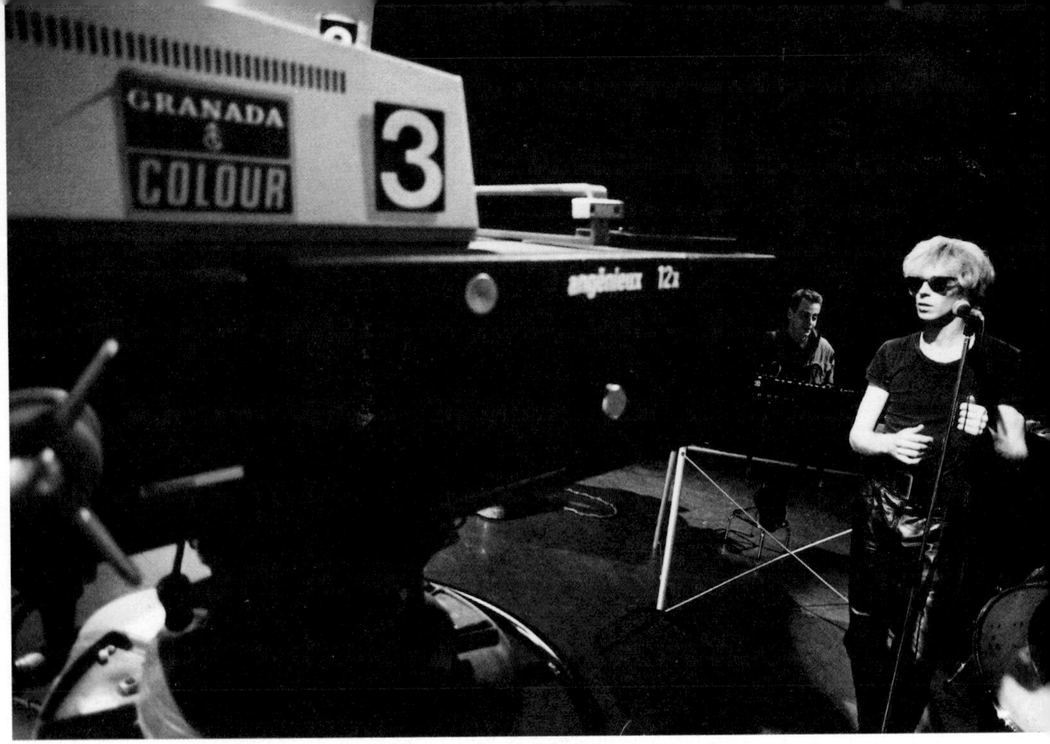

The last Teardrop TV appearance was a performance of 'Tiny Children' for Granada; August 1982. (Photo: Kevin Cummins)

Julian Cope and Dorian Cope on the final and aborted three-piece British tour; October 10th, 1982. (Photo: Kevin Cummins)

The last photograph of The Teardrop Explodes;
October 1982. (Photo: Kevin Cummins)

against this huge '50s Coca-Cola fridge in the corner. It was so beautiful and horny looking, the way that she did it, that I shifted in my pants. She had big tits and stuck her ass out in the coolest way. Also, she had pink ankle-socks over her stockings and the cutest pink high-heels. She looked so good that I got pissed off.

I got up and walked out of the dressing room. I talked to the road crew back in the main room, then sat with my feet dangling over the edge of the stage. I was sad. Girls like that one in the dressing room really existed. *She* was my type, my shape, my favourite clothes, everything. Shit.

I sat there for a while, pissed off. Then I saw my two girlfriends leave the dressing room and head for the exit. Shit, I can't let them go. I have to at least talk to the one in pink. But they were about 10 yards away and I don't know how to start conversations with strange. . .

"Hi. Did you enjoy the show?" I just spoke. I *could not* lose her.

"Yeah, it was great." They turned and smiled. They were both great looking, really were. It's just, well I'd seen God. And she was dressed in pink with the cutest everything. She even smoked in a cute way and I hate women smoking. Somehow, on her it was cool.

We talked and we talked. They were from Manhattan. They'd driven 150 miles to Albany. They were big fans. They'd met Bill Butt the night before at the Ritz, on 14th Street. They were in the dressing room because Bill had left their coats there, for safety.

I stared at the cutie in the pink dress. Her hair covered her eyes. She looked about 17. And I'm 23. And married. Shit.

"I'm Dorian and this is Patty," announced my dream woman.

It suddenly hit me how far they had travelled. In my stupor, the whole journey had only seemed like 30 miles.

Wow, it was different then. A hundred and fifty miles? I hadn't noticed. That worried me. There were too many things I no longer noticed. Now, in my tunnel vision, all I could see was this young girl I wanted. I mean really wanted. And me a married dude. Shee-it!

They had to go, but said they were coming to the next day's show. We made our sad and tender goodbyes, and I reluctantly let them go. I watched them leave the club, then I trailed back to the dressing room.

"Dorian . . . Dorian . . ." I repeated over and over in my head.

We drove the 150 miles back to the super Taft in wonderful Times Square. We arrived back at about 4 a.m. I staggered into bed and thought of the girl in the pink dress. Then I got too horny, so I jerked off and went to sleep.

TAKE IT NOW

The following morning, I woke early and thought about the previous night. I thought about the girls I'd met in Albany and I couldn't get one of them out of my head. She said her name was Dorian. What if I don't see her again?

I left the Taft Hotel with Dave Bates and walked the five yards to the stretch limousine. Bill Butt stood on the corner and filmed this unusual event, whilst I put on my "This is every day" expression. I had radio interviews in New York all day. Later we would record a live concert at My Father's Place on Long Island.

I was learning that weird American phenomenon known as the schmooze. This is a Jewish term and inevitable business condition. It means, perhaps, a lunch or drink with someone, or an overfriendly first meeting with someone that you need on your side.

Of course, I had no intention of schmoozing anyone. I was quite convinced that it was a gross and un-English piece of bullshit that any true artist could get around.

The morning went smoothly but as Dave Bates and I made our way out to Long Island, the snow began. Down it came in torrents. Far more than any British storm. Wow, I thought. Now we'll see New Yorkers in action.

The roads out to Long Island were packed with commuters rushing home. I was surprised and disappointed. I thought that New York would be used to this weather. (Over the years, I've discovered that New Yorkers are used to this, but love to panic and appear unprepared.)

The Long Island Expressway was jammed. We were on our way to WLIR, the hip alternative Long Island station. We crawled along for miles and miles.

Running very late, we jumped into the elevator up to the radio station. A weird back-woodsman type spoke to me. "Hi, I'm Wild Bill Larsen."

Sure, I thought.

"I'm a big fan of yours, Mr Cope."

He was about the same height as me, around 6'2", but built like a brick shithouse. He wore a kind of Canadian shirt and lumber-boots, and had a mass of red hair and a big beard.

"Could you put me on your guest list, Mr Cope? I can bring you some fine mescaline for the show."

I told him that was fine. I hadn't taken mescaline yet, but I was very interested. We did the radio station and I promptly forgot about Wild Bill.

My Father's Place is a very cool bar in a wealthy little town called Roslyn. Its owner, Epi, had a reputation for bringing good and unlikely music out to the Island.

Bates and I arrived at the now snowbound club to find the whole group

and road crew off their heads. Epi passed me a fine grass spliff and soon I was as gone as the others.

Technicians from WLIR walked around, but we couldn't help them. The two new guys, Alfie and Jeff, got pissed off at our easy attitude, but I didn't care. I wanted to see that girl again and it preyed on my mind, the only thing that would *not* go away.

The hours passed. The club was empty. No-one would be out tonight, said Epi. Long Island is snowbound. Where's the frontiersman spirit? I thought. And what if that exotic girl I'm so uptight about doesn't turn up?

There was a knock at the dressing-room door. It was Wild Bill Larsen.

"Hi, man," I said. "How you doing?"

"I brought the mescaline for you." He opened his palms to reveal four tiny pink tablets.

"Great. I'll take them after the show." We were on stage in under an hour.

Bill looked at me through half-closed eyes. "Take them now."

"Yeah, WPLJ, that's the song we wrote. We wrote this song, too. It's a cover version of one of my own songs. Thank you, thank you."

I was rambling on and on. I was high on mescaline on live radio, but I was happy as hell. The little girl and her friend were here again. The club was empty, maybe 80 people at most.

I was too crazy to dress tonight, so I had jeans on and a white shirt. The show was great. I was given a tape of it and we were beginning to sound the way I wanted. The songs were getting stretched and trippy, and my little girl stood at the front looking up at me all through the show.

Back in the dressing room, I was glowing. Mescaline is a devil drug. It gives everyone strange elfin features. It can be very scary. I have a friend called Dan who tried to take a bus home from the centre of Liverpool. Every time he tried to board the bus, phwooosh, the Devil would rise up in front of him. He tried all the way up Hardman Street and eventually gave up.

Anyway, I was much happier than that. I waited for my friend and her pal and eventually I ushered them in from outside the dressing room.

My girl looked more beautiful tonight. Last night, she was an adorable pre-teen vision, but now she was elegant with her white skin and an evening dress and her hair piled up and messy.

I felt bad about my feelings towards her. I was married. Shit, she only wants to be friends. Why do I have to spoil it by wanting her so badly? I felt shit, and guilty about my wife at home.

I started to talk to her friend, Patty. She was also pretty damn gorgeous, so I felt less guilty if I concentrated on her. We ranted on and on, my trip accentuating everything great about my little exotic vision in the corner. I found out that she lived on East 13th Street in Manhattan, but her parents were in Port Washington, only five miles from the club.

That evening, I was more intoxicated than ever. Back in the Taft Hotel, as the trip wore off, I lay shaking and sweating with the effects of the drugs and her total incredibleness.

Shit, man. What a dude for getting married.

HEAD-ON

"Don't you find it's hard to keep your feelings in your own back-yard?"

Sky Saxon

The whole situation was deteriorating around me. The group was looking to me for advice, but I was out of my mind. Gary and I were sharing a room, but we just tripped out and I thought about my marriage and how it would now come to pieces.

See, Kathy and I were pals. That was the whole basis of the marriage. I never wanted to jump on her, nor she me. Now I had fallen for someone else. Someone I did want to jump on. Even if she didn't feel the way I felt, I knew it was so extreme that I could never go back to such bland feelings again.

Our main New York show was at the Ritz on 14th Street. We got there early and hung out with Dorian and Patty. We smoked and talked for hours, and I felt aching and want all the time.

Patty booked the bands at the Ritz, so Dorian and I were left alone at one of the tables. We looked goo-goo at each other and rubbed noses, but the tension was so extreme.

I felt bad. Dorian knew that I was married, but I was being one of those assholes who just wants to forget shit like that.

That night, we were great. The Teardrop Explodes was hot shit at the moment. We'd had press constantly and all the hip New Yorkers were there.

It's weird, you know. I dug New York like mad, but I felt less hip than anyone there. I was freaking and bouncing off things, and screaming and dancing, grovelling at the front of the stage, down and down again. I felt so exposed. We were hip northern cool. People in London didn't understand us. How could New Yorkers? It was good to feel like that. I guess it's the only way I operated in front of alien audiences. Also, we played a lot of stuff from the next album. Stuff that was longer, more rambling. Sometimes we sucked shit, but the audience couldn't tell.

That night, I was surrounded by American women. I loved them all. Awlright, I'm the leader, no problems. Yeah, I can be a pin-up, no problem.

Dorian wore a white lace dress. It was the first time I noticed her shape.

She had great tits. I love big tits. I think my mother breastfed me way too long, that's why I'm obsessed. Mind you, I also loved her pale skin, which was another total obsession of mine. She sat on my lap all evening and I pretended to her that we were just friends. It was out of hand. I told her that she and Patty could not follow us to Boston, as they had planned. She was confused, but I had to clear my mind for a while.

In Boston I heard that 'Reward' was no. 6 in the British charts. Awlright! We played New England, but I rang Dorian all the time. I hadn't rung Kathy for weeks and it was now getting almost impossible. I felt as though that had come to an end naturally.

I was in America and feeling out of touch with any real world. You see, I was expected to act cool and lead the group and all this heavy stuff. You know, it really didn't seem so long since I was the asshole holding everyone back. Now I was dragging everyone behind me and hadn't a clue how to control it.

Every day, I'd teach them new songs. Every day, we'd pull songs to pieces on stage and operate on them. I recorded everything.

If someone said something interesting, I wrote it down. I took in constantly. But I had no real idea what we were doing. It was not exciting to be high in the British chart. I was in New York being hip as hell, man. Fuck the charts, we're going to be enormous *and* get cooler.

"All the English groups act like peasants with free milk."

That's a Mark Smith quote. It struck me hard in the chest.

America is a place to consume. When you first go there, it makes Britain seem Third World. Excitement is so immediate that the turn on is quite different. You don't sit around, like at home in Britain. You get up and go out. All the time. It's so easy to be taken in. To believe it's better. It's not, though, it's just different. That's why I was freaking out. I mean, I didn't know what was normal here.

Dorian and Patty knew so many groups. They were so aware of scams and all the bullshit involved. I was this guy who knew no-one in the music scene, except for people I'd grown with. Man, it churned me up inside. What if I'd fallen for some groupie? I was off my head most of the time, so I really had no judgement.

Then it happened. We consummated our thang.

It was not intentional. No way would I have had the nerve, except in the most extreme circumstances of comfort.

Dorian and Patty and I were hanging out as a kind of threesome. On my one day off, we met at St. Mark's Place, between 2nd and 3rd Ave. I needed to buy clothes, so we wandered round Andy's Cheapies and a few old leather stores.

In March 1981, everything was still ridiculously cheap. I picked up some

cool black ballet pants and we went back to the apartment on East 13th Street to try them on.

Patty made tea and I tried stuff on. Their apartment was a piece of shit, but I dug it. They shared three rooms with another girl, Tanya. Dorian and Tanya had their own bedrooms, as they were both studying at New York University. Patty used part of the living room as her bedroom, with a material partition. There were clothes strewn all over the place, and jars of make-up and stuff piled in corners. Records were scattered round the stereo and they seemed to play hip English music exclusively. You know, stuff like Joy Division, Teardrop, Bunnymen, Bauhaus and Killing Joke.

Downstairs an old Polish couple ranted and raved about the noise all day. Those apartments, shit. If I were an old Polish guy, I would have thought, surely I'd deserve more than this in life. Of course, I laughed at the old couple, along with Dorian and Patty. You do.

Patty went out to buy some stuff from the deli on the corner. I put on some music, and Dorian and I assumed our natural positions, that is, facing each other so close up on the couch that our noses touched. We talked like that for a few minutes, but we were alone. I couldn't let this opportunity slip away. So what if I'm married? I'm not really, not in my heart.

Our mouths were almost touching, in any case. I threw caution to the wind and just kissed her. Very gently. I had to feel her lips, I just did.

She kissed me back! It was alright. We kissed some more and then we got hot and Patty walked in with the tea.

Embarrassment. Patty walked into her sleeping "area". I dragged Dorian into her own bedroom. We fumbled around for a few minutes and then we made love.

It was like the first time. You know how it is when one partner is inexperienced. It makes you feel the same. I asked her if it was her first time. It was her second.

It was messy and beautiful. Sheets all over and clothes pushed up, and indecision and freaking out. And her head done in, and my mind blown, a religious experience, including all the guilt and faith you ever wanted or needed.

I loved her and that was it. Pain. Pain was my life from now on. I was going to cause a lot of pain for myself and everyone around me. The guilt washed over me, then it began to settle.

And that was it. I was not married. I had a new love.

Bill Drummond and I swapped rooms at the Taft. He shared with Gary and I brought Dorian to stay with me. It was a trip, an excursion that I never would have expected. Head spin. Tail spin. Male spin. See the spin I'm in.

Of course, Kathy rang from Liverpool. Bill answered the phone and played it uncool, so she got nervous. Ha, I did not care. I was in heaven.

Breakfasts in diners in Times Square. A girl with so many layers of clothes

on, it was a Catholic guilt trip just to get undressed. The room in the Taft was awash with male fluid and female blood. We crashed and battered each other, and I forgot everything.

I wrote a song called 'Bent out of Shape'. It was her favourite phrase, and alien to me. From then on, the blood we spilt was always significant. I subtitled the song 'I Love You (in Ragtime)'. Menstruation is a total drag for women and a headtrip supreme for men.

In the following days, we drove to Hartford and our New Jersey gigs. We stayed together in Washington and heard that the *Kilimanjaro* album was getting big in Britain.

It was nonsense, though. All I could feel was right now. And now was going to be over, any minute. We cried and wailed in the car, a beautiful silver 1980 Ford Mustang. We drove and fooled around all the time. She finally got round to telling me her last name. It was *Beslity*. A Hungarian name that got changed at Ellis Island. Dorian Beslity. As we drove along, we did each other with our free hands. And time ran and ran. Until it finally just ran out. And I was gone. Leaving a beautiful girl crippled with love at John F. Kennedy Airport. And back to Britain and a host of possibilities that I didn't ever want to comprehend.

I locked myself in the toilet for some of the flight. Other times, I just wept openly and ran my face up and down the plane window.

Eh, fuck it, man. Fuck every single thing in this tiny enormous world. 'Cause I'm going to die without precisely what I need. And I neeeeed!

BAD ONE

At Heathrow Airport baggage claim, my head bulged and weighted down in an agony of 10 million worries. What if I never saw Dorian again? How do I even begin to tell Kathy? Where do I live now? How can any reasonable person expect me to keep it together? Fuck them all, they don't know shit about love.

The drugs in my system were coursing around, scurfing up my veins and distorting my vision of things. By the time I got out into the main terminal, I couldn't hold it down anymore and I ran with my baggage cart out of the customs and down the gangway, where hundreds of stupid idiots were welcoming their loved ones. What about me, you bastards?

I ran and I picked up speed and no-one was around when I got to the wall, so I just slammed right into it. The stupid cart turned over and my bags spilled all over the floor. Then I got up and ran at the wall until I was senseless.

Bill Drummond ran up, just behind two policemen, who asked him if I was on drugs. He said it was far more than that and they said I was to get out of there. They were really pissed off. I thought, You stupid dickheads, what do

you know of any tiny part of this world, and I raged away as Bill and his friend Henrietta whizzed me off to the Columbia Hotel in Bayswater.

I awoke in Room 305, about six hours later. Peaceful now. I was feeling becalmed and beautiful. The room was pitch black and strewn with my clothes and stuff from America.

At the Columbia, I always took the main blanket and tacked it over the window. Then I'd leave the bed-shell in the corridor and sleep on the mattress. The Columbia staff were cool about any shit you did.

At the top of my toiletries bag I found "Little Dorian", this tiny faded Magyar doll with a cream and green dress and hair almost off. A present of true love which the real Dorian had never been without since she was a baby. I clutched at the little doll and jerked over on my side. My stomach. It groaned. I couldn't get away, I slung myself round the bed, kicked the sheets out, pushed my head up against the wall till the pressure and pain soothed me.,

What do I do? What is this? America was the other side of the world. I was a dead man. At least dead. I couldn't even walk or piss. I crawled over to the corner of the room, my mouth dry and my lips chewed to pieces. I stuck my head under the blanket at the window and looked out over Hyde Park.

Then, with just a T-shirt on, I took in the sights of London's coolest park whilst I pissed long and hard into the carpet. I stayed in that one position about two hours. The movement and the intense orange colour of the streetlamps appeased me. My knees became blocks, cornerstones which held me together. I was huge and beautiful, like a large dog at his master's window.

I thought about Dorian in New York, and my bare feet dug into the carpet, and I had to get out of there. But where to? Who can understand this shit? The rest of the group were a bunch of disparate personalities and I had no sense of camaraderie with anyone but Gary. If I asked Troy, he'd be sweet and say, "It's okay, baby." I didn't want that, I wanted the full hugs and kisses understanding treatment right now.

I called my parents in Tamworth.

I sat in an empty first-class compartment of the London–Manchester train. We were still at the platform at Euston station. I didn't want anyone to get in, so I laid my meagre bags around the seats and pretended to be asleep, my legs blocking the entrance.

The train filled and filled. I hadn't washed my clothes so I guessed that I stank, and no-one came in. Then, as the whistle blew, an elderly Irish guy with no luggage got in. He smiled, blew up one of those dumb aircraft pillows that fit around the neck, lay down and went to sleep.

In my corner, I read the address in my lyric book: "La Dorian, 236 E. 13th St. Apartment no. 24, New York City." It was so foreign. How could I keep in touch with someone with that address?

I began to write to her as the train pulled out of the station and into the environs of Londonurbia. Tamworth was 100 miles away. I'd be there in an hour and a half. God, these days never end, they just merge one into another.

I'd arrived at Heathrow at 7.30 a.m. and it was still only 12 hours later. Time sensed that I was confused so it went right on and fucked me up more. In the blackness of the old compartment, I watched the stations I knew so well flash by me, their names so English and quaint to this well-travelled boy who'd been to America and flown two times for God's sake.

Bletchley was soon gone and stupid Milton Keynes, and then Rugby, Nuneaton ... Whizzing through Polesworth, I felt a little calmer. The darkness couldn't obliterate the scene at the Pretty Pigs, the ugliest pub name I knew, and I flashed by, barely a mile from Tamworth. Or "Tarm-warth" as my wife called it when she goofed on my supposedly posh accent.

Yeah, you dickhead. You're married.

I sat in the kitchen at my parents' house. It was home, my home for 18 years until I'd left for Liverpool. Now I was 23 and a failing son-of-a-bitch. Bad. I felt major-league double-dog shitty as bastard hell.

I told my parents, in a roundabout way, that I was in love with a new woman. My father looked at me and said, "Listen, old son, your mother and I knew you weren't in love with Kathy. We understand. That's why we felt so awful at the wedding. You couldn't listen."

I understood for the first time. My parents live in a cocoon of their own making. They adore each other and only let people into their thing if it won't rock their boat. I'd always admired that, but now I knew I was a product of them. They didn't even persuade me to see Kathy.

That night, I lay on the sofa with my mother and we drank tea and talked about love and how it turns you into an inert gas that just lies there, and I was closer to them than any time in years. I resented the things they couldn't know about me. And I knew that they could never understand the drugs or the hurting myself thing. We talked until about 2 a.m. and they put me to bed in my old bedroom. I felt like a five year old and a very old spirit at the same time. Oh God, this is a bad one.

SMASH HITS BOY

It was two days later and we were walking through the streets of Sheffield. My parents had driven me up to a show at the university. It was being recorded for live radio.

We walked around, oblivious at first, but there was a trail of people behind

us. Eventually, on the university campus, we were caught in a kind of pleasant mob who kept us there until security broke them up.

I was way gone and confused by this. My mother dug it, in a perverse way, but I couldn't work it out. We'd gone away as a big cult group. Now, there were shitloads of people recognising me. I hated it. It was bullshit. Girls, young girls about 14, came up and kissed me or screamed. Fuck that.

The two days in Tamworth had chilled me out. I wasn't near drugs and I felt a vague perspective returning.

The folks decided they had better leave, so I said goodbye and waved them off till they were out of sight. Then I walked back to the stage, where I was offered a huge spliff by Bob Proctor.

The show was wild. The hall held about 1,800 people, but it was overflowing and packed with asshole girls cheering for me. It seemed as though Dave Bates was right. I was a pin-up.

I peaked out at the audience and a girl grabbed me. She and her two friends started to neck me as hard as they could and their friends screamed around them. Bob Proctor shouted, "Fuck off, you bunch of slags!" and hauled me back to the dressing room. We had some small lines of cocaine to straighten me out and everyone tried to vibe me up, as I was having trouble breathing.

I sat chewing my lips in the toilet under the stage. My stomach bayed and howled. I farted a big one and Gary and Troy went hysterical. "So that's how you inflate those things," Troy laughed, pointing at my brown leather jodhpurs.

We could hear the stamping of the crowd above our heads and looked at each other. What is this? We've had a hit, that's all. So what is this shit about?

The *Kilimanjaro* album was at no. 26 in the British chart. It had been around there since late November and now 'Reward' was helping it along.

We put it off as long as we could. Finally, the instrumental strains of our intro tape faded. The rest of the group grooved into 'Like Layla Khaled Said' and Bob Proctor prodded and pushed me onto the stage.

This was my ultimate nightmare come true. I danced and cavorted. I spun and smiled. I did every uncool thing I could think of and still they smiled. Alfie started his dumb new-wave dance and I wanted to twat him.

We came offstage and I refused to do an encore. Fuck them, they wouldn't know a good group if it drove its entire PA up their collective asses.

Outside, the hall raged. Crazyland. And my kind of crazy it was not. Collectively, they sucked more shit than any audience I'd ever seen. I could have hung from the lighting truss and wanked over them. It would have had the same effect.

Bob Proctor said he thought we should do an encore. The rest of the group agreed. I wouldn't entertain the idea, but they hassled and hassled. Fuck them and fuck you all. I reached in my bag and took out a little jar. I took one tiny hit of acid and walked towards the stage.

"'Great Dominions'," I said. The slowest tune we had. See if you dig this for an encore.

That night, at the Hallam Towers Hotel, the acid flowed over me and I wanted to die. There were girls in the foyer and in the elevators. They even enjoyed 'Great Dominions' as an encore. I had been beaten. Seemed as though I was your well-loved boy whether I wanted it or not.

I lay in a fever of brain sweats and pulsations long into the night. Fame. Ha. It *can* be overcome. I lay, giant-size, on my bed and watched the dawn through crackling radioactive brain-cells.

At 6 a.m. I hosed myself down in the bath, put on my filthy pink and cream nightshirt and went down for breakfast. I sat drinking endless tea until the place filled up.

Dorian Mary Beslity, my little Magyar–Greek vision, was 3,500 miles away in New York. We were even on different times now. I don't know, how d'you ring the US? Isn't it like £10 per minute or some shit?

I sat like a hollow man by the window. Gradually, the seats around me filled up with the rest of the group and road crew. Some girls, schoolgirls, came by in search of autographs on their way to school.

"Ay, cute boilers," said Alfie, in the brazen London-lad twang that I so detested and mistrusted.

Soon they were over at the window handing up schoolbooks for us to sign. I smiled at them. I did my bit. It was okay really. If you're into being adored by flat-chested pre-menstrual virgins.

Over Snake Pass and out of Yorkshire we drove, Troy to a hotel in Liverpool and Gary and me to our homes. We would rest a couple of days and be busy again soon.

Now I had to face reality. A wife. A woman indoors, man, not the thing for a cheating, tripping fool. We had consoled ourselves with another mild acid trip that morning and as we wound up over the rolling hills and tight V-shaped valleys into Lancashire, Gary told me about the legend of Ichomobothogogus, a two-headed goat that he'd just invented.

We rolled around the back seats about it until we hit the outskirts of Liverpool. When we dropped Gary off at home, I was on my own.

"... so I can't go back to Kath's, no way." I sat in Paul Simpson's front room in Prince's Road. I had sneaked home mid-afternoon, when Kathy was still at work, changed my clothes, then whizzed round to Simmo's about half a mile away.

He said I could stay there, but he was a big friend of my wife, too. That evening, I walked back to the Devonshire Road flat and tried to confront the situation head on. I told Kathy that my head was done in by the American trip and our weird new success over here.

"I've got to stay at Simmo's. Everything's just too weird to think about," and I was gone. She accepted it, no questions, nothing. I thought she was stupid for that. Huh, this'll be an easy separation.

I roamed around Liverpool in a stoned drughead stupor. A hollow man in an inflatable leather outfit. I was stared at and hassled by long mac types and young girls. The brown leather flying-jacket and pants, which had been my joke, were now a famous proposition, I could tell, but it didn't change anything. I'd had these clothes on since early October and they stunk to high heaven. My hair was filthy and matted. That was the only way I could achieve such a shape to my hair. I was obsessed with Scott Walker and Jim Morrison. I wanted that elegant "short" pre-hippy longhair look. I loathed the bloody long-mac greyness that our scene had inspired. It was spring 1981 and the ugliest, most beautiful, uncomprehending time I'd ever known.

ACID DROPS, COPING WITH LIFE AND ALL THAT MISERABLE SHIT

Crappy punning headlines and easy one-liners. Journalism at its basest, un-purest form. Coverstar. Good copy. He'll say anything you want. Get him now.

I was a stinking sameclotheseveryday bullshitting bad-attitude Peter Noone teenangel dustbust my o-so personal life Aled Jones acid-nobody. I fucking sucked the runniest shit and I was beautiful.

Sleeping on the floor at Dave Bates' Lisson Grove flat, in Marylebone. Sleeping in my A&R man's living room and doing TV and glamour shots all day. Did *Top of the Pops*. Had ass kissed all day. Slept alone. Did acid. Talked about myself to some female writer. Slept alone. Rang Dorian. Slept alone. Avoided my wife's phone calls. Slept alone. Slept alone. Slept alone.

I sat cross-legged in Bates' bedroom. He had the biggest record collection in the world. Four copies of 'Little Johnny Jewel' by Television. Two copies of The Spades' single from 1965, with Roky Erikson. Give it Me! A copy of the International Artists boxed set, still sealed! Give it Me! He had all the cool shit I couldn't afford. He didn't listen to them, just had them. We'd wade through piles of stuff I wanted to kill him for.

I'd do a hit of acid and Bates would do cocaine. He was in charge of making the tea and I made compilation tapes. We made eight volumes called *Total Drugs Music I–VIII* and danced around in a new friendship frenzy.

Batesy's flatmate, Droyd, would sit quietly and skin up endless spliffs. Droyd had a name, John Wilson, but he was so chilled out in every way that Droyd *was* his name.

I rang Dorian for hours each night, using 11 false credit card numbers that

she had given to me. I was a grooving popstar, but I was still an own-nothing £35 pounds a week Zoo employee in whatever the real world was.

In Liverpool, my wife told everyone I was just weirding out. She'd ring every so often but I couldn't make any comment. I couldn't tell her. What was she? Dumb or something?

I was presented with a silver disc for 'Reward'. It had sold 278,000 copies. Awlright! They gave me a gramme and a half of coke sealed in a little glass phial as a gift and I laughed at the cliché of it all.

Mid-afternoon, high on cocaine and a small hit of acid, I roamed around record shops with Batesy. It was like Simon and Garfunkel on that famous record sleeve. Batesy was walking fast and assertively in front, whilst I staggered and drooled behind.

We met Droyd and they took me to a small club called Dingwall's. We sat secretively in the corner and I watched as my hands turned into chicken legs. In about an hour, the quiet table was surrounded by women, all talking to us. I couldn't figure out why they were here. The trip made them scary and birdlike. Carrion-crows waiting to swoop.

"Wow . . . my hands, man . . . Chickens a-gaaain. . ."

I spoke to no-one by myself. A blond girl in the mêlée reached for my outstretched arms and said, "They're the hands of an artist, Julian."

I looked at Batesy. Did she really say that? Do people say things like that? Bates nodded. Yes, she had told me that I had the hands of an artist. Aha ha ha ha ha ha ha ha ha ha ha ha ha ha ha ha ha ha ha ha ha ha ha ha ha ha ha ha ha ha.

I slobbered all over Droyd and we slumped into the corner of the seat. We had to leave. Now. It was a bad scene we got out of. Ten more minutes and I'd have been scared to fart.

We rolled on around streets and into taxis. I found myself thrust into a dungeonous club full of hip knobhounds. Propelled into the main room, I ran for the wall and clung to it tenaciously.

Women in black clothes and gaping red mouths motioned to me as they dreamed past me. Faces closed in on me until I started to suffocate in the wall, its softness sucking me in like some shagpile carpet. I heard alien voices whispering "Julian Cope" and eyes would dart quickly towards me and then, just as quickly, dart away again.

Bates told me I was famous. Uh? I lurched ungainly back and gesticulated dramatically. Me? Ha ha ha ha ha ha ha ha ha ha ha ha ha ha ha ha ha ha ha ha ha ha ha ha ha.

As I questioned the fame thing, I stared into another large room. On stage and reading from a lectern, Richard Jobson was a poet tonight. Fascinated to see true Renaissance man in action, I stared from my bush-baby cling in the doorway.

Richard Jobson AKA Jobbo was in full form. Rich and sonorous, he played

the post-punk McGonnigle with style. Through my mean snivelling hyper-everything I was sickened and left the room.

Immediately, I was seized and gripped by Paul Morley from *NME*. He said something idiotic and my head spun and swirled and carried me faster and faster towards the stairs and out of the club, into the street and a taxi which took me far, far away from people and expectations.

I was woken from Batesy's doorstep a few hours later and put to bed. We had TV the next day.

I didn't want to do TV. I wanted to get fucked up and rehearse. I wanted to be full of drive and sass, knocking out classics steadily. I didn't want to do TV.

I'd been away from home now since before we went to America. I had no clothes but the stage stuff and I was accumulating bullshit at Batesy's flat. Albums, books, trinkets and stuff.

I was getting hassled all the time, so we booked a house in the country. I wanted to record all the new songs and we would hire a mobile studio to do it.

The night before I left, I sat playing board games with Bates and Droyd. Droyd had some blotter acid, so we combined it with some Southern Comfort and grass. About 11 p.m., my brother rang me from Liverpool. A distant, distant voice from another star spoke bad words down the phone into my ears. Joss had read my lyric book, found Dorian's address, told Kathy and was now confronting me in the middle of a trip.

I copped right out for a while. I couldn't comprehend what was being implied. Then I told Joss anything he wanted to know because I felt so guilty. I told him I was off to Bear Shank Lodge in the middle of nowhere and put the phone down.

A second US tour was booked, but had been put forward. If Dorian met me in Texas, we would only be apart about nine weeks. I drove up to Northamptonshire in Bob Proctor's Chevrolet Camaro. The most starlike I'd felt, thus far, was arriving at the cool, cool Bear Shank Lodge in that car.

The farm was a paradise at the end of a long winding track bordered on two sides by enormous and beautiful yellow rape fields. It was five miles from a village called Oundle and the countryside was as flat as the Low Countries.

We were a group of sweet-tea drinking, fried-breakfast loving carnivores. We were served macrobiotic food and the phone had a lock on it. The guy was a dickhead and only gave in after a heavy and concerted push.

I rang Dorian every day with the credit card numbers and we rehearsed like mad. Journalists were also around. We got front covers all over, just from interviews in that place. It chilled the journalists out. They'd come up and we'd roll around together, and they'd go away loving me because I was friendly and interested in them. They had not yet realised that I was interested in everything.

We recorded the new songs. They were crap performances. Gary was way too out of it and I had no voice. It didn't matter too much. In fact, it was better in a way. If you do something good without thinking about it, you invariably find it impossible to recapture the first raw snarls.

The recording straightened me out for the direction of the second LP. We had already tried to record a song called 'Passionate Friend' but it was all over the place. A good song with no arrangement.

With no new single ready, Dave Bates chose to re-release 'Treason', a song over a year old. We remixed it and Bates and I did a deal. I wanted to change the album sleeve, dump the ugly tripping fools and replace it with a simple image. Bates wanted to add 'Reward' to the album. That's cool. We did both.

The album got even bigger and 'Treason' stopped at no. 18 in the British chart. We did *Top of the Pops* and I was cute as hell.

At Bear Shank Lodge, I received a phone call from my father. "Hello, old son, we're bringing Kate down to see you."

They didn't want to do it, but they felt they had to make an effort. Kathy, or Kate as she now seemed to be known, was very close to my parents. She always came to them in emergencies.

I cleaned my act up for the Gloomy Sunday and checked that everyone else was cool. My parents drank tea while Kathy and I walked around. They left an hour later. It was all over. That was obvious.

The weeks away from Dorian crept on. The US tour was put back and I drifted into a maudlin haze out in the country.

In Rockfield, the Bunnymen had completed their second LP and were gaining ground. I'd spend weekends in the Columbia Hotel, which was becoming more and more rock'n'roll every day. Pam Young had informed The Human League and other Sheffield and Liverpool groups came down. The rules became less strict with every band who stayed there.

The Columbia was *our* hotel. It was the first post-punk hotel. You didn't have to step over heavy-metal groups or members of Buck's Fizz, because it was our thang.

The press was going crazy over The Teardrop Explodes. We were a two-hit group, yet we had more coverage than Adam & the Ants, who had hits every eight weeks.

I was expected to write new singles every week. Eh, who can get *that* together? If we had a new release, all I worried about was getting a cool B-side together. You know, give people some other reason to buy the thing.

One week, the letters page in *Smash Hits* magazine was three quarters filled with Copey/Teardrop stuff. We were big. Publicly, we appeared far bigger than our sales or output. Journalists found out about my lax attitude towards hygiene

and the hedonistic debauched side they didn't want to be involved with but were fascinated by.

Time crept on. In the middle of 1981, when the press was still gripped by Cope-rophilia, we left for Texas. We'd rehearsed to a standstill and needed to get out of there.

Britain is a closet when you want to be left alone.

LEWD DID I LIVE & EVIL I DID DWEL

I stood on the tarmac at Dallas Airport in full black leathers and mirrored shades. The temperature was 95 degrees, almost body heat. Taxiing down the runway, I had been determined to present my alien culture to these cowboys. For God's sake, we're in Texas. The place where my favourite group, The 13th Floor Elevators, were escorted to shows by state troopers to stop them getting near drugs.

I wore force 11 sunscreen to retain my paleness and we drove around like dudes-supreme. We were picked up by weird women at our hotel. They drove Camaros, Thunderbirds and Corvettes, and were upfront about wanting to fuck us.

Our first show was under a freeway, on a stage with wire across the front, like the *Blues Brothers* movie. We got major league fucked up and strolled on to the stage. "Hi, we are The Teardrop Explodes from Liverpool, England."

I janged into the 'Layla Khaled...' riff on my new Fender electric 12-string and watched in delight as the audience, to a man, began to beat 10 shades of shit out of each other.

Behind my smile, my head observed these goings-on from a distance. The riff janged along and I felt no need to stop it or even interrupt its flow with a chorus. After a while, Alfie nudged me and I realised I should sing. The rest of the show was the same – about 250 people bottling each other. Troy timed our opening song at 17 minutes.

All these tanned sun-worshipping Texan dudettes hung out with us. One, a very cute one, asked me if I wanted a lift back in her Corvette. I was too fucked up to trust myself and was missing Dorian, so I declined.

Back at the hotel, women were all around. My little Corvette girl was there and I found her in my room. She wanted us to screw and do methadrine. I told her that was out of the question. She went into the bathroom, shot up the methadrine and lay there crying. I walked into Bob Proctor's room.

"Some girl's off her head in my room. Swap rooms, Bob. I can't handle that shit."

•　　•　　•

Dallas to Houston and on to Austin. One day, we arrived outside a hip record store. There were loads of people and we got to sign a guy's VW Beetle.

The scene was always the same. Bob Proctor sat in the front seat, driving. At his feet was his tour manager's case. It contained hash, grass, speed and any cocaine that Bob could get. I sat next to him, my leather legs up on the dashboard, wearing my mirror shades, like Peter Fonda in *Easy Rider*. Gary sat between us but behind. I refused to roll joints. I couldn't anyway, so they took it in turns.

Right at the back of the van Troy sat with a case of beers and Tequila. He got in the van every morning and got fucked up until he passed out. He never made sense but he was entertaining as hell.

Caught between the front and the back were Alfie and Jeff. They were both straight and easy to freak out.

As a heavy Bible reader, Jeff found Bob Proctor very hard to take. Bob would find the page that Jeff had finished at, tear the page out and roll a huge spliff with it. I liked that a lot. I was very into forcing my thing onto others at that time.

I kept control of the acid. I was paranoid if I didn't have any on my person. Gary and I were tripping every few days at this time. The enormous distances we had to drive were so new to us. You know, it's like driving up and down Britain over and over and over.

We'd get bored and play "Sock". Gary would sit in the middle of the seat with me on one side of him. I would put a sock over my head, climb out of the van window, over the roof and in through the other window. The only rule was that I was not allowed to fall off the van or I'd be killed.

We'd played this game in Britain before, but it was scarier in Texas because Bob Proctor drove so fast. I never got killed but it was a stupid game, you know.

While we played to between 100 and 250 people per night in Texas, we were getting bigger and bigger in Britain. I was still quite unaware of that. We were so removed from it all.

Bill Drummond could never be phoned and Bob Proctor was broke. We had no money for food after two weeks. One time, whilst we waited on Bill, Bob Proctor took Alfie's credit card to pay for our rooms. It was the only way we could get out of the hotel.

The rift between Alfie and Jeff and the rest of us was widening every day. They shared a room and we spent each and every day off our heads and hassling the shit out of them. We didn't care. By the time we got to Tucson, Arizona, Bob Proctor actually beat Alfie up before we went on stage.

The shows were totally inconsistent. I'd be brilliant one night and utter triple-dogshit the next. Or I'd pick just one girl and sing all the songs to her, and slag off her boyfriend.

•   •   •

We worked our way up the West Coast to Los Angeles. We did two shows at the Whisky-A-Go-Go. Awlright! We hung out in the dressing room and were bombarded with drugs and good wishes.

I took a small hit of acid and walked out on to the stage. All the great performers I was following on to that stage. Think about it. The Doors, The Seeds, Love, Janis Joplin, The 13th Floor Elevators, Tim Buckley. . .

My head spun and so I spun. I was a spinning-top in my leathers and matted blond mane. Between songs, I muttered and intoned, sometimes gibberish and sometimes great wisdom. Then I was off again, throwing myself on to the floor, falling into the audience and grinning, always grinning.

We had a new song, 'The Culture Bunker'. It was a comment on my meanness and inability to get off on the success of the Bunnymen and Liverpool in general. The open bitchiness of the song assuaged some of my guilt and the chorus refrain was aimed straight at Mac: "I feel cold when it turns to gold for you."

On stage, 'The Culture Bunker' was merciless. It dipped and swayed and finally dropped down and down and down, until there was just me grunting quietly into the microphone.

I sat on the floor in the far corner of the Whisky dressing room, away from the rest of the group and doing my own intense thing. The first show was over and there were girls at the stage door. I could hear West Coast voices saying, "But we have LSD for Julian," but Bob Proctor was having none of it.

I sat on my black leather jacket, hair and shirt plastered to my head. I didn't wear socks, so the leather of my boots was soaked and a fixture of my feet.

Troy swept up to me, a bottle of Tequila and a glass in his hand. His smile was manic and his eyes were glassy. "I think there's someone you should meet, baby."

The rugby scrum at the dressing room door kicked and shrieked with hip women and a few guys. Bob Proctor held them back with a constant stream of "Fuck offs" in his normal manner.

"Her name's Lydia Lunch. She wants to meet you."

I knew her name well. She played open wound music with her mouth and guitar in a group called Teenage Jesus. Yeah, I was totally into meeting her.

Troy walked back to get her. He returned with this fascinating woman in the tightest black dress, with bright red lips and a mane of black hair. She sat down right next to me and gazed right into my head. "Watching you on stage was like masturbation."

Wow, that was the heaviest line I'd ever been hit with. I smiled through the hallucinogenics and our eyes were caught in the same beam of light. We sat transfixed. Then she took my hand, guided me into the small guitar-tuning room and shagged the ass off me.

A street-musician skated by down Sunset Boulevard, wearing my T. E. Lawrence sheikh outfit. Across the street, a group of policemen ringed a strange

situation. It involved four guys on angel dust or some similar "size of an elephant" drug, pushing an enormous '70s Cadillac down the road, sideways.

After the show, we stayed at the Tropicana. I was sure I had the room where Sam Cooke was shot. There were bullet holes in the ceiling. But then I found out everyone else had bullet holes in *their* ceilings too.

Lydia left around 7 a.m. and we drove to San Francisco.

UNSAFE AT ANY SPEED

In San Francisco, we *were* a psychedelic group. All the older journalists came out to meet us. They said I wrote like Arthur Lee and championed us loudly.

I staggered around the streets, confused and happy and guilty at everything I did. I hung out on my own on Haight Street and bought loads of second-hand biographies.

My phone-calls with Dorian were so inconsistent. Sometimes I was charming. Other times, if Dorian said *anything* wrong, I would become silent and motionless and look straight ahead at the floor of my hotel room. I'd stare and stare until my eyes saw only directly in front of me, and darkness would cloud the edges, and a tunnel would form and I'd slip into a mood of total and inert psychosis.

I had all this blotter acid from Los Angeles and during an interview a middle-aged woman called Sheila gave me a clear plastic bag full of "sherbet".

"It's pure California Crystal," she said. "A thousand trip bag. I live out on the rock and the Dead sent it for you."

We crossed the Golden Gate Bridge, out of San Francisco and on our way to Boulder, Colorado. It's a 1,200-mile journey. We had to do it in two days in our crappest of crap Dodge Ram van.

We resumed our positions and I cradled my 1,000-trip bag in my hands. It was the size of an ounce of rolling tobacco and clear.

Bob Proctor said we had to break the speed limit all the time, just to get to the show on time. Fuck it, I thought, let's make this an epic of epic journeys.

I evaluated my situation. I had seven trips in either blotter or tablet form. It was around noon. I had two days of intense hell ahead of me. Better take them all.

I scooped up the blotters. They were between an eighth and a quarter of an inch in size. They had colour cartoons of Disney characters printed on them and I took all seven of them with a swig of beer.

Gary looked at me, his air of resignation to the fore. If I was going to be

in a state, he figured he should fuck up too. I took his forefinger in my hand and dipped it lightly into the bag of crystal.

"Lick your finger, Gary. Right, that's one trip. Okay?"

Gary stuck his finger in the packet five more times. Right, it's like that, is it? Over the next half hour, I added eight more fingerfuls of crystal acid to my dose of seven blotters.

Nothing happened quickly. Alfie and Jeff looked apprehensive, but I settled down to read at the front of the van. I had bought the autobiography of Blaze Starr for 25c on Geary Street in San Francisco. She was a stripper, but I mainly loved her name.

The coastal breezes were soon far behind. The hills gave way until, through the intense heat and the haze, we were over the state line and into Nevada.

"Ay, fuckin' shuddup, will yer?" Bob Proctor asked for the tenth time.

"Sorry, Robert." I had started to make truck noises as the trip came on. Errrrrr Urrrrrr ... It was hard to stop, especially when someone kept asking me.

I looked up. A VW Beetle was travelling towards us down the highway, about two feet above the ground.

"Alfie, look. Look, Alfie. Look, look, look! Looook."

He looked. The Beetle passed. "So what?"

So what? I couldn't believe it. The single most amazing thing in my life, thus far, and Alfie doesn't care. Suck thine shit and then suck mine, Alfredo.

And then it happened. My 15 trips came on. I looked at Gary.

"Faaaaaaar Ouuuuuut! Garfield, you're the bloody family dog."

I sat bolt upright. He was too. Sitting between Bob Proctor and myself, Gary Dwyer sat, paws 'n' all, as canine now as he had been feline in Rockfield. He stuck out his long wet tongue at me and panted.

I brushed my filthy matted hair luxuriously by the open passenger window. It streamed out behind me, the wind from the enormous open gash buffeting and massaging me. I was huge. I was totally huge. My breathing was strong and virile. I looked around at everyone, my nostrils flared and equine. I felt Godlike and beautiful. Huh, I'm Mercury and you can all fuck off.

With the temperature around 100 degrees, we were not yet fully into the desert. The towns became fewer and fewer and soon we alone raced across the vast and giant white sand, like a tiny slot-car, across Nevada.

Occasionally, a convoy of chromed and shining Peterbuilt and Kenworth trucks would appear, endless miles in front of us. We would catch them up in minutes, sometimes trapped behind their vapour trails, then dip and sway before vrooming past them. I stared transfixed at their tiny rollerskate wheels fighting to support the enormous weight thundering through the dazzle and the heat.

Troy Tate stood, sagging and with great effort, at the edge of a Nevada truckpark, a beer in one hand and a brace of iced imported lagers in the other. We were

filling up with petrol at one of the zillion 76 truckstops on these highways.

We had eaten our fill at a roadside diner called Middle of Nowhere outside Cold Springs, Nevada, then danced with a couple of old guys. Before we left, I'd helped the waitress's son with his homework and she had given us all sun-hats with the placename on it.

Now it was midnight and the frying pan that was the van roof had begun to cool slightly. Gary and I stood, vacantly and immobile, at the gleaming and spotless all-night coke-machine, looking out into the mountains.

We ambled slowly over to Troy at the far edge of the truck park, my hearing too acute in the sibilance and the treble of the jetblack and insect-laden night.

This place. This place and this frame of mind. I was solid and separate from everything. The road went on forever. And these roads. They weren't even real roads. Nature threatened to reclaim them at any minute. Like an elastic band stretched round a tennis ball, it felt as though I could cut through them with a gigantic razor blade and send them spinning off into space.

Bob Proctor rounded us up and packed us back into the van. I had bought a family pack of marshmallows. A huge $3 bag and nothing else. The others had bought quite sensibly and I looked longingly, trying pathetic attempts to do swaps. A marshmallow for a Hershey bar? No way. A marshmallow for a can of coke? Fuck right off.

As we pulled into the hotel for the night, the acid was hotter and clearer than ever. It was 3.30 a.m. We had been travelling for 16 hours. And I had spent the last hour pressing white and pink marshmallows, alternately, into the ceiling of the van. They stood out like huge candy rivets in patterns along the roof panels.

Bob Proctor told us to stay in the van whilst he checked in. Eh, we thought. It's cool to leave the van. We staggered, crazed and slobbering, into reception.

It was a cowboy town. Behind the reception was a casino and the carpets were deep pile red. Like raging bulls, we were sucked towards the dynamite red.

Around us, a Western movie was unfolding. I could not believe it was real. I could not believe that the town sheriff was gambling only about five feet from me. And he wore the most enormous hat. A gigantic stetson. It was white, a creamy white which reminded me of coagulating milk. As I was drawn into the thick of the casino, Bob Proctor jerked me back hard.

"You bloody dickhead. Are you off yer bloody head? We're not in Liverpool now, yer clown. They'll kill us if yer pull any shit."

"B-but this is for *us*, Bob. The sheriff's wearing his best *hat*, for God's sake."

I just couldn't believe that this was normal. My brain seethed with ideas, but Bob Proctor had made me paranoid. I grabbed the key and fled upstairs with Gary.

That night, sleep would be impossible. What are we stopping for, anyway? We could drive forever. Huh, bloody Alfie and Jeff need to sleep.

I consoled myself in endless baths, but Gary was restless. Finally, he hauled me out of the bathroom. It was 5.30 a.m. and we had been awake for over 19 hours. We couldn't tell. We were fuelled and ready to go.

There was no room service and nothing to do. We watched some repeats on TV but Gary had to go out. As the sun came up, we both took just a couple more hits of the crystal and set off to walk around the town.

It was six hours later, around mid-morning, when we pulled up at a desert store, full of cowboy boots, moccasins and far-out regalia. We had seen large signs announcing the place alongside the highway for about 50 miles.

I drooled over a pair of tan suede Indian boots. I paid $15 for them, then spent the next hour cutting all the fringes off.

We crossed into Utah and soon Nevada was left way behind. Gary and I lolled comatose and vacant in the two front passenger seats. I was nowhere. I'd been strung out right across the journey, a part of me still in San Francisco, the rest littered at regular intervals across the desert. The accumulation of the trips, the weeks of little sleep and the situation with my marriage, all this and travelling across America in a van, were beginning to take their toll. Eh, I thought. People do this shit for years. Don't wimp out now, you plank. You've got a show tomorrow night.

Bob Proctor still had a lot of cocaine left over from San Francisco. Normally, he and Troy were the only takers, but today, we stopped at a roadside diner and had a few lines each.

Cocaine isn't a nice drug. It's a bullshitter and that's a fact. But I needed to straighten up. The LSD was so much a part of me that I could only just hear my natural mind, raging away down some lost tunnel, screaming, "Remember me, remember me."

The highway through Utah was like some sunbaked open coalfield in South Wales. The sand was grey by the sides of the road and we travelled for mile upon mile alongside dusty freight trains and open-haulers. The railway lines were parallel with the highway for ages at a time, then they would suddenly shoot off.

My pal, the freight train, would then ride about a mile away before snaking back to the road and we would remain, side by side, cutting through the desert together.

We had maintained an impressive average speed on the journey. Bob Proctor had figured that we had to break the speed limit by 20–25 mph for most of the time, just to give us space to eat. But every day we fell a little behind.

We caught up with a convoy of trucks belching smoke, crawling along and in no hurry to let us past. Gary and I screamed out, "Overtake, overtake, overtake." Bob checked his CB radio, but there was nothing happening. He tried to pass a couple of times but the oncoming traffic was just frequent enough to make it difficult. Then, he suddenly pulled out. To the *right!*

We raced down the hard shoulder on the inside of the convoy, the sand and the dust pouring into the open windows. We choked and cackled as we bounced around inside the van.

Yeah, yeah. Past the first container wagon, awlright. Past the second container, awlright, on and on and on, past the seventh container wagon and ... right past the patrol car which had obviously been the reason for the convoy's delicate speed.

As the patrolman strode towards us, Bob Proctor fumbled his briefcase out of sight. It contained my 1,000-trip bag, a large bag of grass, the San Francisco cocaine and all the tour receipts.

Be normal, I thought. Concentrate.

"This is fuckin' Utah, right?" snarled Bob Proctor. "They lock you up, you pull any shit."

Normal, normal, normal. I sat looking gleefully and psychotically normal, trying to understand the seriousness of the situation.

"You realise you were doing 83 miles per hour, sir?" The patrolman looked stupendous. So law-enforcing that I had a problem not complimenting him. I beamed at him. Hope I look okay, yeah, I'm cool.

"Yeah, sorry about that. We've gorra get to Boulder dead soon."

Bob's Liverpudlian twang interested the guy, but we weren't getting off completely. He told us that overtaking on the inside on dirt at 83 mph was dangerous to other people and us as well. Yeah, we know, dead sorry, etc., etc., etc.

He fined us on the spot, then we had to follow him to the nearest post office. He couldn't take our money. He had to watch us post it to the king of fines.

And we were off. No arrests, nothing. I got severely booed for being over-friendly, but what's new?

The Salt Lake City signs became more frequent. One said 225 miles, then 130 miles, then out of nowhere I caught the glint of something golden on the horizon. In just a couple of miles, the dust grey earth became green and lush like the English countryside. The glint came from the dome of the capital building. Each US state capital has a dome. The Mormon state capital in Salt Lake City has a golden dome. It figures.

The unreal and spiritual building reached out to me but in an instant we were gone. I had only seconds to think of Brigham Young, Donny and the guys, and we were leaving this green and idyllic oasis far behind.

Bone-weary, brain-weary and utterly fucked, we entered the state of Colorado. Are we there yet? Are we near? No, we're not even close. The day was coming to an end. No way would we get to sleep in Boulder tonight. Shit, another half-day of travelling tomorrow.

Troy had collapsed in the very back seat, his system totally caned by the

weight of beer and the intensity of spirits. Jeff and Alfie were hunched up together, their hellish journey still in full flight.

In the front seat Gary and I kept Bob Proctor alert. He'd driven thousands of miles since our arrival in Dallas and was more psychotic than anyone.

I was starving. Let's stop, man. We waited for a diner, a truckstop or some such to appear, but nothing did. There was no food in the van, not anything. Sweet-wrappers and tobacco and trails of two weeks driving littered the floor. In my haze, it looked wonderful. I searched on my hands and knees for a morsel, but to no avail.

The night wore on and the temperature plummeted. I put my feet up on the dashboard and lay back. My eyes caught a feast, a complete feast. On the ceiling, petrified from the heat and filthy from the dust, were the pink and white marshmallows that I'd so carefully stored two days before.

I pulled them off the ceiling, one at a time, like a farmer picking fruit, and hungrily chewed them up. Gary was revolted, but soon he was eating too.

Around 3.30 a.m. we pulled into a tiny town called Dinosaur, checked in and fell into oblivion. For Gary and me, even the acid could not halt our crushing and inevitable slumber.

"Now look, Pam. Yer've gotta find him *now!*"

Bob Proctor and I stood at the only pay-phone in Dinosaur, Colorado. We were broke again, to-*tally* skint. We had $17 between us after we had paid the $55 for the rooms. Bill Drummond was not in Liverpool and Pam Young couldn't seem to clear any money for us.

I wasn't concerned, though. The trip was still in full swing and I was only interested in one thing, a huge church-sized fibre-glass Brontosaurus that stood in the middle of this dust-bowl of shacks and roadside diners. How had we missed this thing last night?

I wandered back to the motel, still transfixed by the fake dinosaur, and topped up the trip with a couple more fingerfuls of the crystal. The motel was three long domestic trailer caravans and a reception hut. We had booked the entire place for $55!

An hour or so later, we were back on the highway with the promise of money soon. The shape of the Colorado countryside had changed entirely. We climbed high up into the Rocky Mountains, on and on around winding treacherous passes. The hours passed and I fell into my first real sleep for days. I slept, fitfully and hunched, in the front of the van up to the very top and, after hours and hours, I felt us begin to make the descent into Boulder.

That night, The Teardrop Explodes played a very unartistic and average show. I wore my new suede Indian boots to make me feel good, but I was truly gone. All spent.

SAME INITIALS AS CHRIST

"A night on fire put out all traces of feeling."

'The Great Dominions'

On and on and up and round the US map we rode. Danger on all sides, but mainly danger from our load. Each show saw a new side to The Teardrop Explodes, until we bore little resemblance to the group which started the tour.

In Denver, Colorado, we made a personal appearance at Waxtrax Records. Three people came. The owner was embarrassed for us and I left with shitloads of free albums. Gifts of guilt.

That night we played to a bar full of Midwest punks. By the middle of the set they had left in disgust, to be replaced by the Deadheads and yippies at the back.

I guess we disappointed a lot of people. They came to see a post-punk beat group and got Buffalo Springfield. I had long sun-bleached hair, a tan suede outfit and a Gibson electric 12-string guitar. The songs went on forever, littered with personal put-downs and insults for the audience.

The 1,000-trip bag was regularly attended to as we peeled away the miles upon endless miles. Out of Colorado, through Lawrence, Kansas, where our dressing room was actually *next* to William Burroughs' headquarters. (Gary and I broke in to search, unsuccessfully, for the original manuscript of *Queer*, his then unpublished and notorious classic.)

In Chicago, the entire PA broke down as 'Kilimanjaro', our intro music, was playing. I wandered on and played a couple of acoustic songs, fuelled by the club owner's uncut and wonderful cocaine.

The rest of them learned to improvise on one chord during my more and more frequent escapades on and around the stage. I explained that they could do what they liked, so long as it was always on one riff. No clever stuff. No blues. And no solos.

In Detroit, the crew and PA arrived on time, whilst we were late waking up. We broke down 200 miles from the gig. The police helped us, the AAA helped us. The van was just fucked. We'd bought it from Bob Proctor's mate in New Jersey. It was a piece of shite. Gary and Troy and I got completely fucked up at the side of the road. "There'll be no gig tonight." And what do you know? We made it. With minutes to spare, we arrived at the stage door. The house manager said it was too late to start any show. I agreed. I didn't care and I was too crazy to sing. Bob said we had to play or we'd forfeit our money. So we piled on stage and played, oblivious to everything.

The Canadian border at Windsor Bridge is a very heavy crossing. The authorities *know* what's going on. Everyone does their huge accumulation of American

drugs down the road, in Detroit, then travels through the border, wired, amped, skulled and generally with a hell of an attitude.

On the back of our crew-truck, behind the Detroit club, we set up a frenzied chemical picnic. I yelled and screamed but Bob Proctor insisted that I dump my beloved 1,000-trip bag. There was no way we could keep *anything*.

By the early hours of next morning, we passed into Canada, our mouths forced into amphetamine smiles and our lips chewed and red raw. We checked into the Toronto Sheraton at 8 a.m. and sank into oblivion.

Of all the staff writers at *NME*, Adrian Thrills was the most reasonable. That was the only thing about him that I didn't like. He was small and skinny with a Mod-head full of ideas of how things should be. As one of the early champions of The Teardrop Explodes, Adrian was concerned that we were becoming a bunch of cocooned acidheads of state. He was right, I guess, but I'd recently realised that I had the same initials as Jesus Christ, and that changed everything. No more apologising for *this* dude.

Late afternoon, around six, I got a call. It's Adrian Thrills. He's been waiting for you all day. Sorry, I didn't even know he was in Toronto.

I arose into the chaos of our room. Gary had been farting like a bastard all night. My clothes were all heaped together in one damp wedge of solidifying matter. You remember finding filthy week-old sportsgear at the bottom of your bag when you were at school? Well, that was my clothes. The whole room stank of damp, shit, stale tobacco and old fruit, the only thing available to eat when we arrived.

I wanted to make at least a reasonable impression on Adrian, but that was ruined when he knocked on our hotel-room door, unexpectedly. I had just taken a bath. To piss Gary off, I'd locked the door from inside and closed it behind me as I left. Adrian's first introduction to the tour was watching Gary punching and kicking a hole in the bathroom wall. I made vague explanations and we went down to the club.

I think we were shit that night. We did two sets; one was unremarkable and one sucked big logs. I rang Dorian from a stupidly unattended telephone and missed her more and more as our separation drew to a close.

Out of Canada and down into New York State we came. I never understood how big it was. New York State stretches from way up at the Canadian border halfway down the eastern seaboard.

Adrian Thrills was with us all the way. I didn't want him there. I liked the guy and didn't want him to see us cracking up. I had this couplet spinning round in my head. It went:

"I'm a Turner sky and I look from above.
It's alright for now, but how do I get down?"

WE TALKED FOR HOURS, EXCEPT FOR THE FAINTING

And so we arrived in Albany, New York State's capital, 150 miles north of New York City and the place of my first visitation from Dorian, 13 weeks before.

For this reason and also because of the lack of pressure at such a small gig, Dorian and I had decided to rendezvous here for a second time. I had a night off and, maybe, time to decide whether this was real or puppy love. But I was worried in case I blew my first meeting with Dorian in three months.

I was sitting in the Howard Johnson's residents' bar. I wore jeans and my leather camo belt, a white T-shirt and these terrible scummy grey suede boots that I got in Toronto for $3. I had washed and aired my filth and sweat ingrained clothes in honour of Dorian's arrival.

What if I didn't fancy her? Or what if we've got nothing to say? Or maybe it was only a holiday romance. Shit. I worried and worried until I realised I just had to wait. The hours passed and I began to wonder if she would come at all.

And then, from my place at the bar, I saw the most beautiful vision. She was standing in the hotel foyer and wore an exquisite and very old off-white chiffon strapless dress. It had delicate red leaf patterns and an enormous red taffeta bow around the waist. Her wide crinoline underskirt accentuated her gorgeous shapely legs. She wore red high-heels and her black lacquered and crazy hair fell over her eyes.

I knew she was Dorian immediately. I just had this problem accepting that she was here for me. This was the woman I'd been rude to on the telephone so many times? I strode up to her.

Shit, man, she's incredible. We stared at each other from about four inches away, just like a dog sniffing around some long-lost pal. I found it all vague and unbelievable.

I took her hand and we walked outside and up the steps to my room on the balcony. We locked ourselves in there, pushed the two double-mattresses on to the floor and made love all night.

Pressure on. No matter how much I tried, I couldn't help feeling that this wouldn't work. The odds were so totally against it. I started a fight during the night. "I can't sleep in such a confined space." Bullshit. It was more space than I *ever* had.

Gradually, I eased myself into this new and all-important situation.

It was the next morning. Dorian and I ate breakfast and drove into Albany's centre. This was the stuff I had dreamed about doing. You know, the real little unimportant shit. It seems like you yearn more and more for this stuff if your life becomes extreme.

I get so pissed off when dickhead rock'n'roll artists pretend to be angst-ridden and fucked up all the time. Don't you know how rude it is, you planks? Falling for the artist trip is the most dumb-ass thing ever. It proves you're a hollow shell. Being off my head around the world was a small consolation. I wished every minute for peace and simplicity.

We flicked through the record racks in some collector's shop. Dorian bought me an original copy of the first 13th Floor Elevators LP. A prize! We hung out and made our way, slowly, back to the motel.

Kid Gambino, our sound guy, had been with us since our last US tour in early March. Everyone had commented on how particularly crap he was. Of course, I really dug him, so no-one could get rid of the dude. Walking out of my Howard Johnson's motel room, I noticed Dave Bates, my A&R man, with a weird-faced guy. He had long black hair and a hooked nose. Bob Proctor told me he was the new sound man. Gambino's out.

What? How fucking rude. No way! We got to the soundcheck and I freaked out at the idea of someone being foisted upon me. Kid Gambino sucked up to me and tried to persuade me to keep him. I didn't care about that. I was just pissed off at not being asked.

I ignored everyone and left. It brought me right down. I sat in my room and just glowered. My moods were becoming increasingly twisted.

I always wanted emotions to hit at precisely the right moment. If someone turned up unexpectedly or left without warning, I was a real mess. A stupid self-obsessed dickhead.

"Er and um and um, er and um and um, this is serious, this is serious, this is serious. Er and um and um, er and um and um, this is serious, this is serious. . ."

We were stuck in the elliptical and timeless riff of a song called 'Poppies in the Field'. Ranting away, I'd been caught in this falling-leaf pattern before. No-one ever dared to stop me since Balfe left and now I was pissed off as all hell.

The Gambino affair was well worth spoiling an entire show for. Especially as we'd played a brilliant set in Albany only three months previously.

That night, Bates stayed away from me. Dorian was scared to put a foot wrong in case I told her to go home. Everyone was on edge.

We left for Philadelphia the next day. I told Dorian I'd see her in New York. Far from Britain and so far into the tour, nothing made sense.

I'm in love with a girl who has the most dresses and shoes in the world. She knows *nothing at all* about love and I have a wife at home who's freaking out.

I veered between total guilt and complete rage at the situation. I consoled myself in the sheer *chaos* of LSD and found that it prevented me from lashing out too much. Instead, I was looking inwards for some sense of peace.

I would walk my mind down a long corridor away from my eyes. The world outside was drifting away and away until it was a ship going over the horizon and a black tunnel would appear around my world, whereupon I would slip into a mood of total inert psychosis.

Meanwhile, our New York show was a stupid and mistaken "double-bill" with U2 at the Palladium in Lower Manhattan. In Liverpool, we thought that U2 were a bad joke, a record company's idea of a northern group. They talked of passion as though it was their exclusive right. Ho-hum. Down the eastern seaboard, U2 had sent the Teardrop messages. The final one was a tape of Sparks' old 45 'This Town Ain't Big Enough for Both of Us'. I really dug that. Maybe Bone-head and Co. weren't Bad Company after all.

Double-bill, huh? We went on first, did really well and left. I'd seen U2 in the soundcheck. Led Zep, man. Uncool. But they were dead sweet and a bit younger than us, so we gave them some leeway. They weren't gonna do *shit* anyway. To quote Gary Dwyer, U2 were really called the Hope Brothers. "'Cause they've got two hopes of making it: Bob Hope and no hope."

In Britain, my absence was contributing to our ever-increasing size. The little girls could only see my pictures and the rumours were still coming only in dribs and drabs. Had they been able to smell me or hear the new songs, then the bubble would have burst immediately.

And so we left these verdant pastures and great new world of possibilities. Yes, it was time to face the brutal old world with its real problems and its tight reins, close fitting and cutting hard into my expanding skin. No leeway and no forgiveness.

Between the Devil and the deep blue sea.

Between post-punk and absolution.

MY FIRST NAME IS PLANCIS, BUT YOU CAN CALL ME PLANK

Back to the purgatory of Britain for the summer. Oh, fun, fun, fun. I can be a pop singer, ho-hum.

In London, I couldn't even enjoy a stoned day in the park. I was constantly recognised by 11 year olds out with their parents. Room 311 at the Columbia Hotel was my home, my refuge and my inspiration. I moved all the unnecessary furniture into the corridor, brought posters, tapes and a guitar into the room, and slept on my great-grandmother's 90-year-old quilt.

Summer '81 was the first heyday of the Columbia as a rock'n'roll hotel. Musicians who hated it were just bitter because they thought they were late on

the bandwagon. But this scene, disparate as it was, needed some place that was a reaction to the old-style chrome and deco palaces that charged £150 per night to shit like Thin Lizzy and the Geezer fraternity. In the Columbia, Soft Cell, Cabaret Voltaire, Heaven 17 and the like talked to the Bunnymen, The Wild Swans, The Pale Fountains. The only cool old dudes were Slade, whom everyone loved in any case.

"Meester Julee, he never leave heez room ... He like the smoke, you know." Francisco, the bartender, was there every night giving me a good rap to people.

Troy Tate, still a resident of London, would drink his evenings into oblivion, the link between the Sheffield and Liverpool camps.

One evening, I'd been on a radio review programme called *Roundtable*. I'd danced and fallen off tables in the control room, screaming and laughing throughout the show. Then I called The Human League single "kack" and got out of control and got banned.

You know, you get asked to do shit TV and they get surprised when you fuck up. I mean, just simple psychology would tell you not to ask people like us to do it. Like, say, Adam Ant was around and really good at his thing. So people like that should do the shit because they do it well. I didn't even care about the stuff, so it's hard to take it seriously. What record companies never sussed was that if I'm forced to do something through circumstances, as soon as I come out the other side, I'll fuck them royally up the ass.

That's not a threat. I don't feel proud of that. It's just in me and I've got to do it to stay alive and feel that I exist.

We started our first tour of Britain since our hit singles. In America, we were still just culty as hell. I was used to drugged women and psychedelic heads. Suddenly, I was confronted with innocence. My natural reaction was one of revulsion. My brief confrontation as a trainee teacher with five and six year olds in Liverpool had reminded me to ignore anyone still at school.

We walked out for the first show and I freaked. Yukk! What a total right-off drag. Stupid lickle teeny girls a-fussing and a-fainting and a-paying no heed to the single-mindedness of our one-chord space-grooves.

Alfie bopped like a dude born to be uncool. He was the Personification of New-Wave Man. Girls held up banners. I saw one that said "ALFIE!" Soon, that one seemed like hundreds. What were we becoming?

I took more of everything to help me get through this obnoxious and cissified routine. Psychologically, I felt compelled to remain dirty, no, get dirtier, yeah, be filthy. It was the middle of summer '81. I wore only my leathers and refused to change them. They were the symbol of the fame I was so detesting but I thought, fuck everyone, I'll be way beyond all of them. I'd think gross thoughts.

I wanted to run up to little girls. Give them my autograph. Force it on them, you know.

"Here you are, stupid asshole girl. You don't know me but you'll want it anyway."

Halfway through the tour, the Nottingham show was a chaotic teeny affair. I could feel all the long mac brigade retreating to the back of the hall.

We played the hits and the big radio songs from the album and they went crazy. We played stuff off the forthcoming album and they went crazy. I couldn't faze them at all. They loved it. I was on some great metaphysical acid trip. The direct descendant of John Donne, T. S. Eliot, Jim Morrison and Patti Smith. Boy, I must have been fooling someone. I was bloody Peter Noone.

The Nottingham audience got more teary and disgusting. I called to them, "You little bitches can piss your lickle panties . . ." I railed on about their stupid parents waiting in the stupid cars outside for them. And how they wanted to fuck me and how they didn't have the attention span of a butterfly and all this miserable stuff that they hadn't come to hear, and Duran Duran didn't do this unprofessional stuff, did they?

John Taylor, from Duran, said in *Smash Hits* that summer that their only competition was from The Teardrop Explodes, "If Julian Cope can keep it together." Yeah, *no* problem. I had the audience. Now, I just needed to convert thousands of pre-teens into doubtful understanding followers. I just needed faith and an attitude.

David Bates, A&R man and one-time friend, got up from the dressing-room floor. I rushed out of the room and down the stairs of the Coventry Odeon, Droyd in pursuit. . .

Bates had arrived at the soundcheck with a new Teardrop single. One that I'd not even been consulted about. They had edited it and released it with my manager Bill Drummond's permission. The song, 'Ha Ha, I'm Drowning', was the *fourth* single from the *Kilimanjaro* album. That was way too much. Now Bates was telling me for the first time. Well, fuck that. I had knocked Bates to the floor and was now fleeing to the stage with Droyd in pursuit. He told me Bates was dead upset and knew it was a bad thing.

"Listen, man. He brought you to placate me. Batesy is record company. He's just proved it."

Bob Proctor was totally into the skirmish. He drove me to my parents' house in Tamworth. It was only about 15 miles away. I said I would stay there until Phonogram Records withdrew all the copies of 'Ha Ha, I'm Drowning'.

Bill Drummond hounded me at my parents' house. He said it was just hurting *my* career. Bullshit. My career is nothing when a gesture has to be made. We can always reschedule the shows.

After two days, I had lunch with the managing director of Phonogram. He was really nice. He acquiesced and agreed. He also told me that the single had entered the chart at 66 with only three days' sales. I said I was sorry. It was a principles thing.

Soon we were back in London. We played a dreadful show at the Hammersmith Odeon, mainly through my hang ups, and Gary and I were back at our favourite hotel. The Columbia had no room service and a shit phone service. The rooms were boxes with badly put together unit furniture and floral wallpaper. It was cheap as hell and they brought the rates down if you stayed all night.

I'd been back at the Columbia about a month, ringing Dorian every night and running up massive bills, when I got a call from the guy on the front desk.

"Julian? 'Allo. Listen, you know you call America all the time?"

I listened intently. He had a proposition to make. If I gave him a fiver for each call, he wouldn't list any of them. I said that was cool. For as long as that guy worked there, I got cheap international rates.

It came at exactly the right time, as well. I had to be careful with the fake credit card numbers. I stopped using them for a while when they caught on to me.

Midsummer, I took some time off to write songs. Bates and I made up and he told me that I could use the flat while he was away. I phoned Dorian and got her to fly over within the week.

A flat and a month together would give us a real chance.

CHRIST V WARHOL

It was high summer and sticky heat as I packed Dorian and her umpteen suitcases into the taxi at Heathrow Airport's Terminal 3. We sped along through the outskirts of London and got caught in the traffic at Hammersmith.

In the back seat, we couldn't believe it. She was here. She felt unreal to my touch. Each time we met, I had to relearn her body and her head. At last, we had space and time to ourselves.

Bates' flat was now home to me. Each night I took the sheets and made up my bed on the couch in the front room. We had a routine. Droyd would skin up a final joint and I'd make the last tea of the night. Bates was exempt as it was his house and he was doing shitloads anyway. Now I was with Dorian in Bates' flat.

I love that speedy feeling that you get when you meet someone at an airport off an early flight. You intend to go to sleep early but it inevitably becomes

2 a.m. and you're not even sleepy. Waking up at 6 a.m. and running on pure and ugly adrenalin, your body is soon travelling out of the city and through the suburbs, watching commuters still scrambling for breakfast in their houses overlooking the railway line. By the time you pick up your friend, you feel jet-lagged yourself in a weird kind of way. Back home by late morning and already you've done a day's living.

I carried Dorian into the main bedroom and plopped her on to the bed. She felt so new, so brand new. Wow. I thought these were the women you never get to touch. I'd been with pretty girls before, but it seemed to me this was different. She had so much sexuality oozing out that it took my breath away. And the most outrageous underwear.

I pulled gently at the clasp on her belt and removed her dress, then we lay down and tripped out over the beauty of each other. I felt as worshipped as she did. This total piece of amazing ass with the brains of my weirdest friends all wrapped up in acres of the sexiest material and the palest, milkiest, most female shape this lickle planet did know.

We cavorted for hours. It felt like no-time and no-place.

It was the next morning. I had introduced Dorian to Droyd and we lay around Bates' bedroom, smoking weed and listening to psychedelia.

Droyd and I took Dorian out to breakfast at the Sunshine Café on Lisson Grove. It was about 20 yards away and as we left I bought a selection of British chocolate. I piled her up with Toffee Crisps, Cadbury's Caramels, Curly Wurlys and Yorkies. These things are so rich compared with American candy. American chocolate is shit. It's all chocolate-flavoured candy, man. Hershey bars? Candy. Mr Goodbar? Candy. There's a load of great American traditions, but believe me, the sweets suck.

Back at the Lisson Grove flat, we listened to the first Pink Floyd LP. I hadn't played it for months and now it was sounding great. When we reached a song called 'Lucifer Sam', I just played it and played it and played it. There's something about the way that Syd Barrett sings, "But that cat's something I can't explain . . ." and the guitar riff, which is disjointed and snaky. Barrett. He was looooose.

That evening, I told Dorian and Droyd that we were going out. It was weird for Dorian as Patty was in London hanging out with Killing Joke. They had grown apart after we had met. Before that time, they were inseparable, but Patty had developed a kind of "crush" on me that forced them both apart.

Around six in the evening, we dropped a tab of acid each. I knew that Dorian was still exhausted from the jet-lag, but I thought what the hell.

For some inexplicable reason, we arrived at the Venue, a shithole of vaguely gigantic proportions. As the trips began to take effect, I heard a tannoy announcement from what seemed like 2,000 miles away.

"Wow, I think The Television Personalities will be on soon."

Neither Droyd nor Dorian had heard the announcement, so they both thought I was the oracle when, sure enough, The TV Personalities trooped onstage.

My breathing became forced and deliberate. I watched the group on stage but I was not calm. They had a monkey playing the drums. A monkey in a cage. I must be mistaken, I'm tripping and that doesn't happen at the Venue. Still, they *are* The TV Personalities so they can do what they like.

Dorian was getting younger and younger all the time when something happened that almost sent her back to the womb: the group began to play 'Lucifer Sam' by Pink Floyd. No. Is that weird? Is this a weird thing to be happening?

I asked Droyd. He didn't think so really. I asked people around me, but they were too intrigued to see Julian Cope on acid to answer the question.

Dorian thought that it was way too weird and began to cry. She said they had control of our minds and that really scared me. I looked over to Droyd and screamed, "Is she okay?"

Droyd stared at the dishevelled and miserable little girl. Her make-up was all over her face and she was crying uncontrollably. It was deafening in the place.

"Yeah, I think she's fine," he said, smiling blandly.

Oh, that's good. I felt pleased that Droyd was in charge and appeared to know what was going on. It *was* weird. Of all the songs they could play in the whole world, of all the unusual cover-versions, they pick that one. Still, in a way it fitted together so well that we couldn't question it for too long.

"Yeah, and wouldn't it be cool if Patty turned up?"

"Don't *say* that. It would be too much," squirmed Dorian. Her head was lifting off at the very thought and already I was putting her through too much. I forgot that she was younger and stuff. You know, you put your woman through your trip and expect her to take to it.

I walked to the men's room. It took a period of minutes, as I was easily diverted. Women would call "Julian?" and I'd think that I knew them and spend ages staring at their faces, looking for some kind of recognition. Once I discovered that they only knew me from The Teardrop Explodes, I would carry on towards the toilets, only to be stopped again 10 seconds later.

In the toilets, I couldn't tell if I was peeing or not. Had I pissed myself? Was I stinky? There were guys looking at me doing my loopy thang. Were they looking because I was acting weird? Did they recognise me? I realised that I didn't give a shit and that made me feel better.

Eventually, I remembered where I was. There was a club outside. You didn't come here to stay in the men's room. Hmm, I'd better leave.

I strode purposefully into the chaos and rage of the club. I saw Tom Bailey, the singer from The Thompson Twins, and we talked just long enough to be

aware that I was making no sense. I made my way past the bar and a guy threw a pint of beer over me. Hey, that felt *gooood*.

I carried on walking, but a voice of normality tugged away at my senses. Way back in my head, I sensed that throwing beer over someone was not a friendly act. I figured I'd better go back and question the guy about his actions.

"Er, excuse me. Are you the guy who just threw beer over me?"

"Yeah. Wanna make something of it?"

"Er, I just wanted to know one thing. Was it meant in a heavy way? You know, are you being *heavy* towards me? I have to ask you 'cause I'm tripping and I don't know you."

The dude looked bemused. He stared to see if I was joking. As I stood, distant and unaware, I'm sure he realised I was for real, and that totally threw him.

"Yeah, well . . . You kicked Mick Finkler out of the group, didn't you?"

I reached for my past but fumbled it badly. I was just about to say I remembered Mick well, but I checked myself as I sensed that it would go down badly. Especially as he'd still been out of the group for only one year. God, it seemed like forever ago.

"Erm . . . Mick? He . . . he was . . ."

I drifted again, as my eyes lit on the rows of spirits behind the bar. They shone in thick syrupy translucent greens and ambers. Oh God, they looked *sooo* beautiful.

"Yeah. He . . . couldn't write . . . songs and wouldn't let me write stuff on my own so eventually I got pissed off and threw him out. I gave him loads of chances but it was a group decision 'cause we had to . . ." My voice trailed away.

That was enough for my beer-chucker. He was okay, now. We started some kind of dislocated conversation. His name was Wally and he claimed to have been a founder of the Sex Pistols, even though he looked more like a heavy Elvis Costello.

I started to walk back to Dorian and Droyd when I bumped into Patty. She looked great.

"Wow. I told Dorian we'd see you here. Coool."

Patty was freaked out. "Dorian's here?"

I walked her over to our table and Dorian shit. They hugged and it was weird and emotional. Droyd smiled blandly at everyone and figured everything was going fine.

Dorian explained that we were tripping.

"Shit, no wonder my friends thought you were a space cadet, then."

Irony and coincidence, she was with Wally the dude and his mates. She told Dorian they were likely to beat shit out of me. No way, I thought. I could feel their intentions with my super-psychic sensors.

I walked back to the bar to confront them and soon we were all talking in

a group. Droyd decided that Patty was going to sleep with him. Dorian told Patty this. She said no, but came back to Bates' flat with us.

Droyd and I hunched into a corner of his room and tried to understand things. Was it always like this? It seemed that I was tripping *all* the time.

Every so often, Dorian would come into the room in tears.

"Are you okay?" we'd ask.

"No," she'd tremble, then stagger back into the other room.

After about two hours of this, I decided to stand up. I rose gradually and, over a period of minutes, I reached my full height.

I was a cliff-face. Long and high and terrible. I was way too high up. I couldn't bear the vertigo and clasped the mantelpiece before I reeled against the mirror.

I looked down at the countryside miles below. The hills looked like a three-piece suite, only textured way beyond nature's taste. The floor might as well have been the ocean floor. But my main concern was still the cliff-face. I stared pitifully at Droyd for encouragement and ideas. "How do I get down?"

Droyd had no idea. I'd just have to stay there. And stay there I did, until Dorian came to tell me that Patty had left.

Lying in Batesy's bed that night, we were so tripped out that I couldn't handle it. Emotionally, our heads were caned. Also, Dorian was crazy. She didn't believe that she would ever stop tripping. I couldn't give her reassurance. I wasn't that sure myself. Days and nights were becoming one solid wedge of time now-adays. We lay there in tears, thinking that we were forever to be stuck like this. My stomach revolved with the amphetamine that was cut into the LSD.

At around 7 a.m. we fell asleep. It was good to have her over here. She had been in London almost 24 hours. Awlright!

The next day, I was supposed to record a B-side for our forthcoming single, 'Passionate Friend'. I'd listened to the first LP by my friend Pete Wylie's group Wah! It was very disappointing, but there was one image that I really got caught up in. One line said: "You've got 15 minutes, I've got 2,000 years."

That was the battle. It was Andy Warhol-fame versus the eternal fame of Jesus Christ. Yeah. I sat down and wrote a song called 'Christ v. Warhol'.

That was my battle from now on. 'Cause I wanted *both*. NOW.

EAST OF THE EQUATOR

I was troubled. I knew what it was. I had too much control over the group. The friction had gone once Balfe had been kicked out. This was more apparent than ever when we recorded a bunch of songs in Fulham. I supervised everyone

during a song called 'East of the Equator' and kicked all but Gary out for the rest of the session.

Gary and I put down the backing tracks for three songs in as many hours, then piled vocals and ideas on as quickly and as loose as we could get away with. The songs were 'Tiny Children', 'Christ versus Warhol' and a dreary harmonium and brass freak out called 'Window Shopping for a New Crown of Thorns'.

I had gently wrestled control from everyone and refused to delegate.

Around this time, August 1981, Bill Drummond and Dave Balfe began to tell me that I was evil. This was *not* the paranoia of an acid king swanning his trip around his court. They became quite open about it and only a few of my close friends seemed to take my side.

I loved Bill Drummond. I mean, yes he had fucked me around and yes, he was a two-faced swine sometimes, but then, who isn't? I knew for shit damn sure that I was at least as bad at times, although only to minor characters in our scene.

The Teardrop Explodes was more and more like an old B17 bomber every day. Half of the crew and the engines were gone and the man in control had an almost kamikaze attitude towards landing.

I knew that Alfie and Jeff had become encumbrances and they were hassling to become full members. Troy, Gary and Drummond were whispering loudly in my ears about Balfe's rejoining and I was feeling more megalomaniac and guilty every day, what with Kathy's life being ruined and a bunch of people reliant on my not fucking up.

In mid-August, we recorded our new single, 'Passionate Friend', at Genetic Studios in Goring-on-Thames outside Reading. Goring is a beautiful and incredibly wealthy place. It is home to the DeFreitas clan and, as such, partly explained to me why Pete was so peaceful in his head. I reckoned that equal doses of Liverpool and Goring would keep me on an even keel too.

The rest of the group stayed in the Miller of Mansfield, an old tavern in the centre of Goring. Dorian and I chose to remain up at the studio, in a weird chalet bungalow. If we left the doors open, flocks of geese would walk in to visit us.

See, the studio was brand new and all the money had been spent on equipment and technology. Martin Rushent, who owned the place, had made his money from the Stranglers and The Human League. He wasn't interested in comfort.

So here we were, the group, our long-time producer, Clive Langer, our engineer, Alan Winstanley, and a song that we'd recorded before and that had given us trouble.

Clive had rearranged 'Passionate Friend' by knocking out all the bits I had fussed over and concentrating on the hooks. We worked hard and quickly.

I decided not to play on the song, just sing. It made me feel more like the boss, you know? Writing a song and turning it over to the other musicians was a big kick for someone who, months before, was still pleased at being good enough to be on a record. What an inverted snobbery! Especially as I'd played *all* the instruments on the B-side.

At the end of the recording, Bill Drummond said it was the biggest hit so far. I was convinced of it, too. The song had hooks galore and it built and built till it couldn't build anymore. And it was sooo cool!

'Passionate Friend' came out to great reviews. Journalists said it sounded like The Turtles and by the second week of release we were on *Top of the Pops*. Once a group has been on *Top of the Pops* a couple of times, it feels like a God-given right to be on. As though that's it for the rest of your life. We called the show "Toppy" in true Liverpool tradition.

We piled into the "Toppy" studios for what was to be a "live" broadcast. Of course, we were still going to be lip-synching, but it was screened directly to its regular 10 million viewers.

Gary and I took hits of LSD during the afternoon and our dressing room had a vague narcotics lab feel about it, what with Droyd and Bates and the head of Phonogram TV punishing large quantities of powder.

We lurched over to our set. I was going to perform the whole song on top of a grand piano, in bare feet with leather pants and a shit embroidered top that I'd made from a Columbia Hotel pillow-case.

I climbed onto the piano and freaked. No way. I could barely stand up on the ground. Up on the piano, I felt like Basketball Jones, the cartoon kid from the Cheech & Chong video who keeps getting bigger and bigger.

I looked up into the ceiling of the studio. The lights twinkled like distant stars. From my elevated position on the piano, studio technicians and members of other groups looked grotesque. The acid heightened the fake tans of everyone in the room and only accentuated the paleness of the Teardrop members. Of course, if they'd had the chance, Alfie, Jeff and Gary would have been sun-worshippers, but I had to keep those bastards in check.

We ran through the camera rehearsal and loped back to the dressing room. The next few hours were spent smoking spliff, with everyone trying in vain to dissuade me from wearing the orange pillow-case.

"Okay, Copey . . . Five minutes and you're on."

Uh? Wow, Batesy was right. I sat head down with the front of my leathers undone. Sweat coursed down my belly and I mopped it up with my shitty top. I was paranoid as hell. The BBC make-up women had scared the shit out of me. They had asked me if I'd just come back from the Bahamas and said they loved my tan. Of course, irony is lost on someone who's tripping his brain out, so I figured that I must be turning brown.

"I'm not too dark *really*, am I?"

"Fuckin' 'ell, Copey. You're dead pale, honest."

Gary was trying to make me feel better, but what did he know? He was tripping too and I didn't want people placating me.

It was time to go. I wasn't ready. We had to go. I wasn't ready. Why aren't you ready? I don't feel tall enough. Well, you're gonna be standing on top of a piano. Is that tall enough for you? Eh?

They led me reluctantly out to the studio floor. It was total chaos out there. People were running around and freaking out and winding everyone else up. I suddenly felt very becalmed.

A group called Buck's Fizz was doing their thing on the other side of the studio. They were a two-boy, two-girl fun group with cutesy expressions and dance routines. We were to follow them.

I watched, fascinated, then, as time moved slowly on, I felt sucked into their scene. God, they were brilliant. I wanted to be in Buck's Fizz. I rushed over to Gary and hit him with the idea. The two of us should join. Imagine an acid-soaked dance group with showbiz routines, it would be incredible.

It was two minutes to our performance. We had to be exact as it was live, so no mistakes. Bates dragged me to the grand piano. Shit, it's like an ocean liner. The piano was exquisite and moved gently past me as I walked around it. Little girls ran over to me as I climbed aboard it. I smiled my most ridiculous and inane grin and, after much manoeuvring, scrambled to the top of this vast and polished plateau.

The finish of the piano was unbelievable. I waded in its high-gloss black syrup, my bare feet sinking deeper and deeper into the surface like hot wet tar on a newly completed road. It was all I could think about.

"Don't jump around too much, Copey. It'll cost us a fortune if you wreck that thing."

Oh, thanks a lot, Batesy. Thanks fucking loads. That's just what I want to hear when I'm tripping on live TV. The boom camera swung away from Buck's Fizz as their song faded out.

Everyone was in position and I forgot to duck as the camera crane whizzed past my head, nearly knocking me from my dubious perch. Okay, I'm not in Buck's Fizz. I'm not. Better remember.

"The friend I have is a passionate friend, but I can't see you buying . . ."

'Passionate Friend' doesn't have an intro or anything. It just *starts* – vocals, drums, guitar, everything. All together. In a split second, I was fighting for my life up on the piano.

I looked back at Gary, who was off his head. His blond quiff was hanging straight out over his face, jiblike and starched and strong like a newly creosoted fence. I wanted to climb onto it and walk along its length, like a sailor walking the plank.

Around me, the song waged war with itself. So much going on. How can I keep this together? Who cares, I'm doing fine. I looked down at Jeff, thousands

of feet below me at the piano keyboard. He looked ridiculous to me, like the Phantom of the Opera or some such shit.

Now, 'Passionate Friend' is also one of those songs that has a reprise. See, the whole song builds to a climax, then we come to a stop and start the whole thing again. Suddenly, I was miming, *"The friend I have is a passionate friend, but I can't see you buying. . ."*

Hold on, I thought. What's all this? My mind did double-takes and I battled for some sense of reality. Maybe this was the real start of the performance. Maybe I'd imagined the first half of the song. What the hell is going on?

I felt the song disappearing into a tunnel. It was fading out and the *Top of the Pops* audience was cheering. I felt as though I had been up there for days. But I'd done battle and I seemed to have won.

In the next couple of weeks, that single went up and up. Ha. The weirdest thing was *how* it went up: one place at a time or even sticking at the same place for a week.

I figured it was time to get rid of Alfie and Jeff. I told Bill Drummond to do it and we played *Top of the Pops* two weeks later with Balfe on bass and no keyboard player. We were back to the same line-up as 10 months before.

The Bunnymen had already released *Heaven Up Here*, their second album, whilst we were touring our asses off in America. I had all the songs written for our second album. Balfe, Troy, Gary and Clive Langer sat in a London rehearsal room, swapping instruments and rearranging my songs. I sent Dorian home to give me some time to concentrate on the recording, the group holed up in the Columbia once more and Dave Bates booked us into Air Studios in Oxford Street.

MORE BY LUCK THAN JUDGEMENT, HERE AM I

My hotel room at the Columbia stank. My clothes stank and I stank. It all came down to a lax attitude towards hygiene and a chemical enlarging of my skin pores, March to September in the same clothes and a general inability to hose down anything other than my body.

Rumours of the group's imminent demise had begun months before, but the sacking of Alfie and Jeff brought cries and letters from the teeny girls I was trying so hard to piss off.

In *Record Mirror*, a cartoon Cope with huge bags under his eyes was seen shitting in a shower. Under the caption was a story, precisely what had happened in Candy's room over four years before, but written as though it took place only yesterday.

After the long US headtrip, I had let my hair grow and grow until it was

crazy and matted and bleached by the sun. I wouldn't wash it for months on end in case it lost its shape, but it was so dirty by now that I could mould it into place with my hands.

When Dorian was around, she insisted that I use deodorant and hairspray to hide the smell, but now she was back in New York. I needed to start 'The Great Dominions' without romance and women adding to the confusion. I had a semi-beard over my sunken cheeks and was convinced I looked Messianic. The leathers were gone for the moment, replaced by black para-military gear and Bob Proctor's mirror shades.

Air Studios at 214 Oxford Street is one of the best in London. It's situated on the top floor, overlooking Oxford Circus, and only artists with some kind of reputation seem to get booked in there, as it costs a fortune.

The first day, we all piled into the reception, smoked a few spliffs and lay in a heap in front of the manageress's office. Gary and I awoke to see Paul Weller and Co. easing past us, muttering "Hippies" under their breath.

The Jam were recording down the corridor and had just released their 'Absolute Beginners' single. Ha, they call us hippies but they're not averse to ripping us off, I thought. That brass sound was patent Teardrop and everybody, including the press, agreed.

Japan were just finishing their *Tindrum* LP and Patty, Air's manageress, was having a thing with one of them. Of course, now they were leaving and Troy quickly stepped in to fill the breach.

Troy baby was in love all day and every day. Women adored him. In fact, so did men, you know. He was so into everything. Every day, Troy would look at me and say, "Hey, baby, is this Bliss Street or what?" Then he'd raise his eyes to the heavens and look 10 million times more cartoon than I ever could.

We began the recordings with a Scots engineer called Colin Fairley. We intended to use a different bass player for most of the songs, but Gary and I laid down the basic tracks. Other songs didn't have rhythm tracks; we just built them up over loops of grooves or synthesizer pulses that Balfe and Gary had worked on.

There was no set formula. Compared with *Kilimanjaro*, the new album was not even made by a group. Clive Langer would play guitar, Balfe made all the weird synth noises and I played most of the piano and organ.

Sometimes it became total bloody hell. Balfe and I were taking a lot of speed and our judgement became severely impaired. Amphetamines tend to make a person grossly over-confident and everyone told me that I was very threatening. I disagreed. Balfe's the threat, man.

Songs changed drastically once we jammed them. One song, called 'Seven Views of Jerusalem', started life as a kind of acoustic Tim Buckley country ballad. Balfe said it was shit and wrote an entire marimba and percussion groove for it. He was *right*. I started to trust him again.

My favourite song on the album was 'The Great Dominions'. We had toured it on just piano, but it sounded too pompous to me and I wanted radical changes. Balfe built up a loop of synthesized breathing and scraping by sellotaping the D notes down on his Prophet 5 and just playing the buttons. I added organ and we recorded Gary's drums in the huge Studio 1 with just one microphone suspended from the ceiling. Troy baby played one solitary and mournful guitar and I added a lumbering Duane Eddy bass.

Over the weeks the album took shape, but never without major freak outs. One time, I got paranoid that Balfe was getting control, so I caught a midnight train to Liverpool and moaned and bitched the whole weekend away with Pam, Zoo's long suffering secretary, and anyone else with Balfe grievances.

Dave Bates wanted killer singles on this album. He heard the basic unfinished version of a song called 'Colours Fly Away from You' and told me to get it finished as quickly as possible. I hated that pressure. I agreed with Bates that it would be a brilliant single, but no way was I going to tell him. Without Dorian and with the added Bates/Balfe intrusion, the early ease of recording began to slip away.

"Hey, Ringo, are you still alive down there?"

I looked up from the floor of reception and saw Linda McCartney walking down the corridor. I prodded Gary, who was lying half on top of me and half on the couch.

"Hey, Garfield, Linda McCartney called you Ringo."

We'd been calling Gary "Ringo" for about a year. He *was* like Ringo. But for Linda Mac to give her approval? For the next month, Gary Dwyer *was* Ringo Starr.

Now that The Jam were gone, Paul McCartney was recording his 10 billionth album at Air. We started hanging out together. Awlright, I'd finally see how the Establishment had got that way.

I expected to hate McCartney. I'd been fed a diet of the *Let It Be* film and Dave Bates' Beatles bootlegs. In both, Paul McCartney came over like some uptight twee-boy. He wasn't like that at all, though. I dug him; he was pretty hard. Also he smashed Balfe at pool, which was worth shitloads.

My 24th birthday came right in the middle of recording. Linda Mac gave me a copy of her *Linda's Pictures* book, and McCartney gave me his book with a cartoon and an inscription in the front. Ha, I finally had something to give to my mother to prove this business was not all illusion.

I celebrated by giving Linda Mac a copy of *Fire Escape in the Sky*. This was a compilation of Scott Walker recordings which we had released on Zoo Records. Bill Drummond and I had licensed the tapes and I'd picked my favourite stuff. We even designed a plain grey album sleeve; I wanted all those post-punk dudes and dudettes to buy Scott in droves.

• • •

The album dragged on. *Kilimanjaro* had cost £20,000 to record. We were only halfway through this one and Bates said we'd gone over £40,000 already. Huh.

My nerve was going. I still tripped for days at a time, but the recording had brought it pretty much to a standstill. My throat was so sore with the raw rough-cut yellow amphetamine that we got from Liverpool. I sang along to a song called 'Falling Down Around Me' and Clive Langer said it sounded great. My throat was so painful that I could only manage two takes, but we got it, no problem.

The rest of the time was not so simple. I'd sit on my own at the organ in the big room, staring through the glass into the control room. Balfe, Clive, Troy and Colin Fairley sat motionless and uncommunicative, sometimes for hours at a time.

Every day, journalists and record company people were around. The new album was big news and the teeny girls were still expectant.

I called Dorian back from New York to give me some sense of normality, but it wasn't normal. I mean, we were expected to act like stars and stuff but the whole group was still on £35 per week. I couldn't even pay hotel phone bills. Clive Langer had to take us out to eat pretty much every night, as he had money from his string of Madness hits, which were still coming thick and fast that autumn.

Also, because of Air Studios' location, we were stuck in the tourist make-a-fast-buck heartland of central London. If I walked more than 100 yards from the studios, I became hopelessly lost. The same with Gary. So we had to pork out in the expensive eateries where most people just come to graze and be seen.

Torino's became our hang-out. Torino's? I mean, what a shit name. That's like having a café in Rome and calling it Coventry's. They hated us there. We hated them, but we were stuck with it. A quiche and cappuccino nightmare, you could spend a week's wages on just the smoked herring salad! Gary would sit with his balls out and I would stare glassily round, dressed only in my nightshirt. I felt like Lawrence of Arabia, only *after* he'd gone off the rails.

I had my first LSD flashback there. The whole restaurant pulsated orange and the colours ran into my eyes, stinging like shampoo. It scared the hell out of me and Clive became paranoid as a bastard. See, his older brother had suffered brain damage from *one trip*. He still lives with Clive's parents, it's such a sad, sad thing. So Clive spent the rest of the album trying to convince me off the stuff.

Pressure on. We need the album *now*. We need it for Christmas and we need a single ready in two weeks. Phonogram Records had already taken advance orders for 100,000 copies of the new album.

Dave Bates was still insisting on 'Colours Fly Away from You' as the next single. I wanted 'Bent out of Shape' which was much classier and far less obvious.

Bates kept on at me how he'd let me take my time and how he'd allowed me to make the record *my* way, and all this miserable stuff. After the sneaky and shabby release of 'Ha Ha, I'm Drowning' that summer, I was paranoid as hell. But I was knackered, off my head and not well supported by my management. Finally, and working against intuition, I conceded. Fucking give him 'Colours . . .' and be done with it.

In two weeks, with the single pressed and ready to go, Dave Bates decided that I was right, 'Bent out of Shape' would have been a better 45.

All around me, I felt the machinery engaging once more. The album was not yet ready, but that was *my* problem. They had a schedule and this album had to be the biggest Phonogram release of the Christmas period.

Dave Balfe was not yet fully operational; he was still excited at being back in the group and right now his head was in art mode. Great. The longer he stays like that, the better.

Balfe was obsessed with the word "empirical", which means to judge the world *only* on one's experience. In other words, don't trust the theory types. I could dig that in a big ass way. I had left the education system for the same reason – it was full of "teachers" who had done sod all in the outside world.

Balfe and I both believed in following intuition to its end. I had avoided drugs all through the peer pressure days of school and adolescence. Now I had embraced them, I felt utterly devoured with an "I'm taking this because I want to take it" attitude. I wanted to fuck me up, and Balfe seemed to want to come too. We had no time for assholes who said what they felt people should hear. Rock musicians are notoriously under-educated gauche lucky shits . . . but I saw that as a strength, not a weakness.

BAD TO THE BONE AT CLUB ZOO

So *Wilder* was finished. Thank God for that. These things start so sneakily and then drag on for the rest of your life.

The main thing was that it sounded the way I felt. I didn't know if I liked it. I'd stopped caring whether I liked our music, really. All I was interested in was getting precisely what I felt onto tape. See, there was this creeping gloriousness entering rock'n'roll, and I'd been at least partly responsible. I had pushed against the icy metallic late-punk thing. My voice was finally getting strong, but it could get out of hand. Mac's singing on the Bunnymen's *Heaven Up Here* LP had become a Teardrop joke. It was pompous and old-fartish, like some crap Victorian actor reducing Shakespeare to a series of postures and declamations. I hated music that wished to impress. If you want to impress

people, run the 100 metres. Music is there to touch people. If you pretend you feel more than you do, you're just being rude.

Evil was seeping around me by now. What had started as a simple fear from years ago was becoming bigger and scarier all the time. Bill Drummond told me that I needed to reduce myself still further. It was not enough just to let Balfe back in the group. I drew a black "X" on my belly, to ward off evil. Magic marker stays on fairly indefinitely but needs to be touched up from time to time.

Bill had booked a five-storey club in a back street in Liverpool where we could play every night. The idea was a multi-media place called Club Zoo. On each level of the club, various shit would happen simultaneously.

One one floor, we'd run full-length cult movies.

One another floor, the ever-changing support group would play.

On the third floor, a bar for everyone with games and shit.

On the top floor, a haven for the group and their entourage to do their thing.

Finally, in the basement, The Teardrop Explodes would play two sets per night, three nights a week for six weeks, and, in the words of Bill D., "They'll be so bored, they'll have to get good."

After the summer nightmare of Odeons and theatres filled with pre-teens, this appealed to me in a big ass way. The club was in Temple Street, a tiny back alley, and was run by real nice Liverpool mobsters. Colin Butler, whom Bill had brought in as a surrogate manager, having given himself over almost entirely to the Bunnymen, turned them on to speed within days of our arrival and, combined with his "excellent grass", soon had everyone eating out of his hand.

The first night was a shambles. About 50 people came. No-one would believe that we would play in such a shithole.

The next night, a few more people arrived. Most of them couldn't even find the place. I didn't care. I was in Liverpool again and away from the strain of being successful.

We were staying at the New Manx Hotel on Catherine Street. It was a nice clean shithole run by an older faggy guy called Jim who drank himself slowly into oblivion each day. Jim loved us all. He was used to comedians and vaudeville types, so his rules were lax as hell. Breakfast finished at 1 o'clock, or when he ran out of eggs. The dining-room walls were covered in 8" × 10" photographs of stars in varying degrees: Billy Dainty, Sarah Vaughan, Max Wall, Aimee McDonald, Brian Cant, Ida Lupino . . . on and on. And each one had a story, a story that was endlessly repeated to each newcomer to the hotel. Oh yeah, and Jim was Santa Claus! I didn't pay much attention to that one the first time round. I figured I'd just misheard it. You couldn't ask Jim to qualify things that he said; no-one in this world has that much spare time.

Club Zoo began to pick up pace. In two weeks, we had a regular clientèle. But you know all that stuff about losing the star-trip? It was bullshit.

One night, I spent half an hour refusing to let Pete Wylie in for free. I'd send messages down from our "chambers" that "everyone must pay". Of course, I let everyone I felt like in for free. Boxhead, Bernie Connors, Timmo, they all piled in for nothing. I made a point of letting Johnno in because he was my mate and also Wylie's guitarist in Wah!

So the club just enabled me to carry the bitching right into my own back-yard.

The top floor was our inner sanctum. But in the far corner was my *inner* inner sanctum. We draped it with flags and muslin and low lights burned up from the floor.

I would lie, propped up, on a bed and "see" people. Balfe and Bill regularly told me it was out of hand, but they enjoyed it as much as everyone else.

That autumn, whoever was playing in Liverpool would hang out afterwards in Club Zoo. I would never see them unless I already knew them. I couldn't handle being with anyone more successful than me, it just drove me crazy. The Human League came down one night; I just pursued Suzanne with a camera, I couldn't even face her without the lens separating us. Phil Oakey, the singer, didn't come down. I was sooo relieved.

As the weeks passed, the club became my whole life. I rang Dorian less and less. I took more of what people gave me. The far-out became more and more commonplace.

One couple returned again and again. The boy was pretty and about 21. He wanted me to sleep with his girlfriend. I thought that was weird, but they both wanted it a lot. I didn't like that.

Two young kids from Birkenhead, Liverpool's New Jersey, told me how they stood for hours gazing at the city lights and listening to The Teardrop Explodes, whilst the LSD transformed their empty space into something romantic. Every week they brought me something new to try. One night, I gobbled down a tablet, as usual without asking, only to be told that it was methadone, a heroin substitute. We were between sets and I had an hour to come down. I sweated and snorted. My breathing was way too much and I felt my respiratory system giving way. I rushed into the ladies' room and threw up a trail of mud-brown soup across the floor. Then I lolled my head into a bowl and passed out.

When I awoke, I had five minutes before stage. Colin gave me some brown speed and I was alive and ready to go. Everyone in the dressing room was laughing at me. They often laughed. I was a cliché in full battle-gear. God, though, I was so sad. I hated the thought of what I was becoming, but I couldn't see any way around it. It was in the stars. I was bad, and even the people around me knew it.

There was a song by Armand Schaubroeuk called 'King of the Streets' that I played all the time. The chorus was my life:

"I'm going down, down the road, the road to hell. Lord, I'm going down. . ."

It made me so sad. I wanted to be good. I wanted the goodness of Jesus Christ and everything bad to be banished from me. But I felt as though my fate was carved in stone and there was no way out.

We waited for the inevitable *Top of the Pops* performance for 'Colours Fly Away', which I was not looking forward to. We had already spent too much money on a Bill Butt video shot at a chemical plant in Bristol. We'd hired a helicopter for a whole day and spent from 6 a.m. until 2 o'clock the next morning trying to get all the shots. The most exciting part was hanging out of the open door, which had been removed to give a better shot. The rest was just a drag. The whole group had taken a lot of amphetamine to keep awake. The result was five guys with the bug-eyes of life, Dave Balfe even more than usual.

Anyway, in the cocoon of Club Zoo, the progress of the single was noted with yawning disinterest. That is, of course, until it was not a hit. Not even close. It stayed at no. 54 then slid down and out.

Wow. I wasn't expecting that. Where was the *Top of the Pops* pisstake which I was so used to detesting? Who fucked up? Find a scapegoat.

It angered me that my desire for success was still there. I prided myself on not caring, but I was fooling myself. I had cut my hair short to get rid of the teenies, abused them constantly on the British tour and in the press, recorded a second album that was in no way a follow-up to the *Kilimanjaro* LP and still expected them to buy our records in droves.

The *Wilder* album was Phonogram Records' flop of the year. It was expected to be huge and they had shipped 120,000 to the shops. Even the press dug it. No matter, 50,000 were sent back to be stored and destroyed and in three weeks the record was out of the Top 100 and history.

Letters flooded in to *Smash Hits* magazine. Young girls said I was an asshole with a bad haircut. All the hip alternative dudes hated me for my vacillation between pop star and Scott Morrison Wannabee. The best joke I'd heard in years arrived in November 1981: "What's the difference between The Teardrop Explodes and a cow?"

"A cow has horns at the front and a twat at the back."

I sort of shacked up with Gary Dwyer's cousin Sharon at the New Manx. She was married and a close friend of my ex-wife, so we had to be secretive. Of course we weren't, so everyone hated me even more.

The shows became outlandish and everyone took it for granted that I would at least rip my arms open on the rough pillar in the centre of the stage every

night. Sometimes I would bay like a hound and wade into the audience, singing entire songs hidden from view. Dave Hughes, from Dalek I Love You, filmed the majority of the shows. We'd watch them each night and laugh.

If anyone talked during a quiet song, I would stop and single them out, then refuse to sing any more. The black cross on my stomach became bigger and bigger, and I'd spout what Balfe termed "streams of unconsciousness". I'd argue with songs, explain lyrics, do "face-solos" and give away my clothes from the stage. We filmed a *Melody Maker* session at the "Sputnik" Catholic cathedral. I climbed up one of the 45-degree buttresses, then fell off and broke my ankle.

The rest of Club Zoo's performances were done in a leg-iron.

We filmed a Christmas *Top of the Pops* in which I wore just my flannel nightshirt. We played 'Reward' and I felt as though we were history. We were.

At 8 p.m. on Christmas Eve, I left the New Manx Hotel and hailed a taxi. He didn't want to take me to Tamworth, as it was 100 miles away. I promised him a £10 tip and he grudgingly took me.

My parents' house was an oasis of normality for a week but I was back in the New Manx Hotel for New Year's Eve. Sharon and I rang in the new year in room no. 5, high on LSD and champagne.

LONG GONE AT McGONNIGLE'S

When we took Club Zoo to Dublin in January '82, Bill Drummond was conspicuous by his absence. Colin Butler was now in full charge of operations and the whole group noticed an immediate improvement in the quality of drugs we were taking.

Mick Houghton, our soft-spoken and deep publicist, was there to coordinate the huge amounts of press and photo sessions expected. The group was still big news, as the failure of the album hadn't been completely realised yet.

We set up home at Bailey's Hotel, the line between hangers-on and road crew becoming less and less defined all the time, especially with Tempo, Robbo and Jamie Connors in our actual road crew now. Besides, the Liverpool scene was different. One night, when I came to my room to sleep, Mick Aslanian and Bernie Connors were both tucked up in my bed.

"Fuck off, Copey. Don't be such a star."

Hmm, maybe they were right. This'll keep me in my place, I thought, as I dragged the cot mattress into the corridor to sleep.

•   •   •

The first show at McGonnigle's club was a lot of fun, but a little off the wall. People expected me to be the way I appeared in the press and, as I didn't feel too inspired and we'd never played Ireland before, I gave them pretty much what they expected.

There was a double-album Teardrop bootleg around at that time called *Petulance*. The title sums up perfectly where my head was then at. It wears thin pretty soon, actually. It even gets to be a drag if you are the perpetrator.

After the show, I walked with Mick Aslanian, Jamie Connors and Kevin Connolly to a pub to try Guinness. Kevin and I had taken a great many magic mushrooms in the dressing room and I began to piss everyone off. I was enthusiastic about everything. I saw a busker who was kneeling down playing the flute. I was convinced he was a leprechaun and hassled the guy vigorously. By the time I had finished, Kev and Jamie had fled, leaving the ill-equipped Mick Aslanian to accompany me. Mick is like Ed Norton from *The Honeymooners*. He's sweet and full of good intentions and easily freaked out. His Liverpool nickname was Partial. I thought it was because he behaved like a man with no direct link between his body and his brain. The other stories sounded like urban legend, and highly unlikely.

At Bailey's Hotel, a party was in full swing in Kev and Jamie's room. A young girl with a dark feather cut sat in the biggest armchair, dispensing pills to everyone. She said she was 16 and her father was a road manager for The Grateful Dead. She said there was a picture of her on the back of the *AOX-OMOXOA* album at nine years old. She was completely off her head, the first person I'd met who was almost intolerably crazy.

Alison and Aishling, the girlfriends of Bono and the Edge, disrespectfully, were also ensconced in the room, obviously checking up on what the bad guys get up to.

Partial and I arrived into the middle of a scene. Neither of us could work out what was going on. We had been stuck in O'Connell Street for 30 minutes as I tried to give all my money away to girl guides, until Partial reasoned with me long enough that if anyone deserved it, he did.

Troy arrived, stayed just long enough to call everybody "Baby", then left with a secret stash of women.

Dave Balfe sat, eyes blazing, fully upright on the bed and told me that I must try the Adolescent's acid. I told both of them that I'd taken mushrooms instead, but this only fired her up more.

"Please take my stuff," she wailed.

Okay, I'll try some. But only if Kev takes some, too. I told the Adolescent that if she was so concerned with dosing us up, she should have some as well.

"No way," wailed the Adolescent. "On acid, I could never handle that you're more famous than me."

"But you're not famous at all," I blurted, confused by her reasoning.

"Well, don't fucking rub it in!" she howled.

Wow, even in my solipsistic, egotistic, Odinistic acid one-ness, the self-possession of that last outburst double-took me to the core. Right on.

Six hours later, Balfe, Gary and I sat in Colin Butler's room, freaked out. The U2 girls had treated us like the Devil himself and weird shit had happened. Now we wanted to be normal, and quick.

Balfe carelessly played with a spilt sachet of coffee complement on the glass table-top. All Colin's powders had long since been snorted, but he still handed a blade to Balfe, maybe out of wishful thinking.

Two minutes later, Troy and his posse of females piled into the bedroom. He saw the mound of coffee complement which by now had been chopped into four lines by Dave Balfe.

"Hey, baby, is there enough for me there?" Troy's nostrils flared in a macho post-coital kind of way.

"Sure, Troy. Take the biggest."

Balfe caught my grin, but managed to suppress his own. Troy would surely discover the deception in seconds.

Troy Tate carefully took his cleanest, largest Irish note, rolled it lovingly into a neat thin stem and held it delicately but firmly over one end of the white lines of powder. He looked around at his adoring girlfriends, flashed us his best James Bond smile and, with perfect and unconscious comedy timing, said, "Too much of this stuff can make you stupid." Then he put the whole lot up his nose.

Balfe, Gary and I were down the corridor in a second, screaming in disbelief, hysterically crying. We ran and we ran and hoped Colin would sort it out.

DOWN

I loved Colin Butler. He was our salvation. He made everything fun again. He didn't hassle Gary and me with business shit, he just kept us high and happy.

Dave Bates, Pam Young, even Bill Drummond, they just wanted to make me miserable. Not Colin, though. He was *our* man. He was for *us*. I think his greatest dream was to go to Australia.

My belongings were strewn over many cities by now. I'd left all my US tour stuff at Dorian's apartment on East 13th Street in Manhattan to give her an everyday feeling of me. Other clothes and a vast amount of records were back in my old bedroom at my parents' house in Tamworth. The room was depressingly different in every other way, though. Gone was the psychedelic purple wallpaper from 1972 with the Faust manifestos and the posters pasted everywhere. And gone, too, was the class of '77 additions which I had brought for Joss when he

took the room over. At Dave Bates' flat in Marylebone I still had stacks of LPs, boxes of cassettes and shit all over Droyd's room. But the saddest place was my old flat in Devonshire Road in Liverpool. When my ex-wife moved out, I had asked Pete DeFreitas to move in. Even at my most paranoid, I trusted Pete pretty much completely. But he wasn't the tidiest dude in the world.

Our crazy Adolescent guest had been staying in and around the Teardrop camp for months. She paid her way with consignments of drugs sent by her father from the West Coast. But she was finally beginning to blow our minds. She was everywhere. There were a lot of strange people around the Teardrop at this time, but every minute of every day the Adolescent would be screaming long and into the night. I rang DeFreitas and told him that I was sending the Adolescent up to Liverpool to stay with him at my old place.

"Cool, man. Simmo's here, too. He's trying to avoid someone."

We sent the Adolescent up there, went off to record and play a British tour, and promptly forgot about it.

I had written a beautiful new song, on organ, called 'You Disappear from View'. It was a wistful love ballad to an unseen girl, the kind who would not come running every time I called. During the Club Zoo dates, the group had turned it into a kind of Earth, Wind & Fire funk workout, syncopated brass stabs and a real dude supreme of a bass line from Ronnie François.

We returned to Genetic Studios, with a reluctant Clive Langer, to record the song as the next single. Everything went fine, but Balfe and I were unhappy with the result. I liked it but felt it wasn't the kind of direction we should be going in. Balfe just detested it. We went off on tour and left Clive Langer to stew over it, remix it and come up with the goods.

It was two months later when we arrived in Liverpool for our first show since Club Zoo. The smiling Colin Butler was still keeping us happy, but his desire to go to Australia was becoming a passion.

Simmo had rung either Balfe or me almost every day. We didn't take his calls, though, as we guessed it was about the Adolescent.

The group all checked into the New Manx Hotel and I walked the half-mile down Prince's Road to my old flat. The place looked like a Beirut tenement. All my clothes were piled in one corner of my spare room. Under my clothes were a few of the toys I had kept since I was a child and the Victorian crockery which my grandmother had given to me. I waded through the lot trying to sort things out.

In the kitchen was a mound of unpaid bills, final demands written in red and addressed to Mr J. D. Cope, including an electricity bill for £266. I was still on £35 per week and broke.

In my grandmother's Victorian sideboard, in the vast yellow and red living room, were the Echo & the Bunnymen tour accounts, chequebooks, bank

statements and about 20 unmatching black socks. This kind of relieved me. At least the Bunnymen were chaotic as well, more so really. I mean, giving DeFreitas responsibility for all *that* shit?

Simmo pleaded with me to take the Adolescent away. "She's off her head, Copey. She's been selling acid to Kev Connolly for 20p a tab. Her dad sends it from Los Angeles with *your* name on it."

Even DeFreitas, a man normally known for his capacity to chill out in the most extreme situation, was worried. He told me that we had to stop her right now. About six packages of acid and MDA, each package containing 200 tablets, had arrived at *my* home with *my* name on the envelopes, in the last two months. With my burgeoning reputation for LSD in the press and the Adolescent's increasingly loud mouth, we had to catch it whilst we could.

Balfe and I sorted it out the only way we knew. We were already fighting the rest of the group and the record company over the release of 'You Disappear from View', which still sounded like shit to us. We took the Adolescent and her friend on the rest of the tour and decided that we *would* follow Colin's intuition and go to Australia after all.

SPIRAL

It was warm spring weather and the English countryside looked particularly beautiful as I sat in the back of a car speeding towards Heathrow Airport. It was still very early morning and I was half asleep.

Colin Butler was driving and his weird friend Martin was skinning up a huge grass spliff in the passenger seat. From the stereo, blasting at full volume, was the ever-present major-league drag known as 'You Disappear from View'.

"I still say you're crazy," beamed Colin. "This sounds like a hit to me, if ever there was one."

"Fucking hell, man. *You're* the crazy one. It's total fucking kack." I refused to be drawn into this stupid bastard conversation *one* more time.

"... and you disappear from view, very unlike the other ones..."

Colin enthused over music the same way he enthused over the cricket or over scoring some particularly fine weed. Everything was so bloody jolly all the time. I really dug the guy, but he knew shit about music.

In the front seats, Martin was causing chaos. He'd dropped the open grass tin on to his lap and now Colin was trying to retrieve the situation by swerving all over the place and panicking. At that moment, we entered a town called Tring. Now, even I knew that Tring was not on the way to Heathrow.

"Come on, man, get your shit together," I yelled. "We're not even going the right way. You two are acting like you're fucking tripping."

Colin Butler turned half around and smiled.

Oh, great. We're off to Australia and the manager's tripping. At that moment, I yearned for normality. Couldn't *any*body act like a reasonable human being?

In the front seat, Colin and Martin cackled and guffawed, their faces gleeful and drooling. They were both small, each around 5'6", and I felt as though I were being driven by two psycho-hobbits.

I persuaded them back on to a route that would actually get us to the airport, but I was resentful as hell at having to take charge. Martin and I swapped seats, I put a Tim Buckley album on the car stereo and threw the cassette of 'You Disappear . . .' out of the window.

It was four hours later. From the window of the 747, I could see cobwebs stretched over a carpet with an ever-changing pattern. My face sagged. I had Oliver Reed's face. My jowls were blue, they must be. My eyes drooped and I was that dog, the one out of the cartoon.

"I'm that dog," I said to Balfe, who was staring at an in-flight magazine.

"Uh?" he said, unaware that I'd even spoken.

"I'm that dog . . . you know, the one out of that cartoon."

"Droopy," said Pip, our lighting guy, leaning in from his seat next to Balfe.

"Bloody hell, Pip. Why don't you lean a bit more?" Balfe was irritated, I could tell.

Whenever Balfe got irritated, I could feel a "Wind-up Balfe" mood immediately begin to build inside me.

The shit had really hit at the airport. The road crew had loaded everything, equipment and all, onto the plane. They were all pissed off at Colin, who placated them with the suggestion that we *all take acid.*

Now, I was *not* into that. Couldn't we behave for once? I really wanted to be good, after my recent revelations. I started a totally unconvincing rap, which the group and the crew laughed at.

Gary took some. Then Balfe took some. Then Ronnie François, Ted Emmett and Mal, our guitar guy. Pip had some and so did Mark Napier, our 17-year-old sound technician. I was actually the last to have any.

We had a 32-hour flight to Sydney, via San Francisco and Hawaii. There were 11 people in the party and 9 of them boarded the plane high on LSD.

Oh well, if shit happened, we could still rely on Troy Tate and our sound guy, Neil Levine. Ho-hum.

For the first few hours, I was consumed with an hour-long cassette of Throbbing Gristle called *Beyond Jazz Funk*. It's hard to describe their music, really. At worst, it's just rubbish, and at best, it's the product of genuinely sick people. I played the tape over and over. It got so that I didn't feel I was listening to anything at all, just the sound of my own amplified brain.

I plopped the headphones over Dave Balfe's ears for a reaction.

"Copey, yer fuckin' twat. What's that shit?"

I had intruded and that was good enough.

I got up and scanned the rows of people, looking for Colin. He was engrossed in some newspaper and was smoking a long luxurious-looking joint. I squeezed past people and walked up to him.

"Is that cool?" I asked him, pointing at the spliff.

"Sure," he said. "Just do this," and he put his right arm above his head and wafted the smoke around.

I stood in the aisle and took a few tokes, but I was paranoid as hell. People were looking at me, so I passed it back to him.

At the back of the plane, a scene was developing. Gary and Ronnie were looking out of the last emergency exit. I was back in my place and listening once more to Throbbing Gristle. I had tried to interest an old lady in the tape. I was extremely polite about it, but she looked more scared than anything.

Meanwhile, up at the back, Colin had joined Ronnie and Gary and they were smoking another joint. One of the older stewardesses, a blonde Scandinavian, was talking to them. I got jealous of their scene and rushed up to join them.

"If we 'ad Jacob's ladder, we could hang it out of the plane," said Gary. "Then we could climb down it and dive in one o' them lakes."

Thirty-five thousand feet below, the weird outline of Newfoundland could be seen.

The blonde stewardess was getting on well with Colin. She told him to be careful with the spliffs and did we have any coke? I couldn't believe it. Colin Butler led a charmed life. No-one acted this cool when he was not around. I stared at the stewardess, right up close.

"What iss he on?" she asked Colin.

"Oh, he's just tripping like the rest of us."

She smiled at me and I figured I must be safe.

It's a 13-hour flight to San Francisco. As the passengers began to get restless, there were always at least nine people on board who were fascinated by *anything*.

Our friendly stewardess handed me a white US immigration form which I sat and smiled at for about two hours. I couldn't hope to fill it in in my present condition.

Time passed. The trips slowly began to wear off. Our party all looked frayed and distant. Except for Gary, that is, who just looked totally disgusting. He sat bolt upright and in pain. His quiff was droopy and his face dark and glowering. I was about three rows behind and I could hear him moaning loudly.

"Our" stewardess helped him into the galley, where he stayed for the rest of the flight. She told Colin that Gary should see a doctor as soon as we landed in San Francisco. We had a four-hour layover, so it shouldn't be a problem.

• • •

It was Mal who realised Colin Butler's error: we needed temporary US visas for the layover. I didn't have one and neither did Gary, Balfe nor Pip.

We were totally pissed off when we landed. Thirteen hours of tripping at 35,000 feet and then straight into a "holding tank". The San Francisco authorities politely escorted us down to a room with no facilities, miles away from anyone. Then they locked the door and came back 45 minutes before it was time to take off.

The rest of the dudes had been hanging out in the cocktail bar, eating oysters served on two enormous seashell plates and drinking wine. I told the official who was in charge of me that I'd never eaten oysters before. He gave me two minutes to eat the leftovers, so I drank down 12, one after another, in a mix of bravado and hunger. The effects of the LSD were long gone and I had made an uneasy peace with my stomach.

This ceasefire came to an abrupt end as we boarded the plane for Hawaii. The oysters had the same consistency as the contents of a spitoon and I threw up throughout the flight.

Plane journeys, man. Thirty-two hours is a long haul. You can watch zits come from nowhere. Skin dehydrates and lips fray. The adrenalin and the sense of timelessness; bowel movements start at your shoulder-blades and end at your knees.

All that free alcohol at 35,000 feet multiplies its sea-level power several times. Troy Tate had begun his quiet session as we left London and was still punishing spirits when we landed in Hawaii.

The last half of the journey was made in oblivion. I vaguely remember watching Gary buying a Hawaiian shirt and staring out wistfully into the dry-heat sunset of Maui . . . then we were gone, and landing in Sydney, half a day later.

We had come the wrong way, to save money. This way we flew into the sun and lost a day.

On the tarmac, at Sydney Airport, the authorities committed their final indignity whilst we were in their control: guys in white industrial suits crop-sprayed us as we sat inert, confused and farty.

Then, at last, we had arrived.

OF *DANGERMAN* & EGG ON TOAST

As they hoisted me out of the water, my knees and feet dragged over the rocks, the white skin on my legs became pinstriped with red rivulets of blood, and I felt invigorated and alive.

I had heard about the seventh wave before, but I'd really had no inkling of

its awesome and devastating power. I lay back in the sun and tripped out on my experience.

The Cosmopolitan Motor Lodge, on Bondi Beach, is strictly second division rock'n'roll. It's ideal for a group on their first Australian tour, especially if that group has no reason to be there but vibrations.

Bondi Beach is the big surfing paradise in Sydney. So much so that even I was drawn on to it. We'd go down amongst the muscle boys during our copious free time, my pale and skinny body larded up with force 15 anti-tanning lotion; whale-blubber, as Gary termed it.

My beachwear comprised a long-sleeved black T-shirt, black shorts, black Chinese slippers and socks, and a black felt hat. The rest of the group was happy to fry, so we played long and hard on the headland just out of sight of the motel.

It was the Australian grass which had lured me onto the rocks; I felt so clear-headed I didn't even notice that I was stoned. I climbed down, shoeless and unafraid, to a jagged shelf and stood completely still. Of course, the tide began to drag me and rip my feet, then buffet me and rip my knees, until Gary realised I was in trouble and panicked, then I panicked, and the water was swirling around my shoulders. Gary, Balfe and Ronnie dragged and eventually hoisted me out.

Sydney was cool, a very cool city indeed. Why the Australians allow themselves to be perceived abroad as lager-obsessed retards is beyond me.

I walked alone through King's Cross, *the* heavy porn and drugs district, at 2 a.m. wearing a nightshirt, parachute boots and a heavy ammo belt. *No*-one laughed, no-one *gave* a shit.

Colin Butler spent his time at the Mansell Rooms, a low music-biz haunt. He and Troy would get shitfaced, dance on the tables, knock everyone's drinks into their laps, throw down money for laundry bills and buy the whole club drinks.

Colin would tell me, "Oh, no work today," so I'd take a trip, hang out on the balcony and, just as the trip came on, Ingrid from the record company would arrive with an interviewer and photographer.

"Didn't you know? There are five more after this."

And that was the tone of the entire tour. There was never any formal meeting of band or crew. We arrived in Sydney and Colin took off to do his own thing.

Roadies and technicians are not used to this looseness. They want dates, times, itineraries, lists, etc., and rightly so. They were all hanging out and no-one knew what the hell was going on.

Our first show had been the night after our arrival. We were so jet-lagged that Balfe fell asleep on stage. Colin bought speed for the crew, but every venue was a product of his inconsistency. Some places were huge, others were local pubs.

Our first two weeks were just in Sydney. Eight shows in one city. The first show was Paddington Town Hall. Its 1,500 capacity was crammed wall to wall, with kids flocking around outside. The next venue was a pub called the Railwaymen's Arms or something. When the Teardrop first arrived, there was a genuine buzz. People were all over. But by the end of two weeks, when we had played every hall, hut, garage and church in Sydney, no-one but the most devout fans could be bothered.

I didn't really care about this. This was as close to a holiday as we would get. I was happy just to be out of Britain and everything that was expected of me there.

Besides, I was into watching *Dangerman* on Channel 7 at 5 o'clock every morning. Gary and I would wake up, smoke a spliff and make egg on toast in the kitchenette. Then we'd go back to sleep till 8.30 and order a huge breakfast on room service.

One afternoon, we piled into Colin Butler's room straight from the beach.

"You know Paul King, everyone," beamed Colin.

Oh, yeah. He's the new manager guy. I'd seen him before, when we were on tour in Britain. Paul had flown over from London for a meeting with Colin about some crisis or another. It seemed weird for a dude to come all the way for a meeting. I thought no more about it.

It was on this tour that Dave Balfe really hit his sexual peak, in both the quality and the amount of women that he fucked.

No-one had ever seen the Balfe come-on. We were fascinated and a little in awe. One day, he managed to fuck this really sweet 17 year old who was waiting for my autograph in the foyer. I was outraged, but there was no getting around it, Balfe was good.

Everyone was confused. Balfe was so ugly that most of his partners would be laughing about the idea right up to when it happened. *And* most of these women were really good looking, *and* Balfe never remembered their names *or* where he met them. That was a side to Dave Balfe that I could really enjoy; it was a genuine gift of badness, one of which he took full advantage.

Two guys from a group called The Church brought some grass down to one show. Steve, their singer, asked me if I wanted a magic mushroom. A mushroom?

He handed me this luscious hunk of psilocybin, about 2" in diameter. I ate it up and got ready for the show.

Forty minutes into the set and I'm beginning to levitate above the audience. The people at the front are the edge of a forest and as they stretch back, I am confronted by a tropical jungle.

I looked down at the full length of me, way down to the southern-most tip of my boots. God, I was so beautiful. So black and shiny. The crotch of my

leathers was sculpted and polished in the pale red arc lights, and there was, at that moment, nothing so beautiful as a man.

We were caught up in the glow of a song called 'Clamentis', a loose, loose groove built over a loop of marimbas and single recurring bass line. Balfe had attempted to recreate the voodoo of Dr John's 'I Walk on Gilded Splinters', which we used as intro music to each show. Sometimes it didn't work at all, but tonight I stretched the song to its fullest and most sinewy conclusion. On and on it went, down and down, until it was just a series of wood-blocks and clicks.

I assumed my favourite pose at the front of the stage, a pose I had lifted from a painting in my grandmother's house. It is sunset at a desert watering hole. An exhausted horse is drinking in the semi-darkness. On top of the horse, his bare feet stretched towards the beast's neck, is a majestic and bowed Red Indian brave.

I stood becalmed and silent at the front of the stage, my head also bowed, but my right arm outstretched. The breathing rhythm, which Dave Balfe controlled, became smaller and smaller yet never entirely faded.

The crowd was still. I was still. The air was thick and expectant and my mushroomed mind transported the event and its witnesses back to the primordial soup.

Down and down we went. And down and down, and utter silence. Nothing. . .

and . . . in my head . . . I knew . . . that I . . . could stay . . . like this . . .

all . . . night . . . all night . . . all night . . . all night . . . ALL night . . . ALL NIGHT. . .

. . .AALLLL . . . NIGHTTTT. . .

My head was an equatorial jungle. I stood awed and silent.

In the dressing room and a half-hour after the show, we sat, still drained and saturated, chain-smoking endless joints. My soaking leathers were a part of me, stinking and tightening around my ass and legs. The constant nightly assault of human sweat from the inside and of blistering heat from the stage lights outside was rotting the very fabric of the leather. I had not worn any kind of underwear for years and a hole was appearing below the zipper, through the chemical reactions of urine and heat on animal hide.

Lying on the floor of the tour van, on the way back to the hotel, I was amazed at the luxury of our travel. Two weeks of driving around Sydney and cigarette-butts, roaches, old magazines, empty cans and chocolate-wrappers littered the floor of the van. In my mushroom stew, I was oblivious. It *looked* beautiful to me and I lolled my head back against Gary's gargantuan black size-12 parachute boots, snuggling my body into the floor. I looked up at the faces of the group and crew, caught in the amber glow of the streetlights, miles above me like an animated Mount Rushmore. I purred. It was that same safe

feeling that I'd had as a child curled up on the back seat of my parents' car, travelling back to Tamworth after a long weekend with Nana Todd, my Welsh grandmother.

"Ay, Copey, geddoff the floor, you plank, it's filthy," said Gary.

"Yeah, you fuckin' dickhead," Balfe couldn't resist. He wasn't tripping and I was.

In the front of the van, Troy was groaning. He had done his usual full day's drinking and had decided to entertain me. I listened to the moaning turn into gentle complaints, and told Balfe and Gary how happy I was.

"Fuck off, Copey. He's fuckin' dead ill."

It registered not one tiny bit and I hauled myself up to the front of the van. Troy was leaning into the seatbelt, the palms of his hands applying a heavy pressure to his belly. Wow, this was pure entertainment, and I told him so.

"Er, not now, Julian," beamed Colin. "We're on our way to the hospital."

Awlright, I thought. Some action. I started to sing sweetly about Troy's being ill, and how he was the coolest, and how beautiful everyone was. I flailed around inside the van, beaming at each and every one of them. Happy.

Oh, happy, happy, a-happy happy happy. . .

"Fuckin' shut the fuck UP!" Dave Balfe exploded.

He snarled at me, a pig of a man with bulging eyes. Around me, the rest of them caught me in the united glare of their eyes and I shrank back against the van door, then down and down into a heap on the floor, my chin on my knees. I was terrified. I shut up whilst we dropped Troy off at the hospital and was too scared to utter a sound until we arrived back at the Cosmopolitan Motor Lodge, 45 minutes later. It was around 2 a.m. and the trip was still in full swing.

In the foyer, I was drooling and alone. Everyone had grabbed their keys and fled. I knocked on Balfe's door. He wouldn't open it and Gary was hiding in there.

Eventually, I walked slowly to our room. I sat on the edge of my bed and tried to think. I had so much energy left, I couldn't possibly sleep.

I turned on the TV and flicked through the channels. Nothing, nothing, nothing, then . . . awlright. A film. A classic film. It was *The Loneliness of the Long Distance Runner*, an early '60s British film starring Tom Courteney. I'd seen this film countless times and I loved it. It's all about a prisoner who finds his freedom in cross-country running. There are endless scenes of him pounding through the kind of English wood that my mind had cried out for earlier in the evening.

Quickly, I stripped off my leather pants and boots and put on my long black shorts. I moved both Gary's and my bed into the centre of the room. And then I began to run. Round and around the room.

Tom was *my* man. Someone had come through for me.

That was me: the long distance runner.

HOLY JOE'S MANHATTAN HOLE

"The Great and Most Essential Lord of the Lights and Artistic Genius Supreme, Monseigneur Moshie Manhattan of Sydney, Australia, and the World Does Welcome and Applaud the Most Regal and Most Beautiful Lord Julian Cope . . ."

The illuminated address, in all its infinite and delicate detail, sprawled on and on down the page. It was handed to me by a great-looking man of about 45, dressed in full leathers, jacket, boots and pants.

Moshie Manhattan was an extravagantly dressed man of around 70. He wore a white summer suit and a large white Panama hat. According to the girls who hung out with us, he had been to every show and the leather guy was his boyfriend.

This peculiar couple followed us to Melbourne, but were extremely careful to keep their distance. Every other day, a new illuminated letter would arrive. I would read it and file it as a precious gift, but I never knew whether they wished to get closer; they seemed quite happy forever 10 yards away.

Melbourne is as different from Sydney as Liverpool is from London. I had been loath to leave Bondi Beach and the sanctuary of our routine, but really, I was happy anywhere.

Within hours of our arrival, Troy had surrounded himself with a new gaggle of females, Ronnie François had burned himself badly, Gary and I had taken some acid, walked down the strip and become hopelessly lost.

Now Neil Levine and Colin hung out together. It was a weird combination and Neil started to freak. The girl they were with was a heavy heroin addict. She was always on the tour bus. One time, she was so strung out and oblivious of everyone that she just pushed her pants down and did herself with both hands.

As soon as we arrived in Melbourne, those three went off to score heroin. They waited outside the house, then lost their nerve, then said, "Let's do it," then . . . two police patrols and an unmarked car screamed out of nowhere and raided the house as they sat indecisively.

Poor Neil was mentally caned, he couldn't handle it at all. He was beaten about the face by a million "what ifs".

Still, in Melbourne, we all lost it.

I was developing a bad habit on stage. It was called "lack of pace". I would go berserk from the moment I opened my mouth. In Melbourne, I stripped most of my clothes off and wedged myself into the filthy ceiling, between water pipes and electric cables. That was fine until a song like 'Tiny Children', which is so delicate and small. Sung by a half-naked asshole way above the audience with soot and grime over his torso, the song lost its considerable impact.

'Sleeping Gas' had hit its peak at Club Zoo, a 9–10 minute freeform blitz,

truly transcendental and epic. By this time, though, it was at least 15 minutes long and completely shapeless. I thought, and so did Balfe, that the longer it was, the more of an art statement it became. Absolutely not. After the first Melbourne show, I walked into Ronnie's room. He was listening to a cassette of the performance. At the end of 'Sleeping Gas', with the house lights on and the audience embarrassed, all that can be heard is my never-ending and ridiculous scat singing: ". . . *Splurger-burger-burger-burger-burger-burger-burger* . . ."

The Teardrop Explodes group and entourage were like a badly organised parking-lot. The cars were still there, but someone was stealing things – hubcaps at first, but then wheels and even engines.

Colin Butler's skin was changing colour. He helped me to blow out any interview. It got so that I'd only do fanzines.

Our videos were on TV, projecting an image that not one of us could live up to. I saw a video by a Sydney group called The Laughing Clowns and thought it was brilliant. They had a fine atonal brass section and their song 'Holy Joe' was like the theme from some Berthold Brecht musical. I met their drummer, Jeffrey, and bought all their albums. I was a man obsessed. They had a great sense of balance.

There was too much disparity between the Teardrop live and the recorded version. I was either stripping and smothering myself in honey or singing choirboy songs. We *needed* that balance.

Finally, after what seemed like forever, we left Australia and headed for New Zealand. Ronnie François was broken-hearted; he'd fallen in love with a beautiful woman called Wendy and was inconsolable.

Auckland was like England 1962. There were three TV channels which shut down before 11 p.m. The outskirts of the city were filled with second-hand hi-fi and thrift shops. The middle was like Cardiff, all arcades and boutiques. One street cut through the city as though it belonged in New York. It was a weird combination and I didn't like it.

Some guys had driven up from Christchurch, 800 miles away, to see us. I wasn't interested in talking to them, though. I didn't give a shit.

My greatest memories of New Zealand? The bag of grass that the promoter gave us the night we arrived and finding a copy of *Stand* by Sly & the Family Stone for $1.40. Oh, and one other thing: I finally witnessed Dave Balfe's mythical come-on technique first hand.

We were at a private party thrown for us by the promoter. Balfe and I hung out for a while, but nothing was happening at all. We decided to leave and had actually got to the door when Balfe saw this girl sitting on the reception table.

"Are you coming upstairs?" he asked.

"Yeah, okay." And they were gone.

That was it? Nothing more? No diddle-iddle-ink like Samantha in *Bewitched*?

I waited around for 10 minutes and Balfe bounced down the staircase, red-faced and grinning.

"Sorry I was ages, I met her mate on the stairs."

Ho-hum.

My mood swings were getting frequent now. I was having trouble maintaining my Babbling Fool stance. Half the time, I didn't even know what was going on. I'd sit, eyes heavy-lidded and swollen, and do whatever anyone asked.

Balfe was usually good at maintaining momentum, but even he had problems lifting us. Why were we here? He had been with Kate St. John from The Ravishing Beauties for a while now and would occasionally break down in tears.

I had been in Sydney for five days before I could work out the time difference and ring Dorian in New York. Gary could never ring his fiancée, Lynn, in Liverpool. It cost him too much and it was night-time there whenever we were awake.

On the last day in New Zealand, Colin announced that we had no US work permits or visas. Of course, we had a tour ready and were expected in two days.

I was seized with panic, overwhelmed by it. New Zealand is as far from home as an Englishman can get and we didn't even have the right papers to get out of there.

I hung around outside the US embassy all day. God, it was sooo far away. Not just Britain, everything. Thousands of miles and shitloads of gigs before we could have any peace.

As the tension built, Colin was of no use at all. He was the same sweet dude and maintained a vicious self-belief, but he was glaringly lacking in psychology. We all milled around the Pan-Am desk and prayed to get out of the place.

And then, with about an hour to spare, Colin Butler and his beaming smile walked into the departure lounge. He handed each of us our passports and said, as we got on the plane, "Pretty cool, eh? A US visa stamped in New Zealand. Not many people will have one of those."

UNITED STATES OF MIND

Bombardment. I was being bombarded by everything. It all sucked shit, the whole fucking lot. I figured that it was probably the natural growing pains of an evil soul. I was starting to feel pretty damn evil most of the time.

The flight from New Zealand was a major league drag. The US customs in Hawaii checked *every* one of my 100 cassettes, every page of my lyric books, every part of my anatomy, every hair on my head.

Los Angeles was a wash-out and a let-down. We were stuck in the shitty Beverly Sunset hotel, so I reclused out and got in a foul black mood.

I rang Dorian and felt so far away from her that it killed me. I was removed from the people I loved and I just had to wait. A woman called Marcie rang. She was a friend of Lydia Lunch but I didn't give a shit.

At 3 a.m. Balfe and I put on our leathers and walked up Sunset Boulevard to Ben Frank's for Eggs Benedict. On the way back, a bunch of rednecks called us faggots and I got totally anti-American.

The guy on the hotel desk was Argentinean. It was the time of the Falklands crisis and we were supposed to care. We didn't give a shit and rolled him a spliff as a goodwill gesture. Of course, British joints have tobacco in, so he thought we were taking the piss.

We played a nondescript show at a place with no vibes and left. A total right-off drag.

In San Francisco, I began to hang out on my own. Everyone's minds were caned and we had nothing to say. I took some acid and met some young female fans in Union Park. They showed me around and I bought a few cheap biographies on Haight Street.

We played a club called the I-Beam, an old psychedelic cinema. The audience was receptive but I was energy-free. I did my trance-out with a perfunctory professionalism. Ho-hum.

Then, halfway through the set, a beautiful little girl, who had spent the evening in rapt attention in front of me, called out gently, "You're the king of psychedelia."

It was a cute but dumb thing to say, and it made me feel like a phoney and a loser. At least I worked harder after that, but the performance was no better really.

I had started to write a thing called "Krankenhaus". It was a kind of play in pidgin German, with songs and poems and a central character called Krank.

Krank was a throwback. The rest of the human race had developed into weaners with huge heads, whilst Krank was tall, straight backed, blond and beautiful. This made him an outcast, so he spent his life running and fighting with his friends, Hellmouth and Joker.

It was a horrible, mean-spirited and nasty piece of work, but it reflected my state of mind and kept me alert during the asphyxiating tour schedule.

My favourite poem was a tender little piece called "Fuck Muscle Beach (Los Angeles)":

"Fuck Muscle Beach (Los Angeles)
Fuck the tough and the tanned
Stay pale; white as the driven snow.
Honest, it's best."

I was fascinated by translations. It had always struck me as oddly correct that when Mort Shuman translated a Jacques Brel song, it retained all the bile and contempt of the original. Yet, when Rod McKuen translated the Brel song 'Ne Me Quittes Pas' it was reduced to the drippy '70s Las Vegas blandness of 'If You Go Away'.

My brother Joss had introduced me to nine poems by a Russian dwarf called Metranil Vavin. On leaving Leningrad for Paris, he had translated the poems into French. The versions which I knew were translated once more, from the French into English, by an American poet called Clayton Eschlemann. The charm of these poems, besides the strange subject matter, was their unwieldy structure and archaic phrasing. With a head full of hallucinogenics and armed with the Metranil Vavin poems, I aimed to turn "Krankenhaus" into a multi-level artpiece, stuffed full of songs, poems, rants and games. It was the perfect antidote to the road.

Dave Balfe's art-statement film got as close to reality as any road-film could. It was long and boring and impenetrable. The US section was just endless shots of highways, intercut with me looking deadly and lost.

On and on the tour went. I felt lessened by each successive gig. This version of the Teardrop was the strongest and most creative yet, but I was inconsistent and easily fooled by the audience. Other times, I would be jealous of the rest of the group.

In Detroit, I was really moving. I felt goood. The audience dug me the way I wanted and I was loving them back. Then, out of the corner of my eye, I noticed something slightly off-putting. In front of the organ, rising out of the chaos of dancing freaks, the cutest girl in the audience was staring long and hard at Dave Balfe, with her tongue hanging out of her mouth. Balfe was grinning wildly from behind the organ and making equally vicious sexual faces.

I freaked out completely. What the fuck is going on? I'm giving it loads at the front of the group and an ugly plank like Balfe is turning on all the women from behind his keyboard.

The rest of the set was rubbish. I felt self-conscious and stupid. I couldn't even stare at any female in the audience; as far as I was concerned they all wanted Dave Balfe.

After the show, Balfe gave the girl five minutes of lovin' and, as it was Detroit, we sat in the back of the truck and finished all the drugs, in honour of the approaching Canadian border.

Colin Butler was pissing me off. I loved the guy but he couldn't keep it together. His skin had begun to change colour once more. It was a pale flaky grey. He kept complete control of the drugs. Balfe, Gary and I were quite poor at this time. That was the reason why I took so much LSD – it was extremely cheap and transported me for 10 hours at least.

Troy, Ronnie and Colin had spent shitloads on cocaine all across America.

It really helped when the van broke down, as the coke contingent would immediately jump out and stand around, nostrils flared into a macho grimace, and order each other about.

On these long, long drives, I developed a great respect for Dave Balfe's ability to skin up. He would sit on the back row of the bumping, jumping and swaying Dodge van, Gary hounding him on one side, me hounding him on the other, the darkness and the wind from an open window buffeting his concentration and *voilà*, a perfect spliff would appear from nowhere. Every time.

I even reintroduced "Sock", our old game, where I would put a sock over my head, climb out of one window, scramble over the roof and in through the other side. It still didn't put him off.

In Ottawa, we played a show in the conference room of our hotel. The audience was a mixture of rock'n'rollers and salesmen from a furniture convention. A huge black guy hung around Colin all evening. Who's this dude? Oh, he's going to sell us some acid cheap. Why, man? We're off to New York tomorrow.

Colin could not be dissuaded. He bought 200 microdots from the guy "because it was such a deal". We all said he was crazy. Especially as we were all flying and he had to drive the truck across the border at Rochester.

I wasn't interested in the stuff anyway. I was going to see Dorian and meet her parents on Long Island. You're losing your marbles, Colin.

This tour was grinding the fine edges off everyone. If I was happy for half a day, I'd think I was back to normal. But then the sinking blackness would return and my all-pervading gloom would take over.

It was wonderful to see Dorian. Lynn had stayed with her on Long Island and she and Gary were now holed up in their hotel room. It was an oasis and I was going to be fine.

The Ritz was on 14th Street. It was an old ballroom with a balcony all around the dance floor. The dressing room was on the left side of the balcony, so it was easy for people to get backstage. A curtained window in the dressing room gave a great view of the audience and a steep old iron staircase led down on to the backstage.

I peeped out at the audience from behind the curtains. There was no-one there. Nonsense, said everyone, it's early. Besides, they're all hanging out at the bar.

Time went on. There was no-one there at all.

Rubbish, you dickhead. It's going to be packed.

I didn't believe anyone. Sure there were people. But there could be more. There's room for more. Loads more. My head felt bad and I started to retch. I was forcing it, but people took notice. I told Colin that we couldn't go on. He explained that we'd signed a contract that had to be fulfilled. Besides, I couldn't let down all these people.

What people? No-one's here.

Colin pulled Troy over and said, "Talk to him." Troy baby explained that the place was fine, there was a good audience and he wouldn't go on if it was that bad. Hmm. . .

An hour later, I was panicking. It was past showtime. I really could *not* go on. My breathing was erratic and sweat coursed down my body. People started to get angry. Of course there's a crowd. Yeah, but that wasn't the point anymore. I'd built myself up so much, I couldn't come down. Shit.

I thought maybe I should act crazy. That'll convince them. I had been leaning against a metal strut in the dressing room. I started to rub my arm against it, very slowly and imperceptibly. I worked my shirt up my arm and, whilst nobody noticed, gently applied more and more pressure until the skin began to tear and a tiny wound appeared. This is perfect, I thought. I worked on, quietly and carefully opening the wound some more, then suddenly, "What's all this shit?" Balfe screamed at me. I was found out. "Don't be so fuckin' selfish, you twat. You've got Dorian here now, so cut it out." He ranted on and on about how much he was missing Kate St. John, but how we had to be professional.

Everyone raged around the room, looking for bandages and stuff. Dorian tried to calm me down, but I *was* calm. My mind was fixed on its one goal: to get out of the performance.

By now, everyone had their eagle eye on me. It had become a contest. I saw them conspiring in the other room whilst Mal and Dorian kept hold of me.

I started to develop breathing problems. It was so hot. I was so cooped up. I couldn't stand it. I tell you, I'm going to beat these bastards.

"I'm gonna sit on the stairs, okay?"

Okay. So long as I kept the door open so they could check on me. "Fine," I said, and sat at the top of the iron stairs.

Everyone said that I threw myself down the staircase because I'd argued with Dorian and I was tripping. Not at all. For a start, I didn't *throw* myself down. I just stood up and kind of let myself fall. Also Dorian and I were quite happy. And I wasn't tripping either. I just did it to make them *think* that I was crazy. I didn't know it would come to this. But it was them or me. Also, I knew myself well. If we had played that night, I would have been so shit that Teardrop fans would have dropped like flies.

They carried me out and I got my way. I wasn't even that badly hurt. And it was a small price to pay for saving our reputation.

EMPTY CATHEDRAL

We drove down the Long Island Expressway, just the two of us, in Dorian's silver Ford Mustang. I was finally going to meet her parents and her dog. Out of the tour's clutches and a chance to get stable.

Everyone was cracking. The morning after the Ritz fiasco, we'd found out that Colin had shit out and dumped the 200 acid tabs half a mile from the US border. What a dude! Then Chris Ayres, who had joined the crew in Los Angeles, was busted for marijuana two hours from New York.

Mr and Mrs Beslity lived in Sands Point, an exclusive village near Port Washington. It was only a 40-minute drive from Manhattan and I was desperate to meet them.

We left the LIE at exit 36 and drove the 15 minutes to Sands Point down the tree-lined road with its houses set way back in the woods, one every 300 yards or so. As we passed through, I felt a little awed. I was stinky and crazy and used to slumming it. Best behaviour, I thought. Sands Point had its own private police force, but at least we didn't have to show ID at a checkpoint, like so many of those little fascist states in America.

We rounded a bend and I was confronted by Long Island Sound, a huge stretch of blue water with enormous and luxurious houses dotted at irregular intervals along its length.

The Beslity house was a huge flat-roofed ultra-modern place built into the side of a hill. The front was all on one level, but the driveway at the side fell away steeply. The back of the house was two-storey and all glass, the lawns went way down, almost to the water, and there was a secluded beach. Bloody hell, I thought.

An hour later, I was happy. I could stay here forever. My visa lasts for almost a month and we only have a few more shows.

Helen, Dorian's mother, was incredible. She was a real Greek goddess with an amazing figure and a film-star face. And, best of all, she seemed to understand me. We had often talked on the phone and now we had so much to babble about.

I was a little nervous of Dorian's father; Steve had a heavy reputation and I'd seen a photograph of him doing a handstand on the railings of the Brooklyn Bridge. He had got crazy during the '50s and lived only to extremes – either they were wealthy as hell or they were close to bankruptcy. The family had just had to get used to it.

This all helped me to feel at home. They didn't treat me like a weirdo. They didn't think I was. And I felt pretty normal after some of the stories I heard.

We stayed in this idyllic spot for two days and I hated its ending.

We were off to Boston. What a horrendous drag. Still, I could come back in a week. That thought kept me high as Dorian drove me back to the Tour of Hell.

In Boston. Who cares? It was like I'd never been away. I felt myself going down again. Shit, I've got to beat this thing, it's not for very long now.

The routines fell in once more. The soundcheck, hanging around, an interview, hanging around and photos in a parking lot, waiting, a meal, then waiting. I spent my life waiting.

I started to feel sorry for myself and moped around in my room. I didn't want to see anyone at all, let alone go on stage.

There was a knock on the door. I ignored it but they were persistent and a voice bellowed. It was Colin Butler. He said Balfe was freaking out and wanted to go home.

Dave Balfe sat hunched over with tears streaming down his cheeks. His eyes were completely closed up and he was inconsolable. After about 40 minutes, he managed to tell us that we had to finish the tour now. This minute.

I had freaked out so much during the last tours that this was standard. But not from Balfe. And they always managed to persuade me back to work in the end, using guilt-trips, or threats, or sometimes even reason.

This time, it was different. Dave Balfe was gone in the head. While people had been worrying about me, he had flipped out. It took ages for Colin to understand.

The last show we played was in Ottawa. Colin would take a lot of shit for letting the group fall to pieces on the East Coast. Dorian and I drove Balfe to Kennedy Airport, 200 miles in silence.

Two days later, I sat in my old bedroom at my parents' house, up in Tamworth. I still had three weeks left on my US visa, but Colin Butler had insisted that we were going to be busy immediately.

We weren't busy at all. We had nothing to do for weeks. I sat around the house vacantly and tried to relax. I needed to ring Dorian all the time, but my parents were always phobic about overseas calls. However much I explained to them that I would pay for the call, they still couldn't imagine it could be less than £50. So every evening, I would walk up to the phone box and feed endless 50p pieces into the slot.

One day, as I sat talking to Hutch, one of my oldest friends from school, I felt surprised when he said I was doing well. As far as I was concerned, I had failed more than anyone I knew. I was back in the bedroom that I'd left in 1976. The record collection leaned up against the same wall as in the old days. My marriage had failed. I had nowhere to live. It was May 1982 and I was 24.

I felt like an empty cathedral, right after a coronation.

GROEDIPUS

I was fed up. I was fed up and hollow inside. Why be in a group? It just keeps unnecessary pressure on. I have to worry about the rest of them getting paid, so I have to write songs at a reasonable pace, with a single every five or six songs so we can stay in the charts and compete with shit who would sell their ass, their mouths and their souls to any dickhead record company who will fuck them off as soon as they drift from the formula.

I loved pop music. I wanted to make pop music. I refused to hide behind some art trip. Trivialise your trip. Don't fall for the art statement, that's total garbage.

But all this was falling on stony ground. Groups were appearing with ridiculous attitudes. The punk thing that I believed in so much was being torn down. And I'd helped to do it. I'd appeared like some nice boy with the blond fringe and the big beat, and I'd confused the whole issue. I'd been greedy. I still was greedy. I had nearly a whole album of songs ready to record. Well, not really. But I'd told everybody in the press, so I'd better get writing.

I was jealous of Echo & the Bunnymen. Jealous as hell. They had no need to get crazy on drugs or fuck themselves up. Mac was quite happy to go out night after night and pretend. They would appear to free-form on stage, but it was worked out down to the last aside. And Mac would do his "I'm high" bit and everyone would believe it.

I was so angry at this. But, then again, I was angry at everything. And my focusing was a way off.

The evil was in me. I believed that much. I had to trust Dave Balfe, really. I knew I couldn't trust myself; if I was evil, I had to force a democracy on the group. Give my power up and suppress my own opinions.

I played some of the new songs to Balfe. He said they didn't sound like The Teardrop Explodes. I looked at him like he was crazy. Have you even heard *Wilder*, Balfe? *That* sounded nothing like the Teardrop, until we did it.

But this time, Balfe would not acquiesce. My new songs were "rock", according to him, and I should do a solo album as well as the new Teardrop LP.

"And I'm gonna write some songs for a change. Why should you get all the fuckin' publishing?"

I'd never heard it put so bluntly. Balfe never wrote songs. I couldn't see why he wanted to take on such a task. But, like a lot of musicians, he seemed to think that a song was just a bunch of music with some lyrics over it.

I guessed that I just had to trust him on this one. Maybe I was prejudging him. Maybe he's got the muse.

BLURRED MAN OF ALVECOTE

I had nothing to do. Nothing at all. Balfe was in London writing and recording songs for the third album. Gary was up in Liverpool with Lynn. After such intensity on tour, the let-down forced me into an inert state. It was at this time that staying with my parents became such a help. After a few days, their sense of order at least gave me something to focus on.

I would wake early at my parents' house. Such was the strict routine there that at 7.30 every morning I would find myself eating bacon and eggs in the kitchen with my father.

I needed that routine. I needed severe normality. My parents wouldn't take my weirdness and it forced me to act like every other human being. Joss was away at Essex University, so this time in Tamworth gave us an opportunity to rebuild our thang.

My father had worked as an insurance agent for the Prudential for what seemed like forever. His clients were scattered around the Tamworth area and, as a child, I had loved to travel with him when he made his calls. Now, around 18 years later, I was doing exactly the same thing. When he called on a client, I would sit in the car and read, waiting for the door of the house to open and his smiling face to appear. I felt so terribly lost, I needed to recreate as best as I could.

Although Tamworth is a real pig to look at, it is surrounded by some of the most beautiful villages I know. We would drive through Seckington and Newton Regis, Austrey and Hopwas, all these places that flooded my memories and irrigated my soul.

Over the next few days, the whole area started to make sense. Maybe my familiarity with it had been lost. Maybe my travelling had given me a new perspective. Maybe you do need to travel to appreciate what you have at home.

Whatever it was, Tamworth was beginning to grow in my head. I had nowhere to live and no roots anymore. Liverpool was out of bounds, as my ex-wife lived there. London was no good; it drove me crazy and I couldn't even bear to walk down its streets.

I began to warm to my old town. Hell, if this place was in the American Midwest, I'd love it. So love it, you bloody snob.

One day, as we were going home via Polesworth, I asked my father to drive down the road where we used to pick blackberries. We turned right down a winding lane and went on towards a weird place called Alvecote. The hedgerows were gone now but everything else was much the same.

Alvecote is built on the main railway line between London and the north west. We followed the lane for about two miles until we came to the priory.

Alvecote Priory is a ruin. Supposedly, it was the scene of the vile rape and

execution of nuns during the Dissolution of the Monasteries. Now, all that was left of the walls was an enormous arch like a curved and inverted 'V'. There was a deep and dangerous crater, about the size of a large empty swimming-pool. This had been the basement of the priory and its floor was now littered with huge blocks of stone where the walls had collapsed inwards over the years. I was entranced by the place.

I walked the 20 yards to the canal. The old wartime pill-box was still there, its concrete construction almost hidden in the undergrowth. I scrambled and scraped my way onto its high roof and stretched up on to my toes to survey the area. My father left me there to explore for a while. . .

It was over an hour later and I was standing high, high up above the canal looking out across the counties. I had explored the entire area: the tow-path, the railway line and the narrow twisting lane. At one point, they all ran parallel to each other and pointed the way out through floodlands up to a barren mound rising out of nowhere. As a child, this was the swamp and its Anglo-Saxon funeral mound. It held great significance for my brother and me: we thought this ancient tract of land was inhabited by a spirit world and would tread carefully.

Returning now, as a confused shell of an adult, the place seemed just as special. I was sure it had power. I stayed on the mound for a considerable time, then, as dusk approached, I began the four-mile trek home.

For the first time, I considered Tamworth as a possible home. It was directly between Liverpool and London, and only a one and a half hour train journey from both cities. Also, it was cheap and it was far from prying eyes.

In a couple of days, my mind was made up. I rang Dorian to tell her the news and began to look for a three-storey house. It had to have three levels, it just did. I wanted a house with an upstairs living room and hardly any garden.

In a couple of days, we'd found the *only* three-storey house that was for sale. It was right in the centre of Tamworth and cost £15,000. It was 400 yards from the train station and 300 yards from the shopping mall. I made an offer and got accepted and waited to move in.

I was going to have a home, a bloody great home.

FALLING DOWN AROUND ME

In London, shit was happening. Paul King, our new manager that nobody knew, was assessing his situation. He called me down for a meeting and it was then that I found out that we would be supporting Queen at two stadiums! He'd mentioned it vaguely during his 24-hour visit to Sydney, but I hadn't been paying attention.

Still, that seemed like nothing compared to the main thing: our debts. They were enormous. Colin Butler had taken Bill Drummond's small debt and built something all of his own from it, something huge and special. This was a real drag, especially as I wanted to split the group up.

The debts continued to mount up over the next weeks, but they soon became overshadowed by Balfe's plan. He wanted to sack Troy Tate and Ron François.

That's cool, I thought. That's one step closer to splitting up. Awlright.

I felt no compunction about the move, it washed right over me. But wait until after the Queen shows, I warned Balfe. And *you* can tell them, this one's your idea.

Back in Tamworth, I waited impatiently for the house contracts to be signed. I fought with my father about it. Come on man, when am I in there? I needed a place, I needed Dorian over here, I wanted to fuck off from everything.

In London Dave Balfe recorded song after song. One time, I played him a thing on acoustic guitar called 'The Greatness and Perfection of Love'. He refused to use the same rhythm that I'd written, but liked the song. He also turned 'Metranil Vavin', a gentle eulogy to my Russian poet, into a funking swamp thang. When I returned, a month later, both songs were impossible to sing. Ho-hum.

We played the Queen shows in late June. I didn't try to escape, just came on all ugly. I found my oldest, shittiest, most creased hand-dyed piece-of-shit shirt from the bottom of my closet in the Liverpool flat. It was damp and stunk of mildew, kind of like old oranges.

At both Leeds and Milton Keynes, the audience were incensed that we were playing. Ha-ha, this was fun. We were bottled mercilessly from beginning to end by heavy-metal bum-boys who shouted, "Fuck off, you queer!" at me. Wow, they dig Monsieur Freddie and they call *me* queer. So much for the workings of the average mind. I blew them kisses and stuck my ass out at the audience. They hit it full on with a coke bottle.

One guy missed my head with four consecutive bottles. I grinned at him with my puppy face, all tongue and drooling. His fifth shot made perfect contact with my right cheek, Fuccck Offf! The audience applauded wildly. I applauded too, but I was red-faced and hurting. I had a certain respect for a hatred so blind.

Then Queen arrived in a helicopter as we played 'The Culture Bunker'. It was a low trick. But it was their show and what were we doing there in any case? Besides, low tricks are the main act's prerogative.

I cared nothing about The Teardrop Explodes. The sooner we die, the better.

In London, Dave Balfe told us that he had an LP ready to record.

In London, I told everyone that I had half a solo LP to record.

In London, Paul King got me drunk at the Coconut Grove and told me that we owed over £90,000.

In London, I spent an afternoon answering mail that had built up since Liz Atkins' fan club had fallen to pieces. I made hundreds of photocopies of my face and wrote the same message on each one: "Dear so-and-so, Julian is dead. He died yesterday. I'm sure he would have hated you anyway. Love Liz."

Then I put a handful of assorted heavy-metal badges in each letter and mailed them off.

In Tamworth, I finally moved into no. 1 Mill Lane. Miss Dorian Beslity flew over at one day's notice. I bought a mattress and a toaster, and moved my shit from Liverpool.

We holed up for a few weeks to get stoned and reason the situation through. My mind was brittle as hell. I was lucid most of the time, but felt my attention lapsing in long conversations.

Finally, I agreed. We'll do the third Teardrop album, then I'll be free.

Two weeks later, I sent Dorian home. I've got to be professional about this; I don't want *any*one to have reason to call me weird.

Yeah. Maybe life's course would run smoothly for a change.

WHIRLPOOL

"And perched in such domestic worldliness as this
Just plan to pull the rope at any sign of bliss."

I'd been screaming my head off the whole journey. That was part of the fun. We were swerving all over the place and these country lanes were far too narrow to give much margin for error.

I knew that Gary had no license, but I couldn't drive at *all* and anyway I trusted him well enough. He didn't really want to *kill* me. That was just a game. So if the worst came to the worst, I knew I could always bang on the roof and he would stop. Anyway, since Balfe had banned us from the studio a week before, we had to have *some* fun.

The only way to stay on the roof of a car, at real speed, is to keep your head down and assume a crucifix position. We had a rule that the car's front windows had to be open. That way, I could stretch right across the roof and lock my fingers around the edges of the doors.

Gary and I were now on our third lap. It was a circuit of around four miles, avoiding all local villages except this one tiny hamlet without a name.

Kingsley Ward, the owner of Rockfield Studios, had lent us this ancient beaten-up Cortina estate, which we nicknamed "Old Yellow" on account of its vile paint job. For the first few days, we had driven everywhere with me on the roof. It was only after that got boring that we hit upon the idea of the game.

And now? Now we were locked in the struggle of our mechanical rodeo, with Gary in charge of the beast below and me the pale rider, shrieking and howling and hanging on for dear life.

Down into the vale we thundered, my mouth tight-lipped as Chris Evert, avoiding the tiny flies that rushed into my hair and my eyes. Then up the other side and up and up and over the hill we went. A slight bend and, take it carefully and, more carefully, Gary, then out of the curve and wow.

We passed a car on a wide stretch. Ten seconds earlier would have been a disaster, ha ha. Not a problem. Have you seen this guy? The rubber man. There's no way anything could happen.

I loved to taunt fate. Come on, come on. You're not going to kill me, you're chicken. Not you, Gary, fate.

We hurtled into a three-hill roller-coaster, up and wheee! DOWN! Up and wheee! DOWN! Up and wheeee!

Gary beat on the ceiling of the car, bam, bam, then he wound up the window on the driver's side, trapping my right band.

"Hey, Gary, heyyyyyyy." (I kick the car with my boots.)

"Gary, fuckin' Garyyyy." (I beat the roof with my head.)

At this point, Gary is a dead man once he stops. He is 6'5" and thick as shit if he doesn't suss that fact.

On the way down the final hill, Gary winds down the window, I free my right hand, a red car appears from nowhere, we brake like fury, miss the car and ... slide gracelessly into a ditch.

I was lying upside-down in a thorn bush. I wasn't hurt, it was too funny. I could have fun with Gary, I really could. We didn't even haul the car out for a while. It looked fine where it was. We skinned up and lay in the back, laughing our heads off.

The record being made had nothing to do with me. That fact was only now beginning to hit home. Dave Balfe and Hugh Jones had been holed up in Studio 2 for a week now. In that time, neither Gary nor I had even been invited down. In fact, we were positively unwelcome.

Hugh had been a good friend and ally. He had recorded more Teardrop stuff than anyone else and normally we sat side by side making decisions. But now, though he did not know it, he was fast becoming the enemy.

Dinner was at 7.30 every night, and Balfe and Hugh would leave their studio cocoon, haul themselves up to the white house on the hill and sit there, confused and irritable.

Occasionally, Sally, Hugh's girlfriend, would arrive with their stupid Dalmatian, who would retrieve old bacon covered in hair from behind the cooker, then lick everybody. Then Balfe would wait patiently whilst Hugh and Sally retired to their private room to scream at each other. Gary and I would ask how it was going and for a while, over an after-dinner spliff, we were friends again.

Then they'd be off into the night, and we'd settle down for another evening of endless drugs and videos. We watched *Animal House* constantly. We rented it six times and I then went out and bought it.

Gary and I started to buy a half ounce of hash every day, dropping half of it on the patterned carpet and leaving half-smoked joints all over the place.

Lynn, Gary's fiancée, was doing all the cooking. This kept us both a little more balanced, but I rang Dorian every night, freaking out at what The Teardrop Explodes was becoming.

A little while later, Balfe let us into the studio. We listened passively to the series of whirs, clicks, loops and endless synthesized noises that constituted our next album.

I filled up the electric kettle as full as possible and made coffee in each of the 12 mugs. I put 10 sugars in each of the coffees and then dropped Maryland cookies and digestive biscuits into each mug until they overflowed with soggy, sweet and disgusting mess. Then I poured the contents of the sugar bowl into the coffee jar, emptied the box of tea-bags into the half-empty kettle, surveyed the pathetic microcosm of chaos and walked out of the room.

I believe that my little protest reflected the stature of Balfe's work perfectly. Mine was a tiny and concentrated vandalism against a narrow-minded and artless dry-wank.

The days limped by. A blurred routine of nothingness. At the end of each night, I staggered up to my bed and slept a numb, dreamless sleep. Around 10.30 the next morning, I would surface for a huge farmhouse breakfast from Lynn.

My bedroom was hung with drapes and flags from home, and my clothes hung on nails over the walls. My blaster and tapes were all that I cared about.

Occasionally, Dave Balfe gave me a reference tape for me to judge the album's progress. I never listened, I was too sad. Instead, I played rough tapes of my new songs, over and over. Now, these will never come out. And they feel. They really feel. Even if you hate them, at least they live somewhere. On this album Balfe was excluding me from, the songs had no natural place *any*where.

Gary and I did less every day. Sometimes we played "Bottle". You line up milk bottles on a wall, walk back about 15 feet and then try to scare the bottles into falling. I always won – after half an hour, Gary would lose his temper, throw stones at the bottles and forfeit the game.

Kingsley Ward was concerned; once he found us lying in the town square in Monmouth. We'd been there for hours. What else was there for us?

Kingsley was crazy. He was famous for being unbalanced and he hated his brother, Charles, who co-owned the studio. So one day, to make us happy and to put the fear of God into Charles, he bought us a double-barrelled shotgun.

Now even I thought that was strange. Stupid, really.

As soon as Balfe heard about it, he dropped everything and came up to the house. The two of us ran out into the trees and shot wildly and indiscriminately at everything we saw. We set up a clay-pigeon shoot.

The next day, I heard shots on the opposite side of the valley. I ate breakfast and skinned up a joint, got dressed and walked in the direction of the noise.

Up in the open fields behind the studio, Gary Dwyer stood, gun in hand, reloading for the umpteenth time that day. Mark Parle, Lynn's brother, let another clay-pigeon go. Swwwupp!

Bang! Gary missed. He cursed under his breath. And now I was here to wind him up.

"How many's that, Garfield?" I asked casually.

"About 80," said Mark.

Gary was pissed off. He had not yet hit one of the things.

"I'll show you what to do," I said, not knowing the handle from the pipe. Mark let one go and I fired into the air. I missed. Gary laughed.

I told them that I knew my problem: I should be treating the shotgun like a beautiful woman. Men in films always talk like that. Mark let go another clay. I shot. Swwwuppp! Smash! I hit the thing.

I handed the gun back to Gary and said, with a dreadful sigh of boredom, "That's how you do it, okay?" and walked off down the hill.

I was walking down the lane when PK 354 pulled up. It was Paul King's British racing green E-type Jaguar. He had come to see how we were doing and tell us about the autumn tour. I wasn't interested at all. The front of the Jag reminded me of a dolphin's face and I insisted on riding on the hood, at 5 mph, up the hill, so gently and with so much power.

Paul was concerned. Nothing was happening. Really not anything. The tour was looming large and the recording was not close to being finished. Hugh Jones was off the rails and Balfe had this blind belief that, should we finish it, the record would be a classic. He wanted to call the album "Be Prepared to Become a Whirlpool". Ho-hum.

A few days later, we were tripping to escape from the prison of the album. Gary and I were happy and I even persuaded Balfe to chill out with us. Bill Butt was down to film some of the recording and suddenly everything was fine.

Gary and I were playing "Brick", this game we'd invented where you stand about 15 feet apart and try to knock the other guy out. Every time I threw a brick, the unleashed energy would propel me on to the floor and I'd become a hysterical slavering dog.

It was a slow game. The acid in my system was cut with some weird amphetamine which gave me that drug feeling that makes your veins feel like a bunch of electrical cables.

Whenever the brick came my way I could see its vapour trail immediately

from Gary's two-handed throw to the arc of its flight towards me. One shot mesmerised me so much that I stood petrified, the brick cutting through the air like a *Twilight Zone* space-freighter and hitting me fully in the chest. A shudder echoed through my body but there was no pain. I was gargantuan, beautiful and indestructible.

Then Balfe decided to play. What a knobhound! We'd had this cool elegant scene going, like croquet or something, and this maniac starts in on us.

First, his brick missed me by inches. Then his next brick missed Gary by inches. Then, out of nowhere, another brick hit Gary on the side of his head. Blood poured down his temple and I rushed up to help. Bloody hell, I was so angry.

Behind the hedge, Balfe's head bobbed up and down, scared stiff but smiling that dumb-ass grin.

"You're fuckin' dead, Balfe!" I screamed. I ran to the cupboard under the stairs and grabbed the shotgun. I gave it to the still groggy Gary and helped him outside. Dave Balfe began to remonstrate and protest hopelessly. No way, man. You are the Dead Dude of Rockfield.

And off down the hill Balfe ran, with Gary in slow elegant pursuit. John Wayne as Rooster Cockburn in *True Grit*. Right on.

I had no sense of time. It felt like forever, maybe it was an hour. Bill Butt and I stood at the entrance to the roof of the white house, surveying the opposite side of the valley with his binoculars. Two tiny dots moved across the landscape and the occasional shot rang out. It reminded me of those *Tom & Jerry* cartoons when Tom is defenceless and has to reason with a Jerry mouse who is armed and furious.

A half hour later and I was filling up buckets from the septic tank in the field. I lined up the buckets, then filled one with clean water.

Gary soon arrived, wild-eyed and happy. "The twat's disappeared. I think he's in the woods."

I showed Gary the rows of shit-filed buckets and explained my plan.

When Balfe finally dared to come near the house, he was sooo reasonable, so careful and so freaked out. We stood at the door of the house and I picked up the bucket of water. Then I poured it over my head and smiled.

"You've gotta let us do that to you, Balfe, you twat."

Dave Balfe bobbed about for a while and finally forgot the danger. He was tripping heavily and dorked up to us with his most slappable expression on his face. Whoosh. . .

Whenever Balfe got it, he really got it. He stood there covered in cow-shit and septic-tankness and smiled. Gary and I walked back into the house with our empty buckets and skinned up like mad.

DEATH RATTLE

"If we do this, though, Kingy, the whole thing will've been for nothing. I mean, we'll be just like all the other shit."

I sat in the dressing room of Liverpool's Royal Court Theatre, tears of grief and disbelief coursing down my face. I had tried and I had failed. The tour must go ahead. If not, Paul King would go bankrupt and we didn't want to put him through that as well.

I'd given up on the album. It would never get finished. Balfe could scream his head off for all I cared. He still needed me to sing the fucking tunes.

Now it was the tour. The total right-off tour. A sensational drag of epic proportions. And here we were on the first day of rehearsal, pleading with Paul King not to make us do it.

See, Balfe had decided that we could tour as a three piece with tapes. I had said yeah, yeah, yeah, to *any*thing, just to keep him busy and me in Tamworth. Of course, now I had to sing to a bunch of synthesized tapes and Gary had to mime half a set and play bullshit over bullshit for the rest of the time.

Even Paul King didn't want us to do it. He told us it sucked shit the minute he heard 'Reward' played too fast on a dinky bum-boy synth. But we had to.

Julian David Cope was going to sell his ass to stop his manager, Paul King, going bankrupt. This sale was made easier for me in the knowledge that Paul would have been solvent and happy had Colin Butler not one day walked in to his office with stories aplenty.

We had to do this. We had to do this. Shit, what an empty incredible feeling.

Walking on stage knowing that you can not be better than total crap is a headtrip. Knowing that makes you think so-what to everything.

I tried to shut myself off on stage. There was scaffolding for me to prance around on and different heights of staging so I could be a showbiz dude. I hadn't helped design anything on the stage, but that made me feel more guilty. Ignorance of Balfe's crimes against the Teardrop was no defence. Had we been a political regime, I would have been shot alongside him.

This was it. This was the end. Fans saw the show and said, "What happened? You've lost it." I was transparent. I could not hide my feelings. After every song, I'd apologise and announce the next one. I was used to total freedom, freedom to groove and stumble and trance out. On this tour, I was so burned that I couldn't concentrate one minute. I missed vocal cues all the time, the tape would be in the wrong place and I'd throw Gary and Balfe. I'd have tantrums when the tape snapped, of course I would, anyone would. You feel so foolish, the audience has their sense of disbelief whipped from under them.

At Manchester, the tape snapped during 'The Culture Bunker'. Then it went into auto-reverse. Then I kicked the eagle motifs off the main stage in disgust.

Then I kicked the lights off the highest stage so they were hanging by their wires in mid-air. I kicked off my boots and ripped off my shirt and hurled them into the audience. I threw my electric 12-string off the stage, the monitors, the mike-stand, the whole lot, all the time screaming apologies and saying how shit we were.

I thought about taking my leather pants off, but really, so what? The stage was a perfect metaphor for bad sex without introducing another soft dick into the proceedings.

An hour later, the audience was still outside our dressing-room window, baying for blood. They deserved it, too. We finished the tour with the press on our heels. Julian Cope had been too cocky for too long; they finally found out how much I really stunk.

I didn't discuss it with anyone. I just did it. I split the group up. It was November 1982 and we were old news.

Dave Bates had played me the Blancmange album and told me it was like Scott Walker. Fuck off, no way. Blancmange were this terrible middle-class duo. The singer sung heavy fake depression songs, but smiled on TV like it was a joke.

At home in Tamworth, I burned the album sleeve on the cooker, then skated around the kitchen on the record before taking a knife to it. Then I pinned the whole mess on the wall, where it stayed forever as a symbol of my guilt.

Officially, we split on November 15th 1982, four years to the day after the first gig with Echo & the Bunnymen. No third album, nothing. That was the bloody end of that.

The Cast of *Head-On* in 1999 ᴄᴇ

DAVE BALFE sold Zoo Records, created Food Records and signed Blur. Then he sold the lot for millions. He is married to Helen and has two children, Gabriel and Isabella.

DAVE BATES runs his own London-based record label.

RITCHIE BLOFELD This Prescot College madman and occasional Hungry Types singer is now headmaster of a Newbury school. He lives with his wife Joan and son Tom.

IAN BROUDIE The Big in Japan lead guitarist has eclipsed everyone in recent years with his Noel Harrison/'Windmills of your Mind'-styled Lightning Seeds. His soccer anthem 'Football's Coming Home' is clearly the new 'You'll Never Walk Alone'.

PETE BURNS Someone showed me recent TV footage of *Rock Goes to Collagen*, in which Pete claimed that he was nowadays unheard of here but 'Big in Japan'. Looks better than he used to and will always be a legend.

COLIN BUTLER Whereabouts unknown.

JAYNE CASEY The former Big in Japan singer is Director of Humanix at the Bluecote Chambers in Liverpool.

GEOFF DAVIES Still manages Probe Records and '80s legends Half-Man, Half-Biscuit.

PETE DEFREITAS Echo & the Bunnymen's darling drummerboy is dead. He left behind his common-law wife Johnson and daughter Lucy.

BILL DRUMMOND Writes Patriarchal literature with the '80s video-biker Zodiac Mindwarp.

GARY DWYER The former drummer for The Teardrop Explodes drives a forklift truck in Liverpool.

ROGER EAGLE The founder of Eric's and the Liverpool scene died of cancer in May of this year (1999 ᴄᴇ).

RONNIE FRANÇOIS The Teardrops' former bass player lives in Australia with Wendy, whom he met on the fateful Teardrop tour of 1982. They are happily married and he is still making music.

ALAN GILL The co-writer of 'Reward' is in jail.

CHRIS GOODSON The other member of my 1977 experimental band Hungry Types is a bearded village elder and relief sheriff in Kurdistan(!) He is married

to a member of the nomadic Pathickey tribe and they have seven daughters. He never answers my postcards.

MICK HOUGHTON is still my publicist and still a recluse, but still exerts a low key force on the outside world. When Rob Dickens, MD of Warner Brothers, signed us to the publishing company in 1980, he said to Dave Balfe and me: "Come and meet Mick Houghton, he's the only other person in the world I know who still uses the word 'shag'." Nowadays, "shag" has become a cool term the world over, whereas in 1980 it was less street than "front bottom" – and it's all because of Mick Houghton's insidious subterraneous cultural burrowings. I've even heard it suggested that it was Mick who brought the phrase "Skin up!" to the south, which seems possible, as I never heard the phrase in London before 1981, and then only from other northern rock'n'rollers.

CANDY JAMES My college roommate lives in Halifax with her husband Steve. I saw her for the first time in 20 years on the *Modern Antiquarian* tour in November '98.

HOLLY JOHNSON Nowadays, Holly has re-emerged from self-imposed her-mitdom to be embraced as a mightily deserved '90s Gay Icon.

IAN McCULLOCH had to reform Echo & the Bunnymen recently without all the original back members. During the lean early '90s, when the Bunnymen opted for a less '80s singer, McCulloch fronted a Doors/Love retro-styled group called Elektra-Fiction and refused to play any Bunnymen material whatsoever.

DAVE PICKETT The original drummer for The Teardrop Explodes is an artist living in Kent. He still looks uncannily like his old self and recently reminded me that though 'Sleeping Gas' was my music and words, it was his title.

PAUL SIMPSON The original organist with The Teardrop Explodes and leader of The Wild Swans is married to his long-term partner Jeanne, who is a successful designer. His '80s Wild Swans singing-style has been successfully appropriated by Ian McCulloch for the sound of the New Bunnymen, Paul nowadays records instrumentals for a Gloucestershire label with ex-Christians/Yachts organ guy Henry Priestman.

SMELLY ELLY This seminal Liverpool-scener AKA Paul Ellerbeck has lived on Peckham Rye estate, in south London, these past 17 years and called me out of the blue in 1997 CE to ask if I had a tent he could borrow.

TROY TATE Became the lead singer with Brummie automatons Fashion during the mid '80s. The self-styled 'International Dosser' and third Teardrops guitarist now lives a quiet life and works in a theatre in York.

THE ADOLESCENT grew up.

PETE WYLIE Became Liverpool's most successful misogynist – he even named his daughter Mersey! Still successful in all his rigorous undertakings and success-fully tours parts of Scandinavia with Wah Pete! The Georgie Porgie of Rock!

PAM 'PAMMO' YOUNG The First Woman of Zoo is the second most rock'n'roll woman I ever met after my wife Dorian. She's still gorgeous and lives in Liverpool with her daughter Velvet.

INDEX